ATTIS

THE AUTHOR

Tom Holland was brought up near Salisbury and now lives in London. He has written extensively for radio. His first novel, *The Vampyre*, was published by Little Brown in March 1995 to huge critical acclaim.

ATTIS

Tom Holland

a&b

First published in Great Britain in 1995 by
Allison & Busby
An imprint of Wilson & Day Ltd
179 King's Cross Road
London WC1X 9BZ

Copyright © 1995 by Tom Holland

The moral right of the author is asserted

This book is sold subject to the condition that it shall not, by way of trade or otherwise, be lent, resold, hired out or otherwise circulated without the publisher's prior written consent in any form of binding or cover other than that in which it is published and without a similar condition including this condition being imposed upon the subsequent purchaser.

A catalogue record for this book is available from the British Library

ISBN 0 74900 213 1

Typeset by N-J Design Associates
Romsey, Hampshire

Printed and bound in Great Britain by
WBC Book Manufacturers, Bridgend, Mid Glamorgan

For Sadie, my dearest love, without whom this novel would never have been started, still less finished.

Animae dimidium meae.

Also by Tom Holland

The Vampyre

As the outer shell of the city grew, so to say, its interior likewise expanded: not merely its inner spaces, within the sacred precinct, but its inner life. Dreams welled up out of that interior and took form; fantasies turned into drama, and sexual desire flowered into poetry and dance and music. The city itself thus became a collective expression of love.

Lewis Mumford. *The City in History*.

> dea, magna dea, Cybebe,
> dea, domina Dindymi,
> procul a mea tuus sit
> furor omnis, era, domo:
> alios age incitatos,
> alios age rabidos.

> *Goddess, great goddess, Cybele,*
> *Goddess, mistress of Dindymus,*
> *All of your frenzies keep far*
> *From my house, Queen Cybele:*
> *Summon others to your madness*
> *Others to that fury drive!*

Catullus. The prayer of Attis.

CATULLUS

SUMMER

I
CATULLUS

It was far too hot, that August afternoon, to be walking along the old chalk road. Too hot, and too dull, too choked by the dust that hung filthy in the air, and smudged all it touched, the tufts of grass, the odd line of scrub, the humped and barren downs. Even the track blurred away in the end, its white line dissolving into distance and haze, and it was a dispiriting sight for the young man, as he paused on the ridge and stared ahead, that afternoon, that hot afternoon. He shifted the bag slung over an aching shoulder, and shaded his eyes as he looked ahead again. Still nothing, only the shimmering horizon, and disappearing road. He sighed and plunged his hands deep into his pockets. Then, head bowed, he trudged wearily on.

The afternoon darkened slowly into twilight. The young man flung himself onto the side of the path and dusted off the powder of dirt that had gathered on his trousers; then he leant back, and with his head resting on a discarded shoulder bag, shut his eyes. He was soon fast asleep; when he opened his eyes again, it was evening, and the sky was almost purple, and he was still on his own by the side of a track. He climbed to his feet and peered into the distance. No change there. Heat and darkness, and a vanishing road. The young man sighed. He turned, and looked behind him. The road disappearing again. Clouds of dust refracting the sunset. And then he saw it – a something – a tiny dot. Emerging from the red haze of the distance behind him. And heading, presumably, for the distance straight ahead.

The dot disappeared, down behind a ridge. Then it emerged again. It was a carriage, the young man could see now, drawn by horses. They were trotting at a fair speed. The young man picked up his bag, and as the carriage rumbled ever closer, he began to walk slowly along the side of the road, glancing over his shoulder to admire the equipage and fresh paint, all gold and shiny black. The horses broke into a sudden canter; the coachman yelled at them and reined them in, and the carriage, with a lurching shudder, slowed down, then stopped. The young man waited by its side on the edge of the track.

"Are you going to see Troy burnt?" a woman's voice asked.

A carriage door opened; the young man walked towards it and clambered in. A sharp command, the door was shut, and the carriage started to move again, away towards the distance.

At the same time, two men were tuning violins in a forest. One sat hunched over his instrument; the other, leaning against a tree, looked sweaty and miserable, wiping back long hair from his eyes and swearing softly to himself. Both men looked too clumsy for their delicate work; both were dressed in high leather boots and green breeches.

The first man rolled up from his haunches. In the twilight, it had been impossible to see his shaded face, but now, as he packed away his violin and turned to stare at his companion, the violent white make-up of a clown glowed unmistakably, framing the deep pits of darkness that were his mouth and eyes.

"I don't want to play it here," the other man said. "Not just for people's entertainment. Not here of all places."

The clown stared back at him, then turned and began to walk.

"He must be planning something. He never fucking stops."

Still no reply.

"Hey, wait a minute. I haven't even done my make-up."

The second clown gathered up his belongings, and started to chase his companion down the path.

"You never let me forget, do you? Never!"

Silence answered from the darkness that soon had swallowed them both.

Elsewhere, by a high white wall, three men played with heavy sticks. They slouched easily in their uniforms, self-consciously even, feeling, perhaps, their lack of guns. A couple of ladies, riding past the salutes of the men, and flicking their long skirts as though disconcerted by the stares, glanced uneasily at each other.

"I didn't know there would be sentries," one whispered to the other.

"It's probably to keep people out. Probably part of the game," the other whispered back.

"But of course it's part of the game. What else could it possibly be?"

The ladies spoke no more but, like others behind them, cantered up the gravelled path towards distant lights, and the sound of far-off music.

By now, it was fully night. In the blue darkness of the sky the stars burnt, prickling like drops of sweat. In the forest, a light breeze had begun to blow.

The young traveller could feel the cool against the sweat of his face. He continued to stare compulsively out through the window; it was a long time now since he had been invited to climb into the carriage and join its mysterious occupant; still he had time only to gaze out, at the passing landscape, and the contours of its change. He wondered about the Troy that was waiting to be burnt. The lady had assumed that he had been heading there; but the young man felt too tired to confess that he had never heard of it, and risk being flung out for his ignorance; he couldn't face it, no, not now it was dark, and they were on a strange road. So he continued to stare at the landscape outside and not ask his hostess about where they were heading, who she was, why she had stopped to pick him up.

Occasionally, he would steal a glance at her. She sat in the dark of a far seat and it was hard to see her face; her dress, like the shadows, was black; her arms, pale; that was all he could distinguish. He didn't object to her silence, he realised. If the lady were to speak, or if he were to lean over to try and make her speak, he felt vaguely that a spell might be broken, some enchantment. He smiled, and rubbed his eyes. He felt as he did when drunk, or very tired, straining to capture a significance in objects seen every day, imbuing them with meaning, but unable to understand them. He looked at the lady again, and her pale arms. She continued to stare away from him. The young man picked at his lip and turned back to look outside.

They were passing through a forest. The darkness was dense with trees and twilight shadows. Even when the traveller leant out of the carriage window and strained his eyes, it was hard to distinguish anything much, except for the road, still straight and ghostly pale, leading away into the forest gloom. Occasionally, the clatter of hooves could be heard; once or twice, a muffled horseman galloped past. The young man heard a rustle of skirts; the lady, on her side of the carriage, was also leaning out and straining to look ahead.

Suddenly, the road was lit by torches. The surprise was so great that there was barely time to focus on the scene illuminated by them, in great pools of orange, a high white wall, and the shapes of men waving and running towards the road. One gave a cry but straight away it was lost, as the carriage hurried under a large archway and returned to the dark. The horses began to trot more slowly, then whinnied, and there was a shudder. With a final crunch of gravel, the carriage lurched to a halt.

"You'd better get out here."

It was the lady, speaking at last.

"The party's over there." She gestured vaguely. "You can't miss it."

With a nod of thanks, the young man gathered together his coat and bag, and scrambled out through the door. The moment his feet had touched the gravel of the path, the carriage started to move away again. Within seconds, it had rounded a corner and was gone. The young man stood alone, in the middle of the road, and wondered what to do.

He looked around. There was no one to be seen. There was a party – but where? At Troy – but where was that? He cursed himself for not having spoken in the carriage, for not having found out even the lady's name – what would he say when he reached the ball? He sighed and shouldered his bag. He could hear a faint sound of music. He decided to follow it, and the lady's instructions, down a narrow path. But the path soon began to disappear, and eventually petered out altogether in a dense confusion of trees and bushes. There was no light, and without even the sound of music to guide him now, the young man could only stumble and swear, his face scratched, his trousers torn, his hope of ever escaping the forest's clutches seeming to evaporate by the minute. He blundered on uselessly; finally, in despair, he threw himself onto the ground and called for help at the top of his voice. At once, as though in answer to his own cry, he glimpsed something in the distance, and jumping to his feet, he stumbled eagerly towards it. A cottage, almost buried beneath nettles and clumps of weeds – the quickest way, the young man decided, would be just to climb in through the window. He reached for a ledge and pulled himself up; inside was a darkness too deep to pierce. He strained his eyes; he counted to ten; he jumped.

"Ow, fuck!" shouted something as he landed on it.

"Ow, fuck!" it said again, as the young man leapt to his feet in alarm. "Ow, my leg, fuck!"

"Sorry," said the young man. He wondered what else he could say. "It's not as if I meant to jump on you."

"That's hardly the point, is it? Fucking look next time."

"Sorry."

His adversary grunted, and the young man could hear him moving over rubble and smashed tiles, distinguish him as a faint silhouette pushing at something in a far corner. The shape turned and stood up again, and the young man, whose eyes were slowly adjusting to the dark, saw that what he had at first thought to be just pale flesh was in fact the mask of a clown, luminous, heavily painted, with stars for eyes and an ugly wide red smile. The face looked back at him, and its smile creased even further upwards.

"Looking at something?" the clown said bitterly. "Like the make-up, do you?" He swore, under his breath, and bent down a second time to push at a bundle in the corner. "Come on, Lud," he said. "Time to be off. We'll be late otherwise." He pushed again, and there was a faint stirring as, slowly, a second clown stretched and climbed to his feet. The young man felt too numbed already to feel much surprise.

"So what are you doing here, then?" the first clown asked him. "The ball isn't here."

"I know. I got lost."

"Oh." The clown seemed uninterested. "You'd better follow us then. We're heading that way."

"Are you..?" The young man stopped, embarrassed.

"Yes?"

"Are you... Your make-up...I mean...is everyone meant to be wearing it? At the party?"

"The ball."

"Yes, of course. The ball."

The clown stared at him coldly. "You haven't been invited, have you?"

The young man stared back. "No," he admitted, after a pause.

The clown laughed mirthlessly, and began to pick up his things. "Well, that's one thing to be said for you, I suppose. You know something?" He stood up suddenly, and pushed his face up close against the young man's. "I was really getting to hate you." The young man stared back, at the clown's unblinking eyes, and the thick drops of sweat forming slowly on his brow, paint bubbles, greasy with white. Neither man said anything. Then the clown laughed, a second time, and walked across to a doorway. "Because you haven't been invited, I'll do you a favour – I'll show you how to get to a road. But only because you haven't been invited, right? It's still not as though I like you." He waved and disappeared through the doorway. The second clown flitted after him and the young man, making his way carefully across the shattered floor, followed the clowns out into the forest again.

"Where are you?" he shouted. There was silence. "Where are you? Please." Still there was silence, and then he heard laughter and a slow scraping sound from the dark ahead of him, and then suddenly, beautifully, quite unexpectedly, music, a short movement, one violin rising and holding a single note, while the other rose and fell, and danced around it, until, together, both finished and there was silence again. The traveller stood, amazed, and then clapped his hands. The two clowns re-emerged from the dark, holding their violins. One bowed, but the other, the one who had been so angry just a few minutes before, came up to the traveller and took him by the arm.

"You see," he said, "we're not guests either, we're just here to play the music. Isn't that right, Lud?"

The second clown nodded, and smiled coldly.

"He's called Lud. We were in the war together."

"You're soldiers?"

"Killing machines, we were once." He leered.

"And now you're clowns?"

Beneath his make-up, the man began to frown. "I told you – we're musicians," he said at last. He flicked his hair back from over his eyes, careful, as he did so, not to brush and smudge the heavy black paint. All of a sudden, he looked exhausted. He glanced at Lud, who began to walk away.

"We're off," said the first clown, turning to follow his friend. "Come with us, and we'll show you the road."

The young man chased after them. "You've been here before, then?" he asked.

"Once."

"And that was for a ball too, was it?"

The clown nodded.

"So is there anything I should know about this place? About what's going on, I mean?"

The clown shook his head slowly. "Look," he said, "we just play our music. We try to keep out of everything else. I'm sorry."

He walked on. The young man stood, staring after him. "What's your name?" he shouted.

"Pollo," said the clown. "My friend's called Lud."

"Thank you, Pollo, for all your help."

"Not at all."

"My name's Catullus."

"Not at all, Catullus."

The clowns vanished, past a curve in the road, and the young man was left alone, more bemused than he had been before. Silence, as dense as the forest all around, stifling, like an illness, he had forgotten just how stifling in his attempts to escape it, and now it was returned, as bad, no, worse, more oppressive even than it had been before. The young man began to run down the path, hoping to catch up with the clowns, but the paths split and he was soon lost again, taking a wrong turning, stumbling and jumping over rough land. Then he found a tiny footpath, snaking up a sharp ridge, with bowers and rough stone arches marking its way; the young man took it, running all the time, even though he was sweating, and his side had begun to hurt. Ferns brushed against his legs; he felt them and was suddenly conscious of their touch as though they were emblems of the strange place he had been brought to, of his entrapment in its night. He shivered and continued running, on up the slope.

He reached the crest and stopped straight in his tracks. He could hear voices from below. Cautiously, he looked ahead and then down, at a sheer rock face, and a small temple, hollowed into its base. Outside the archway two carriages stood; one of them he recognised, the other not, but a man passed in front of the second with a torch, and the traveller could see that it was larger and heavier than the carriage he had ridden in, with a gold emblem painted on its doors, an eagle framed inside a wreath. Three women stood on the path by its side, all dressed in wide, flowing skirts, and with their faces cast into shadow by riding hoods. One shook another's hand before kissing and embracing her; then she kissed her other companion, longer, and on the mouth, before climbing elegantly into the heavy carriage. There was a muffled shout, and the horses began to break into a canter. The two women left behind dowsed their torches, and then climbed up into the same carriage that the young man himself had been riding in just an hour or so before. There was another shout, and a shake of the reins; the second carriage too began to rumble away. Catullus stared after it and stood, lost in thought, as silence returned. Then, slowly, he scrambled his way down to join the empty road.

The ball was a triumph, a marvellous success. Everyone seemed quite agreed about that as they sat on cool night-time grass, or whispered in punts; many, of course, didn't have time to agree, because they were too busy enjoying themselves, which was wonderful, of course, and what the night was all about. High on the watchtower in the heart of the gardens, two lovers were stroking and kissing each other, but if they had stopped and looked around, they would have seen the ball spread out below them in all its fevered life, swirling to the lake, and far beyond. They would also have seen that morning was still a long way off. Not something they would have minded much.

There were, of course, a few people, not many, but a few, who minded the lack of morning a great deal indeed. One of these was His Excellency Gnaeus Pompeius, President of the Republic, and popularly known as Pompey the Great. He had always hated social occasions. They made him feel boring. He knew he wasn't good at them, and that he always ended up being ignored by people who were. He also knew that there was a cruel irony here, since he was only forced to attend functions in the first place because he was important, and it didn't seem fair that people should then spend an entire evening rushing past him as though they didn't even know who he was. And even if they did, they plainly didn't care. Pompey shifted uncomfortably in his seat, and sighed.

"Ghastly event, Metellus," he muttered.

Metellus, a tall anguished-looking man in black, nodded his agreement. "Yes, Your Excellency." He nodded again. "Ghastly."

Pompey grunted with satisfaction. The ball was being held in Metellus' name, and officially, he was only there at his Minister's request. It gave him momentary gratification to think that his host was having, if anything, a worse time than himself. It seemed only just.

A party of ladies and young men rushed past them, laughing and screeching on their way down to the punts. One, a girl in a broad pink crinoline, tripped on her petticoats. Her companion, an exquisitely attired fop with an enormous wig, helped her to her feet with a flourish, and gave her a dainty kiss on each breast. There was a tremendous shriek of laughter and then they were running off again, hand in hand, down to the lakeside.

"Ghastly people, Metellus."

"Yes, Your Excellency."

"Where on earth did you find them all? Never realised you were such a sociable sort of fellow."

"Your Excellency is joking. You know full well that this is only nominally my party. I don't know a soul here. In fact, I wish I were a thousand miles away. Damn." Metellus' wig had fallen over his eyes. He pushed it back up and rebalanced it on his head, which was bald, and shaped like a cone.

Pompey watched his deputy and instinctively patted at his own wig. Then he gazed with gloom down at the brocade waistcoat stretched over his stomach, and wondered if he hadn't repeated Metellus' mistake by choosing a costume that drew attention straight to his most unflattering feature. Pompey didn't like to think of himself as fat, and usually managed not to – and yet tonight, there it was, unmistakable, a great bulge of stomach, slumping out from his frock coat. He felt lumpish and unhappy.

"I'm fat," he said suddenly, hoping to be contradicted.

He was.

"Not at all, Your Excellency. Damn."

With a sigh, Pompey clambered to his feet and watched as Metellus fiddled with his wig again. Pompey patted at his stomach. There was another long pause.

"So where is your brother-in-law?" Pompey asked eventually.

"Clodius, Your Excellency? Heaven alone knows."

"He was supposed to be here hours ago. That was the agreement. He knows we're only here so we can talk to him. Who the hell does he think I am, to be kept hanging around here like this?"

"Most unfortunate, Your Excellency. Sadly typical."

"How dare he? How bloody dare he?"

"I did advise you not to come here tonight, Your Excellency, if you remember. Clodius' manners are hardly to be be relied upon." Metellus stared at the President coldly. "In that, of course, they are like the man."

Pompey clasped his hands over his stomach in mute rage, and then hurriedly unclasped them again. "I'm going for a walk," he said after a pause.

"Oh yes? Where, may I ask, Your Excellency?"

"I don't know. Anywhere. But I'm going. I'll be back soon."

Pompey walked out of his tent and looked up. There was still no sign of morning in the sky.

Meanwhile, Catullus had discovered the ball. For the first time, he was on a road that led somewhere, and he could hear music again, faintly at first, then ever more clearly. Through the blackness, flecks of light began to glimmer. Suddenly, the avenue of trees fell away and Catullus stood enraptured by a glittering of whites and oranges and reds, splashes of light, scarcely dancing on the waters of a lake deep enough to still them, but with their gleam unextinguished, burning on. Like a grindstone, the ball scattered sparks throughout the night.

Catullus began to jog. The path had left the forest now and begun to follow the shoreline of the lake, but a high wooded cliff still obscured everything that was not the lake itself, the lake and one small island, floating, it seemed, on a blaze of light, with a wooden castle decorated with pennants and hung out with lamps. Tiny figures could be distinguished on the battlements, so far away that there was no point in shouting out and asking them how they had managed to cross the lake, or where there were boats to be found. Catullus continued to trot, and half-hope, half-fear that he would meet someone soon.

"Who's that?" a voice asked from ahead.

Someone was coming along the path.

"Come on, own up, whoever you are," the voice called out again. "Don't be naughty with mumkins."

"It's me," Catullus shouted back.

"You? Ah." The voice sounded unsurprised. Catullus trotted a few paces forward and the owner of the voice emerged, a young woman, striding purposefully towards him.

"I was just walking along the rocks," Catullus explained unnecessarily.

The woman studied him. She had an enormous lower lip, so pendulous, so glossy, so brightly painted, that Catullus realised he had been staring at it in amazement, and had to check himself. The lip began to shape itself into a broad smile. The woman behind it took a step forward, arms outstretched, and embraced Catullus in a haze of scent.

"Darling," she swooned, "you've been so naughty, haven't you?"

"I have?"

She waved a finger. "Oh, come now, you know you've been just the naughtiest, and Mummy Camilla isn't going to stand for it. No, you naughty boy, no excuses, I'm just the lividest. Where have you been all night? I've been here getting simply too bored for hours, and no one even said you were here!" She slapped Catullus playfully on the hand. Then she linked her arm around his, and began to lead him down towards the lake.

"Now then, since you're plainly a major party tart, you're going to come with me over to the island, okay? There should be a boat down here, oh yes, there it is, see? – at the end of the pier." She tugged at Catullus' arm. "Come on."

"I've got to row it?"

"But of course, I'm a petal." Camilla jumped into the boat; Catullus followed her. He picked up the oars, and Camilla nestled up against his lap. "All right, I'm ready now," she said. Catullus heaved at the oars. With two clumsy splashes, the boat began to move away.

Camilla nestled down even more snugly into Catullus' lap. "Now tell me where you've been hiding all evening," she demanded.

Catullus shrugged. "Oh, you know. Here and there."

Camilla's lip quivered suddenly. "Do you know, it's red face city, but I *absolutely* can't remember your name." She buried her face in embarrassment against Catullus' groin.

"Catullus," said Catullus. Camilla slapped him playfully on the arm, and pealed. "Of course it is! Of course it is! Swear pozzo it won't happen again! But you're naughty too, turning up late, just so you can make a late entry and get everyone talking about you, no, don't argue, I can read you like a book, do you really think you can pull that old one on me, young man?"

"No, actually, I don't know anyone. I haven't got the faintest idea what's going on. What is going on?"

Camilla laughed. "Don't play the hick with me!" She kissed him. The lip felt as it looked, damp and soft. "I like the castle," Catullus said hurriedly, turning in his seat, trying to escape a second kiss. Camilla smiled indulgently, and also twisted to look ahead. "You're joking," she said. "Or you're majorly ignorant about good taste. I think its *foul*. Big-sore-on-the-eye-ville. Poo-ee. I'm just breathing a big sigh of relief they're going to burn it down."

"What?"

"Burn it down." The indulgent smile returned. "Big bonfire. Don't say you haven't heard about it? Burning down Troy? You must have done."

"Well, yes, but..."

"It's the castle. That's what they're going to burn. *Big* bonfire. Major fun."

"Why do they want to burn it?"

"How can they have a Trojan party without burning something down?"

Catullus thought for a second. "So this is a Trojan party?"

"Two hundred percent it is."

"Why?"

"Because they wanted to burn something down, I guess. I don't know, why would you have a Trojan party?"

"I don't know."

Camilla laughed uproariously. She kissed him again and rested her hand on his chest. Catullus wondered what to do. The woman was clearly well-connected. He pecked her on the cheek, then looked hurriedly ahead again.

The far shore was no longer obscured by cliffs. Catullus could see great coloured marquees and lawns rolling down to the water's edge; there were more stone follies, and lights and banners everywhere, and crowds, sitting, or dancing, or strolling through the courts. "Whose party is this?" he asked involuntarily and at once regretted the question. But Camilla didn't seem to find it odd; "Clo's," she said. "And Clodius'. You really don't know them?"

"Not very well. No."

"I'm just the munchiest with them. Clo especially. We're just two fingers in the same glove together. She's a very lovely person, very. I love all my friends." Camilla began to run her fingers up and down Catullus' thigh. "Don't you think it's important? Loving your friends?"

Catullus looked at her. "Oh, I don't know. I hate most of mine."

"Now you're just saying that to be fashionable." Camilla winked, so heavily that she left mascara smudges over the top of her cheek bones. She smiled, and her lip glistened all the more as she gently squeezed Catullus' balls. "Surely you love your friends?"

There was a crash from behind them. Catullus leapt to his feet, and saw that the boat had run into the island's landing steps. He groped towards them and was beginning to pull the boat in when, suddenly, there was a shriek from behind him, so piercing that he almost fell into the lake with surprise.

"Clodius!" It was Camilla. "Munchkins! Come to Mummy!" She leapt to her feet and clattered up the steps. "It's such a *seriously* amazing party!"

Catullus looked up. Above him, on the end of the landing pier, stood – what? A woman? – or a man? The face was painted, beautiful even, in a heavy way, but no, it was too heavy, despite the thin lips and cheeks, which were both painted red, obscenely red, so yes, obviously a man. He was dressed as a man too, Catullus could see now, in a wig and frock coat, both very elegant, and he clutched at the wig as Camilla embraced him. "Who the hell invited you?" he asked rudely, pushing her away. "Or did you just smell it out as usual?"

Camilla ignored the question and kissed him expansively on his cheeks. "Clodius darling," she said, stepping back, "you look lovely." She slapped her lips together. "Munchy."

"Well, it's no thanks to you, slobbering over me." He brushed her away. "Now, if you don't mind, I've got a night's entertainment to oversee."

"But Clodius, we've only just met."

"Exactly."

"But Clodius..."

"No. Go away, Camilla, I don't want you. Shoo." He began to walk down the pier steps, towards a boat which was rocking gently in the breeze. "But I do need those clowns," he said suddenly, looking back behind him. "Where are they? Clowns!"

Lud and Pollo shimmered out from the dark. Neither glanced at Catullus, but scurried past him, down the steps. Clodius looked at them shortly and nodded; both clowns scrambled into the boat, and after settling their violin cases down by their feet, each one picked up an oar and hunched himself over it. They only looked up when Catullus, eager not to be left stranded on the island, ran down to Clodius and asked him for a lift.

"Who are you?" said Clodius, looking up at him.

"He's Catullus," shouted Pollo at once. "And he's a gatecrasher."

Clodius stared at the clown, and slowly shook his head. "Did I ask you for your opinion?" he said at last. "No. So keep your mouth shut – at all times. Understand?" Pollo nodded mutely. Clodius turned politely back to Catullus. "Now then – you want a lift?"

"If it's no trouble."

"But you've only just arrived here." Catullus shrugged. Clodius stared at him, then glanced at Camilla. There was a second's silence. "All right then, get in. But hurry – the night fades into morning even as we speak." Clodius settled himself down into the boat and Catullus scrabbled to join him. As the boat pulled away from the pier, Camilla blew it a kiss and waved; Catullus smiled, even though he could see that Clodius was sitting motionless, staring at him, frowning. When Catullus looked round a second time, Camilla had gone. He smiled again, and trailed his fingers through the cool water.

"So," said Clodius, leaning forwards, "you're a gatecrasher."

"Yes. Up to a point."

"Only a point?"

"Well, it was inadvertent. I didn't mean to come here. I got picked up."

"Oh?" Clodius sounded suddenly interested.
"In a carriage. I don't even know whose it was. I just got in."
"How remarkable."
"Maybe."
"Oh, it is, it is. It's very odd." Clodius nodded and leant back. "I don't often have gatecrashers, so I'm terribly flattered to have found one at last. I'm intrigued. Tell me everything, please." He rested his chin on his clasped fingers and waited. Catullus, wearily, began to talk.

In fact, everyone was weary now. But it was quite all right: you could yawn and talk about being dead on your feet, and even wish that the ball would end, because being tired was all part of the fun and made you realise just how late it was – or early, as people were starting to put it now, looking across at the first red streaks of morning in the east. Not that the night was over yet – no, it just meant that you could relax a bit, that things weren't quite so frenetic. The party swept on, in pools of light and noise. No one went to bed.

Some said they wanted to and meant it, but they just felt all the more excluded. Pompey, studying the early morning sky, could also see, from where he was standing on rocks by the lake, the dark rim of forest, an impenetrable band of darkness strung out between him and everything he was used to, busy streets, official papers, people who respected him and knew who he was. Catullus too, lying in the boat, imagined the woods as strange frontiers to a world he didn't understand and should never have reached. The figures on the far shore, for instance, dancing and jerking like tiny marionettes, made him feel even lonelier than he had been in the emptiness of the downs, and watching them, he slowly realised how tired he was, how heavy and slow his limbs had become. So tired. He began to struggle, desperately, to marshal his thoughts, all he had seen and heard that night, into some pattern that would explain them, link them at least; but even as he tried, he knew that it was no good, for he could feel a haze of tiredness dulling his mind, so that memories were left distinct but unassociated, dashes of colour on shifting grey. Each sound he heard – the rhythms of far away conversations, the splash of oars through the water, his own voice talking about all the things he had seen – was dimmed and echoed. Everything seemed so far away. Catullus looked and listened, with a furious concentration, as though he were trying to understand a foreign language spoken too fast, but it was no good, no, he was too exhausted by his efforts, he would have to give up. The night outside began to dissolve and reform. Catullus wondered if he was dreaming that he was awake or imagining his sleep.

Clodius began to talk. His painted lips minuetted delicately, red against white. "Isn't that odd," he was saying, "you coming to Troy by accident? Like Achilles – long haired, beautiful, doomed Achilles. Doomed to die, so that Troy might burn. Do you think that's you?" He laughed, and Catullus blinked, and tried to understand.

"I'm not Achilles," he heard himself say.

Clodius laughed again, delighted. "Did I say you were? I was wondering, spinning a fancy, that was all." He lowered his blackened eyelashes and smiled. "You know," he said, looking up again, "I've never been able to fathom how the Trojans got taken in by that stupid horse. They were such a clever race, by all accounts. In fact, I don't think it's possible. The Greeks must have lied. It must have been the Greeks who were burnt. Can you imagine it? The horror in their faces as they answer Helen and hear the flames being lit? Exquisite." Clodius nodded, and his eyes gleamed as though he were drunk. He looked suddenly at Lud. "What do you think? Don't you think it's exquisite?"

Lud made no answer. Pollo too, after glancing quickly round, froze his face back into passivity. The two of them, white masks gashed with black and red, seemed hideous parodies of the man they served; all three faces glowed palely at Catullus from the far end of the boat, so that he imagined, as his tiredness deepened and the water around them became darker and ever more still, that they were all passengers on some unreal ship of the dead. By now, the boat was slipping past black rocks, into a tiny unlit cove, the splash of oars echoing increasingly above the strains of music that could still, just faintly, be distinguished over the lake. At last, an oar scraped something; there was a crunching of shingle from under the keel. The clowns stopped rowing and Clodius leapt to his feet.

"Well, go on," he shouted at Catullus. "Pull us up. I don't give you free lifts just so that you can sit there all night."

Catullus did as he was told. He had imagined, all the way across, that his limbs would be unliftable, but in fact, as he climbed onto the beach, hauled up the boat, made his way up the rocky path, he felt as though he were made of air, as though his body scarcely existed at all. From the crest of the rocks he looked out over the lawns and courtyards spread out below, and saw them, like his own thoughts, swimming away.

"Come with me," ordered Clodius, seizing him by the arm. "I want you by my side. You two – stay here." Lud and Pollo sat themselves down on a rock and stared up mutely. "Be ready with that piece you played earlier. I'll call you when I want it."

Clodius pulled Catullus up a higher path. He stopped at the top of a cliff and looked around. There was a clump of ash trees and in front of them, sitting on the rocks that looked out over the lake, a large man in a gold brocade waistcoat, with his shoulders hunched against the dawn. Clodius walked up behind him and coughed.

"Your Excellency."

Pompey turned round, surprised.

"Who..? Ah, Clodius, it's you. About bloody time." His eyes narrowed. "What are you doing made up as a woman? Isn't that a bit excessive?"

"I don't think so. Not in the circumstances."

The man frowned suspiciously. "Well – if you think it's necessary."

"It makes the point." Clodius paused. "I like your waistcoat."

"Do you? I don't. I think it makes me look fat. Metellus assures me it doesn't, but how can you trust someone who insists on wearing a wig when he's got a pyramid for a head?"

"Ah, my dear brother-in-law. Where is he?"

"Over there, sulking in the trees. He kept tagging me around. I got fed up with it. Told him to leave me alone till you were ready."

"Well" – Clodius gestured with his arms – "I'm ready now."

"And?"

"All in good time. Come on – why don't we sit over here and wait for the fireworks?" Clodius led Pompey to a bench further along the cliff, looking out over the island. "Will this do?"

"Lovely." Pompey eased himself onto the bench and Clodius turned to shout into the trees. "Come on! We're ready!" There was a rustling and Metellus appeared, still clutching his wig firmly onto his head. "Good morning," he said stiffly. He pointed at Catullus. "What's he doing here?"

"He's my gatecrasher," said Clodius, introducing him. Catullus shook hands, first with Pompey, then with Metellus. He looked at the bench, slumped onto it, and curled up. Pompey stared at him in some surprise. "Is he all right?" he asked. "He doesn't look it."

"He's fine," Clodius assured him.

"Looks as if he's been having as good a time as me." Pompey grunted to himself. "You'd better have what I want, Clodius. I need a pick-me-up. It's been a bloody awful evening."

"Oh, I am sorry to hear that. I thought you'd find it all wonderfully apt."

"Apt? Bloody tasteless, I'd have said – in the circumstances. Hmm..." Pompey stroked his stomach meditatively, then looked up. "Good – well – to business. What have you got for me?"

"Well – a decision really. That's all you wanted, wasn't it?" Metellus stirred uneasily but Clodius ignored him. Gently, he began to stroke his powdered chin. "I face certain problems," he said smoothly. "You understand that. As leader of the Republic's main association of unions, I have a duty to consider my supporters' legitimate interests. These are hard times. My supporters have a lot of legitimate interests."

"Oh, for God's sake!" said Metellus indignantly. "I don't know why we're bothering to sit here, and listen to all this talk again. It's just the same old story, isn't it? Legitimate interests, more money. The Government can't afford it. The country can't afford it. What on earth are we doing here?"

"Listening," said Pompey, "listening. So shut up." He nodded at Clodius, and Clodius, nodding back, continued.

"I looked at the papers and reports you gave me." Metellus stirred again uneasily, but Pompey stilled him with a lazy swish of the hand, and Clodius carried on. "I'm quite prepared to accept everything that the studies are saying. I hadn't realised things were quite as bad as they obviously are, and I needed to. I have about as much interest in seeing an economic freefall as you do. So – up to a point, I am quite willing to accept your proposals. The whole committee is."

"Up to a point?"

"Yes, of course. We need to have something if we're going to call off an industrial dispute that we're on the verge of winning."

Pompey sighed and threw his hands up in the air. "But I thought you'd accepted that no one was winning."

"Oh, yes, I have. You have. The various committees that run things have. But my followers – they haven't really had the chance yet."

Pompey snorted. "Well? Go on, then. What do you want?"

"Okay – we'll abandon industrial action against wage freezings, devaluation, your austerity measures, whatever. But – in return – we need a negotiated minimum wage, and representation on any commissions and unofficial planning boards. We can specify which ones exactly later, if you agree in principle now. Reasonable?"

"What else do you want?"

"Complete confidentiality."

"Of course. What else?"

"And..." Clodius stretched, and smiled. "And... There are certain parties... who won't welcome our – what is it? – our partnership – however excellent and patriotic our motives."

"Such as?" said Metellus at once. "Who do you mean?"

Clodius frowned and waved his hand. "You know who I mean."

"This is outrageous."

"Not at all. You know as well as I do that they're on virtual suspended convictions. It's just a matter of clearing up a few judicial anomalies. It should be no problem. And it has to be done."

"You'd drop all your demands to keep wages on a level with inflation?" Pompey asked slowly.

"Yes."
"You could guarantee it?"
"Yes. Of course."
"Hm."
Pompey stared out at the lake in silence. "When do the fireworks begin?" he asked after a long pause.
Clodius took a watch out from his waistcoat pocket. "Any minute."
"It wouldn't do at all to talk through a fireworks display."
"No, Your Excellency."
"Bad form."
"Yes, Your Excellency."
"Hm."
Pompey looked out towards the island again.
"You may have noticed that there were some men outside the gates this evening."
Clodius shrugged. "It had been brought to my attention."
"I thought it might be wise to have them there. Just to keep an eye on things. Keep a check on people. For everyone's good."
"Of course."
Pompey nodded to himself. "Well – they've been removed. Earlier this evening." He turned back to Clodius. "I see no reason to regret that decision." He pointed out to the lake. "Is that the fire starting? Over there by the castle?"
"Yes, so it is. Right on time. The fireworks will be leaping into action any moment too." Clodius climbed to his feet. "Your Excellency – will you excuse me? Just for a few minutes."
"We'll need to talk."
Clodius shook his hand. "I give you a gentleman's agreement."
"I'll want a damn sight more than that. Still – it can wait. Should I wake your friend, do you think? It would be kind, wouldn't it? I'm sure he'd hate to miss the fun."
"That would be most considerate." Clodius bowed. "Your Excellency. I think this is going to be an agreement neither of us will regret." He bowed again, then turned and began to walk away. Pompey shifted in his seat and gave Catullus a heavy nudge in the stomach. Catullus woke up, immediately. A face was staring down at him – hadn't he been introduced to it, just before he'd fallen asleep, or had he seen it from somewhere before? It was familiar. "I thought you might like to watch the fireworks," the face said. "Thank you, thank you very much," replied Catullus blearily. He sat up, and his eyeballs were stung by a blaze of light. It was from the castle. They were burning it, and the gates and battlements were collapsing under the flames. Great areas of the lake looked as though they were boil-

ing beneath the reflections, and sparks flew like midges over the water.

Catullus rubbed his eyes and yawned. He opened his eyes again; there was a sudden explosion of colour in the sky, and a vast cheer from behind the trees as the ball-goers applauded the first hail of fireworks.

"They're good, aren't they?" Clodius had come back, and stood leaning on the bench behind his guests. "I think I prefer the bonfire, though. I've always wanted to see Troy burn. It should go on for hours."

It did. Long after the final scatterings of gold and pink had trailed away into early morning light and the cheers from the gardens faded and died, the castle blazed on with undiminished fury. The crash of falling timbers and steady crackle of burning wood began to blend with the first scattered songs of birds and become, in the minds of all those gazing towards the eastern skies, an overture to the rising day. Catullus listened and shut his eyes and allowed his thoughts to drift, so that he didn't at first hear other sounds, music, from behind his back, where Pollo and Lud had been ordered to play, quietly at first, the notes hanging over the rocks, then the theme forming and gradually deepening, becoming ever more complex, rising in the end, as Clodius had wished it to do, to pattern the morning and the dying flames. Catullus wanted to listen but he was sleeping again, and he could feel himself falling, even as he struggled to open his eyes; soon even his memory of the fire had been dimmed, surely he was asleep now, yes, he could remember nothing now, he was asleep, but still the music played, and Catullus could hear it, hanging over his sleep, and its theme was playing through his mind, and it kept on playing, even as he dreamed, and it rose and shaped, and it continued to be there.

He woke suddenly. The music had gone. Everything was silent. The sun felt hot on his eyeballs and the light too clear, too harsh. He looked out. A wide stain of black was smoking on the island; by his feet, the grass had been trampled; otherwise, there was nothing, nothing to suggest that the night and its enchantments had ever existed, or not just melted away on the first second of morning. He ran his hands through his hair. Disgusting. Everything about him felt disgusting. He stood up, and felt even worse.

"I didn't wake you, did I? Sorry if I did."

Catullus turned in surprise. A woman had been standing behind the bench – bare arms, black dress. The woman from the carriage.

"Hello. What are you doing here?"

"Nothing much." She sat down on the bench. "Why, does it matter?"

"No." Catullus stared at her stupidly. "I just thought everyone had gone, that was all."

"Of course they haven't. It's only six o' clock." She pointed towards the trees. "Though they'll be going soon, I suppose. That's why I'm here, actually – I don't want to go until everyone else has left. I don't want to have to speak to them. I hate it, having to talk to people this early in the morning, it gets me in a bad mood for the rest of the day."

"Aren't you afraid you'll have to talk to me?"

She grinned. She was much prettier when she grinned, Catullus thought, much prettier. Why was that? Because she looked too tired when she didn't. She had plump cheeks, and her hair was very black and glossy, and her eyes were lined heavily with black as well, but when she didn't smile she seemed too small for her own face, too fed up with her own attractiveness, because she was attractive, there could be no doubt about that, even though she was tired and plump and all her make-up had smudged. He was staring at her too much, Catullus realised, but he couldn't help it, and not just because he found her so attractive. No, he felt a sudden pang, now that the sun had risen and it was a day just like any other day, and everything seemed ordinary again. He needed to identify the odd snatch of memory, identify and capture it, so that he would have a bulwark against looming ordinariness, and all the nights when something magical would not occur. Only the woman beside him was left now, a final echo of the enchantment as she had been its harbinger, and Catullus stared at her greedily in the way that anyone, about to leave a place rich in memories, studies it for a significance he discovers he has neglected, and is now aching to understand and preserve.

"You do remember me, don't you?" the lady asked suddenly.

Catullus smiled. "Of course I remember you. You brought me here, to this" – he searched for a suitable word, and gave up – "place."

"You enjoyed yourself then?"

"Sort of. I was a bit afraid people would know I was a gatecrasher."

"How could you have been a gatecrasher?"

"I wasn't invited."

"Don't be silly, I invited you."

"When?"

"When I picked you up. Surely that was obvious?"

"You didn't say."

"You didn't ask."

"No. I suppose not."

The woman turned, and raised her face to meet the sun. "Anyway," she said suddenly, "you spent all evening with Clodius, didn't you, and he knew you weren't a gatecrasher."

"You know Clodius?"

"He's my brother."

"Really?" Catullus tried to remember if he had been told anything about Clodius' sister. Something Camilla had said? "Are you Clo?" he asked, remembering.

"No. I hate being called Clo. I'm Clodia. Clodia Metella. You met Metellus as well, I think. My husband. He was with my brother."

"Which one? There was a fat one. Oh – sorry. But he was *fat*."

Clodia laughed, and her eyes sparkled with delight. "No, not the fat one. The thin one. With the pointed head. He's my husband. Can you believe it?"

Catullus shrugged. "I don't really remember him."

Clodia laughed again. "I have the same problem." Her smile now, as she threw her hair back and closed her eyes against the sun, had a curl of lazy feline grace. "Why can't you look more cheerful?" she said at last, when she saw that Catullus was still staring at her. "Look happy. You don't look happy at all. Life's a ball. Smile."

Catullus smiled, briefly, through his teeth. "I'm not happy," he said. "I've got too much to do."

Clodia kissed him on the cheek. "Tell me about it," she whispered.

"I've got to get to Rome."

"And that's where you were heading yesterday? Oh God! I'm sorry. I brought you miles out of your way, didn't I?" She reached forward, and kissed him on the cheek again. "I suppose you're angling for another lift."

Catullus stared at her. Her smile was soft again, as soft as her lips had felt against his skin. "Yes," he said at last. "I suppose I am."

Clodia shook her head. "Sorry, I've got to stay on here, I'm afraid." There was a rustle of skirts as she stood up from the bench. "But I tell you what – why don't we go and find someone else?" She held out her hand. "Come on."

Catullus didn't bother to conceal his disappointment. "I'll walk, thank you."

"What, to the station? It's a long way. You didn't meet anyone else last night, did you? Who we could ask?"

"Camilla?"

"Camilla? You met Camilla? God, you really bumped into them, didn't you? Metellus and Camilla. Oh dear." She shook her head, then glanced at her watch, and took Catullus' arm. They began to walk across the lawns.

"Thought of someone?"

"You can go with the showmen. They'll be off now. I'm sure you'll find one who's going to the station." She pointed to a road by the edge of the lawns, where men were busy packing up trucks and vans. "Over there. Ask them."

"Are you off?"

"Afraid so." She looked at her watch again. "Got to get everything tidied up." She kissed him quickly. "I hope it was all worth the coach ride."

Catullus nodded.

Clodia turned, then glanced back at him, and suddenly took his hand. "I'm sure we'll meet again," she said. "I would like that, very much." She nodded, and the sun caught the gold of earrings, four or five of them, gleaming against the deep black of her hair. She reached up to kiss him, on the lips at last, then turned again, and Catullus watched her as she hurried away across the lawn. He realised that he had forgotten to ask her about the men they had seen by the entrance in the forest, about the second coach with the eagle on it, about a whole legion of mysteries, and his ache to understand what he had seen seemed suddenly confused with his thoughts of Clodia, as though both were objects of the same desire. Looking around him, at the lights and marquees being taken down, dismantled before his very eyes, Catullus felt almost that he had been given a text to read, a poem, an imposition of meaning on the night that he had nevertheless failed to understand, and now it was morning, and the sun was in his eyes. He searched for Clodia, but she had gone, as though melted by the light. Catullus swore to himself. Time for him to be off as well.

He walked up to a man who was loading a small stall onto a van.

"Please could I have a lift?" he asked.

The man looked at him.

"Where are you going?"

"The station. For Rome. I'd be vastly grateful."

There was a pause. Then the man gestured with his thumb. "In the back. But I'm going now, all right?" Catullus nodded. His head had begun to thump in time to the hammer blows from the lawn, and he barely noticed how uncomfortable the tarpaulins and wooden frames in the back were, as he clambered over them, and nestled himself down. The driver turned his ignition key and the engine slowly choked into life. Catullus listened to it as the van started to move, rolling and bumping its way down the track, taking him from the ball. With one last sudden effort of excitement, he craned his neck out of the back. He could see the island, and the lake, and all the lawns spread out before it, and then the van turned and swung into the forest, and Troy and the estate were left behind.

II

ROME

The train swung and creaked past fields becoming suburbs. Catullus could feel excitement gathering within him. Rome couldn't be far now. Even the air felt heavier. When Catullus moved up from his seat, the leather would suck at his back and a hot blast from the window pound him on the face. He was moist with sweat, and wondered if he looked crazed. Not that he could give a fuck either way.

"Tickets please."

A guard had come in from the far end of the carriage. Catullus watched him as he moved slowly past each passenger, glumly taking tickets, stamping them, then just as glumly handing them back. Catullus felt sorry for him. There was no magic in the name of Rome for him. Had he ever travelled to the great city for the first time? Had he enjoyed it? Catullus pressed his face to the window again, with the anxiety of a miser who needs to touch all he owns, penny by penny, and still worries that something, somewhere, is being frittered away.

"Ticket."

Catullus handed it over.

"When do we arrive in Rome, please?"

"Four twenty, next stop after this."

The guard stamped the ticket, and handed it back. Catullus returned to the window. The hot blast from the windows was fading now; the train was slowing down. Suddenly there was a rasp of brakes, a jolt, and then stillness. The platform outside was small and tatty; litter, flattened by the heat and commuters' footsteps, hugged the stone; warm paint glistered; a large poster thanked people for using Rome Regional Railways. 'Fuck Rome Regional Railways,' someone had added underneath.

A few passengers sloped past Catullus into the carriage. They smelt of heat and overwork. To Catullus, though, they seemed privileged beings, people who lived just a single stop from Rome, and excited by the thought, he looked back at the platform and read the station's name out loud, redeeming it, melting it into the promise of the city it announced. There was a sudden jerk – the train was moving again. Moving – towards; Catullus rolled the sound on his tongue and savoured it as though he were tasting a sherbet ball; Rome. Rome. He could say it now, as often as he liked, now that he was almost there, he could think about it as luxuriantly as he wanted to, about all he had ever read and imagined, about the men who had lived there, governing, writing, inspiring, fighting, about its history and dark beauty and cruel scenes; so much poetry in just the single word; he rolled it again; Rome. As the city neared, so Catullus could feel his imagination soaring to meet it. He leaned forward again, and this time pressed his nose right up against the window pane. He rubbed it up and down, then checked himself, smiling. What was he doing? Frigging himself? No need. No need.

Gradually, the train began to quicken again. However intently Catullus tried to study the city as it loomed past him, he could feel it slipping his eyes and understanding; he discovered, to his shock, that even though he was now looking at Rome, it seemed as unreal as it had always done from the isolation of his room at home. Hunched streets and houses appeared, then went, piles of rust and tyres, people walking on pavements, standing, talking, not looking up as the train with Catullus on board sped past them, and on, through Rome's outer wards now, their names glimpsed briefly on station boards, Corolla, Cestius, Quirinale, colonising grey streets with the richness of their sound, each syllable belonging there, only there, nowhere else. There was a whistle and a thump, a tunnel, then out again, past new towers sleek this time, and white, high and regular over the tangles of wire and litter still running along the side of the tracks, and then the train was dipping down between two walls made from dirty red brick and it was obvious, when the walls fell away again, that the towers had been sentinels on the ancient limits of Rome, for between more towers and rows of houses, Catullus could now catch occasional glimpses of water, a river, and of course Rome had only one river, and everyone knew where that flowed, right through its heart! Then at last, a heavy lurch and the train had swung away from the inchoate mess of buildings and was actually running along the banks of the Tiber, following it as the river bent away towards the Senate House. Catullus knew what lay beyond that great curve – bridges, domes, crane spiked wharves, lining the river as far as Ostia and on, out to the sea, he knew, he had seen so many pictures, and now here he was. His stomach tightened and so did the brakes. The train began to slow, and for a brief moment the great sights of Rome stood framed between the piercing still blue of the sky and the muddy Tiber waters, and then the train swung away and the famous view was lost.

The train creaked slowly up to its platform. Catullus could hear departure times sounding from the intercom now, and read a large sign in red and white plastic, 'Welcome to Zama'. In a minute he would be standing on Rome's concrete, smelling its air, feeling its heat on his brow; he would never again come to Rome for the first time. The train stopped. Catullus swung open the carriage door. He had arrived in Rome.

Caelius felt pissed off, and since he'd been desperate not to feel pissed off that afternoon, he felt more than usually pissed off about feeling pissed off. He'd been eating a doughnut and a large blob of jam had dripped out of it onto his jacket. The jacket was new, bought especially to impress Catullus shitless, and now it had a bloody massive dollop of jam smeared right across it and to make matters worse, two girls had seen it happen, and started laughing, and whenever he looked up at them they started giggling again. Caelius licked his finger and tried to rub at the jam stain without being noticed; he glanced up; one of the girls tossed her hair back, and the other slowly cracked up into giggles again, and started tossing her hair back too. Why did they all do it like that, that sort of girl, the sort that was always richer than him, and younger, and had lived in Rome all her life, and spoke three languages probably, the bitch? Caelius kicked at a bin. Pathetic. He wandered off, and when he looked back over his shoulder, the two girls had been joined by their boyfriends and were no longer watching him. The boyfriends were rich and beautiful, of course. God, life could be cruel.

So where was Catullus? Caelius glanced up at the arrivals board. It was his friend's fault he'd had to come to the station in the first place, and now the fucker hadn't even been able to turn up on time. Caelius wondered if the looming reconciliation would be an embarrassment. A year was a long time to be separated, after all, a lot could change in a year, an awful lot, and no doubt it had. Yes – no doubt. Caelius smiled at the thought of his friend. He'd be so deliciously naive. First time in Rome, with a crap archaeology degree and literary leanings. Caelius wondered if his friend still had his literary leanings, and hoped that he did. His smile broadened.

There was an announcement. Catullus' train was approaching the station. Caelius began to wander down the platform, nonchalantly – he didn't want to go too far, it would be very undignified to be at the wrong end of the train and then have to come running back. His luck held. As he stood there, striking a raffish pose, a look of bemused indulgence gracing his lips, the carriage door opposite him swung open, and out stumbled Catullus.

Catullus stared at his friend. Then he reached out to hold him, to kiss him on the mouth, but Caelius turned his head and Catullus was forced to brush his lips across the cheek. He flushed, and took a step back. Caelius began to smile.

"You've got jam all over your jacket," Catullus said at last.

"I know."

"Still. Hasn't spoilt it too badly."

"I should hope not. It's actually very expensive."

"Is it really?" There was another brief pause. Catullus looked about him. "So this is Rome," he said eventually. "Wow."

"Yes." Caelius rubbed his hands together. "Want to head off and see it, then?"

"You've found a flat?"

"Yes."

"And there's still a room for me?"

"Of course. Only I've nicked the best one."

"Oh, naturally, I'm naive and rural, you just push me around as much as you like." Catullus picked up his shoulder bag and began to walk. "Let's go."

He glanced at his friend, and felt a prickle of pain. All right, so Caelius wanted to play it cool – fuck him. There were plenty of other factors that made this moment precious. Catullus gazed up and around him again, concentrating hard, determined not to fritter his first experiences in Rome – they were far too valuable, flecks of gold, to be panned by his consciousness, then lingered over and stored up in his memories. He walked past the platform and out into the main station; high above his head, girded flights of metal arched and soared; Caelius spoke to him but he was too rapt; he looked round, to ask Caelius what he had said, and Caelius pointed with his arm. Catullus turned back and saw a small man in a hat running straight towards him. He put out his arms and shouted, but the small man was running too fast, and didn't notice Catullus until he had collided with him, and been sent sprawling onto the station floor.

"Oh dear, I am a clumsy great oaf," the man laughed, scrabbling around for his hat while staring up at Catullus. "Like an elephant, wouldn't you say, with concrete boots on? Ha ha ha. Or perhaps I'm being unfair to elephants. I wouldn't know, I've never met one. Ha ha."

He took Catullus' hand and pulled himself up. "Ha ha ha," he rocked, "oh dear, oh dear." He stared at Catullus in sudden silence. Then he jabbed a finger out and prodded him in the chest. "You were at the ball, weren't you?"

Catullus frowned. "The fancy-dress ball, you mean? The Trojan ball?"

"Yes, yes, last night. And now here we are, meeting up again. What a coincidence!" He smiled knowingly. "Or is it? Ha ha ha. What do you think?"

"But I've never met you before. At least I don't think I have. Have I?"

"Well, ha ha, that raises a number of interesting philosophical questions, doesn't it? If you think you have never met me does that provide a subjectivity that is the only knowable reality and is that reality therefore in turn something that is more than purely phenomenal? What's your opinion?"

"I haven't the faintest."

"Ha ha! A pragmatist!" The small man leant forward and winked. "But of course, we are both men of the world, and we have to admit that the beauties of philosophy, sometimes, fail to fill in every detail. For instance, ha ha – I might have seen you at the ball, and yet you not have seen me, simply because it is my role in life never to be seen." He nodded. "Now what do you say to that? It is not, ha, *profound*, but as an explanation it serves. Wouldn't you say?"

Catullus stared at him. "You've been spying on me? Why?"

The man grinned. "Well – I'd never seen you before."

"So?"

"So? You were in the company of a beautiful and celebrated lady. I was intrigued."

"You mean Clodia?" Catullus asked, and felt his heart leap stupidly as he pronounced her name.

"Yes, yes." The man nodded, so vigorously that his Adam's apple seemed to bounce in and out. "Were the arteries pattering? Cupids chirruping?"

"No," said Catullus, a little too insistently. He turned to Caelius. "She just picked me up."

"Oh, did she?" The man cocked his head, like a bird scanning a grub. He tittered. "Picked you up?"

"No, not like that."

"No?"

"No."

The man looked disappointed. "Oh dear, I am sorry. It's my besetting fault. Always hoping to find tender hearts, wherever I look. Ah well." He chuckled to himself and looked up suddenly. "All right, then. What about Clodius?"

"The transvestite?"

"Ha ha ha! Yes, if you like. That's the one."

"No, I'd never met him before either."

The man blinked. "Really?"

"Yes, really. Why?"

The man clapped a hand up to his mouth. "Well, that is puzzling!" He began to laugh again, so uncontrollably that he had to wipe a sludge of gummy tears from his eyes. "What were you doing there, then?" he finally gasped. "Why on earth had they brought you? It's all most strange! Ha ha ha! Quite a riddle. Do you like riddles?"

Catullus shrugged. "There's a time and a place. This isn't it."

"Now, now." The small man patted him on the back. "Whatever befalls, you must always keep your sense of humour. Ha ha ha." He tapped the side of his nose, then picked up the bag he had dropped in the collision. "I must be off. I hear time at my back, ha, *delightful* though our little chat has been. And I hope you've enjoyed it too," he added, turning to Caelius, "although I'm afraid I know nothing about you and so, ha, have nothing *directly* relevant to contribute to you personally." He shook hands. "Just remember, the two of you, always keep an eye open for the amusing side of life. That can be so important." He shook hands again, and tilted his hat. "We'll be meeting again soon, I'm sure. In the meantime, goodbye. Goodbye."

The small man started to hurry away, nodding all the time like a jogging ostrich. He had soon disappeared, and Catullus and Caelius were left staring at each other and shaking their heads.

"What a strange man," said Caelius. "What the hell was he on?"

Catullus stared at him. "Haven't the faintest," he said at last.

"Well, what was he talking about?"

"I don't know."

"What was this ball?"

"You heard me say. I don't know."

"But you went to it? And you fell in love – with a woman, did he say?"

"Don't, Caelius." He stared into his friend's eyes. Nothing there, just an amused gleam. Catullus turned away. "It's not important. Couldn't you tell he was just fucking me about?"

"No. It sounded like instead of turning up in Rome last night, which don't forget you were supposed to do, you went off to a ball given by someone rather important, which I thought sounded an interesting thing to have done, and so I wanted to know what happened. Surely that's reasonable? Don't be so fucking grumpy about everything."

"I'm sorry. It's just..." Catullus yawned. "I'm too tired."

Caelius shrugged. "All right. I can wait. No need to start fighting yet. We've got plenty of time for that later." He pointed towards the Underground. "Come on. One last train, I'm afraid. Then you can go to bed."

"I'm not in a bad mood."

"Of course not. It's just it's your first time in Rome, isn't it? Come on."

He wrapped an arm round Catullus's waist and began to steer him across the platform. Catullus glowered in silent resentment. He'd forgotten how infuriating Caelius could be, how superior. So what if he'd been on the Underground thousands of times? – the whole point for Catullus was that this was his first time and he didn't want to be made to feel inadequate, he wanted to relish the novelty, so he would just have to concentrate and not let Caelius get to him. He smelt the air and looked about deliberatively – black-stained steps, ticket barriers, the outer rim of a new and untested pool of experience which loomed unknown, waiting for him, as other strange pools, in the forest, by the lake, in the ancient heart of Rome, had also loomed and waited unknown. He broke free from Caelius and walked up to the barriers, then cursed himself when he heard Caelius laughing, and turned to see him pointing at a ticket machine. Catullus paid his fare and when he saw Caelius waiting for him again, by the head of the escalator, with a fat smirk on his face, Catullus walked past him with only the wateriest of smiles and began to move down the escalator, not looking behind to see if Caelius was following him. He stared into the distance ahead, and heard wild chords from some hidden musician soaring through the dark, reaching high over him and all the countless other travellers, shaping itself to the groined shaft arching above, emptying Catullus' mind of Caelius and all other thoughts and noise, so that the music, rising and falling, unbroken by pause, seemed not only to heighten but become a wholly new feeling of strangeness. He passed a sweaty, badly dressed man with a saxophone, and tossed a few coins onto his coat; then he followed a sign into new tunnels and the music began to fade on the air, dimmed out by the clash of thousands of feet on the metal flooring, from ahead and behind him, round corners or down yet more flights of stairs, so that it seemed to be sounding from everywhere, an endless metal rhythm, beating the approach to the platforms like a drum.

"If you go handing out cash to every wino you see, you won't have any left and then you'll have to become a wino yourself," muttered Caelius as they waited together for a train.

"I liked the music."

Caelius shrugged. "So? Doesn't mean you've got to pay for it."

The tunnel walls shuddered. Catullus glanced at Caelius despite himself, and Caelius nodded back. The train came to a halt, and the two friends pressed themselves aboard, then waited, for two, five, ten minutes. Still the train didn't move. Catullus groaned. He peered through the window, at the posters on the opposite wall; one showed an observatory, silhouetted against a blaze of stars, but before Catullus had had time barely to glance at it, he heard the slicing of doors, and the train lurched away. The poster was lost.

"Here you go," said Caelius, shoving a newspaper against his chest, "that's probably what all the delays are about."

Catullus twisted his neck to study the headline, 'TRANSPORT AND EMERGENCY SERVICES STRIKE ADDS TO ECONOMIC

GLOOM.' Catullus glanced up at his friend. "A total strike?" he asked. "So we could all get burnt to a crisp and no one would even lift a finger?"

"Read it."

Catullus sighed, and scanned down a column of newsprint. Misery piled up on misery in each successive paragraph. Selective strikes in all emergency areas. Demands in the Senate for the army to be brought in. Calls for a vote of no confidence against the Government. Other news – a further catastrophic fall in productivity. Further job losses. Bullying comments from Caesar. Disaster, disaster, disaster. An unfunny cartoon. Catullus shook his head, then handed the paper back.

"Aren't you interested?"

"Not really. Not at the moment." He felt depressed. So papers looked just the same in Rome as they had always done back home in Verona – they were still full of bad news, the shit economy, tensions with Caesar, the endless strikes – there was no change at all. Somehow, irrationally, Catullus felt disappointed. He had been hoping that in Rome itself the news might seem a little less dispiriting, that it would be impossible to be in the capital and still believe in all the stories of failure and decay. No, he hadn't really hoped that, he realised, it was just that in his excitement, he had forgotten that all the stories described a shabby, declining city he didn't want to know about, not yet at least. That was why he hadn't wanted to read the paper. How typical of Caelius to have given it to him. Catullus looked outside as the train pulled into another station. They were beyond the central zone now, he could see from the map. The platforms were black, and rotting posters hung half torn from the walls.

"Feeling more cheerful?" Caelius asked.

"Not really."

"What's the matter, baby?"

Catullus stared at him. "I'd like you to show me some affection, actually. Is that too much to ask for? It's been a long time, Caelius. Or at least it's seemed that way to me."

Caelius smiled. "Sorry." He reached for Catullus' hand and squeezed it. "Really, I'm sorry." He paused. "Tell me about this ball."

"Don't change the subject."

"Did you really meet Clodius?"

"You know him?"

"Of him. From my uncle. He's a most newsworthy character."

"Then why haven't I heard about him?"

"You probably have. He's..."

"What?"

"I can't remember."

"Why not?"

"I'm prone to these fits of forgetfulness."

Catullus shrugged and turned away. Caelius pulled him back round.

"This evening. We'll talk then. When you've slept."

"Really talk?"

Caelius stared at him, then inclined his head. "Yes, if you feel we have to."

"I do." Catullus nodded. "All right, then. Tonight."

"Good. Because actually, I have to be frank, you need some sleep. You're not at your best right now. Wake up nice and refreshed. Also, it means we can put the introductions off till you're in a better mood."

The words slipped unnoticed past Catullus' mind. Then he suddenly woke up to them.

"Introductions? Who to?"

"To whom. To all the people you're going to be living with."

"Fuck."

"Exactly. Since I know them, I can concur with the use of that word."

Catullus picked gingerly at his lip. "Okay. Go on."

"Okay. The prize arse is Tubbers. He's our flat mate, I'm afraid. In fact, thinking about it, don't bother meeting him, put him off for as long as possible. But even if you do skip him, there's no respite. Because you're still left with Mummy Dugbal, a hideously fat crone who lurks with her brood on the ground floor and who unfortunately happens to be your landlady. She's got a husband who's mad, and two loathsome children. That's the lot, I think."

"Oh. Goody."

Caelius snorted. "Why did you ever come here? Why did I ever come here? It's such a shit hole. Boo hoo hoo. I want to go home."

"The green, green grass of home."

"Yes." Caelius looked up, as the train began to slow. "And what do we have instead? The brown, brown shit of Rome." The train stopped and the doors slid open. "Come on." He led Catullus out onto the platform and stood with his arms uplifted. "Home!" Then he sobbed and bent down over his bag.

There was no one to see him, except Catullus, who stood and listened to the dripping of water from bare, far off tunnels. He could imagine them, black, heavy, smelling of condensation and paper, like the platform he was standing on. "Everything's so fucking squalid, isn't it?"

Caelius frowned at him, looking suddenly annoyed. "Well, what did you expect for the rent you're going to be paying? It's probably best to think of it as being vital. I may go on about it, but it's not too bad really. Promise. You'll learn to love it."

"I feel so depressed."

"Don't be. This is Rome. Ornament of the world, matchless Rome."

"I know."

"Just give it time. This is the most exciting city in the world, don't forget." Caelius turned and began to head down the platform. Catullus followed him, into a tunnel, and then on, up dark winding stairs. With each step, he could feel his excitement of the afternoon fading away, and imagined it to be the echo of a heavy bell, a sounding memory of something real, but dying at the same time into thick silence. Really, he couldn't hope to enjoy squalor on two hours sleep.

"What's this place called?" he shouted after Caelius.

"Tallowfield."

Catullus walked out through the Underground entrance and looked down the High Street.

"Nice."

"It's a very up and coming area actually. Give it a couple of years and it'll really arrive."

"So why did we have to be early for it?"

"Stop whingeing! Stop it, this instant! Where the hell did you expect to be living? The Palatine? If you don't like it, you can just fuck off back to Verona."

"Why's there so much litter?"

"Because there is. This is Rome. Come on, down here."

Caelius swung into a blank-looking side street. There were blobs of tarmac everywhere, dolloped over the road and sticky in the heat. Catullus prodded one gingerly with his toe. It felt spongy. So this was a coming area. Everything was boarded up, and there wasn't anyone around – it was lonelier than the Downs, Catullus thought, and he felt a lurching sickness in his stomach as he remembered the cool luxury of Clodia's carriage. Well, that was lost to him now, and Clodia with it. Catullus sighed and hurried to keep up with Caelius. Still no one to be seen, and although the occasional roar of a lorry from the High Street could be heard, the deeper Catullus wandered into the tangle of back streets, the more he imagined himself to be lost in the petrified remains of some abandoned world frozen into stillness before anyone had had the time to take in the washing, or empty the bins, or clear up the rubbish bags stacked against the walls.

He heard a noise. Excitement. It was a dog, limping over a mound of flattened newspapers, its ears cocked suspiciously, as though it were surprised to see anything else wandering through the empty streets. Catullus watched, and felt a glow of empathy as the dog began to pee against the kerb side. Caelius absent-mindedly skimmed a can at it, and the dog yelped with pain as it backed away.

"You can't do that," Catullus protested. "Not when the poor thing was having a pee."

"Sorry. Reflex."

"It had a limp. And now you've given it another, you heartless bastard. You really are turning lawyer, aren't you?"

"No alternative, I'm afraid. It's the steely expression of my will to win."

"Dog eat dog?"

"Exactly." Caelius stopped by a door. "Here we go."

He took out his keys and Catullus admired the paintwork. It was green and fresh and shone out from the drabness of the rest of the street.

"Mrs Dugbal," said Caelius, nodding at the door. "Well, not Mrs Dugbal, Mr Dugbal probably, or a Dugbal infant, but Mrs Dugbal was the inspiration. She's very keen on spick and spannery."

He pushed the door open and stood listening for a second. "All clear," he announced; "come on."

He led Catullus up a staircase and onto a brightly decorated landing. "Our floor. I'm in there." He pointed at a door. "Tubbers is down there. It's the smallest room and he's paying just the same as us, so we're on a winner rent-wise. He's an economist, so just feel free to rip him off whenever you need to. It's like stealing from the blind." He pointed down the corridor at a third door and nodded. "That's yours. It's quite small, I'm afraid, but it does have a view, so you'll be able to enjoy the dawn traffic." He swung the door open and waved Catullus in. "Like it?"

Catullus looked around and nodded slowly. "Very nice," he said, dropping his bag. "Ascetic."

"Yes, maybe. But you can tart it up."

Catullus nodded again. "Later, I think."

"Fine, fine. You get some sleep. We'll sort it out later."

"Okay."

Caelius stood for a moment, and Catullus waited, for anything, some sign from this man that he was really not a stranger. Caelius smiled, then clapped his hands. "Right, see you this evening. Sweet dreams."

"Yes. Thanks."

"Not at all. What are friends for? Sleep well."

Caelius blew a kiss, then shut the door after him. Catullus threw himself onto the bed and buried his head under a pillow. Within seconds, he was asleep.

He woke again with a start, thinking that his brother was behind him. His first instinct was to turn; then he realised that he was in a strange room, no longer in his dreams, in the wrong place, and alone.

He turned. His brother wasn't there, of course. Instead, there were long shadows everywhere, and the room looked sickly. It was the light, it was the evening, framed by the casement window, it was everything. The table, the unfriendly chair. The walls. There was a noise from downstairs; the clattering of a pan, so familiar a sound that it made Catullus sick. Again, he wished that he hadn't woken up. But even as he stirred to look down on his pillow, he could feel the mattress all lumpy beneath him; it was no good; he hated the mattress as well. Was this all that Rome was going to be? – it had seemed so massive from the train. Why did it seem so small now? It had shrivelled up and become his bed. And the bed was ricketty and uncomfortable, and he hated it.

He swore, to break the silence. Then, with a effort of will, he stood up, and walked to the window and stared outside. He didn't know what he had been expecting to find. Something vast, he supposed, something panoramic, shrouded in the twilight as his own small room was shrouded, with the casement window a point of intersection, so that the gloom of the room would cease to be a mark of tiny separateness and instead become a quality shared with the entire city, and then Catullus might feel that he belonged in Rome, really was a part of it, and he would become excited again. But there was no view. He could see a single road and some blocks of buildings opposite him, but there wasn't much else to look at, no skyline, no expanse of people and bustling streets. Catullus rubbed his eyes and leant further out from the window. He felt heat dusty against his skin. That was one thing to be said for his room, he supposed, at least it was cool. It had always been the other way at home in Verona, the room hot, and the evening outside fresh against the face. He suddenly realised that there was a pain from his hip, the catch driving into it, and that too reminded Catullus of leaning out from his bedroom at home – there had been a catch in the window sill there too, and it had driven into his hip in the same way. He had minded less then – he had had to lean out, if he had wanted to see beyond the lawn. There had been trees, lining the nearby lanes, their boughs dipping and sometimes sweeping the walls marking out the garden. When they had been young, Catullus and his brother had been forbidden to lean out and look, and so they had always enjoyed doing it, listening to the soft stillness of late summer evenings, and imagining what it would be like to run through the woods and find hidden lairs in the cool dark of the trees. One night, Catullus' brother had gone to find out. He had jumped from the window, onto the dampening grass below, and scouted his way through patches of dark, up to the gate and then beyond into the woods. He had been gone for hours. Catullus had counted every second, paralysed by fear and admiration, and the catch had left an ugly testimonial in his hip, a purple bruise that had stayed for days but faded quicker than Catullus' awe at his elder brother's exploits. He never found out what had happened. His brother never spoke about what he had seen or done, but at first, Catullus hadn't needed him to; he had just accepted that his brother had proved himself, and done something great. Then the next day, Catullus himself had gone to the woods and wandered through them, but he had felt upset all of a sudden and left out, for they had changed, he'd realised, and whatever his brother had seen had long since faded. Catullus had pestered him and begged him to say what had happened; even better, to take him along the next night; in the day, it hadn't been frightening to ask and hope that his brother would agree. But his brother had just shaken his head and smiled, and kept silent. Catullus had been so angry that finally he had reported his brother to their parents, and managed not to feel guilty for several hours afterwards.

Catullus shifted and tried to make himself comfortable. His eyes had become better adjusted now. He realised, as he studied the wall opposite his window, that what he had at first imagined to be the front of a warehouse was in fact a temple. The mistake, though, had been understandable, for the wall was black and stained, and Catullus, looking at it, found it hard to decide whether or not the entire building had been abandoned to a similar state of dereliction. It seemed haunted by its stillness. Catullus continued to stare at the black-streaked walls, and out, at the empty road. Somebody had to come. This was Rome, after all, erstwhile largest city in the world – where the hell were the people who lived in it, all wiped out in some universal plague? Still no one passed, and Catullus began to breed strange fantasies in his mind, that the whole of Rome had been stilled, that he was the only person left living in the wreck of the dead city, that its vastness was his to do with as he wished. He decided to wait until someone came. His reward? It would mean that things were about to look up. And if no one came? Then he was doomed to stay miserable. Catullus waited, then sighed. He didn't have the time to play such a stupid game. He turned, and as he did so, saw a dark figure approaching the temple.

Catullus swung back and stared out through the window. There was a man, slim, dressed in black, a coat on his shoulders and flowers in his hand. He pushed at a huge wooden door, opened it, and disappeared into the darkness beyond. The door thudded shut, and the street was empty again. Catullus stretched and felt a foolish sense of relief. He picked up his jacket, and was just about to call Caelius, fortified, when the door crashed open and the light was switched on.

"Oops. Major blunder. Didn't mean to. Sorry."

Catullus looked into a pair of glassy saucer eyes. The eyes winked and refocused back at him. Catullus looked the rest of the voice up and down; it came from a tall, fidgety young man in a striped shirt and bow tie, with a mouth that hung slackly like a fold of damp canvas.

"Manners breakdown, I'm afraid," the apparition said at last. "Hello."

"Hello," said Catullus politely.

"Damn glad to meet you, damn glad." He offered a hand, which Catullus took. "Bit hammered, I'm afraid. Bloody shame. Poor impression, and all that, sorry." He lurched forward and had to lean against a wall. "Who are you?" he asked eventually, trying to stand up again.

"Catullus – Caelius' friend."

"Oh, great, great! Caelius, eh? *Rarly* good bloke."

"Yes."

"Rarl pal of mine."

"You wouldn't be Tubbers, would you?"

The young man hiccoughed. "No," he said, stifling a belch. "Hugo. All my chums call me Hugo."

"Tubbers!" Caelius' voice bellowed from the next room. "Have you woken Catullus up?"

Tubbers giggled. "Sorry," he said nervously. "Blotto. Too much of the nectar, flooded out the bloodstream. Made apologies though. All okay."

"You tit," said Caelius from the door way. "I tell you not to wake him up, and so what do you go and do? Wake him up. You tit."

"I was already awake," said Catullus. "Really, it's all right."

"Well, he's still a tit. Look at him. Pissed at half past seven." He glanced disdainfully at Tubbers, who had collapsed back onto the bed. "You've introduced yourselves, have you? Good, well that spares me the embarrassment. Might as well get the rest out of the way while we're doing it. Come on."

Caelius turned to leave the room, but Tubbers, staggering to his feet, lurched after him and grabbed at his shoulder.

"Going out tonight?"

Caelius stared at him. "Possibly. Why?"

Tubbers smiled uncertainly. "Oh, you know. No reason."

"Do you want to come with us? Is that what you're trying to say?"

"Out on the razzle. Have a rarl laugh."

"I think not."

"Why not?"

"Because Catullus and I have a lot to discuss, and you're pissed, and all in all, I don't think it's a recipe for fun."

"Chunder. Always feel fine after a chunder."

"I'm sorry," muttered Caelius to Catullus. "I feel so embarrassed."

Tubbers pushed past them. "Right," he said. "See you later. Have some *rarl* fun." He staggered towards the loo.

"God," said Caelius, "to think I've been seen in public with him."

"Is he all right?" Catullus asked, following Caelius down the staircase. "He looked rather unwell."

"He's fine."

"Are you sure?"

"Of course. He's just got a terminal case of being a complete arse, that's all." Caelius stopped outside a door. "And talk of frying pans and fire, here we are – Dugbal zone." He pressed his ear and listened. "Bad luck. She's in." He knocked. There was no answer. He knocked again, louder.

"COME IN!"

Caelius patted Catullus on the back. "Good luck, old chap." Then he opened the door, and Catullus was ushered into a steam-filled kitchen. A vast woman loomed through the haze like a tug berthed in early morning mists; a steady slapping sound beat through the steam; the woman's fists pumped up and down, walloping a shirt with great piston blows, pausing only to hang it up and reach mechanically for another, then returning back to work with a power as awesome and undiminished as it had been before. There were mounds of laundry everywhere. The woman looked up from her washing board, frowned, and pointed at Catullus.

"Who's he?"

"My friend. From Verona. You said you'd like to meet him."

"Well, don't they have manners in Verona?"

Caelius pushed Catullus forward. "Say hello," he whispered.

"Hello," said Catullus. He held out a hand. Mrs Dugbal looked at it without interest, and took another wallop at a wet shirt. Catullus looked round and pointed at the door questioningly. Caelius shook his head.

"Little bit of manners, that's all it takes," said Mrs Dugbal, looking up at last. "That's all I ask for. Doesn't take much. We'll forget about it now, shall we?"

"Yes. Thank you."

"Now then. Just the one house rule." Mrs Dugbal held up a podgy finger. "If you see Mr Dugbal in your passageway, you are in no way to disturb him."

Caelius nodded. "That's fine, Mrs Dugbal. Fine. Isn't it, Catullus?"

"Oh yes. Definitely."

Mrs Dugbal grunted suspiciously. She swept away a mound of washing, then, picking up a dry shirt, plunged it violently into an enormous bowl of soapy water and shook it as though she were drowning a cat. Realising that Catullus and Caelius were still watching her, she looked up in surprise and shooed at them with her hands. "Well go on, what are you standing around for? Go and introduce yourself to the children."

Caelius pointed at a side door. "I think she likes you," he whispered as Catullus pushed it open. "No, really."

Catullus said nothing, just looked around. After the steam and noise of the kitchen, the new room he had walked into seemed muffled, almost heavy with silence; for a second, Catullus couldn't work out why, and then he realised that the walls were thick with hangings, carpets, flowered sheets, with scarcely a breathing space for the plaster beneath them. Books were piled up everywhere, there was an old pram in a corner, and more carpets had been draped over mounds of clothes, old radios, ancient picture frames. There was a single table and a young girl was working at it, concentrating so intently on the book propped up in front of her that she hadn't even noticed the door opening and shutting behind her. On the floor, a small boy, younger than his sister, was ripping up pieces from one of the rugs and carefully wrapping them round a doll. He jumped to his feet when he saw Catullus entering the room, and stared up aggressively, his thin legs like splints, splaying out from his shorts.

"Hello," he said. "You've got big ears."

"No, I haven't," said Catullus indignantly, and felt them with his hands.

"Oh well, it doesn't matter," the boy replied in a bored tone, as though Catullus wasn't worth arguing about. He picked up his doll and handed it over. "I'm doing pharaohs at school," he said. "Do you know anything about pharaohs? I do." He started to chant in a sing song voice. "Ramasses, Thuthmoses, Hatshepshut."

Catullus inspected the doll. "What's this?"

The boy stopped his chanting immediately and gave Catullus a look of withering scorn. "God, you're thick. Don't you know *anything*? It's a mummy. When pharaohs died they became mummies. That's why he's wearing sheets. You're really *stupid*, you are."

He started to chant again, jumping up and down as he sounded each syllable, sometimes stopping to repeat and linger over any name he particularly enjoyed. Then, suddenly struck by a thought, he stopped his dancing and turned to Catullus again.

"Pharaohs were really into torture," he said, speaking the final word with such relish that his face twisted up. "Torture!" he said again, and smiled happily. "Because you know, they'd get someone they didn't like, like a slave or something, or maybe even someone important, and they'd put him in this box and then they'd chop bits off of him, so that by the end there'd be nothing left, and he'd die in horrible agony. And then they'd pour vinegar over him."

"Why vinegar?"

"'Cos then he'd die in even worse agony."

"Jez." The girl had finally looked up from her books.

"Yeah?"

"Can't you stop it?" She sounded bored and tired. Catullus looked at her and suddenly realised that she was very beautiful, blonde and open faced, with blue eyes so pale they seemed to be drops of transparent glass. He wondered how she had found herself related to Mrs Dugbal.

"Sorry." The boy spun round again. "Vanessa says I'm not allowed to talk about torture. She says it's horrible. But that's only because she works all day and she's *mad*."

"Have you heard of insect tortures?" Catullus asked.

"Insects?"

"You tie a man down, and you put him in a box, and then you pour insects through a hole until he suffocates."

The boy thought for a moment. A look of deep appreciation slowly dawned over his face. "That's really good, that is," he said at last, grudgingly, as though reluctant to admit the value of anyone else's contribution to what he evidently regarded as his own private field of study. "Do you know any others?"

"Jez, will you stop it?" The girl had been staring, unblinkingly, at Catullus ever since he had spoken. He was glad when she turned away. "Dad," she asked, "can't you stop him? – he just goes on and on, and I *hate it*."

A vague stirring came from what Catullus had assumed to be a pile of rugs, and a hand appeared from the side of the mound, feeling for a tasselled cap that had been lying on a table by the side of the chair. There was a sudden convulsive twitching, and a face appeared from the rugs as they fell away, long and very delicate. Slowly, and with great dignity, the man placed the tasselled cap on his head and then smiled uncertainly at the room around him. He turned to his daughter. She stared back at him, coldly, her eyes so pale now that they seemed to shine, and said nothing. Startled, Mr Dugbal turned to Caelius.

"Good evening," he said, taking Caelius' proffered hand, and nodding stiffly as he shook it. "And your friend?" he asked, turning to Catullus.

Caelius introduced him.

40

"You, er... You have met my wife?" Catullus admitted that he had, and Mr Dugbal nodded sagely, as though a secret bond had been forged between the two of them. He shook Catullus' hand a second time. "Good, good." He stroked his porcelain chin and stared out into space.

All this time, Jez had been watching his father frantically, hopping from foot to foot, twisting sheets tightly around his mummy. "Dad," he asked suddenly, hanging onto the rugs that still swathed his father, "Dad, have you heard about insect tortures?"

"You see what I mean?" Vanessa said. For a moment, Catullus thought she was about to cry. "*Stop him*, Dad!"

Mr Dugbal looked startled, like a deer caught in the headlights of two oncoming cars. He fluttered for a second with his hands, then shrunk even further back under his coverings.

"What do you want?" he asked Jez feebly, ignoring Vanessa altogether.

"Have you heard of insect tortures?"

"Insect tortures." Mr Dugbal took off his cap and stroked the tassels gently, gazing out again into nothingness. "Insect tortures." He frowned. "Do you know," he said suddenly, looking into his son's face, "that in the land of the Circassians, when a child is born, his mother will catch any insects that land on him while he's asleep, and dip them into gold? And then, when he's older, he wears them round his neck. Did you know that?"

Jez looked bored.

"It's true," said Mr Dugbal hurriedly. "This cap is a Circassian cap." He looked up at Catullus and nodded. "And look." He fumbled inside his shirt and pulled out a small chain that had been hanging from his neck. Catullus bent over to look at it. Mr Dugbal nodded again and pointed to a tiny grasshopper, dangling from a link, delicate, made from gold. "This too is from Circassia."

Jez stared at it. "So where's the torture?" he asked.

"Oh. There is no torture."

"Bore-ring!" Jez threw his mummy onto the floor in disgust, and Mr Dugbal, with a look of pain on his face, snatched the tiny grasshopper away from Catullus' gaze and buried it once again beneath the rugs. He said nothing more, but sat slumped and miserable, staring at his daughter. She looked up once, then returned to her books. Jez still squatted hopefully on the floor, but otherwise, the room had resettled into total stillness. Caelius looked at Catullus and nodded. They both said goodbye, and then, as reverentially as they could, backed out of the room and shut the door behind them.

In the kitchen, Mrs Dugbal was still hard at the washing.

"Do you like crab?" she asked Catullus as he passed.

"I've never had it before."

"You can have some tomorrow, then. I'll cook you breakfast. You look as though you could do with some good food inside you."

"Thank you. I'll look forward to it."

Mrs Dugbal snorted, and wrung out a sheet. "Mind you don't smoke in your beds," she bellowed after the two friends as they shut the kitchen door behind them. She snorted again, scratched herself, then returned to her sheet.

Upstairs, Caelius lay back on his bed and smiled. It had gone all right, he thought, the reunion. Catullus was moping a bit, but there'd been no embarrassments. No, he was sure, things would be okay. Caelius smiled again, and lit a cigarette.

Catullus, in his empty room, was thinking of nothing. His mind moved over and over the layers of all his new experiences, which he could sense, even as he tried not to think of them, shifting endlessly beneath his tiredness, not patterned neatly, meeting sometimes, fusing, mixing to form new and even stranger compounds, or just cracking, to leave fragments which still, like dying sparks, continued to glow in their isolation. Catullus didn't want to have to remember, stared instead at his room. As before, he saw the table, the dirty walls, his bed. But suddenly, in his imagination, he could also see Caelius' eyes, glaring coldly at him with a strange, deep luminosity, and the web was torn, irreparably, so that Caelius' eyes became the pale skin of Clodia, and the darkness of her dress swayed and rustled like the forest his brother had explored, and the trees that shadowed the carriages when the three women had met, and kissed each other. Images, constantly mutable, succeeding and confusing each other, swept through the mental void that Catullus had been trying so hard to preserve. He swore, suddenly, and leapt to his feet.

He needed to talk. Shouting out Caelius' name, he picked up his jacket and turned out the light. Then, without pausing to wait for his friend to join him, he hurried down the stairs, back into the street, and into the night.

III

VARNEY

The pub was dirty and hot, and it seemed that all Tallowfield had crowded in round its tiny bar. It was still only early in the evening, but the air was already so soggy with beer that Catullus wondered why people were bothering to buy drinks, when all they had to do was breathe in heavily and feel the alcohol dew their tonsils. He gave his order though, when asked, and reluctantly handed over money to pay, even though he'd bought the last three rounds, and now here he was again, the sucker, suckered by the city slicker. Caelius was in the far corner of the pub, chatting smoothly on the telephone; Catullus studied his friend, so poised, so beautiful, so arrogant, and felt jealousy starting to lap at him again. They had been apart for a year – no wonder things had changed, he thought gloomily, he should have prepared himself. How long before he caught up? Would he ever? Catullus stared round the bar, at the faceless crowds, and felt sick with a sudden sense of loneliness. Come back to me, he thought, sensation, lips and skin touching, surprising my blood even now, in this place, surprising me with physical memories. He took his change, and picked up the drinks, and made his way back to his empty seat.

Someone had taken Caelius' place. Catullus lowered the glasses onto the table and sat down. He looked at the man beside him. "Shadows walk the streets," the man muttered in a slurred voice, "and their name is fear." Oh great, that was all he needed, stuck next to a fucking drunk. "I...you're not...been here before?" the drunk asked.

"Why? That obvious, is it?"

The drunk looked at him. "I was born here. Lived here all my life. Hasn't done me much good." He shook his head. "On the streets are shadows!" he screamed suddenly. "There can be no forgiveness from them!"

"Really?" said Catullus, staring at him with distaste. The drunk was dirty. He wore a greasy yellowish waistcoat, the colour of his skin, and when he wasn't talking, his long jaw hung open and dribbled, mottling it. He swallowed. "You think I'm – shit – *shit*! – do you?"

Catullus stared into his drink.

"Well, now you're in Rome, you've got to understand, that if you judge people on appearances, they've got you. Got you!" The drunk snapped his fingers. "You know who I mean?" He waved with his arm. "Them! Them!" He nodded earnestly, and leant over, breathing whisky into Catullus' face. "Let me tell you this – Rome is no place for happiness. It's the most terrible of cities, accursed, that's what it is! But I've got my hopes, that I'll see its streets cracked open, and trees breathing at last amongst its towers, because it is coming. I have seen the signs."

"What signs?"

"Signs of the reckoning. I have worked them out, and you will see. Pride, crumbling like ash into the dust."

The drunk's muttering suddenly offended Catullus like a stench, and he looked at the face before him with hatred. "What are you talking about?" he asked furiously. "What the fuck do you know about anything?"

The drunk looked up blearily. "I know a lot about history," he said after careful thought, and stared at his whisky glass. He began to mutter to himself. Catullus recognised the rhythm of dates. The drunk smiled as he continued his murmurings, as though he were chanting, keeping the world at bay. He looked up and stopped his mantra. "Let me tell you about the Civil War. The Civil War," he said loudly, "the bloody Civil War, it was the reason I lost my job. Amazing isn't it? I lost my job because of the bloody Civil War!"

Catullus smiled hopelessly, and motioned him to carry on.

"I have to tell you the truth," the drunk said unsteadily. "I don't actually have a job at the moment, because I'm unemployed. I'm not saying that because I'm ashamed or anything, just so you know I'm not keeping anything back. All right?" The drunk nodded to himself. He began to tap on the table and as he finished another glass, he became more and more excited. His eyes glittered and sudden drops of sweat formed on his brow. He tapped louder and louder.

Then he began to talk again, almost shouting, as though he were desperate to convince everyone else around him that he was speaking with bravado, that he didn't care what they thought about him. "I worked for a property developer," he said. "A big one, the biggest of them all, he shat buildings all over Rome. Concrete shit!" The drunk's eyes glittered, and he shivered. "There was a secretary, in the office I was in. She didn't like me. I filed mostly, did what she said. I didn't give her any trouble, and I just got on with my job, but all the time I was thinking thoughts to myself, but Miranda, she could see what I was up to, and though she couldn't do anything, she didn't like it and she was jealous." He leant forward. "And let me tell you this. There isn't *anything*, not anything, that compares with a jealous woman." He sat back groggily. "Nothing."

He drank and coughed. "She came up to me one day, when it was late and we were all alone. 'I've got a secret', she said. 'Can you keep a secret?' And she'd found out about how this land was going to be for sale, it was just round from our office, just down the road, and this girl, Miranda, she'd found out all about it. And she'd gone and told the boss and he was ready to buy it, before anyone else, you see, because that would stop the price going up. And she told me where it was, and I was amazed, because it was the very land where I'd decided Marius fell in the battle against the King, because I'd worked it out for myself, even though you'll remember, no one had known where he fell. And I told her. She looked at me, all odd, and then she said, who was Marius, was he important, and I didn't actually say anything, but I did laugh." He smiled slowly. "I did laugh." He looked far away at nothing, and then suddenly frowned.

"My life wasn't worth living after that. She never said a thing, of course, but I could see she'd decided I'd have to go." He hushed his voice again, as though he was suddenly afraid of how slurred it might sound, and tugged on Catullus' sleeve to make sure that he was still listening. "The next day, the manager came into the room where we all had our lunch break and he looked around, and he came over to me! I can still remember feeling the sweat under my collar, and thinking to myself, oh no, here we go, it's all going to happen now. But he was very kind. He asked me how I was, and whether I was enjoying the work, and then he asked me if it was true I was interested in the Civil War. Well, I didn't say anything, but then Miranda spoke in her nancy stuck-up way, and she just looked at me and said, 'Oh yes, he's very knowledgeable about the Civil War, he knows all about that.'" The drunk tried to impersonate her, but his voice was too hoarse and scratched, and the attempt to sound like a girl was so embarrassing that Catullus couldn't bear to look at him. The drunk carried on with his mimicry. "'He knows all about the Civil War.'" He waved his hand with a fake delicacy, and coughed on his memories and indignation. "So the boss asks me if this is true. What could I say? He kept going on about it, about Marius and the siege of Rome, and this land he'd bought, and how he was sure Marius couldn't have died there because he'd always thought Marius had died in a battle. And that was when I spoke, not because I wanted to show off, but just because I knew he was wrong and so I just said, no, no one knows where Marius died but it was in a scuffle, and I think it was at this spot, this bit of land he was buying. Then he said, why did I think that, and I said, research, and then I went bright red. But the manager just laughed and says he's very impressed, and everyone else laughs too, so I laugh along, but I could see that Miranda was laughing the loudest and her eyes were all horrible and bright. Horrible eyes, she had, catty."

"I don't understand," said Catullus. "What did it matter?"

"You mean you can't see?" The drunk leant forward urgently. "It meant I'd shown them up. Me! Who they'd all thought was stupid and poor, and a drunk, that was me you see, just a poor old drunk. But now I'd shown them up!"

Catullus shrugged, but the drunk seemed not to notice him.

"There wasn't much I could do now. Nothing except wait, because I knew she'd got me, and it was only a matter of time. I was so scared, I couldn't sleep. You know how it is. I lived a long way out, so I had to get up early if I was going to get to work on time, but I was always awake for hours before and I'd just lie there, listening to my alarm clock tick, tick tick tick, on it would go, and I knew eventually it would go off, and then it would be even worse, and I'd have to get up and catch the train and go to the office. It was hell." He shouted. "It was fucking hell!" He shivered and muttered to himself; then he picked up his whisky glass, peered at it and shoved it under Catullus' nose. "You know, drink is the portal to freedom from these streets. We must have portals, we must find them and keep them open, or the streets will freeze us. They will, you know. The streets here are the freezing coils of hell." He gulped the whisky down and wiped at his mouth. "But you mustn't think I'm asking you to feel sorry for me, because I'm not and I want that clear, but the only reason I started on the old bottle was that bitch Miranda, she'd got me boxed in." He pointed a finger down at the table and began to count words off with it. "If I was going to get through each day then I needed to sleep. If I was going to sleep then I needed to drink. And if I was going to drink then I couldn't...well, you know. I just couldn't." He slumped forward and tried to think of a phrase that would enable him to express everything he had been hoping for. He kept silent.

Then he shrunk even further into his chair. "I had tried, you know. My landlady, she'd realised how much I'd tried. She'd look at me, as I'd become all...a whole lot dirtier...and she'd say I should stop looking so nervous all the time." He laughed. "Nervous. Of course I was. Because it was then I'd begun to understand the signs. And so I knew that chaos was approaching, just as I knew I was going to lose my job."

Catullus frowned. "Chaos? What were these signs?"

The drunk trickled a grin. "Oh, you'll recognise them, all right."

"When?"

"No." The drunk shook his head. "I want to tell you about my job first, how I lost it. Miranda the bitch. She got me in the end. I made a mistake, I admit that, but she pushed me." The drunk nodded to himself. "I was tired one day, and cold, and a little drunk, because I'd had some whisky at lunch, and all I wanted was to be left on my own and get on with my work without being disturbed, but she wouldn't, oh no, she could tell, and she just wouldn't leave me alone. On and on she went. 'Found out anything else about Marius?' she said, and everyone else tittered, stupid bastards, that's all they were, and suddenly I couldn't stand it any more and I started screaming at them. Then other people started coming in, and finally the boss came in too, to find out what was wrong. I screamed at him as well. And the moment I'd done that, well – that was that. So I just said everything I thought, because it didn't matter by then." He paused and his eyes moistened. "I told them everything. I told them that a lot of things were very wrong. I told them that the time of flames and retribution was approaching. And then they sacked me, and I had to go, and that was that."

He sobbed chokingly, staring into Catullus' face and breathing whisky fumes on long, aching sighs; Catullus stared back. Frightening. And shit, the man stank. Catullus sniffed at his own jacket. Had he been infected? With a smell that might be his own anyway in forty years? Would Caelius notice and be witty about it?

Catullus got to his feet and reached inside Caelius' jacket. The wallet was still there, which was something at least. Catullus took it, slipped it inside his own jacket pocket, and wondered if he should take all Caelius' belongings, just to be on the safe side, but it hardly seemed necessary. The drunk lay below him with his head on the table. God, he was foul. Catullus turned away, then paused. He took the drunk's shoulder and pushed at it, gently at first, then with increasing violence, until the drunk had woken and raised his head to stare up blearily. "Do you want a drink?" Catullus asked roughly. "Whisky," said the drunk at once. Catullus took his glass, then shook the drunk by the shoulder again. "And these signs?" he asked. "You keep mentioning them, but you never say what they are. They're signs of what?"

"Ruin," muttered the drunk.

"And how do we recognise them?"

The drunk stared up at Catullus' face. He smiled. "Fire and blood," he whispered. He nodded. "Blood." Then slowly, his head sank back onto the table, and Catullus turned away, in frustration and disgust, at the drunk, and at his own sudden longing to share the vision of ruin, to see the pub with its crowds of strange unfriendly people, and the city beyond, all of it, consumed by fire, its buildings toppled, its monuments wrecked, everything abandoned totally.

Someone laughed in his ear, a girl. Catullus glanced at her, longing for her, then pushed hurriedly through the crowds to find Caelius.

He found him propped against the bar.

"Where the hell have you been, you bastard?" Catullus shouted over the din. "You've been hours."

"Sorry. I got caught. Actually, I was going to buy you a drink, but I seem to have left my wallet behind." Caelius laughed lightly. "Silly me."

"And not so silly me." Catullus handed the wallet over. "Same again please. And one whisky. Large."

"You can't have two drinks. That's greedy. Ooh! Or have you made a friend!"

"Sort of."

"Well, go on. I'm excited."

Catullus smiled weakly. "It's a drunk, and before you start complaining, no, he's not my friend, but I couldn't get rid of him because I didn't want to lose our place, and since it was you who spent all that time on the telephone, I reckon it's your fault, and not mine. All right?"

Caelius shrugged. "All right. But why've we got to buy him a drink?"

"You're buying him the drink."

"I'm not. If you want to waste money, why don't you buy some condoms or something?"

Catullus grinned forcedly. "I told him I'd get him one. It'd be cruel to disappoint him now. Don't be so tight. Buy him his whisky."

Caelius grumbled as he waited for his order. "You don't half have a knack of attracting weirdos. I've lived here for over a year and met barely a fruitcake, and now you've turned up and they're crawling all over the shop."

"It's only one wino."

"And there was that mad one in the station. The one with the Adam's apple. How does the wino compare with him? Ratings out of ten?"

"Eight and a half. He's smellier."

"Oh great." Caelius picked up the drinks. "Let's give him the whisky and then he can fuck off. Or does charity run to listening to those you get pissed?"

Caelius started to make a furrow through the crowds, and Catullus followed him. Over by the table, the drunk had climbed to his feet; Catullus pulled on Caelius' shoulder and pointed, as the drunk swayed uneasily and stared about him, a look of bewilderment on his face, as though he had lost something precious. He didn't seem to recognise Catullus, but grabbed at the drink when he was offered it, and took a short rasping gulp. He swayed once again, rocking back onto his heels as though he were reaching for something just beyond his reach, and then fell, heavily, with such a thud that a few people even heard it above the roar of the pub's conversation, and looked around to see what had happened. One man, thin and wearing a light overcoat despite the heat, came over and helped Catullus to lift the drunk back onto a chair.

"He can't stay here," the man said.

"And what are we supposed to do about it?" asked Caelius rudely.

The man stared back and shook his head. "He can't stay here," he repeated.

Catullus crouched down by the drunk and slapped him lightly on the cheeks. "Where do you live?" he asked. No answer. "Listen. We need to know where you live." Catullus slapped him again, and the drunk murmured. A light froth of spit hung like a meniscus between his lips. "He's out," said Catullus, standing up again, and ignoring the man in the raincoat as he turned back to Caelius. "What the hell are we going to do?"

"Why have we got to do anything?"

"We can't just leave him."

"Course we can. Bung him in the urinals and he can sleep it off there."

The drunk began to moan softly and twitch his jaw.

"No. We can't. We'll have to find out where he lives."

"You're joking. He probably doesn't even have a home."

"We'll take him in a taxi." Catullus took his friend's arm. "Please." He stared into Caelius' eyes. "I could do with clearing my head. Please, Caelius."

Caelius shook his head. "Look, I'd love to oblige, you know I would, but where the fuck do we go? We can't just dump him."

"He lives in the Zenoria Road hostel," the man in the overcoat said unexpectedly.

Catullus looked at him in surprise. "How do you know?"

The man shrugged. "It's my job, knowing things." He smiled. "And if I was you, I'd be more careful about the quality of acquaintance you keep. This isn't Verona, you know."

He smiled again, bowed his head imperceptibly, and then turned and disappeared, slipping through the throngs of drinkers bunched around on all sides. Caelius and Catullus were left staring at each other in amazement.

"Well, I'll be fucked," said Caelius. "What is it about you? They all come swarming after you like flies round a cow's arse. Who was that one?"

"Haven't the faintest." Catullus shook his head. "Never seen him before in my life. And it's not funny. How the hell did he know I'd just come from Verona? Really, I've never seen him before. Maybe he was at the ball too, like the other one, though what he's doing hanging around in a shite hole like this I don't know. Not the sort of place you'd expect to bump into ball-goers."

"Don't be a snob. You're here, aren't you? Why shouldn't others be?"

Catullus shrugged. "Just seems strange."

"Yes. And there was me looking forward to hearing all about it. And instead it seems we have a jolly night of drunk-dumping ahead of us. Heigh ho." Caelius sighed. "Look at him. Too comatose even to finish off that whisky you made me get him." He swallowed it and made a face. "I hate whisky too. Oh well, I feel absolved from having to do good for the rest of the week." Caelius stared at Catullus. "We really have to go?"

Catullus nodded. "We need to be on our own." There was a pause. "You did promise."

"All right then." Caelius made a face. "But only because you insist. Come on – let's get it over with."

The two men dragged the unconscious man through knots of chattering people. Out on the pavement, they saw a taxi coming and waved it down. The driver looked round uneasily as his nostrils caught the smell of drink. "I'm not having some bastard throw up in my cab," he said. "Zenoria Road," replied Caelius with a lack of concern. "Right place for him," the taxi driver muttered, looking round again as the drunk began to moan and quiver in his back seat. "Shouldn't be allowed out of there either. Bloody disgusting."

Catullus soon realised what the taxi driver had meant. It wasn't far to Zenoria Road, but as the taxi left the streets that had knotted their way through the houses and office blocks of Tallowfield, as it turned to drive slowly past a waste of gutted buildings stained deep with pools of black, the noise and light of the pub began to seem an eternity away, and Catullus found that he was regretting his philanthropy. The drunk, as though he could sense the darkness outside, began to moan more loudly, the shadows that flitted over the car passing too, perhaps, across whatever dreams were troubling him through the fumes of his stupor. The taxi pulled past a few peeling dirty buildings, then stopped in front of a large house. Windows cast weak light onto the pavements and tarmac of the road below. A small sign, freshly painted, announced the hostel. "Zenoria Road Refuge. Welcome."

Caelius paid the driver while Catullus bundled the drunk out from the back seat. "Want me to stay?" the driver asked. "No, no, we'll walk," said Caelius. "Suit yourself," the driver replied, and drove away. The night suddenly seemed very empty.

A large, old fashioned door chain hung by the entrance; Catullus pulled at it and waited. Behind him, the drunk began to shake through all his body, and then vomit uncontrollably. He was still retching as the door was answered, by a small stoutly built old lady who peered aggressively at Catullus through thick half-moon spectacles.

"Yes?" she asked.

"We've brought...um. We've brought – him." Catullus pointed down at the drunk, who lay spreadeagled against a step, still spitting gobs of vomit from his mouth. The old lady took off her spectacles and gave him a quick glance.

"Oh, Mr Varney. I was wondering if he'd been getting up to mischief." She nodded sharply at Caelius, who was standing by the drunk on the steps. "Well come along, don't just stand there," she ordered brusquely. "Bring him in!" She turned and marched back into the hallway. Caelius looked at his friend, made a face, and then the two of them tried to lift the prostrate but now conscious Mr Varney up from the steps.

"Don't dilly dally, shilly shally!" the old lady shouted from the top of a staircase as they dragged the drunk through the hostel doorway. "Up here!" Mr Varney turned to Catullus, murmuring apologies, but he was still far too weak to make his own way up the staircase. He was heavy, and his clothes were stained with vomit now as well as with all the earlier dirt and drink.

The lady showed them into a badly-lit dormitory. It was filled with iron beds, bodies hunched up on them. Catullus was conscious of eyes staring at him from the dark. "That's his bed, over there," the old lady told them. "Well, go on." The two men dragged Mr Varney across the floor to his bed and dumped him down onto its rumpled sheets. Mr Varney stared up at the three faces gathered around him; he looked frightened and confused, and he began to shout.

"Shut up!" the old lady said briskly. "I've told you about this before. If you're going to go out and drink yourself silly, you'll be getting no sympathy from me." She turned to Caelius and nodded. "You have to be strict with them. 'Strict and firm, you'll have a happy home', that's my motto. I've always lived by it, and I always will." Caelius nodded sagely, and began to introduce himself.

"No, no, I can't stand around here and talk to you all night," said the old lady. "'Talk and fun, no work will get done.' And there's plenty of work to be done here, that's for sure." She nodded accusingly at Caelius and Catullus, then turned back to Mr Varney and jabbed at him with her finger. "And as for you," she said, "you just behave yourself for once. I want no more nonsense from you, you understand? There'll be trouble otherwise."

She turned and walked briskly out through the dormitory. Caelius and Catullus began to follow her, but Mr Varney, behind them, moaned and beckoned Catullus to come near him again. Caelius shook his head urgently, but Catullus, holding his nostrils, turned back to the drunk and bent down by his side. Mr Varney mouthed something, then started to fumble about under his pillow, pausing every few seconds to lie still and breathe in slowly. At last, he found what he had been looking for, a small battered book, which he pressed to his chest and then handed up to Catullus. He nodded, with a look of pain, and turned onto his side, head hanging over the edge of the mattress, hand clinging tightly to the iron of the bed frame. He lay motionless, staring at the floorboards. Catullus thanked him and even brought himself to touch the drunk lightly on the shoulder. Then he turned, and walked out through the silence of the dormitory. Again, he was conscious of eyes following him from the shadows.

"What a fucking horrible place," said Caelius when Catullus had joined him back out on the pavement. "Just think, you could have ended up in a place like that, so there'll be no more whingeing, and a bit more gratitude, please."

Catullus nodded. "Oh yes, thank you, Caelius."

"And that old lady. Talk about poisoned dwarves. Not a word of thanks from her."

"I don't think I'd be wild if you dumped Mr Varney on my doorstep."

"No, I suppose not. What did Fashion Victim have to say?"

"Not a lot. Gave me this." Catullus looked the book over. It was so worn, the fibres of its cover so frayed, that it was only by moving under the light from the hostel and peering at the gold lettering still faintly legible on its battered spine that Catullus could decipher the title at all. "Marius the Dancer and the Great Civil War", he read. He smiled. "What a nice present." He turned to Caelius and explained. "Mr Varney was very interested in the Civil War."

"Really? Odd thing for a wino to be into."

"He was telling me all about it. He seemed quite knowledgeable."

"Just shows where a little learning can get you, I suppose. Actually, you know, there's a statue of Marius in that temple opposite the Dugbals'. Is he buried there? I think he might be."

"No. No one knows where he's buried. That's the whole point."

"Oh. Well, there's a statue of him anyway. You should go and look at it."

Catullus remembered the young man in black. "Maybe I will. See the sights and all that."

Caelius nodded. "Oh, it's a thriller. Or so I'm told." He began to walk down the pavement. "Come on."

"Where are you going?"

"Back to civilisation."

Catullus watched his friend as he turned and beckoned. "Come on!" he shouted. "You were the one who dragged us out here! I thought you wanted to talk."

"Yes." Catullus stood where he was. Suddenly, encouraged by Caelius, he felt paralysed. His hopes, his thoughts of all that he had been intending to say, seemed pointless, as they had done since his arrival in Rome, chilled by Caelius' flippancy, and the solitude of the dark street had not brought them together, as he had hoped it might, but rather provided a setting worthy of their separateness. Catullus wanted to talk; he wanted to; but it was impossible. He stared around him, and felt a sadness that was like the night, empty and impenetrable, with Caelius standing alone at its heart.

"Come on!"

Catullus walked. Caelius watched him, a smile curling faintly on his lips. "Nothing to say after all?" Catullus stared into his friend's gleaming eyes. So clear, so piercingly blue. He reached for Caelius' hand, but it was pulled away, and Caelius began to walk down the pavement again. He glanced round, to check that Catullus was following him, then shook his head. "All right – if you've been struck mute, I'll ask the questions. This ball – tell me about it."

"I don't want to."

"Bollocks to that. Tell me."

So Catullus did. And as he spoke, he found that his memories of the previous night were consoling him, not banishing the sense of sadness, but transmuting it, into something rich and almost sweet, as the smell of the trees at midnight had been, and the touch of the air on his arms, and the physical presence of Clodia. And remembering Clodia, Catullus smiled, and felt his sadness starting to fade quite away, and his own words, describing her, as he listened to them, seemed suddenly like flares sent up into the night.

Then, in the distance, something caught his eye. He stopped, and pointed. "What's that?" he asked, and Caelius turned to look. There was a fire to their left, a large bonfire, blazing away on the waste land into which the line of roadside buildings had finally crumbled. Both men stared out at the scene. The flames were rising high enough to cast twisted patterns of shadow through the black smoke, over the dereliction all around them, and out into the Tiber, which lay vast and silent, a band of deep darkness between the fire and the lights of tower blocks twinkling feebly from the far bank. The fire choked on a large piece of rubber and the flames spurted, casting the site in a brief wash of orange.

"I can't see anyone," said Caelius, shading his eyes.

"Were you expecting to?"

"Of course. Dropouts. More friends for you."

"Why would anyone need a fire? It's sweltering enough as it is."

"True." Caelius thought. "I don't know."

Catullus began to walk slowly on down the pavement. He continued to gaze out at the fire, the second he had seen in two nights, he realised suddenly. Then he peered ahead, into the darkness of the street that led back to the pub. Nothing. He stared back out at the fire.

"What's this place called?"

"Zenoria Road."

"Yes, I know *this* is Zenoria Road, but what about that, the place where the fire's burning? It must be something."

"Not necessarily. Doesn't look very much like a something to me." Caelius glanced around. There was a sign standing crookedly on the edge of the road. Caelius wandered over to it and peered at the words. Then he smiled and read the notice out. "'Fairlawns. Ancient gardens of the kings of Rome. Trespassers will be prosecuted.' How charming."

"'Ancient gardens of the kings'," repeated Catullus to himself. He looked out at the rubble, and the mounded tips of earth, and the rusting skeletons of cars caught and reddened in the light of the flames. "'I have heard the sayings of the king. What are his habitations now? Their walls are destroyed, their habitations are no more, as if they had never been.'"

Caelius stared at him. "What?"

"Lament of the harper of King Inyotef. Egyptian."

"Oh."

"It's poetry."

"Yes." Caelius pulled a face. "I guessed as much."

Catullus smiled. From the fire, there was another sudden spurt of flame. A shower of sparks arched and fell through the dark. Both men watched as, unexpectedly, a single figure rose up from the shadows and danced, silhouetted against the blaze, his arms waving clumsily, and his head thrown back. Caelius and Catullus gazed on in silence for a while; then Caelius made a gesture with his hand. The two men turned and began to walk, then run, back to Tallowfields, and the crowds of the pub.

"It's all very odd."

"Oh yes," nodded Catullus. "Very." He closed his eyes. He'd had enough. But Caelius, as though compensating for all that they had failed to discuss on Zenoria Road, was worrying the topic of the ball to death. He pursed his lips and rocked forwards on his bar stool. After a minute's thought, he looked up. "It's weird."

"Is it?"

"Yes, of course it is. You just agreed it was."

"I said it was odd. I don't really see that it's weird."

Caelius waved his hand impatiently. "Odd, weird, what's the difference?"

"Well, it's odd that there should have been such a massive party on the night I was travelling past it, and that I should have been picked up by the hostess and taken to it. That's *odd*. But I don't really see that it's weird."

"Because... because... because. Because."

"Because?"

"Because there are so many reasons why it's weird I haven't got time to go into them all."

"Is this some lawyer's trick? Do I have to pay you before you actually talk?"

Caelius stared up at the pub ceiling and slowly ran his hands through his hair. "Where can I begin?" he said. "Surely you can see that it's weird? I mean, all those people. Clodius and Clodia. Metellus. He's a fucking minister for God's sake. In the Government."

"So? I don't see why that's particularly weird. Surely even ministers have time off now and then?"

"But together like that?"

"Of course. They're all related. Metellus is Clodia's husband. It's hardly weird."

"It is weird, because Metellus wouldn't be seen dead at a party with Clodius, and even if he was, he certainly wouldn't be seen sitting down with him having a friendly little chat. And vice versa."

"Why not?"

"Because Metellus is a stuffed shirt and Clodius is a gangster."

"He's not really a gangster, is he? I thought that was just the newspapers."

"He is. He's a thug. And a union leader. And therefore a class traitor. None of which makes him go down well with Metellus. Get it?"

"But they're relatives. Surely they have to meet up sometimes?"

Caelius gave him a look of carefully manufactured scorn. "You don't know anything about relatives, do you? Or politics."

"And you do?"

"Well, more than you, evidently." Caelius leant forward and smiled a superior look into his beer glass. "I do have to admit something, though. I've actually been doing a bit of insider dealing on you."

Catullus looked at him, surprised. "How so?"

"I happen to know for a fact that Metellus would not be seen with Clodius, no way, absolute fact. And I also happen to know, absolutely definitely, that the whole ball is weird, but I'd want to check on my sources before elaborating."

"Really? Quite the little barrister you're getting, aren't you?"

"Don't forget I'm Cicero's nephew."

"Are you? *The* Cicero?"

"Ex-President and Greatest Living Roman? Yes, that Cicero."

"You never told me."

"Well, I didn't really know him. I was never much partial to uncles as a youth. Before I came to Rome, that is."

"And decided to become a lawyer."

Caelius shook his head. "Don't be cynical. Actually, he's a large pile of shite influence-wise. Pity. He's so out of fashion politically that I think I'm just better off keeping quiet about him."

"He can't be that out of fashion."

"Oh, he is. And it's all to do with Clodius, you see. That's how it ties in."

"What does?"

"This ball being odd."

"Sorry, I'm lost. How does Cicero fit in?"

Caelius leant back. "Do you remember his prosecution? Of Clodius? No, well, it was all quite a long time ago. I just assume everyone must have heard about it because I've been told the story so many times. By The Great Man himself. Maybe I should get him to tell you personally. I'm sure he'd love to be given the excuse."

"Really?"

Caelius nodded slowly. "Oh yes. I think so. And especially to you, if you were to swap it for your account of the ball. God, all those anecdotes. But I think you two at least would find them mutually interesting."

"Why don't you just tell me yourself? I don't want to meet Cicero."

"Bollocks, you've obviously got a knack for mixing with politicians. Why worry about Cicero when you've been hob-nobbing with brand leaders like Clodius?"

"Yes, but I didn't know it was him at the time."

"His face *has* been in the papers quite a lot recently."

"Not in drag. You can't blame me for that. Don't you think it's a bit – well... weird, I suppose is the word I'm groping for. I'll grant you that, the labour leader in drag, that does seem weird. I'm not even convinced it was him."

"It was him."

"How can you be so sure?"

"Just wait and see."

"Why not tell me now?"

"Because I want you to tell Cicero everything before you know what it all means."

"Well, thanks a fucking million. Where are you going?"

Caelius had stood up. "To phone Cicero. Get us an invitation to dinner."

"Wait, you can't do that. Caelius, wait! You can't titillate me like that and then not tell me."

"Ultimate fulfilment will be all the sweeter for it."

"No, wait! I told you everything."

"Well, you're a foolish virgin for having trusted me then, aren't you?" Caelius counted out his change. "Keep my seat this time, will you? I don't want you making any more friends tonight."

He turned and pushed his way towards a passage leading away from the main bar. There was a phone there. "The first drunk I see," Catullus shouted after him, "your seat's his." But Caelius had gone. Catullus stared morosely into his drink and drew a pattern with it on the table.

"Ayerooo!" shouted a voice from behind him.

Catullus looked round.

"Ayerooo!" It was Tubbers. Catullus waved at him and Tubbers waved back. "Ayerooo," he explained, "drinking call of the best bloody drinking club in town! Come and join us! The Wild Batchelors of Tallowfield! Have some *rarl* fun! Ayeroo!" Catullus walked across, and settled himself uncertainly into a spare seat. Tubbers gave him a thumbs up, and beamed. "Bloody good fun," he said. "Bloody good laugh."

Catullus sneaked a glance at the other Wild Batchelor. He was large and broad-skulled, and had a flattened nose; an occasional fizzing sound came from the inside of his mouth as a small pellet of tobacco was sucked from one molar to the next. Catullus coughed and stirred; as though reminded, Tubbers raised his head and his eyeballs rose and sunk like a snowstorm shaken up in a glass toy.

He creased his brow earnestly. "How are things, then? Settling down?"

"Fine, thank you."

"Oh right, right, great news. Like Tallowfield?"

"Very pleasant."

"Bloody nice place. Bloody nice pub too."

"Yes, it's lovely."

Tubbers nodded, and shook his head to the juke-box. "They're opening a club here soon. Should be bloody good fun." He pointed his finger in and out as the rhythm quickened. His jabbings bore no relation to the beat of the song. "Ayerooo," he shouted again, "the Wild Batchelors! Bloody hell, eh, what a laugh! Want to meet my pal?"

Catullus glanced at the pal, and shook his head.

"Great bloke," Tubbers whispered heavily. He turned to his

companion, and slapped him on the back. "Ayeroo, Bulldog!" he said. "This is the Bulldog. Bulldog – Catullus."

"Nice to meet you" said Catullus.

"All right?" nodded the Bulldog.

"The Bulldog's a snooker player," said Tubbbers excitedly. "Aren't you, Bulldog?"

The Bulldog gestured modestly with his hands. "It's been known. Screw and side, yeah. Same again please."

He pushed his glass forward. Tubbers beamed and climbed unsteadily to his feet. "Bit of the old nectar?" he asked Catullus, but swayed towards the bar without waiting for an answer. He was back almost at once, proudly balancing three glasses. "He's bloody good too," Tubbers confided, handing the glasses out. "Not much going on though right now. Recession. Bloody bad news. Isn't that right, Bulldog?"

The Bulldog nodded. "I'm as happy as a load of shit in a bucket."

"Bloody right, bloody right. So actually that's why we're here, the Wild Batchelors of Tallowfield, ayerooo! Trying to get him a job."

"What sort?" Catullus asked.

"In the club."

The Bulldog leant over and winked heavily. "We'll still use the old snooker cue, know what I mean?" He winked again. "Keeping order, and that."

"Heard of Crassus?" Tubbers asked.

"No."

"*Marcus* Crassus," the Bulldog added with emphasis.

"No. Never."

"Bloody rich bloke," said Tubbers in hushed tones. "Coins it in."

"He's sharp," said the Bulldog. "Like the edge of a fucking broken bottle."

Catullus shrugged. "Okay, I get the picture. What about him?"

Tubbers explained. "Owns this pub, you see. Club bound to do well. Get in on it, bloody good move. Ayeroo. Here we are."

"Crassus, he's a rich wanker," said the Bulldog. "Anyone in his way" – he brought his fist down suddenly onto the table – "like bluebottles." He looked at Tubbers. "Same again please."

"More of the nectar? Bloody good idea!" Tubbers swung up. "Ayeroo! Caelius! Over here!"

Caelius had returned from the phone.

"Hello," he said shortly. "That'll be fine," he added to Catullus. "Tomorrow."

"*Tomorrow?*"

Tubbers slapped Caelius on the back and interrupted him as he was about to reply. "Having a bit of a piss-up," he said loudly.

"Then I think I'll give it a miss, if it's all the same to you."

"Go on. Have a drink. Nectar on me."

"Isn't it always?"

Suddenly, the Bulldog stood up. "I want to see the club," he announced. Tubbers was taken by surprise.

"But, Bulldog, it's shut. Trespassers prosecuted, and all that."

"I want to see the club."

"Tell you what – have a drink."

"I want to see the club."

Tubbers stared at him. "All right," he said, after a pause. "Why not? Bit of a laugh."

"What is this club?" asked Caelius. "Where is it?"

"Under the pub," Tubbers whispered back. "Come and see it. Please." He turned and saw that the Bulldog was being swallowed by the crowds. "Please," he whispered again. "Please. For me."

"Great," said Caelius as he watched Tubbers push his way through towards the passageway. "What a perfect end to a bloody magical evening. Poking our way round some half-dug hole." He rose to his feet. "Come on, then."

Tubbers had disappeared through a door in the passageway. Caelius and Catullus followed him. As they began to make their way down a winding staircase, a light was switched on from below, and they could see the cellars they were heading for; high vaults, fresh masonry, a powder of dust unswept from the concreted floors. From above, the dull roar of conversation sounded, surging dimly like waves heard through a cave's wall. Even more insistent was the silence of the catacombs leading into darkness away from the central chamber. The Bulldog moved towards one of the entrances.

A sign barred his way. He stopped and tried to read it aloud. "KEEP OUT." He grunted and kicked it over; then he made his way past it into the darkness beyond.

"Should you be in there?" Tubbers asked nervously.

"Bollocks," said the Bulldog from the darkness.

"Oh. Right!"

"There's a body here," the Bulldog announced suddenly.

"A body?"

"Yeah."

"Golly." Tubbers turned back to Caelius. "Did you hear that? There's a..."

"I heard." Caelius pushed his way past and walked into the shadows towards the Bulldog's voice. "Where?" he asked. "Are you sure?"

"Yeah." The Bulldog pointed. "There."

It took a few seconds to adjust to the dark, but Catullus could see the shape of the body as soon as he had walked into the catacomb. He walked up to it and squinted. Then he felt it. It wasn't a body – well, it had been a body, once, but now it was just a skeleton, ages old, Catullus would have guessed, so old that the hard yellow bones seemed to have been chiselled out from the rock of the floor. Catullus bent down again and studied them; they had been cemented in. Strange. He looked about. There was something strange on the wall as well, a carving. He could just make it out when everyone else stood away from the light: a dancer, his legs apart, his arms in the air, his head thrown wildly back. "Like the man by the bonfire," Catullus whispered to his friend. Caelius frowned and said nothing.

"Your round," said the Bulldog to Tubbers. Then he walked out from the catacomb, and everyone else followed him, back up the stairway and into the bar. No one seemed to have noticed their trespass; Crassus would never have to know about it. Only the man in the coat who had spoken to Catullus earlier in the evening looked up, but this time he kept quiet, not moving from his stool beside the door. "I need something to fortify me," whispered Caelius, very quietly, so that no one else would hear him. "Want a drink?" Catullus shook his head, then stared at Caelius who had begun to pat desperately at his jacket. "What's the matter, have you got scabies?" Catullus asked. "No, it's my wallet. My fucking wallet. It's gone." Caelius frisked himself again, then swore violently. "What am I going to do? It must have been that sodding bastard cunt wino we took in the taxi." Catullus shrugged. "Go and ask him for it back." He pulled Caelius on the arm. "Come on, you can't get a drink now. Let's go."

On the street, Caelius hesitated before accompanying Catullus back towards their flat. "I ought to do something," he said. "I think I will go back to that hostel."

"Go in the morning."

"He'll have slipped it to his fence, or something equally vulgar and low-life like that."

"Was there much in it?"

"No. But it's the principle of the thing."

"Oh, come on, Caelius." And Catullus reached for his friend's hand, and began to pull him down the street. Away from the lights of the pub, he suddenly took Caelius in his arms, and kissed him long on the lips, with passion, his fingers stroking the curve of his back, holding him tight. Catullus felt Caelius' tongue as it touched his own, and then his friend had broken free and was staring at him, wiping his mouth.

"No," said Caelius eventually. "No. I thought we'd decided."

"You'd decided."

"No – we'd decided."

"I had to do it once, Caelius, just for old times' sake, but now – that's fine – enough."

"It is better for both of us this way."

"Yes, if that's what you think, all right. I was expecting it, I suppose." Catullus paused. "And we're still friends?"

"Of course." Caelius sounded hurt. "Best of friends. I'd never have invited you here otherwise, would I, you tit?"

"I'm sorry."

"So am I." Caelius held his friend in his arms. "We like each other far too much to spoil it with sex. It was just a stupid fling, wasn't it? It should never have happened."

"But it did."

"Yes, it did. But baby – it was a long time ago."

"And now we're in Rome, and everything's changed." Catullus smiled. "Yes, you're right. Of course you are. Best of friends."

Caelius took his arm. "Best of friends." They walked back to the flat, and Caelius didn't mention his lost wallet, preserving an amicable silence instead. It was only later, when Catullus was asleep, that he finally made up his mind to go for it. Noiselessly, he crept out of the flat, then began to hurry back along the street.

IV

MARIUS

The next morning, tentatively, Catullus pushed open the Dugbals' kitchen door. There was no laundry left, but vast metal pans were still massed around the room on various shelves and sideboards. One was perched on a cooker, rocking and shaking as water bubbled away inside it. Mrs Dugbal stirred at something, then turned round to face Catullus as he walked across the room.

"Do you like your crabs with or without eggs?" she asked, but didn't wait for an answer. Instead, she fished out a crab from a neighbouring pan, and waved it. "This do you?" she asked. Catullus nodded dumbly, and watched as the crab, its claws waving in ponderous desperation, was dropped into the boiling water.

"Well, go on," said Mrs Dugbal, not looking round. "Sit down."

Catullus smiled with embarrassment at the other three Dugbals as he took his place. Mr Dugbal buried his face in his newspaper; Vanessa didn't look up; only Jez seemed enthusiastic about seeing him. "I was thinking, you know," he said at once, not bothering to finish his mouthful and spattering the table cloth in front of him with crumbs, "I was thinking, wouldn't it be a totally safe idea, if, you know that insect torture you were going on about last night, if instead of insects you got someone and you used snails." He nodded with excitement and banged his fork up and down against the table. "You're tied down, you see, and you feel snails crawling all over you until you can't stand it any more. And then someone puts one on your eyes and you die." Jez smiled happily.

"Why would you die?" asked Catullus, watching distractedly as Mrs Dugbal scooped out a crab and began to hammer at its shell with a large mallet.

"Because they've got a deadly poison, stupid, which they inject into your eyes so you die in agony. Eeeugh." Jez screwed up his eyes and rolled his head about. "Like that. They're all covered in *slime*. Don't you think it's wicked?"

Mrs Dugbal prevented Catullus from agreeing by shoving a steaming mess of crab and eggs under his nose.

"Go on, then," she ordered. "Eat it up."

"Do you like them?" Jez asked.

"What, snails?"

"No, crabs."

Catullus prodded at the pink crab meat, and dipped it into his egg yolk. "Very nice" he said, swallowing it.

"I think crabs are stupid. They ought to get eaten. I don't like rats either."

"You eat rats?"

"No, *thicko*, they're horrible. Do you know, if you feel a rat's tail, that's covered in slime too. There was one in our cellar. Do you think that's why you don't have them for breakfast, because all the slime might make you sick?"

Catullus stared down at the egg yolk as it congealed around the crab, and felt his stomach lurch towards his mouth. He breathed in deeply and looked up to see Vanessa staring at him, her eyes as cold as they had been the day before.

"I've got to go now," Jez said, pulling on his sleeve. "I've got to go and clean my teeth for school. See you." He pushed his chair back and got to his feet. Vanessa followed him, but as she turned to leave the room, Mrs Dugbal lunged at her shoulder and caught it, spinning her daughter round to face her. "Aren't you going to eat your crabs?" she asked, eyeing the mound of pink flesh left heaped on Vanessa's plate. "That's God's food you're not eating."

Vanessa stared back at her mother and her eyes narrowed.

"You know I'd die rather than eat it. I'd rather eat you than eat a crab, and it makes me sick just to look at you! They were alive, Mummy, you boiled them alive!" She turned and ran, slamming the door after her. As the kitchen walls shook, Mr Dugbal began to wail, trembling violently, and followed his daughter out of the room. Mrs Dugbal stacked his empty plate away, and for a second, just a second, wordless misery clouded her face. Then the kitchen door slammed a third time, and Catullus was left alone with his plate of crab.

The whole dish was tepid now. The crab had only partially been drained, and the lumps of its carcass felt clammy in the pools of salt water. Catullus looked at it and thought about how expensive crabs were, how proud Mrs Dugbal must have been of cooking him such a meal. Bracing himself, he dipped a particularly large and rubbery piece of flesh into the thickening egg yolk. He bent his head down, pulled the meat off with his teeth, and swallowed.

There was a crash from behind him as Mrs Dugbal walked back into the room.

"Enjoying your food, are you?" she asked approvingly. She reached into her pot and ladled out more. "There you go. Have as much as you want."

Catullus smiled bravely at his plate. "Is Vanessa all right?" he asked, looking up.

Mrs Dugbal snorted. "How would I know? I've got better things to do than stand around worrying about her. The world's never how you like it to be, she'll learn that soon enough. Which reminds me – I must be off to work. Money doesn't grow on trees." She picked up her bags. "Mind you clear the table."

"I will."

She watched as he tidied up the plates and stacked them by the sink; as he began to pour water into the bowl, she grunted a final time and left, slamming the door behind her as violently as before and thumping her way out through the hall. Catullus bent his head against the window to try to cool his headache, and saw that it had begun to rain; it fell softly as Mrs Dugbal hunched herself up and begun to trudge slowly away from her own neat porch, through the dampened litter of the rest of the street. It began to rain harder, and Mrs Dugbal was soon lost in the grey of the thickening downpour.

There was a click from behind as the kitchen door opened; Catullus turned, thinking that maybe it was Caelius at last. But it was Mr Dugbal, smiling timidly and playing with his cap, dancing from foot to foot until finally, with a cough, he plucked up the courage to ask Catullus if he would make him a cup of tea at some stage in the morning. "You see," he said, as though he had been accused of something, "I am partial to a cup of tea while I do my work."

"Really? What do you do?"

A look of panic froze over Mr Dugbal's face. He began to twist violently and click his tongue against the back of his throat. Like a moth startled by a sudden light, he seemed dazed by his own terror, and it was only after Catullus had taken him by the arm and stilled his shaking that Mr Dugbal could bring himself to speak. "I couldn't possibly tell you that, I'm afraid," he stammered. "Out of the question." Catullus apologised, and Mr Dugbal gradually calmed down. He nodded and shook Catullus' hand, then drifted back out through the door, like a large feathery insect, Catullus thought, the sort that brush against your knees in dark dank woods, and make you long to break out again into fields. But then he remembered that he wasn't in the country anymore, and he wanted Caelius to wake up and show him the sights of Rome.

But Caelius was still nowhere to be seen, and it was raining outside. Catullus wandered upstairs, thought for a minute or two on the landing, then settled himself into the kitchen that served the first floor. He had left Mr Varney's book there the previous evening; he reached for it and settled down. Away from the smell of dead crab, he already felt more cheerful.

He didn't open Mr Varney's book straightaway. Instead, he ran his fingers over the cover, as though he were a blind man reading braille; the surface was rough in patches, but mostly well worn; the book had clearly been opened a good deal. Catullus read the title again: *Marius the Dancer and the Great Civil War*. Then he flicked the book open and began to turn through the pages until, his eyes caught by a chapter heading, he stopped page hopping and began to read.

"How Marius defended Rome from the armies of the King," the chapter was titled. The print was thick and rounded, and seemed to sink into the texture of the page as though it were a chain of weights slung over white sludge. The words stared up at Catullus and as he stared back, trying to work his mind round the first sentence, he suddenly found that the words seemed totally unfamiliar, that they scarcely seemed words at all, in fact, but just a meaningless jumble of strokes and curves. He blinked, and looked at the sentence a second time; then he read it out loud, and even though he could hear his voice pronouncing sounds, the words themselves seemed to be skimming off his mind like pebbles flicked across a lake. He blinked again, and spoke the sentence again. Suddenly, as though in compensation, he found that not only could he understand what he was saying, but it was as though the book were reading him, so that he too, like the words, was sinking into the page itself, was being pulled along so fast by the sentences that soon he was oblivious to their very presence, as they dissolved themselves into a meaning finally deciphered and grasped. And so Catullus scanned on, with an eagerness he found hard to understand. "Imagine the feelings of terror and panic," he read, "when the citizens of Rome heard the threats of the king. Through the great gates of Westbrook the royal herald had ridden, past the deserted pleasure gardens and palace of Fairfields, over the Tiber, and on, up towards the Senate House. Rome echoed to the ring of hooves, and seemed already a dead city.

"'Senators, not worthy of the name, traitors to your royal master the King,' proclaimed the herald. 'Hear the terms of peace that are graciously allowed to you. You are to open the gates of Rome and surrender the keys you have kept for so long from their rightful possessor. You are to relinquish all those powers and abuses won by trickery with which you and your forefathers have attempted to rule the kingdom and keep from His Majesty the power that is rightfully his. All seditious discussion and thought, all pamphlets and books which have argued for the overthrow of the divinely appointed ways, are to be banned and utterly destroyed. On acceptance of these terms, you will be permitted to live, and your families, and your servants, and the City will be preserved from the ruin of siege and destruction. These are the words of the King. The King has spoken.'

"Silence greeted the ending of this speech. Silence deep and terrible, so that no one could guess, as the herald turned and left the hall, what thoughts might be passing through the minds of the senators, what words would be spoken once the debate had begun. The great doors slammed shut and the senators were left alone. Still there was silence. Slowly, Caecilius rose to his feet."

Catullus turned another page and leant back in his chair to study a picture, finely drawn in black ink, with the single caption "Marius before the Senate." With the profile of a Greek god and the vaguest hint of a halo around his head, Marius had been given full military uniform and a look of suffering nobility to distinguish him even further from the blur of blank faces behind him, the senators not sparse as in the text, but plentiful like leaves on an autumn lane. There was a smudge on the corner of the page, a thumb mark, so deeply indented into the paper that it was clear the picture had been a favourite of the book's previous owner.

Catullus read on, through the high sounding rhetoric of the debate in the Senate House. In impassioned terms, senators argued for accepting the terms, for bowing to the inevitability of defeat, the chapter insisting on their nobility even as it was glowered at sternly by the hero on the opposite page. Catullus started to become impatient; he began to skim faster and faster, until, turning a further page, he saw that the first sentence of a new paragraph had been underlined and a star pencilled in on the margin. More evidence of Mr Varney's taste. Catullus stopped skimming and began to read again.

"All seemed inclined to accept the terms," the paragraph began, "until, during a moment of rare silence, the voice of Marius boomed out that he wished to speak. Hush greeted the great general as he took his place, and the House seemed frozen, waiting and wondering what he had to say. Marius gazed around him, and fire blazed in his deep-set eyes. 'I cannot deny,' he began, 'that we are in great danger. The enemy has, by cunning and cruelty, succeeded in destroying our last remaining army. His forces sweep ever on towards us. He is many – we are few. Never, perhaps, has our country known greater peril.'

"He paused, and, we are told, in the silence, that his every limb seemed to expand and glow.

"'And yet!' He brought down his fist. 'Yet! Are we not still Romans? And are we not most Romans when the odds seem most cruelly stacked against us? Do we not have the record of a thousand triumphs, a thousand victories, to cheer us, won by that people whose stock is not yet exhausted? Can we know, can we *feel* this, and still talk of surrender?'

"A murmur began to ripple through the assembled ranks of senators. Marius stilled it with a single glance of fire.

"'We have nothing to offer our people but struggle, and blood, and the terror of knowing that they may face total ruin. And yet I believe – as surely as I have ever believed anything – that they will welcome the fight, and curse us forever if we deny it to them. Who here will accept that curse? Who dares to brave it?' Marius nodded, and waited, and then spoke on. 'Let all the corners of the world look to us and know, that our ancient courage and our love of liberty are not yet dead. The king will come – yes, he will come, and on the walls of Rome he will meet the people, and he will feel the shock, and he will know that he cannot win through. The greater the danger, the greater the triumph! Let us fight, and we will dance on the ashes of tyranny. I say, let us fight, and triumph, and live to dance as free men!'"

So, there it was – Marius the Dancer. Catullus turned back a few pages and studied Marius' profile again. It certainly had the right nose; anyone would have been taken seriously with that sort of a nose – you could have spoken any old shit and got away with it. But Catullus couldn't imagine Marius dancing, and certainly not on hot ashes – it would have been too undignified – and thinking of hot ashes reminded Catullus of the strange dancer that he and Caelius had seen the night before, and he wondered at the coincidence and decided not to put the book aside. But he had had enough of Marius' speechifying; he skimmed over the rest of the call to arms, the applause and approbation, the Senate's rejection of the King's terms, its determination to fight on. At the start of a new paragraph, Mr Varney had pencilled in another star: "Never give up," he had scribbled in the margin, and Catullus stopped skimming to read the annotated passage. "Storm clouds gathered over the capital that evening" – the sentence had been underlined. "To the citizens gathering in the square beneath the now lightless towers of the Senate House, and on the ancient city walls, and in any of the streets and alleyways of Rome, it seemed as though the very skies were darkening in anticipation of the coming struggle. Guards, standing that night on the Westbrook gate, and hearing dull rumbles from far away, did not know if they were the rolls of thunder, or the cannon of the enemy as they drew slowly closer to the city walls. But all knew that the hour of struggle was at hand."

Catullus turned the page, and there was another picture: "Marius greets Claudius Pulcher on the battlements." Once again, the granite-faced Marius stared nobly in profile, his arm sweeping out towards enemy banners and tents, while by his side a second man stood, gazing with a parallel nobility at Marius, his hand grasped firmly on the handle of his sword. It seemed familiar, and Catullus wondered why. He looked again at the sweep of Marius' arm, and recognition flitted tantalisingly just beyond the bounds of his memory; then he looked at the arm again, and suddenly, he remembered – of course, the picture had been in a book his brother had owned and scribbled all over, that was where he had seen it before. Marius had been shaded in and given fangs; a handle-bar moustache had sprouted on his lip. Claudius had been given a massive prick, so large that it had blotted out the sword handle and finished up under the firm grasp of his fingers. A happy grin had been inked in over the face. Catullus smiled, and tried to remember how old his brother must have been. Nine, ten? Anyway, he hadn't been very interested in Marius, and Catullus, reading the book of someone who was, suddenly found that his own interest was making him feel uneasy, as a sudden dull fear settled over him that the person he had once been, laughing at his brother's drawings and admiring them for their nerve and skill, feeling happy because the joke had been explained to him, was now quite gone, had been dead for years in fact, and in its place there was only – what? Catullus thought of his brother, and then of Mr Varney as he had puked up his evening's drink on the hostel steps, and he shivered, afraid that maybe he was changing and becoming all the time more like the drunk he had rescued from the pub, and less like the brother he had always so adored and admired. He looked down at the book, and sniffed at it. No smell of drink, at least. Catullus watched as the book, so old and well thumbed that its pages refused to rest flattened under the cover, gently opened back out again, like an anemone which, brushed inadvertently, slowly fills the pool where it has been lying and proves, with the soft movements of its opening frills and spines through the water, its hitherto unsuspected life. The pages finally came to rest. The book was open again at the picture of Marius and Claudius Pulcher.

"Claudius Pulcher," whispered Catullus to himself. The ancestor of Clodius? How odd. Of course he was, this noble-faced line drawing, he was the ancestor of the Clodius that he, Catullus, had been sitting with just a day and a half ago, hearing the splash of oars, and looking out over the torch-lit lake. He studied the picture again, and it was so plain, so basic, that he suddenly felt that its simplicity could only be a delusion, that it contained some clue or code that he couldn't quite pin down, some hint of the mysteries he had sensed at the ball. Suddenly he remembered, as though the recollection were something he had deliberately avoided until then, that if Claudius was the ancestor of Clodius, then he would have to be the forefather of Clodia as well; touching the page, Catullus felt a dizzying thrill rise in his stomach, and the book, which had seemed so depressing just a moment before, now seemed dyed with a pleasure he could barely understand. He stared at the picture;

then, afraid to pursue his unexpected sense of joy any further in case it disappeared altogether, he leant back in his chair and started to read again.

The next chapter described the arrival of the king's army and the preparations for the siege. Catullus skimmed quickly through it, but the word "Fairfields" caught his eye, and so he paused again, to find out what Marius had done in the royal gardens, where Mr Varney now lived, and strange fires could be seen, blazing through the night. "Marius stood on the Westbrook Gate," he read. "In front of the walls lay the King's armies, encamped in a great horde; behind, the gardens where in more peaceful times, the King had once wandered. But since the flight from his enraged capital, the beautiful lawns and flowers of Fairfields had been decaying. No one had thought to preserve what were seen only as monuments to tyranny. Yet Marius, we know, loved to wander through such wilds. We may well presume that in the ruined arbours and thick tangles of undergrowth he found a stillness that was a refuge from the chaos of war. Certainly, his journal is full of many eloquent testimonies to the beauties that he found. There is a loveliness in ruin, sometimes, that not even the most skilled gardener can create.

"It was also in the gardens that the episode of the Hooded Dancer reached its climax, an event so remarkable that it merits being told in full. We have narrated it below. If anyone does not believe what he reads there, he has only to turn to the journal of Marius himself. In it he will find the same story, and see that we have merely chosen to repeat what is told more fully there. Let the disbelieving think then what they will."

A small heading followed: 'The Hooded Dancer.' Another dancer, Catullus thought, and wondered why he had never heard of the story before. He read on.

"In the streets that month, a curfew had been imposed. After sunset, across the whole of the great city, the only light came from distant flames burning beyond the walls in the camp of the king. Through the deserted alleyways, Marius would sometimes make his way. He would be disguised, so that no one could recognise him, and only when challenged by a patrol would he reveal his identity. Otherwise, he stayed cloaked and hooded, unknown to those with whom he talked, comforting and cheering even those he found who were breaking the curfew. Above all, he loved to talk to the common soldiers, to learn their grievances, and fill their spirits with a new courage. Through the streets Marius would slip, as though he were truly the genius of the anguished city.

"One night, he was walking by the cross-roads of the Aventine. Standing there, he saw a figure as it passed in front of him, then disappeared down a narrow back alley. Marius called out, softly. There was no reply. Hurrying after the figure, he saw it as it darted down another alley, and Marius called after it again. Still it ran on, and Marius resolved that he would follow this figure who refused to stop. And so began the chase.

"The quarry was elusive. The streets were dark and narrow. Often Marius feared that he had lost the object of his pursuit, only for it to step out for one brief second from the shadows it had been hurrying through. Once, the figure was cast into sudden light by a burst of artillery fire, and Marius could see that it was cloaked, as he was too, but also stooped and hunched in the shoulders. Ghostly it seemed, and strange. Marius has written of his fearful imaginings, and well can we believe them! Yet he was not the man to slacken his chase, and he pressed ever on, his footsteps ringing heavily on the cobbles, while ahead of him, more faint, could be heard the echoes of the creature he was pursuing.

"At last, Marius stopped. His quarry was nowhere to be seen. Desperately, he searched down each winding street, and then again, yet there was nothing to be seen. His disappointment must then have seemed indeed overwhelming! Still he wondered what it was that he had seen, and why it had chosen to flee from him.

"'Why do you pursue me?' a voice asked from behind him, suddenly. 'Do you too wish to destroy me?'

"Marius turned, but could see only deep shadows. 'No,' he answered clearly. 'No, I do not wish to destroy you.'

"Slowly the figure stepped out from the dark, to face Marius as he stood waiting by the corner of the crossroads. The cloak of the strange figure had a hood, and still Marius could not tell what lay beneath. But he could see, more clearly than before, how strangely the shoulders were hunched, and Marius sensed something strange and fearful waiting to be shown. His thirst to fathom the mystery grew the more it was denied.

"'Come with me', the figure ordered suddenly.

"'Show me your face', Marius commanded, unabashed, in reply.

"The figure slowly shook its head.

"'Come with me,' it repeated. Then it started to move. Marius followed, having to hurry, staring all the time at the cowled head of the figure by his side. They passed a tavern. It seemed open, despite the curfew, and a group of men, standing outside it, looked up as Marius and his companion hurried by. The men all shouted after them and one hurled a stone. It hit the cloaked creature on his shoulder, but the creature just bent forward all the more, and began to run. A woman saw them, then two soldiers. They too all shouted and hurled stones, and Marius tells us that he was amazed to be with someone known by everyone but himself. And he wondered all the more at what lay beneath the hood.

"It seemed as though they had been running for the whole night. At last, however, they stood outside the ruined entrance way to the Royal Gardens.

"'Do you know who I am?' the figure asked. Marius shook his head. 'Then behold,' said the figure. Slowly he pulled away the hood from his face, and Marius saw, he writes in his journal, that beneath the cowl was the head of an eagle! 'Come quickly.' Marius was pulled against his will along the twisting garden paths. He could only stare in horror at the sight revealed to him. The man stopped, and his eagle's head turned. A wind began to blow, ruffling the golden feathers of the eagle's head as it strained to hear, faint at first, then a deepening murmur, the sound of hundreds of voices coming ever closer towards them. The eagle's eyes, darker than the night, blank and pitiless, turned towards Marius, and even Marius, bravest of men, felt his soul begin to quail.

"'Are you there?' it asked, seeming not to see him. 'Are you with me?' But the creature did not wait for an answer. The breeze now had become a mighty gale, and the two of them were swept on it through the gardens like fallen leaves. Behind them, rising ever above the scream of the wind, could be heard a veritable chaos of voices.

"By the banks of the Tiber, the creature turned to face Marius again, and released his arm.

"'I cannot escape,' it said, and its voice sounded like metal being scraped across a stone. 'Wait and watch.' Then, drawing closer to the river, it began to dance. Marius watched as the creature suddenly raised its head and opened the cruel scimitars of its beak to scream an unearthly sound. Looking behind him, Marius saw that gathered around the creature was a great multitude of people, men, women, children, all carrying staves and clubs. The creature screamed once again. There was a silence. Then with answering screams, the people surged forward and the creature, seeing them advance, began to run. But he stumbled, and the people fell on him, tearing his body to pieces – or so Marius avouches in his journal. What was left of the corpse was flung into the Tiber – but Marius, even the dauntless Marius, could not withstand the horror of his vision. He fainted. When he woke again, it was past dawn and the gardens were empty.

"What are we to make of such a story? We cannot believe that an eagle-headed man really lived – and yet Marius was never known to lie. Perhaps his dream of it had been possessed of a truth greater even than that of reality. What lesson does it teach us? That a single monster, be it never so terrible, can be overthrown by the will of a united people. What man fitter to be assured of that truth than

Marius, even then fighting for Rome's liberty and life against the armies of the king? And, lest people should still choose to scoff, we know also that when Marius ordered the Tiber to be dredged on the following morning, a badly battered corpse was found floating amongst the marsh reeds of the lower gardens. The skull had been sliced in half, from top to bottom. *No one could tell what the face might have been.*"

Mr Varney had added a small note to this sentence. "Here," he had written. "The sign of ruin. Even, odd, even." Then there was a word, written in Greek letters, but not sounding Greek – "Sirephtok". What the hell did that mean? Catullus shook his head. Even, odd, even? He shut the book and put it down. Tea. He listened to the kettle boil, and thought how odd it was that he had never heard of the story before. It was outside his period, of course, but even so, he knew about the Civil War, he'd read books about Marius, but he was sure none of them had mentioned the Hooded Dancer – he would have remembered it if they had. He looked again at the book, its pages still rustling and stirring under the cover. So what had he and Caelius seen, out there on the tip that had once been Fairfields? An eagleman perhaps? Catullus sat down again, and took a sip at his tea. Then he remembered that he had promised Mr Dugbal a cup, and as he wandered back over to the kettle, he decided that he had had enough of reading, and needed to get out. He listened. The rain sounded lighter on the roof. He would visit Marius in the temple opposite. He picked up the book, took it to his bedroom, and then, with Mr Dugbal's cup of tea, made his way downstairs.

Outside the sitting room door, he knocked and waited. There was no answer. Gingerly, Catullus started to turn the handle, and as he did so, there was a sudden sound of crashing furniture and a scuffling from the room behind the door. As Catullus walked in, he saw Mr Dugbal scooping up an armful of tins and then, suddenly startled, throw himself against one of the wall tapestries.

"I was just – just asleep." Mr Dugbal smiled unconvincingly and straightened his cap. There was a pause. He smiled again at Catullus and started to twist the tassels on a blanket.

"Brought the tea then, have you?" he said at last.

Catullus nodded, and held the cup out.

"Aha," said Mr Dugbal, taking it. He smiled again. "I expect you heard the, um..?" He pointed towards the tins, where they had been dropped again by the far wall. "Just – please – don't mention them to a soul. Our little secret?"

"Yes. If you want."

"Thank you." Mr Dugbal blinked, and then suddenly scurried back to his favourite armchair. Catullus watched him as he burrowed under yet more blankets. The chat was evidently over. Catullus turned, whispered goodbye, and left the room behind.

By the Tiber, Lud and Pollo, the two violinists, were walking along a path.

"I have to say it," said Pollo. "Of all the cuntiest places in the world, this is the fucking cuntiest." He stopped and looked around. There wasn't much to see: mud along the river, nettles on the path, emptiness in the waste land stretching out between him and the road a few hundred yards away. There was only the shell of a car and a dampened circle of ash to show that anyone had ever been there at all.

"It's got a bad feel to it, this whole place," muttered Pollo to himself. "Varney was right, it is evil." He grinned at Lud, and pulled his mac tightly round his body as a sudden blast of wind skimmed across the water. "Come on. Let's get out of here."

The two musicians trudged slowly on. The wind screamed more shrilly, and it began to rain.

In the temple, Catullus too could hear the rain as it began to fall again. His first sight, walking in through the doorway, had been of a shaft of light cutting through the darkness, but as the door slammed shut after him, so also had the sun's brief ray been submerged beneath cloud, and Catullus was left in gloom. He stood where he had walked in, at the back of the temple behind the pews; the only thing he could see was the faint glow of marble from a far corner. He walked up towards it; a statue; Marius, of course. Larger, chillier than the drawings in Mr Varney's book had been, but just as dead. The general's eyes were blank; his arm, again, swept out in an implacable gesture of command; the stone folds of his tunic fell uncreasable. Catullus read a small plaque attached to the statue's base; 'Gaius Marius, Friend of Roman Liberty. This statue has been erected to mark the site near which he is supposed to have been buried.'

Catullus turned and walked back towards the pews. His footsteps echoed round the temple's naked stone, over the drumming of rain on the roof above, and it was only when he had taken a seat that he saw that there were two other people with him, both seated a few pews ahead. One of them was an old man, hunched up in a battered jacket, with his hands in his pockets and rain dripping from his nose. The other, sitting well apart, was younger, and Catullus realised suddenly that it was the man he had seen the night before, still with flowers, still in black, exactly the same. He remembered how pleased he had been to see him, and the memory made Catullus feel proprietorial, as though he already knew the man. He walked to the front of the church and nodded, but only the older of the two men stirred and nodded back. "Can't hear the rain now, eh?" the old man said, pointing at the roof. He made his way slowly over to a side door, and pushing it open, stuck out a hand. "Oh yes, it's cleared up now," he said, "look. And all that soil, it'll be soft and givey. Digging weather."

"Why, what are you looking for?" Catullus asked.

"Graves," said the old man with a sniff. "I dig them." He held the door open. "Coming out?"

Catullus followed him. The rainstorm had died into a soft drizzle, which made everything seem grey and dull except for the graveyard itself, which glistened and sparkled, and astonished Catullus, who had never expected to discover such a beautiful stretch of grass amongst the slate and chimneys he had been gazing across the evening before.

"It's wonderful," he told the old man, who nodded appreciatively.

"It's got balls," he said, "that's how I put it. I've always said, there's nothing like a good corpse to give a stretch of turf some balls. We've both got testicles in working order, me and my turf." He nudged Catullus and wheezed. "Wouldn't you say?"

Catullus shrugged. "I wouldn't like to comment on yours."

The old man cackled. "You're staying with Mrs Dugbal, aren't you?"

"Yes. In the flat above her. How did you know?"

The old man laughed again. "You get some crabs this morning, did you?"

"Yes."

"Good, good." The old man paused to get back his breath, exhausted by his laughter. "I got them," he said at last. "I always do, whenever Mrs Dugbal wants anything. Oh, she's a fine woman, she is."

"Where do you get the crabs from?"

"Sea, of course. Back of sea-going lorries." The old man chuckled wheezily again. "It's easier with snails, or strawberries, or anything that can actually grow here, of course. Now then, come and look at these."

He led Catullus down a path to a grave nestled up against a far wall. He pointed. "Look. Beautiful, eh?"

Catullus looked. There was a cluster of mushrooms, rising like bubbles over the grave. The old man knelt down, and delicately picked a few, then dropped them into a paper bag.

"Give those to Mrs Dugbal," he said, handing the bag to Catullus. "Tell her they're from Smallpiece, and remind her – from death comes life." He chuckled. "She'll know what you mean."

"Why, are you having a thing with her, then?"

Mr Smallpiece looked hurt, and Catullus immediately regretted the question. He watched as the old man shook his head and swallowed, trying to recapture his breath. "It's none of your business," he gasped eventually. "But let's just put it like this. She's a marvellous cook and a wonderful woman."

"Yes. I'm sorry."

"That's all right. You just give her those."

"I will."

"Works her fingers off, she does, right down to the bone." He bent and picked up his shovel. "Got a mad husband, you see."

Catullus followed him as the old man began to wander back up the path. "What's the matter with Mr Dugbal? Is he really mad?"

"You live with him."

"Only for one day so far."

"Tell me in a week then, I'll be interested to know." The old man grinned, then began to dig. Catullus was about to say goodbye when the old man looked up again. "He was in the war, I think."

"Which war?"

"The one in Circassia. The one where we went in and won, and then found out that actually we'd lost. That was about four years ago, wasn't it?"

"Yes." Catullus thought about the gold grasshopper he had been shown. "Maybe that's why he's strange, then?"

Mr Smallpiece grunted. He began to dig again. Catullus shook him by the hand, and said goodbye. "Don't forget about the mushrooms," the old man shouted after him.

"I won't," said Catullus. He began to walk away, back up the path. He had noticed the young man in black, standing head bowed by the far temple wall. The man was staring at a newly washed headstone; he knelt and laid his bunch of flowers against it, then bowed his head again, and after a minute's silence, made his way back over the wet grass to the path. As Catullus followed, he glanced at the grave. 'Juventius', the headstone read. 'Memory is the seedbed from which the dead shall live again.' Juventius. Father, perhaps? Son? – no. Lover?

Catullus walked back into the temple. Inside, the dark had been melted into white, the walls everywhere glowing with a pale intensity that made the building seem unrecognisable as the dingy hall he had been huddling in ten minutes earlier. Catullus looked for the man in black, but he seemed to have vanished with the dark. Shit.

Catullus looked around again, and saw Marius, who seemed to be melting away too, the wall behind him gleaming so brightly now that he was virtually indistinguishable from it, and as Catullus went up to look at the statue a second time, he felt its size shrinking under his stare. But then he stared into the empty eyes, and saw that they glowed as remorselessly as before, and as he stared, he found the brightness painful. He turned and looked down; there were some pamphlets scattered on the floor. He walked back to a pew with one and studied the title. 'Welcome to the Temple of Westbrook. Historic place of worship.' This was repeated in three foreign languages – optimistic, Catullus thought. 'The temple of Westbrook is one of the oldest in the capital', the pamphlet claimed. 'It is also called Ricket's Gate, so named after the hospital of Ricket's Gate, which once stood on the site of the present building. At first, it stood outside the city boundary, but when the walls were enlarged, the hospital was torn down and the building you see now built in its place. During the Civil War, Marius "the Dancer" came here to worship, and a statue commemorates the spot near here where he is supposed to have been buried. The temple is still in regular use, but needs substantial funds to be spent on it if it is to be preserved. Your contribution is appreciated.'

Catullus heard footsteps behind him. He put the pamphlet down and glanced round. The young man in black.

"Excuse me!" he shouted.

The man stopped and turned to look at him.

Fuck, what was he supposed to say now? "I didn't know you were still here," he stammered at last. God, how stupid! But the man just smiled.

"I was over there." He pointed. "I've always had a taste for places of the dead." He smiled again, and Catullus, staring directly into his face for the first time, saw that it was deathly pale, offset by a shock of jet black hair. The face was beautiful, with deep-set eyes and delicate bones, and the young man's flesh gleamed like the marble of Marius' skin.

"I haven't seen you here before," the man said after a pause.

Catullus pointed to the statue. "I came to look at that."

"Why, are you interested in the Civil War?"

Catullus hesitated for a second. "Yes. It's not my particular field."

"Oh. A historian?"

"Archaeologist."

"Really? That's fascinating." The man's pallor was freshened by a faint glow of interest. "You must come round and visit me."

Catullus smiled. The young man was really very handsome. "I'd love to."

"What are you excavating?"

"We start next week. A prehistoric site."

"In Rome?"

"Yes. At least, we hope it might be a prehistoric site. The other side of town."

"There is a certain darkness, a certain cruelty, I have always imagined, that flavours our prehistory, and which stains this city even now. What do you think?"

Catullus shrugged. "We might find some darkness but I don't think there'll be much cruelty. In fact, I'm afraid it'll all be extremely dull."

"I hate dullness." The young man pointed at him. "Come and visit me. Promise."

"Give a date."

"Next Thursday. I have a friend, he would love to meet you."

"Oh." Catullus wondered if his face had fallen. "Right."

The young man smiled. "In fact, I must be off now, back to him." He held out a hand, which Catullus shook, then glided out through the temple gates. "Don't forget," he called, looking back over his shoulder, "next Thursday. You'll enjoy it. We all will."

"I'm sure."

"And there will be dark mysteries. I can feel it. I have faith in you. Look and you will find."

Catullus shrugged and smiled. He waved the young man goodbye, then crossed the road himself and pushed open the door to the Dugbals' flat. Well, he'd certainly been beautiful enough, if a little sepulchral, Catullus thought as he climbed the staircase, and it was only when he reached the landing that he realised that he hadn't even asked the young man for his name, and certainly not his address, and then he had to wonder if he wanted to. Maybe, maybe not. It all depended, he supposed. A lot of things could happen in the space of a week.

Tubbers was in the kitchen, reading the paper. He looked up and smiled as Catullus walked in. "Bloody horrid weather, don't you think. Sleep well?"

"Not really. I've been up for hours, temple inspecting."

"What, that old one across the road?" Tubbers wiped his nose. "Never seen it myself. Not a temple sort of chap, really."

"It's interesting."

Tubbers nodded, and asked him if he wanted a cup of tea. "I had a bloody ropey night," he said, when Catullus had nodded. "Rarly sick. Chunder and all. Why I'm off work." He poured out the tea. "Seen Caelius about?"

"No."

"Isn't he meant to be showing you around?"

Yes, thought Catullus. My best friend. My oldest, newest best friend. "He lost his wallet last night," he said casually. "Maybe he's gone to find that."

Tubbers shook his head and pointed at the table. Catullus picked the wallet up. He flicked through the cards inside, then shrugged. "The bastard. So he must have been up for hours." He dropped the wallet, then reached for the spare section of the newspaper and scanned through the headlines. "Fresh gloom for the Government," the title read. "Deficit widens, inflation grows, Ministers to lead emergency debate."

"Shouldn't you be out fixing these figures up?" he asked Tubbers, pointing at the headline.

"I'm no good. No one's any bloody good. Another reason I'm sick this morning."

"They're really that bad?"

"Oh, worse. Total pig's ear."

"Really?"

"Bloody hopeless, whole bash. Longer you work at it, more you give up. Whole ministry just waiting to go sick."

"Oh, I see, you actually work at the ministry. Caelius didn't tell me that."

"Worst bloody job in the world."

"Surely not?"

"Bloody well is, times ten."

"Things won't ever get better?"

Tubbers thought. "No," he said with eventual decisiveness. "Not unless Caesar or someone takes us over, but the Government won't let that happen because then they won't be running the show anymore. But don't know why they want to run it, actually. Time to give up, I'd have thought, say we're sorry, whole thing bloody over."

"Oh dear." Catullus felt a chill in his stomach; he had been joking about Rome for years, but he didn't want to be told that his country was really as shit as he had always pretended it to be. "There must be something we can do?"

"Don't know what. Screwed up in a unique way, you see, so all a bit tricky."

"Well, that's something, I suppose."

"What is?"

"We're still setting trends. We invented economic success and now we're inventing economic fuck ups, and that means that we're still at the forefront of things." Catullus looked at the paper again. "It makes you proud to be a Roman."

"You haven't seen a shoe lying around, have you?"

"What?"

"A shoe. I've lost one. Bloody nuisance."

"What made you ask that?"

"Well, I was just thinking, Caelius never asks what I do, and then I remembered, I'd asked him last night if he'd seen my shoe, and he'd said he hadn't, and so I was wondering if maybe you had. You know, just lying around."

"No. How would I have seen your shoe? I only got here yesterday."

"That's when it went missing."

Catullus stared at Tubbers blankly, resenting the diversion of a conversation he had been enjoying. Had he not seemed serious enough? Or maybe Caelius was right, and Tubbers was just a dick. Either way, Catullus felt annoyed. "No, I haven't seen your shoe," he said shortly.

"Oh well, if you do, let me know. Be a rarl help."

Tubbers returned to the newspaper. Catullus watched him, and then glanced at his watch. Still no Caelius. Where the hell was he? The bastard, the bastard. The rain begin to pour heavily again outside. Catullus decided that he couldn't face reading the paper, so he picked up Mr Varney's book from where it had been lying open on the far side of the table, and began to browse through it again. He decided to go back to the first chapter and remind himself of everything that he had skipped. If he had to read about crises, he would rather they were kept safely in the past.

Outside, the rain was falling harder and harder now, and Catullus imagined it as he read, pounding the house and the street, the slate roofs and the concrete, the whole of Tallowfield, and beyond it, Rome. Soon Catullus had become oblivious to the thumping sound on the roof, the rattling of the windows, but down the rain still poured. Small rivers began to trickle, then run, through the gutters of the streets, sweeping away the filth that earlier rain had only flattened; in the abandoned tip of Fairfields, scummy pools of mud began to form; in the water of the Tiber, litter and waste were picked up from the banks and came to mark instead the slab-grey waves. As the river hurried through Tallowfield, large objects, unexpected objects, could be seen swirling in its waters, bobbing and drifting out from the bank, then swept on away beneath the span of a bridge, out of sight, and the waters flowed on, beneath another bridge, and then another, and on towards the heart of Rome.

In the Dugbals' house, Catullus and Tubbers continued to read. Meanwhile, Caelius was splashing his way desperately through the streets, trying to reach shelter.

V

CICERO

He'd had to go to the lecture, Caelius explained that evening. He had meant to leave a message, but he'd been in such a hurry, and he was really sorry, really. The whole of the rest of the week was at Catullus' disposal. Was he cross? Catullus nodded. "I'm furious, actually. I think you're a total shit." There was a pause, and Catullus walked on. "Is it far?" he asked at last, making it as plain as he could that he wasn't interested in the reply.

Caelius pointed. "We're here. Just go right."

Catullus turned into a square. The weather had cleared, and the air was cool and soft, absorbing the sound of their footsteps on the pavements, insinuating the whole square with a respectful hush, leafy, cloistered, beautiful. "Costs a fortune to live here," said Caelius; "you can imagine." Catullus nodded back. Elegiac wealth, he thought, that was the flavour. A soothing brand. Well, he needed it.

"Behold," said Caelius, spreading his arms.

Catullus looked up. "Fucking hell."

"You like it?" Caelius tried hard not to look pleased. "Good. Of course he may have to sell it soon." He ran up the white steps that led to the door. "Best to pack in the visits while we can."

He pressed the doorbell. Catullus heard a ring from deep inside. As they waited for the door to be answered, Catullus tried to think of something nice he could say to Caelius, to show him that he was forgiven. "How long till you'll be able to afford a place like this?" he asked.

Caelius shook his head, and began to say something. Then the door opened. A small figure ushered them in, and the door slammed shut again. Silence returned to the square.

Upstairs, Cicero too had been admiring where he lived. He scarcely heard the doorbell when it rang. The radio was on, but he scarcely heard that either, since he had come to the window to escape it, to lose himself in appreciation of the order and beauty of the square outside, a two-centuries-old oasis of calm, he thought, and at once the square seemed bathed in the mood of elegant melancholia that he had come to recognise more and more as mildew on the margins of his own thoughts, and which he knew to be either mark or cause of a paralysis, without fundamentally being able to regret it, whichever it was. "Things were ordered better then," he murmured softly under his breath, still admiring the square, "things were better ordered." He had been both advocate and politician, so that he could hardly be blamed for his susceptibility to metonymy, yet it was his heart not his head ruling now, as the sun's last rays cast blood red the marble of the square's city mansions, where two hundred years ago enlightened aristocrats had built what he knew could all too simplistically be summed up as an image of that lost, that truly great age, when Rome's proud oligarchy had shaken the world, when the same state that had brought down Carthage had also laboured hard to bequeath revolutions in science, government, philosophy, finance, a golden age in every art, which had left the world to a certain extent Roman even when, as now, Rome herself seemed enmired in a crisis of decline. It was a distant world, the age that had built the square in which he lived. He had bought the house because it had seemed to embody qualities he admired, and which he hoped could be discovered in himself. Dignity. Culture. Calm confidence. Now, he was not so sure.

He walked over to a bookcase. His study walls were massed with them. Never, never, had he met with anyone who owned more books, let alone who had read them all. Politicians now felt no need to be literate, he reflected. The fools! Look what was happening to the country as a result, run by ignorant careerists with no understanding or sympathy for the greatness they were ruining. He pulled out a book and studied the cover reflectively. His own. Written in more optimistic times. The first years of his political life – was the face smiling up at him really from so long ago? Yes, of course it was – the photograph had been taken from his first election poster. At once a lurching sickness clouded him – no, it wasn't a sickness – it was a pain, a *fury* at the betrayal of his hopes by others. Look at what they had set up in his place! Look at the trash, the incompetents, the crooks! He had smiled from that first election poster, but he wouldn't now, for he had come to realise what he hadn't then, that Rome was like a rotten oak, and only insects and noxious vermin could hope to flourish in what remained of its wood, eating it away, until...? Until. It was a nice metaphor.

There was a knock at the door.

"Come in."

A tiny man popped his neck round the door.

"Your guests have arrived, sir."

"All of them?"

"Yes. Should I tell them you're coming?"

"I'm on my way." The door shut. Cicero put the volume of his reminiscences back in its place in the book shelf, and patted vaguely at the knot of his tie. He stood, and wondered why he was waiting. There was something he hadn't done. Note down his metaphor? No, he hadn't been serious about that. Of course. Turn off the radio. He listened, as he walked over to it, and winced. Metellus, the finance minister, announcing a negotiated end to the campaign of strikes that everyone had thought would surely bring down the Government. How had that threat been negotiated away? No. Cicero flicked the radio off. From what his nephew had been saying, the answer, maybe, was waiting for him downstairs below. Perhaps his luck was turning at last. It deserved to. And so – to work. Cicero switched off his study light, and walked thoughtfully down towards his reception room. Had Clodius really been dressed up by that lake a second time? Really? If he had been... Well, no. Wait and see. Just wait and see. Cicero realised that he was feeling very scared.

Downstairs, Caelius and Catullus had become bored. Caelius bounced up and down on a leather armchair, then started pilfering small bottles from the drinks cabinet. He opened one, and wandered over to Catullus. "What are you looking at?" he asked.

Catullus held up a photograph. It showed Cicero as President, in the robes of state, the flags and symbols of the Republic mounded behind him, pure nobility chiselled on his face.

"Vulgar, isn't it?" whispered Caelius. "And he's not even a senator now. You'd never think he'd been forced to resign."

"I've got this feeling I'm not going to like him."

"Your right, I suppose. He wants to meet you, not the other way round." Caelius handed over a bottle. "But do try and mellow yourself all the same."

The door opened, and Cicero came in, followed by a second man, incredibly tall and thin, walking as though his joints were stiff with rust. Introductions were made. "This is Titus," said Cicero, waving his hand at the tall man as though he were a piece of art. "He's brilliant." Titus bowed his head, which was lined and dry, the colour of fading parchment, and Catullus, shaking Titus' hand, half checked himself in case the arm crumbled away into dust. But looking into Titus' eyes, Catullus could see that they were bright, and very piercing – not mummified at all. Titus nodded, but said nothing, and general silence settled over the room. Nobody seemed keen to be the first to break it.

Catullus raised an eyebrow at Caelius. Caelius raised one back.

"Shall we go and eat, uncle?" he asked softly. Cicero didn't seem to hear. He was standing by a window, his back turned on his guests, staring at the gathering twilight outside. Caelius asked his question again. Cicero turned round, looking vaguely surprised. He stared at Caelius for a second, then nodded.

"Yes, why not? You must excuse me. I was miles away."

"I'm hungry."

"Yes, of course you are." Cicero nodded his head again. "And you, Titus? Are you hungry? And you, Catullus? Good. Then to business. Please follow me."

He began to lead the way out of the dining room, then stopped.

"Strange times, my friends. Evil times." He nodded. "What are they up to, the forces of chaos, out there?" No one answered. Catullus and Caelius looked at each other. Titus played with his fingers, as though they were long skewers onto which he was slipping pieces of meat. Cicero shook his head. The others followed him out of the room.

There was a large grandfather clock in the dining room. It ticked slowly, sombrely, each second passing away on a dull monotone, so that it did not take long to become quite oblivious to it. Once the door had been shut, the passage of time itself began to seem a nonsense, the more the seconds ticked away, forever ticking on. Candles had flickered as the guests had walked in; all other signs of life seemed to have been embalmed. Everything was still, formal, frozen, as though it had been there for ever. The guests sat down and were served. They begin to eat, off cold blue china, sitting politely on the edges of their uncomfortably priceless chairs. A further candle was lit by the small servant, where he waited with a bottle of wine, stationed by a vast mahogany cabinet. In the wash of the flame, Catullus could see the dull gold of picture frames, and inside them, the even duller black of old portraits and country scenes. The clock ticked on. Still no one spoke.

At last, Cicero finished eating, and laid his cutlery with a neat tinkle down onto his plate. He sat back in his chair, the first to do so, and stared at Catullus.

"So," he said, "I gather Clodius has been having lakeside chats with Metellus."

Catullus nodded. "Is that odd?"

"I would have thought so an hour ago."

"Why not now?"

Cicero shook his head. "No, I don't want to influence you. Tell me about your night at the ball first."

"It really matters?"

Cicero shrugged. "Why do you think I invited you here?"

"Because I'm charming? Good company?"

Cicero grunted. "Bonuses, I'm afraid, mere bonuses. So please, you have a captive audience. Make our flesh creep."

"It wasn't that bad."

"I hope it wasn't. But how can you tell?"

"I was there."

"Exactly. Which is what makes me confident that you haven't a hope of understanding the precise significance of anything you saw. So please, just narrate, and leave the exegesis to me."

Catullus stared at him coldly. He was going to say something, but it must have been obvious, because he felt a sudden kick from under the table. Caelius, telling him to get on with it. So he did, but resentfully, for he objected to the pilfering of the right to interpret his memories – they were his, after all, not Cicero's. Yet in fact, he discovered that he could now scarcely recognise the experiences he was describing as his own; he was just a witness in a mystery thriller, the man too stupid to know his own story's end. He caught his reflection staring back at him from a candlestick. The metalwork was twisting his face, breaking it up as the candle flame shivered it. He felt unreal, just a voice. In the candlelit gloom, in the strange timeless pale of the ticking clock, he felt like a spectre, talking to other, equally presentless, spectres. The thought made the sound of his voice seem too strange to listen to. He hurried to the end of his narrative, and the story trailed away. Cicero stared at him. Catullus suddenly noticed that he was shaking. Or was it just the candle light, playing another trick?

"Well," said Cicero at last, "all very worrying."

"Really?" Caelius leant forward. "You think I was right to get Catullus to come and see you?"

Catullus laughed. "I feel overwhelmed. My own humble experiences. Such a fuss and bother. Who would have thought it?"

"Who indeed?" Cicero sunk his head onto his hands and thought in silence for a few seconds more. "I suppose I owe you an explanation," he said eventually, nodding to both his guests. "You haven't heard the news? No? Not surprising, it's only just been announced – the strike's over."

"Which one?"

"All of them. Metellus has just been up announcing it to the House."

"But that's wonderful. Who won?"

Cicero gestured helplessly with his hands. "Not democracy, I fear. Not Rome. Not the country I have loved and been trying to serve these past thirty years. From what you have just been telling me, it sounds as though we have all lost. But..." He nodded and trailed away, expostulating with his hands in a well-practised gesture of dismay, like an actor discovering the truth of something he had always thought confined to the stage. "I think, more than anything, it's a disaster for me. So whether it's also a disaster for the country – well – I'm bound to seem a little biased, aren't I? So perhaps you should be forewarned. Remember who's speaking." He laughed softly in a single breath. "After all, healthy doses of bias are what makes a democracy thrive. Just so long as you remember that all language is bias."

"Catullus is a poet, uncle, I don't think you need to patronise him."

Cicero waved his hand apologetically. "Nothing further from my mind. Just thought I was being modest, that was all. So sorry. Know I'm not very good at it." He gave a soft chuckle. Catullus smiled politely. "What exactly are you going to be biased about?" he asked in the ensuing lull.

"Clodius, I should think," answered Caelius at once. "Clodius, uncle?"

"Oh, certainly."

Catullus nodded. "I want to know about Clodius. He's a union leader -"

"A mob leader."

"Whatever. So what was he doing made up as a woman throwing a massive ball by a lake?"

"Well – that is the question. The most disturbing question of all."

"Oh, really? Why?"

"It was a warning. A code, if you like."

"Go on."

Cicero shook his head. "After the next course."

"Why not now?"

"Because as with any good code, you'll need to understand what's being cracked, and that may take some time, and I'm feeling too hungry to wait that long. Aren't you hungry?"

"Excellent salmon," said Titus, speaking for the first time that evening.

Cicero nodded back and smiled. The small servant began to clear away the remains of the first course, and Catullus fiddled with his napkin as Cicero talked to Caelius about law schools and exams. Catullus started listening to the clock again, as it ticked despite the world of politics and government cabals, feeling it draw him into its own muffled world of timelessness, until he realised with a sudden start that there was a fresh dish in front of him, and that Cicero had stopped talking to Caelius and was waiting.

"Sorry," said Catullus. "Were you saying something?"

"Yes. I was suggesting, if you've woken, that we renew our discussion."

"Oh yes, please. Go on."

Cicero nodded approvingly, and then, like a cat, seemed to expand until he had filled his chair. He stretched out his hands, extending his fingers as though they were claws, and stared upwards into the dark above the candle flames. "Clodius," he said. "Clodius." He breathed out in a long hissing sigh, and then stared directly at Catullus. "Clodius Pulcher is a fag end, the butt left in a full ash tray that the cigarettes of history and tradition always seem to leave."

"I've heard you spin a better metaphor," said Caelius.

"No, but I like it. It works. Think about it. Clodius – he is the repository for centuries of aristocratic vice and stupidity, he is the triumphant culmination of centuries of in-breeding, he is a great boil, a great explosion of pus that has been curdling away under the skin for centuries, and now it's out, growing and festering for all to see."

"Now you're mixing your metaphors. You can't have cigarette butts *and* boils."

"I can and I will, because the one is a metaphor and the other is a simile, and put together they form hyperbole, which is what you need when discussing the really livid pustule on the body politic that is Clodius. No, I'm being serious." Suddenly, Cicero looked it. "He has it all – fecklessness and greed from our upper classes, brutal yobbery from the proles, a remarkable combination, and one that manages to embody just about everything that is odious and wrong in our society today. And that is saying a good deal. He is a menace. You don't look convinced."

Catullus shrugged. "I wouldn't know. But I thought he was fighting to make sure that the poor didn't just go under during the present crisis."

Cicero shook his head. "No. What he is doing is ensure that we all go under during the present crisis. In fact, he is the present crisis. You think he really cares about the unemployed? You think that's why he surrounds himself with gangs of toughs to stop them from taking jobs even if they could find them? You think he has any empathy with them? Any understanding? The man was an aristocrat until four years ago. He only renounced his title then. And do you know why? So that he would have the chance to go outside the channels of government, the democratic channels. That's why. His aim is nothing less than the overthrow of the accepted political establishments of this country."

Catullus must have looked doubtful, because Cicero scarcely paused to take a sip of wine from his glass.

"How can he possibly be motivated by a genuine concern for the poor, for the working classes? Just ask yourself how he managed to get to his present position, within four years, an ex-member of the aristocracy, with – well, you saw it, his estate. That's not the sort of background for which redundant transport workers make a habit of voting. Then ask yourself another question. Is it easier to intimidate the members of a union or the members of an elected national house? If you wanted to bully your way to the top of either one, which would you choose?" Cicero sat back, shaking his head, his arms folded.

"I've forgotten," said Catullus. "What reasons did he give for renouncing his title?"

"Oh, the usual ones. You can imagine them. It was after the war, the one in Circassia. He'd fought in it, and then when he came back, he made a great song and dance about giving everything up."

"Like Mr Dugbal. Our landlord. Did you know that, Caelius, that Mr Dugbal had fought in the Circassian War?"

"Did he? But he didn't give anything up. Having Mrs Dugbal must be a good deal worse than being lumbered with a title, you'd have thought. But he's still got her."

"No, but maybe that's why he's mad?"

"What, having Mrs Dugbal?"

"No. Shell shock or something. He can't have been mad if he was in the army. Well, not as mad as he is now."

Frowning like the conductor of a badly disciplined orchestra, Cicero tapped his finger on the table. "I want to tell you a true story about Clodius as a child, the child, of course, being father to the man. It also, by the way, disproves the theories that something happened to Clodius in the war that transformed him into a psychotic. He was always a psychotic. He was what his mother called 'imaginative'." Cicero laughed. "These stupid upper class parents and their – 'imaginative' – children. Any other class, and he would have been institutionalised."

"Is all this stuff about childhoods strictly relevant, Uncle?"

"Of course. It has rabbits thrown in too."

"Rabbits?"

"Yes. As a child, Clodius was obsessed with rabbits. And because his doting mother always liked to spoil her baby, he was duly allowed hundreds of the animals. Even at an early age, however, Clodius carried things to excess. The gardens became so full of rabbit hutches that eventually, when they were placed together, they came to seem like one enormous city, with rabbits roaming round the makeshift streets and drinking from specially constructed fountains. Clodius would spend hours in this town he had built, whispering into the rabbits' ears, taming them, much preferring their company to that of his friends or his family or other humans. Not a definite proof of madness, I grant you, not in the light of his family anyway, but that was before he became fed up with rabbits, and began to assassinate them instead."

"Assassinate them? How the hell do you assassinate a rabbit?"

"Easy. Give each one a state funeral. Obvious when you think about it. You have a multitude of rabbits, you go off rabbits, what do you do with them? Find something new to do with them. Kill them, experiment with death, crucify them, blind them, break their limbs and leave them to the cats, slice them into pieces. No, not pleasant, not pleasant at all. But that was what Clodius did. One by one, one each day, and when the rabbit was dead, he would arrange a spectacular funeral, and persuade his sisters to take part in them, and his mother would pay for them, and all in all, it turned into a very expensive and time-consuming hobby. I saw him at it once, when I was visiting Clodius' father. I looked out of the window and there were the children, all gathered round the pond, where Clodius was ceremonially drowning a rabbit. I couldn't bear to watch it. The way the poor thing struggled. The children were all giggling. A proof of their 'imagination', I suppose.

"Then, gradually, Clodius became bored with killing rabbits one by one. So? Again, easy. One vast immolation. One vast blaze of eradication and sacrifice. All the remaining rabbits were herded into one of the large cages, packed in tight, and then they were set on fire. His mother found him among the wreckage of the hutches, the air thick with smoke and the smell of burning fur, and Clodius himself clutching onto one last baby rabbit, and crying and crying as though he would die."

There was silence. Caelius frowned. "Even if it's true," he said at last, "what does it prove?"

"It's entertaining."

"Maybe, but I think actually Catullus wants to hear about the ball. Remember? You promised you'd say what was so frightening about the ball?"

"And isn't that just what I've done? Yes, you see, Catullus is nodding, he's the one who saw Clodius' last bonfire, he knows that inference can sometimes be as relevant as fact. The point, Caelius, the point is this." He brought his forefinger down onto the table. "How did Troy fall? Go on, tell me."

"You're being serious?"

"Deadly."

"Well – it was captured by the Greeks and burnt to the ground."

"And how did they capture it?"

"With the wooden horse. They hid inside."

"Correct. It was a deception. And how was Clodius able to capture his rabbits, when he locked them in their hutch and burnt them?"

"I don't know, they were tame, I suppose. They'd have just let him pick them up."

"Correct. Some suggestive parallels, wouldn't you say?"

"Not really, no. What are you saying, that Clodius burning down Troy is the same as him incinerating rabbits? So who are the rabbits?"

"I think I can make a guess at that. Assuming as I do that the entire ball was written in a code that certain people were supposed to be able to read easily. I think I can make a guess as to who the caged rabbit is. Or the fooled Trojan. I think a number of people could. You could."

Caelius looked surprised. "Me? How? I don't know Clodius at all. I don't know any of these significant stories you seem to have been told about."

"You've heard enough about one. One story, about Clodius, you've heard from me. Think about it. When you phoned me last night, what was it you said had struck you about the account of the ball?"

"What he was supposed to have done, you know – what he was accused of at the trial. Oh! Is that what you're talking about?"

"Brilliant."

Caelius thought, and then leant back. "Yes, I see. Of course."

Catullus cleared his throat. "Look, I don't want to seem rude, but will you please tell me what you're talking about. I was the one who saw it all, I think I deserve to know."

"Of course, of course." Cicero leaned forward, an expression of indulgent concentration on his face, like a chess master about to demonstrate a move to a novice. He wagged a finger slowly.

"I'm assuming," he said, "that you don't remember the details of Clodius' trial."

"Not really, no."

"Well, it was a fairly long time ago. Even though it was fairly extensively covered, Clodius being involved – and myself."

"It was, when? About three years ago?"

"Yes. Not so long ago that certain people would have forgotten about it. I think, when I remind you of the details, you will find the echoes of what you saw a couple of nights ago quite unmistakable. And therefore, since Clodius seems to have been responsible for this second ball, offensive as well. To certain people, highly offensive." He paused. "You met Clodia, didn't you?"

"Yes."

"She's an equally unpleasant piece of work, by all accounts, but I don't want to bother with her right now – the brother's quite enough as it is. Nevertheless, it was Clodia who started the whole affair off. In a manner of speaking. You remember I told you that

Clodius had fought in Circassia?"

"Yes."

"You'll remember, while he was out there, some hapless Roman pilot had dropped his hardware on the wrong target?"

"The hospital?"

"Yes. It was a hospital. Terrible, of course, terrible. And provoked the predictable backlash here, everyone frightfully shocked, everyone terribly keen to do something about it, and one of those people, whether because her brother was in Circassia or whatever, was Clodia. There she was, keen to demonstrate her solidarity with the poor mangled women of Circassia, and so how did she do it?" Cicero began to chuckle. "That's right. She threw a party." He choked and began to laugh again. He tried to speak on, but the moment he had repeated "party", his words were swamped with a great bubbling of laughter, and he had to bury his face in his hands. He looked up finally and shook his head. "Dear, oh dear. I am sorry." He caught his breath. "As I was saying. Yes. Clodia wore her heart on her sleeve, and decided, once her brother had returned from the war, that she would throw a party. For charity. It came with two really conscience-tweaking twists. One – the theme. Circassian. Food, dress, music – Circassian. And two – this would be a party for women only. Absolutely no men allowed. No bombing, woman-battering bastards allowed. So that was how it was worked out – the whole thing to be held by the lake in the thick forests of the Claudian estate, the same estate you were taken to the other night. That evening too, it seems, everything looked thoroughly impressive. The guests arrived, and were met by the gates to the park. They were invited to enter a litter. The litter was then carried by men, dressed as Circassian slaves – these were the only men permitted into the park for the evening. Even the horses were geldings. Clodia – well – she had a way of making a point. Much like her brother. Humiliation as vehicle for political activism. You see?" Cicero smiled mirthlessly.

"So. The guests. They arrived. What sort of women? Radical, obviously. Some rich, roped in to help with the cash accumulation. The majority, not very – a lot involved on the fringes of artistic activity, tee-shirt painters, nipple-piercers – you know the type. On the island in the centre of the lake, a group of these people had built an exhibition centre devoted to woman's self-expression – which meant their own, of course, in practice, but as the evening developed, so also were all the guests encouraged to row across and make their own contributions to a large mural, express yourself for the Circassians, that sort of thing. The mural was then to be sold and the money given to an apposite charity. The exhibition hall that had been built around it became known as the Shrine, and this was the whole point of the ball, you see. Worshippers at the Shrine. Maenads. Which made what later happened all the more ironic. But I mustn't jump myself."

Cicero stood up and walked over to the mahogany chest on the far side of the room. He pulled out a drawer, and after rummaging through several files, came back to the table with a worn newspaper-clipping. He looked at it for a second, then gently laid it down by his plate. "Also there," he whispered, "also there – a woman of no particular interest. No particular quality. Would probably never have been there at all had she not also been the wife of a man it had already, three years ago, become inopportune to ignore. Julius Caesar had only just left Rome, hadn't yet set himself openly against the Roman Government, but he was already a man to watch, and wait for, and fear. Which meant that when the wives of Pompey, and Crassus, and anyone else considered to be absolutely unsnubbable, went along to Clodia's bash, his wife was sent along too. And so off she was duly packed."

Cicero picked up the small newspaper-clipping and unfolded it. "This gives a good impression of what she looked like," he said, handing it over. Catullus studied it. A face was peering up at him, but the newsprint was so grainy and indistinct that he couldn't make much out at all. Then he noticed her dress. "Look," he said, handing the photo to Caelius. "Her costume. All striped and patterned, like the rugs Mr Dugbal's got. They're Circassian, are they?"

Caelius shrugged. "I suppose so. If he was in the war as you said he was."

Cicero took the clipping back. "Yes, that's Circassian. That's what she was wearing the night of the ball. You can see that it had been been torn." He folded the clipping back neatly, and slipped it inside his jacket. "So – that's who you have to imagine, arriving at the estate as you did. The sudden explosion of light and music, the tents and swarms of people, the first sight you have as you round out from the trees – it can all seem very impressive, overwhelming perhaps, and Caesar's wife, like you, had never been to Clodia's estate before. So she was dazed as soon as she arrived there. That's what she said. She had spent the whole evening in a daze, for hours, way before she joined the boat trip across to the island, and it wasn't – how can I put it? – she didn't find it unpleasant. Indeed, she seems to have become quite drunk on it – Caesar can only have been taking her out to the dullest of politicking dinners, and so she clearly let rip like some school girl behind the bicycle sheds. That photo I showed you – you've got to remember that a part at least of the horror on her face was due to one hell of an almighty hangover." He chuckled, then stopped. "Not all of it, of course. Not all." He paused, and stared into his wine glass, and took a meditative sip before beginning again.

"At a quarter to midnight – approximately – there was a specially composed concerto echoing themes of Circassia..."

"On violins?" Catullus interrupted.

Cicero thought. "Yes, I think so."

"Were the violinists men?"

"They may have been."

"So there were other men?"

"Yes, but the whole point was that they were menial. They were being employed. Why, does it matter particularly?"

"I don't know."

"Should I carry on?"

"Please."

Cicero cleared his throat. "Eleven forty five. The concerto on Circassia. Midnight. The statutory explosion of fireworks. Twelve fifteen. Dance music, and all the women moving to it faster and faster when a voice over the tannoy reminds all those who haven't yet made their contribution to the mural to get over to the Shrine as soon as they can and make it. Caesar's wife, with a whole group of others, hurries down to the lake side, where there's been a wooden pier running out, lined with torches and Circassian hangings. Boats are waiting at the end, behind an arch of fire, manned by gondoliers wearing demon masks – all maybe just a little too overwhelming now. Because something affected Caesar's wife on that trip across the lake. Something seems to have frightened her and quite dampened down her earlier mood of euphoria. She never said what it was, probably nothing specific, but the effect of being rowed across that lake by demons must have unsettled her, surely? It would have unsettled me. And when the boats reached the island and everyone had disembarked, the other women began to realise that Caesar's wife was no longer with them, but had quite disappeared. It didn't worry them particularly – why should it have done? What could possibly have happened to her? So all the other women went up to the Shrine and left their artistic droppings, and it was only when some of then went back to the boats and began to settle themselves for the trip back across the lake that they began to grow worried. But even then, not seriously.

"In fact, what had happened was that – well, first of all, Caesar's wife had decided to go for a walk. She had felt sick, she said, and so she hadn't wanted to go into a crowded tent with all the other women. Instead, she had made her way along the island shore, along a small path, intending to walk right the way round the island. It wasn't long – Catullus, you'll remember how small the island is – it would take you maybe fifteen minutes. But that night, she never made it. About half way, when she was on the dark side of the island, she was called, by someone running up from behind her. So she turned round, to see who it was, and she stopped. And that was as far as she ever got.

"Running lightly towards her through the dark was a figure dressed in the ornaments and soft silks of a Circassian priestess. I've said that it was on the dark side of the island – the only light came from the flames of torches, and so even that was flickering. As such, it was quite impossible for Caesar's wife to make out the figure running towards her with even the remotest degree of accuracy, and so she just stood where she was, quite still, and waited until the figure was actually standing in front of her, and she could look into the face. It wasn't one she recognised – heavily painted, very stylised, definitely a woman. It didn't cross her mind that it might not be. The two stared at each other, the stranger smiling with bright red lips, Caesar's wife open-mouthed, and neither said a word. Then, with a sudden clanking of bracelets, the stranger slapped Caesar's wife, stingingly, right across the face, and as she fell to the ground, he picked her up in his arms, and pulled open her dress, and then he stuffed her hair into her mouth, so that she wouldn't be able to scream any more. I said "he" – Catullus, you've probably guessed by now – this was no priestess. No. This was a man, determined to inflict a rape that was peculiarly horrifying, a rape quite out of the ordinary. No, I shouldn't say that..." Cicero's voice died away, and for a couple of seconds he stared reflectively into his wine. "Of course, every rape is out of the ordinary, but for that poor woman, it must have seemed – nightmarish. Literally nightmarish. Don't forget – she was still drunk. All evening, she had felt as though she had been drifting into dream. Ten minutes before, two minutes before, even while she waited for the strange painted figure to come running up to her, all that time it had seemed like a dream and now – did she still feel that it was unreal? I think she did. But that can hardly have been a relief. Imagine it. Looking up at a woman's smile, while she herself felt her back being scraped to and fro, along the stones of the track. Which hurt more? That woman's smile or the – what she felt – what she could feel moving in and out of her? I don't know. She wouldn't tell me. And to tell you the truth – I don't think she could have done." Cicero shook his head. "I should never have pressed her."

"The woman?" asked Catullus, breaking a silence. "The woman was Clodius?"

Cicero flung his hands up in the air. "Oh, no doubt. No doubt at all. Who else could it have been? It was almost all too clear. Caesar's wife had been found in the path, lying where she had been left, screaming with a – no, not a scream – a moan, high pitched, without a breath or pause, quite incapable of saying a word, and she stayed like that, in a state of certifiable shock, for the rest of the night. But the first thing that people had found, pressed into her hand, was Clodius' signet ring; then, as the crowds began to gather round the body of Caesar's wife, scattered reports also began to gather of a woman, seen being rowed alone across a lake, and of a figure dressed as a woman and running like a man through the woods of the estate, and several actually went on to identify the figure as Clodius. The next day, Caesar's wife did the same. She had recovered by then, and had no hesitation in identifying her assailant as Clodius. And then people began to remember comments that Clodius had made about Caesar, and one speech in particular, in which he had opposed Caesar's appointment to Gaul, and built up a whole argument based around Caesar's supposed homosexuality, and boasted that he'd be able to give his wife the best fuck she'd ever have – his words, by the way, not mine. Things had become quite unpleasant between the two, and there had actually been a scuffle – but then things were supposed to have been settled. Which hadn't been popular with Clodius' followers. They enjoy seeing their leader bait public figures – as I've discovered to my own cost. And then the final link in the chain came when it turned out that Caesar had given an interview to one of the Roman papers a week before in which he'd repeated an old rumour about Clodius' own supposed homosexual practices in Circassia. It was due to be published the day after the Circassian charity ball, but Clodius must obviously have known about its existence. In the circumstances, to rape Caesar's wife was an extreme but undeniably effective way of spiking the interview. No doubt – in fact definitely – a lot of Clodius' sympathisers found it all highly amusing. Which is still one of the most disturbing things about Clodius' sympathisers I've been able to come up with, despite three subsequent years spent trying to dig up the dirt on them. Clodius rapes – *rapes* – a woman, and it's seen as proof of charisma. Now, no one tell me he isn't an evil man. And his fellow thugs too. It's not too strong a word. That man is evil. Evil."

Cicero paused. Catullus wanted to say something – he wondered if he dared. "I don't doubt you," he said, after a long pause, "and obviously, well, I don't really remember all the details – but wasn't Clodius found not guilty?"

Cicero laughed balefully. "He was acquitted, yes. But with Roman justice in its present state, that scarcely proves a thing. In fact, just the opposite. Clodius wouldn't have bothered intimidating witnesses and bribing the jurors if all the evidence hadn't been so stacked against him. That may seem an unduly cynical observation, but I don't think that it's an unjust one. And there wasn't a lot I, or anyone, could have done about it. We hadn't realised how – rotten – the system had become. That was our mistake. That was my mistake."

"But I don't see how it could have happened?"

"Hold on. I need to tell you why we decided to prosecute first. Now, I think, when the details of the case became clear, that there was a good deal of shock in government circles, a realisation about the sort of person they were up against. Of course, they had always known that Clodius was a demagogue, but they had to understand now that he wasn't playing things according to any accepted or known set of rules. Not at all. And with that realisation also came the sudden sense of excitement, that perhaps with this case we could really nail him, that this was our big chance. And so I agreed to take on the case. I accepted the prosecution at Pompey's personal request. He had just been voted in as President, and since at that point he still thought that reform was possible, he didn't want Clodius getting in the way. And because I supported his stated aims, I decided that I would brave all the inevitable intimidation I'd be bound to receive, partly out of a sense of duty to the government of which I was a member, and partly because I was horrified by the details of the rape. And so I compiled an unassailable case against him. Unassailable. The only thing Clodius had in his favour was a clumsily constructed alibi that it was the matter of a few hours' work to demolish. The evidence was water tight. The most conclusive case I have ever argued for. And result? Not guilty. Can you believe it? Not guilty. Well, what could we do? Clodius walks off scot free, while I'm left the object of a bitter campaign of intimidation. Within a year, some nonsensical quibble of a past case is raised up against me, and instead of receiving the support of the House, I am actually forced to resign. *I* am! Clodius' retribution, of course. But if I have reason to fear for my safety, then so too does the Senate House, so does the Government, so does the country. Already, enough people in the House are more frightened of Clodius and his thugs than they are of the example they set the country by expelling me, when everyone knew that I had been prosecuting Clodius only to uphold the rule of the law. Their law. I don't think it's far-fetched to say that they were voting for their own extinction when they dismissed me. And as for Pompey and his reforms – well, he gave me the prosecution, and then he let me go, and the whole country was witness to the spectacle of a government that had lost its will and its right to rule. I suppose that it was only a matter of time before they surrendered completely."

"You think that's what they've done?"

"Of course. That's what your ball was about. Can't you see?

Wholesale, abject surrender." He pushed his chair back and got to his feet. "Now tell me again. Who did you see beside you when you were with Clodius? Above the lake. This is important."

"Clodius, Metellus, a fat person I hardly remember. I was too tired and he was wearing a wig."

"Think you'd recognise him with the wig removed?"

Catullus shrugged. "I was in such a daze."

"Let's see if I haven't got something that might jog your memory." He turned and walked out of the room. His three guests were left in silence, Catullus and Caelius staring at each other, Titus motionless and folded, looking, in the candle light, like a benign grasshopper. Cicero hurried back. He was holding a photograph.

"Look at that," he said, handing it down to Catullus. "On the left. Recognise him?"

Catullus looked. "Yes, of course. It's Pompey."

"It is indeed Pompey. Now look again. Is it possible – just possible – that he was your fat man in a wig?"

Catullus looked again. He put a finger over the top of Pompey's head, and tried to remember the face he had woken up to on that cliff above the lake. "I suppose it could be," he said at last. "Yes. I'd say it almost certainly was. Yes."

"Well, that's it then. All over." Cicero rubbed his eyes and sat back. "I can distinctly remember, you know, the moment in my life when I first discovered that Rome was not in fact the most wonderful and powerful country on the earth. I was twelve. It was the day I read my first newspaper. Up until then I had been weaned on large glossy picture books, in which the Romans always won, and it seemed just as natural that we should be number one nation as that I should be the son of rich and happy parents and live in a nice house. That was just the way things were. It was a rule of life. And then I looked at that newspaper. If I hadn't, I might well have carried on quite ignorant. I might never have had to sit here now, and face up to the prospect of a complete collapse. Rome's collapse. Our country's. It hardly seems possible, does it? The Roman state about to collapse? Unimaginable. And true. Too true."

"Because Clodius met Pompey by the side of a lake?"

"No. Because the elected head of the state met an unelected enemy of the state, and sued for terms. Surrendered centuries of – of democracy. Rule of law. Political accountability. That is what I think happened."

"Just because they met? Surely they've got the right to do that? And anyway, Clodius isn't unelected."

"I'll let that pass. But look, if you still don't believe me – two points. One. A government's legitimacy can only ever be sanctioned by a people's willingness to put up with it – yes? Without that willingness, systems become fissiparous – the greater a crisis, the greater the pressures for change. And surely we have now reached that crisis point. Rome is – what? – nothing, a shell, a decaying, deindustrialized, bankrupt hulk – it's hardly surprising people are kicking at the walls and finding they're so rusty that they just give way and break in. And at the end of the day – now rapidly approaching, if not already arrived – what stake does anyone not in the present government really have in perpetuating the political frameworks as they exist at the moment? I've despaired of them – and I would consider myself to be the most historically literate conservative in Rome. I don't say this lightly... because, after all, let's not forget, these structures have made us, in their time, the most successful state in the history of the world. Let me just remind you of what the state structures of Rome achieved. For centuries, they protected us from conquest. They won us the largest empire mankind has ever seen, they fathered the first great industrial and economic revolutions, they preserved us from the social turmoils that overwhelmed all other states. And now... How can we have fallen so far? From such greatness, to such bankruptcy? Such poverty. And what can come from economic crisis, but political crisis? I'm not surprised that Pompey met Clodius – who better placed than the state president to stare into the abyss? What does he see there, do you think, our state president? What is there to see? Nothing! That's our crisis! Where history and habit have told us that there are uniquely dignified, comfortingly sovereign structures of state, we discover to our shock that in fact there is nothing, there is just a hole, a terrifying blankness, the vortex of a whirlpool sucking us ever in. We don't know where we're going. We don't know what's going to be spat out on the other side. Above all, we don't really know what can we do to try and influence it. Probably nothing, but a drowning man always feels that he should struggle at least. Which leads me neatly onto my second point.

"You say that there needn't be anything ominous in the meeting between Clodius and Pompey. But surely, in the very fact of meeting Clodius, Pompey is saying that he has reached his decision."

"Why? What decision?"

"Caelius, come on, you were the one who noticed it. Surely you can recognise what you first brought to my attention?"

Caelius shrugged and looked blank.

Cicero stared at him. "Come on. The reason you phoned me. Go back to that again."

"Because the ball had such weird echoes of the one where – you know – Caesar's wife..."

"Yes. Caesar's wife. Caesar. Caesar. Now do you see?"

God, he was such a patronising bastard, Catullus thought, and again, he hugged his memories close. They were his, they weren't the dirty linen of the entire fucking country, they were his, but when an image of Clodia floated up unbidden into his thoughts, he could feel that there was already something less magical about it, as though a rare and secret form of pleasure had been spoiled. Still, Catullus thought, maybe Cicero hadn't penetrated the whole of his mystery. The women kissing each other outside their carriages – who had they been? One had been Clodia – but the other two? Trying to fathom an answer, Catullus woke up again to the conversation going on beside him. Caelius was still floundering under his uncle's proddings.

"Surely it's obvious," Catullus said impatiently. "Caesar wants Rome integrated in the federation he's developing in the rest of Europe. But according to you, Pompey is negotiating with Clodius, and so that involves risking a confrontation with Caesar. Correct? He can't appease them both?"

"Almost. Not bad." Cicero frowned. "But I wouldn't have thought Pompey would have wanted deliberately to aggravate Caesar. He can't afford to do that. We need the rest of Europe far more than it needs us, so we're in no position to be caught sticking our tongues out at it. And yet by attending a very obvious parody of the one episode to have really hurt and infuriated Caesar, this seems to be precisely what Pompey is doing. Which is strange, and makes me think that it must be Clodius' responsibility. Which in turn shows just how desperate Pompey must be. That ball – it wasn't just intended to humiliate Caesar. No. It was meant to humiliate Pompey. And therefore the whole Government. Remind them that if they wanted his support, then they would have to be a part of his snub to Caesar. Really rub their noses in it." He stared into the distance. "And they took it," he said at last. "They took it. They dragged in their wooden horse, and now we've got to sit around and wait for it to open."

The phone rang.

"Please, serve the coffee," he ordered the tiny attendant. "If you'll just excuse me." He got to his feet. "I won't be a minute."

He left the room. Catullus kicked his friend under the table.

"We should be going," he hissed under his breath.

Caelius nodded and motioned him to be quiet. All three guests sipped at their coffee in silence. When Cicero returned, Catullus saw that he was shaking again. His face looked waxy and moist with sweat.

"Who was it?" Caelius asked.

Cicero shook his head. "Don't know. Didn't give his name." He took a swig of wine, and tried to smile. "Just a drunk, I'm sure." He stared at the flickering of the candle flame. What was he listening to, his hearing troubled in the silence of that room?

Something rising from the streets of the city outside?

Caelius pushed back his chair. "Uncle – we really should be off."

"What, so soon?"

"We'll miss the last train."

"Train! When are you going to buy yourself a car?"

"As soon as I've got the cash. But in the meantime..."

"Yes, yes, of course. You too, Titus? Ah well. The party breaks up. Thank you all so much for coming. And thank you for bringing such – interesting – news. I hope you felt that it was worth it."

Catullus shook Cicero's hand. "Thank you for explaining so much."

"Not at all, not at all. You must come again. You're living in Rome for good now, aren't you?"

"Well – for as long as my job lasts. So hopefully, yes."

"Ah. Caelius told me you were a poet. You have to leaven your literary leanings with lucre, do you?"

"Lucre? Hardly."

"So what is this job?"

"Digging up ancient observatories," said Catullus with a shrug.

"How fascinating. No, really, why are you looking embarrassed? It sounds fascinating. You're an archaeologist then?"

"Yes. This will be my first post. I'm looking forward to it. It'll be nice, feeling that the qualifications have translated into something real at last."

"I'm sure. And good luck. I hope to see you again soon."

"Yes. Thank you."

"Oh, by the way. If you're digging up ancient observatories – does that mean you have any interest in modern ones?"

"Yes. I suppose so."

"Well, you should talk to Titus, then. He's an astronomer, aren't you, Rome's leading astronomer?" Titus cracked his knuckles. Cicero smiled. "Sorry we didn't get to talk much. But thank you so much for coming. I hope you weren't too bored with all the little problems of life here on planet Earth."

"It was fascinating," Titus said. "But it does remind me to keep my eyes trained firmly on the stars. And thank you for the meal. It was delicious."

He followed Cicero to the front door. His voice, like a rusty motor that had finally managed to choke itself into action, now seemed keen to keep itself ticking over. "If you are walking, I will accompany you," he called out to Caelius and Catullus, who were already disappearing down the steps into the dark blue night of the waiting square. The surprise of being talked to by Titus was enough to make them both stop in their tracks; they waited as Titus walked down and joined them. On the steps, Cicero waved, then shut the door. The square seemed suddenly very still.

"Damn," said Caelius suddenly. "I should have told him to look after himself."

"He wasn't exaggerating?"

"What did you think?"

"Probably not. Always hard to tell though, isn't it? – with politicians, I mean."

"Yes." Caelius grunted. They both relapsed into silence. Only footsteps sounded now, as they walked on, past the pale stained elegance of mansions and high walls, the trees lining the pavements, the moonlight and shadows. They rounded a corner, and there was a faint sound of music. It took Catullus a few seconds to realise that it was the same theme he had heard the clowns playing two nights before, while Troy had burnt. No, it couldn't be. It was coming from a window on the other side of the street, high up, a single cube of orange on the black front of the house. It *was* the same music. And after they had been talking about the ball all night – how very strange. Catullus wondered if the theme was the same that Caesar's wife had heard, waiting alone on the island path.

He dawdled while Caelius and Titus walked on. Someone appeared faintly behind the orange cube. Who? Clodius? Clodia?

"Do you know who lives there?" he shouted down the street.

No one answered. Catullus ran to catch up. "Do you know who lived back there?" he asked again.

Caelius shook his head. "Sorry. I'm not very good on the Palatine – yet."

Titus pointed. "There is a very fine view from over here," he said. Catullus looked. There was a row of iron bars running alongside the pavement as the road made a sudden swing. He walked over, and leant his elbows between the railing spikes. Below them, Rome sprawled away messily, in patterns of dark and light, fading eventually into a haze of orange where both lights and stars met to dissolve into each other. Caelius joined him, then Titus.

"Is it not fine?" he asked.

Catullus agreed that it was.

"For someone who spends his life gazing at the distances of space, to be reminded of the very different vastness of a great city is salutary." Caelius and Catullus both turned to look at him in some surprise. "I find that this view restrains my more arrogant ambitions, and tempers the yearnings of my spirit of inquiry. It prevents the wax of my feathers from burning."

He gazed out placidly, and nodding slowly to himself, expounded.

"Strangely, one can feel smaller here, I think, than one does when under a telescope. For instance, you see the Tiber, over there, see how black it is. Impenetrable it seems, would you not say? Dense with vacancy, as though the mass of the entire universe had been crushed and compressed into it? Then look at the stars." He pointed. "Up there, you see, that patch of deep darkness there. The galaxies contained within that darkness, the trillions of stars, are so far away from us that we can only measure, not imagine the distance. From that patch of darkness, we have been dead for eternities. And yet – despite all that – looked at from here, I would say that the darkness of that distance seems less profound than that of the Tiber. Astronomers need to be reminded that they too share in tinyness. And it is because I sometimes find myself forgetting this that every so often I come back here and lean on these railings." He looked at Catullus. "It would make for a fine poem, would it not? A poem of science. There are not many that have been attempted."

"What – you've written one?"

"Not finished yet." He paused. "And so you are a poet too?"

Catullus wished that Caelius wasn't there to hear him agree. "Yes," he said softly, then shook his head. "A poem of science, though..."

"You think it's strange?" Titus looked suddenly nervous and insistent. "Arrogant, perhaps?"

"Ambitious."

"Why?"

"Because our language has no great tradition of poetry. It's so hard to force it into the metres of the Greeks."

"And yet you try."

"Yes."

"Why?"

"Because – what is poetry anyway, but..." – Catullus gestured with his arms – "the expression of the inexpressible in an unnatural form? So really, the primitive quality of our language only focuses the task that I set myself. That's what we've all got to hope, I suppose, we Roman poets. That we can earn our language its flexibility after all."

"To express what?"

Catullus smiled. He glanced at Caelius, face profiled against the darkness of the city below. He remembered moments of happiness, jokes shared with his friend, ephemeral snatches. Unexpectedly, he remembered Clodia.

"To express what?" Titus repeated his question. "In your case?"

"To express whatever happens to me, I suppose. Whatever I think, feel or see. To find the right form for a fragment of experience. Nothing more."

Titus cracked his knuckles together resoundingly. "I think it would be easier to write about science. The Greeks, I have found, wrote in metres that encouraged that." He felt inside his jacket pocket, and handed over a card. "This is my address. If you are interested, I could perhaps show you my poem, and the observatory as well. So that you can understand the descendants of the men you are about to excavate."

Catullus looked at the card in embarrassment. "Thank you. Obviously, I'd love to come and read it..."

"Soon."

"Yes. Of course." Titus took his hand. "Are you going?"

"Yes." Titus shook Caelius' hand, then turned. "My car is round the corner. Good night. It was very nice to meet you both. Oh – and if you want the station, it is far quicker to go down the steps." He pointed to a gate. "Good night."

"Good night."

"You fucking show off," muttered Caelius as Titus walked away.

"I'm sorry, Caelius, if you couldn't keep up."

"Keep up? *Keep up?* It was the utter mundanity that silenced me."

"He couldn't have been mundane. He's a famous scientist."

"Then what's he doing writing poems? Famous scientists don't write poems. I've always thought that was one of the few things to be said in their favour."

There was a sudden roar from the distance.

"Shit. The train."

"Was he right about the steps?"

"Let's hope so. Otherwise we're going to have a very long walk back home."

Caelius pushed open the gate and began to run. Catullus followed him. From the shadows, a figure stepped out and watched them disappear. A second figure joined him. They both saw Caelius and Catullus make it to the platform below, then watched as the train pulled out again, and creaked away into the night. The two figures rested motionless for a few minutes, leaning against the railings. One spoke to the other; then they too disappeared back into the dark.

VI

PORTO

"Bed," said Caelius, pushing open the door. "Tubbers. What the hell are you doing?"

Tubbers was hopping up and down the hallway, swearing under his breath, and clutching at his left foot.

"Trod on a bloody pin," he said, pirouetting round.

"Oh." Caelius took off his jacket and hung it on a hook. "Try wearing shoes. They're useful at preventing such accidents, I'm told."

"I've lost them."

"What – both?"

"Yes."

"Rather careless of you, old boy."

Tubbers stopped hopping, and peered anxiously at the sole of his foot. "Keep an eye out for them, won't you?" he said sadly. "Absolutely my favourite pair. Both completely awol. None of the Dugbals the slightest bit interested."

"Neither am I, I'm afraid. And now, if you don't mind, I'd like to go to bed."

"Oh, but you can't. Meant to tell you. Bloody filth's turned up."

Caelius turned slowly round. "Do you mean the police?"

"Rather. Bad news, eh? Wants to see you both." He smiled nervously. "Bit poor really, this late at night."

Caelius sighed and climbed wearily back down the stairs. "Any idea what it's about?"

"No. Didn't hear. Looking for my shoes, wasn't I?"

"Oh, great. Just great." Caelius pushed open the door to the Dugbals' kitchen. Catullus followed him through. Inside, a man was sitting behind the kitchen table, nibbling at one of the mushrooms picked so tenderly that morning by Mr Smallpiece. It took Catullus a few seconds to recognise him. Of course. The man from the pub, the one who had helped them pick up Mr Varney. So he was a policeman. Catullus watched the man as he peeled another mushroom, then popped it into his mouth. He looked up briefly and nodded. No one spoke.

"I was told someone wanted us," said Caelius at last. "Is that true, or can I please go to bed?"

Mrs Dugbal pointed at her two tenants. "Well, go on," she said. "That's them."

"Thank you." The policeman got to his feet at last. "Yes, these are the ones." He felt inside his jacket pocket, and was just about to bring something out when suddenly the kitchen door slammed open and in ran Jez, barefoot and in his pyjamas. He stood and stared unblinking round the room; then he tugged on Catullus' arm.

"Are you under arrest?" he asked.

"I don't know." Catullus looked at the policeman. "Are we?"

"No, no, nothing like that." The policeman smiled down at Jez and tousled his hair. "What on earth gave you that idea?"

Jez gave a look of disgust, and jerked himself out of reach. "Their friend told me. You know, the stupid one, he is stupid, isn't he, Dad?"

Mr Dugbal, who had been sitting unnoticed behind his wife, gave a mild tremor. "Now come on, Jez," he muttered, flapping his hands feebly from his seat. "Don't be rude behind people's backs. I think you should go back to bed."

"No way!" Jez shouted loudly. "No way! I want to hear what's going to happen to them." He took Catullus' hand and looked up hopefully. "Do you think you'll get tortured now? Do you?"

Catullus looked quizzically at the policeman, who shook his head. "We don't torture people in the police force, you know."

"Oh yeah! Tell another. I know all about tortures and things, you don't have to pretend. Do you put electric shocks to people's eyeballs?"

In his excitement, Jez picked up a knife from the table and waved it in front of Catullus' face. "Bzzzzzaouh!" he yelled, hissing out volts of imagined energy through his teeth. The policeman turned to the Dugbals, and gave a mute gesture of appeal; Catullus, seeing it, suddenly laughed; the policeman had seemed so sinister before, and now there he was, floored by a child. "What do you want exactly?" Catullus asked with invigorated rudeness. "Is it important?" The policeman didn't answer; Jez's knife had buzzed unnervingly close to his nose. Catullus watched him blanch and appeal again to the Dugbals; Mrs Dugbal looked unyieldingly back.

"Do you want him sent to bed?" she asked eventually.

"I think that might be a good idea, don't you? We can't have the little fellow getting over-excited."

Mrs Dugbal nodded shortly. "Bed," she ordered Jez.

"Oh, Mum."

"Bed."

"Mum."

"Bed!"

"But Mum, I want to hear about the tortures, can't I please, can't I, just for a bit, please?"

"Get him to bed," she ordered her husband, then turned away to skin the mushrooms. Mr Dugbal shooed vaguely, but Jez refused to let go of either his knife or Catullus' hand until he had been firmly promised that he would hear the full details of any tortures Catullus or Caelius might have to undergo.

"You promise?" said Jez in an agony of disappointment. "You're not keeping your fingers crossed?" He stood in the doorway and danced from foot to foot, looking as though he were about to lose a present he had only just been offered. "Hope to die if you are keeping your fingers crossed?"

"Hope to die." Catullus showed him his two hands.

Jez quivered and nodded, and reluctantly allowed himself to be shepherded out of the kitchen by his father. Catullus watched him stumping sadly up the staircase; then he turned back to the policeman.

"So are you going to tell us what this is all about?"

"Frisky youngster." The policeman nodded towards the staircase. "Quite a character." He chuckled. "I've got a youngster just like him. He can be a right handful too." He chuckled again.

"Listen," said Caelius, jerking suddenly awake from a half doze. "I'm not interested in your fucking family. I want to go to bed."

"I'm afraid that won't be possible. Not just yet." The policeman fished out a card from the inside of his jacket. He showed it to Caelius. "This is my warrant, which allows me to take you anywhere I want to for twenty four hours, and keep you there. Now come along sir, you're a lawyer, you'll know there's no point in kicking up a fuss."

"How the fuck do you know I'm a lawyer?"

"Oh, we know lots about you."

"God, that little brat was right. You are a torturer. This is it – the midnight knock, the police state."

"Really, sir, you're getting as excitable as the young lad."

"Well, I'm not coming. You'll have to arrest me first."

"You want me to? I will if you like."

Catullus caught his friend's eye and shook his head. Caelius shrugged, and gestured the policeman to lead on. "But I'm going to be an important legal figure one day," he shouted. "If I ever get on a police pay panel, you'll regret this." The policeman laughed and, thanking Mrs Dugbal, walked out of the kitchen and back into the street outside. God, it had grown quite chilly, Catullus thought, as a cool wind sliced across his neck, and he shivered. He followed Caelius into the back seat of an unmarked car. Suddenly, from the pavement outside, Catullus heard a gurgling scream; leaning out, he saw Mr Dugbal running past, down the street. Mr Dugbal screamed again, calling out Vanessa's name. The sound was lost on a sudden gust of wind, and the policeman, just a black shape hunched up in the front seat, switched on the ignition, and the car's engine began to hum. They pulled away from the kerb. Mr Dugbal was left behind.

It was to be a long night. Instead of taking the main road towards the centre of Tallowfield, the car turned, and began to follow the signs for central Rome. Catullus leaned forward. "Are you sure there hasn't been some mistake?" he asked the policeman. "I've only been here a couple of days." The policeman just shook his head, and told him to enjoy the views. Catullus crumpled back wearily into his seat. He looked out of his window, but by now they had driven off the flyover, and any views seemed to have disappeared. Instead, a stained concrete wall flashed past, then another; bodies were leaning against them, or lying huddled on the pavements. Catullus wound down his window and peered back; arching high above the concrete he could see great spans of steel, and he realised that they had just passed the station where he had first arrived at Rome. It disappeared, as they swung past another concrete block, and then came the famous view, the Rome of postcards, the Rome that Catullus had seen for that brief moment through his carriage window. They drove up towards it, over the Tiber and the darkness that had so preoccupied Titus; then past the Senate House, and the shadow of its giant clock tower; a sign flashed by, "Welcome to the heart of Rome!"; along a mall and a pompous square, and they were back into narrow alleyways. The car began to slow, then stopped, and shuddered to a halt. The policeman got out, slamming his door behind him, and as he opened Catullus', he peered inside. "Here we go," he said. "Let's get this over as soon as we can."

"Too right," muttered Catullus as he fumbled his way out. Caelius followed him. Both looked around for a police station. Catullus stared up at the building they had parked by, but it was ancient and faceless, and ready to collapse, it seemed. "Where's the station?" Caelius asked. The policeman smiled, and tapped at a small bronze plaque attached to the wall. Caelius and Catullus peered down to look at it: 'Police Complaints Department', they read. Caelius shrugged, and followed the policeman through a door. Catullus chased him.

Inside, the policeman had already almost vanished. There was an endless corridor, which seemed to be pulsing and quivering in time to the strip lights on the ceiling. Furniture was stacked high along the walls, office detritus, tables, chairs, shrouded typewriters, filing cabinets. Catullus began to run. He didn't want to be lost in this place. He followed Caelius up a flight of stairs, and then up a second. On the third storey, there were yet more corridors leading away, with yet more stacked chairs, and shut office doors, but one of the doors, at last, was open, and the policeman was standing by it with a smile on his face.

"Took your time," he said jovially. "You, sir." He pointed at Caelius, then gestured through the open door. "If you'd like to wait in there."

"Wait?"

"Not for long. The quicker you're in, the quicker you're out."

"Oh, well, in that case." Caelius walked through the doorway. The policeman shut it behind him, then led Catullus further down the passage. He stopped outside a second door, identical to the first, and unlocked it. "In there please, sir," he said. Catullus walked in, and heard the door being slammed, then locked on him. He rattled the handle; nothing; he couldn't get out. Hurried footsteps were fading away. Catullus was left alone in silence.

Then he listened, and realised that it wasn't silence after all. There was a low, constant, electronic hum. It was coming from behind a green telescreen, which stared unblinkingly at Catullus from the far end of the room, where it sat on a desk and was surrounded by stacks of papers and files. Catullus walked across to the computer and tapped gingerly at its keyboard. There was a sudden belch of green static; the word 'Danger!' bounced up across the screen. Catullus looked around nervously. Then he heard the door behind him click open.

"Hello, hello, hello!" said a voice he recognised. "What are you doing in the dark?" A light was switched on, as watery and weak as the strip lights outside had been, and fading into the green glow of the computer screen, so that when Catullus turned round to face the strange man he had bumped into at the railway station, he found that he was staring at a face dyed dull emerald. The face beamed back at him, nodding backwards and forwards as though it had just been tapped. "Well, ha ha. Just fancy, meeting again so soon!" He beamed again. Then he picked his way over the vast stacks of papers that lay mounded across his room, and sat down behind his desk. "Now then – this is all wonderful, ha ha, quite exciting. We have had the most terrible accident, you see!"

"Is that why I'm here?"

The small man ignored the question. "A terrible accident," he continued imperviously. "Quite grisly. Blood, and even a bit of brain. Ha ha. Tragic. We both thought you might know something about it."

"Both?"

"Myself, and Porter. The man who brought you here tonight. He had a hunch. We were both sitting there, talking about you, when whoosh! Ha ha. A hunch! It had crept right up and was on him! So we acted on it, and that's why you're here. Does that clear things up?"

The computer gave another spasm, and Catullus felt his mind contracting and spurting in time to the screen's flickerings. "Hold on," he said slowly, trying to marshal his thoughts, "hold on. Who are you?"

"Oh, I am sorry, how unforgivable of me, how very lax! I am Porto. The Great Porto. So called because I can always pluck out the things that must be plucked, sniff out the things that must be sniffed. And also," he laughed diffidently, "to distinguish me from my assistant, Porter, who's less good on the plucking and sniffing side of ship. Porter you have already met, I believe? Yes, of course you have, you met him in your local tavern, did you not, and then he brought you here tonight? So there you are. Porter and the Great Porto. It has, ha ha, a certain ring to it, don't you think?"

"Sounds like a circus act."

"Oh. Oh ho, very good. Ha ha. I like it, very funny. A joke."

Catullus shrugged. "It's the best I can come up with in the middle of the night."

"Then what a shame you didn't come here earlier."

"Is that my fault?"

"Ah! Ethics! Do we have a responsibility towards those things that are out of our control? Or does assuming that they are out of our control actually remove our ability to control them? What do you think?"

"If I thought I could have avoided coming here tonight, I would have avoided coming."

"The empiricist's answer. How strange. I had you down as an idealist, a believer in the beauty of abstract forms. Have you really no place in your soul for the teachings of the golden-limbed Plato?"

Catullus shrugged again. "Do you know? Sometimes, in the middle of the night" – he glanced at his watch – "at about, say, two forty-five, I wake up, and I lie there, and I say 'Fuck the golden-limbed Plato.' And then I go straight back to sleep. It never fails."

"Ha ha ha! How very droll! So – Platonist only by day, Aristotelian by night. How very pragmatic of you! Ha ha ha!"

Catullus lounged in his seat, and stared hard at the Great Porto. "Do you mind if I ask you a question?" he said at last.

"Please. I would be honoured."

"What am I doing here?"

The Great Porto leaned forward and tapped his bony nose. "Well, now. That is indeed the question we lonely ships on a storm-tossed sea must be forever asking ourselves, without hope of rest. Do you not have any possible insights into the problem yourself?"

"Is it to do with the ball?"

The Great Porto giggled. "Half and half."

"Meaning?"

"Meaning – you remember when we first had the pleasure of chatting together, I mentioned my fascination with coincidences? Now, to have a coincidence, ha ha, it takes two to tango. You can't have a coincidence with only one strange event. Ha ha, no – you need two."

"So what's the second one? The tragic accident with the brains?"

The Great Porto winked, and turned to his computer. He pressed a button, and shapes on the screen fizzed and swayed, like mud shaken up in clear water. "Damn it!" The Great Porto gestured helplessly at the screen. "I want my list. The one with you in it."

"I'm in a list?"

Catullus thought the Great Porto would die of mirth this time. "Of course you are!" he bellowed, the words bobbing up and down on his roar of laughter as it surged and broke. He dabbed at his eyes. "That's quite the most amusing thing I've heard in ages! Why do you think you're here if you're not on a list? Why would I be bothering with you? Ha ha ha ha ha!" Suddenly, he sprang to his feet, and with his long jerky stride, began to wade through the mess of papers and files scattered across the floor. Catullus watched him as he rummaged through a stash of purple binders, pulling them apart, ripping out sheets of paper, sending them scattering across the room in clouds of dust and biro tops. The dust began to itch in Catullus' eyes; the light was still flickering, and the computer humming, and he could feel his eyeballs dry beneath his lids. He longed to feel a breeze on his face. The Great Porto went on rummaging.

"Ha!" he shouted at last. "Ha ha, here we are!" He waved a few scraps of paper in triumph, then studied them with a show of great interest as he made his way back to his desk. "If you want to keep something safe, keep it on paper, then you can touch it, you can *feel* it, you know it's there. Don't you think? How can you touch what's in one of these?" He tapped the side of his computer. A picture of Catullus flickered up on its screen. The Great Porto ignored it.

Instead, he smoothed out one of the papers on his desk. "Now, here we have the coincidence. And it's a good one, too! I see you at a ball, I meet you at a station, I get to know you. And then, last evening, you go to a pub – correct?"

Catullus nodded. "Hardly a coincidence."

"Wait. There's more. Much more." Porto skimmed through his sheet of paper again. "Because after you had been in the pub a while, you then proceeded, I put it to you, in a taxi cab, towards a hostel on the Zenoria Road, from which you then proceeded to return by foot. Did you not? Eh, ha ha?"

"And what if I did – are they crimes?"

The Great Porto stared at him with a look of great seriousness. "I think not," he said at last. "I think probably not. But it's all most surprising."

"Why?"

The Great Porto waved his piece of paper. "This is my friend Porter's report on you," he said. "And this is the report of a gentleman downstairs I'd like you to meet at some stage this evening." He waved a second piece of paper. He placed it on the first, and then spread his arms out wide. "Abracadabra! They fit! And they in turn fit with something else. Ha ha. It's all rather like a jigsaw puzzle, isn't it? Do you enjoy jigsaw puzzles?"

"I did when I was five."

"Ah, ha ha, I've never grown out of them, you see. I love jigsaw puzzles." He nodded, and stroked his Adam's apple, which bounced and quivered to the touch. "Now – look at this." He leant across to his computer, and tapped out a formula on the keyboard. He beckoned Catullus. "There." He pointed. "That's your file. Just gone in tonight. And now – if I press this button," – he pressed it – "there, you see, you vanish into this little folder here." He pointed. There was a picture of a file on the screen, with the word 'Troy' underneath it. The Great Porto chuckled again. "There you are, quite snug and secure, and there's no way you can get out of it. And do you know, you can be summoned up by other machines all over the city, and you're quite secure in them as well. I don't know how you get to them – I always imagine, ha ha ha – I always imagine you travelling *down* the flex, and underground, along all the grids, and then up another flex, and then onto the screen that wants you, and it's all so safe and convenient, I'm sure you agree, because you don't have to be got out of bed every time it happens. So we're all winners. Technology, you know, ha ha." He tapped at the screen again. "But sometimes, the you in here just isn't enough, and that's what makes me feel that maybe we are indeed more than just bundles of observed facts. Who knows? – maybe there is an irreducible core of personal identity hidden somewhere, out of fashion though such a heresy may make me in the groves of academe. Ha ha ha. Who am I to say? But the significant fact is this, you are in this file, and I want to know what you are doing there. In bed, as it were, with your bedfellows."

"Who are?"

Porto shrugged.

"Clodius? Clodia?"

"Why do you mention them?"

"You did – the last time we met."

"So I did. Ha ha! But only to find out if Cupid's dart was in your heart. It rhymes, doesn't it? Dart, heart. Would I make a poet?"

"No."

"Not like you, eh? Ha ha. Poetry for you means never having to rhyme!"

Catullus stared at him balefully. "What is it I've done that makes me so interesting?"

"You took a ride in a carriage. You sat above a lake. Why? Eh, eh, why?"

"I've told you, I don't know."

"No. And neither do I. But I will, oh yes, I will." Porto pressed his nose against the computer screen. "Because I always sniff things out. And that file, with you in it – there's something whiffy in that, isn't there? But is it you? Well – time will tell, ha ha!" He hit a button, and a second file appeared. "You see, you're in this one too. Now, maybe that is even more whiffy, what do you think? Or is it indeed, as we have both suggested, just a coincidence? Dark questions, my friend, to which we require some answers."

"Well, maybe I could help if you'd tell me what the second file's about."

Porto smiled, and showed him. "It is codenamed 'Slicer'."

"And what's in it?"

"Not much yet."

"Then how can I help you?"

The Great Porto sprang to his feet. "By coming with me."

"Have I got to? Where are we going?"

"To meet the gentleman I referred to earlier in the evening. A medical gentleman. I think you'll find it all most interesting, if a little unpleasant. But what is a little unpleasantness to a wanderer through the shoals of life such as yourself?" He snapped his fingers. "A mere scratch on your bows!"

"And this unpleasantness – it's to do with 'Slicer', is it?"

"Oh, yes!" The Great Porto chuckled as he switched off the computer, and made a cutting gesture with his hand against his palm. "Come on!" he said, holding open the door. "The night is young. There are secrets to be seen!"

"But you won't tell me what they've got to do with me?"

"No! Not yet! But then, as I said – that's because I'm not absolutely sure myself. Time will tell! Ha ha ha!"

Catullus sighed, and began to trudge wearily after Porto, down more corridors, down a long, long staircase. It seemed never to end. At last, though, Catullus felt basement concrete under his feet. He looked around. "Down here!" the Great Porto's voice called. Yet another corridor. Catullus peered into it, but it was even murkier than the ones upstairs, and he couldn't see a thing. He walked uncertainly along it. The whole thing was made of concrete. It was like walking through a subway, Catullus thought, it seemed so dead and dark. He could hear the sound of the Great Porto's footsteps when he listened for them, receding; he began to run, then he stopped; no footsteps now. "Hello!" he shouted. "Hello!" Nothing. Only the silence of the masonry above him, all those flights and flights of building, pressing down. "Shite," he muttered, "shite!" He hurried on, and then he realised that he had been walking for almost ten minutes. He must have left the building altogether now, so where did the corridor lead to? Somewhere medical, the Great Porto had said – a hospital, a morgue maybe? Catullus peered on ahead, into the murk. There was something ahead of him at last. A box. No, a large filing cabinet, a row of filing cabinets, serried up against the wall, like sarcophagi stored in a museum basement, left to gather dust a second time.

"BOO!"

Catullus leapt out of his skin.

"Ha ha ha, sorry, did I frighten you? Ha ha ha!" The Great Porto climbed out from behind one of the filing cabinets. "Just one of my little jokes. It never fails to amuse. You look as though you've seen a ghost. Ha ha ha."

"It's not surprising, is it, people leaping out on you, it's hardly what you expect in a fucking police station!" Catullus wiped at his brow. He could still feel his heart thumping.

The Great Porto laughed even more. "It's psychology, ha ha. Very sensible. Anything else you see now will seem that much less of a shock. Come on, we're here." He pointed to a door that Catullus hadn't noticed, in the opposite wall. The Great Porto pushed it open. "In we go."

Catullus followed him. There was a short passageway, quite different from the corridor they had just left, clean and almost humming with white plastic. It led into a large, almost empty room, even whiter than the passageway had been. Caelius was already there. He raised his hand, and made a face. Porter was standing next to him, and in front of them, by a table, stood a third man, the medical gentleman presumably. He was small and bald, and had his arms wrapped closely around him, as though he wished that his body were a shell into which he could withdraw.

The Great Porto didn't bother with any introductions. Instead, he giggled, and peered under a sheet that had been draped over the table. Fuck, it was a body. It had to be. The Great Porto giggled again, then turned to the medical gentleman. "Well, Doctor. How's your patient?"

"Dead," said the doctor shortly. "Very dead. Oh, no doubt about it, he's very dead indeed."

"Can I unveil him? For our two guests?" The Great Porto went up to the table and played with the edge of the sheet. "Are you ready?" he asked Caelius and Catullus.

They both nodded.

"Sure?"

"Yes."

The Great Porto began to shake with giggles. He put his arm round Catullus' shoulder. "Now then, ha ha ha, let's see what lies – under the sheet!" He whisked it off with a flamboyant sweep. "There you are! Ha ha ha! What do you make of that?"

Catullus looked down at the slab. Then he stared back up at Caelius, and looked right into his eyes, and saw that Caelius was staring back at him, and it was obvious that they had both had the same idea, they were both trying to reassure the other that none of this was real, that they weren't really standing in a mortuary, they hadn't really just looked down at the corpse of a man who had had his skull sliced right open. But it was real. Catullus forced himself to look down at the mess again. It was horrific. The wounds looked juicy and overripe. What had the body been washed in? It seemed so scrubbed that the flesh appeared remote from its own colour, as clean bodies always do after a good soaking in a bath, and in fact, if Catullus hadn't seen the place where the face should have been, he would have said that the thing laid out on the slab was actually just someone asleep on fresh sheets, someone who'd had a good bath and then been too tired to climb into his bed, but it did mean not looking at the head, which he would have to force himself to do again, he would have to look at it, he couldn't avoid it any more, so he turned back and looked. He felt sick. The chemical smells and – everything.

"Who is it?" he asked.

"You don't know?" The Great Porto shook his head. "Oh dear. We were rather hoping you might identify it for us."

"Well, how the fuck can I identify it if it hasn't got a fucking face?"

"Good point. Well put."

"Is it someone I know?"

"Sort of."

"It doesn't look like the sort of person I'd recognise naked."

"Ooh. Very good. You're getting warm."

"Please. Just tell me."

"You have no patience. Ha ha. How can you play these sort of games without patience?" The Great Porto looked into Catullus' face, and smiled; then he nodded to his assistant.

"We think it's the tramp you took home last night," Porter said. "Varney. All we really want to know is if you think that might be a possible identification."

"We only met him that once."

"Yes. But as far as we know, you were the last people to see him alive." He paused. "Apart from the murderer, of course."

"Oh." Catullus could feel his heart starting to pound again. "I see."

"Take another look."

Gingerly, Catullus lifted up the sheet. His finger accidentally brushed against flesh. It was so cold, and there was just the faintest smell of shit. He looked the body up and down.

"It could be him, I suppose." He looked at Caelius, who nodded and shrugged. "There's nothing that makes me think it isn't. But you should ask the landlady, the woman who ran the hostel. She'd know better than us."

Porter smiled.

"We spoke to her this afternoon."

"And?"

"It's him. She said there was no doubt about it."

"Well – there you are, then."

Porter smiled again, and paused. "She also suggested you two as possible suspects."

"What?"

God knew what his face looked like, but it must have been very funny, because the Great Porto was almost beside himself with merriment.

"You don't believe her, do you?" Caelius asked. "This...we – I mean, we're not really under arrest after all?"

"Ha ha ha ha ha! Of course not!" The Great Porto shook his head good-humouredly. "We just needed to know the time of your movements, that was all, which I gather you have given us. Very helpful of you, much appreciated. You see," he went on, turning to Catullus, "you had much the best deal. Chatting about – other things. Statements can be very dull. Give me a nice friendly chat any day. Happy?"

"No. Why drag us out in the middle of the night if all you wanted to do was take a statement?"

"Dear, oh dear, there's no pleasing some. Would you be happier if we had arrested you? Would you have felt it was all worth while then? I thought you'd be grateful. You can go home soon, and not get banged up. Some people would be relieved."

"But why get us out here in the first place? Just to make a statement?"

The Great Porto reached out and patted Catullus gently on the shoulder. "My dear young friend. Point one. In all police work, we must have speed, speed, and speed again. No time to hang around. Time's chariot draweth near. All that, you see. And point two, the evening wasn't just for anything as uncouth as a mere statement. No, no, no! A friendship has grown up between us this evening, a symbiosis if you like. Surely that was worth losing a few hours sleep for? I understand you now, and you understand me. Better for all concerned, don't you think?"

"Maybe, except that I don't understand you at all."

"Ha ha ha! Ever the fate of the philosopher. You would prefer facts?"

"In the circumstances, yes."

"I'm not the man for facts. Speculation, yes. Facts, no. I can't help you."

"Won't help me."

The Great Porto laughed and wagged a finger. "True, very subtle of you. You're quite right – in a sense, I suppose, it is my responsibility to keep you in the dark, ha ha! I feel like a doctor who may have diagnosed cancer in you, or may not have done. Either way, I'm not telling."

"Well, it all leaves me feeling thoroughly fucked off."

"I'm sorry to hear that. Ha ha, I know! Why we don't we make you feel a little less irate, and tell you about what happened to your late friend, Mr Varney? Take you into our confidence, you deserve that for having been so good. Lots of lovely facts there. Would you like that?" He nodded eagerly, as though willing Catullus to agree, but Catullus just glanced at the corpse and turned away, while Caelius yawned and asked if he could go home now.

The Great Porto shook his head.

"No. I want you to know what happened."

"Why?"

"To see if it jogs your minds, of course." The Great Porto fished around in his pocket, and took out a pen and a scrap of paper. "Now, as I said, I'm not a facts man, but Doctor – you're always ready to give a diagnosis. Give us your diagnosis on our friend on the slab."

The doctor nodded to himself. "The cause of death," he murmured gently, stroking the corpse as though it were a pet, "was undoubtedly a perforation of the left lung." He pointed to a slash mark. "There. There was also severe bruising, two broken ribs, and look–"; he picked up the two hands. "Severe lacerations on the palms. He knew he was being attacked. These wounds come when someone tries to stop a knife or something sharp." The doctor nodded happily. "I think it was probably an axe. It went straight through his body. It must have been heavy."

The Great Porto had been staring down at the slab, fascinated. "Heavy, eh?" he said, looking up. "Heavy enough to chop off a face too, that's what we all want to know, isn't it?"

The doctor shrugged. "Presumably."

"A hack or a chop?"

"A chop."

"Clean?"

"As a whistle. Straight off."

"So – a real craftsman, eh? And performed after death, you think? Like a botanist with his scalpel – needed to pick his plant first. Ha ha ha! That would make sense, wouldn't it? Perfect sense." The Great Porto rubbed his hands together, and craned over to peer at a form the Doctor was studying. "And when exactly do we think the face was chopped?"

"Almost at once. The moment the murderer was sure he'd killed his victim, I'd have thought. Or probably murderers. From the angle of the wounds, I'd have said there were at least two of them."

The Great Porto looked up at Catullus and Caelius and winked heavily, then glanced back at the doctor's form. "And when was the body thrown into the river?"

"Straightaway."

"Well, this is all most impressive. A kick, a slice, and then, into the river. Very efficient processing, wouldn't you say?"

"He was found in the river?" Catullus suddenly asked, as a thought settled like ice into the pit of his stomach. Marius. That story in the book...

The Great Porto was nodding at him. "Oh yes. A shame, isn't it, that the Tiber is so filthy, because it must have been his first bath for months and months. Ha ha ha! But at least he's clean now, and that's the main thing, eh? End up clean, that's the ticket! A scrubbed corpse is a happy corpse!"

"Where was he found?"

"By the Senate House. Near here. Under the bridge. By a boy on a school expedition – I wonder what he was studying? Probably not anatomy, ha ha ha! All very educational though, I'm sure. Something to put in his report, eh?" The Great Porto giggled hysterically.

Catullus waited until he had calmed down. "And you haven't got any idea where he might have – where he was killed, I mean?"

The Great Porto stared at him, and rocked back on his heels. "What do you think?"

"You tell me. You're the ones with the clues."

"Clues!" The Great Porto rubbed his hands. "We don't need clues! Look at Porter, look at his mind, his mighty mind, turning endlessly, sorting out his thoughts, winnowing and sifting – he doesn't need clues. No! We deduce! Deduce!" He took a piece of paper from Porter's hands, and waved it in Catullus' face. "Your friend's testimony, given just now while we were having our little chat. I've only flicked through it, but already my mind has deduced tremendously. It's quite easy. Let me give you a shove. You want to know where our mutual friend might have met with his, ha, accident?"

"Yes."

"Well, we know he didn't cut himself shaving. Ha ha ha! And how?"

"Because you don't shave with an axe."

"No, no, no! How do we know he wasn't shaving in the first place?"

Catullus thought. "He was too drunk."

"Yes! Exactly! He was, ha ha, blotto. And so if he was found dead the next day, we can deduce that he died quite near the hostel, can't we? Easy, you see."

"Yes." And Catullus shivered again, as he had done when he had first imagined Mr Varney floating dead in the black waters of the Tiber, which he and Caelius had seen illumined, the night before, by a great fire on a wasteland tip. "He was murdered on the Fairlawns, wasn't he?"

"Yes. Perhaps." The Great Porto darted a look at his deputy. "What makes you think that?"

"Deduction."

"Ah ha! Go on."

"There was a fire there last night, and someone dancing in front of it."

"Yes. Your friend mentioned it. So?"

"So – Mr Varney was very interested in history. The Civil War, particularly. If he'd heard about a strange figure dancing on the Fairlawns, he would have wanted to go out and watch it. He would have braved a hangover or anything to go out there."

The Great Porto frowned, and rubbed the side of his nose. "Why?"

Catullus smiled. "Surely it's obvious, isn't it? Marius. Marius the Dancer."

The Great Porto frowned even more deeply. "Your deductions are a little, ha, esoteric, I'm afraid, even for me."

"Haven't you heard the legend? Marius saw a strange figure dancing on the Fairlawns. Mr Varney identified very strongly with Marius. That must have been why he was staying in that particular hostel."

"Well, that's most interesting." Porto scribbled something down.

"Is it any help?" Catullus asked.

"Oh yes. Just goes to prove how helpful these little night time confabs can be. A most interesting deduction. Very good."

Catullus glanced at the hole where Mr Varney's face had been, and remembered how Marius' soldiers were said to have dredged a corpse with similar mutilations from the Tiber. Should he mention it? No, they'd hardly been helpful, why should he be? And anyway, the Great Porto was leaving the room.

"Come on," he called by the exit. "I've got something else to show you."

Caelius stared at him bleakly. "We can't go home?"

"No, no! Come and look at these first. You'll like them. Come on."

He disappeared. Catullus and Caelius followed him out, through the corridor, and then back into the long concrete passageway. The Great Porto was busy walking down the long row of filing cabinets, peering at the labels on each one, until at last he found what he had been looking for, under one of the irregular strip lights, and he turned and called everyone to gather round.

"You asked about clues," he told Catullus. "Well, we do actually have the odd clue. Key please, Doctor. Let's show our young guests the goodies. Ooh, they are fun." He started to fumble with one of the locks, giggling occasionally, and then pulled out one of the drawers. It was crammed full with glass jars of various sizes and colours. Catullus peered down at them; he had never seen so many different coloured liquids. "Fascinating, eh?" the Great Porto chuckled. "Ha ha, it's quite like a birthday, so many goodies. You're a lucky man, Doctor – all these beautiful liquids to look at, and you get paid for it too, oh yes, you're a lucky man." He bent over, and gently picked out a large jar. "WAAAGH!" he yelled suddenly, flashing it into Catullus' face, giving him just enough time to see a hand and ear as they floated ponderously in a straw coloured liquid. Then the jar was stashed back into its place in the drawer, and the Great Porto was winking and grinning, and pulling Catullus by the arm. "The Amazing Hand and Ear Mystery," he whispered conspiratorially, "one of mine, a tremendous success. Unsolvable, they said. Ha ha ha! But not strictly relevant right now, and I'm sure you're in a hurry."

"Too fucking right," muttered Caelius. The Great Porto ignored him; instead, like a magician drawing an egg from a woman's ear, he plucked out a second jar, stared at it, and then held it up to the light. "There," he whispered again, "what do you make of that?" Catullus watched, as a black sludge, disturbed from its resting place at the bottom of the jar, floated gently up through the thick liquid preserving it. "Just look at it! What a sight, eh?" The Great Porto held his jar even closer to the light. "It looks like the mess left by biscuits, don't you think, at the bottom of coffee cups? Ha ha ha! What do you call this liquid, Doctor?"

"Formaldehyde."

"Yes, that's the stuff! Never dunk your biscuits in formaldehyde, eh?"

"What's the gunge?" asked Caelius.

The Great Porto's giggles spluttered to life again, as he gave the jar a fresh inspection. "Poor Mr Varney's face," he said after a pause. "Ha ha ha! He has lost his looks, hasn't he? Ha ha ha ha ha ha!"

"Not really," said Caelius. "Now you can't recognise him at all."

"Not quite true, I'm afraid." He pointed. "Look, there's an ear, see it? Oh, there's two." The Great Porto gave the jar one last loving look, and then placed it delicately back in the drawer. "What a treat, eh? Worth staying up for." He grinned triumphantly. "Key please, Doctor."

Catullus watched as the cabinet was locked, and the remains of Mr Varney's features incarcerated once again behind the wall of blank grey that stretched without break into the passageway's far darkness. "What do they prove?" he asked. "Those bits of face?"

"Well," said the Great Porto, leaning against a filing cabinet, "they prove he had half his head chopped off, but then we knew that already. Ha ha ha! But I thought you might be interested to know that we – well, not we – Porter found bits of the face on Fairlawns. Isn't that right, Porter? Ear and there. You get it? Ear and there. Ha ha ha!"

"Next to a large circle of ash," said Porter. "Still smouldering, so you're probably right, that's what he went out to see."

"Perhaps you should join us in the Force. *Then* you'd be able to read your files." Porto clapped his hands merrily. "Good. But that's it for now, I'm afraid. The night's entertainment is over."

Caelius looked up. "We can go?"

"Be my guest. Run along. The land of nod beckons, I'm sure."

"It certainly does." Caelius began to walk down the passageway, as though his tiredness was something that had to be waded through.

"Stop!" shouted the Great Porto. "You'll get lost. How will you ever find the bus stop?"

Caelius stopped dead in his tracks. "Bus stop?" he repeated slowly.

"Yes, the bus stop. It's not hard to find, actually. You want to go back out the way you came, turn right out of the street, then it's five minutes walk to the Aventine Crossroads, and the stop for Tallowfield is opposite there. You can't miss it, as they say."

"Bus stop?"

"Yes." Porto smiled patiently. "Where you catch buses from."

"You expect us to wait by a fucking bus stop? After all this fucking time? What about him?" Caelius yelled, pointing at Porter. "He drove us here, why the fuck can't he drive us back?"

"He's got to get to bed, poor man, he's tired. Been up all night."

"He's tired? What do you think I am?"

"Pretend you've been out at a night club, or something. Young chap like you, ha ha – just the ticket. Good night."

"Fuck you!"

"Ha ha ha!" The Great Porto waved genially as he walked over to the mortuary door.

"*Bastard!*" shouted Caelius as the door slammed shut. "Fucking, fucking bastard!" Then, pulling Catullus by the arm, he carried on walking down the corridor, swearing furiously under his breath. Catullus followed, stroking Caelius' palm.

"Well, at least his directions were right." Caelius looked at his watch. "No fucking bus, of course."

Catullus glanced round at the Aventine Crossroads, as Marius was said to have done however many centuries ago it had been. There were no ghosts now, though, just black-windowed shops, and litter everywhere, and a single cleaner in orange overalls, sweeping sadly. Catullus heard footsteps from behind him, and swung round, but still there was no muffled figure coming out from the shadows, just Lady Camilla. She recognised Catullus, and stopped in her tracks.

"Screech!" She threw her arms out wide. "Absolutely shrieks-ville! You old tart, *imagine* meeting you here!" She clattered down the pavement, arms out wide, and buried Catullus in a slobbering embrace. "Darling, you're just the gooiest! What are you doing here?"

Catullus tried to think up an interesting lie, but needn't have bothered, since Camilla was only interested in talking about herself. "Munchkins," she said, pawing at his chest. "Munchkins, listen." She whispered. "Don't tell me I'm a heartless old hag, I'm not, honestly, I love you very much, but munchkins, listen, I am *wiped*."

"Really?"

"It has been a *rough* night." She trilled fetchingly. "Do you know who I met in the lavatory tonight?"

Catullus shrugged.

"Someone so famous it would bleach your hair out to hear it."

"Who was it?"

"Darling, I don't mean to be rude, I don't want you to feel just the teeniest bit that I don't love you dearly, but I'm afraid I can't tell you. And do you know why? Because I respect his privacy." She dug inside her handbag. "Look," she said, pointing to a entry in her address file. "His fax number. Personal."

Caelius peered at it over Catullus' shoulder. "If this fax number belongs to a man, what was he doing in a women's lavatory?" he asked.

Camilla stared at him.

"Oh, this is my friend Caelius," muttered Catullus. "Caelius – Lady Camilla."

"Of course I know who he is, silly." Camilla kissed him. "Now, Caelius. Remind me what you do?"

"He's a law student."

Camilla smiled understandingly, and shook her head. "Oh well, then. To understand is to forgive. Darling, there are things people get up to in lavatories that a law student wouldn't even be able to imagine." She swung herself off Catullus' chest and onto Caelius', from where she gazed up at him unblinkingly. "And do you know something? I think you're better off that way, I really do. Stay in your safe legal job, and don't ever pry into what people miscall a world of glamour." Camilla laughed sadly. "Glamour! Only someone who didn't know my world would think it was glamorous!"

"What is your world?"

Camilla tossed her hair back again, as though to apologise for her own success. "I don't want to talk about it."

"Why not?"

"Because you'll just be so terribly jealous, and you'll think that I'm an enormous cry baby to keep going on about how actually, it's just so absolutely dullsville." Suddenly Camilla burst into tears, and shook uncontrollably all over Caelius' chest. "Do you think I'm an awful cry baby?" she asked, panting her words out between great heaving sobs.

"No, no, not at all," said Caelius. He stared at Catullus, who just shrugged. "Of course not." He patted her on the shoulder, and made murmuring sounds.

"You see," she choked, "I've actually just had the most terrible news. The Number One Worst." She waited for Caelius to ask her what it was.

"What is it?"

"The Big C."

"What?"

Camilla looked up at him, and her eyes were drowned beneath a new welling of tears. "Cancer!" she managed to shriek out before the tears really began to flow. "I'm going to die!"

"Oh dear," said Caelius. "How terrible for you."

"All the doctors say there's nothing they can do. I'm quite doomed." She stared up into Caelius' eyes again. "So you see, I may not have long to live, and you, you wicked person, you haven't even been keeping in touch with me."

"I'm sorry, but have I met you before?"

Camilla laughed. "These students! Their alternative sense of humour!" She stroked his hair playfully, and pointed at Catullus. "You too. Keep in touch. Where do you live?"

"Tallowfield."

"Taffuld? There's a new club opening there. Sounds serious fun. We should maybe meet up there some time." She began to wander down the street. "I'll bring Clo."

"Clodia?"

"Yes. She thought you were sweet."

The night bus swung round the corner, and began to brake as the driver saw Caelius jumping up and down in the road. Catullus waited until it had stopped.

"She remembered me?" he shouted. "Clodia?"

"Thought you were mmm," Camilla yelled back. "Mmmmm!"

Caelius was beckoning from the bus. Catullus wanted to know more, he had to know more, but Camilla was already almost gone, and the bus driver was waiting. So Catullus clambered on board, and paid for his ticket, then joined Caelius, who was slumped on one of the back seats. The bus lurched up a gear, and swung away from the corner; Catullus saw one last glimpse of Camilla, tottering wildly down some street, and then the bus accelerated, and she was gone. The bus turned down the mall towards the Senate House.

"Well, fuck," said Caelius, hunching even further down into the leather of the bus seat. "Fuck, fuck, fuck. Am I fucked off, or what?"

"Sounds like it."

"Good. I don't want there to be any possible doubt about the matter. I am fucked off. Well and truly fucked. What a fucking ghastly fucking night."

"Yes."

"Fuck."

Caelius stayed hunched, his arms folded, then suddenly he squirmed and swore again. "And you know what the worst thing is? I don't even feel sleepy any more – I can't even look forward to going to bed, thanks to that fucking woman. Who the fuck was she? Patronising me like that. God, I wish I'd hit her in the face."

"I thought you were getting on with her quite well. Giving her a manly shoulder and all that."

"What, all that cancer crap? I hope she has got it."

"Charming."

"Well – I mean. What a bitch. How did you meet her?"

"At the ball."

"Ah, that fucking ball. It keeps cropping up, doesn't it?"

"It certainly does. I think it explains why we were at that police station tonight."

"Sorry?"

"What did you talk about? With Porter?"

Caelius thought. "What we'd done last night. What we'd seen, that sort of thing. How we hadn't done the murder. You know."

"Did you pick up that I didn't even discuss Mr Varney? I wasn't told about him till I'd seen him laid out on that slab."

"So what did you talk about, then? The ball?"

"In a roundabout way. He couldn't work out what it was I'd been doing there, but since I didn't really know either, I couldn't help him much."

"Did it get political?"

Catullus thought. "I suppose so. I'm not actually sure."

"They're contemptible when they try and get political. They start thinking they're clever, when really all they're good for is beating up innocent suspects and kicking the shit out of blacks."

"Who do you think did it?"

"What?"

"Killed Mr Varney."

"Don't really care. There were two suspicious characters seen hanging around apparently, so they'll probably arrest them and trump up some confession, and then that'll be that."

"They didn't suspect us, you don't think?"

"No. Why the hell should they? It must have been someone quarrelling over the meths, who else would want to kill him? They could see we were gentlemen – not the types at all."

"Well – I hope you're right."

"I expect they just wanted to shit you up, and tell you to steer clear of Clodius, or Pompey, or whoever it is they're dirty-tricksing at the moment. Tick you off their list. You'll be okay, now they've realised you're just a harmless simpleton."

Catullus smiled bleakly. Caelius nestled down, and announced that he felt sleepy again. Catullus was glad to hear it. He turned and looked out of the window at the sun rising over Rome's concrete suburbs. Suddenly, the road they were driving along became warm with fresh daylight. Catullus shut his eyes. The sounds of early morning dropped into his mind slowly, spreading out like ripples to fill his thoughts, and then vanish into them. Catullus liked the image, in a groggy way, and thinking about the ripples, forming and forming and disappearing outwards, he felt himself being lulled even deeper into sleep, and all the time, the sounds of morning kept dropping into his mind, falling and rippling, until soon they weren't even sounds any more, but colours, and Catullus was riding them, a blaze of colour, and they stayed colour, but now they were also music, and the music was being played on violins. It was carrying him past rows and rows of deserted houses, towards a fire, or was the music just a tributary of the fire, flowing back towards it, Catullus wasn't sure, but Lud and Pollo, the two clowns, were dancing before it, furiously, as though they wanted to exorcise the heat, and Catullus could see them silhouetted against the blaze. He reached out to touch them, but it was no good, he knew that he was slipping away, so he jerked back and clawed at something, and found that he was in a darkness so total and unexpected that his mouth wanted to shape itself into a scream, and without actually being ready, he began to call out. "Clodia!" Catullus opened his eyes. Caelius was shaking him, and the morning light was glowing in his eyes. He looked out, and saw the walls of Ricket's Gate. Caelius shook him again. "Come on, sweetie, our stop. Wake up."

They clambered out. Inside the house, Mr Dugbal was sitting on the staircase, his head in his hands, his clothes creased and unchanged.

"Morning, Mr Dugbal," said Caelius cheerfully.

Mr Dugbal flinched, and looked up. He hardly seemed to recognise Caelius, who was busy trying to clamber past him. Caelius had almost made it when there was a sudden clattering of bare feet up the stairs, and Jez catapulted himself into his father's lap. Mr Dugbal shook; then, mouthing words inaudibly, he brushed Jez's bony legs from his hips, and slunk away downstairs like a wounded cat. Caelius and Catullus stared after him as he went; Jez seemed quite unabashed. He jumped up and punched Catullus in the stomach.

"Hello," he said cheerfully. "Did you get tortured?"

"No."

"Oh well. But I expect they'll torture you later, and it'll be in public, and I'll be able to go and see you having all your nails pulled out, and oil poured down your throat, and snails and stuff. Did you know Vanessa's gone missing?"

"Really?" said Caelius, sounding surprised.

"Yes. Dad found out last night, just after he sent me to bed. He went mad."

Catullus remembered the screams he had heard, dying on the wind. "He doesn't really look as though he's recovered."

"Yeah, he's in a bit of a mood."

"Where's Vanessa gone?"

Jez looked up shyly, and twisted the tassels on his dressing gown cord. "Screwing."

"Screwing?"

"Yeah, you know. Screwing. What girls do. That's what Dad thinks, anyway, and it can give you babies if you're a girl, so that's why he's been out looking for her all night."

Caelius yawned. "I'm going to bed. I feel too tired to be worrying about other people. Philanthropy becomes morbidity without a good night's sleep."

"That was good," Catullus said.

"Did you like it? One of my own, I'd been saving it up for weeks."

He nodded. "Good. See you, then. Night."

"Morning." Catullus watched as Caelius stumped his way up the staircase. He turned back to Jez. "Don't you think you should go back to bed as well?"

"Don't be stupid, it's school soon."

"Really?"

"Well, quite soon. Going to bed's boring. Don't you want to play space invaders with me?"

"No, I want to go to sleep. I haven't been to bed yet."

"But you're a grown up."

"Grown ups go to bed too."

"Dad doesn't."

"He must do."

"No, he doesn't, hardly ever. Mum does, sometimes, but she's a woman. Oh, go on, please."

Catullus realised to his surprise that he no longer felt very sleepy. Maybe he had mislaid his tiredness on the bus. He looked at Jez, who was staring up at him with eager, glowing eyes. He shrugged. "All right. But not for long."

"Oh, wicked!" He took out his game from beneath his dressing gown. "Look. It's safe, isn't it?" He started playing. "You've got to kill all the aliens, and then when you've done that, you go through these gates, and then you have to kill more aliens, and you go on like that till you're dead. It's really great." He demonstrated. As he manipulated his space ship through gates that had been designed to look like a pair of woman's legs, the computer gave a happy moan. Catullus smiled.

"What's funny?" Jez asked.

"Nothing. Let me have a go."

Catullus was wiped out three times within a minute, but at last he managed to get the space ship through the gates. The computer gave its moan again. Catullus found himself thinking of Clodia, and when he finally made it to bed, he continued to remember how she had looked, in the shadows of the coach, or beside him the next morning, laughing, flirting with him. As he drifted into sleep, he thought how strange it was, to remember a woman so vividly after only a single conversation. Catullus began to slip into dream. But Clodia remained, a phantom presence by his side.

LESBIA

AUTUMN

VII

BOOT

The rain began to thicken. Catullus stared down at his feet and noticed a can; he kicked it, and watched it arc and splash into a puddle. It sat there next to another can; the whole site was still full of rubbish, even after a week spent clearing it, and looking around, Catullus found it hard to believe that there could ever have been a time when there hadn't been rubbish on the site. Was that what the Trojans had done, when they had first landed – dropped litter everywhere? It wasn't the sort of place now where anyone would choose to settle. It was a shit hole, and in the rain it looked even more of a shit hole. Everything seemed derelict; there were a few cranes in the distance, further down the river, but even they had been abandoned; on the far side of the site, the houses looked barely inhabited, though sometimes boys had stopped in the street on their bikes, and shouted at him to fuck off, so he guessed that they had to live somewhere near. It was hard to feel passion when surrounded by such crap.

Catullus glanced at his watch. It was getting late. Evening was creeping up through the rain, and the darker it became, the more Catullus felt that it was time to be heading home. He peered through the drizzle for Doctor Gower.

The Doctor was such a vast man that it should have been easy to keep a track on him, but he was excitable, and inclined to run off without warning. Catullus picked his way up a mound of bricks and looked over the site one final time. He was just about to leave, give in to the rain, when he saw someone standing by a road-side wall. Catullus strained his eyes. Yes, it was Doctor Gower, he'd recognise the bulk anywhere. What the hell was he doing? Polishing something? Catullus skidded down the brick pile and across the site towards the wall.

"Come and feast your eyes on this!" bellowed Doctor Gower, hearing him. Catullus bent down and peered as the Doctor continued to scour furiously at a stone set in the wall. "Now, what do you make of that?" he asked triumphantly. "Victory, that's what it is. Victory!" Catullus peered again, but still couldn't see anything remarkable. He said so. The Doctor snorted.

"Just notice how different it is from the others. Notice the blue. Now look, when you polish it, the dirt comes off, and it becomes even more blue." He tapped one of the bricks. "But this is quite different," he said disdainfully. "Red, utterly common. Now look at our stone again. Unusual, and quite beautiful. Clearly not from a local source of rock at all." He stood back, and then darted forward to polish it again. "Victory! I knew it was here!"

"But how can you know that the stone is from the observatory?"

"The stones were said to be blue, weren't they?"

"Yes, but..."

"Yes, but? Yes, but? Don't shrivel up this moment for me with any yes buts! It's sacred! No yes buts, I won't tolerate them!"

"But..."

"No!"

"Okay." Catullus nodded. "Okay." He paused. "I just want to know how it got into this wall."

Doctor Gower's frown creased out into a smirk. "My dear boy, if that's all your buts amount to, then dolly me up some more." He pointed over to the waste site. "That's where it came from. Out there. The very site on which I said the stone circle would be found. And now we have the first hard archaeological proof that I was right." He bent down and kissed the stone. "We must set about prising this beauty out."

"But this wall must be, what? – only a century old?"

"Yes."

"And the last authenticated record we have of anyone seeing the stones is about four centuries old?"

"Yes. So?"

"You really think that the stones would have lasted three hundred years before being used?"

"Of course, of course. Because this just shows what I've always said, that the circle wasn't wholly destroyed. Remains of it survived and still survive, and it's only been a matter of finding the site. And now we know we've got it – the Great Dance of Stones! We've got it! The oldest site in the whole of Rome! It's ours!" He threw his arm out in a wide arc. "Buried out there are the first yearnings of our ancestors. 'There is a place, called the dance of stones, sometime a famous place of worship of the heavens. And the people who live by it know nothing of it save that in times long gone, it was much cherished by our forefathers, the Trojans.'" The Doctor gestured a second time. "The antiquarians were right. I was right. The Dance of Stones does indeed lie out there!"

Catullus peered through the curtain of rain. The only stone circle that he could see was the ring of decaying storehouses mouldering into rubble on the boundaries of the tip. "I still don't see that we're going to find anything." He pointed at the rubbish heaped across the site. "How many foundations must have been thrown down there over the past four hundred years?"

"None."

"None?"

"Not a brick."

Catullus smiled in disbelief. "Something must have been built there."

"Why?"

"Well – I mean – this is Rome. There isn't a square foot of Rome that hasn't been built on. And the old city walls ran just back there. It must have been garrisoned – in the Civil War, at least?"

Doctor Gower shook his head, sending a shower of droplets from the few remaining wisps of his hair. "It doesn't follow. Not necessarily."

"It must do. There must be Civil War buildings. It was just after the time when the stones were last seen. Why else would they have disappeared? How else?"

"You seem remarkably keen that we should find Civil War foundations. Forget the Civil War. It's unimportant."

"I'm just drawing on what I've read about the site."

"And what have you read? Dextrar's book? Eh? Is that what you're basing your theories on?" The Doctor laughed loudly, and bent down to pick up his bag. He rummaged through it, and then drew out a book. "*Archaeology of the River Tiber*. That's what you've been reading, isn't it?"

Catullus shrugged. "Amongst other things."

"Well, let me tell you that *Archaeology of the River Tiber* is a load of bollocks." He ripped out a fistful of pages. "And let me also tell you that Professor Dextrar, DPhil, Chair of Antiquities, is also a load of bollocks." He tore what was left of the book in two. "There. That's what I think of Professor Dextrar, DPhil, Chair of Antiquities. And his appalling book." He tossed the confettied shreds into the air, and watched as they were flattened by the rain into the dirt by his feet. "Don't ever let me catch you reading it again."

Catullus shrugged. "Is it really that wrong?" he asked, as Doctor Gower took him by the arm and began to lead him towards the shelter of his car. "Or do you not like him because he's the established authority?"

The Doctor shook his head, and didn't smile. "I don't like him because he's a shoddy researcher, and because he's blocked the fruits of my own research for what seems like half a lifetime. It's been a bitter experience. To feel so close to something so important, and yet to have been blocked all the time by obstructionist, pen-pushing, pig-ignorant councillors and their lackeys in the University."

"But why were they blocking you?"

"Philistinism." Doctor Gower's already fleshy face deepened an extra shade of purple. "Undiluted philistinism. What you have to expect nowadays, I'm afraid. Potentially the most exciting site in Roman archaeological history, and they see it as real estate."

"Who does?"

"The council. And whichever shady developer is hanging in the background waiting to build his insurance towers here. And all backed up by Professor Dextrar, doling out exactly what everyone wants to be told."

"It seems very political."

"Oh yes. Archaeology is built up on the heaving terrain of politics. How could it not be, when its function is to present the past to the future? Two of the most political of concepts, and especially now, when we seem to be throwing them both away." The Doctor grunted gloomily. "So what we will find here will also be political, and Professor Dextrar's book is also political, and that is why you must never read it again."

"So hold on – he was saying that there was no need to preserve the site, because even if the stone circle had been here, there'd be no traces of it left? And so it could be sold to the developers?"

Doctor Gower nodded. "That was the drift."

"But what about you? I still don't see how you can be sure yourself. Not meaning to be rude."

They had reached the car. Doctor Gower unlocked one of the doors. "Get in," he said. "There's something I want to show you." As Catullus climbed onto his seat, the Doctor looked around. "Where's Boot?" he asked. "She's gone already, has she?"

Catullus shook his head. "I don't know. I haven't seen her." Boot was the assistant on the site. She had a friend who worked in a café a few streets away, and she'd told him that she was going to stay there until the rain stopped. "I know she's around somewhere. Why, do you want her?"

The Doctor shifted in his seat, and coughed apologetically. "Well, not exactly. She's not trained, you see, so I don't want her getting involved in all this, so if – you know – when you see her... Keep things quiet. Just to play safe."

Catullus felt a sudden prickling along the back of his neck. "What have you got, then?" he asked softly.

Doctor Gower smiled. "Let's not run before we can walk, shall we? First things first." He swivelled himself round awkwardly, and reached for a briefcase and a small package wrapped in newspaper. He placed the package tenderly by his feet, then clicked open his briefcase. "Now then." He took out a sheet of paper and looked at it. "I want to read you this. You'll probably know it. It's from one of the early Republican histories." He cleared his throat.

"'The Trojans'," he began, "'watched over by the gods, sailed on until at last they saw new land. And this was the land where the city of Rome was destined to be built, and a new empire raised up from the ruins of that which had been lost. And as they sailed, they saw an eagle flying ahead, and they remembered the prophecy, that they should see an eagle, and wherever it led, there should they go, and wheresoever it landed, there should they build a shrine to the heavens. And the eagle led them up a great river, and it alighted on the bank, and the Trojans prayed to the gods and gave thanks, that they had been safely guided through so many travails, and they landed, and they burned their ships. A strange facility of magic was in them then, that they might do as they had been commanded by the gods, and build rock upon rock, stone upon stone, and so they reared up a great circle which was open to the heavens, and men could read the patterns of the stars in its form. This was the circle which in later times was known as the Dance of the Stones, and where it is now, no man can say. For a time had come when men began to fear the stones, and forget what they had been, and then it was that the stones seemed built on haunted ground, and were not meant for men. Whether that be true, I cannot say, for we have forgot what our forefathers brought, and have almost forgot the stones themselves. But the place where they stood is still deserted and lorn, and no man builds there.'"

Doctor Gower rested the sheet of paper on his knee. "Now then. What do you make of that? As a topographical pointer?"

"Well...the deserted – what is it? – the lorn place where no man builds anything – that's our site, I suppose. But it's hardly accurate as history, is it? – it's a string of stories. That bit you've just read, for instance, all that stuff about eagles and Trojans. You're not saying the Trojans did come here to found Rome? Surely that has to be a myth?"

"Well, does it? But you're going too fast – let's just hold on and leave the Trojans out of this for now. Because this sentence here, this last one –." The Doctor pointed down at the sheet of paper, but he quoted from memory. "'The place where they stood is still deserted and lorn, and no man builds there.' Now, that isn't referring to the Trojans, he's talking about a contemporary superstition, and so I thought that it might just conceivably be useful to check the land records, and see which plots in Rome hadn't been built on at the time."

"But there must have been any number that hadn't been built on, surely?"

"Not within the city walls. Not within streets or areas of obvious conurbation. No, I'm exaggerating, there were a few, but if you looked as far back as the records went, then there was only one site that seemed absolutely immune to the building going on all around it, and this was the period when Rome was first really expanding, don't forget, there were little straggling settlements developing and growing everywhere, everywhere except one place, and do you know where that one place was? Here. And did you also realise that when you go to the records and look forwards instead of back, there's an even more remarkable thing? During all the centuries when Rome grew to become the largest city in the world, right up to the present day, there was one area that was still not built on. Just one area. And that, I'm sure you'll agree, is really extraordinary." He wound down his window, and gestured at the bleak expanse outside. "If I hadn't researched that wilderness out there into the ground, I would scarcely believe it myself. But as far as I can tell, that site hasn't been built on for at least six hundred years. At least six hundred years. For some reason, what we have out there is virgin ground, absolutely untouched." He tapped at the sheet of paper on his knee. "And I think our historian here gives that reason. That, at any rate, is what we have set ourselves to prove."

Here? And by what power? By what power had it remained uninhabited for all those however many centuries? It seemed too fantastic, too unsettling almost, to be really true. Catullus stared out through the blotted windscreen, as Doctor Gower flicked a switch, and the first thud and wheeze of the wipers began to smear across his view of the wasteland outside.

"Do we have any other evidence?" he asked.

Doctor Gower frowned, and shifted in his seat. "We have the evidence that I've just given you. Don't wonder whether we should be here now, wonder why we weren't here years before. Surely you can recognise that faith can exist as evidence, indeed, that faith is often its own best evidence, if it has been inherited. It certifies its own historical pedigree – you don't have to radio-carbon faith. The legends of Rome lie as deep any artefact, under every street. You have to dig for them, but they're there, waiting to be found. We are going to dig."

Catullus shrugged. In the half dark, and the after-thrill of wondering if an old legend might really have been true, he could almost accept this. And of course, he wanted to, he realised, the seeming mystery of this ancient spot, the imagined ghosts of Trojan ships, beached on the Tiber mud flats where there was nothing now except litter and shit. It had been the hope that ghosts might be real which had first guided his interest in the past, the thought that maybe the past touched the present sometimes, in some places, and redeemed it, though he could remember that he had been reluctant to acknowledge this, for while he had never been as thrilled by a sense of mystery as when he found himself hoping that maybe it was true, yet it had to catch one out, it had to be a surprise, for otherwise the mesh of common sense would never allow it through.

Doctor Gower had been picking up the small bundle he had put down earlier by his feet. He handed it over to Catullus. "Maybe this will satisfy your professional doubts," he said. Then he sat and watched expectantly, like a mother waiting for her child to open a present, as Catullus unwrapped the newspaper. Inside was a tiny black figurine; Catullus stared at it, and felt the same chill that had gripped his stomach the week before, when he had been staring at Mr Varney's faceless corpse on the slab. Then he shook his head; it was a stupid connection to make, just because the tiny chipped figure had an eagle's head. The statue could hardly be from the Civil War – it was far too primitive. Catullus held it up to what was left of the light. From one of the old eastern empires? Yes, probably. But not a style that he could pin down with any certainty.

"Well?" said Doctor Gower eagerly. "What do you think?"

"I don't know. Circassian?"

"Exactly right! Well done! Do you know much about Circassian myth?"

"Not enormous amounts." Catullus looked at the figurine again. "If it is Circassian – well, I don't know. The eagle was the divine bird, so if it's combined with a human body, I suppose... Divine made flesh, god made man, that sort of thing? I don't know. Not really my speciality."

"You're on the right tracks, though." The Doctor beamed, and only the need to speak prevented his smile from floating up towards his eyebrows. "Now listen to this. The eagle was the goddess of the heavens, of knowledge and peace, who brought fire and language and medicine and all sorts of things to mankind – there are obvious parallels in other pantheons. But the twist in the Circassian version is that, after a while, mankind began to discover that there were drawbacks to civilisation, since those who had received the eagle's gifts were more liable to be bullied around than those who had kept their savage state intact. And so the people who had embraced civilisation began to complain that they would have been better off without it, and that the eagle's gifts hadn't brought peace, as she had promised they would, but only bloodshed and weakness. Well, when the eagle got to hear about these complaints, she decided to come down from heaven to face them personally. She arrived at the city where civilisation had first taken hold, and which she had always especially loved as a result. But as she walked through the streets and market places, people began to see her, and gradually they began to attack her, and more and more people joined in, until the eagle thought that she was going to be torn to pieces. In her desperation, she did what she had first done to capture man's attention, she danced, a beautiful, haunting dance of love. But it was no good. It only infuriated the mob all the more. But at the very last moment, just when she seemed doomed, she was rescued by the ruler of the place, who was aghast at his people's ingratitude, and announced that the whole town should gather to hear the eagle's explanation of why peace had brought only further suffering. But the eagle couldn't give a reason. She said that peace should breed peace, and civilisation civilisation. But she had been wrong, and she didn't know why, and her sorrow was so great that if the townspeople wished to kill her, she would accept her fate without protest or complaint. But the ruler of the town wept with her, and kissed the goddess on her beak, and prayed that he could join with the eagle, so that peace could live with war and be in the same body. The king of the gods heard his prayer – the man was fused with the eagle, and the result was the figure you've got in your hands there. The eagle-king – who was also a queen, of course, as well – was the greatest ruler that the world has ever known. He won every war he fought for his people. But he also guided his country until it became the home of freedom and prosperity and all the arts that the eagle had first taught mankind. But the human half of the soul was mortal, and so when it died, the goddess was left on her own again, and returned to the heavens. The world she had abandoned crumbled away to its former state. And the only hope that the people had left to them was a promise made many years before, that though the eagle king would have to die, he would also one day come back. And hence the cult of Sesostris Aetos, the eagle king, whose statue you are holding in your hands." The Doctor sat back, and his smile bobbed up again. "An interesting legend, I think, in the circumstances."

"And this statue came from the site out there?"

"Yes."

"What the hell was it doing there?"

"Aha!"

"It's genuine, you've had it dated?"

"Oh, yes. It's over two thousand years old, Circassian, but distinctively from the western seaboard of Asia Minor, which may have explained your uncertainty earlier in identifying it, since style varied quite considerably from region to region. The cult of Sesostris was much stronger on the western coast."

"The western coast. Where Troy stood."

"And from which the Trojans are said to have escaped approximately two and a bit thousand years ago, guided here, the legends have always said, by an eagle."

"And where they built a temple to the heavens, and the eagle in Circassian myth was the goddess of the heavens." Catullus whistled. "How many people know about this?"

"As many as it took to get the funding."

"So that's what we're looking for? Evidence that the legends of the Trojan foundation are based on memories of an actual colonisation by the Circassians? But... the orthodoxy..."; Catullus paused, and thought about the mounds of books he had had to devour for his exams, the vast structures of scholarship he had been forced to bow down before, and now, on his first post, he was inching his way under them, and each trench he dug would be a tiny mine, and when the time came, he would stand back and watch as the whole dusty edifice was blown up into the skies. If the Doctor was right. If... "But the orthodoxy is that early Roman culture was autochthonic. The stone circle, the one you think is here, I thought that had always been accepted as true because it associated the earliest Romans with the other stone circles around here, and they're surely the product of an aboriginal culture? There's nothing like them in Circassia, so far as I know. What are we expecting to find out there, then? – a Circassian structure, not an indigenous one at all? But that would revolutionise...well – the whole basis of our understanding of Roman history. Surely the Trojan migration has to be a myth?"

"Why?"

"Because...oh, God. Because the legends are so comparatively late, because there's always been such an insistence on the indigenous character of our culture, because it seems impossible..."

"It's far from impossible. For instance, has it never struck you? – the legends of the Trojan arrival, they only really begin to flourish when Roman writers are starting to insist on the autarky of their cultural heritage. That seems a paradox – unless the Trojans were chosen as a more acceptable, a more Roman name for a remembered *Circassian* migration that was now becoming an embarrassment. The Romans couldn't deny that their civilisation had originated in the East – but they could at least palliate that sense of obligation. In Homer, there is always the sense that the Trojans are racially akin to the Greeks, and the Greeks are much more acceptable ancestors than the Circassians. I don't know, I can't be certain about that. But we can dig, and wait, and keep an open mind. Who knows what we will find? It's very exciting. Because I really think there's a chance we might – just might – be on the verge of rewriting all the orthodoxies about the beginnings of Roman history. We can only wait and see."

Catullus looked down at the figurine he had left lying in the shadows of his lap. It had the blackness of the past it had been buried under for so long. Yet if the icon had been lost, what had the god been doing, walking centuries later through the streets of Civil War Rome? What was it Marius had believed he had pursued and seen ripped to pieces by the baying mob? Catullus held the statue up to the light, and ran his finger gently over the curve of the beak. The god had kept his face, not like the eagle man Marius had seen, not like Mr Varney either, both dead... This time Catullus did shiver. He stared out of the window, and thought that he could see a single fire burning deep from within the blackness of a distant warehouse.

"Where exactly did you find the statue?" he asked.

Doctor Gower pointed. "Over there." Catullus shifted back to look; Doctor Gower was pointing at the warehouse. There was nothing there now, just darkness. He must have imagined the fire. "In front of that building?" he asked.

"Yes." Doctor Gower nodded. "You probably can't make it out in the rain, but there's a tip been dug, just recently. A couple of tramps had been camping there, and they found traces of a strange brickwork, which they told me about, because they'd seen me around and knew I'd be interested."

"And is the brickwork still there?"

"No, demolished already, I'm afraid. A digger came and enlarged the pit, and just – " Doctor Gower gestured sadly with his hand "– all gone. But I did fit in a preparatory survey, with a few volunteers, and, presto, after a couple of days, there we found it." He picked up the statue from Catullus' lap, and stared at it in silence. "Sesostris Aetos." He kissed the beak. "If we found you with just an exploratory strike, what are we going to dig up this time round, eh? It sets my mouth watering, it really does." He looked round suddenly. "Who's that?"

There was the sound of footsteps coming up the road outside. Doctor Gower reached down frantically for the newspaper wrappings that had been left scattered by Catullus' feet, and started to fold them round the statue again. There was a click from behind as the back door was opened, and Doctor Gower slipped the half-wrapped statue into his pocket.

"Ah – Boot," he said, looking round.

"It took me enough time to find you," said Boot, slamming the door behind her. "You might have told me you'd be going off, I've been looking for you everywhere." She sneezed violently, and wisps of dank hair were left plastered over her face. She picked them off, and then began to squeeze the water out of her sodden jersey sleeve. She wiped her nose, and sneezed again. "Can I go home now?" she asked.

"I do apologise," said Doctor Gower. "I assumed you already had done."

"No. I said – I was looking for you, wasn't I?"

"Well, I'm terribly sorry. Do please accept my apologies."

Boot sneezed, and nodded, and sneezed again. "Oh God," she said, as she shut her eyes and tried to get her nose under control. "I'm so soaked, and now I'm blowing snot all over myself, and I'm getting even more soaked. Could I have a lift to the main road, please? I think I need a drink after being out on that bloody dump all these hours."

"Of course, of course. You too?"

Catullus nodded. "Why not?" He looked over his shoulder at Boot. "You don't mind?"

Boot shrugged, and shook her head.

"Afraid I won't be able to join you," said Doctor Gower, patting the bulge in his pocket. "Things to write up back at home. A splendid day today, though." He nodded at Boot over his shoulder as he began to negotiate the car through the mud. "Really quite exciting."

Boot sneezed into her sleeve again. "Oh yes?"

"Yes! Everything's set up for what promises to be a tremendous week next week. I'm very thrilled."

"Great."

"Oh yes, there'll be some sweat shed next week!" He began to sing. When he'd reached the main road, he pulled the car over, and slapped his hands happily down onto the steering wheel. "Well, here we are! Have a good weekend! See you on Monday!" He waited until Boot and Catullus had both shut their doors behind them, then began to sing again. A last cheery wave, and he was off. As he drove away, the back wheel of his car pulled out through a puddle, and an arc of water slooshed up over Boot.

"Oh, piss! Piss, piss, piss!" She flapped her arms up limply in the air. "Look at me, I'm such a bloody mess. I'm so horrible and ugly and wet, I can't bear it." She looked up at Catullus. "Do I look really horrible?"

"No, not really. Like one of those adverts, you know, where someone has an awful day and then they go back and have some tea or something. Like that."

"I want something a damn sight stronger than tea." She took Catullus by the arm. "Come on."

"Where are we going? The place where your friend works?"

"Yes."

"Is it nice?"

"Not really, but it beats being stuck out on a rubbish tip in the middle of a storm. And the drinks are free, and you get some quite nice other things thrown in as well."

"Like what?"

"Wait and see." She stopped outside a tatty white door. "Here we are." She pushed the door open. A bell rang, and a girl in a white shirt and short black skirt stood up from a table where she had been reading a paper. "Oh, hi there, Boot," she said, looking round. "Did you find him?"

"Eventually. Took me bloody hours, though. He'd gone and hidden himself in his car. Can you believe it?"

The girl smiled. "That's what jobs are like."

"Seems so." Boot sat down beside her. "Except this one, the bloke seems more pissed off with me when I do turn up than when I'm sitting in here. I don't think I'll bother turning up next time, it might keep us all more mellow."

"Yes, except you'll probably get sacked again." The girl nodded at Catullus as he sat down opposite her. "She's always getting sacked, aren't you Boot? She used to work here with me, you see, only she never turned up to that either, so that's why she got the boot. That's why she's called Boot, boot, get it?"

"Oh, I see," said Catullus. "Really?" Boot nodded. "So you've only started coming here now you've been sacked?"

The waitress giggled. "Yes, that's a point, Boot. I hadn't thought of it like that, it is a bit odd."

Boot shook her head. "It's just I've realised this place had certain perks."

The girl giggled again. "Like what, Boot? What perks?"

"Like free whisky."

"Nothing else?"

"I don't think you're doing your job, Mona. You've got two clients to serve, who are both waiting for their freebies."

Mona smiled, and got to her feet. "Do you want whisky too, then?" she asked Catullus. Catullus nodded. "If it really is free."

Mona nodded. "It is unless anyone else comes in, but no one ever does." She waited, and fiddled with the hem of her skirt. "What do *you* do on that rubbish tip, when it rains?"

"Suck up to anyone who's got a car."

Mona stared at him, wide-eyed, then began to laugh. "You suck up to them?"

Boot sighed, and lit a cigarette. "Are you going to get that whisky, Mona? I'm dying of hypothermia here."

"Yes, yes." Mona turned, and went out through a bead curtain at the back of the café. Boot didn't say anything, just wrapped her arms round herself and sneezed. Catullus could see little droplets, glistening all over the formica of the table top. He wiped them up with a paper napkin, and offered a second one to Boot. She blew her nose on it, then blocked off one of her nostrils and sniffed up the second despairingly. Catullus could hear the snot refusing to budge.

"Why are you doing this job if you hate it so much?" he asked her.

"It's a job, isn't it? Why are you doing it?"

"Amazingly enough, it interests me."

Boot's laugh was swallowed up in a sneezing fit. "I shouldn't laugh," she said, when she'd recovered. "I expect I'd be quite into it if it didn't rain so much, and we actually found things, but it's just I'm getting a bit pissed off with all this shovelling shit from one bit of dump to another. Stone circles and things, if we found a stone circle, I'm sure I could get interested in that."

"Stone circles?" said Mona, coming back into the room with an almost full whisky bottle. "Is that what you're digging up? They're centres for cosmic power, you know. Look, I've got a necklace."

"What do you mean, cosmic power? Where did you pick up that crap?"

"No, it's not crap, Boot, a bloke was telling me all about it."

"What sort of a bloke?"

"A musician. He comes in here sometimes. They're linked up, stone circles, all over the country, with lines that give them power. Look." She reached down inside her shirt, and pulled out a necklace chain. There was a tiny piece of blue rock attached to it, framed inside a pendant. "See, it's nice, isn't it?"

Catullus looked at it. "Where did you get it from?" he asked.

"The bloke gave it to me. The musician I was telling you about. I think it's beautiful. It's meant to give you luck."

Boot picked it up from Mona's chest and peered at it. "How do you know it's real?"

"It doesn't matter if it is or not."

"Yes, it does, because if it isn't real, you won't get any power, will you?"

Mona shrugged, and tucked the necklace away. "It feels nice," she said. "And that's the most important thing." She clasped her breasts, and hummed softly to herself. Boot watched her, and slowly rounded out her lips to blow a smoke ring. Then she turned back to Catullus.

"Do you think this thing we're looking for out on that rubbish tip is real?"

Catullus shrugged. "I don't know. That's what we're digging to find out, isn't it?"

"But what do you think?"

"Maybe."

"Oh come on, don't keep it all clenched in, what do you think?"

"We might find something. There's a reasonable chance."

Boot smiled. "Has he shown you that little statue thing he's got?"

Catullus stared at her. "Yes," he said slowly.

"Was that what you were doing in the car?"

"Yes. Because he said he didn't want to show it to you."

Boot laughed and sneezed at once. "He needn't have bothered," she said, wiping her nose again on her sleeve. "As if it matters who knows."

"But how have you seen it?"

"You're not gay, are you?"

"Why do you ask?"

"Because Doctor Gower's been going around all week with this bloody great big thing sticking out of his pocket, and if you'd been gay, you'd definitely have noticed it."

Catullus shook his head. "Could be I just don't fancy men when they're fat and sweaty."

Mona giggled. "You don't, do you, Boot?"

Boot shrugged. "Maybe not. But this bulge *really* sticks out, I mean, we are talking *grotesque*. He kept on stroking it and looking happy, and sometimes he'd go off to his car, and come back ten minutes later looking even happier – you must have noticed it, surely?"

"Sorry. As I said, I really don't fancy him."

"Yes, that's fair enough. Shit, maybe I do, after all? What a frightening thought. Well, anyway, I was getting more and more interested to know what it was he kept down there in his pockets that was so wonderful, and so one day I followed him, and looked in through his car window, and there he was with this little black statue, just stroking it, you know..."

"It's actually a Circassian cult symbol."

"Yeah, well – takes all sorts."

Catullus laughed. "How funny."

"It is, isn't it? And I know all about it anyway, because my uncle tells me what's going on, so I don't know why he's bothering trying to keep it all a secret."

"How does your uncle know about it?"

"Well, he knows Cult Dick quite well. Actually, he was the one who got me the job in the first place."

"He's an archaeologist?"

"No, not at all, he runs a magazine."

"Which one?"

"'Alexandrian.' Have you heard of it?"

Catullus stared at her. "Of course," he said slowly. "The poetry journal."

"Well, it's not just poetry, because otherwise no one'd ever buy it."

"But poetry is what it's famous for."

"Maybe, I've never read it." Boot stared at him. "Are you a poet then?"

"Yes, of course."

"Why of course?"

"Well, because otherwise I'd never have heard of the magazine, would I?" Catullus raised an eyebrow in careful inquiry.

Boot shrugged. "You'd have to be good. He wouldn't look at your stuff just because I'd given it to him."

"Yes, of course, but he's got to look at it first, so he can decide whether it's crap or not, hasn't he?"

"So you think it is good?"

Catullus wondered what to say. Yes, of course he thought it was good. "It's not what I think that matters, really, is it?"

Boot smiled. "All right. Fine. I'll ask him. But everyone writes poems, you know. Well, everyone like you, anyway."

"What do you mean, everyone like me?"

"Nothing. You know what I mean."

Catullus looked at her. "Maybe." He shrugged. "But you'll let your uncle look at them?"

"Yes, yes, I've said I will."

"You don't have to sound so pissed off about it."

"I'm not sounding pissed off. I've just said I'll give them to him, haven't I, what more do you want?"

Boot reached for the whisky bottle, and poured herself out another glass. There was an awkward silence. Catullus was just about to speak, say anything, when he felt a tap on his hand and he looked round. Mona. She was staring at him. He stared back. "Could I give you a blow job?" she asked.

"What?"

"A blow job."

"Here?"

"Only if you want it."

"What is this, part of the service?"

Mona giggled. "Not always. It depends." She smiled at him, and stroked his hand. "Tell him, Boot, tell him how much I like it."

Boot didn't say anything, just sent another smoke ring slipping out from her lips. Mona bent down and crouched under the table. "We'll do it here, shall we?" she asked, looking up.

Catullus shrugged. "Fine." He felt Mona's fingers as she unzipped his trousers. "Oh look," she said, "he's not gay. Look, Boot, he's not gay."

"It doesn't prove I'm not gay at all," said Catullus. "Put your fingers round him. Yes, like that. You see, up he goes. He does it even when I touch him, and I don't fancy myself at all."

"Oh yeah?" said Boot.

"Do it again," Mona ordered. "One, two, three." Catullus clenched his sphincter, and Mona squealed with delight as the prick bounced up off her palm again and brushed against the top of the table. "Keep him there." Mona gave the tip a quick dab with her tongue, then looked up. "What do you call him?" she asked. "Has he got a name?"

Catullus laughed, and jerked his prick up against the table again.

"You ought to call him Bouncer," said Mona. "He's like a naughty dog. Down Bouncer. Bad boy. Come here, I want to stroke you."

"Bouncer. Fucking hell." Boot stubbed out her cigarette, and shook her head. "And I've got to work with this guy." She leant back in her chair, and watched as Mona lowered her head, and carefully placed Catullus' prick inside her mouth. Catullus drummed his fingers on the formica table top. Fuck, if he felt her teeth even skim the glans, he'd have to pull it out, it really sent shivers down his spine just thinking about it, it was like hearing finger nails going down a blackboard, but still, he hadn't felt any teeth yet, so maybe he should just stop worrying about it, yes, he'd lie back and relax, because it was lovely, really lovely, there hadn't been any teeth at all, only the soft flesh of her lips, and sometimes the tip of her tongue, there, she was lapping with it now. Catullus drummed his fingers again.

"Do you want me to come?" he asked.

"Mmm." Mona nodded urgently, then allowed his prick to slip out of her mouth, and gulped for air. "Yes," she said, "yes, I want lots." She wiped her mouth, and took another deep gulp of air. "Give me a finger lick, Boot, please, give me a finger lick." Then she took Catullus' prick and began to suck on it again with long desperate pulls. Boot didn't move.

"You'll bring the poems sometime next week then, will you?" she asked.

"What?" said Catullus, turning to look at her at the very moment a particularly strong spurt of pleasure ran like a shock down his prick and up into the pit of his stomach. "Yes," he said, nodding in time to the feel of Mona's lips, "yes, sometime next week."

"Good." Boot stared at him. "And if he likes them, he'll probably want to meet you, I should think. He's a bit domineering, but very nice – you'll like him."

Catullus nodded vaguely. He could feel himself coming, it would be any minute, all that stuff waiting to shoot up the pipes.

"Actually, he's the only relative I like," said Boot. "He must be fifty, but he's young at heart. He still wears his leather trousers."

Catullus came. Whoosh. He left his prick where it was, waiting for Mona to take it out herself. She sucked, and as the hardness slowly softened, the pulse in his groin began to beat again – more sperm oozing out. At last, Mona opened her mouth, and as she sighed, Catullus could feel his prick slithering out over her bottom lip. It fell limply onto his balls; must stash it all away, he thought, waking up again to the fact that he'd just had a blow job in a café. He fiddled with himself, and watched as Mona slowly slipped herself into the seat opposite him. She wiped her mouth, and then rubbed her hand over her hair. "Mmm," she said, "mmm. It makes your hair grow glossy, did you know that?" She reached down and felt herself. "Pour me a drink, will you, Boot?"

"Was there lots?" Catullus asked.

"Why do men always ask that?" said Boot as she handed the drink over.

"Because I thought that was the whole point – she said she wanted lots. I don't know how capacious my bollocks are, do I? How am I meant to measure them, I've never been able to suck myself off, have I?"

He stared at Boot, and Boot stared back, while Mona stroked her face and continued to smile. Suddenly, Boot laughed and shook her head. "I was just being jealous, I'm sorry." She reached over and took Mona in her arms. "I'm sorry," she said again, turning back to Catullus. "I didn't mean it. You know how things get."

Catullus watched her as she began to comb through Mona's hair. "I'd better go," he said, getting to his feet.

"Oh, don't," said Mona. "Please stay."

Catullus looked down at them both.

"No, I'd better go." He smiled at Mona. "Thank you. It was lovely. Thank you very much."

He turned, and pushed open the café door. It was still raining outside.

"Goodbye," said Boot. "See you on Monday. Goodbye."

"Goodbye." Catullus turned, and blew two kisses. Mona and Boot lay hunched up against the wall, cradling each other in their arms. Catullus pushed on the door again, and walked out into the evening gloom.

He had begun to feel a lot happier about going home. For the first few days, his room had seemed so empty and unfamiliar that Catullus had made a habit of walking in, looking round, and then spending the rest of his time out or in Caelius' room. Then he had decided that this couldn't go on; taking Caelius along as a moral prop, he had gone out on an orgy of shopping, and spent a weekend fine-tuning what he had bought into a room that at least seemed more friendly than it had done before. Others agreed. Sometimes Catullus would walk in and find Jez waiting for him, sitting on the bed, killing aliens or eating cereal, or doing both. Catullus would humour him for a while, then chase him out.

That evening, Jez didn't have a game. "Vanessa's back," he said as Catullus walked in.

"Really? I didn't know she'd gone missing again."

"Oh yes. Last night."

"Was your father upset?"

"Yeah, he always is, he goes really spasmo. But I don't know why, I think it's stupid."

"It's not very nice for him, his daughter running off like that all the time."

"Yeah, but if he's so worried about it, why does *he* keep going off? I know he does, 'cos I've seen him, he gets up in the middle of the night. Vanessa's only following him."

"Where?"

"Don't know."

"Why don't you ask him?"

"No, stupid, how could I ask him, he'd go *mad*."

"Why?"

"'Cos look how mad he gets with Vanessa."

"Because he thinks she's following him?"

Jez made a face. "Yeah, I was just saying that, *stupid*."

"Why should she want to do that? I thought he thought she'd been out getting pregnant."

Jez looked at him with scorn. "Get clued, man."

Catullus shrugged and turned away. "Sorry. I'm obviously out of date."

He folded out his newspaper. He could feel Jez staring into his back, but he didn't look round. He read the headline instead: 'Unions agree to austerity package.' He began to skim through the article printed beneath.

"This room's really boring," said Jez suddenly.

Catullus didn't answer.

"Why don't you do some painting on the walls, that'd make it less boring. You could do someone dying, really *horribly*, with loads of blood going everywhere, and it'd be all red."

"I can't paint."

"My dad can. He's really safe at painting, he is. He did a whole massive great one once, and it was really great, only it got lost."

"How did it get lost? If it was so massive?"

"Dunno. But it did. It just went. We looked everywhere for it, and Dad got really mad at Mum, 'cos he said it was her fault, 'cos she'd wanted to get rid of it."

"Why?"

"Dunno. But I helped him look for it, 'cos I really liked it. That was when he built me the tree house."

"What was it a painting of?"

Jez swung himself off the bed and wandered over to the window. "Oh, loads of things. There were temples, like that one out there. What was your best subject at school?"

Catullus thought. "History. Why?"

"Well, that's okay then, only you've got to be really good at history to get Dad's paintings. There was this old town, you see, and it had loads of really weird buildings and things, and it looked wicked. You should have that on your wall, I'll paint it for you if you like."

"You?"

"Yeah!" He stared up and his eyes widened. "Oh go on, please! I'm really safe at art, I am, promise!"

Catullus looked round the room. "I don't think I want it done up."

"I'd only do it in one corner if you liked, look, I could do it over there, just this one teeny bit, promise, and I'd only do any more if you liked it. Promise."

Catullus looked round again. "What about your mother? What would she say?"

Jez clapped a hand over his mouth. "Oh no! I've got to do my room, and I'd totally forgot, and if she comes back and I've not done it, she'll go *mad*. I'd better go. Bye." Without another word, he scampered from the room, and Catullus heard him clattering down the landing towards the stairs. He'd left the door open; Catullus shut it, then realised that the window had been left swinging open too, and the rain was soaking the edge of the carpet. He walked over to close it. There was someone in the street outside, walking slowly towards the house, loaded down with bags; Mrs Dugbal, it had to be. It was. She dropped her shopping onto the pavement by her door, and began to fumble in her handbag for the key. Jez had gone to tidy his room just in time. On the other side of the road, the door to the temple creaked open, and a white-haired head popped out.

"Evening, Mrs Dugbal," said Mr Smallpiece.

Mrs Dugbal looked round, and grunted.

"Lovely evening," said Mr Smallpiece, trying again.

Mrs Dugbal snorted, and picked up her shopping. Then she barged her way through her open front door, and slammed it shut. Mr Smallpiece was left staring out into the empty street, a look of anguished admiration on his face. Catullus waved at him, and he waved sadly back, continuing to stare at the Dugbals' front door.

Catullus hadn't been back to the temple since that first day. He felt guilty. After the invitation from the young man in black to visit him and his friend, Catullus hadn't made any effort to track him down, and now it was too late. In fact, he had only seen the man once since, still clutching flowers, still dressed in black, and Catullus had deliberately avoided him then and kept out of his sight. But even though Catullus hadn't returned to the temple, Ricket's Gate continued to streak his thoughts, like the black stains that ran down its outer walls. On some evenings, the temple seemed to still the street outside with a sense of desolation so strong that Catullus was almost tempted to draw his curtains against the presence brooding at him from the other side of the road. And when he slept, he sometimes found that his dreams had been infected; that night, he lay and imagined that he had woken up, and when he opened his eyes, he saw the death mask of Marius painted on the ceiling. The lips were clenched tightly together to prevent a cry of pain, as the shadows hollowing out the features of Marius' face began to run and disappear into streams of black. Catullus woke up with a start, and couldn't be sure that the face hadn't really been there, lost on the pale light filtering through the curtains.

The following week, at the excavation site, Doctor Gower also began to find the Civil War weighing on his mind. Sinking a preparatory trench, the labourers had found the first traces of a brick wall. They began to clear away the soil and dirt, and the more they dug out, the larger the structure they had found began to seem. On the Friday morning, Catullus arrived to find Doctor Gower staring glumly down at the trough they had been digging round the brickwork all week; his hands were plunged deep into his pockets, and he didn't even look round as Catullus walked up to join him.

"It's Civil War," he said miserably. "No doubt about it. It shouldn't be there, but it bloody well is. Damn it. Damn, damn, damn."

Catullus had prophesied the existence of Civil War structures the week before. He wondered if Doctor Gower remembered. "It may not be too extensive," he said, trying to sound supportive. "We're only on the edge of the site."

The Doctor threw his arms up in despair. "It doesn't make any difference. It shouldn't be there, that's the bottom line. Why isn't there any record of it?" He picked up a stone and flung it into the pit with all the force his disappointment could muster. "Go on, then," he said after a mournful pause, "dig it up, and let's know the worst. Concentrate on demarcating the foundation boundaries." He picked up a trowel, and jumped down into the trench. "Let's try and get it finished before tonight. I don't want it hanging over me all weekend."

Everyone set to work. Boot had turned up for the day, and worked next to Catullus, sweeping and smoking. She'd relaxed, Catullus thought, since he'd left her last week in the cafe with Mona. She wasn't as pissed off all the time, and when she wasn't pissed off, she laughed a lot and became funny. Catullus liked her when she laughed, though he never relaxed – he was always waiting for that something that might make her snap, because even though he could make her laugh now, he still hadn't worked out what made her stroppy, still felt that he hadn't really sorted her out. He hadn't asked her yet either about the reception of the poems he had given to her for her uncle to inspect; once, he had opened his mouth, to mention them, only to find that he was talking about something quite else. And so the afternoon passed.

"Eureka!" shouted the Doctor suddenly. He leapt out of the trench, brandishing a chart triumphantly over his head. "Look," he said, running up to Catullus, "it's nothing serious, I don't think we're in trouble." He creased out the site plan and jabbed at it with his forefinger. "See? We're not on the projected site itself yet, and look, if you stand here..." He dragged Catullus round to look at the wall he had finished uncovering. "Look, you see, this building, it's self-contained. There's no way that wall goes on, it stops there, and that means it never cut across where the stones themselves were. And still are, almost certainly. Thank God, eh? Our golden goose is still out there, waiting to lay its eggs. Thank God, thank God." He mopped at his brow with a handkerchief, then scrambled back into the trench he'd been digging. "Look, you can feel it," he said, rubbing his finger up the side of a cornerstone. "Absolutely smooth. Odd-looking thing, isn't it? What do you think? Mausoleum maybe?" He patted the stone. "Well – whatever – it can wait. Let's go and have a drink, shall we, have a little celebration? All this sweat I've been shedding, it needs some replacement. Come on, you two, let's get the sheeting on, stake this place out, and then we'll repair to a local watering hole for some refreshment." He clambered up out of the trench. "Capital, eh, absolutely bloody capital! Thank the stars above, that's all I can say! Or should I say heavens, ha ha ha!"

He was still booming cheerfully as he led the way to the nearest pub and started ordering his rounds. "You know something," he whispered loudly to Catullus over a sixth pint, "this thing we've found, it might actually turn out to be a bit of a godsend. I mean – not bad, is it, digging up something that shows nothing's been built there since at least the Civil War? And anyway, a Civil War building, not many of them left around." He raised his glass: "Cheers! One Civil War mausoleum, notched up straight off, and confirming the hints of bigger fish still to come. To triumph! To the truth! To our own stone circle!"

Doctor Gower downed his pint, then staggered back up to the bar.

"I've got to go," Boot whispered. "He's an embarrassment."

"It's always good for the soul, seeing the respectable about to fall flat on their arses."

"Any minute now, though, he'll start reaching for mine, I know it, I've been a waitress. You develop a sense for these things."

"Your arse? You told me he was gay."

"Then he'll go for yours, won't he, and are you sure you want that, a great drunk professor with a beard groping you?"

"It might help my career."

"Yes, but only if you're going to be enthusiastic about it."

Catullus shrugged. "If you put it like that."

"I do. Come on. Let's go."

They both climbed to their feet, but Doctor Gower reached for Catullus and slapped a hand down onto his shoulder. "Come with me, laddie!" he bellowed, "come with me!" Then he took Boot by the arm, and dragged them both out of the pub and through several streets, until he had led them back to the wasteland under which the Stone Dance was supposed to lie buried.

"Insects!" shouted the Doctor. He stretched out his arms and stood swaying on the edge of a litter dump. "Insects, that's all we are, we're just bloody insects!" He stretched out an arm again, and staggered forwards a few steps. "Look at our shit, it gets everywhere!" He staggered again, and fell over a pram frame. He clambered to his feet, and pointed at Catullus. "All shit. All hopeless. Flush it away. Flush it away..." His voice died, and he sat down on an oil drum. Tears began to trickle down his purple cheeks.

"So sad," he whispered, looking up. "So sad." He stared a mute appeal, as though Catullus were some embodiment of historical destiny. He beckoned him down, and whispered heavily into his ear. "We're insects digging up giants, you know. Out there..." He pointed. "Out there are the true giants, buried beneath the shit. We need our giants, because what else do we have? We're so sick, so dead, so very, very dead. You understand?" He pulled Boot by her sleeve, and whispered in her ear as well. "You see what I mean?" Then slowly, his eyes glazed over and his legs swung in the air; with a feeble moan, he overbalanced, and fell into the mud.

"Well," said Catullus, "you were right. We should have left earlier."

"Come on," said Boot. "Let's get him a taxi."

They each took a hand. A small object fell out of one of Doctor Gower's pockets. Catullus bent down to pick it up, and unwrapped the newspaper in which the object had been swathed. Sesostris Aetos. Of course. Catullus frowned, and slipped the statue into his own pocket. Then slowly, he and Boot dragged the Doctor back through the dirt. "Taking it to Mona?" Boot asked. Catullus shook his head and smiled. They dragged the Doctor on through the dirt, and tried to work out where the main road was.

VIII

CAESAR

Caelius pulled his sports car into the kerb, and reached for the street map. An area of dereliction, that was where Catullus had said he was working. Not much use as a description – the whole place was derelict. But then Caelius saw that there was a large open space down by the river – he'd try there. He was about to toss the street map into the back seat, when he remembered that he didn't have one – of course not, no sports car had a back seat, tee hee hee! Caelius pummelled the steering wheel gleefully, then placed the street guide on the seat beside him. He glanced down at it; the book was covering a copy of the evening newspaper. Caelius folded the newspaper over, so that the headline was staring up. Then, shades on, arm hung out. The car began to purr down the street.

Catullus had just given up his attempts to shift Doctor Gower when he heard the soft pulse of the engine coming down the road behind him. "Hey," shouted Caelius through his window, "hey, worker of the world!" Catullus looked round in surprise. Caelius waved at him. "Picked up another drunk?"
"Where the hell did you get that car?"
Caelius reached out and stroked the framework. "Nice, isn't it?"
"Very. Whose is it?"
"It's on permanent loan. So it's mine, near as damn it. Don't look so pained, your friend might think you're feeling jealous."
Caelius climbed out and introduced himself to Boot. Shit, she didn't like him, Catullus could tell. How embarrassing. Her eyes had glazed over straight away, and Caelius thought that he was being witty – how *embarrassing*. "You want to avoid going round with him," he was saying, "he's lethal. Everywhere he goes, weirdos of all sizes and descriptions just fall into his path, all dying to vomit up on you." He turned back to Catullus. "What were you planning to do with this one?"
"Get him in a taxi. Pack him off to the university."
"What? He's not your boss, is he?"
"Yup."
Caelius looked down at the Doctor as he lay motionless at his feet. "God, I ask you. Intellectuals."
"Why don't we just take him to Mona's cafe, and dump him there

to cool off?" Boot suggested. "We could stuff the Professor in the front seat, I could squeeze in behind him, and you could drive us there."

"What about me?" asked Catullus.

"You could walk."

"I'll get lost."

"Course you won't. Come on. Let's get him in. I've just about had it with professor-shifting."

Catullus did get lost. All the time, he was worrying about what Boot and Caelius might have been saying to each other, and worse, what they might have been thinking about him. That was the true issue, he realised, as he finally found and recognised the street that led to Mona's café, he was afraid that seeing the sort of person he was capable of liking might damage him in the eyes of both Caelius and Boot, an unworthy worry, he knew, but there it was – he couldn't help human nature. And Mona – he didn't want her embroiled in some quarrel. He remembered her face, and the feel of the nylon on her thighs, and her lips, yes, those lips. He put his hand in his pocket, and stroked himself. Then he pushed open the café door.

Well – there were no raised voices, no chairs flying round the room. Doctor Gower was slumped over one table, and Caelius was leaning back from another, talking about something or other, and Boot and Mona were both laughing. Catullus had never imagined that they would actually get on. He could feel his stomach knotting up.

"I'm here," he said loudly. "At last. I told you I'd get lost."

Mona squealed, and came running up to him. She gave him a big hug and then kissed him; those lips, they were *so* soft. It could have been worse – he could have come in and found her sucking off Caelius' prick. Or maybe she'd already done it. No, her breath would have smelt. He kissed her again, just to make sure, and then allowed himself to be led to the table.

"I was just saying," said Caelius, "we should go to that thing they're opening up tonight."

"What thing?"

"You know – that thing we went wandering round with Tubbers, the place under the pub."

Catullus stared at Caelius as he lounged in his chair next to Mona. "No," he said after a pause. "I don't think so. I thought it looked shite."

"Oh no!" said Mona, reaching over to press his hand. "I really want to. Oh, go on, *please*."

"Well. Maybe." He stared straight into her face, and she smiled back, her lips wide but not open. He shrugged, and turned to look at Boot. "Are you going to come too, then?"

"Don't know. Don't know if I'm in the mood." She stared away into the distance as cigarette smoke drifted out lazily over her tongue. Catullus stared at her in desperation. He wouldn't want to go unless she went too. Just himself, Caelius and Mona, with himself the reluctant one, no, it would be a disaster – Boot had to come. He'd rather have Mona a dyke than fucking Caelius any day.

"Give me your number. Then I can try and persuade you nearer the time."

Boot stared at him, then shrugged, and reached inside her bag for her pen. "Here you are," she said, scribbling down some numbers onto a sugar sachet. "But you'll have to be very persuasive."

"Oh, I will be. Smooth tongued."

Boot smiled. Good, Catullus thought, she'd got the joke, a nice private one between himself, her and Mona – he savoured the flavour of renewed intimacy, and decided that it would be a good moment to leave. He climbed to his feet.

Caelius looked up. "Off already, are we?" He smiled at Boot and Mona. "Well. Nice meeting you. See you tonight, maybe."

Mona nodded enthusiastically and reached up to give Catullus a kiss. "Bye," she said, turning to Caelius; then another "bye" to both of them, as Catullus held open the café door, and ushered Caelius out into the street. Boot hadn't said anything, but Catullus blew her a kiss anyway. "I'll phone you tonight," he called, as he shut the door.

"Nice girl," said Caelius, as they headed over to the sports car. "Have you both been copulating?"

Catullus looked at the car's paint work, and hoped that someone had scratched a key along it. No one had. Caelius opened the door for him cheerily, then climbed into his own seat. "Only, you see," he said, as he reversed his way back down the street, "all that stuff about tongues, it's usually a complete give away, isn't it? Whenever two people sit there and have a little smirk about tongues, it invariably means copulation."

"But I was talking about tongues with Boot."

"Yes, the fat one. Who did you think I meant?"

"She's not that fat, she's plump."

"So you are copulating?"

"No, of course not. She's a dyke."

Caelius shook his head. "No."

"She is, she's a fucking dyke. I think I should know, shouldn't I?"

Caelius shook his head again. "She's a fake."

"Caelius, you're talking shite."

"It's not shite, it's common sense. The only dykes who dress like your fat friend are the sort who wouldn't even stop to wipe you off their boots, let alone talk to you, and so the fact that you and her are sitting there having cosy little jokes about fellatio leads me to suspect that even if she's pretending to be a dyke, she isn't one really. There you are, you see. Common sense."

Catullus sat back in his seat, and wondered whether he should try and laugh the whole argument away. He sighed. "Let's just change the subject," he said, turning back to face Caelius. "I don't want to talk about it."

"Sure?"

"Yes."

"All right, all right. I'm sorry. I didn't mean to piss you off." Caelius paused, then turned round to face Catullus again. "So – you haven't been having oral sex, then?"

"What – with Boot? No. Not even vaguely."

"Oh well, there goes my tongue-conversation-equals-oral-sex theory."

There was a lengthy silence. Caelius tapped his fingers on the steering wheel as they waited in an immovable traffic jam, and glanced at his watch. "Shit!" he said suddenly. "Of course!"

"What?"

"The reason I came to find you. All this dyke chat, I'd completely forgotten. The most appallingly terrible thing has happened."

"Really?"

"Yes. Look beneath your arse. I laid it out for you specially."

Catullus reached for the newspaper. He read the headline: 'EX-PRESIDENT CHARGED'; beneath it was a large photograph of Cicero. Catullus turned the page; inside, there was a second photo, Cicero with a jacket round his head, being bundled into a police car, with assorted people jockeying round.

"When did it happen?" Catullus asked slowly.

"This afternoon."

"Why?"

"You remember what he was going on about that evening, when we had supper with him? About Clodius? Well, looks like he's been got at last. Well and truly nobbled."

Catullus tried to remember. "Refresh my memory."

"It all stems from that rape trial he did, when he prosecuted Clodius. You remember that?"

"Yes, and then he got dismissed from the Senate, and it was all Clodius' doing. But I can't remember what it was he was accused of. Cicero, I mean."

"Property scams. The big one. The one that refuses to go away."

"I don't think I've ever heard of it."

"That's because you're a sad, provincial, other-worldly type, who doesn't get turned on by things like deals, and vast amounts of cash, and stuff like that."

"I am quite. Just not enough to go in at six each morning and have my arse cleaned out by some spiv who's five years younger than me, that's all."

"Yes, but isn't it sexy? Don't you think?" Caelius smiled. "The financial world. It gives me this tightening feeling round my testicles."

"I notice you're not going into it either."

"Oh, but I am, sort of. Law's the same thing, really, only you get even more cash, and you don't have to sink too obviously into the shit."

Catullus flicked at the photograph of Cicero. "He seems up to his neck in it."

"Good point," Caelius conceded with a short nod. "Very good."

"So – what's it all about, then?"

"The scandal? Where were we? Well – it all begins with Crassus."

"Goldfinger?"

"That's the one. You know about that development he did along the Tiber waterfront?"

"When he pulled down the old city walls and four listed buildings, yes."

"Of course! – there were old buildings, weren't there? So you're bound to remember it. There were loads of houses and entire communities uprooted as well, but I guess they're less important on the scale of things. But yes, you'll remember all the fuss, and how it seemed to go on and on forever, no one able to decide whether Crassus should be allowed to build these office blocks or not, and then suddenly, it was just like that –"; Caelius clicked his fingers; "– this committee saying, fine, yes, go ahead, you build whatever you like. No problem."

"But that was years ago, wasn't it, or have I got the wrong scandal?"

"It was – what? – five or six years ago, but it's been dragging on for ages since then, because all these rumours kept dribbling out about how the committee had been crooked. Not exactly bribed – Crassus didn't leave smoking guns or anything obvious lying around, but it was well – let me think. It was all very complex, but it was something to do with...God, what was it? It was something to do with how there were people on the committee who were able to give assurances that Crassus would only develop a small proportion of the land that was being talked about. You know – a lot of the housing estates and the old communities would be unaffected, that sort of thing. Yes, that's right. There were representatives of the councils, and local businesses, and they all gave guarantees that although Crassus could have the land, they would act as checks, and they were given the legal right to enforce their guarantees, and so it was only after all that had been sorted out that Crassus was given the green light. And then of course, a few years later, all these local businesses started selling out to Crassus, and more and more land got gobbled up, and by then it was too late, and then it turned out that all the local council leaders had bought up shares in the development scheme, and everything started to smell most unpleasantly."

"And Cicero?"

"Well, he'd originally chaired the committee as the representative of the Government, and been very keen that the development should be hurried through. Because, quite genuinely I'm sure, he thought it would boost the local economy, and keep lots of otherwise unemployables off the streets, and – you know – all sorts of good, sensible reasons like that. But when these dodgy councillors came to light, he claimed to be shocked and appalled, and accepted the prosecution brief, and duly got them all convicted. In fact, it was a masterpiece of a case, because the facts and issues involved were all so complex, and he made them seem so easy – in a sense it really established his reputation as *the* leading lawyer around. Above all, he managed to present the evidence without really implicating Crassus, and buggering up the development scheme, which would have really left the government with a white elephant on their hands, and screwed up the property scene to boot, so that was a real plus. It also sidetracked any suspicion away from himself, of course."

"What, he was under suspicion too? Because he'd been on the committee?"

"Yes, sort of, but it was actually much more complex than that, because it wasn't just Cicero who was being whispered about, but the entire Government, and that's why the scandal was seen to be so damaging – potentially. Because the thing was, everyone knew that the Government had always had this real interest in letting Crassus do exactly what he wanted. Not just for straight economic reasons, but because Crassus contributes absolute fortunes to the Government's private funds, and you don't want to go around offending the bloke who hands out the cheques. Not clever strategy at all – even the Government had been up to working that one out. Because when it comes to cheque books, Crassus is Mister Big. Money means power, after all, and Crassus is the only person who's got any of the stuff left. A bull in a bear's world. Ask Tubbers. Ask him whether it was Crassus or the Treasury who's been determining economic policy over the past decade, and I bet you a share portfolio he'll say Crassus. No competition. So that's why this whole scandal, and now

Cicero being arrested, well – its implications are earth-shaking. Government-shaking, probably."

"So what is it exactly Cicero's been arrested for?"

Caelius shrugged. "Where to begin? Almost anything you care to mention. Bribes charges, insider dealing charges, perjury, anything that carries a whopping jail sentence. He's fucked."

"No. Surely not?"

"Why not?"

"Well, what's the point of being a crack lawyer if you can't even get yourself off a few sticky charges? Expertise and self interest, I'd have thought it was the perfect combination. Surely it's just the ultimate refinement of what law's all about anyway?"

"Yes, except that this isn't really anything to do with the law. That's the whole point, that's why it's such big news. In fact, it's such big news that the actual issue of whether Cicero is guilty or innocent, or even whether he ends banged up or not, is rather secondary. I mean, I'm sure he is innocent, but that's not really the issue."

"I bet it's the issue for your uncle, isn't it?"

"No, not even for him. In fact, especially not for him, because he's better able than anyone to see what's going on. Enormous amounts of shit have been flying in from various directions, and they have just hit a very large fan. So it's frightening – *really* frightening. That'll be some comfort for Cicero, I suppose, as he slops out, knowing that everyone else is in it just as much as him."

The traffic ahead began to move, and Caelius stopped talking as he eased the car forward. Catullus looked ahead. The cars at the top of the hill had already ground to a halt again, and now the cars just in front of them, and now they'd had to stop, and they were as wedged in as before, while outside, in the world of the city they were stuck in, shit was hitting fans, and nothing was bunged up at all, everything was shifting, and uncertain, and in the process of dissolving away. But could it really be true? Just because one man had been arrested? Surely not, surely that wasn't how things worked? Catullus felt a crushing sense of his own ignorance, and a parallel sense of fury, that these events and people should be able to affect his life. What the fuck were they to him, or he to them, that they were able to make him feel both trapped and swept away, immovably stuck and helplessly adrift, in a jam and in the shit? He wanted freedom from all that. He didn't want to be sucked in and down, he had the right to define his own world. He swore, softly, and ran his hands through his hair.

"Let me get this quite straight," he said slowly.

"Mmm?" Caelius took off his shades to glance round.

"I just want to sort out why it's so terrifying that your uncle has been arrested. It's like the ball, is it?"

"What?"

"The ball. What Cicero said about the ball. That it was a token of how Pompey had to do what Clodius wanted. I'm assuming that Clodius is publicly associated with the campaign to have Cicero charged."

"Oh yes. Absolutely. But you see, it wasn't just getting Cicero charged that was at stake, it was getting the law changed, that was the real point. That's why it's now public that Clodius has got the Government by the curlies. Cicero couldn't be arrested for what he did on the commission because he was covered by ministerial immunity, and that would only be waived if the President was presented with direct evidence that hadn't been seen before. Now, I've read through the paper, and I've been listening to the radio, and as far as I can tell, there has been no new evidence. Which means that Pompey is effectively breaking the law in having Cicero arrested. So that's one thing. Another is that everyone knows that even if Cicero had got up to dodgy deals, it was all for the Government anyway, and so if he is convicted, Pompey and everyone else will be tarred by association, and should themselves be liable to prosecution. Only they probably won't be, of course, because otherwise Pompey wouldn't have let Cicero be arrested. But even so, it doesn't exactly strengthen him, does it?"

"And I guess, also, it must piss Crassus off a bit."

"Well, exactly, I was just about to mention Crassus – God knows what will happen there. I don't see how he can possibly avoid prosecution – if Cicero is convicted. And that would then mean financial meltdown for the Government, and the property market, and what's left of the economy, and shit – the whole thing is just too grim to think about."

"Just because one man has been arrested."

"Yes, okay, but it's like the Government arresting itself, isn't it? It's the Government saying, publicly, to the whole world, yes, we're very sorry, but we're crap. We have no pretensions about governing Rome any more on our own, we can't do it without Clodius, so we're going to do exactly what he wants us to do, and see if we can't just try and sneak something past him in return."

"The strikes were stopped."

Caelius snorted. "We'll see how long that lasts. And even so, we're still left with a Government that has now semi-officially voted itself out of existence. Lots of people aren't going to like what's popped up to take its place."

Catullus nodded, and stared at the traffic jam as it shimmered in a haze of heat and fumes. He glanced at his watch. "When's the news?"

"Soon. Too fucking soon. We're never going to be back at this rate." Caelius slapped his hands down on his steering wheel, and peered around. "Look. That side road. Where do you think it goes?"

"Nowhere, probably, or other people would be taking it."

"It can't go nowhere slower than this road. Come on, let's give it a go." Caelius indicated, and swerved violently as the other cars began to move slowly forwards again. He sped up a back alley, and smiled at the view of the empty roads disappearing away from him. "Lateral thinking," he beamed.

"Do you know where you're going?" Catullus asked.

"No. But at least we're moving. We must be going somewhere."

"Yes. I expect that's what Pompey's saying as well."

The streets began to lead upwards. "I don't know about Pompey," said Caelius, reaching out to pat the side of the car, "but driving this, you feel that it doesn't really matter where you're heading. What a beauty. Look how steep it is out there, and she just glides along."

"You're still not saying where you got it from?"

"Sorry, old chap. Dash of prostitution involved, so mum's the word, I'm afraid. You know how it is."

"Yes. I expect Pompey's saying that too."

Caelius laughed, and began to pick up speed again. At the top of the hill, the road and houses both levelled away, and Caelius, looking out, suddenly slowed down, and pulled the car in by a pavement edge. Below them, Rome lay spread out, crystalline beneath the blue of the sky, like a frieze painted over pure light, Catullus thought, balanced between afternoon and dusk, between summer and autumn, a wondrous sight. He slammed his door shut, and stared out again at the city buzzing in its thousands of tiny particles below him, never seeming to stop, never seeming to have limits, stretching away into the horizon whichever way he turned. "Impressive, isn't it?" he half whispered to Caelius; and as he spoke, there was a lull, just for a second, as all noise, the grind of traffic, the barking of a dog, even the breeze, seemed to arc and dive, and Catullus felt that he was being shown, in the brief fall-away into silence, the sense of a moment uniquely revealed, a snatch of the time he had always imagined as being frameable only by the Roman air. The ache of what Rome had been and known filled his imagination with an intensity that he hadn't experienced since his first arrival in the city; he felt a longing to make sense of something, but what, or even how, he couldn't say.

Then a stone fell, in one of the streets behind the car. Catullus spun round, and heard, or thought he heard, a brief snatch of music played on a violin. He froze, and there was silence again; then the music returned, more scratchily now, and further away.

Catullus felt an unexpected shiver of elation and fear. "It's them," he whispered, "it has to be." He grabbed Caelius by his arm. "Quick." He began to run after the sound, down the main road and then sideways, into a narrow, empty street.

"Who are we chasing?" shouted Caelius above the echoes of their own footsteps.

"The clowns. The ones from the ball." Catullus held up his hand. "Listen." The traffic could be heard again now, far off, but there was no other sound. Caelius shrugged. He kicked a tin, and watched it as it bounced and clattered down the street, ringing through the emptiness. It came to rest, and then suddenly, barely distinguishable from the hum of Rome rising up through the heat, the music could be heard again. There couldn't be any doubt now – it was the same piece that had been played on the hill by the lake, the same piece and on the same instruments. Surely, then, it had to be the same musicians as well?

"Okay," said Caelius. "What do you want to do about it?"

Catullus shut his eyes. "I think – we should get back to the car," he said slowly.

"All that panic, and you haven't got anything you want to ask them?"

Catullus shook his head. "Sorry," he said. "It's just that suddenly I feel a bit shitted out."

"*You* do?" muttered Caelius under his breath. "*You* do?" They walked back to the car. It was only as they pulled away that Catullus recognised the view they had been admiring as the one that Titus had shown them a few weeks before. He glanced at Caelius. "Do you ever get the feeling you're being followed?" he asked. Caelius raised his hands up, then slapped them back down onto the steering wheel. "I don't know," he muttered. He turned to look at his friend. "I do know one thing, though. If those clowns were at the ball, then you should stay clear of them. I think, right at the moment, that anything to do with that ball is trouble." He kissed Catullus softly on the cheek. "Don't mess with it."

Catullus nodded. "Okay," he agreed. "Yes, okay. You're probably right." He lapsed into silence. On the pavements, pinned to advertising boards, the afternoon papers announced that Caesar would be holding a press conference that evening.

It was well past six when Caelius screeched the car to a halt outside the Dugbals' house.

"Right," he said, slamming his door behind him. "Try not to look too unappetising."

"What, as a rule of life?"

"No, just for now. Tubbers broke our TV last night, the tit, so we'll have to go crawling to the Dugbals. Grim, but there's no alternative, I'm afraid."

"I don't see why it matters that I look appetising," said Catullus, following him. "It doesn't seem to bother Pop Dugbal."

"Yes, but he's not the one who counts, is he?" Caelius cleared his throat and stood to attention outside the kitchen door. "Mrs Dugbal." There was no reply. "Mrs Dugbal!" Catullus pushed the door open; inside, the kitchen was empty, but through a crack in the door beyond, a muffled voice could be heard talking from the sitting room. Catullus pressed his ear to the crack, and tapped gently at the door. "Come in!" the voice bellowed. Catullus peered round the door. "Oh. It's you." Mrs Dugbal stared at him. "What do you want?"

"We were wondering if we could watch the news," said Caelius. "Please."

"It's already started."

"Yes. I know." Caelius smiled, and shuffled his feet. "That's why we came hurrying back. Only, it's just that my uncle's on it. Please."

Mrs Dugbal continued to stare at him. Finally, she grunted and pointed at the floor. "Go on then," she said. "Down there. But I don't want you talking and gibbering like a pair of monkeys, you understand? And it's just this once. I'm not having you in here each and every evening. It's bad enough knowing you're upstairs. Well, go on. Press the button." Catullus reached across to the television; he switched a knob, and waves of black and white bounced across the screen; finally they congealed into a photograph of Cicero. "That's him, is it?" asked Mrs Dugbal. She snorted. "Crook." Catullus sneaked a look at her; she was brushing the hair of her daughter, who knelt in front of the chair, face frozen into a dulled scowl, staring down at the carpet as she played with a bangle on her arm. She only looked up once, to protest as her mother tugged at a particularly tangled knot of hair. "It's your own fault," said Mrs Dugbal, yanking at the knot again with her hairbrush. "If you will stay out all night, you can hardly complain if you have to suffer a bit of pain for it the next day. That's the way of the world. Now, shut up." Vanessa lowered her head again, and as she did so, caught Catullus' glance. Her eyes glowed with hostility, and Catullus looked away.

He turned back to the television; footage of the arrest was being screened. "The former president, if convicted, faces a possible maximum sentence of fifteen years," a voice said as Cicero was shown being bundled into a police car. "A bail hearing has not yet been granted, so for tonight at least, Marcus Cicero will be detained in a police cell. Whether he is moved to a more permanent place of detention will depend on the evidence presented by the Public Prosecutor, due to be heard tomorrow. But whatever the decision of the hearing, it is clear that for the former President at least, the ordeal is only just beginning."

The item ended, and cut away to a newsreader. "Reaction to the news has varied across the political spectrum," she announced; a picture of Clodius was flashed up. "Tribune Clodius Pulcher, who has long campaigned to have the remit of the investigation broadened, hailed the arrest as a vindication of his criticism of earlier government investigations." Film of Clodius, arguing his case, replaced the photograph, and Caelius leant over to dig Catullus in the ribs. "See?" he whispered. "Have you ever seen a larger smirk?"

"Shut up, you two," said Mrs Dugbal.

"It'll be war again," said Mr Dugbal suddenly, who had hitherto been curled up unnoticed under his ball of rugs, but now sat trembling on the edge of his seat. He pointed a finger at the image of Clodius on the screen and nodded desperately round at everyone in the room. "It will be war!" he shouted. "Fire, from the skies and welling up from the earth, I've seen it all before, in the land of the Circassians! There were cities there once!"

"Now look what you've done," said Mrs Dugbal furiously.

"It wasn't our fault, it was the TV," protested Caelius.

"It was you. Shut up or get out." She turned to her husband. "Shut up."

"The flames can burn up even metal."

"Shut up."

"They feed off brick and human flesh."

"Shut up!"

Mr Dugbal stopped shouting and gave a sudden startled blink. He muttered something, and a thin smile, so watery it seemed on the verge of dribbling over his chin, replaced his frown. He shrank back into his rugs, and still smiling, tried to reach out for Vanessa. Catullus turned back to watch the news again.

Clodius was still being interviewed. "This only goes to show, that if the Government had listened to what I was saying, we could have got the whole process of remunerating those people whose lives were ruined by this squalid affair up and running years ago." He paused. "Perhaps in the future, the Government will do me the courtesy of taking my arguments a little more seriously."

There was a soft knock at the door. Mrs Dugbal stared at it in silent fury as the handle turned, and a head inched its way through the resulting crack. "Evening," the head said nervously. It was Mr Smallpiece's. "And a good evening to you, Mrs Dugbal." He chuckled to himself under his breath. "Keeping well, I hope?"

"No thanks to you if I am. What are you doing here?"

"Ah, well." He swallowed, and mopped his forehead with a large dirty handkerchief. "Got something for you, haven't I?" He held up a plastic bag, the effort making him wheeze. Painfully, he began to pick his way across the room towards Mrs Dugbal, who had turned back to the television and was watching Pompey deny that he was capitulating to economic blackmail. Mr Smallpiece paused for breath, took another shuffle forwards, and tripped up on one of the carpets.

Mrs Dugbal exploded. "You fool, you clumsy old fool!" she bellowed, flinging her hairbrush onto the floor. "What are you doing here? Have I ever asked you in? Have I ever? Have I ever asked you to come in and wipe your dirty great boots all over my carpets?"

"Oh no," said Mr Smallpiece, shaking his head with wry admiration. "You've never done that."

"Then for you to come in like this is bad manners, and as you will know, I am very firm on manners. And stop panting like that, it's making me feel ill."

Mr Smallpiece nodded obediently, and patted a hand over his heart, to try and smooth out the rattle in his breath. "Yes, Mrs Dugbal." He pointed to the bag. "I've got you some snails. You like them, don't you?"

Mrs Dugbal reached over for the bag and held one of the snails up to the light, as Mr Smallpiece watched and smiled. "Grave bred," he whispered. "Pedigree."

Mrs Dugbal grunted, and inspected the snail again. "I suppose you'd better sit down, then," she said grudgingly. Mr Smallpiece dropped like a weight onto one of the carpets. "But you're to keep your mouth shut – understand?"

Mr Smallpiece nodded. For the first time, he noticed Catullus, and he smiled and winked. "She cooks a lovely snail," he whispered, leaning over. "A lovely woman altogether. A rare gem." He winked again, and licked his tongue over his lips. "The things she can do."

"Shut up," whispered Caelius.

"SHUT UP!" bellowed Mrs Dugbal.

"Sorry," said Mr Smallpiece. Catullus smiled at him, then turned back to the television. There was a shot of the Senate House, and a reporter's voice was speaking over it. "So it seems certain that the arrest of Marcus Cicero this afternoon must have had the direct sanction of the State President. But what is worrying senators here is that by surrendering one of his own political supporters to the demands of Tribune Clodius Pulcher, Gnaius Pompey runs the risk of seeming little more than a creature of the unions. The President denies that there has been any surrender – but whether his credibility will survive what many are seeing as a severe jolt, only time will tell."

The news cut back to the studio. "Well, one person who has

unequivocally condemned today's events is Commissioner of Gaul Caesar. He has described the arrest of Marcus Cicero today as "a constitutional outrage". Speaking after a specially convened press conference, he told our correspondent at the Commission why."

Caelius nudged Catullus as Caesar's face appeared on the screen. Catullus stared at it. Thin, aquiline. Handsome. The focus broadened; Caesar was sitting behind his desk, not in uniform, but in a stylish heavy suit, his tie knotted with a touch of deliberate dandyism. He leaned forward to answer a question, and a smile played on the edge of his lips, a sad smile, the smile of a man forced to notice something squalid and be reminded that it exists.

"The issue, surely, is very clear. The government in Rome has surrendered to gangsterdom. This won't stave off social and economic collapse. On the contrary, it only makes it more likely. So what is the President trying to achieve?"

Caesar shook his head, and the interviewer made use of the pause to flick through his notes. "Well, as I understand it," he said, looking up, "you've accused him of offering Cicero as a 'blood sacrifice' in return for the unions' agreements to call off their strikes. Do you stand by that?"

"Yes. Clearly something of that order has occurred. The exact terms aren't important, I don't think. Something far graver than the survival of a few politicians is at stake here – we are talking about the possible extinction of Rome herself."

"As what?"

"As a recognisable political entity."

The interviewer looked shocked. "You mean that?"

"Oh, yes. Now clearly, as a Roman myself, I don't want to stand by and watch the place of my birth disintegrate. But there's another factor. I am also the Commissioner of Gaul, and I'm trying to develop a Federation here in Europe that is directly threatened by the meltdown in Rome. Our own economic and social wellbeing is tied in irrevocably with yours. So please – let's remember that the Roman crisis affects the whole of Europe. We are in this together."

"And that's what – a threat?"

Caesar leant forward, and seemed to be weighing the possible sound of words on his tongue. "A warning," he said at last.

"Against what?"

Again, Caesar paused, and when he spoke, did so slowly and with great deliberateness. "Against the assumption that only those involved in the present petty rounds of infighting have the right to determine the course that Rome will take in the future."

"Do you want to expand on that?"

Caesar shook his head. "No. What else is there to say?"

The film stopped, and for a few seconds the image of Caesar was left frozen on the television screen. There was a choking sound. Catullus looked round. He realised that it was the first catch in the throat of someone about to sob. Mr Dugbal choked again, and tears began to slip down his lined cheeks, like water over parched delta mud, Catullus thought, and perhaps it was the effectiveness of the image that made him feel almost relieved to see Mr Dugbal crying so silently, as though he were watering whatever secret anxieties lay dry behind his face. Vanessa shook her head free from the hairbrush and walked over to her father's chair. She took Mr Dugbal's hand and stared down as each tear glistened along the silvery path of its predecessors. Mr Dugbal tottered to his feet. He stared at Vanessa, then at his wife; then walked over to the far wall. Catullus watched him as he pulled back one of the hangings and opened a door that had been concealed behind it. It led into darkness. Mr Dugbal disappeared through the door, and as the wall hanging fell back into place, it was as though he had vanished into thin air.

"Get out," said Mrs Dugbal suddenly.

"What?" said Caelius, who had crawled right up to the television, and was listening to a studio debate with great ostentation.

"Get out," said Mrs Dugbal again. "Get out!" She ran at him, shooing with her arms; Caelius ducked, then joined Catullus in a strategic retreat towards the kitchen. Mrs Dugbal looked round and saw Mr Smallpiece crouched against the wall; for a brief second, her face softened, and she reached down to take him by the hand. She squeezed it. "You understand?" she whispered. Then suddenly, she jerked him up and almost threw him at the kitchen doorway. He went staggering through it, and the door was slammed shut after him, the whole house shaking, and Mr Smallpiece with it. "What a woman," he whispered.

"If woman indeed she is," said Catullus shortly.

Mr Smallpiece caught his breath back. "Oh, she's a woman all right. No doubt about that." He wheezed with laughter and patted at his chest. "And what a cook too. My word, yes. Oh, what a woman!"

"Have you ever actually eaten anything she's cooked?" asked Caelius disbelievingly.

"I should think so!" Mr Smallpiece shut his eyes and smiled. "She does me the honour of coming round to my house sometimes, and cooking up my tea. Those snails – oh, she cooks a lovely plate of snails..." He opened his eyes again. "Ah, well. Better be getting back and doing my own tea tonight, eh?"

Catullus escorted the old man back out onto the street. "Goodnight, Mr Smallpiece," he said, waving.

"Goodnight. See you in the graveyard again, perhaps." Mr Smallpiece paused and turned round. "Oh, that reminds me. That young man you met up with, the one all in black, comes every day – he was asking after you."

"Was he? Oh God."

"He gave me this to give you." He reached inside his pocket and took out an envelope, which he studied and then handed over to Catullus. "I'd almost forgot. Goodnight."

Catullus nodded as Mr Smallpiece shuffled away, then opened the envelope and pulled out a card. An invitation. Drinks. 'Mysteries and the Man of Blood in the Civil War'. A note scrawled; "Know you'll love this." Catullus looked at the date, and worked out that it was for the end of the week after next. He turned the card over, and saw that it had been signed, 'Furius'. Furius. Catullus mouthed the name, remembering the delicate face that had glowed death-pale from the temple gloom. He glanced up the street, but it was empty, so he slipped the card away, and ran up the stairs. Caelius was waiting for him outside his bedroom door.

"Going to come out then, tonight?" he asked.

Catullus stared at him in surprise. "What, you still want to? With your uncle in jail and the country collapsing as we speak?"

"Why not?"

Yes, why not, Catullus thought, what the hell, why not? "It's decadent, I suppose. Dancing in the ruins while the barbarians mass."

Decadent. And Catullus had always wanted to be decadent. The sound of the word triggered a childhood memory, a picture, of brutish cavalrymen sweeping through the gold and ivory streets of some ancient city, its citizens too debased even to look up from their pleasures and realise that destruction was at hand. The barbarians had worn black, Catullus remembered, and the citizens virtually nothing at all, but their flesh had been very rich and pink, and he had enjoyed studying it a great deal, in his bed at home.

Caelius squeezed his hand. "Going to ask your friends?"

"I'll see." Catullus turned, and before he had realised what he was doing, had brushed his finger against the tip of his prick. Thoughts of naked flesh and raped cities billowed up into his imagination again. "I'm just going to have a lie down," he said. "I'll see you later." He nodded at Caelius, and as he opened his bedroom door, felt himself overpowered by rich thoughts of decline and decay, of surrender, of abdication. He drew his curtains, then lay down on his bed.

IX

CLODIA

"I don't know why you told him we were going," said Caelius sourly, as he and Catullus sat on the landing, waiting for Tubbers. There was a crash from the room behind them, and the sound of muffled swearing. Caelius sighed, and glanced at his watch. "Come on!" he shouted. "What the hell are you doing?"

"Sorry," said Tubbers, putting his head round the door. "Looking for the new bow-tie. *Rather* natty. Can't find it anywhere."

"Well, that's it, then," said Caelius, getting to his feet. "I'm not hanging around waiting for someone who thinks he can wear a bow-tie to a nightclub. Come on, we're off."

"No, hold on, guys, wait!" Tubbers patted despairingly at his throat, as though hoping to find that the tie had been there all along, then hurried after them down the stairs.

"I don't know why you bother buying new clothes," said Caelius. "You look a twat whatever you wear."

"No, rarly, it was rarly – you know."

"So that's another thing gone missing then, is it?" asked Catullus.

"Yah, and it's not just me now, is it?" Tubbers looked at Caelius. "His shoes have gone. Probably deny it now."

Caelius aimed a kick, but Tubbers dodged out of the way and laughed, trying to pretend there had been a joke between them. "No, but rarly – bloody odd, isn't it? Bloody odd."

Caelius shrugged, then suddenly froze. "Look!" he whispered, and pointed. Catullus looked.

Ahead of them, in the shadows, were three figures. One was shorter than the other two, and was speaking in a low voice at great speed. The two silent figures, just silhouettes, turned and stared, and as Catullus walked forward, they melted away into the darkness. The third was left staring after them.

"Hello!" said Caelius suddenly. "You're out late – again."

Who the hell was it? Catullus watched as Caelius passed him and walked up to the figure in the shadows. He could see eyes now, glowing. Vanessa. Caelius started talking to her, but she continued to stare after the shadows, and didn't say a word. As Catullus walked up, she turned her gaze on him.

"Have you seen my dad?" she asked suddenly.

"No," said Caelius, slightly nonplussed. "Should I have done?"

Vanessa didn't answer the question. Instead she looked over her shoulder, then tugged on Caelius' hand. "You won't tell him you've seen me?" she asked. But she didn't wait for the reply. With another glance over her shoulder, she let go of Caelius' hand, and suddenly ran down the street, back towards her house. Caelius pointed after her.

"That's the one. That's our klepto."

"Why?" asked Catullus sharply.

"Why? Why's she nicking things? Any number of reasons, I'd have thought. Society. Resentment at being born a Dugbal. Adolescence."

"Oh, right!" said Tubbers. "A sort of crush? You think that's why she's nicking our clothes?"

"Hardly – she started off with yours, didn't she?"

Catullus stared at his friend. "But why her?"

"Well, she's just strange, isn't she?" He shrugged. "Look, it's only a theory, but remember that time when we found Daddy Dugbal sitting up late for her? When we got back from that police station?"

Catullus shrugged. He did remember. "Jez said she was out getting pregnant."

"But she isn't pregnant, is she? So she was probably out pilfering. That's working-class teenagers for you. They're all bloody criminals."

"And those two she was just with then?"

"I don't know. Crack dealers? Clients? Don't worry about it."

"No." But Catullus did worry. As he walked on down the street towards the pub, he found that he was worrying a great deal. For he was almost certain that he had recognised the men who had been talking to Vanessa before slipping away. He was almost certain that they had been the two clowns.

The street outside the pub, when they reached it, was warm with the heat of queuing people and distant noise. Pub regulars stood clustered on the pavement, watching the strange influx onto their turf – no wonder they looked resentful, thought Catullus, staring at two old men as they finished off their drinks, it must be disorientating to see people for whom the night was just beginning. To see people like *him*. The queue shuffled forward. It was really true – he was a part of it, a queue late at night, in a big city, and he was a part of it. Catullus smiled. These were the moments that he had come to Rome to find.

"Seen anyone you recognise?" asked Caelius suddenly.

"Why?" The lurch of nervousness, which Catullus thought he had tamed, ballooned up in his stomach again. "Have you?"

"No." Caelius looked oddly diffident. "Just wondering, you know. It is odd how you bump into people at places like these."

Catullus stared at him suspiciously. Caelius shrugged and smiled. "Your girlfriend coming?"

"Shit! I forgot to phone her."

"Well, do it inside. We'll be there in a minute."

"She's not my girlfriend."

Caelius smiled. "No, of course not."

Catullus was going to answer back, but Tubbers interrupted him with an excited yelp. "Hey, guys! Look! It's the Bulldog! Hey, Bulldog!"

Catullus peered through the entrance to the club. There was a stairway, leading into a thick sweaty darkness, but a few steps down, twirling a snooker cue, the shape of the Bulldog could indeed just be made out. Tubbers started to dance happily. "Ayeroo!" he called out loudly. "Ayeroo," replied the Bulldog placidly, before spitting out a gob of tobacco against the wall.

Tubbers smiled and shook the Bulldog's hand. He began to trot down the stairs, but Caelius and Catullus, trying to do the same, suddenly found themselves being pressed up against the wall, a snooker cue in their stomachs, the Bulldog just behind it. Catullus felt too winded even to speak. He heard some people at the top of the stairs begin to laugh.

"We're with him," Caelius managed to gasp, pointing after Tubbers. The Bulldog didn't say anything, just bent down and stared into Caelius' eyes. Caelius winced at the smell of tobacco-stained breath. "We're very sorry," said Catullus with loud precision. He swallowed. "I think there may have been a mistake."

"Money," said the Bulldog, pointing to a sign. "Hand over your fucking money."

Caelius opened his mouth to complain, but was shut up before he could say anything by the snooker cue's progress further into his stomach. Catullus reached inside his pocket and paid for two tickets. The snooker cue relaxed.

"I'm going to sue you," shouted Caelius, when he felt that he was a safe distance away from the Bulldog. "You just wait, I'm going to fucking sue you." The Bulldog flexed his shoulders back. Catullus reached for his friend's arm, but Caelius broke free and flicked a v-sign back up the stairs. The Bulldog began to twirl the snooker cue again, and eyes in the queue behind him gleamed with anticipation.

"He's a fucking ape, isn't he?" said Caelius loudly. Catullus pretended that he hadn't heard the question, but the Bulldog had, because suddenly he was running down the stairs, shoving Caelius up against the wall, and then pushing him so that he fell and tumbled into the darkness of the club below. The Bulldog watched Caelius disappear, then walked back up the stairs. "Dickhead," said one of two girls just behind Catullus. They pushed past him and giggled. He was going to yell something after them, say that it wasn't his fault, but he knew that doing that would only make things worse, and suddenly he felt furious, with himself and everyone else, with the whole night. He started to follow the girls down the stairs, and found that his heart was beating loudly in his ears.

At the bottom, Caelius seemed annoyingly unperturbed. "That fucking great ape, I'm going to sue him till there's nothing left of him. The bastard. Hasn't he heard about evolution? People like him should still be picking fleas off themselves up trees."

"Well, why don't you go back up there and put it to him?" replied Catullus furiously.

Caelius smiled. "Because he wouldn't know what evolution was. No, I'll just wait till the morning and get him sacked. Come on, let's forget about it."

"You're a fucking arse, Caelius."

"Look, sweetie, don't take it out on me, I'm the one who's just been dumped down some stairs by a missing link, all right?" Caelius patted his friend on the shoulder. "Come on. You probably need to work it off. Let's dance." They wandered across to one of the catacombs. For the first time, Catullus started to look about and become aware of things around him. There was an archway above his head; he passed under it, and suddenly felt the air lie heavy on his skin. Looking up, he saw a vast dome, its brickwork damp and shimmering with sweat, pulsing and then fading like a mirage on hot tarmac, as lasers swept and stabbed across the roof. Through the pools of dark and coloured brightnesses, crowds danced, incredibly fast, Catullus couldn't believe how fast they were moving. Everything seemed unbearably alive, even the walls, even the catacomb roof; it was like being inside the stomach of a dying animal, he thought dreamily, and he was one of the parasites that were writhing and twisting across its pit, maggots, they didn't know why they writhed, they just did. Catullus found that he was dancing as well. There was a pop, and a smell of smoke. In front of him, a man turned and span, and became a silhouette, as green laser beams bent through the smoke. The music screeched and fell, and the man waved a whistle in the air, then blew on it, piercingly, and everyone else began to blow on whistles too, and the whole floor seemed to be shivering, and Catullus felt suddenly happy and relieved. He couldn't believe it. It was such a glorious feeling, as though everyone knew just how he felt, and was happy for him too. But then the music scratched and changed again, and there was a sudden pulse of white light, and everyone's faces disappeared, so that there were just blobs of whiteness, glowing out of the dark, like skulls, Catullus thought, like sculptures of the dead in Tartarus. The man who had been blowing the whistle brushed against Catullus with his arm; it felt clammy, and the moment it had touched his skin, froze him still. He remembered how white Mr Varney's arm had looked, bleached by the Tiber and laid out on the slab. Caelius was staring at him now, looking worried, but Catullus just shook his head. He didn't want to dance any more. He felt disgusted again. A woman brushed past him, then another, and then more people, all dancing, dancing, until he felt as though he were the only person standing still in the entire club, and a flush of humiliation added to the sweat he could feel on his back. He was brushed aside again, this time by two men who clung to each other as though they wanted to share the same skin; they kissed, and laughed. Bastards, thought Catullus. They're happy – I'm not.

There was no point in staying where he was. He turned and made his way back through the crowd. A girl, dancing on her own, swayed in front of him, tossing back her hair and smiling, as though the music was inside her, in and out, screwing her. She saw Catullus and reached for him; he stared back, at her moist lips, but his legs felt too heavy, and the air was pressing down on him, and he felt angry again, so angry that he wanted to hit someone and cause him pain. He pushed past the girl, and walked out of the catacomb towards one of the bars. What was going on? There was an itch, prickling somewhere deep inside him, beyond his reach; he ordered a drink, and as he waited, felt his anger tickle him so physically that he was tempted to rub himself up and down against the seat, anything to stop it. He drank and suddenly found himself outside his anger; it was as though he were looking at himself with someone else's eyes, that girl's perhaps, or anyone's, and he didn't like what the eyes could see. He tightened his grip on the bar ledge, and suddenly, he knew where he could scratch his itch; it had moved to his groin; it had become an erotic pain, grinding from deep inside. He rubbed himself, desperately, and the more he tried to stop the itch the more it seemed to burn him, as he became aware of what he was doing, and felt his sense of humiliation spurt and increase. He stopped, and steadied himself against the bar. His hand reached out and knocked a pen; as he bent down to pick it up, the prickling in his balls ran all the way through his body, and bent him up double with shame, and anger, and a longing for relief. He reached for a pad of paper that had been left on the bar, and began to write, shutting out the thump of the music in the cellars, yoking the words together with a rhythm of his own. He finished the poem, took a sip from his drink, and stared at what he had written. Reading it back over, he felt the itch start to tickle his balls again, but he ignored it this time, just carried on reading. He made a correction, then began to copy the poem with a careful hand, shaping the letters with great deliberation. He felt the itch gradually start to fade away.

"It's rude, it doesn't rhyme, it must be modern." Catullus looked up. Caelius was standing behind him, peering down with interest at the note pad. "Is that all you've been doing? Writing dirty limericks?"

"It isn't a limerick."

"Well, whatever – it's still dirty."

"Maybe, but the fact that it's not a limerick is what gives it its whole point. Its dirtiness is in deliberate contrast to the purity of the metrical control. That's where the tension comes from, because the form and content are there to threaten each other. See?"

"Yes, well, if that's how you like to pass your time." Caelius sat down beside him, then turned to scan the entrance door and the staircase beyond it. "What is the time?" he asked casually.

Catullus glanced at his watch. "Gone twelve." He stared at his friend. "You are waiting for someone, aren't you?"

"No, no, I was just wondering."

"What, when we can piss off and go home?"

"Speak for yourself, I'm having fun." Caelius glanced round behind him again. "Come on, for God's sake, even Tubbers is having fun. Look." He pointed, and Catullus swivelled in his seat. Tubbers was in a far corner, drink in hand, chatting to a couple of girls. The Bulldog was next to him, his arm round Tubbers' shoulder.

Caelius shook his head. "Look at him. What's he doing?"

"Talking to a couple of girls."

"Exactly. He must be off his head."

"Why?"

"Well, would you talk to girls if you were Tubbers? Of course not. But look, they're actually listening to him."

Catullus watched as one of the girls crossed her legs. They were brown and very long, unnaturally long in fact, far too long to be a woman's, Catullus suddenly guessed. The girl laughed, flashing white teeth, and tossed her hair.

"Is Tubbers gay?" Catullus asked.

"I don't know," said Caelius, surprised by the question. "Why?"

"Those girls. You're sure they're not boys?"

Caelius stared at them again, then shrugged. "It would stop him reproducing himself, I suppose. If he was gay, I mean. Well – let's keep our fingers crossed."

The girls had got up. They walked across the cellar floor as though it were a cat walk, away from Tubbers, who had sat down with the Bulldog and was staring morosely after the girls as they began to sway peristaltically within their clinging dresses.

"They're gorgeous, aren't they?" said Caelius. "Look at those arses."

"Plastic."

"I don't care what they're made of. Just as long as they *look* like women." Caelius grinned, and patted Catullus on the hand. "Sorry, babe. Not a sensitive thing to say. But dear, oh dear, what is it about this place?"

"What do you mean?"

"There's you writing rude poems, there's Tubbers actually starting a conversation with someone who hasn't got a beard, and there's me fucking dying because I'm not in the middle of a shag. I'm in my prime. I have needs."

"Really?"

Caelius bared his teeth. "Yes!" He glanced at Catullus' watch. "You phoned your friends yet?"

"No."

"Well, get onto them. Especially that gorgeous one who wanted to give me the blow job."

Catullus swung round and discovered that he was staring very hard at a beer mat. So Caelius had known all along. Catullus picked the beer mat up and began to shred it into pieces. All the anger, all the disgust he thought had been written out of himself into the poem began to itch and tickle under his skin again. Caelius nodded at him, and smiled, and made a slithering sound with his tongue. Catullus tried to remember the feeling Mona's tongue had given him, then imagined her taking Caelius' prick into her mouth, and Caelius coming as he had come. He imagined Caelius fucking Mona, very hard, and laughing at him as he was forced to watch, and to his horror he found that the idea was exciting him and making his skin scratch all the more. He climbed to his feet and had to steady himself against the bar.

"Going to phone them?"

"No." Catullus began to walk away.

"Where are you going?" Caelius shouted after him.

"Outside. I need some fresh air." And it was true. He felt as though he were being smothered by the noise, and the heat, and everyone's excitement. He had to get outside. He had to feel something cool against his skin.

He ran up the stairs. The crowds of people waiting to get into the club were still thick, but Catullus pushed his way through them, and had almost reached the top of the staircase when he suddenly froze.

He was staring into the face of the policeman, Porter. Porter stared back. Neither man spoke. Catullus could feel a fresh surge of anger rising up inside him as he continued to stare wordlessly into Porter's face. Then he shoved him aside, and barged his way up the few remaining steps. He staggered out onto the pavement and began to run. He hurried down an empty street.

In the distance, someone laughed, but then there was nothing, and Catullus felt the silence as though it were the cool against his sweat. He stopped running, and gazed out at the blackness of the city. It seemed menacing and brutish, humped against a star-lit horizon, and Catullus found himself staring up at the sky, as though to escape the threat. The feeling at the back of his neck surprised him; it reminded him quite unexpectedly of a time many years before, when he had been camping with his brother in a forest, and had craned up at the sky to see beyond the trees that had been towering over their tent. He had ended up lying with his head out of the canvas, staring up at the night with its stars and blue sky, and had woken up the next morning unable to move his neck. He laughed with delight at the memory, and the sound was so strange in his ears that he laughed again, to see if he could repeat the shock. He couldn't, but he felt better all the same, and just by discovering that the accidental discovery of a memory had so lightened his mood, felt able to convince himself that the anxieties he had felt prickling him down below, underground, had been nothing more than a metaphor for the sweat under his clothes, and now, under the sky, the blue night sky, as the sweat cooled, so was his anger fading away. Suddenly, Catullus discovered that he couldn't even remember what it was that had unsettled him.

He would phone Mona, he thought. Why not? He felt in his pocket and took out the sugar sachet Boot had given him earlier that afternoon. He went over to a phone, pushed some coins in, and dialled.

The call was answered almost at once. "Hello?" said a voice that Catullus hadn't been expecting. It sounded middle-aged, upper-class, and very cross. "Hello, who is it?"

"Is Mona there?" said Catullus after an embarrassed pause. "Or Boot?"

"Boot? Do you mean Arabella?"

"I don't know."

The voice tsked at him down the phone. "I wish you people would learn that half-past-midnight is simply not an acceptable hour at which to make telephone calls." Then Catullus heard the receiver being dropped onto a table, and the sound of heels disappearing into silence. Catullus watched nervously as numbers flickered downwards on the coin display. He slipped more money in, and continued to wait. Then he heard footsteps again. They stopped. "Hello?" said Boot's voice. "Who's that?"

"Sorry, it's me," said Catullus. "I didn't realise you had guests."

"It's not a guest, it's my mother. I'm at home. What are you doing, phoning me so late?"

"You said you might come out."

"Yes, might. Which also means might not. You really want me to come?"

"Yes."

"Sorry. You're too far away, and I'm too lazy. But thanks for trying."

"Oh well." There was an awkward silence. "I didn't know you were called Arabella."

"We've all got our problems."

"It's nice."

"No, it's not. It's a horrible name. One of my aunts was called Arabella. She was very beautiful apparently, she was famous for it. Whenever I see my other aunts together, they all shake their heads at me and I know what they're thinking. They're all disappointed I'm so ugly. Still, what do I care. Oh, that reminds me."

"What?"

"Aunts – uncles. Hold on." Catullus heard a rustling. It sounded like a letter being taken from an envelope. Boot came back to the phone. "Listen, you know those poems?"

"Ye-es." Catullus felt his heart jump up into his throat.

"Guess what? My uncle really likes them! I've just had a letter."

"Really?"

"Yes. I'd never have guessed."

Catullus believed her. "Thanks a lot, Boot."

"It's amazing. He thinks they're really great. He wants to meet you."

"What about?"

"I don't know. I'll just read you what he says, listen." Catullus heard the rustle of the letter again. "'They are really quite exciting' – that's your poems – 'and I would very much like to meet your friend. Could you ask him if he would be free to come Thursday week, at four o'clock? Please provide him with my address.' So. Going to go?"

"Yes, yes, of course. Hold on, let me just get some paper. Shit, the money's running out." Catullus felt inside his pocket, and drew out his diary. He looked at the date. 'Furius', he had written, just earlier that evening. Well, it was too bad, and he hadn't really fancied him anyway, he wasn't in the mood for delicate types. "Yes, that's fine," he told Boot. "Should I phone your uncle, then?"

"No, I'll tell him. Listen, the address –" The pips started to go. "What's your number, I'll–" The phone went dead. Catullus stared at the receiver, then kissed it. "Yes," he whispered to himself. He put the receiver down and leant against the pay phone. "Yes, yes, yes!" He smiled stupidly, then began to run quickly back down the street.

He hadn't asked about Mona, he remembered. Damn! But something about the alchemy of the night must have changed, because, suddenly, he only had to wish for something, and desire became gold. "Wait!" a voice shouted out from behind him, and even before Catullus had looked round, he knew that it was Mona's. He turned, and Mona came running into his arms, kissing him happily and feeling warm against his body. "How did you know I was coming now?" she asked, but didn't wait for an answer, taking him by the arm instead and pulling him towards the club. "I'm sorry I'm late, but I knew you wouldn't mind." She kissed him again. "I've been getting us presents."

"How kind. I love presents."

"Yes, me too." She beamed, then pulled Catullus into a side door. "Here," she said, taking out a couple of pills from a small envelope. "One for you, and one for me." She watched as Catullus swallowed, then took hers, and laughed happily. "Come on!"

"What was it?"

"Don't worry!" She laughed again, and took him by the hand. "Just have fun. Come on!"

She began to run, and Catullus ran with her, feeling suddenly so light and golden that when he first heard the music coming up from the club, he listened to it as though its beat were something he was going to glide across. Downstairs, the music seemed louder and more exciting than it had done before; the crowds more febrile and happy; the air even more dense. Catullus felt his brain start to swoon and rise upwards, as though his thoughts were incense and his skull a censer; even his smile was bobbing like a cork, he realised, and why not, why the hell not? – he was happy. He felt a terrible energy warming through his limbs; people brushed past him all the time, and his skin sparked at the touch, and sent a charge that reached deep into his bones and ran down towards his toes and fingertips. Mona stroked his arm, and he felt the charge again, lighter, more erotic now. He wanted to move. He had to move, he had no choice. He embraced Mona and found that she was swaying too. He took Mona's arm and stroked it. Then, together, they began to push their way through the crowds.

Catullus felt a tap on his shoulder. He turned round.

"You baby, you!" pouted Camilla into his face. "What are *you* doing here!"

Catullus smiled and pointed through the cellar archway.

"You *total* fag hag! Kissey for munchkins? *Thank* you, darling. And who's your friend?" Camilla didn't wait for the introduction, just reached out for Mona and drowned her beneath perfumed kisses.

"What are you doing here?" Catullus shouted at her.

"Well, there was your little friend."

"What little friend?"

"The student. He asked me to come, and because I'm such a *major* angel I said I would."

"Who?" Then realisation dawned. "Caelius?"

"Yes, and now he's off somewhere, probably taking coke in the loos, except he is only a student of course, and so probably can't afford it, but anyway, net result equals total tragedy, Mumsy's all alone."

Catullus almost choked on his laughter. "Let me get this quite straight – *Caelius* invited you here tonight?"

Camilla winked a mascaraed eyelash, and took Catullus by the arm. "Just the teensiest bit jealous, are we? Well, don't worry, babykin, Mumsy will always love you too. It's just your friend gives top-grade, *seriously* heavy orgasms, that's all, I mean it's not as if he has personality. Not like you. So don't be jealous." She kissed him. "We're still lovey, lovey?"

"Oh, yes, absolutely." Catullus could feel laughter waiting behind his lips again. "You go and find him."

"Kissums first." Catullus did as he was told, then waved and turned. "Be good!" Camilla shouted after him. "And if you see your friend, tell him I'm going to give him a *serious* spanking."

"Oh, I will," said Catullus to himself. "I will." His evening was complete. He punched the air, and ran through the archway, into the cellar beyond, Mona skipping with him, a whistle in her mouth, her finger jabbing forward into the air, up her arm swayed and up, in time to the music, and Catullus followed. God, he thought, how wonderful everything was turning out to be. A sheet of white bathed the dancefloor, then black, then white; faster and faster the strobe pulsed out across the floor, and faster and faster arms punched, up, in, across, out into the air. Catch up with the light, Catullus told himself, move faster than the light, make it serve you. He span towards Mona, who smiled and reached out to touch him, and her body seemed to be rippling as it moved, to be made of nothing except light, and when he felt her fingers on his own, he was almost surprised, because he could scarcely believe that he was made of anything that wasn't light himself, his limbs didn't seem to have any weight at all now, and only the music in his ears seemed real. The strobe stopped, the music changed, and as lasers shimmered across the floor, a cheer and a great sea of raised hands rose to meet them. Mona had found water from somewhere; she drank from a blue bottle, then poured more water over her hair. She laughed and shook her head; Catullus watched transfixed as silver droplets scattered out like mercury beads. He took the bottle, then, as beautifully coloured lights began to play on a screen behind them, he took one swig and helped Mona up onto a raised podium. The lights swirled and shaped, and Catullus danced on, as the patterns changed behind him, and the entire world seemed made of motion and delight.

A girl waved at him. He scrambled down. Mona followed him, but as she jumped, there was a fresh rush on the dancefloor, and she was knocked to the ground. Catullus looked round for her, but the girl who had waved to him was taking him by the hands. He was whirled away and pressed tightly to her, then whirled away again. He broke free, but Mona was gone. A second girl took him, and held him tight. Catullus felt her body damp against his, damp and soft, and then she was swinging away too, shaking her head back and waving her arms, her fingers outstretched, so that light from the lasers seemed to be spilling through them, and her face was left as nothing but a green silhouette. There seemed something familiar about it, but Catullus couldn't make out what. The girl swung closer towards him again, and began to conjure patterns with her hands; she weaved and darted them as the music quickened, and still it was impossible to make out her face. She spun; light caught her arm and the shadow of her breasts, and suddenly Catullus couldn't bear it any longer, all the energy in his body seemed to have become desire, and so he reached out to hold her and press her to him. She breathed softly on the side of his neck, and Catullus felt her cheek brush past his own; as she swung away again, the lights dyed her cropped blonde hair an even more brutal pale, and her face, cast in shadow again, reminded Catullus suddenly of Clodia. Impossible. It couldn't be? He studied her again, and laced his fingers through hers. Gold gleamed in her ears. From high above them, across the sweating vault, a singer moaned; the girl hugged her warm body tight again to Catullus', and he stroked his fingers up and down her back. She wasn't wearing much; Catullus remembered the rich black gown Clodia had worn for the night of the ball, and the thought that the girl dancing with him now might be the same woman made his stomach feel as though it would fly away. The feeling of warmth began to stain its way downwards; the more certain Catullus became that he was indeed dancing with Clodia, the more exciting he found the idea that he could stroke her naked skin, or feel her legs, or run his hand through her now blonde hair, just as though she were anyone. The first time he had seen her, in that cool dark carriage, she had seemed so forbidding that he had felt frozen by it; now they were melting with each other's sweat. He stroked the sides of her breasts; no ice there now. He felt her leg against his; he felt her hand on his arse. He kissed her.

Catullus lost all sense of time. The night was dissolving away around him, but he didn't notice, his limbs were too light, his body too warm. Still the music pulsed on, heavier now, a thudding, remorseless, metal beat, and Clodia, dancing to it, began to grind herself against Catullus, holding him so tightly that he had to stand still. The rhythm quickened, and Clodia screwed herself round, round and round, forcing Catullus backwards until he staggered and fell. "Not here," he whispered, and when he realised what he had said and meant, he felt a muggy warmth gush upwards into his brain. For a brief moment, his mind seemed to clear itself, and he understood that the light of life was too brief, its night too long, for glimpses of joy to expire unattempted, that existence without them was nothing but ash. He began to pull Clodia over towards the wall. "Do you really want to?" Clodia whispered. She laughed. "We can't." "We have to. It's important. We must." "Over here, then," Clodia breathed into his ear. She led him across to an alcove, empty except for shadows. There was a wall on one side; a slab of something on the other. Clodia lay down in the middle. Catullus knelt down in front of her.

"Live, my darling, live and love." The words rose unspoken on Catullus' thoughts, soaring away on the rush of excitement that left him conscious of nothing except for the lips he had reached forward to kiss, and the breasts he could feel against his own chest, and the heat of Clodia's thighs, he could smell them, or was he smelling himself, it was hard to tell he thought, as he kissed Clodia's stomach, a thousand, a hundred, a hundred thousand times, and then down, down, licking, just a quick dart, and then undoing his trousers, and there it was, his own hot scent, merging with Clodia's, and in, was he *really* going to do it? "Come on," breathed Clodia. "We haven't got all night." No. Catullus nudged, then pushed, then, as he became aware of the music again, began to grind in time. He was moving too fast. He was too excited. He had to slow down. He stared at Clodia, but no, he thought, that was a bad mistake, not now, think of anything else, just not her. A shadow fell across him, then moved on; someone walking past. Suddenly Catullus was distant from himself again, looking down, and he couldn't believe it; he was on a dancefloor next to hundreds of people, fucking an aristocrat, and it was wonderful, it really was, he had to laugh. He kissed Clodia on both her burning cheeks, then shut his eyes as he imagined himself dissolving away into the touch of her lips, and he knew that it was safe now, just to melt and enjoy the floods of pleasure. Clodia sighed and scratched at his back; she rolled with him, and Catullus could feel her trying to pull her leg out from under his arse. He arched his back; yes, he half-breathed to himself, lie on top, push me hard, make me come, I can't hold back much longer, give me the excuse. Clodia moaned and gasped, and bent her neck backwards; as she did so, her fingers ran down Catullus, towards his groin, and the feeling sparked straight to the top of his prick. That was it! He came. He thought of himself, beating and pulsing deep inside Clodia. Clodia. Nothing could describe the pleasure he felt on staring at her and sounding her name. He moaned a second time, wishing that somehow he could stay inside. But dampness was already making his groin feel clammy; as Clodia bent forward to kiss him, his prick flopped free. He moaned a third time. Clodia dabbed a finger onto his lips and ssshed him. Then she took him in her arms and pointed at the dancefloor. "Bit late to be worrying about that now, isn't it?" Catullus whispered. Clodia just smiled, and ran her hands through her hair, as she had done above the lake that morning weeks before. Catullus sighed. He broke free of Clodia and pulled up his trousers, wriggling with his arse so that he wouldn't have to stand up. He looked at the wall they had been lying beneath. Still very dark, Catullus was relieved to notice. He wondered how high the slab had been on the other side of them. He turned, carefully, to have a look.

Fuck, there was a skeleton. "What's the matter?" asked Clodia. Catullus pointed. "Even in Arcadia." He stood up, gingerly, looking around. No one gave him a glance. He took a few steps forward, to look at the slab closely for the first time. Its ends were made of concrete, its top and sides of reinforced glass; inside was the skeleton that Catullus remembered from his previous visit. He looked at the wall; the drawing of the dancing man had been left in place as well. There was a sign next to it now. Catullus walked over and read. 'This carving survives from the Marian period, when the cellars were used for religious rituals. Its significance is uncertain. The skeleton in the floor dates from the same period.'

"Does it say what it is?" Clodia asked.

"No."

"Odd thing to have in a club." She stood up and read the sign for herself. "Nice carving though. Cigarette?" Catullus shook his head. Clodia continued to look at the carving. "Why's the man got an eagle on his head?"

Catullus stared at her wide-eyed. "What?" He looked back at the carving. She was right. The man *did* have an eagle's head. How the hell had he missed that?

"It's like the statue my brother's got."

"What, he's got an eagle-man? Clodius?"

"Yes, on his desk at work. Have you seen it?"

"No, of course not, I only met him once."

"Oh." Clodia looked puzzled. "Then how did he know you were here tonight?"

"I haven't the faintest idea. He told you I was, did he?"

"Yes. This evening. He rang me up. I wouldn't have come if he hadn't."

"So, hold on, he wanted you to come and meet up with me?"

"No." Clodia looked puzzled again. "I just thought it would be nice. I didn't know how else I'd get to see you."

"But look, hold on, I don't understand. How did your brother know I was here tonight?"

"I don't know. He just did. But I'd asked him to find you."

"Oh." Catullus stared at her. "I see." Clodia smiled at him, took his hand, then glanced around the cellar. The music had stopped, and striplights been turned on. The crowds were thinning out through the archways. "Well," said Clodia, standing up. "I'd better be off, I suppose."

"What, now? Won't you stay a bit?"

"No, I'd better go." She glanced at her watch. "It is seven. I promised I'd be back." She made a face. "My husband."

"Don't you think he'll have noticed by now?"

Clodia laughed. "Oh, he doesn't mind about that. No, it's just he's ill, you see."

"Oh, well then. In that case. If he's ill."

"Yes." She reached for his cheeks and kissed him. "I'll get in touch."

"Yes." Please, please. He stared up at her, into her tired, blonde-topped face. "Goodnight, Clodia."

"Goodnight."

"It was wonderful, everything. Really."

She nodded. "Yes, it was." She smiled, almost shyly, then hurried across the cellar floor towards the archways. Catullus stared after her, and wished that she hadn't gone. His stomach seemed empty, and his mind numb.

He sat down and stretched. He wasn't in any hurry to leave. His limbs were still tingling with energy, and when he stretched again, he could feel his emptiness starting to glow and heal. He looked around. Where was Caelius? If he could catch him with Camilla, then that would really be perfection. He smiled and shifted, and then suddenly, out of the corner of his eye, he saw what he had been sitting on. That skeleton, he was on that skeleton! Catullus shut his eyes.

He didn't want to look at the bones. They reminded him of an idea that had first struck him a few minutes before, when Clodia had pointed out the wall-carving's head, but though it had made him shiver then as well, he had forgotten his theory since. Saying goodbye had enabled him to bury the idea away. But now there it was, exhumed, brought to light again, like the very bones he was sitting on. He opened his eyes. He would have to look. He would have to see if his idea had been correct. He climbed to his knees, and put his eye to the glass. Then he stared at the skeleton's skull.

Only half of it was there. The face had been sliced off – there was nothing left of it, no wonder the bastard looked so dead. Catullus remembered Mr Varney's corpse, and the wound to its skull. He remembered the dancing man he had seen on the spot where Mr Varney had been killed. He remembered the dancing eagle-man that Marius had seen on the same spot, hundreds of years before. And then he looked at the carving of the eagle-man on the wall above him, and the skull with its wound buried just below. Catullus climbed to his feet. The night had fooled him – all its joy had led only to this, cramping fear. He could still feel the drug in his head, but it was stif-ling him now, and seemed the token of horrors. He began to shiver convulsively. He had to get out. He looked one last time at the shattered skull, then began to run.

From a corner, Lud and Pollo watched him. They had seen everything. They sat where they were for a few minutes, then Pollo stood up and lumbered across to where the skeleton lay. He peered down at the skull and shook his head. He shouted something at Lud, who nodded back and clapped with his hands. Pollo laughed. He began to dance.

X
CLODIUS

Even once you'd gone inside, you could still hear the river slapping against the mudflats, slap, slap, slap, even when you were up against the bar, there it was, like a dull heart beat, and you had to wonder where it was coming from, because outside there was nothing, no river, only the road that had led you there, and rubbish ploughed into tipsites, so that the whole place looked like a city cursed with salt, barren and dying, but still the sound came.

No one was trying to get away from it. No one could. Pale boys sat on the dirty steps, slicing at themselves with razors, very delicately, but very deep. A girl was sobbing at a bully's feet, licking and sucking them through her tears, and she choked, and sobbed all the more, but the bully didn't look down. There were a few old men, staring sadly into their beer glasses, and a beautiful lady, elegantly dressed, was powdering her face. She dabbed and dabbed at it incessantly. No one spoke. The Tiber lapped on against the mud.

"Did you ever finish my book?" asked Mr Varney. "I miss it sometimes. My old friend. That's how I think of it. Did you ever finish it?"

"No."

"There's a pity."

"Why?"

"Ask Clodius."

"What does he know?"

"He knows you fucked his sister."

"Does that matter?"

"Ask Clodia."

"Where is she?"

"She's been here all the time." Mr Varney pointed. "Powdering her face." Catullus looked at the beautiful lady. She had become Clodia, naked. Mr Varney began to laugh. "Her pretty face. Her pretty little face!" He spluttered, and his eyes wept as he laughed more and more. He leaned over the bar, and smashed a bottle onto the floor. It shattered everywhere, and Mr Varney, groping after it, was able to retrieve a long thin shard. With great care, he began to slice open his face, and the bone melted away like hot wax, dribbling down over his frayed waistcoat, and still Mr Varney laughed, a thin damp membrane stretched and flapping over his throat, like cellophane over old meat.

"Why are you laughing?"

Mr Varney's membrane flapped all the more. "You don't know who killed me?" Suddenly, the laughter stopped. Mr Varney whispered. "You need to find out. Maybe it was you?"

The membrane fluttered, then ceased to move. No one else spoke. The Tiber beat on. If only there was a way out.

Slap. Catullus opened his eyes, then shut them again. It was daytime. He was awake. There was another slap. Where was it coming from? The dream was over. Catullus sat up, and opened his eyes again.

"You look really funny," said Jez, who was balancing precariously on a rickety chair. "You look like you've seen a ghost or something."

Catullus stared at him and nodded slowly.

"So you did see a ghost! Wick-id!"

Catullus grunted. "And now I wake up and find I'm looking at you."

"Oh, shut up, you – you – spasmo!" Jez shadow boxed at Catullus across the room, and almost fell off his chair with excitement. He balanced himself, then danced up and down on the spot. "Do you like my painting?" he said at last. "Don't you think it's safe?"

Catullus twisted round to look at where Jez was pointing. He could see fresh streaks of colour, a curving line of blue flecked with greens and browns. "What is it?" he asked.

"It's a river, stupid. Look." Jez picked up a brush and dipped it into some blue paint. Then he clambered back up onto his chair. Slap. The river wound on by a further foot. The paint gleamed thick and glutinous, and looked very wet, as wet as the river into which Mr Varney's corpse had been slung.

"What's it for?" Catullus asked.

"It's going to be this amazing city, like I told you. Like the one my dad did, remember?"

"Rome?"

Jez shrugged. "When Dad painted his city, he'd been to loads of places. If I'd been to loads of places, I'd paint them too."

Catullus looked at the blue line again. It snaked and coiled like a snipping from a gut. "You'd better get on," he said, pointing at the top bank. "You need to get some buildings up."

"I was going to, except you were asleep like a great *lazybones*. That's what people are, my mum says, who don't get up in the morning."

"The reason I'm in bed is because I *was* up in the morning. See?"

"No."

"Too bad." Catullus reached for his watch. "Bugger. Two o'clock."

"Yes, exactly, it is bugger, that's the word, bugger, bugger, because I wanted to start earlier, only Dad wouldn't let me, not even when the man wanted to speak to you on the telephone."

Catullus stared at him. "Man? What man?"

"I don't know. It's all on a bit of paper. Do you want me to go and get it?

"That might be a start."

"All right." Jez jumped down from his chair. "Wait there."

"Come and find me in our kitchen," said Catullus, following Jez out into the corridor. "I need tea."

"Does your mouth feel like it's been dried out for months and months, and then had water poured in front of it?"

"Sort of."

"That's a good torture, that is. I thought of it myself."

"Jez – phone message."

"Could I do tortures on your painting? My dad's one had really great pictures of people getting burnt up by flames, it was really *horrible*."

"Jez, get that message, or you won't be painting anything. Go on. I'll be in here." Catullus walked into the kitchen and slammed the door shut behind him before Jez could say another word.

"I don't know why you encourage the little bastard," said Caelius, who was slumped over the table, waiting for the kettle to boil. "Just tell him to fuck off and leave you alone."

Catullus grinned. Caelius looked dreadful. "Are you all right, old chap?" he asked.

Caelius stared up at him balefully. "What does it look like? I feel fucking shite."

"Oh dear." Catullus' smile broadened. He joined Caelius at the table, and patted him on the arm. "By the way," he asked after a gentle pause, "did you meet Camilla last night? I only ask, because I ran into her, and she was full of all this shit that you'd invited her there." He paused again. "Actually, she said she was on the lookout for you."

Caelius opened one bloodshot eye. "She found me."

"Yes? And did she give you a spanking?"

"What?"

"She said when she found you, she was going to give you a spanking."

Caelius made a face. "Very funny."

"Nightmare date, Caelius."

"Don't."

"What am I meant to think? Dumped for Camilla. The words salt and wounds leap to mind."

"Sssh." Caelius put a finger to his lips. "Keep your voice down."

"What? She's *here?*"

"Yes. In my bed, actually. She kicked me out to go and make her tea. Which I'd better get on with, I suppose." He staggered to his feet and boiled the kettle again. "Look, I don't want you thinking I like the bloody woman," he said, as he fished about in a cupboard for teabags. "But you've seen the car she's lent me, and – well – I'm sure you understand."

"Screwing people for cash, eh? You fucking lawyer-tart from hell."

"It's in my blood," said Caelius, nodding and managing to smile for the first time that morning. "Sorry, but there it is."

Jez came running into the room. "I've got the message," he announced proudly, and handed over a scrap of paper. Catullus looked at it. "Come to Thirty-Eight Golden Quay," he read aloud. "At half past four. If problem, ring." He turned the paper over, looking for a number. There wasn't one. He read the message through again, then looked inquiringly at Jez. "So who's it from?"

"I told you, a man. On the telephone."

"What man?"

"I forgot to write it down."

"Oh, great." Catullus sighed and slapped the piece of paper down onto the table. Caelius reached for it. "Golden Quay is that development we were talking about last night. Crassus'. The one that got Cicero banged up."

"Oh, right. So who the hell wants to see me there?"

"Haven't the remotest. It's full of foreign banks and things."

"Well, that's a great help." Catullus turned back to Jez. "Look, think about this. Are you sure you can't remember who this man on the phone was? Sure he didn't say?"

"It's not my fault," said Jez sulkily. "It was my dad, he answered it."

"Well, did *he* take down a name?"

"No way, because when he picked the phone up he went all spacky and just dropped it, and that's why I picked it up. See?"

"No. Why did your father go spacky?"

"Because he's a spack," said Caelius before Jez could answer. "Look, what does it matter? Just go to whatever it is, Thirty-Eight Golden Quay, and find out that way. What's the problem?"

Catullus remembered his dream, and the severed skull he had lain next to the night before. "Out," he told Jez, who made a face, and had to be shooed away. Catullus slammed the door shut again, and turned back to face his friend.

"So – what's the problem?" Caelius asked a second time.

Catullus tried to marshal his thoughts. "I'm sure you'll think I'm being paranoid," he said after a pause, "but it's just that I got a bit spooked last night." He began to explain what had happened. Caelius looked interested, but also, when Catullus had finished talking, puzzled as well.

"Well, I'm not surprised you were spooked," he agreed, "but I don't see what it's got to do with you going to Golden Quay. You think there might be someone there waiting for you with an axe?"

Catullus wondered if he did. He shrugged. "Seems possible, I suppose."

"Doesn't follow," said Caelius. "Just because you see one person who had his face chopped off a few weeks ago, and another who had his face done up in the same way a few centuries ago, doesn't mean there's a connection. And even if there were, it doesn't mean that it's got anything to do with you."

"But don't you think it's odd, that it's only since we met Mr Varney that we've started being followed?"

"By whom?"

"Well – last night – I'm sure it was those two clowns who were talking to Vanessa, and then later I definitely saw Porter, the one who took us to that police station. It can't be coincidence."

"And you think, what, they're all hanging out at Thirty-Eight Golden Quay, waiting to bump you off?"

"You don't have to make it sound ridiculous."

"I do, because it is ridiculous. Why would any of them want to kill you?"

"Why would any of them want to kill Mr Varney?"

"Because he was a drunken old git. I'd like to have done it. But you haven't got anything remotely in common with him, so what is there to worry about?"

"No, I suppose. You're right. When you put it like that." Catullus nodded, and Caelius nodded back. He reached for some keys that had been left on the kitchen table, and tossed them over to Catullus. "Look, take the car. Go and find out who wants to see you at the mystery address, and set your mind at rest."

"Thanks." Catullus stared down at the keys. "You won't need them?"

"No. I was going to drive over and see my uncle in his nick, but I can do that tomorrow. It's hardly as though he'll be going anywhere."

"All right. Thanks."

"Not at all." Caelius picked up the tray and manoeuvred it onto his hip as he opened the door. "And get things in perspective," he whispered. "Just remember – even if you do meet an axeman – you'll still be having a better time than me."

Catullus trotted down what had once been a wharf, and was now the front of a shopping arcade. He was late, not that that bothered him particularly, but he supposed it was good all the same that he had an excuse. There had been a traffic jam. He had been stuck in it for twenty minutes without moving. Eventually, he had asked a lorry driver what the hold-up was. "Pickets," the lorry driver had replied. "Unions." He had advised Catullus to park his car and walk the rest of the way, which Catullus had done. At the picket line, he had been asked what he was doing, going to Golden Quay. "Haven't the faintest," Catullus had answered, but he had been allowed to pass through the barricades nonetheless. One of the pickets had laughed when Catullus had shown him the address written on Jez's note. He'd pointed with his finger down the wharf, and said it wasn't far.

Not quite true, Catullus thought. He paused, and leant against a lamp post. Offices stretched away behind him along the river front, white blocks of glass and steel, the shimmer of their reflection scarcely ruffled by waters which lay as sleek as anything mirrored in their own silver blue. Stillness was everywhere. The quiet, like the architecture's gleam, seemed chill despite the warmth of the sun. Catullus began to trot past the office fronts again. He felt like a fly crawling over a gleaming new fridge.

He passed Number Forty, a large tower, and then Thirty-Nine. He ran up the steps of the next building, and was about to push his way through the doors when he saw, to his bemusement, that he was trying to enter Number Thirty-Seven. Catullus stopped, to check that he had read the sign right. He had. So where the fuck was Thirty-Eight? He walked back to Thirty-Nine, inspected that building's sign as well, and was about to throw Jez's note away as a hoax when he noticed a small passageway, almost hidden behind a billboard advertising unlet office space. Catullus followed the passageway down a flight of steps, then through a stone arch that seemed to have been preserved from a different era. It probably had been, Catullus soon realised, as he made his way over uneven paving stones, and saw what had once obviously been a small factory ahead of him. Its walls were red brick and streaked with black, but in the shadows cast by the two vast structures on either side of him, Catullus found it hard to work out what might possibly lie inside.

"You're bloody late, aren't you?" he was asked the moment he'd walked through the doors. Catullus looked round in surprise. Voices seemed to be coming at him from everywhere. He was in a reception room, with slogan-crammed notice boards, and angry posters, and men in groups shouting loudly at each other. Although there was nothing in the room that didn't look dingy, its mood seemed charged with something violent and electric. After the marmoreal stillness of the river front outside, Catullus found the change overwhelming. He tried to work out who had been talking to him, and failed.

A hand fell on his shoulder. "You're late, aren't you?" the same voice asked him again, and when Catullus turned, he found that it belonged to a large, tungsten-haired man wearing a denim boiler-suit and a look of pious gloom. "Come with me," he ordered, staring reprovingly.

"Why, who are you? And what is this place, anyway?"

The man snorted wordlessly and began to move off. Catullus hurried after him, still asking questions, then suddenly snapping and insisting he be told. The man looked back at him with contempt. "All right, fuck you, then," said Catullus, and was about to turn when, to his horror, he found himself face to face with Lud and Pollo. He gawped at them, and Lud and Pollo stared silently back. Then one of them smiled, and muttered something under his breath, and they both pushed past Catullus and walked quickly on down the corridor. Catullus wondered whether to follow them, then remembered all the jokes Caelius had made about axemen. "Wait!" he shouted after the man in the boiler-suit. "Wait!" But his guide had already disappeared. Catullus ran down the corridor. There was a door that had been left open. He looked into the room that lay beyond it. The man in the boiler-suit was there, talking to a second man who had his back turned to the room and was looking out through the far window. Catullus walked in, and the man in the boiler-suit, hearing the noise, turned to face him. Then, more slowly, the second man turned round as well. Oh fuck, Catullus thought. It was Clodius.

He smiled. Without make-up, his features had lost their chiaroscuro, but there couldn't be any doubt, it was the same man Catullus had stared at while crossing that revelry-ploughed lake all those weeks before. Clodius offered his hand; as Catullus shook it, he wondered what the hell he was wanted for. He looked into Clodius' eyes to see if he could find any hint, but no, there was a pale glitter, nothing more. Catullus sat down, trying not to feel worried, unsuccessfully.

"Sorry the message I left you was a bit brief," Clodius said, leaning on the edge of his desk. Catullus nodded his head, tried to say something, then stammered and laughed. Clodius watched him, smiling quietly. "Good of you to come, anyway," he said, after a pause. "Got held up by our reception committee, did you?"

"The pickets?" Catullus nodded. "Yes. A bit."

"They're good lads. No trouble from them?"

"No, they were very helpful."

"Good. Because contrary to what you'll read in some sections of the press, everyone here knows that you don't fight for your rights by giving innocent people trouble. We leave that to our friends in the government and police."

Catullus smiled politely, and this time was careful not to gabble. "I was wondering," he said, "about that picket. Because I thought that all the strikes had been called off."

"They have been. That's not a strike out there. That's a protest."

"There's a difference?"

"Of course. You strike if you have a job. You protest if you haven't."

"Interesting semantics."

"Oh, absolutely. You have to have your semantics sorted out in this struggle, you see. You meet fire with fire. You meet force with force. And whatever happens, you have *got* to meet slippery lawyers' bullshit with some thick, stinking bullshit of your own." He leant across to Catullus, and took him by the arm. "Look, over here." He pointed towards a window, and pulled Catullus across to it. "Look out, tell me what you see."

Catullus stared. He couldn't see anything, except for the dark glass of the building opposite. He described it.

"Inhuman looking, don't you think?" said Clodius, nodding. "And you know what? That's exactly what it is. Inhuman. Full of foreign ants you never even see. Infesting the place." Clodius snapped his fingers. "Clear them out, that's what I want to do, and their nests with them. That's what our pickets are for. I'm not breaking any agreement I've made with the Government, because there aren't any jobs left here for people to strike over. But I never made any agreement not to protest for people who've seen their whole community scrubbed off the map. Never. Do you see? It's important you do. Because this is where you are about to come in."

Catullus must have looked startled, because Clodius laughed and nodded to his aide. "You see? Absolute disbelief, at the very idea he might have a part to play." He laughed again, and then suddenly clenched his fist in Catullus' face. "You think I'm joking?"

Catullus stared back. The glint in Clodius' eyes had become a slow burning fire, and his face, so mobile just a few seconds before, was now frozen pinched and white. Catullus shook his head. "No. I don't think you're joking." Clodius smiled back bleakly, and clenched his fist so that the knuckles gleamed. "Good," he said slowly, "good." He rubbed his knuckles gently over Catullus' cheek. "It's important, you see, that you understand."

"Understand what?"

"That in a fight you've got to use your fists." Slowly, Clodius stretched out his fingers. He looked at his palm. "But also, of course, that fists aren't the only way of fighting. You do see?"

Catullus shrugged desperately. "I suppose so."

"No, you don't. Well, you're less intelligent than I'd hoped."

Clodius ran his hands through his hair, then marched briskly away from Catullus and sat down with his feet up on his desk. "What do people say about me?" he asked suddenly. "Go on, don't be nervous."

"Well," said Catullus, bemused by the rapid shifts in mood and topic. "You're well known..."

"No," shouted Clodius, interrupting him, "be rude. Tell me about the shit they write in the newspapers."

"They say..."

"That I'm a thug? That I'm a mindless bully?"

"Yes, that's the drift, I suppose." Catullus paused. "Actually, if you really want to know, they say you're an absolute cunt." He shrugged. "Sorry."

Clodius breathed in heavily. He ran his hands over his face, then stared up again. "In a country where the very institutions are a form of violence, do you think that people who are oppressed by them should have the right to use violence back? If it's the only way?"

"That's an old question. Sorry. I try and avoid philosophy unless I absolutely have to."

"Yes. And so do I." Clodius smiled and leant forward. "Listen. You must be an intelligent person or else my sister wouldn't be interested in you. Try and take in what I'm about to say. Get that establishment fog out of your brain." Catullus opened his mouth, but Clodius silenced him by standing up and wagging a finger. "Sssh," he whispered. "Just listen." He began to prowl up and down the room, stalking Catullus in his chair. "Did you know," he asked suddenly, "that when a corpse rots, there's a gas released? It's the same with government. A political order starts to decay, but there's still power in the air. It never goes. It's a law of physics. As it disperses from one body, so must it transfer to another. And Rome, well, even now – that's one hell of a corpse." His voice hardened over with irony. "Patrician, world-conquering Rome. There's several centuries worth of plunder and brutalization stored up there. But who's it going to go to, do you think, all this legacy of power? Or rather, who's going to grab it? Because that's how you get hold of your corpse gas, you see. You bottle it up as it escapes, and you keep it to yourself, and you don't let other people even near it. And if they try, you hurt them till they stop. And that's what's going on now. Funeral games." Clodius paused. "You look shocked. You haven't heard this before?"

"No, no, that's not it." Catullus shook his head. He couldn't tell Clodius, of course, but he had indeed heard it all before, from Cicero, Clodius' mortal opposite. That was the shock, he supposed – both men convinced of the other's quackery, and disagreeing over cures, to be sure, but both also sharing the one brutal diagnosis. He asked Clodius to carry on.

Clodius nodded. "Who is it we want to hurt, and who wants to hurt us? The Government? No. Not any longer. What can it do? It's too old, too tired, dying on its feet. The only able man they had was that crook Cicero, and fortunately for the safety of the nation he's now locked away – you probably heard?" Clodius laughed with pleasure. "At least now, he's with criminals who have been properly convicted. Sadly, his erstwhile colleagues haven't joined him yet. And even the ones who aren't crooked are rotten in other ways. My brother-in-law, Metellus, for instance. Minister of Finance, and he's got a tumour in the brain. He'll be dead within the year. The cancer cells will spread, and they'll leave him spongiform." Clodius shrugged expansively. "Almost seems too perfect, doesn't it, as a metaphor? Except that it's more than just a metaphor, of course, because the fact that any government is prepared to keep on a near-corpse with a tumour just emphasises the failure of its own collective store of grey cells. Don't you think?"

"Yes. If it's true."

"It is."

"Clodia's husband? Yes, she said he was ill."

Clodius' face suddenly whitened with rage. "The things I tell you don't require my sister to confirm them," he hissed. He bent down and stared into Catullus' face. "Just listen. Metellus is dying. The Government is dying. You don't waste your breath fighting things that are terminally ill. All right? Got that?"

"Yes." Catullus nodded back at Clodius' face. "Okay. And so that's why you called off the strikes, is it?"

Clodius shrugged. "If you like. The benefits of attacking the Government had to be balanced against the long-term economic future that we're going to be inheriting from them. They've screwed it up quite enough on their own without any extra help from us. And anyway, you don't demolish your own inheritance."

"So why the pickets?"

"Because we are not relaxing our struggle, we are simply re-directing it."

"Against Crassus?"

"Just – wait." Clodius held up a hand. "Against two targets. Both dangerous. Both biding their time, both waiting with their flasks to bottle up that corpse gas. And so – irony of ironies – the government and myself find that we are threatened by the same enemies. Only, of course, because I'm cleverer, I can recognise them both, while the Government thinks that one of its enemies is actually its friend. Which suits me, of course."

"They're all hyenas, you see, the ruling classes," the aide muttered. "Cracking the bones of the poor. Or is it jackals?"

"Caesar's no jackal, he's far more dangerous, he's a killer. Even the government, tumour-brained or not, can see that. He's the enemy Pompey knows he has." Clodius paused and gazed into space. He winced at something Catullus couldn't see. "Caesar," Clodius murmured to himself. "Caesar." He smiled humourlessly, and turned his head to stare back at Catullus. "If the papers had wanted a genuine thug, they'd have looked to Caesar. But they're too cowed and stupid. They either won't or can't see what he's up to. That great confederation he's got, and all that talk about common destinies and free trade – it's gangster talk. He's just waiting to pounce. Don't be under any illusions, Caesar will do anything. When he wanted to get rid of me, he got his own wife to pretend she'd been raped. His own wife. And then when the prosecution was thrown out of court, he divorced her. If he's willing to behave like that with his own family, you can imagine how he's going to treat Pompey and all the other incompetents who think they're still in power over here. Look at Caesar's nose. Look how big it is. Do you think he can't smell corpse gas with a nose like that?"

Clodius paused to wipe his brow, and as he did so, Catullus saw that his eyes were glittering with excitement. "I don't want to frighten you," he said. "We'll keep Caesar at bay, don't you worry." He paused again. "But there was a second threat I mentioned – a second snooper round the Roman corpse – a second monster sniffing out the gas." Clodius leant forward. "And this is where you come in, you see. This is your chance. We need you. What do you say? You can do something, something that will help." He took Catullus by the arm. "I'll ask you again. What do you say?"

"I don't know," said Catullus. Clodius' fingers were pinching now. "How can I say when you won't tell me what it is that you want me to do?"

Clodius nodded, and released Catullus' arm. He paced over to the window, and for a while chose not to speak again. "You were right," he said at last, not looking round. "The second threat we all face is from Crassus. Do you know him?"

"No."

Clodius laughed. "He looks like what he is. A slug – a white slug. Tiny, tiny eyes, and a belly full of slime. It's hard to think of him as a person at all. I always imagine him as a mass of white flesh wedged into the top floor of a building like that." Clodius gestured at the tower opposite. "He has to eat people's livelihoods and futures, just to keep him going, and then he shits it all out, and lies in it."

"So let me guess – you don't like him?"

"No." Clodius shook his head. "No, I don't like him at all. There's nothing there. Cicero's got brains, and Caesar's got charisma, but all Crassus has got is money. And what's money? The sum of people who have been screwed." He walked back to his desk and picked up a jacket. "Come with me," he said, taking Catullus by the arm and leading him over to a door on the far side of the room. He opened it and ushered Catullus out. "I want to show you something."

They were in the open, at the top of a flight of old stone steps that ran down the side of the building to a road below. "This is our headquarters here, you probably guessed," said Clodius. He pointed down the road to a brick wall. "You see that? That marks the limit of our property. And then you see beyond? All Crassus', as far as you can see, lock, stock and barrel – there isn't a tiny pebble of it that isn't his. Have a look, tell me what you think."

Catullus stared. More buildings, more cubes of glass, of air and sky, most finished, some not, stretching away. As before, a terrible stillness. The gleaming black roads were empty; cranes stood motionless; only smoke, rising from where Catullus guessed the picket line was, stained a purity which otherwise seemed like death. Undone, he thought, remembering the Alexandrian poet – the vision is fled, our daylight no longer touches it. "A necropolis," he said at last, "full of empty tombs."

"Really? You think so?" In sudden excitement, Clodius took Catullus by the hand and began to pull him down the steps. "That's what it is, of course. You know what lies out there, under all that steel? Homes and memories. Destroy them, and you're half way there to destroying the people who owned them. So yes, you're right, it is a necropolis! And that's what it's going to stay. A place of the dead. A place where nothing living ever comes back."

Clodius pulled Catullus on. "Look, you see." He pointed out through his headquarter's gates. A vast roundabout, just outside, lay abandoned and half-finished. "That's the main traffic junction for the whole of Golden Quay," said Clodius, almost choking on his delight. "They'll never complete it. We're in the way, you see." He gazed happily at a digger, already rusting where it had been left on a bank, then turned to walk back towards his factory. "They never realised that we'd been buying too. It never crossed their minds. So you can imagine their shock. They started building their road, and then we turned up, and announced that the factory was our new HQ, and therefore definitely not for sale. It left them feeling, well – pissed off."

Clodius turned suddenly, and grabbed Catullus by his arms. "I like pissing Crassus off," he breathed, the laughter freezing out of his face. "I like to piss Crassus off any way I can. Any way at all." He nodded, then put an arm round Catullus' shoulders and began to lead him back up the flight of steps. "Do you know something, though?" he whispered softly into Catullus' ear. "It's not just me who's pissing Crassus off. Did you know, for instance, that right at this moment, he's not overwhelmingly turned on by you?"

"Me?"

Clodius nodded slowly, then made a tutting sound. "You're digging, I think, on a site further down the Tiber, on a site rich with archaeological potential? You're digging slowly, and with a no doubt painstaking concern for detail? And you are comforted, I am sure, by the knowledge that it is easier for a property developer to uproot living communities than it is to sweep aside long dead ruins? Am I right?"

Catullus shrugged. "If you choose to put it like that."

"Oh, I do." Clodius smiled, and brushing Catullus free, leant for a moment against his office door. "And it leads me to hope for just one thing."

"Which is?"

"That you enjoy pissing off capitalists even half as much as I do. Because if you don't – well – that would be a shame." He glanced at Catullus. "I hate seeing people waste their opportunities." He held the door open. "Come on."

Inside, everything had become bedlam. The office seemed to have filled to bursting point with talking people, and no sooner had Clodius walked in than he found himself almost submerged by them. "Shut up!" he bellowed at the clamour. "Norris, get them to shut up!" People began to shush, and an uneasy silence fell at last. Clodius pushed his way through to his desk, then turned and nodded impatiently at his aide.

"What's going on? What's this all about?"

"Trouble with the pickets," said the aide, Norris. The corners of his mouth twitched briefly, then plunged back downwards. "Some of the lads have set a lorry on fire."

"The idiots. I told them not to start trouble. Is it serious?"

Norris agreed that yes, it probably was, and again, the corners of his mouth twitched upwards from the jowls. Clodius swore violently. "We can't have trouble out there, we can't afford it." He thought for a couple of seconds, then he bellowed at everyone to get out of his room. Norris lagged behind.

"What I say is, if some of the lads want to burn a lorry or two, then what's wrong with that?"

"Everything," said Clodius. He glanced at Catullus. "Everything."

Norris stared back at him, and then nodded his head imperceptibly. "You'll need to get a move on, though. It's one of your lads from the army who started it. They won't listen to me."

"Then you'd better make them," Clodius whispered palely. "And quick. Do you understand?"

Norris nodded again. He left, and Clodius slammed the door shut after him, leaning against it, breathing in quickly. "You can't blame them," he said, looking across at Catullus. "Times are so hard. Of course you're impatient when you think your family's going to starve." He walked quickly back towards his desk and started to search through piles of paper. "But there are more ways of playing this than just setting lorries on fire. Yes, here we are." He waved a stapled sheaf of papers in the air. "Because once again, you see, the Trojans have their part to play."

"The Trojans?"

Clodius nodded, and held the papers up again. "These are the minutes from one of Crassus' board meetings. Don't ask me how I got them." He glanced at the front page. "And would you believe it? It turns out that Crassus doesn't much care for archaeology. According to these papers, he'd much rather buy up your site and use it for industrial processing."

Catullus shrugged. "I suppose then at least it might provide some jobs."

"Was that a facetious comment, or merely a stupid one?" Clodius stared at him coldly. "I've told you. Get it into your head. We're playing a long term game here. We're going to squeeze Crassus round the neck until his bowels explode."

"Yes. Sorry, of course we are."

Clodius stared at him, his eyes narrowed. "Listen," he whispered, after what seemed to Catullus an eternity of silence. Clodius picked up a second sheaf of papers. "You and I, we both have an interest in keeping that site free of bulldozers. I'm going to be sending a few people, not many, just to keep an eye on things. All right? Now, it's your job to stop your boss panicking about them. If you hear any news, anything that might be of interest, you're to let them know. Otherwise, just keep on digging, and find lots and lots of priceless artefacts. All right? Think you'll be able to cope with that?"

"That's all I've got to do?"

"Yes. For now. Just keep us posted."

Catullus breathed out, then laughed. So that was it. Saving lost ruins and his own job, they were causes he would happily fight for. He nodded at Clodius. The mesh of politics, which he'd feared had been tightening around his throat, hung suddenly slack and loose again.

Clodius picked up a cap, then walked to the door. "Come with me, and I'll see you get through to your car." He ushered Catullus out into the passage. "Tell me what you've found so far," he asked. "Something from the Civil War, is that right?"

Catullus nodded, and described the excavations. To his surprise, Clodius seemed genuinely interested.

"My ancestor, you know, he fought with Marius. Claudius Pulcher."

Of course. Mr Varney's book, with the picture of the battlements. Catullus remembered his nightmare, and how Mr Varney had talked about Clodius too, before stretching for the bottle edge and slicing open his face.

"I admire the men who fought in the Civil War." Clodius had reached the water front. He stopped and looked behind him, up at the glass and steel. "The old republic men, they took on an establishment that hid its rottenness with glitter. And kicked it over. It must have taken courage, being the first to do that. " He started walking again. "No, Claudius Pulcher is one of the few ancestors I'm not ashamed of. Did you know that we'd found his papers recently, in one of the family vaults?"

"Really? Are they published yet?"

"No, we've got someone working on them at the moment. She's very good, I'm told."

"Anything interesting in them?"

Clodius thought, then smiled. "Yes. It's quite a coincidence, actually. Perhaps I should tell you."

"Why, what is it?"

"There was a statue, I think, someone found on your site?"

Catullus felt his spine turn cold. "Yes."

"A man, with an eagle's head? Sosos something."

"Sesostris," said Catullus slowly. "Aetos, the eagle."

"Yes, that's right. My ancestor turns out to have been one of his acolytes. Which is strange, apparently, since the god was Circassian. The woman who's studying the papers was rather surprised."

"I bet she was." Catullus shut his eyes. The image of Mr Varney, face bubbling on the glass shard's slice, was waiting for him. He rubbed frantically at his eyeballs. "Any clue as to why Claudius had been a part of this cult?" he asked, his voice sounding distant and strange in his ears.

"Not really. We didn't talk about it for long. She only mentioned it because she knew I'd been in Circassia."

"During the war."

Clodius stared at him. "Yes," he said coldly. "During the war."

"Your sister mentioned that you had a statue of Sesostris on your desk." Catullus paused. "I didn't see it there today."

Again, Clodius stared at him, and his eyes had frozen to ice. "My sister should learn to watch what she says," he whispered slowly. "The statue is lost." Then Clodius turned his back, and began to hurry again. Catullus, almost running to keep up with him, noticed that a fresh column of smoke had begun to plume in the distance. He couldn't see Clodius' face, but he doubted that it was wise to ask any further questions. So Clodius didn't like talking about what he'd done in Circassia, Catullus thought. Nor about Sesostris. He wondered why.

Suddenly, there was an explosion. Clodius started to run. There was a second explosion, and then another, and above the echo Catullus heard screams and shouting. He could see people running towards them. Clodius hurried on, not pausing until he had reached the road his pickets had been blocking; Catullus, lagging behind, watched him as he stopped and looked around, then disappeared into clouds of black smoke. Catullus followed him. The pickets were still there, he could see now, milling around uneasily behind their barricades, and further down the road, at the head of a long line of traffic, lay the gutted carcasses of two large lorries. There was another explosion, and one of the lorries' cabs disintegrated completely. Catullus watched as flames began to lick across the wreckage. Far off in the distance, sirens began to wail. Otherwise, everything seemed suddenly deathly quiet. Catullus could hear the smoke now, guttering upwards into the sky.

"Who did this?" Clodius' voice. Catullus looked round. There was a crowd gathering in a circle, and Clodius, standing on one of the barricades, was in the middle of it.

"Who did this?" he asked again. Silence. Clodius stared behind him, at the smoking wrecks of the lorries. "Was anyone killed?"

Still silence. Then someone spoke. "No. They got out." "They were going to force the barricade," a second voice said. "It wasn't the pickets who shot at the lorries, anyway," the first voice added. "You don't shoot at men just for doing their jobs."

"So who did shoot?" Clodius asked again. He waited, then screamed at the top of his voice. "Who did this?" He saw Norris. "Who did it? Tell me."

Norris pointed. Hundreds of heads turned. Squatting behind a battered oil canister and with a gun still cradled next to his chest, Pollo was staring into the far distance. Lud was beside him, looking down intently at the ground. Neither of them even glanced at Clodius. Neither of them spoke. Then Pollo began to whistle, and Catullus recognised the tune he had first heard at the ball by the lake.

Clodius leapt down from the barricade. He sprinted over to the canister, kicked it, and sent it rolling noisily across the tarmac. He stared down at Pollo, who carried on whistling, until winded by a kick into the pit of his stomach. As Pollo lay gasping in the dirt, Clodius reached down for his throat and yanked him to his feet. The two men stared at each other, and Clodius began to gouge his fingers deep into Pollo's cheeks. "Why did you do it?" he asked after a few seconds. "Why did you fire at the lorries?" Still Pollo didn't speak. Clodius' fingers gouged deeper and deeper. Pollo groaned, and Clodius released his grip.

"You wanted it done, didn't you?" Pollo whispered.

"No," Clodius hissed back. "No," he said again louder, "we didn't want it done. We don't use violence."

Pollo began to laugh. "*We* don't use violence, *we* don't use violence. How the fuck can you get away with saying that?"

Clodius' eyes narrowed, and his fingers gouged deep again. "Because it's the truth," he said at last. "You'd better understand that. You and everyone."

"Fuck you." Pollo spat. "Like it's the truth you didn't want those lorries shot, but they still got shot. Like it's the truth you don't want all sorts of shit to happen, but it still happens." He twisted his head free from Clodius' grip, and caught sight of Catullus, who had been standing just beside him. Pollo laughed, even more hysterically than before. "Yeah, and it's the truth you didn't want him followed so your sister could go and fuck him, but he still got followed. And your sister still got fucked. Fucked like some slag."

The blood left Clodius' face. He shook. Then he smashed Pollo on the jaw with his fist. As Pollo staggered, Clodius smashed him again, then brought his knee up into Pollo's stomach. Pollo fell with a thud onto the tarmac, and Clodius kicked him, three or four times, and finally turned, leaving Pollo whimpering in the gutter. "Get back onto the picket line," he shouted at everyone. "When the police come, just keep your mouths shut. There'll be nothing they can do."

The pickets roared back a great shout of approval, waving clenched fists in the air as they began to return to the barricades. Clodius clenched his own fist. He called out a slogan, and the pickets answered back, chanting slogans of their own. Clodius watched them, then turned back to stare down at Pollo. Lud was holding his companion, using a handkerchief to dab at the blood flowing from Pollo's nose. Clodius bent down and took out his own handkerchief. He wiped the sweat from Pollo's brow, then lowered his face until the two men were once again staring eyeball to eyeball. "Listen," Clodius whispered, "you mention my sister again like that and I am going to kill you."

Pollo didn't say anything, just stared back up into Clodius' face.

"Don't push things too far, Pollo. We're not in Circassia now." Clodius stood up and tapped Pollo's chest with the tip of his foot. "You watch it. You know what happens to people who push things too far. Ask your friend. They end up with their faces sliced off." He turned and walked away.

As he walked, he heard someone behind him running fast in the opposite direction. He didn't look round. If he had done, he would have seen Catullus, who had heard everything, and was now flat out, trying to get back to his car.

XI

MONA

Catullus sat listening to the sound of his own heart. He had driven miles now, from Golden Quay to the site where he worked, a long way, but still his insides felt soupy, and bloody hell, he thought – why not, why the fuck not? He'd been through enough. There had been Clodius and the clowns, the flight from the picket line, the smoke, and the police cars, and the eerily empty streets, and even now, there in the car with him, wrapped up in paper somewhere in the boot, was the small black statue of Sesostris Aetos. Catullus twisted round and fumbled behind his seat. There it was, in its paper packing, where he had left it the day before. He picked it up, and placed it on his lap. So innocent, it looked. And maybe it was, maybe it was. But fumbling with the edge of its paper wrapping, Catullus felt like a child again, daring himself to stare at something terrifying. Gingerly, he began to strip the paper away.

The curved black beak gleamed up at him. As before, when he had been shown the statue by Doctor Gower, Catullus felt an iciness in his stomach which made his brain feel sick. He swallowed, and tried to clear his mind. Think, think, he told himself. Marius' eagle-god; the corpse found later floating faceless in the Tiber. A skeleton, faceless, in a Civil War cellar. A few weeks ago, Mr Varney, faceless. And now, by chance, Clodius overheard, threatening Pollo with a slice to his skull. "We're not in Circassia now" – that was what he had said, but why? Was there a connection between Circassia and Clodius' threat? Catullus stared at Sesostris Aetos again. A Circassian god. Worshipped by Claudius, the friend of Marius, and Clodius' ancestor. What had the cult of Sesostris involved? Semi-decapitation perhaps? Catullus ran his finger over the statue's beak. It would be easy to find out. Doctor Gower's library was kept in a Portakabin rented on the site of the dig. Catullus felt in his pocket. Yes, his keys were still there. He wound down his window and stared out at the rubbish tip from which the statue on his lap had come, and beneath which, perhaps, lay Circassian stones. Catullus could just glimpse his boss's Portakabin, perched on a far ridge like some ark on a flood.

He stuffed the statuette into the pocket of his coat. Then he climbed out of the car and left the pavement, stumbling across the rubbish tip. As he reached the Portakabin, rain began to fall. "Open, you bastard," Catullus swore, as the key stuck, and the rain fell ever heavier and more cold. Why was it always so vile here, he asked himself, why hadn't the Trojans followed the sun? The key turned and Catullus hurried in, slamming the door behind him. He listened to his heart. Its valves were still working overtime. The noise synchronised with the pounding of the rain on the roof. He took out the statue, and placed it on a shelf by the door, its face against the wall, so that its eyes and the curve of its beak were obscured.

Then Catullus looked around. Books were stacked everywhere, but he knew exactly the section he wanted. He ran his eye over the titles on the spines. There it was: *The Cult of the Eagle in Ancient Circassia*. By H. L. Gower. He took it out, and opened the first page. There was a photograph of a marble carving – an eagle-man, Sesostris presumably, brandishing a sword. Catullus sat down and began to read.

The book was hard going. There were large chunks of a script that Catullus didn't even recognise, and the passages that he could read through seemed too esoteric to be worth the effort. Catullus began to skim through chapters, half frustrated, half relieved, and was about to put the book aside when suddenly he saw a photograph that froze him where he sat. There was a skeleton, half embedded in a floor. Catullus peered at the skull – no face. A caption described the skeleton as the remains of a ritual victim, found in the ruins of an excavated temple, one of several unearthed in the immediate vicinity. A note gave a page reference. Catullus breathed in heavily, then looked the number up.

There was a chapter heading, 'Sacrifice and the Sesostris cult – the evidence from archaeology'. Sacrifice, Catullus thought. Sacrifice? He read on. "Themes of violence and love, then, were always implicit in the cult," the chapter began. "The figure of Sesostris himself, who is both warrior and civiliser, destroyer and creator, man and woman, human and divine, makes this clear. Even before the eagle becomes one with the king, her gifts are shown to bring both peace and violence in their wake. In the most ancient versions of the legend, this tension between the god's two functions is focused in the idea of dance. Dance is what the eagle first teaches humanity in order to reveal the potential beauty of civilisation; but on her second visit to the world, it is what enrages the townspeople, and almost results in her physical dismemberment. There is, of course, no suggestion that the eagle is actually killed; it is the point of the orthodox legend that she is rescued by the king with which she then becomes fused. Nor is there any suggestion that the two halves of the god resulting from this union are explicitly contradictory; the eagle-king is great precisely because his powers to civilise are an expression of those same powers that win him military prowess. How then are we to explain the Greek mythographers, who described Sesostris Aetos as a god in which opposites were at war with themselves, and to whom, they claimed, human sacrifices were made? This sounds nothing like the god the Circassians wrote about and worshipped. Were the mytho-graphers writing propaganda, wilfully distorting evidence they had not understood? Or were they perhaps reporting on a variation of the cult, a variation that did indeed practise human sacrifice? Up until now, the evidence either way has been scanty to the point of non-existence, and historians, not surprisingly, have preferred to conclude that the Greeks were fabricating their reports. Dramatic new archaeological finds, however, now suggest the opposite. Before examining this new evidence, it is worth reminding ourselves of what exactly it was the Greeks did claim.

"The fullest surviving report comes in the *Histories* of Diodorus Siculus. 'In the remotest part of Circassia', he writes, 'is a temple dedicated to a god worshipped by all the Circassians. He is called Sesostris, also known by the Egyptians as Serapis, and he has for his head the eagle of the god known by the Greeks as Zeus. The people who live around this temple claim many strange legends for themselves. They say it was in their temple that civilisation was first given to mankind. They claim, like the Jews, that they are the favourites of the gods, but also, like many of the people of the West, that they are descended from Trojans who fled the sack of their city. Whether this is true, I do not know, but it is what the Circassians say. They also have no kings, because long ago they had been ruled by Sesostris, but when he returned to heaven, the Circassians believed it would be impiety to replace a god with a man. To this end, they claim that all men are equal, and will accept no one who tries to be the master of his fellows. It is for this reason that the Circassians who live by the temple say that they are the most civilised of men.

"'Yet it is the practice of these Circassians to offer human sacrifices to their god, a thing that the Greeks certainly have never done. The Circassians do not sacrifice living men willingly, nor often, but will do it if the omens demand it, as a means of purifying their land. For the Circassians say that their god is both good and evil, light and dark, and can never be at peace with himself. When he ruled as their king, he gave the Circassians peace and then war, and then peace again; now that he has left them, the whole universe is witness to the struggle the god must have with himself, in a terrible conflict that will never end. Yet there are moments when the powers of light are particularly beset, and this is the time, so the priests say, when darkness must be appeased by the sacrifice of men.

"'This is the practice that the Circassians follow when they sense such a moment to be upon them. A priest dances on a sacred spot. This is to invoke the spirit of the eagle who danced, the Circassians say, when she first brought down the gifts of culture from heaven. The next man to cross that spot is then killed, and his face -'" Catullus stopped reading. He gripped the page he was holding, and knew that his face must have turned as white as his knuckles. He read the sentence again, but even before he had finished it, he knew what it was that the priests had done to their victim's skull. "'The next man to cross that spot is then killed, and his face is sliced off with a sword.'" So – he had been right. Catullus patted his hand on his thumping heart, and became aware of the rain again, bulleting down onto the roof above him. He glanced up nervously at the icon of Sesostris, then read on. "'His face is removed to indicate the slicing away of the eagle's head, and with it, the principle of light. The corpse is then offered to the principle of darkness, and is considered to be unclean. This sacrifice is made again two further times, on sites carefully chosen according to sacred calculations, and which are understood only by the priests who make them. The fourth offering is not chosen by lot. Instead, the priests choose the man who is the most capable of doing good to the state, and the most capable of doing evil, for it is a principle of the Circassians that the greatest men are also the most dangerous. The chosen victim is killed, and again his face is sliced off. He is then buried with great splendour, and the Circassians worship him as a hero, for it is believed that by dying, he has glutted the taste of darkness for more blood.

"'One ritual only remains to be fulfilled, before the age of light can be restored, and with it justice and harmony and peace. Although all Circassians share responsibility for the bloodshed, one from amongst them is chosen to accept the guilt. He too is then put to death, and the Circassians rejoice, hoping that the eagle will return to them. And I know what I write to be the truth, for I have been to the temple and seen the graves of men who had been the sacrifices. And if anyone should still doubt me, I challenge him to go, and see what I have seen.'"

Catullus breathed in very deep. Was it possible, really possible, that Mr Varney's death could have had some link with such a strange and long distant ritual, a ritual that might anyway never even have existed? And if it was possible, then how and why had Sesostris reappeared in Rome? Catullus thought again about what he had heard earlier that evening, on the picket line at Golden Quay. Had Clodius talked about slicing faces off because he had come across some remnant of the cult still alive in Circassia? Catullus stared down at Doctor Gower's paper, and tried to think. The chapter he'd been reading, hadn't it mentioned a temple, just uncovered, seeming to corroborate Diodorus' claims? That, surely, must have been in Circassia. Catullus looked down at the page, and found his place.

It was not just a temple that had been found, Catullus read, but an entire hill town, the ancient fort of Dumutsi-Bau. It was, as Diodorus had described it, "in the remotest part of Circassia," and had been left ruined and virtually untouched for centuries. In a series of cellars, skeletons had been found, the bones built into the floor and the skulls half sliced. On the walls, carvings had been distinguished, "typical," so Doctor Gower described them, "of contemporary Circassian artwork, and particularly of the artwork associated with the cult of Sesostris elsewhere in the region." There was a photograph of one of the carvings; it illustrated a dancing man, but otherwise, Catullus was relieved to notice, had nothing in common with the crude line-carving he had seen in the nightclub cellar. "It seems hard to resist the conclusion," Doctor Gower summarised, "that Diodorus' account of the Sesostris cult was based on fact and, in all likelihood, personal observation. Other Greek historians who wrote on the subject all seem to have derived their information from Diodorus, and there are no other known sources; it therefore seems likely that the present excavations at the site of ancient Dumutsi-Bau represent the only realistic chance we have of increasing our knowledge of the cult that once flourished there. If further discoveries are not made in the future, it seems improbable that we shall ever know from where the rituals came; nor why and how they then disappeared."

Catullus closed the book, and put it back carefully with the others on the shelf. So – what was he going to do now? He bowed his head and rested it against one of the Portakabin windows. Outside, the rain was falling as heavily as ever, swept by the wind in great gusts across the wasteland. Catullus could see the mausoleum they had begun to unearth, and the tape strung up round it, flapping in the gale; how strange, he thought, the conjunctions of past and present, the networks of coincidence that seemed to run through time, connecting, impinging, at certain places, certain points... An eddy of rain blotted the window, and with it Catullus' whole process of thought. He felt suddenly very cold. He had to get away. The evening outside was growing darker by the minute.

He stood at the top of the Portakabin steps. He felt like a swimmer about to dive. He ran, but after a minute he was wet through, and so he slowed down and began to walk. He had reached the pavement when suddenly the thought of everything he had seen and read struck him with a feeling of unbearable horror, so that he felt overwhelmed by it, and began to imagine that there *was* something walking up behind him. He walked faster, then began to trot. There *was* something! Should he run? No, he was being ridiculous. Of course there was nothing there. Then he felt something touch him, lightly, on the back.

He spun round.

"It's me."

Mona. Catullus breathed in deeply, then laughed. He reached out to hug her, to hold her tight.

Mona smiled at him. "Did I frighten you?"

"No, it's just – well – I didn't think anyone else would be out here in this."

"I love the rain." Mona pirouetted, then ran her hands through her hair. "Doesn't it make you feel beautiful?"

"Not me, no. I can't get away with it." But Mona could. Catullus watched her. He suddenly realised that his fright had left him a lot of energy, tingling in his muscles, waiting to be used. Mona's short dress was so soaked through that it clung to her.

"Do you want to come back to my place?" she asked suddenly.

"Really?" Catullus discovered that he did, desperately. He wanted pleasure, contact, an experience of joy – anything that might untrammel lowering circumstance, restore him to himself.

"Please." Mona laughed, and started dancing again. "I thought you'd come back with me last night, but I lost you, and I had nothing to do. So you owe me."

"You don't want to be with Boot?"

"No. We had a row. She's gone back to stay with her parents." Mona took Catullus by the hand, and started to lead him on down the street. She looked up at him shyly. "I think she fancies you."

"Boot?" How odd – that was what Caelius had thought too. "Surely not?"

"Yes, I think so. You see, that's what we were talking about. When we had our row."

"But I thought – you know – she – you..."

Mona stared at him. "Yes. She does. But I think she loves you too."

"How do you know?"

"Because she's upset. She takes things too seriously. She's not like me."

"Because you don't give a fuck?"

Mona glanced up at him again, and started to giggle. She pressed his hand tightly. "I don't care about anything like that. I just like being happy."

She led him down a side street. Catullus pointed back at the car and offered to drive, but Mona shook her head. There was no need, she said, she only lived a few minutes away. And so Catullus followed where she led, and they walked on down the street. If there had been anyone watching, back on the main road, he would have soon seen them swallowed by the unlit night rain, fade and then vanish altogether.

The next afternoon, when he arrived back home, Catullus found that Caelius had been waiting for him, and was in a vile mood.

"I very generously lend you my car, out of the goodness of my soul, and not only do you leave it parked in the middle of a fucking riot, but you then also fail to bring it back until three o'clock the next day. What the hell have you been up to?"

"I had to go to the site."

"Oh yes? Why?"

"None of your business. Look, I've said I'm sorry. Was Camilla annoyed?"

"Bugger Camilla, what about me?"

"Sorry, what about you?"

"You knew I wanted to go and visit Cicero today."

"Oh, yes, sorry. I forgot."

"You think they build prisons that are all nicely linked up to the public transport system, do you, just in case any of the lags want to pop out shopping? Well they don't, they build them miles from fucking anywhere."

Catullus paused. "You managed to see Cicero, then?"

"Yes, but that's hardly the point."

"Was he all right?"

"Yes," said Caelius decisively, "he was, actually. He was very pleased about the riot. He'd been up all night listening to the radio reports."

"Really? What happened?"

"In the riot? Not a lot, as far as I could see. You ran away, the police turned up, they had a chat with Clodius, and then they pissed off as well. But Cicero was in clover. I couldn't stop him giggling."

"Why?"

"I don't know. As I said, he just kept on giggling. About the only thing I got out of him was that he wanted you to write a report, about all the things you told him that evening when we went round to see him. You know, about the ball and everything. I told him you were hardly in a position to refuse."

"Why?"

"Going off with my car, not bringing it back, that sort of thing. In the circumstances, I felt you owed me a favour."

Catullus thought. It didn't seem particularly clever, promising to report things to Clodius one day, then writing out reports for Cicero the next. "When does he want it by?" he asked.

"Soon as possible. I told him you'd write it tonight."

"And supposing I've got better things to do?"

"Have you?"

"No."

"Well then, be off with you. Go and get stuck in to it at once."

Catullus sat silent. He remembered his terror of the day before. If there were strange processes threatening him, he thought, perhaps it might help him to transcribe his memories and fears, perhaps the written word might even kill them off. "All right," he agreed. "I'll get it to you by tomorrow morning. But, please, just for now, I've had a fuck of a weekend. No more hassle. Caelius – no."

He left the kitchen, sloping into his room and lying down, to rest and think. Jez had been working again with the paint brush, he noticed. A large swathe of the river had been completed, and a high tower, half painted, streaked up the wall. Catullus stared at it, and remembered the watchtower he had seen at the ball, before he had met Clodius, or come to Rome, or even heard of Sesostris Aetos. He began to piece together memories. Faces and events began to melt. He tried to keep a grip on the images floating in his brain, but it was too difficult, they kept slipping his comprehension, and soon, before he had even realised it, he had fallen asleep and begun to dream.

He was late up that afternoon, and had to work until the early hours to complete the report. His writing took possession of him, not pleasantly, but like a fever, and even once he had put it away and returned to sleep, his dreams seemed full of happenings that he knew to be important but could not understand. He found himself in a cemetery of glass; when he looked at the tombs, it was not his own face that was reflected back, but the mutilated features of other people, Caelius, Mona, Boot. Clodia. Somehow, he knew that he was being held responsible for the injuries, and he wanted to shout out that, no, it wasn't him, but still the accusations scratched inside his skin and then he could feel them hatching, all over his body and his every limb, as though they were insects being born from tiny eggs. He began to run, down a path of white steel, and suddenly everything seemed muffled, dead, and the itching stopped. A man stood ahead of him, his back turned. Catullus knew that it was Mr Varney. Slowly the man turned round. No face, just a terrible gash. "Did you ever finish my book?" he asked, as he had done before. "No," said Catullus. Mr Varney shook his head sadly, then held out an arm. There was the slow, heavy sound of wings beating. An eagle, so beautiful that Catullus wanted to cry out with pleasure at the sight of its dignity and power. The eagle landed on Mr Varney's arm, and fixed Catullus with an unblinking gaze. Mr Varney reached up to one of his eyes. With a slow, gurgling plop, it was pulled out and tossed into the eagle's open beak. The second eye followed. "My eyes!" screamed Mr Varney, "my eyes!" He staggered and fell, and when he stood up he had been transformed into Clodius, his face restored, but his sockets still gaping and black. The eagle beat its wings restlessly on his arm. "Blind!" Clodius screamed. "Who did this? Who is responsible? Kill him! The ritual demands it!" The eagle beat its wings faster and rose. Catullus watched it coming towards him. Its talons were outstretched. They were coming for his face. Closer and closer the eagle came. His face, what could he do? Catullus screamed and shut his eyes tight, then opened them again. He panted for breath and looked around. He was awake.

It was early, but Catullus couldn't face the idea of returning back to sleep. He climbed out of bed and got himself ready for work. He'd be at the site long before anyone else, but so much the better – he would have time to look over Doctor Gower's library again. As he walked out through the door, he caught sight of Mr Varney's book. He remembered his two dreams. "Did you ever finish my book?" Mr Varney had asked. Catullus glanced back at it, shrugged, and picked it up. Then, slipping it into his bag and leaving his report for Cicero outside Caelius' door, he left the house and set off for work through the early morning streets.

When he arrived at the site, he found, to his surprise, that Doctor Gower was already there. "Vandals," the Doctor said, glancing briefly round at Catullus, then staring back glumly at his excavations. Catullus looked. The marking tape lay flattened in the mud, and all the signs and boards had been smashed. "Couldn't it have been the storm?" Catullus asked. "It was very bad a couple of nights ago."

"No." Doctor Gower shook his head and pointed. "Look, you see. Footprints, everywhere. And over there, the entrance slab. Someone's forced it." He walked slowly across to inspect the damage, still shaking his head, then bent down to rub his fingers over the chipped stone. "Someone tipped me off early this morning," he said, not looking round. "So I came hurrying."

"Any idea who?"

"No. Rough sort of voice. Never heard it before."

"Odd thing to do, if it was one of the vandals. And how did they know your phone number, or even who you were?"

"I don't know. Don't really care either. To be honest with you, all I'm really worried about is the state of our excavations. Such *mindlessness*." Delicately, he flicked away more powdered chippings, then lumbered back slowly onto his feet. "Well," he said, looking down at the entrance slab, "there doesn't seem much point in hanging around now, does there?" He glanced at Catullus. "What do you say? Shall we go in? See what's waiting for us?"

"Yes." Catullus nodded slowly. "Yes, of course, we must."

"Good man. You first."

Together, they heaved away the slab. Beyond it lay a tiny opening, and steps, descending Catullus couldn't see how far down, down, into blackness. Doctor Gower switched on his torch and handed it to Catullus. He nodded and gestured towards the opening. Catullus nodded back, then squeezed his way through.

He shone the torch, but the steps still vanished into blackness.

"It must be very deep," he shouted back. "I can't see where the steps end."

Doctor Gower just grunted heavily. There was a pause. "I think I'm stuck," he said eventually.

"Stuck?"

"This damned hole, it's so -"; he grunted again. "Damn the thing, I am stuck."

"What shall I do?"

"Go on without me. I can't get through."

"You're sure?"

"Yes, yes, of course. But just be careful. Don't damage anything." There was another grunting, and Catullus guessed that the Doctor had pulled himself free. He looked back up at the daylight, then slowly began to descend. "Good luck," he heard boomed down after him. The echoes sounded in his ears, then disappeared away into the darkness still waiting for him beyond the torch's beam. Catullus walked slowly on.

The air was thick and musty, as he had expected it would be, but as he descended further, his nostrils began to find the heaviness spiced with something sweeter, something rich. He swung his torch about. The roof of the stairway rose ahead of him, and the darkness seemed to have become even deeper, absorbing all his light, waiting desolate and vast and unexpectedly cold. A chamber, Catullus guessed. As he stepped towards it, he could hear the sound of flies buzzing. He murmured a few lines of Aeschylus under his breath, and thought of the darkness-haunted gold found in Agamemnon's tomb. Who was he trying to fool? This was no Mycenae; there would be no gold. Catullus stood where he was, at the bottom of the steps, and pointed the torch forwards to see what he had found.

He was in a chamber, hollowed upwards into a dome. There was a tomb, just in front of him, and then beyond that, shadows becoming blackness. It was from the dark that the flies were swarming. Catullus took a step forward and noticed that the odour, the strange sweet odour he had first smelt while coming down the steps, was now so strong that it was almost overpowering. It too, like the buzzing of the flies, was coming from the darkness ahead. He put his hand over his nostrils and walked on. He watched the torch light as it swept across the walls, spilling over the uneven brickwork. There were lines carved on the bricks, he suddenly noticed, and daubings of what looked like red paint. No, he thought, no, a fraction of a second before his eyesight confirmed what he had already guessed. There were images of dancing men on the wall.

"Blood," Catullus thought, lines from the tragedian rising in his mind, like bubbles from a drowning man, "the stones bear witness to an act of blood. Hidden within the entranceway, a scarlet flood – a body hacked into carrion." He was in a dream, a trance of madness sent by the gods. When he moved, his limbs seemed slow. He pointed his torch down, into a far corner. There was something there wrapped in black polythene bags. It was a body – the head was sticking out from one of the bags. Catullus looked down at the face. Nothing. Only a red mess, still oozing. The smell, the rich sweet smell, rose from the pulp, and it was so thick that Catullus could almost believe that he was being held up by it, as he leant forward and felt his insides heave, and then began to puke and puke and puke.

He gasped desperately and looked away. He saw the tomb. The slab on the top had been left undisturbed. He ran over to it and tried to shift the slab, but it was no good, he'd never do it on his own. "Come down here!" he shouted. "Come down here!" From far away, he could hear Doctor Gower start to protest, but Catullus screamed, bellowed, started to cry. "Do anything! Knock the fucking wall down! Just get down here, *please!*" He kept shoving at the slab, and shouting, screaming. Minutes passed, an eternity. Then footsteps at last. "What is this?" said Doctor Gower, holding his handkerchief to his nose. Catullus pointed at the bundle in the far corner, smiling through his tears, then started to push again at the heavy marble slab. "You must get out," said the Doctor. "Get out at once." Catullus just pushed. The Doctor looked at him, then walked over to join him by the tomb. Together, they heaved at the slab. Nothing. Another heave. It began to shift. A third heave, and at last, it moved, and the two men pushed, and the slab was lifted right up off the tomb. Catullus leaned forward. He pointed the torch down into the coffin, and there it was, the skeleton he had been expecting. Its skull, like that of the corpse in the corner, had been sliced in two, and its face removed.

Porter leaned against the door of Doctor Gower's Portakabin.

"He'll see you in a jiffy," he told Catullus. "He's just got someone with him at the moment. Won't be long."

Catullus glanced around. Teams of policemen were fanning out across the waste land, sorting through the litter and clumps of weeds. Over on one of the roads, demonstrators had gathered and were chanting slogans at the police. Catullus wasn't sure, but he guessed that they were Clodius' men. He breathed in deeply and stared at the sky. Thank God for the sun, he thought, and fresh open air.

The door behind him clicked, and someone came out. It was Boot. She saw Catullus and smiled at him faintly. "I'll wait for you," she whispered. "I need you, I'll be waiting."

"In you go," said Porter, holding open the door.

Catullus glanced back at Boot, then he walked up the steps, and the door was shut behind him.

"Ah ha!" chuckled a familiar sounding voice. The Great Porto had leapt up from his chair, and was stalking across the room to shake Catullus by the hand. "Once again, I'm afraid, ha, once again, we meet in sadly unpleasant circumstances. Alas! But then what are circumstances, after all, but the fruit of our functions in life? An upsetting thought, ha ha, but true none the less!" He beamed and looked anything but upset by the idea. "Won't you sit down?" He chuckled again, sat down himself, and switched on a tape recorder. Then he leant forwards.

"Now then. You've been taken down again to look at the, ha, what shall we say, cadaver?"

Catullus nodded. Yes, he'd been taken down again. That smell of blood, and the weight of earth overhead. Never again.

"And you identified the body?"

"Yes."

"The naked body?"

Catullus swallowed. He knew that beads of sweat were forming on his brow. "Yes."

"No difficulty this time? Still, I suppose, she must have been a prettier sight naked than poor Mr Varney. Eh, ha ha? Your colleague, the young woman I've just been chatting to, she seemed to have no difficulty in recognising our victim's naked body either."

"Well?" Catullus shrugged. "They were lovers."

"And you?"

"Me? And Mona, you mean?" Catullus remembered how warm her body had been, how beautiful her face – no, no, don't even think, leave it all buried in some dark part of the brain. He looked up. The Great Porto was staring at him expectantly. "Sometimes," he said. "Yes, once or twice."

"She liked to sleep around?"

"You don't have to put it like that."

"But she enjoyed, what can we call it, she enjoyed intercourse, she enjoyed fucking, eh, eh?"

"Yes. I suppose so." Catullus thought, and again, he couldn't prevent memories from coming back. Mona's mouth, round his prick. No mouth left now, only a bloody hole. No, no, no. "She liked being happy," he tried to explain. "And she liked making other people happy as well."

"This must have made you jealous?"

"No. I never loved her. But I liked her."

The Great Porto nodded earnestly. "So when did you last, ha, express this – affection – for her?"

"A couple of nights ago. The night of the storm."

"I see." Porto nodded again, and jotted down a note. "You are aware then, are you, that as far as we know, you were the last person to see her alive?" He studied Catullus' face attentively. "Apart, of course, ha ha, from the murderer?"

Catullus tried to stare back at him coolly. "So? What are you saying?"

"Nothing, nothing. Just pointing out the coincidence."

"Coincidence?"

Porto sat back in his chair and laughed long and loudly. Then he leant forwards, and his head bobbed slowly as he stared at Catullus. "The coincidence, my young friend," he whispered, "that you were also the last person to see Mr Varney alive, before he too got stabbed and had his face sliced off. Remember?"

Catullus stared back at him, trying not to betray any emotion. In other words, he was looking as guilty as fuck. But what else could he do?

Suddenly Porto winked, and chuckled to himself. "Coincidence? – maybe. Ha ha ha! That's what they say, isn't it? I believe we talked about coincidences the last time we met, didn't we?"

Catullus nodded. "I believe we did."

"Have you been in contact with Clodius again, since that little chat we had?"

"What?"

"Clodius. Have you been in touch with him?"

Catullus frowned, then shrugged. "Yes."

"When? The last time."

"A couple of days ago. But I don't see what it's got to do -"

Porto raised his hand. "A couple of days ago?" Catullus nodded. Porto stroked his chin, then jabbed forward a long bony finger. "So – let me work this out. You meet Clodius – when? The afternoon? Yes, good, the afternoon. And then in the evening you come here, and then in the night, you are, ha – friendly – with our murderee. Is that correct?"

"It wasn't me." Catullus couldn't stand it any longer. He stood up and shouted. "It wasn't me! I was the one who found her, for fuck's sake! You think I'd go back down into that pit on my own, if I'd already killed Mona and dumped her down there? Have you seen it? Have you smelt it down there?" He stopped suddenly, and sat down again.

The Great Porto stared at him unblinkingly. "Down there," Porto said after a pause, "it is like, ha, Plato's cave, is it not?"

"What?"

"The cave mentioned by the immortal Plato, surely you remember it? Where all we poor mortals lie, chains around our waists, seeing the shadows of objects that are behind us, and mistaking such shadows for reality. I thought, when I was down there, now then, am I watching shadows here, or am I glimpsing reality? You see?"

Catullus stared at him. "I wouldn't actually have thought there was anything much more real than the corpse of a mutilated girl."

"Your reproach is, of course, justified. But I am afraid that it is often a policeman's job to abstract the personal."

"Oh? Like Plato."

"Yes, very good, ha ha, just like Plato. Doubtless you find his philosophy too, ha, a little inhumane. But it was his calling – he had little choice. I too, in my own very different profession, must perforce be guilty of a certain chilliness as well. Once in a while. But you can be sure that I do it, like Plato, ha ha, all in the name of a higher cause." He laughed at his own witticism. "Oh dear," he choked, "oh dear. But you see my point? I look at poor Mona and I see, of course, a savagely murdered girl. Of course. But I also see, ha, I see a shadow. Cast by the fire on the wall of the cave. But what is behind me, what is making this shadow? At the moment I can't be sure. Ha ha, I remain chained, although I am twisting and turning. But I know one thing."

"And what's that?"

The Great Porto stared at him. "You're standing there somewhere in front of the fire. One of those shadows on the wall is yours."

Catullus shook his head, very slowly. "You're wrong. It wasn't me. I've said. It wasn't me."

Porto shook his head, smiling. "You know my pedigree. I am, in my own way, a philosopher. I would not be so presumptuous as to say that anything can be certain. But I deal with probabilities. And I say that even if you were not the murderer yourself, then it is highly probable, at the very least, that you are implicated in all of this somehow." He nodded and tapped the side of his nose. "And I will find out. I always find out. I am the Great Porto."

Catullus breathed in and out, very deeply. There seemed to be a weight over his heart. "Will I be allowed to go from here?" he asked slowly. Porto stared at him. Silence. Catullus wondered what he would do if Porto said no.

"Yes," said Porto. "Yes, you can go. For now."

Catullus breathed in deeply. He felt like a drowning man who had found a plank. He was almost happy, for the first time since, well, since he had pointed his torch at Mona's corpse. Oh God. Mona's face, carved away. How could he have forgotten, even for a second? Mona was dead, and her killers were still out there, uncaught, unknown. Stalking him, perhaps.

"I'm between Scylla and Charybdis, aren't I?" he asked.

"Ha ha," chuckled the Great Porto. "Are you?"

"Yes. Hasn't it crossed your mind that they're after me? You think I might be a murderer, but whoever it is who's doing these things, they might have me down as someone to be murdered. Don't you think? Which would leave me fucked, wouldn't it, if you and they were both after me?"

The Great Porto sucked in his lips and scratched at his nose with a pen. "It would," he agreed after a pause, "definitely. *If* someone was after you. Ha ha, that's the point though, the big if, isn't it?" He nodded. "*If.*"

"Well, look, I'm telling you, it's nothing to do with me."

"So who is it to do with?"

"I don't know, that's your fucking job, isn't it?"

"Help me then." Porto leaned slowly forward. "Help me. Who do you think is doing it?"

Catullus wondered what he could say. When you're accused, always keep your mouth shut, that was what the lawyers advised. And God knew who Porto might actually be working for, he was clearly shady as fuck.

"You asked about Clodius," said Catullus slowly.

"I did," agreed Porto, reaching for a pen.

"Why?"

"Ha ha! If you don't know that, you can hardly expect me to tell you. But why did you bring him up?"

Catullus shrugged and again, wondered what he could say. "You know he served in Circassia?" he said at last.

Porto's whole body stiffened. "Yes," he said. "So what?"

Catullus pointed to a shelf behind his head. "There," he said. "Behind you. There's a stack of books, pass me the one on the top." Catullus found the chapter he had read two nights before. "There," he said, handing it to Porto. "I don't want to say anything that you might use to get me into shit. So just read that. And then when you've finished, go and look at the skeleton in the coffin next to Mona. And then try and work out what the link is between Circassia, the Civil War, and whoever it is who's out there now with his meat cleaver.

And leave me alone." Catullus got to his feet. "I want to go now."

Porto glanced up from the book. "Go then," he said.

Catullus waited for him to say something else, but Porto returned to the chapter and didn't look up again. Catullus shrugged and turned, and slammed the door shut after him. He pushed his way past Porter without nodding, then began to run across the litter and mud, looking for Boot, and the chance to get the hell away.

But the hell away where? Catullus tried to think, and realised with an increasing ache of desperation that everything his life had previously been now seemed grotesquely warped and changed. He was a person who had discovered a murder; he was a person who was suspected of a murder; he was a person who might be the victim of a murder. Like mirrors in a funfair show, each one of these thoughts cast reflections back so twisted that he could scarcely bear to recognise them. He wanted to escape, he wanted his old reflection back, but the mirrors blocked him in on every side. They would fade, Catullus hoped, they would fade; mirrors gave reflections, after all, not reality. But as he stumbled on over the rubbish piles, he could imagine a hall of them stretching ahead of him, far into the distance. Whichever way he turned, he had a long way to run.

All the more reason then to meet up with Boot, and perhaps share the journey. But she was proving to be almost as elusive as peace of mind itself. Where the hell was she? She had said she would wait. She needed him, that was what she had said, just as Catullus needed her. To talk about Mona, to hallow their grief. And then – of course – Catullus realised where she would be. Why hadn't he worked it out before? Too self-pitying, that was what he had been, and the very idea that he was guilty of introspection comforted him, reminded him that he wasn't necessarily alone. He turned a corner, and headed down the street, towards the café where he had first met Mona.

He looked through the window. Yes, Boot was there, sitting at her old table, drawing on a fag. Catullus pushed the door open and Boot leant back in her chair to look up at him.

"You took your time," she said, getting to her feet.

"There were things to discuss, weren't there?" Catullus muttered.

"It gave me time for a few funeral fags, I suppose. It's what she would have wanted, I'm sure." She laughed, and Catullus watched her, impressed by how quickly she seemed to have recovered; if there was still pain in her eyes, she was keeping it veiled. Out on the street, Boot took his arm, and again he was surprised; she had hardly ever touched him before. It was almost as though she were trying to behave like Mona; and then Catullus realised that, of course, that was exactly what she was trying to do – it was the finest tribute she could pay to her friend. They had left each other on bad terms; "too serious," that was what Mona had said about Boot. And now Boot was going to take things lightly, even the death of Mona, because that was surely how Mona would have behaved. She would have been delighted to see it, Catullus was sure.

"Where are we going?" he asked, as Boot led him on.

"The Underground. And then – I don't know."

"The Underground?"

Boot looked at him sharply. For the first time since he had met her in the café, she gave up fighting her expression of pain. "It's where Mona is," she said shortly. "After all." She let go of Catullus' arm and walked on a few paces. Then she turned back to face him, and took both his hands. "I did love her, you know. I really did. She showed me what life was for. That's not being extravagant, I don't think, saying that. And now she's dead."

Catullus stared into her eyes. They seemed very deep, but still with no hint of tears. He pressed her hands.

"Thank you," she said. She turned and began to walk on again. "And I hope they catch him. Whoever did it. I hope they catch him soon."

"Yes," said Catullus weakly. And of course he hoped they did too. He more than anyone. And now Boot wanted him to go underground, deep underground, where the dead lay. Where he had promised himself that he would never go again.

On the train, he discovered that he was shaking. He held tight onto Boot's hand, so tight that she turned to look at him with surprise, but he couldn't help it, he felt light with nerves. The train stopped and people climbed on, normal, everyday people, who just sat down and didn't give him a second glance, and there he was, a man who had discovered a murder that morning, and no one was even able to guess. There was a buffet as the train entered a tunnel. Catullus looked out. Black brickwork was flashing past. There was nothing else to see, just black brickwork, arching up above them, around them, closing them in, bearing the weight of tons of earth. He couldn't stand it. He got to his feet and staggered as the train swung round a dark bend and then began to slow. "I've got to get out," he told Boot, smiling ruefully, like a drunk man trying to reassure himself that he can still think straight. But when the doors slid open, he leapt out and began to run, not caring now how strange he would be looking, and he kept on running until he had reached the escalators. Boot followed him, running as well. As he stood to catch his breath, she walked up behind him and silently took his hand.

Back up on the streets, she began to talk again. About Mona. About how much Mona had taught her. About the importance of acknowledging love, and enjoying it, of being happy. Catullus nodded occasionally, but otherwise hardly listened – he didn't want to have to put up with talk about Mona now, he couldn't stand it, he just wanted Boot to shut up. He had been wrong – it wasn't helping him being with her, not the way she was going on now. He walked on aimlessly, not knowing where he was, or where he was going, and ignoring Boot as she just talked and talked. He needed someone who would take his mind off things altogether. Caelius perhaps? No. Well, someone else.

"I've got to leave you here," said Boot suddenly. She pulled Catullus round to face her and he noticed that she was crying now. They stared at each other in silence; then Boot reached for Catullus and pressed him to her, hugging him so tightly that he thought she would never let go. But she did, eventually; wiping away her tears, and then sobbing uncontrollably with long choking gulps, she kissed him, on his lips, his cheeks, his lips again, so that her tears were left wet all over his face. She broke away at last; "I've got to leave you here," she said again, and began to run. "Don't be unhappy, my love," she shouted, turning, then turning back and running on. She disappeared, and Catullus was left staring at the empty street, stroking his cheeks as they slowly dried.

He felt a bit stunned. He looked around. Where was he? The houses seemed familiar. Then he realised. He was on the Palatine, where he had come that first time to visit Cicero, and then again with Caelius, when they had heard the clowns. So where had Boot gone off to in such a hurry? Rich people lived here. People like Cicero. People like Clodia. And it was as he was thinking of her that he first noticed Clodia coming towards him, wandering across the street to reach the pavement where he had been left standing by Boot. "Hello," she said in an unsurprised tone. "What are you doing here?"

"I came to visit you, of course," he said, composing himself.

"How nice." She smiled, then pointed on down the road. "Do you want to come and have a drink or -"; she tried to think of an alternative. "I don't know, something?"

Catullus nodded slowly. "Yes. That would be lovely."

"All right then." She offered her arm. Catullus took it. With a feeling of relief that lightened the very depths of his stomach, he allowed himself to be led towards her house. Perhaps things were turning up, he thought to himself. He glanced at Clodia, and felt a sudden, magical, unexpected thrill of joy.

XII

LESBIA

As Catullus lounged in the bath, he studied his face in a shaving mirror. An attractive face, he decided, looking younger, perhaps, than it really was; strained, weary, not surprisingly, of course, yet also with the hint, apparent even through the steam on the mirror front, of something not immediately identified. Yet it was there, the emotion, in his eyes, his smile, his lips, which were pretty and almost feminine, and which Catullus, admiring his features dispassionately as though they belonged to some girl, realised suddenly were shaped by a desperate hope. Thoughtfully, as though conducting an experiment, he puckered a kiss; he remembered Mona, how she had met his lips, and at once black horror, visions of her annihilated beauty, swarmed his mind, like the demons let loose from Pandora's box. Yet the word 'hope' still hovered undimmed in his thoughts, and Catullus knew that it could not be allowed to fade, to be extinguished, for an impulse bridled was a form of death, and life was what he needed now, life and vision, touched, held, loved. Catullus studied his face again; and saw his chance. Such chance might keep the world at bay. Catullus stretched himself slowly along the length of the bath, and began to mould a penis out of bubble bath foam.

The door behind him opened.

"I can feel everything soak away," Catullus called out, not looking round. "The morning and everything, just soak away."

There was a brief silence. "Who the hell are you?" a voice asked.

Catullus jerked his head round in surprise. There was a tall thin man with a pointed head standing in the doorway. He had a dressing gown on, and looked vaguely familiar.

"Have we met?" Catullus asked.

The man took a step forward and almost shook with rage. "I wouldn't have thought that was likely," he said, and his voice almost cracked. "Now sir," he said, fiddling furiously with the end of his dressing gown cord, "now sir! Would you mind telling me who the devil you are?"

Catullus gave his name. The man didn't seem pacified. He stopped playing with his dressing gown tassel, but began to pat and fiddle with his hair instead. There was another anguished pause. "Did you know," he asked suddenly, "that I am the owner of this house, and that I want a bath? Now, this very moment?"

"Oh," said Catullus. "I am so sorry." And he demolished his foam penis at once.

"Where's my wife?" the man began to mutter to himself, "Clodia!" Of course, Catullus realised – Metellus. Oh fuck, how embarrassing. "It's my bathtime," Metellus suddenly shrieked. "I want my bath! Clodia, where are you?"

"Here, darling," cooed Clodia from behind his back. She put her arm round him, and began to steer him away from the bath as though he were a little child. "Now come on, let's get back to bed, shall we?"

"But he's in my bath."

"Don't be selfish, you can use the one upstairs." She ushered him out through the door, then turned her head. "Sorry," she said to Catullus. "He's a bit funny. I'll be back soon." She closed the door behind her, and Catullus stared at it, then shrugged, and sank back into the foam. He began to build himself two large breasts.

After a few minutes, Clodia walked back into the bathroom and sat down on the lavatory seat. She stared sadly at something in the distance, then shifted, and looked at Catullus. "Sorry," she said again. "It's his illness, it makes him like this."

"I'm very sorry."

"Don't be, please. I've had enough of people being sorry."

"Is he very upset?"

Suddenly, Clodia smiled. "Oh no, not about you, if that's what you mean. No. It's only because he's used to having his bath where he wants it, and when, on the dot. He's a polite man, usually, but he does like to have his own way." She made a face. "All important men are like that. You're not important, are you?"

Catullus shook his head.

"Good, then perhaps that's why I like you."

Catullus smiled. "Yes, perhaps."

Clodia smiled back. Beneath the cropped brutality of her blonde hair, her face glowed with sudden warmth. She leaned forwards to kiss him. "Do you want to have sex now?" she whispered. "With me?"

Catullus shrugged, then nodded. "Why not?" Clodia kissed him again, and Catullus wondered if she had noticed his prick, which was gradually slipping up through the bubbles like a periscope. "Don't let me put you out, though."

"Oh, I am sorry, I've been awful, haven't I?" Clodia suddenly rained a shower of kisses on him, then paused and looked solemn. "It's just –" She trailed her fingers through the bubble bath and started to stroke his thighs. "Well, you know, I just think it's better to warn you that sometimes I can be a bitch. A real bitch. I don't know why, I can't help it. But if I tell you now, then maybe when I do start to become awful, you'll understand, and still like me. What do you think?"

"Well, how are you awful?"

"Oh, I don't know." She shook her head. "There's one thing that men don't like, and that's that sometimes, when I'm having sex with them, I do fall asleep."

Catullus laughed. "God, if that's all, I'm used to it."

"Really?" asked Clodia interestedly.

Catullus wondered whether to lie, then allowed his vanity to get the better of him. "No," he admitted.

"I didn't think so," said Clodia, starting to play with his prick, "because that other night, you were actually quite vigorous and manly. I didn't even think about going to sleep, which is quite unusual for me."

"I was on artificial stimulants."

"Were you? Oh well, that explains it then. Perhaps you aren't quite as manly as I'd thought." She stared at him closely. "Don't worry though, there's no reason why that should be a problem. I'm often attracted to unmanly men."

Catullus smiled. "Me too."

"Really?" Clodia raised an eybrow. "That might be convenient." She dropped his prick suddenly, and stood up. "Undress me. But slowly. Respectfully." She pointed at herself. "You see my body, how round and beautiful it is? Well, you mustn't touch it until I say you can."

"Why not?"

"Because it turns me on, the idea that I'm making you wait."

"Cruel anticipation," whispered Catullus, standing up and drying his hands.

"Cruel anticipation," nodded Clodia. "Exactly."

With careful grace, Catullus began to play the lady's maid. He unzipped the back of Clodia's dress, and slipped it down over her legs, right down to her boots, which were heavy and black, and tightly laced. Catullus bent down to untie them; masochistic thrills fluttered through his testicles; there he was, naked and kneeling, respectfully fondling an aristocrat's boots. He looked up at Clodia, and the nakedness he could now see between and through her underwear; she'd been right, it was indeed beautiful and round. With the lightest of gossamer touches, he began to roll down her tights, and as he stroked them gently past the curve of her belly, he found that his desire to touch her skin, even for the fraction of a second, just to feel her beneath his fingertips, was torturing him in the most exquisite way, he couldn't wait, he couldn't possibly wait. But he did. Clodia arched one of her legs and Catullus bent down again, tugging at the delicate gauze of the tights, very softly.

"Do you like it?" Clodia asked, smiling down at him.

Catullus didn't say anything, just pulled at her tights one last time, then sent them falling gently onto her dress.

"You're very good. I'm dying for you to touch me, can you tell?"

Catullus glanced up. He nodded.

"Most men are crap at sex. They haven't got the patience. Women are much better, I think."

Catullus stared up again. "And I suppose it's easier for you to go to sleep while they're fucking you."

Clodia began to laugh. "Don't," said Catullus. "How can I get these off and not touch you if you're moving about all the time?" Clodia laughed even more. As Catullus levered the knickers down, one of his fingers brushed inadvertently against the inside of Clodia's thighs. He felt her start, and then reach down to stroke him, and he thought, shit, it's just as though I've come too soon, and so he pulled the pants off quickly, without worrying about not touching her legs any more, and then knelt up to kiss her, desperately, as though he really could feel his sperm seeping out, and he had to hurry, to catch up with his pleasure before it peaked and went. But he hadn't come, and as he began to stand up to kiss Clodia on her lips, he suddenly felt her hand round his prick, holding it tightly and forcing it downwards, so that he had to fall back onto his knees. "Naughty, naughty," she murmured softly, shaking her head. He looked up at her. She touched his lips with her fingertip, pushing at them gently so that he had to bend his neck slightly back. She reached for a small silver bottle. Oil. She took out a stopper and bent the bottle forward. Catullus breathed in sharply as he felt a cool touch drop onto one of his nipples, then onto the other, and he stared at his chest as the oil began to trickle slowly downwards like the twin courses of heavy tears. Clodia smiled, watching him, then leant back onto the lavatory and opened her legs. "Come slowly," she ordered. Still kneeling, Catullus pushed. "Now out." No, it was too lush, too rich, he couldn't. But he played by the rules, and did as he had been told. The air felt freezing on his dampened skin. "Now in again." There was a long hissing moan. Him? Her? He couldn't tell. He was lost. "Pick me up," Clodia whispered. "Quick, just pick me up!" "But I've never done that," Catullus thought. "Suppose my back goes? Suppose I'm not up to it?" But he was. As he grappled with her legs, Clodia pushed at him, her hands on his shoulders, shoving him against the wall, her thighs wrapping round his hips, her pelvis grinding harder and harder against his own. Their two bodies began to slip against each other, as the oil, and their sweat, and the steam from the bath, all mingled and sealed them within a single skin. "Is this how fish do it?" Catullus wondered, as he slithered down the wall tiles, Clodia's body sucking at his, and following it down. "I feel like a herring." The idea briefly intruded through the mists of his pleasure, but it couldn't survive them for long, not now, nothing could. This is it, Catullus thought, this is it. Then he stopped thinking altogether. He was sensation, there was nothing else. He could vaguely feel Clodia as she began to laugh and cling to him more tightly, but even she was a blur, and when he saw her, he wasn't sure if his eyes were open or shut. At last, although time had long since lost any meaning for him, he felt all control, everything, just slip away, there was nothing else for it. He groaned, and then, perfectly, like a pilot landing a plane, he allowed himself to come. "Oh God," he thought, and held Clodia tightly. "Oh God, oh God. And she didn't fall asleep." He kissed her happily, snuggled up against her, and then realised that she was already flat out. But he was too exhausted and satisfied to care. "So," he wondered, "is this joy?" and then fell asleep himself.

There was another routine of sex and lazy sleep that evening, and then another the next day, but for most of the time Clodia preferred to talk. She'd never really liked sex that much, she explained; did Catullus think she was odd, because lots of people did, or could he see what she was going on about, because it was disgusting, really, all that sweating and panting, it was *vile*. If she ever became particularly vehement, then Catullus would lie back and wait, because the more Clodia denied that she liked something, the more keen she would suddenly seem to experience it, and would reach out to kiss him even as she insisted that she was going to stay celibate for the rest of her life. "You must hate me," she would tell him, "I'm so crap at being nice to people, and making love. I'm so lazy." Well, it was true that she was lazy, but if she told him that she was crap at anything – well, he was getting to know her now – it almost certainly meant that she wanted to be good at it, and Catullus would feel a thrill of excitement, knowing that he was the object of such a resolution. At such moments, happiness warmed him in a protective embrace. It was hard to believe: Mona was still dead, a killer was still loose, he was still a suspect in a murder inquiry. Nothing had changed – he knew that. But sitting on Clodia's bed, drinking her whisky, listening to her talk and laugh at his jokes, he could almost convince himself that he didn't care. If anything, in fact, his fears fed his calm, which blazed like a hearth-fire in a haunted wood.

And so Catullus found it easy to fall in love with Clodia. He felt safe staying in her room, surrounded by the hangings on her walls, the carpets on her wooden floors, the plants, the tank full of fish, the pens and brushes and books scattered everywhere, the comfortable furniture and the wide empty spaces, the tall arched windows and the golden light. He felt safe being next to Clodia herself, the magic palladium at the heart of the sanctuary, now wholly beautiful in Catullus' eyes, and as compulsive as she was beautiful, so that her obsession with herself had become one that Catullus was quite happy to share, and did, encouraging her shamelessly, listening and making her laugh, and wondering all the time if she reciprocated his careful affection. She had to, surely – could she ever have had a better audience? Catullus lay stretched out on the bed, and Clodia would talk happily on. About herself, about how wicked she had been as a child, what a tear-away. About how she had married Metellus when she had been very young, just before his cancer had been diagnosed. About how she still loved him, but faintly now. About his tolerance, his kindness. About how they had never had sex. About how she liked to have sex with women. About how she hated to have sex with women. About every topic under the sun, so long as it had some connection with herself. On the rare occasions when her conversation stalled, Catullus would prompt her. Tentatively, he brought up Clodius' name. Did she see much of him, he asked, waiting for some sign of self-consciousness, some hint that she was privy to her brother's confidences, but Clodia just laughed. "No, he's so self-obsessed, you know, he's only got time for his own interests. Don't you think?" Catullus smiled to himself, then mentioned how he had been to see Clodius a few days before. He asked her about Circassia. "He went on about that again, did he?" said Clodia, raising her eyes. "It's so boring. You're not meant to say that though, are you? When it was all happening, you know, the war, I thought it was awful, and I did things to help, but now it's finished, what's the point of going on about it? Did you see his friends?" "Friends?" "You know -" Clodia coughed. "His 'friends'. Those two soldiers who'd been in the war with him. You must have done, they were at that ball where I met you. Listen, they played this." Clodia sat up and rummaged through a pile of records she had left scattered in a corner. She found what she had been looking for, and put it on her turntable. "It's very old, but it's beautiful, I think. It always reminds me of people I love. Clodius, other people. Do you have music that does that to you?" She lowered the needle. "It's Circassian. Listen." And Catullus did listen, as the familiar notes began to sound; they wouldn't remind Clodia of him, he thought with a slight pang, but they reminded him of Clodia, of mystery, of night air. "I heard you play this once," he told her, "when I was walking in the street below, and I looked up and wondered if this was your room." "Did you? And was it?" Catullus walked over to a window and looked out. "Yes. I think so," he said slowly. He felt distracted by the unexpected beauty of the view. He had never seen colours so intense, so sharp. The blue of the sky, the white of the marble houses across the road, the autumn reds amongst the leaves of the trees, and then, down the hill, the many coloured vastness of Rome as it stretched into the distance, a composition of abstracts, too vivid for any other sense to be made of them, given coherence only by the warm oak of the shutters that served to frame the view. Catullus listened to the music as it rose higher and higher, keeping his fancies company.

"What are you thinking?" Clodia asked.

"How beautiful the city looks. Too beautiful to be real, almost."

"And the music?"

"Oh, that's real enough. But it still has to be played by someone, hasn't it?"

"So?"

Catullus shook his head and stared back out at the colours beyond the window. "I hadn't realised that your brother and those two violinists were – close," he said at last.

"I don't know if they're really *close* close." Clodia swung herself up off her bed. "I don't know what they all got up to in that war. He never talks about it."

"How much do they see of each other now?" Catullus stared up at Clodia as she walked over to stand next to him. "Have you got any idea at all?" Clodia shrugged, then kissed and embraced him. Catullus rubbed his cheek against the softness of her skin, but never stopped looking out through the window, at the still street below him, and the great city beyond it. There was a long silence. "Could I stay here, do you think?" he finally asked, turning back to face Clodia. "Not for long. Just until things blow over."

"Of course. I thought you were going to anyway. Stay as long as you like."

Catullus smiled. Until what things blow over, she could have asked. But there was no point in dangling conversational bait in front of Clodia's mouth, and that was why he wanted to stay, after all, so that he wouldn't have to think about himself, and the knots of circumstance threaded by the blank world outside, he wanted to absorb himself in Clodia. He allowed her to pull him down onto a pile of cushions, stacked high against the wainscot so that they reached the window sill. Catullus nestled up against Clodia's body and hugged her tightly, then turned back again to stare out at Rome. It still looked unreal, not an abstract now, but the city a dreamer might have painted from his memories. Was this wealth, Catullus wondered, having windows that could play such tricks? He stroked Clodia's cheeks, and glanced at her, and was astonished to see that she too seemed to have changed, to have revealed an aspect of her appearance that Catullus had never suspected of existing, for he hadn't seen the shade on her skin and the angle of her face suggest such a precise erotic charm before, precise, yes, tantalisingly precise, and yet at the same time leaving Catullus to wonder how many other forms Clodia could take, what endless other shades and angles were waiting to be combined. Catullus pressed himself desperately against her. A beauty that was infinite would always be slipping away from him, he thought. Or was it only in this room, where light seemed to be so various and rich, that everything, from a city to the face of a beautiful woman, was able to metamorphose so rapidly? If that were the case, then it only increased his longing to stay. He felt like an initiate, seduced in some ancient sanctum by the promise of flickering beauties and insights. He looked at the sunlight falling onto the open wooden floor, at the plants flourishing by the alcoves, and then, inevitably, he thought of his own bedroom, back in Tallowfield, and wondered, with unpleasant clarity, if that was all his high feelings amounted to, just a peasant's cringe. All of a sudden, everything seemed clear. He was no initiate. He wasn't Clodia's lover, she didn't want him to stay, he was being an embarrassment, just go! Down in Rome, there was still Mona's ghost to appease.

"Stay," whispered Clodia, stroking his chest. "I want you to stay."

"How did you know what I was thinking?"

"You tensed. You looked round the room and went stiff, like Metellus trying to dance." She kissed him and ran her hand through his hair. "Poor darling. Don't be miserable. Stay here, I need you."

Catullus stared at her and thought, just for a fraction of a second. Then he kissed her and laughed. "Of course I'll stay."

The next morning, he phoned Caelius. "I'm at Clodia's house. She's putting me up for a bit."

There was a short pause. "You mean, *the* Clodia, the one who lives on the Palatine?"

"I do."

"You bastard." There was another short pause. "So what am I meant to do about it?"

"A favour. I was wondering if you'd bring over some of my clothes. I'm starting to smell."

"Piss right off and die."

"Please. You have got the car. And you could visit Camilla."

"Ooh, great."

"You two not getting on?"

"Let's put it like this – the moment I can afford my own car, I'm out."

"How sad. And there was me thinking it might really be love."

"Ha!"

"Oh well, forget Camilla. But look – I'm over here, you haven't seen me for a couple of days. And the Palatine's beautiful at the moment. Are you sure you wouldn't like to drive over?"

"Quite sure, thanks."

"Go on."

"I'm busy today."

"Tomorrow."

"How long are you staying?"

Catullus thought. "I don't know."

"You're not in hiding, are you?"

"Why?"

"I read about what happened to that poor friend of yours. And there's a phone message here from that policeman, the one who wanted to see us before."

Catullus breathed in deeply. "What does he want this time?"

"Just to see you. I told him I didn't know where you were."

"Good. He's the detective. It's up to him to track me down."

"He wants to see me too, actually. Don't know why. Anyway – you stay where you are. Just hold on a minute." Catullus heard the phone being put down, and Caelius rummaging through something. "Hello? Sorry about that, I was just looking for the other messages. Okay, yes, there's the one from Porto, but we've agreed you're going to ignore that. And there's one from Doctor Gower saying that all excavations have had to be cancelled for at least this week, so that's good news, isn't it? And then there's one from Boot, saying please phone, and she's left a number. Got a pen?"

Catullus scribbled the number down. The exchange was the same as Clodia's, he noticed. A Palatine number. So Boot moved in high circles as well.

"You're sure you won't come over?" he asked Caelius.

Caelius paused. "Oh, all right," he finally agreed. "Late tomorrow evening, would that be okay? It won't leave you smelling too much?"

Catullus smiled. "I'll wash a lot."

"Yes, you do that. And look after yourself as well."

"I will. Thank you. Thank you, Caelius." Catullus kissed the receiver. "Goodbye."

He lowered the receiver. If not a lover, then a friend, yes, a friend it was perhaps now no embarrassment to love.

"Was everything okay?" shouted Clodia from the kitchen.

"He'll bring some stuff round tomorrow." Catullus wandered down the corridor. Clodia was sitting by a table with two friends, both of whom he'd been introduced to earlier; Marghi, one of them was called, a bullet-haired woman in leather jacket and trousers, and the other one's name he couldn't remember, Ariana perhaps, something like that, Marghi's absolute opposite, blonde and willowy, and dressed in long skirts. Catullus had hoped to come back and find them gone. He smiled dutifully, nevertheless, and sat down.

"If your friend can't bring you any clothes till tomorrow," asked Clodia, "what are you going to wear till then?"

"I don't know." Catullus shrugged. "I'll have to improvise."

"But Clodia, he'll have to borrow some of yours," said Ariana, who had the habit of drawling her vowels so extravagantly that even the most banal of her comments would have sounded suggestive. She lit a cigarette and smiled pruriently. "Marghi would approve of that, wouldn't you, Marghi?"

"You could borrow mine. Would you like that?" Marghi took off her jacket and tugged at the string vest she was wearing. "You'd look manly enough in this, wouldn't you?"

"I haven't really got the body for it," said Catullus politely.

"Yeah, you're right, you need a pair of tits to look good in a string vest, don't you, eh?" Marghi nodded and laughed raucously.

"I'll ask Metellus," shrugged Clodia. "He must have something wearable somewhere."

"Have you met Metellus yet?" Ariana asked.

Catullus nodded. "He found me in the bath."

"Did he?" Ariana's grin stretched and became even more feline. "Was he furious?" She leant forward and her eyes glittered. "Do tell me all."

"He was fine. I'm sure he's got much more important things than me to worry about, anyway."

Ariana shook her head, and her grin reached almost to her ears. "But important men always like to bother themselves with affairs of the flesh." She tossed her hair back coquettishly. "Don't they, Clodia?"

"Do they? How would I know?"

"Oh, she's wicked, isn't she, wicked, making comments like that about her poor husband! And all these other stories, as well – oh, she's *wicked!*"

"What other stories?" asked Clodia idly.

"Promise you won't get upset?" Ariana stretched out her long fingers, and brushed them against Catullus' hands. "It's just that – no, I can't, Clodia. Oh, very well." She smiled. "I've heard you're having an affair with your brother."

Clodia smiled back faintly. "Says who?"

"An unimpeachable source." Ariana nodded, and almost licked her lips with pleasure. "Camilla."

"No!" said everyone simultaneously, and they all began to laugh.

"You've heard about Camillas, have you?" Ariana asked Catullus.

"Camillas?"

"Tamperings with the truth."

Catullus smiled. "Well, I've met Camilla. Has her cancer been cured yet?"

"No, no, it was an abortion she had, not cancer," said Marghi.

"An abortion and cancer," said Ariana.

"And a brain tumour," added Clodia. "She had all three. At the same time."

"And when she's not dying, what else does she actually do?" Catullus asked. "I've never actually been able to find out."

"She's a secretary," purred Ariana.

"Really?" said Clodia, sounding surprised. "But she's rich."

"Inherited. She doesn't actually earn it. You remember she said she had an important job in the Senate? Well," – Ariana stretched – "it seems she was sacked from this important job for not being able to type fast enough. Oh, and I met a film producer too, who'd employed her as his receptionist. That was her movie career." Ariana grinned sleekly across at Clodia. "You can imagine how desperate I've been to reveal all this."

Catullus mentioned Caelius's description of Camilla, which amused Ariana enormously, as Catullus had known it would. "Caelius," she gasped in between her fits of laughter, "he's your friend, is he? Camilla told me he was an officer in the air force." And she and Clodia both laughed until tears came into their eyes. Catullus watched them, and felt pleased with himself; if making bitchy remarks about people was the route to social success, well – he'd had months of practice at that with Caelius. But even as he chatted on, he found that his feelings of resentment against Clodia's friends were still rankling, that there was something not quite right, even if he was making Ariana laugh. Clodia. That was it, he wasn't making Clodia laugh. He didn't know why, but it seemed suddenly impossible. There had been no problem earlier, just the opposite – his conversation had sped along. But now, if he wanted to talk to Clodia, it was as though his mind was having to run through sand to come up with things to say. Everything felt so forced. He burnt to be alone with her again.

At last, long last, Ariana and Marghi left. Clodia led the way back up to her bedroom.

"Did you like them?" she asked.

"Oh, definitely," said Catullus.

"They liked you. I was getting quite jealous."

"Really?"

Clodia laughed. "No, not really."

"Pity." But at least she'd noticed her exclusion from the

conversation, Catullus thought. Good. "So do you see them much?" he asked, trying to keep the note of jealousy from his voice.

"Not often. But you know how it is," said Clodia. "You meet people in a crowd, and you just keep up with them, don't you?"

"And what crowd is that?"

"Oh, Marghi, she runs a club. I go there sometimes. It's a bit of an effort, though. Most of the time, I'm like you."

"What's that meant to mean?"

"Well – someone who likes lounging around being lazy."

"I'm not lazy."

Clodia hung herself round his neck. "Yes, you are, sweetie, of course you are." She rolled him onto some cushions and sat down on his chest. "You'd rather stay in and talk, wouldn't you, for instance, than go out?"

"What, right now? Yes."

"Well then, there you are. You're lazy."

No, thought Catullus, I'm not lazy, but I'm greedy and possessive, and I don't want the Clodia I know to become a different Clodia, I want her to stay mine. For Catullus had realised now that his earlier anxiety, when he had felt inhibited about talking to Clodia in front of her two friends, had been a result, not of jealousy, not of a fear that Clodia might become another person's lover or companion, but rather that she had already become another person herself, one that Catullus could only recognise faintly, as though he were looking at her through smoked glass. Indeed, sitting by the window where he had first dared to imagine Clodia as being just a succession of points in time, flickering past all efforts to synthesize them, Catullus found it hard to think of the woman he was holding in his arms as having a personality at all, at least a personality that he could comprehend and be certain he had fathomed, for Clodia's character, like her beauty, seemed infinite, and to mirror the infinitude of all the different moments of which her life was made. That was the problem, Catullus realised, that was why he was in such agonies at the thought that she might meet other people, and do different things, and lead a life in which he wouldn't even have a part; he couldn't bear the idea of her becoming someone he might fail to recognise, someone who might in turn, of course, not recognise him. And so when Clodia damned her friends and old habits for being tedious, Catullus encouraged her, not brutally, but with care and subtlety, so that Clodia was always able to arrive at conclusions that could then seem to be her own. She would agree that she loved him more than anyone else – of course she did, otherwise she wouldn't be with him, would she? Catullus believed her; he didn't doubt that when she made such assertions, she was convinced of her own sincerity, and that she really did love him, for Clodia was never less than transparently honest, and when she thought something, she always said it, without ever bothering to check herself. But even so, Catullus wasn't much comforted; after all, he reasoned, Clodia's honesty was what made her so selfish. When she went somewhere without him, he worried, she would discover that she was just as happy as before, perhaps even happier, and then she would be able to admit that she didn't love him at all, and yet still be telling the truth, for Clodia's most fervent vows, Catullus knew, would only ever be as though written on wind and running water. And so Catullus did not try to force them out of her; he knew that there would be no point. Instead, because it was achingly clear to him that Clodia needed to feel unhedged, to be free to do or behave as she liked, Catullus forced himself never to hold her down to anything, and tried to persuade her that he too disliked being bound by promises. He never denied that he loved her, and he never stopped encouraging her to laugh at that large part of her world which was not centred on him. But if, as she frequently did, Clodia chose to rejoin it, then Catullus did not complain; he knew that by not clinging to her, he was ensuring her ultimate return And when they were together again, he found his pleasure at having her beside him once more renewed and fulfilled.

But it was the nature of such a pleasure that it had to be bought at a price. For a long time, after the ball, when Catullus had first thought of Clodia as being a woman he found attractive, the idea that he might one day fall in love with her had lurked reassuringly at the back of his mind, not with any great obsessiveness, but tingeing his thoughts with an occasional warmth, in the way that an anticipated holiday sometimes can, or the knowledge of savings kept unspent in a bank. He had never had to bother with close analysis of such a vaguely imagined prospect, for his idea of Clodia had hovered too close to the margins of fantasy to require it, and Catullus had never even stopped to wonder about what Clodia might represent to him, still less about why she should represent anything at all. But now, when he could hold Clodia in his arms every day and sleep in her bed every night, Catullus found that the more familiar her touch and feel became to him, the more obsessively he began to abstract her back into a dimension of imaginings, where, for all his efforts, he would soon start to feel her slip away again from his grasp. Catullus realised, to his discomfort, that he loved Clodia for the very qualities that most anguished him, and Clodia, he suspected, loved him in turn because she could never have had a lover so tolerant of her vagaries, one who could understand them as being a part of what he desired, not a distraction away from it. Was he flattering himself, Catullus worried, and was he perhaps mistaking Clodia's ability to understand the nature of the love he was offering her? He didn't think so, or at least not often, for the less he talked to Clodia about the quality of an affair they were both still casually pretending was free of emotional intensity, the more full of meaning what they refused to say became; he could tell, he knew it, from the way she looked occasionally, from the way in which their conversation sometimes seemed to be operating as a strange game, fluidly evolving its own rules and codes of conduct, obeyed by both without prior discussion or agreement, they both just understood, that was how it happened, lovers' telepathy. At its happiest, conversation with Clodia struck Catullus as being like a delicate trellis frame placed over untouched depths, and he and Clodia would both waltz across it, occasionally snatching glimpses at the vastnesses below. Did she have similar conversations with other people? Catullus didn't think so. He saw her with others, and he heard her talk about them, and he didn't recognise the love that he knew she was accepting from him. He couldn't be sure of course – but then, wasn't it precisely such uncertainty which explained his passion's urgency? As anxieties churned round and round in his mind, there were times when he felt that he could almost welcome them. Did Clodia suffer from them too, Catullus wondered. Even if she did, she wouldn't tell him. But what was good for him had to be good for her as well, and so sometimes he would go out with Clodia and not talk to her at all, just concentrate on trying to be amusing with her friends. If she went out on her own, he would always make a point of seeming occupied, as though the idea that he should even remotely miss her was a ludicrous one. He knew that he was unconvincing, but then, that was part of the point. He knew that she knew that he knew it. And all the time, he would be hoping that Clodia missed him even half as much as he did her, and wondering when, if ever, she would admit to it.

It was to try and encourage such an admission that he would sometimes go out himself, quite casually, perhaps slipping a mention of his plans into a conversation, but never drawing attention to them – after all, he thought, you don't, do you, not when you're just popping out? In particular, he saw Boot, who like him had no work to go to, and whose parents, it turned out, lived just down the road, in a mansion that seemed vast even for the Palatine. Of course, it had been impossible for Boot to go back to the flat she had shared with Mona; instead, she would meet Catullus in her parents' garden, and occasionally they would both talk about their dead friend, but not often, not after the one occasion when Boot had cried, clinging to Catullus for what had seemed like hours, just sobbing and sobbing. The next time Catullus saw her, Boot seemed to have become her old self again: tough, funny, unsentimental. She never mentioned the time when she had kissed him outside Clodia's house; Catullus began to wonder if it had ever happened at all. But no, he thought, Boot was proud, she would never admit to anything that might make her look ridiculous. After all, wasn't that why she had never let on about her parents' wealth? Rich little wannabe dyke, that was what Caelius had called her, cruel, but it was true too, Catullus supposed; how the hell had Caelius guessed? – his ever sniffing nose for people's stashed away shit. Still – it didn't matter; Boot remained Boot. But Catullus, already suffering vague pangs of guilt as a result of his affair with Clodia, found that he couldn't resist feeling sorry for her; it helped to mollify his admiration, and blunt the stabs of attraction that still surprised him occasionally as he lay with her in her garden, or watched her laugh. If he ever thought about it, and he tried not to, he generally had to admit to himself that Boot deserved much better from him. But she wasn't Clodia, and whenever he compared the two, the light from the one left the other blotted out.

He didn't want Boot to know this, of course. He didn't want her to know that he was having an affair at all. He never actually lied about it, just implied that he was single, and Boot, for whatever reasons, seemed happy enough to believe him. Or at least, she chose not to press him about his ambiguities. It turned out that she had never met Clodia, only heard rumours about her. "She's odd, isn't she?" she had asked once. "That's what people say."

"Do they?"

"No. Correction. That's what people like my father say. And he thinks I'm odd. So actually, it's probably a good sign."

"Well, what does your father say?"

"Nothing much. And it's not really her he hates anyway, it's her brother."

Catullus had asked why. Boot had made a gesture of boredom, then reached for a cigarette. "Oh, you know. Clodius is Clodius. And my father is a businessman. They're natural enemies." She had begun to smoke vigorously; Catullus didn't ask her anything else. She still didn't like talking about her parents, and so it didn't seem fair to press. He didn't even know what business her father ran. One that made a lot of money, he guessed, looking round the lawns. Poor Boot. It must have been dreadful, coming from such a privileged background.

As for himself – well, he was certainly getting used to privilege, he realised, as the days slipped by. Clodia entertained him lavishly; if her selfishness seemed prodigious, then so too did her generosity, not surprisingly perhaps, Catullus thought, since she spent money as she did everything else, with an instinctive regard for her own enjoyment. "So I'm a tart," Catullus thought. "Who gives a fuck?"

He began to enjoy going out with Clodia more, and hitherto distant vistas of pleasure started to come into focus as he understood what it might mean not to have to worry about money. He felt happier now, even when he was on his own in Clodia's room; as with all the other delights he had been introduced to, the enjoyment of living in a vast and beautiful house unencumbered with Dugbals seemed to grow rather than diminish with familiarity. Metellus he never saw; he could have baths, do anything in fact, whenever he wanted to; it was as though he owned the place. Sometimes he would think about his poverty-cramped rooms back in Tallowfield, and feel uncomfortably like a beggar made king for a day; he couldn't live with Clodia all the time – supposing she became bored? But then he would glance round her room and see some of the clothes that Caelius had brought round for him; he had been out with Boot at the time, but when he had come back, there they had all been, dumped down in Clodia's room, a wonderful sight, almost as though they had been there forever. And so with the familiar and the beautifully unfamiliar blended in front of him, Catullus began to relax, his love for Clodia touching his love for her room, and his love for her room reaching back again, and gilding his love for her still further with enchantments and associations.

Lying in his favourite alcove, savouring the flavour of such emotions, Catullus would often start to feel that their taste was lightening his whole body, as though they were drugs, designed to give him the energy to pursue more experiences, and perhaps to understand them. Well, at the very least to confront them, Catullus thought, since in moods of particular confidence he would sometimes find himself ready to exhume memories that he had deliberately interred, and which he knew, even as he renewed his autopsies, would continue to baffle him. After all, wasn't that why he had originally tried to put them to rest, because he hadn't understood them, because horrors were always the worse for seeming to lie beyond explanation – wasn't that always the case? As though he were probing a barely healed wound, Catullus would recall his descent down into the tomb, towards the dark and the buzzing of the flies; he would repeat it again and again in his mind; always the darkness, and the buzzing of something just out of reach, and the truth a corpse without a face. In an attempt to glimpse some of its missing features, Catullus dug out Mr Varney's book from his bag. That dream, asking him if he had finished the book, had it been trying to point him anywhere? In a last resort, become superstitious, Catullus thought – it might just work. But it didn't, not at first. He read through the whole book, and couldn't find a single further reference to eagles, to murders, to anything. So that was that, Catullus assumed: don't believe in dreams. Then a tiny note scribbled in the margin caught his attention. 'Point this out', Varney had written, next to a paragraph describing Marius' death on an unidentified stretch of the city walls. Just underneath had been added the name and address of a development company, presumably the one that Varney had been working for, and then under that were three words: 'even, odd, even'. Even, odd, even. Hadn't that been written somewhere before? Next to the description of Marius' dream, perhaps? All of a sudden, Catullus felt the hairs on the back of his neck start to rise. He flicked back through the book's pages. Yes, there it was, Varney's scrawl again, 'even, odd, even', just by the description of the faceless corpse dredged from the Tiber. Well, well, Catullus thought; perhaps the old drunk had been on to something after all. Catullus reached for his note book and copied the words down onto a blank page at the back. Even, odd, even, though? What the hell did it mean? Something, please, Catullus thought; the idea that it might just be gibberish was too frustrating even to contemplate; he didn't *have* any other clues, for fuck's sake. And so Catullus solemnly promised himself that he would worry at the words, ponder them endlessly, tease their meaning out whatever it took. The idea of having something to track all of a sudden thrilled him. He began to pace around the room, and felt so light with energy now that he thought he would have to run somewhere fast, just to stop himself from floating away.

But he stayed where he was, walking up and down. He tried to calm himself, to think rationally about what the words might mean, but he was so excited now that he couldn't actually bring himself to concentrate on his discovery at all. He reached for his note book and stared at the words he had written down, as though the sight of a few marks on a sheet of paper might somehow ballast his interest in their meaning again. But it was no good – his excitement now was for desire, for life. He scribbled out the first line of a possible poem, and then another, and as he wrote, he felt as though he had caught the topmost curve of a wave. He finished the poem, and read it back through. He laughed. It was obscene, really obscene, but good too, and funny, and hendecasyllabic. He began to correct, the excitement still alive.

Clodia came back. Catullus kissed her, then pulled her over to the bed and began to caress her, up and down, passionately, talking all the time at a furious rate. "Are you on speed?" Clodia asked. "Have you been taking things?"

"It does feel a bit like it," said Catullus, massaging her feet. "You noticed?"

"Yes. Hard not to."

Catullus vaulted himself forward and clung to her. "I know. It just sort of happened. You know the way it does. All – mmm." He shivered and shook his head, then kissed Clodia deliciously on her lips. "Mmm," she answered back, "mmm." Then suddenly, she broke away from him and stood up. She walked back over to her bag and picked it up. "It's because you're famous, isn't it?" she asked.

"What?"

"You being like this. It's because you've become famous." She felt inside her bag and pulled a magazine out. "There," she said, throwing it over to him. "You hadn't seen this?"

Catullus shook his head. He stared at the magazine. 'Alexandrian'. And then he understood. Boot's uncle – of course!

"First page," said Clodia, joining him back on the bed. Catullus looked. And there they were. His poems, in printer's ink. Catullus glanced up. "Did you just buy this?" he asked.

She laughed. "No, I was given it." She kissed him. "But I would have bought it if I'd known, promise." She looked over his shoulder. "Are they good?"

"What, the poems? Of course they're good."

"They seemed to be. I just wanted to check. I did read them, but I'm stupid, I don't really know much about poetry."

"There's not much to know. It doesn't make you any money, and the people who write it are romantic and have a tendency to die young – you know, all that stuff."

"Metellus writes poetry."

"Well, there you are. He's dying."

"Yes, but he's not young. And he's not romantic, either."

"He must have hidden depths, though." Catullus flicked a finger at the magazine. "He was the one who bought this, then?"

"No. Crassus had it."

"Crassus? The millionaire?"

"I think he's a billionaire, actually."

"Yes, but it was still *the* Crassus, the one your brother's been busy leading strikes against? You've just been out with him?"

"Not just him. There was Pompey too, and others, oh, you know. Men in suits." She made a face. "Blagh. Metellus' friends. He made me go. I didn't want to, but I thought that since he'd made this great effort to get up out of bed, I'd better. I didn't want to give him a relapse. He was looking really dead, you know, all pale. Perhaps I should have stopped him going, I hadn't thought of that."

"Well, how did he look when he came back?"

"I don't know. I left him there. I had a row."

"With him?"

"No, with Crassus." As she thought back to it, she clasped a hand over her mouth. "Oh God, I was so awful. You know how I can get.

I can't believe how rude I was to him."

"Why, what did you say?"

"Oh, just that I thought he was obnoxious."

"And that was all?"

"That and a bit more. But he deserved it. He kept going on about what a fucking superstar he was. On and on and on." She made another face. "He thinks he's so wonderful, just because he makes all that money, and I told him I thought he was a shit. Which made him cross."

"I'm not surprised."

"But he is a shit, don't you think?"

"Probably, if he's a billionaire."

"Exactly. I mean, he must know that himself. I expect he's proud of it, really. So I don't see why he has to be uptight about it."

"Yes, but telling someone he's a shit, I mean, it's not exactly incisive, is it, as financial analysis goes?

Clodia laughed. "Oh God, who cares what he thinks?" She stretched languorously, then looked up at Catullus and smiled at something she had just remembered. "He did ask after you, though."

"Me?" Catullus stared back at her in surprise. "I've never even met him."

"He definitely asked after you, though. They all did."

"But I don't know any politicians."

"Well, they all seemed to know you. Or about you anyway. And they all liked your poems. They were raving about them, in fact."

Catullus shook his head in disbelief. He reached for the copy of 'Alexandrian', and opened it again. What was wrong, that a party of government ministers should think his poetry so good?

"Beloved." Clodia knocked the magazine out of his hands with a tired sweep of her hand.

"What?"

"Be romantic."

"I'm not romantic. I'm a neoteric."

"Well – whatever you are, suck my toes."

"I'd rather write."

"Later."

"I feel the muse's fire."

Clodia moaned. "I don't want to lie here and watch you writing a fucking poem. I want you to suck my toes. And then I want you to love me. And then I want to go to sleep. If you've got to write poems, you can do it then."

Catullus kissed her. "Have you washed your feet?" he whispered.

"Yes." She moaned again, and stroked herself gently. "Please."

Catullus smiled, and dropped the magazine to one side. But later, when Clodia was fast asleep, Catullus reached for his note book and opened it again, staring at the blank sheet of paper and then down, at the gently breathing woman who lay curled up beside him. Her lips, just open, could never have looked softer; her cheeks never have seemed quite as smooth; the shadows on her face and breasts lay so calm that it was as though Clodia, by falling into her deep sleep, had become a single person at last, the countless succession of her personalities stripped away, and left scattered, like her clothes, to wait for the morning. Catullus reached out to stroke the curve of her back. This naked, she was his. She couldn't escape him. He shifted, to watch the silhouette of her breast; it moved, gently, up and down, in time to her breathing, but the rhythm was that of sleep, and therefore of Catullus' possession of her. He shifted again; new shadows lengthened across her body, a new silhouette began to rise and fall, but still she stayed his, a single Clodia, a nude Clodia, his Clodia. He could feel his testicles starting to tighten again.

But of course, he couldn't wake her, not if he wanted to be sure that she would stay his, passive and framed by her owner's eye. Catullus began to stroke himself as he realised the paradox in which he had become enmeshed; the fulfilment of his fantasy required its frustration; play the master and he would lose his slave. He stroked himself harder; the idea that he might be trapped excited him. He stared at Clodia's naked body again, and listened to the soft undulations of her breath; the calmness now seemed so unbearable that Catullus was almost tempted to shatter it, anything, he thought, to find some relief, but no, it was impossible, he couldn't bring himself to part with the sight of Clodia asleep, and so his own desire prevented him from taking her, bound him so firmly that it might have been rope. Catullus still stroked himself, but with the knowledge now that it was the very impossibility of the climax he had been imagining that was keeping him excited. He ran his fingers delicately through Clodia's hair, and sighed. He would never get to sleep now. "Clodia," he whispered, "Clodia." Unwilled, a few lines of Sappho rose into his mind. He bent low and murmured them into Clodia's ear. Then he trailed away. He could only remember half the poem. He repeated the opening lines, and wondered if Sappho had done the same thing once, whispered the poem and not been heard, found out the truth of what her verses had claimed, that the greatest love can leave a lover paralysed, feeling like a god, no, more glorious even than that, more glorious than a god, but unable to move, slowly burning up from inside, and so almost near to a death as well.

Catullus reached for a pen, carefully, so as not to wake Clodia. He wrote her name down on his empty pad, then circled it. He could still feel his frustration tickling him deliciously. He murmured

Sappho's poem to himself again. Had writing about the symptoms of her passion helped her to calm them? Was that why Sappho had reached for her pen, to stop her finger tips from itching to be elsewhere, to leave them spent once the poem was done? No. Impossible. Sappho had written to perpetuate her desire, not to exhaust it. In her poem, she had created a lover from words, one that couldn't be touched, held, enjoyed. She had loved, and then shown her love transforming its object out of reach, into fantasy, tormenting, tantalising fantasy. Catullus stared back down at Clodia. Fantasy. That was what he too had created, from her sleep and his own gnawing desire, an unreal woman, a woman he couldn't hope to possess. If he wrote about her, he would have to admit this; and yet the recording of such an admission would also surely be its own best excuse, for passion was rarely able to fulfill itself, and frustration had its own erotic thrill – wasn't that what he had been discovering all night? He stroked himself, harder and harder the more he longed to touch Clodia. Then he reached for his pen again. He began to write.

He dedicated the poem to its inspirations, his desire for Clodia as she lay asleep beside him, the similar desire he had found in Sappho's lines. All that he could remember of her poem, he translated; the rest he composed himself. He tried to imagine Sappho, writing like him, somewhere remote in the past; next to an olive skinned girl, perhaps, lying in bed, gazing through a window at the rocky shores of Lesbos, and beyond them, at the burning blue Aegean sea. Catullus glanced down at Clodia, so real by his side, distilled into squiggles on the sheet of his pad. Tomorrow was Thursday. He would be visiting Boot's aunt. He would give her the poem, and perhaps she would publish it, and then, perhaps, a few people would read what he had written, and wonder how he had written it, and imagine a new Clodia who would then become theirs. Catullus reached out to stroke the breasts of his Clodia – the real Clodia. She moaned and stirred, but didn't wake. Catullus watched her as she felt for a pillow and hugged it, like a tiny girl clutching a doll. He would wake her, Catullus thought, he would do it. He had written his poem now, amber encasing memory. But first – Catullus looked at Clodia's name, where he had circled it at the top of his writing pad. He thought for a few seconds, then crossed it out. Lesbos, Lesbian, Lesbia. Lesbia. With himself the new Sappho? – perhaps. But Lesbia, yes. The perfect choice. He found Clodia's name where he had written it in his poem, crossed it out and carefully inked in 'Lesbia' instead. Then, with that decided, Catullus closed his writing pad, tossed Lesbia aside, and reached out, at last, to wake up Clodia.

XIII

CLAUDIUS

The next day it was cold. Catullus and Clodia went for a long walk, hand in hand. We look like children, Catullus thought, as they stood by a park pond and stared at their reflections. They were both pink-faced and muffled against the chill. As they talked, the autumn air against their cheeks made their intimacy seem to glow all the warmer. Catullus kissed Clodia; she smiled back at him, and took his arm. They walked on, and the light began to fade. The margins of the park were lost in mist. Clodia held Catullus tighter, then hugged him as she walked, and the soggy darkness seemed lit by a shared sense of joy.

Back home, Clodia made a fire and they both nestled down in front of it, curled on thick cushions. Clodia started to draw; Catullus reached for a paper and skimmed through the headlines. Caesar had begun to dump vast reserves of Roman currency; the stock exchange was melting; Clodius had led a protest against rocketing food prices. From outside, there was a sudden scudding of rain against the windows. Catullus put the paper down and lay back, listening to the patterings of the rain and the crackling of the fire in the hearthplace. Shadows leapt and danced across the room. Catullus watched Clodia as she drew, her hands cast white, her face and hair orange by the light from her reading lamp. She looked so solemn, so abstracted. The artist. Another unsuspected Clodia.

At last, she tossed her sketch aside and stood up. Catullus reached across for the notepad and studied Clodia's drawing.

"Is it good?" he asked after a pause, deliberately echoing the question she had asked him the night before.

Clodia smiled lazily. "A drawing's only as good as its subject."

"And what is the subject?"

"You, of course."

"Really?" Catullus studied the sketch again. "Is it modern?"

"Oh, very." She pointed at a canvas propped against the wall. "See? Everything I do is thoroughly modern."

"You painted that?"

"Yes."

"But it's wonderful."

"Of course it is. I have to sell it. I'm a painter. That's what I do."

"I had no idea." Catullus stared at the canvas again. It was – wonderful – whatever. He felt inadequate to describe what he liked about it, and realising that, he felt ashamed. All the time, he had been thinking that it was he who was the artist. He looked at Clodia with a renewed desire, born of envy and admiration.

Did she realise what he was thinking? She bent down to kiss him and blew softly on his neck. Then she pointed at the sketch she had drawn. "I wanted to thank you for your poem."

Catullus brightened. "You found it? You liked it?"

"Yes. I thought it was lovely. And *very* flattering."

Catullus smiled and bent his neck back to kiss her. "Only, there is just one problem. I don't understand paintings and you don't understand poems, so what do we do about the language barrier?"

"I don't want to *talk* about them. I can't be bothered with that sort of shit." She shook her head, and padded softly back into the shadows. "They're gestures, aren't they? That's why they matter."

Catullus shrugged. Carefully, he tore off Clodia's drawing from the pad and laid it to one side. Then he reached for a pencil. He looked at Clodia. She was staring into her fish tank, occasionally dabbling her fingers into the water, or puckering her lips at the fish as they swam past her face. "Look," she said. "There's a Clodia. And there's one who looks like you." She glanced round. "Write a poem about him."

"Why?"

"Why not? I don't want people thinking that you and I just sit around having sex and high-minded feelings about each other. It would be nice for them to know we do other things as well."

"Like watching goldfish?"

Clodia stood over him. "You know what I mean. Like now. Don't you feel happy? It's nice and warm and that's all it is, it's not profound or anything, but it's – you know. And to have that sort of feeling with anyone..."

"Yes." Catullus stared into her eyes. Then he glanced over at the fish tank. "So – no sex, no profundity. Impossible."

Clodia reached for a bottle and poured out a measure of brandy. "Drink that," she said, handing it over. "And sit next to the fire." And so Catullus did, snuggling comfortably into a cushion while Clodia stroked his hair and stared dreamily into the patterns of the darkness. "There," said Catullus, when he had finished writing. "Fish with no sex." Clodia peered over his shoulder and read the poem. She began to laugh. "You can't go on about fish like that. You can't. Not if you're trying not to be obscene." "Really?" "Yes." Catullus reread his poem and understood. The brandy made him feel heavy with the joke. He reached for Clodia, and felt so lazy and happy to be holding her that he wanted time to stop, so that he could fall into his experience of the moment like a stone, feel it washing over him forever. Clodia kissed him, and Catullus opened his lips as he laughed, and pulled her down on top of him, and his limbs felt dull with erotic warmth. "How can I finish the poem now?" he asked, stretching slowly as Clodia began to stroke him. "No excuses," said Clodia. "And remember – nothing obscene." She handed him the writing pad, then reached for a stocking and used it to gag him. "Total silence. I want that poem. Just write."

And so Catullus did. The fish became a bird, stroked and petted in Lesbia's lap, the object of her affections as it was of the poem itself. As Catullus wrote, the laziness he could feel inside his bones flickered into a golden haze of sexual delight, but he stayed true to his word and kept the poem untouched by what he felt, Clodia's touch against his skin, the warmth of the fire and her body against his. As with the night before, the sense of being restrained aroused him even further, his passions heightened by the very requirement to keep them in check, the stocking in his mouth and the bird in his poem both delicious symbols of discipline. "Is it innocent enough now?" he asked Clodia through his gag once he had finished the poem and handed it up to her. Clodia read it through and nodded. "But I haven't got a bird," she muttered. "Still, is that the point?"

Catullus nodded back at her. "It made the poem all the more exciting to write," he tried to explain, untying the gag. "Even more than the one I wrote last night. That one left me feeling emptied, because I could write about what I felt. This one, I still feel..." His voice trailed away.

Clodia nodded and re-read the poem, then handed it back to Catullus. "Come out with me tonight."

"Where are you going?"

"To Marghi's."

"The leather dyke club?"

"You don't have to be a dyke."

"And what about the leather?"

Clodia shrugged. "Suit yourself." She stretched luxuriantly and curled up again in front of the fire. "I'd have thought you were in the mood for it, though."

Yes, maybe. Catullus stared at her longingly, and tried to picture her as a leather dyke. "I've got to go out first," he said slowly.

"Come along afterwards, then. Phone when you've finished." She turned and sat up to face him. "What are you doing, anyway?"

"Meeting my friend's uncle. The one who edits the poetry."

"Won't it be dull?"

"I don't know. Depends how wonderful they think I am."

Clodia grunted. "Sounds boring to me. But you go if you want." Catullus was delighted. Was she feeling cross? Did she want him to stay with her? He glanced at his watch. Time to meet Boot. And time to leave, now that he could pass an evening imagining that Clodia was missing him. "I'll be taking those two poems I wrote to you," he said, slipping them into his bag.

"Good," said Clodia, staring into the fire.

"Doesn't it flatter you? All of them wondering who Lesbia is?"

Clodia poured herself a brandy and sipped at it. Catullus smiled. He walked across to the door and looked back at Clodia, who was still curled up in front of the fire's orange glow. "See you tonight, then," he said. "Miss me," he added in a soft whisper. He left the house content.

The warmth in his stomach survived the rain, and it survived the tube journey out from central Rome, his first since that fateful day when he had discovered Mona's corpse. Beyond the tube exit, it was still raining. As he splashed along the pavements with Boot, Catullus felt the brandy warmth in his veins suddenly sicken and chill. He squeezed Boot's hand. She stared into his eyes, and smiled sadly.

"Are you thinking about Mona?" she asked.

Catullus nodded. "How did you know?"

"The streets round here." She gestured, at bars and cafés humming with the wind-up towards night. "It's the sort of place she liked coming to. It reminds me of her. That's all." She took Catullus' arm. "But let's not talk about it. Please."

"No. No, of course not." Catullus walked on in silence, Boot beside him. He tried to forget about Mona, and think about the evening ahead of him instead. But it didn't make him feel better. He suddenly realised, as though for the first time, that he was about to meet someone who really mattered, whose taste was unsparing, influence unlimited, and that he had chosen to bring, what? – love poems. Oh, to be sure, artificial constructs, in neat unsparing metres, all very Alexandrian, all very Greek, and yet, and yet – something more as well, to him at least, distillations of his longings, his own sensations, the most precious possessions a memory can have, not to be scattered blindly like jewels into mud. The cold weight in his stomach began to churn. He was swept by a desperate longing to be back with Clodia, who didn't give a shit about poetry and objective opinions, and only liked his poems because they were about her. That was the sort of readership he wanted. Not mocking sophisticates, passionless.

"What's it going to be like tonight?" he asked.

"How should I know?" said Boot, surprised. "I've never been to this sort of thing before."

"Why are you coming now, then?"

"Because you're going, of course."

"Your uncle's that frightening, is he? – you can't send me in alone?"

Boot shook her head and laughed. "No. You've just got to stand up to him, that's all. He's a little military in manner, but it's just eccentricity now."

"So he was in the army once?"

"Yes, in Circassia."

"Oh?"

"He had a boyfriend I think, other ranks, anyway, all rather difficult."

"What, he got drummed out?"

"No, no, I don't mean that, I mean I think the boy friend died, got shot or something, blown up. I don't know, it's still very raw, I've never asked about it. Never dared." She stopped by an elegantly porticoed doorway. "And here we are," she said, ringing the bell. She smiled. "You'll be fine. Don't worry. He may be eccentric, but just remember, he does know what he's talking about."

"I know." Catullus hunched his shoulders gloomily. "That's what's worrying me."

The door opened. "Oh, wonderful. You did come." A young man, in antique clothes, high shirt collar below his bloodless face, a vampiric frock-coat, long and black. Unmistakably the man from Ricket's Gate – the man Catullus had thought he was standing up. What was he doing here? "Aurelius is upstairs," the young man told Boot. "With his acolytes." He turned to Catullus, and tugged softly at his sleeve. "A word," he whispered, "I have an apology to make." He drew Catullus across the hall.

"What is it?" Catullus asked.

"This." The young man brushed back his hair, his long thick hair, as though tired of its weight, and the heavy lids of his eyes drooped low. "Aurelius – my friend, I think I mentioned him – he is not an enthusiast for the Man of Blood."

"Man of Blood?"

"Yes, this evening, our talk. It was on the invitation."

Catullus remembered. "Yes, I'm sorry. Of course."

"I love Aurelius very much. I love him with a profound, ripe, unappeasable yearning, which is eternal, I'm sure. Nevertheless," – the young man paused, and stretched his fingers out – "this evening, it so happens, Aurelius has behaved like a bitch. With deliberate obstructiveness, he has organised one of his literary gatherings, here, tonight." The young man's cheeks pinched his narrow bones. "It will be dull, dull, dull, and I hate it, it's desecration!"

Catullus wanted to laugh. "Don't worry on my account. I'm very fond of poetry."

"Are you? Well, I am not." The young man suddenly hissed with rage, and bit his lip, so furiously that blood began to smudge his skin. He darted out his tongue, and swallowed, and his face seemed to twist and flicker at the taste. With some effort, he recomposed himself. "It can't be helped, I suppose," he said, taking Catullus' arm. He dabbed at his lip again, with his finger, then sucked at it daintily. His face softened, as though with sudden remembrance. "But I love Aurelius all the same. And so must you. He is a wonderful man, despite everything. Come with me and meet him now."

Catullus followed the young man up the stairs. "Are there many poets coming tonight?" he asked.

"Two, I think. One's here already. He claims to be an astrophysicist, so as you can imagine – he's dull. The second's yet to arrive." The young man opened a door and glided Catullus through. "But he'll be dull as well. They all are, all dull."

"Ah! My poet!" A stentorian voice, with just the faintest rise at the end of each word. Catullus looked round and saw a large-muscled man bearing down on him. Aurelius, it had to be – he was wearing the leather trousers that Boot had described, and his body and hair, cropped very short, were still those of a soldier. Catullus offered his hand – it was crushed in a vice. "Good to see you," said Boot's uncle, wringing his arm, "damn good. My poet," he added, gesturing.

"No, Aurelius, wishful thinking, I'm afraid." The young man in black took Catullus' spare arm. "He's mine."

"No."

"Yes. He's my archaeologist."

Aurelius shrugged, clearly quite unsurprised. "So? So? May be yours, Furius, but he's my poet as well, and so I guess we'll just have to share him, won't we, eh?" A clipped laugh, and then he yanked Catullus free from Furius' grip. "Come on! Let's get things moving! This way, come along!"

He frogmarched his guest into a second room, pushing the door open as though shoving his way through a crowd. Catullus looked around in silent astonishment. He was in a morgue for dead gods; statues were laid out everywhere, full statues, torsoes, legs, even, in one corner, three large toes and the fragment of a foot. The necropolis was massed by the side of each wall; in the centre of the room, barely illuminated by the candles dotted around on various plinths and marble slabs, was an arc of elegantly arranged antique chairs. Catullus' fellow guests were all sitting perched on them. Everyone seemed to be studying a copy of Pheidias' Zeus. Then Catullus realised that they were watching a television screen.

"News," Aurelius explained. "This damn crisis."

"Why, what's happened now?"

"Well may you ask! Never bloody seems to end, does it?" He peered at the television. "Oh, it's Caesar. Demanding Clodius be handed over to him. That's right. Started some run on the currency markets, interest rates gone up, something like that. Ask my brother, he's a businessman. I find it all damn incomprehensible."

"Why didn't you tell me who you were?" whispered Furius softly in Catullus' ear. "You are evil." He draped himself on a chaise. "Here, sit down beside me and make amends." Catullus cleared away a few Egyptian gods, then joined him; Aurelius perched awkwardly on a pedestal, his hand on Catullus' back.

"Know everyone, do you?" he whispered boomingly. "There's Horatio Gower, of course, you've met him." Oh yes. Catullus lifted his hand. "What about Titus?" Aurelius asked. "Know him? Brilliant man. Astrophysics, written a poem about it, can you believe? Wanted you two to meet, think you'll find each other interesting."

"I think we already have met, if he's the man I'm thinking of. Is he here?"

"Yes, behind Saturn Defeated." Catullus peered. There he sat, Titus, as wrapped in silence as he had been before in Cicero's dining room. His eyes were almost shut, and he was playing, as before, with the long skewers of his fingers. Catullus nodded to him, but Titus didn't look up, continued to stare into whatever depths his thoughts were charting. There was a sheaf of papers waiting on his lap.

"And then, just next to Furius, that's his star guest, Marcia." Aurelius pointed. Marcia was large and round, with a kind smile and warm eyes, and looked rather out of place. "Our expert on the Man of Blood," Furius whispered. He gestured at the television. Clodius was being interviewed. "Him, Clodius, she's been reading some of his papers. Family records, only just found, from the Civil War. The results" – his eyes narrowed as he hissed the word – "fascinating."

Catullus breathed in deeply, as he realised what Furius was talking about. "These papers," he asked after a slight pause, trying to sound nonchalant, "would they have belonged to Claudius?"

Marcia overheard him, and nodded. "Claudius Pulcher," she mouthed.

"Very impressive," said Aurelius, a hint of annoyance in his voice. "How did you know that? But of course – you're working with Horatio, I forgot. So you'll be playing on both sides of the field this evening, literature and that damn Civil War. But don't forget – I'm the one who's publishing you." He rose to his feet. The news had ended. Aurelius crossed to the television set, and pulled the plug out, decisively. He began to goad a conversation into life. The business of the evening was formally under way.

Catullus glanced at Marcia, and wished that he could talk to her about her work on Claudius' papers. He looked round the room for a Sesostris. There had to be one. He found it eventually, in a dark corner lit by a single candle, only a small statue, but entire, and since it was surrounded by fragments of arms and sliced thighs, it looked like a scavenger perched on a butcher's slab. Catullus remembered Doctor Gower's book, and its chapter on blood sacrifice. What rituals had Claudius Pulcher practised? And what about Marius? He needed to know. Lives might depend on it. His own included, he thought.

Aurelius was discussing literature, and the publisher's role. "They're ungrateful bastards, writers," he coughed. "Can't write if you're not going to get published. What's the damn point? No damn point at all. Writers write, but publishers produce. Don't you think, eh?" He nodded at Catullus.

Catullus bowed his head imperceptibly. He could see his chance. "You don't always write *only* to be published."

"Nonsense. Sentimental cant of the worst kind."

"You think so? But often, isn't writing just a need, like any form of expression, almost a relief? It can be so private an impulse, sometimes, that even the thought of publication would be sacrilege."

Aurelius snorted. "That how you feel, is it?"

"Sometimes, yes, it's usually a passing fit admittedly, but I wasn't actually thinking of myself this once." He turned to Marcia. "The papers you're looking at for Clodius. The ones his ancestor wrote. Were they private? They must have been."

"Oh yes," said Furius at once, "do tell us about them. Marcia, please. The Civil War! That cruel, dark time." His eyes narrowed as he smiled. "Stir our blood."

"Well..." Marcia looked uncertain. She glanced at Aurelius. "We were talking about literature. I don't want to..."

Furius silenced her with a delicate wave of the hand. "Yours is a narrative of mystery and dissolving time. Can that not rank as literature?" he asked.

"Certainly sounds intriguing enough," said Doctor Gower.

"Yes, remarkable," agreed Catullus.

"But not literature," boomed Aurelius. He stared harshly round the room. Marcia swallowed nervously; then Aurelius threw his arms up in the air. "Oh, yes, go on, why don't you? Tell us what you've found, Marcia. I'm sure it's *fascinating*."

"Well – I hope so. I mean, I find it fascinating, but, well, I don't know..." She blinked through her glasses. "If you really are interested. I don't even know how much you all know. Perhaps it would be best if I just started at the beginning. If you'd prefer that? Aurelius?" Aurelius sighed and waved his arm limply. With an apologetic cough, Marcia began to set the scene.

Catullus listened alertly, even though, to begin with, he had already learnt most of what she was talking about. Marcia sketched a brief description of the career of Claudius Pulcher, his early sympathies with republicanism, his refusal to stand by the King in the Civil War, his close association with Marius, his military genius, and his subsequent role in helping to establish the Republic. She touched on her own career as a historian of the period, and she mentioned two of her books, one on Claudius himself, and one on the underground cults of the time. She described her excitement on first handling the papers, and then, as though she were telling a ghost story, began to describe what she had read and found in them. Catullus leaned forwards. Doctor Gower, he noticed, began to stir uneasily as well.

It was well known, Marcia explained, that Claudius had always had a profound interest in the underground hermeticism that had begun to flourish during the breakdown of more conventional structures of belief in the Civil War. But what she hadn't realised – and what no one had realised – was the depth of that interest, nor, she added, the specific and remarkable character that it had taken. She didn't want to sound certain about anything – the papers were too disorganised to allow that, and too many of them were written in an arcane language that bordered on a code. But, and Marcia repeated again that it was a large but, if her first assumptions were correct, then their contents had revolutionary implications for studies of the whole period. For not just Claudius but Marius as well, it seemed, had been devotees of a hermetic cult that could possibly, just possibly, have underlain many of the most central tenets of their republican beliefs.

Marcia cleared her throat and turned to Doctor Gower. "The origins of the cult were very remote," she said. "It must have been present in Rome before the Civil War, but it has been difficult to find traces of it. In fact, before I started looking at these papers, it was hard enough finding traces of it in the Civil War records, and that's the period in Roman history when it seems to have been most popular. Up until now, though, historians had always assumed that even that popularity wasn't very extensive. So when I wanted to find out more about this cult that Claudius was writing about, I had to turn to a historian from a quite different field. Doctor Gower, it is a great honour to meet you here tonight, for that historian was yourself." She felt in her bag and drew out a book. Catullus recognised it. The one he had read in the Portakabin. "This was the best account of the origins of the cult I could find." She turned to everyone else. "One of Doctor Gower's classic studies of Circassia."

And what about Marius, Catullus thought impatiently. Marcia needed prompting. "So the cult," he asked, "the one that Claudius imported from Circassia, that must have been what – Sesostris?"

"Yes, that's right. You know Doctor Gower's book?"

"Of course, he employs me." While everyone laughed politely, Doctor Gower frowned and shook his head. Catullus understood. Don't mention the statue. But Catullus wasn't interested in Circassia, he wanted to hear about the Civil War.

"I only know a little bit about Sesostris," he said, speaking to Marcia again. "He was the god who inspired the blood sacrifice, wasn't he?" Marcia nodded and agreed that he was. Everyone else began to look more interested, even Aurelius, despite himself. Amazing what a mention of blood can do, Catullus thought. As good a time as any, then, to press onwards to the crucial question.

"So what are you saying?" he asked. "That Claudius and Co. were busy sacrificing people, in the middle of the Civil War, in the middle of Rome, to some strange Circassian god? Is that what the papers prove?"

Marcia rocked backwards and forwards, thinking about the question. "Well – let's put it like this. You have to remember the context. The Sesostris cult was brought to Rome as a pseudo-philosophy. Sesostris himself was worshipped less as a god, more as the founder of a new way of thinking – that was why his adherents worshipped him as divine, because the nature of his insights seemed to suggest that he had to be divine. You see?"

"Yes," said Doctor Gower, nodding. "Like the Egyptian god Thoth, or the Jewish Moses. They were seen as lightning rods, connecting the divine and the human, the personifications of wisdom." He shifted in his seat, as though preparing himself to deliver a long lecture, and cleared his throat. Catullus saw his chance, and interrupted him.

"I'm sorry," he said to Marcia, "I'm being ghoulish here, and probably naive as well, but I still want to know if Claudius went around sacrificing people."

"Yes," said Furius, licking at his lips, "that's what we all want to know."

"Oh dear." Marcia shook her head. "You're forcing me into conjecture and sensationalism, which is what you want, I suppose. Oh dear, oh dear." She furrowed her brow, then shook her head again, vigorously. "No. No, Claudius didn't sacrifice people. I'm certain of that. Not in the sense you mean 'sacrifice', anyway."

"So what sense do you mean?"

"Aha. That's the question, isn't it?" She laughed uncertainly, then turned to Boot. "I wonder, could you please pass that little figurine there, the one just next to you?"

Catullus watched as Marcia was handed the tiny statue of Sesostris. The scimitar of the eagle's beak was silhouetted against the lamp, and the rims of its eye were lit a dim orange. It looked cruel and alien, and very strange.

"Now, Doctor Gower will correct me if I'm wrong here," said Marcia, "but in Circassia itself, Sesostris himself had a dual personality. You can see it reflected in this little statue – man's body, eagle's head. This idea that the god represented a tension within himself was brought to the West, and it rapidly became the focus of the entire cult, at least as it developed in Rome. It was claimed that Sesostris had founded civilisation and culture – the very standards of human behaviour and achievement that Rome herself was now claiming to embody as well. But the Circassian legend also contained a warning. If Sesostris was worshipped as the founder of civilization, then he was also to be feared as its potential destroyer. Let me quote Diodorus, and again, Doctor Gower, you may have to correct me here." Marcia shut her eyes, and her knuckles whitened as she clutched the statuette even tighter. "'The Circassians say that their god is both good and evil, light and dark, and that it is impossible for him ever to be at peace with himself.'" She opened her eyes again, and looked round her audience. "You see? The cult only really became popular when the Romans were starting to believe that they were a chosen people. But this was also a period when many of the more intelligent people in Rome were starting to feel a deep pessimism about the implications of their own achievements. They were worried that success was rotting away its own foundations. They worried that they were becoming brutalized, corrupt. Many people began to fear that civilization – by which they meant their own, of course – was unable to progress without also retrogressing, that this process was inherent in its very nature. And so the teachings associated with Sesostris began to fall on fertile ground."

"Why?" asked Furius. "And what has this got to do with blood sacrifice?"

Thank you, thought Catullus. Marcia bobbed her head nervously and smiled.

"Well – according to Diodorus Siculus, the blood sacrifices were a Circassian tradition. That had always been a bit of an embarrassment to Sesostris' adherents in Rome, not surprisingly I suppose – it wasn't really the sort of thing they wanted associated with their philosopher-god. So the more sophisticated followers of the cult began to abstract what had originally been a literal report, and say that the sacrifices symbolised man's need to cast out his own evil, that kind of thing. Because Sesostris was both eternal and mortal himself, and a part of him had had to die before he returned to heaven, he was cast as an example of this kind of a sacrifice – he became a prototype, I suppose, rather than a god to be worshipped. Similarly, the need for sacrifice itself was enshrined as a moral rather than a purely religious requirement. So this was what the Roman adherents of Sesostris ended up arguing -"; Marcia raised her hand, and began to count off points on her fingers. "They said that the universe was founded on an eternal conflict. They said that any gain had to be paid for by a loss. They said that civilization erected its pillars on blood. And having argued all that, some then concluded that the world of order generated its own shadowy inverse, and that certainty itself could only be maintained by acknowledging that nothing was certain. In the more mystical of tracts, this came to be seen as the ultimate sacrifice – the admission that order *was* chaos. And hence in turn, a further paradox – by acknowledging chaos, the hope was raised that order could be restored."

"Did they really believe that?" Titus asked suddenly. He tapped gently at the papers bundled on his knees. "How remarkable." He nodded, repeated his observation, then lapsed back into his customary silence. No one else spoke. Catullus thought, in the stillness, about what Marcia had said. A memory rose in his mind – a disturbing memory, a memory of a pattern of words, scrawled in the margin of a tattered history book. "I wonder," he said suddenly, "whether this world of order you've been talking about, and its shadowy inverse, was this expressed by any sort of mystic configuration of numbers or mathematical values?" God, everyone was looking at him strangely. Did his voice sound odd? He carried on. "Because mathematics was important to a lot of those hermetic sects, wasn't it? Pythagoras, obviously, even Zeno, I suppose – I mean, didn't they see numbers as the key to the architecture of the universe? Numbers, and the patterns they could make – that sort of thing. I was just wondering," he trailed off lamely.

Marcia smiled and nodded. "That's an interesting question." She nodded to herself again. "If I could, I'd like to postpone answering it, just for a minute or two, because I wanted to say something about Claudius himself that will lead into that very subject." She stared briefly at the statue in her hands, then looked up again. "You see, what's exciting about these papers I've been looking at is that they prove quite categorically that Claudius was an adherent to the Sesostris cult. In one sense, I suppose, I wasn't very surprised. The Sesostris cult had always been attractive to anti-royalists. Even way back in Circassia, it had underpinned a form of republicanism – that was why it had originally had to stay underground in Rome, you see. But increasingly, the cult was also used to sanction overt rebellion. After all – it claimed that disorder sometimes had to be fought with even greater disorder, that otherwise chaos might come again, that the blood of the few occasionally had to be shed for the good of the many. And in a way, it was because people believed something very similar that they ended up choosing to fight a civil war. People rose against the King because they wanted to avoid the threat of an even greater conflagration later on. So – you can imagine – Claudius wasn't the only one who used religion to justify his actions.

"But –"; Marcia paused, and beamed over her glasses. "But – Claudius' devotion to Sesostris seems to have been literal, and therefore rather bizarre. Very bizarre, in fact."

"What do you mean by that?" asked Doctor Gower, leaning forwards and staring at her intently.

"Well, Doctor, you will know better than anyone how literal the Circassians once were with their religious practices." She smiled at Catullus. "Yes, and you too, judging by your look of eager relish."

Hardly relish, Catullus thought, it's my nerves, my fucking nerves. But he forced himself to smile. "So there *were* sacrifices?" he asked.

Marcia shook her head. "No, as I said before, not sacrifices, not to the god. But maybe something even more interesting."

"Involving blood?" Doctor Gower asked. Catullus studied him. So what had he been thinking about for the past fortnight? What had he been making of that slice through Mona's head, and the identical wound they had found on the skeleton in its Civil War tomb? Something, but nothing like an answer, judging by the perturbed look on his face. Well, thought Catullus, go on Marcia, tell us what you've come up with. See if you have an answer.

"This is what I discovered in Claudius' papers," said Marcia, picking up the statue of Sesostris again, and angling it so that its eyes caught the candlelight. "I discovered that Claudius himself was something far more than just a conventional devotee of Sesostris. He was a philosopher, a mystic – he was fond of describing himself as a guardian of eternal truths. Now – I can't be certain about this – but I think it's pretty clear that Claudius felt able to make this claim because he had been initiated into the cult's highest and most dreadful secrets – and that, I can assure you, made him one of a very, very select few. Other hermetic texts have come down to us – but apart from Claudius' own papers, only one other collection of writings has survived which betray a full initiate's knowledge of arcana. But Claudius himself, of course, was much more than just an initiate – he was also an important man, a man of real power. And it is that which makes his papers so uniquely exciting. They aren't just a record of beliefs – they are also the record of beliefs translated into action, into affairs of the state.

"For instance – one mark of Claudius' status is the title he gives to Sesostris. Lower initiates always referred to the god as 'Korephtis' – the Greek word for dancer, of course. But in the two advanced texts we possess, Sesostris is named 'Sirephtok' – and in Claudius' papers too, this is the title that the god is given. So what is the significance of such a word?" She turned to Doctor Gower. "You remember how in the original Circassian myths, the dance was the symbol of the civilization that Sesostris brought, and its accompanying blend of violence and peace? Well, this symbolic value survives in the texts of the Roman mystics, and reaches a sort of macabre apotheosis, I suppose, in Claudius' own writings. Dance, for Claudius, is a pattern of movements imposed on chaos – at its profoundest, it is capable of mimicking the tensions that form the universe, and, perhaps, even of overcoming them. And this –"; she turned to face Catullus; "this is where the two points you raised, about ritual killings and about the patterning of mathematical values, meet and coalesce. Because, you see, in Claudius' writings, both are referred to as answering the same need, and the need, in Claudius' case, was nothing less than the salvation of the Roman state."

Catullus sat back in his chair. Oh God. "How many murders do you think Claudius was responsible for?" he asked slowly.

"Four," said Marcia promptly. "And do you want to know why I think that? Well – as I said, the secret is in Sesostris' title. 'Sirephtok'. Think about it. It is both an anagram and a cryptogram, a standard hermetic conceit. Take the Greek word 'Korephtis', translate it into our script, and you have nine letters. Nine is an odd number – it can therefore be used very effectively to symbolise the value of a world in chaos, where even is odd, and odd even. Subtract an even number of letters from both the start and finish of the word – say two – and then invert them, to suggest the presence of order within chaos. You see? And then, having done that, you leave the middle five letters as they are, to suggest the exact inverse, the presence of order within chaos, and lo and behold! – 'Korephtis' has become 'Sirephtok'. You have a typographical representation of the pattern formed by the universe, with symmetry and asymmetry framed and all astruggle. And what is more, you know where to commit your murders."

"Even, odd, even," muttered Catullus to himself.

"What did you say?" asked Doctor Gower sharply.

"Even, odd, even," repeated Catullus, his voice suddenly rising. "Isn't that right? Isn't that the pattern? You murder someone, it doesn't matter where, anywhere, you just kill him. You repeat the murder, maybe – I don't know – a fixed distance away, anyway, one that's capable of being divided by an odd number. Then you impose the pattern you've just been talking about inside those two points. Yes?" Marcia nodded. Everyone else looked bemused. Catullus thought that he was going to break. "Don't you see?" he asked Boot, trying to calm his voice. Mona had been her lover, after all, she had a duty to understand. "Even, odd, even. Yes? The killings are like the specially arranged letters, an imposition of symbolic value onto the world. Doesn't that make sense?" His voice began to rise again. "Aren't I right?"

Doctor Gower shifted. "Well, yes," he agreed, "that's certainly how the Circassians interpreted the sacrifices they made. You can tell from the graves of the victims. They're all lined up in fours, with an even distance between the first and second graves, and then the third and fourth, but an odd distance between second and third." He stared at Marcia. "Are you saying that the same pattern was repeated in the Civil War? That people were actually murdered according to it?"

Marcia nodded. "That's certainly what Claudius' papers seem to suggest." She turned to Catullus. "You see what I meant, when I said that he hadn't actually been sacrificing people – well – at least not to a god?"

"But he was offering his victims up to the state, wasn't he?" asked Catullus dully. "To Rome."

"Yes. I suppose so." Marcia thought. "If you care to put it like that. But it was something more as well. It was a literal attempt to invoke chaos and thereby dispel it. It presupposed that the symbolic could have a significance that would then be able to affect the real. Certainly, I have no doubt, from the evidence of his papers, that Claudius believed wholeheartedly in the value of what he was doing."

"Not much of an excuse though, that, was it?" said Doctor Gower slowly. "Ironic really. That the Roman mystics should have allegorized the need for sacrifice, while preserving the old primitive belief as a revelation to be awarded to their most privileged initiates. Don't know quite what that says about religion – something depressing though."

Titus nodded his head vigorously at this, but Marcia frowned. "No," she said. "I think that Claudius was exceptional. He and Marius."

"Tell me, then," said Catullus. "Marius – he believed the same thing, did he?"

"It's hard to be certain," said Marcia. "But I think he did. He is referred to by name in Claudius' papers, sometimes with a Circassian surname, the name of the king in the original legend, you know, the one who blended with the eagle goddess. Do you remember that old story, the one in which Marius met an eagle-headed dancer and then watched him being torn to pieces?" She held the statuette of Sesostris to the lamp again. "Well – if you assume, as Claudius seems to have done, that Marius was an initiate, then the whole strange story seems to make sense."

"Because it refers to a murder that Marius commited himself?"

Marcia shrugged. "Well – one that he at least sanctioned, he and Claudius. Remember where and when it took place. In the king's gardens, at the very height of the siege, when Marius must have been terribly afraid that the royalists were about to capture the city. I think that the murders, if they were indeed committed, were born of desperation. Marius was willing to try anything. And we know for a fact, don't forget, that a body was found in the Tiber the next day, complete with the ritual wound to the skull. Something must have happened."

Boot's knuckles had turned white. So she had noticed the reference. She looked up and stared into Catullus' eyes. God, he thought, if I look half as pale as you do, I must be looking very disturbed indeed. And I am disturbed, I am.

"So let's get this straight," he said, staring intently at Marcia. "This story about the Hooded Dancer – that refers to one of the actual killings, you think?"

"Well – it seems a possible explanation, put it that way."

Catullus nodded. "And are there any, um – any suggestions as to where the other killings might have taken place?"

"Unfortunately, no. Not in the records, anyway."

Boot began to hug herself. Doctor Gower shifted, and scratched his head. But Catullus kept calm, and his voice stayed measured and slow. But he could hear his heart beating loudly in his ears.

"Presumably," he said, patting at his chest meditatively, "if you could find out where a second murder had taken place, then you could use the coordinates to work out where the other two murders had been committed as well – couldn't you?"

Marcia thought about it. "No. You'd need three murders. Two wouldn't be enough. You'd know where one and two were, or three and four, or whatever, but you wouldn't then be able to use those coordinates to extrapolate the remaining two. The values of odd and even aren't fixed, remember. You'd have your straight line, of course – you could get a map, and then just draw it between the two points and extend it either way. Then you'd know that your two other murders were somewhere on that line. But, as I said, to find out where exactly all of them had been committed, well, you'd have to have three of the murders pinpointed before you could work out all four."

"I've had enough of this," said Aurelius suddenly, rising to his feet. "We're running out of time, and I want to hear some poetry. If we've got to hear about formulae and figures, then let us please listen to Titus. This was meant to be an evening devoted to verse."

"No, darling," said Furius, stretching langorously, "this was an evening devoted to the mysteries of the past." He smiled. "The Man of Blood, the figure of our dreams, haunting the cusp of things living and dead."

"Well, you've had bloody bucketloads of that, it's my turn now." Aurelius stabbed with his finger. "Titus! Your poem! I want to hear an extract at once." Then he glanced at Catullus. "And I hope you've brought something along too. That's what you're here for, to read your verse, not sit there and gibber."

"I'm sorry," said Catullus suddenly, standing up. "I've got to go."

"What? But you can't! He's going! He is, he's going! Stop him someone, dammit, stop him!"

Catullus ignored all orders. He pushed his way past Doctor Gower and through a clump of bronze divinities, but his heart was beating so fast that he felt as though he were made of rippling water, and could flow through anything. Outside, in the next room, he leant against a wall. He breathed in deeply and shut his eyes. Oh God. God, oh God. Why him? What had he done to get mixed up in such shit?

Someone tapped him on the shoulder. He opened his eyes. Boot. They stared at each other. "Did you understand all that stuff back in there?" he asked.

Boot ignored the question. "You can't go," she said.

"I've got to. I can't just sit here. I've got to do something."

"About what?"

"About Mona. Perhaps you didn't understand after all, but those people Marcia was talking about, the ones who got killed in the Civil War, they all had their faces sliced off. Yes, that's right, Boot, just like Mona. And like someone else as well, an old man I knew. Which makes two. Which makes two more still to be killed. Which means that we should do something pretty urgently, don't you think?"

Boot stared at him. "Like what? You can't go to the police. They think you did it."

"*What?*"

"Well – they think you might have done it. I told them to piss off, but you know what they're like. They'll pin crimes on anyone who's to hand." She hugged him. "I'm sure you're right, probably what Marcia was saying does have some relevance, but you can't be certain, can you? And I just think that till you are certain, you don't want to go near the police. Please. I don't want Mona's death to lose me a second friend." She pressed him tighter and stared up into his face. "Please."

Catullus shut his eyes and ran his hands through his hair. "So what the hell should I do?"

"I said. Go back."

"What, in there? Why?"

"To read your poems. That's what you came for."

"I can't."

"Why not?"

"I just ran out."

"No one will care. You're a poet – you're highly strung. You're allowed to do strange things – even talk all evening about things which bore your publisher. But if you do go without reading him a poem, especially when he's been looking forward to it so much, he'll never publish you again. So think about it."

"All right. I've thought. I'm convinced." Catullus breathed in heavily. "Boot..." He took her by the hands. "Boot – thanks."

Boot smiled slowly. "No. Not at all. Just – you know – well..." She made a face, and pressed Catullus' hands even tighter. "Anyway, you see – I want to hear your poems. I want to find out if they're really any good. Not that I'd know one way or the other, mind you."

"How funny," said Catullus. "That's what someone else said." But they had already walked back past the statues by now, and into the inner circle, so he didn't have the opportunity to expand. Boot took her seat, Catullus took his, and Aurelius, watching them, nodded curtly to Titus. "You can start now."

Titus smiled at Catullus. "I don't think you will like this, from what I have read of your own work," he said, "but I think that you will be interested in it. I would very much appreciate your comments, anyway, whatever your thoughts. I was just explaining –"; he gestured to his audience; "that what I have brought along to read here, is not actually so very remote from the topic we were all discussing so animatedly a few minutes ago." He tapped at the sheaf of papers he was holding. "I have here a poem, about time, and space, and the nature of belief."

He began to read. Catullus tried to concentrate, but it was impossible, of course. Listen to Titus, he thought, it's rude not to, but it was no good, and soon his mind was wandering again, like an exhausted bird searching for a perch, and finding only swamplands and darkness instead. Concentrate, he told himself, concentrate. He stared straight ahead. The candles were guttering. The reflections they cast onto the bronze bodied statues were starting to fade, and shadows were flickering outwards from the gods' dead eyes. Catullus shivered. A large Poseidon was staring at him. Its face was blank, pitiless, like that of Marius in the temple at Ricket's Gate. Catullus flailed desperately for something else to think about, and once again found himself listening to Titus's voice. And as he listened, he at last began to associate the sound of words with meaning, and he clung to the meaning with urgency.

"'There is no purpose, no god – only space,
Infinitely falling away from itself
Into pointlessness.'"

Oh, very comforting, Catullus thought, as Titus paused to turn over a page. But the sentiments suited the bleakness of his own mood, and having found himself able to listen, Catullus was relieved to have the chance to concentrate at last. Titus read on. His theme seemed to be nothing less than the nature of the entire universe, so fucking hell, Catullus thought almost resentfully, nothing modest there – talk about jumping in at the deep end, most poets kick off with stuff about love. And that reminded him of his own poems, scribbled out on two slips of paper and stashed away in his bag, with not a mention of the cosmos in either one. Only love. Only terrestrial, bollock-bound love.

But the more he listened to Titus's poem, the more fascinating he found it, fascinating and appalling. He didn't understand it, not the details, but the poetry was strange and beautiful, and the sheer vastness of its pessimism began to shrink Catullus' sense of his own worries, until at last he felt that everything he was and might become was nothing, just a particle of dust, blown on the winds of an empty eternity, a pointless accident like the universe itself. Titus talked about the brain-melting infinity of space and time; he talked about matter and its microworld, where electrons swerved, and protons sometimes died, and afforded the universe an unglimpseable foretaste of its own fate. "Uncertainty is all, and intrinsic in all"; Titus paused to nod, and then repeated the line. "Uncertainty is all, and intrinsic in all." Catullus was soon lost again, but through the haze of his bafflement, he was sure of two things, the extraordinary ambition of Titus's project, and his own sense of utter dislocation. He couldn't understand the arguments, but he could understand the conclusions, coated in poetic honey, as Titus himself had put it earlier in the poem, and the taste made him feel vertiginous and lost. Realities were multifoliate; universes infinite; everything that could have happened, had happened, somewhere, and if it seemed impossible, well, Titus thought it wasn't, and he should know, Catullus supposed, after all, he was the physicist, he had set out to reveal the truth, that was his manifesto, to reveal the truth about the nature of things. Titus paused, then began to suggest the realities there would be in other worlds. A Helen left unraped. A Troy unburnt. An Achilles dying of peaceful old age. The Greek ships burnt at Salamis. Rome never built. And a Clodia riding past me on a dusty chalk road, Catullus thought suddenly to himself, and for a brief dizzying moment, he could believe that it had actually happened, that he had never met Clodia, that he was just a compound of atoms, given sentience for a fraction of a second, that he was nothing but the product of a flitting cosmic joke. But the second passed, and he could still think, and he knew that Clodia had stopped her carriage for him, that she loved him. Suddenly, to his amazement, Catullus was happy. He reached inside his bag, and felt confidence in his poetry rise with his certainty of Clodia's love, and he knew that there was nothing he wanted more than to read his poems out. Language, he knew, was only a trickster's soulless tool, and passion a passing chemical trick – the Alexandrians, the wise and witty Alexandrians, had taught everyone that. But now, somehow, things seemed changed, for Catullus wanted to believe that within the metrical frames, scandalously, was life, his life. Was it true? Could he be so gloriously, so richly naive, as to say that the moments of joy that his poems enshrined gave the lie to Titus, to the theoreticians of the Greeks, to his own restless doubt, his cynic's *need* to doubt? Catullus stroked a stiffening erection through his pocket. Clodia, he thought, Clodia, dearest, desirable, beautiful Clodia. What insights you give me into the nature of things.

And the insights survived, and when Titus finished reading, Catullus found that his comments on the poem seemed inadequate to the fever of what he wanted to express. He praised Titus' poem, discovered indeed that he could hardly praise it enough, for it had opened him to strange feelings and thoughts, dazzlingly strange, and yet, he insisted, Titus had to be wrong, for there were antidotes in life, to be felt if not set out, to the despair that the poem had eulogised.

"But it doesn't eulogise despair," said Titus, shaking his head. "No, you misunderstand it. For if my poem does have a moral point to make, it is that the measure of human worth is the capacity to *outface* despair. You see? Not to ignore it or believe that it can be palliated. We have no purpose but to come to terms with our lack of purpose. That is what I argue. Therefore – to acknowledge the inevitability of despair need not be to celebrate it. You do see?"

Catullus nodded. There was so much that he wanted to explain, but he suddenly felt overwhelmed. "Yes, I do see," he said with a helpless shrug. "I just don't agree that despair is inevitable, that's all." He caught Boot's eye. She raised an eyebrow and smiled. He would have smiled back, but Titus was speaking to him.

"And what is this premise that enables you to argue against despair?" he asked.

"It's not a matter of having a premise, don't you see? Premises, premises – look for them, and maybe despair is inevitable, but happiness doesn't exist because there's a premise for it. Happiness, feelings of exultation, moods of desire and devotion..." He paused. "I don't know," he said. "I can't explain. Maybe that is my explan-ation. I don't know."

Titus smiled. "Read your poems, then."

"Yes," said Aurelius, his eyes bright. "Read." He reached for Furius and held him in his arms. "Read to us about devotion. Affirm happiness for us against despair."

So Catullus read. Both poems were enjoyed, genuinely, perhaps because they weren't very long, Catullus thought, recognising that he could afford such self-modesty, confident within himself of other reasons. At the end of the evening, as the party broke up, Aurelius promised Catullus that the two poems would both be published in the next edition of his magazine. He had seemed more moved by them than anyone, almost disturbed, it had seemed. "Who is Lesbia?" he asked, staring piercingly at Catullus and Boot. "Anyone I know?"

"I don't think that matters," said Boot hurriedly. She paused, and turned to Catullus. "Does it?"

Catullus shrugged. "I'm surprised you ask," he told Aurelius.

"Oh? Why?"

"You edit 'Alexandrian'. All we Alexandrians know that authors don't exist." "How stupid," said Boot. "What do you mean?" "There is only the poem, the text, words defined exclusively by other words. Lesbia cannot exist outside the poem. Similarly, the feelings for her that I describe have no real autonomy, they are only a response to circumstances that betray my ideologies and assumptions, they're all quite mechanistic, in fact."

"Bugger that," said Aurelius with sudden vehemence. "Bugger literary clever talk." He squeezed Catullus' arm. "I just want to know – does Lesbia exist?"

Catullus smiled slowly. "Oh yes. Of course she does."

"Good." Aurelius nodded, almost with relief, it seemed. "Good. And you love her?"

Catullus felt Boot tugging at his arm. Aurelius watched her, then nodded again. "Goodnight," he said suddenly. He turned and hurried away without another word, and Boot and Catullus were left to walk down the stairs. But they had scarcely reached halfway before Aurelius had reappeared, a bulky silhouette against the light from the upper floor. "Wait," he said, pointing at Catullus, "you." He walked down the steps with slow, measured steps. His face was blank and expressionless. "Do you really think..." he said, then broke off, as though what he had to say lay beyond the resources of the soldier's mask he had moulded carefully across his face. "Do you really think," he said again, "that the happiness of a moment can survive the dissolution of that moment by the passage of time?" He stared impassively ahead. "What I mean is, I suppose – can memories of what is gone still bring us happiness? *Real* happiness? What do you think? Can we use these fragments of joy to escape present pain?"

"I don't know," said Catullus. "I hope so."

"I'm glad," said Aurelius. He tilted his head imperceptibly. "Goodnight." Catullus stood silent, listening to the sound of his footsteps disappearing, then stared at Boot.

"What was that about?" he asked her, as they began to walk on down the stairs.

"His dead soldier friend, I suppose. The one I told you about."

"Juventius?"

"Yes. How did you know?"

"I met Furius once when he was visiting the grave."

"Oh God." Boot shook her head.

"Why does Furius go?"

"Because Aurelius can't bear to see the grave, and yet he can't bear to think of it being unvisited."

"So he sends his new boyfriend?"

"Furius doesn't seem to mind."

"No." Catullus remembered the grace with which Furius had worn his coat. "He almost seems to enjoy it."

"And maybe Aurelius does too." She stopped. "No, sorry, that's an awful thing to say. But I do think..." She turned to look at Catullus. "Well, don't you think – you can mourn for too long? I hope, I mean, Mona..." She stopped. Oh no, Catullus thought, she's going to cry. But Boot controlled herself. "It is difficult though, isn't it?" she said at last. "Mourning for someone. Feeling guilty. Worrying about what you can say or do, or when it's right to do it. Do you feel like that?"

Catullus thought back to the day when he had found Mona's faceless corpse, and then gone on to slide naked down bathroom tiles with Clodia. He nodded. "Yes," he said. He paused, and took Boot's arm. "But you're right," he told her at last, "mourning can't be allowed to destroy the mourners' lives. It's bad to feel – too much guilt." And I haven't even felt guilt, he thought silently to himself, I love Clodia so emptyingly that guilt hasn't even crossed my mind. And then he remembered that he hadn't phoned Clodia yet, and it was getting late.

"What are you doing tonight?" he asked Boot. "I'm going out, so I thought, maybe..."

Boot shook her head. "I've got to get back to my parents. They're laying on some big do next week, and I promised I'd help them. They've been so kind to me about Mona and everything, you know, that I just don't think I can fuck them around at the moment. I'm really sorry, you know I am." She stared at him. "But what about you? You were in such a state earlier. What are you going to do about the police?"

God. Claudius. Marius. He'd forgotten all about that. How could he have done? How could he even think about going out? But no, he had to see Clodia. Clodia in leather, Clodia the dyke. He felt longing start to burn again, and faintly, so faintly, the dimmest fever-hint of anxiety. "I've got to go out," he told Boot. He stood by a bus stop. "So if you're still heading back, we'd better say goodnight here."

"Yes." Boot stood silently, staring at nothing very hard. Her face looked bruised.

"Would you come to this party?" Boot asked suddenly.

"What, the one your parents are organising?"

"Yes. Would you? You'd come and keep me company?"

Catullus hugged her and laughed. "Yes, of course. I'd love to."

"It won't be fun. It's going to be shite, actually, stiff-necked and suited, full of important people who are dead, only no one's noticed." She smiled briefly. "But you'll still come?"

"Yes, I'll really look forward to it." A bus was drawing up. Catullus looked round. His number. "Phone and give me the date," he said, snatching a quick kiss, and jumping on the bus. "And thank you for coming with me tonight," he called out. "You've been so kind. Really, Boot. I'd have had a breakdown without you."

"It was nothing," said Boot dully.

The bus was drawing away. Catullus lurched to the back and looked behind him. Boot was still standing where he had left her, staring at nothing. He waved, but she didn't notice. Then the bus swung round a corner, and Boot was left behind.

XIV

CYBELE

Catullus left the bus at the Aventine Crossroads, and ran to find a phone.

"Hello?" a thin voice answered after several minutes. It sounded weak, and male – Metellus. Shit.

"Um." Catullus paused. "Is Clodia there please?"

"No, but she left you a message," said Metellus shortly. There was a rustling of paper. "She's at somewhere called 'The Thiasus of Cybele'. It's at the Aventine Crossroads."

"Which is where I am now."

"How very convenient for you." There was a pause. Metellus coughed. "If you do see my wife, will you please remind her that she did promise me she would be back soon." He coughed again. "Remind her that I am feeling none too well."

"Yes." Catullus swallowed down a sense of guilt. "Of course."

There was another pause. "I enjoy your poetry," said Metellus unexpectedly.

"Oh," said Catullus, nonplussed. "Thank you very much."

"You have a great talent." Catullus could hear Metellus breathing deeply, painfully. "Yes," he said at last, "a great talent. A great capacity for..." His voice trailed away. There was another silence.

"I'll pass on your message," said Catullus eventually.

"Well, then. Good night." There was a click and the phone went dead. With it went the faint traces of Catullus' remaining sense of guilt. He left the phone booth and scanned round the Aventine Crossroads, looking for 'The Thiasus of Cybele'. There was no sign, only a number painted discreetly on a blank wooden door, but once he had reached it, Catullus found that he recognised the entranceway. It was next to the bus stop where he and Caelius had met Lady Camilla, that night after the interview with Porto. Catullus pushed at the door. It opened, onto a badly lit corridor. There was a pay desk at the end, and a couple of men in leathers, and then, just beyond them, a further black door. It swung open. Catullus had a brief glimpse of crowds of people, and the sweep of coloured lights. The door swung shut again, and the person who had opened it began to walk down the corridor. Catullus smiled in surprise. It was Caelius.

The two men embraced. "Where are you off to?" Catullus asked.

"Home, I'm afraid," said Caelius, disengaging himself, and

grinning broadly. "I've got a job to go to now, you see."

"Really? What is it?"

"What is it?" Caelius repeated the question with heavy sarcasm. "Pig-farming."

"When did you start?"

"A couple of days ago. When my company heard I'd passed my exams, with flying colours, I might add. And that's it, no more learning law books, just professional status, snappy suits, and pots of cash. Goodbye poverty."

Catullus smiled wanly. "Congratulations. If that's what you want."

"Oh, it is. It is." Caelius grinned back. "And you know the best thing of all? It means that I can now afford to buy my own car, and therefore don't need Camilla's, and therefore can tell her to piss off and fuck herself, herself being, I should think, the only person she hasn't fucked. Actually, I've just been finishing with her now."

"What, in there?" Catullus pointed down the corridor.

Caelius nodded. "Yes. There seemed to be a certain symmetry about it. This was where I first met her, do you remember, so I thought – what better place for the exorcism?"

"I hope you weren't unnecessarily shitty."

"Not unnecessarily. She deserved it." Caelius glanced at his watch. "Look, I must be off. Leave the night to you under-employed men of leisure. What are you doing, meeting Clodia?"

"Yes. Did you see her?"

Caelius smiled. "Oh yes. Fleetingly." He squeezed Catullus' hand. "Goodnight. Have fun." He turned and left, and Catullus walked on down towards the two men in leathers. Shit, I'm underdressed, thought Catullus, staring at them – I'm not bald, and I haven't got anything looped through my nipples. He coughed, and one of the men looked round. "Evening," said Catullus, trying not to stare at the chains sewn across the man's forehead and cheeks. "One please."

"Catullus!" a voice drawled. "Hiiii!" Catullus peered into the club. Ariana. She glided up behind the two leather men and beckoned to Catullus with a long, satin-gloved finger. "It's all right," she told the men, "he's with me." She reached for Catullus and kissed him on the lips. "There," she said, "branded, with glacier red." She glanced down at his clothes and shook her head. "It's really nice to see you making such an effort. Here, come with me." She pulled him into the club and up against a wall, then felt inside one of her pockets. Catullus stared at her trousers admiringly. They were leather, festooned with black pom-poms, and cinched in tightly with a heavy buckled belt. "Pucker your lips," she ordered, unscrewing a lipstick. "Glacier red?" Catullus asked. "But of course, what else?" Ariana nodded back. She finished applying the lipstick, then added mascara to his eyelashes, and painted round his eyes. "Beautiful," she said, stepping back to admire her handiwork. "Clodia will be proud."

"She likes tarts, does she?"

"Oh yes, she does, take it from me." Ariana hissed a grin. "It is important to look the part here. If you want to have fun, that is."

Catullus stared over her shoulder. The place was full, and yes, there was the odd glint of a chain or two, the odd sheen of rubber. But Catullus was disappointed – after his glimpse of the doormen, he had been expecting more. "It doesn't measure up to my anticipations," he murmured.

"Oh, it's hardly started yet," smiled Ariana. "It's early days. And anyway, this is only Elysium."

"Elysium?"

"Home of the blessed. If you want real decadence, you want Tartarus. Upstairs. Home of eternal torture and delight."

"Sounds much more the thing."

"Oh, it is. And Clodia's there too."

"Tortured or torturing?"

"Having a drink when I last saw her. And complaining I'd laced her up too tight into her corset."

"A corset?" Catullus moaned. "Oh, I'd never dared imagine she'd be wearing a corset. Where do I go?"

Ariana pointed across the dancefloor. "You see that door over there?"

Catullus couldn't, but he nodded and said that he was sure he would find it. "But aren't you coming?" he asked.

Ariana held up a Sinex bottle. "I need to fortify myself. A quick trip to the gentlemen's loos."

"Watch out for Camilla," Catullus warned.

"Why?" Ariana's eyes glittered delightedly. "Does she enjoy hanging out in men's lavatories?"

"That's what she told me once. And she'll need a new man, of course, now that Caelius has chucked her."

"He hasn't? No? Really?" Catullus had never heard syllables drawn out quite so far. He smiled and nodded, and told Ariana that he would see her soon. He left her still grinning contentedly, like a crocodile given a baby goat. Remember, Catullus told himself – never row with Clodia while Ariana was in the room. And the thought of Clodia, laced upstairs, sent roseate flutters along his prick.

He reached the far wall, and looked for a door. Shit – there were two. So which one had Ariana been talking about? There was no way of telling. There was a sign on one, a quotation from Homer, 'Sing, heavenly goddess, sing of pains beyond counting.' Well – that sounded like an advert for Tartarus. Catullus pushed at the door. It opened easily. He walked through, and shut the door behind him. The thump of the music suddenly seemed a long way off. Ahead of him there was a passageway, dimly lit, with red paper velour slapped up badly on the walls. Yes, Catullus thought – this is a corridor to hell.

There were some steps, leading downwards. Catullus took them. The corridor bent round, and he saw that there were doors on his right hand side, running all the way along the wall. He tried to open one of them – locked. "Hello?" he shouted. "Hello?" Nothing. He peered ahead. Still the same velvet gloom. He walked on towards it, and began to make out a further door, straight ahead of him. He reached it, and tried the handle – locked again. Unbidden, a memory fell across his mind, of the last cul-de-sac he had entered, and the surprise he had found waiting for him at the end of that descent.

There was a scream. Very short, very sudden. Catullus froze, then his heart began to pump again, the sound echoing dully in his ears. He took a step forwards. As he did so, there was a second scream, longer, rising and gurgling slowly away, and Catullus ran back along the corridor, towards one of the doors he had passed while coming down. There were more screams, then silence. Catullus slammed himself against the door, twisting the handle desperately, even though he knew that it would be locked. But to his surprise, the handle turned easily, and the door swung open. Catullus fell into the room.

There was a man standing there. Pollo. He was blindfolded and gagged, and there was a chain running from his nipples down to the tip of his foreskin. Otherwise, he was naked. Strips of flesh were bleeding all across his body, and there were ochre piss streaks spattered down his legs. He was hanging from a wooden frame, like a joint of pork on a butcher's hook, and he whimpered through his gag as he struggled helplessly to move. Catullus stared at him, appalled, then reached out to touch his bleeding side. As he did so, he noticed Clodius.

His first thought was to wonder which of them looked the more surprised. Then he noticed Clodius' enormous prick, purple and stiff, and he realised that Clodius was holding a riding crop, black and thin and wet with blood. As Catullus took a step backwards, Clodius tossed his crop against the wall, then ran to try and slam the door. But he was too late – Catullus was already hurrying down the passageway. "You," Clodius shouted after him, "I've been looking for you! I want some answers, you bastard!" But Catullus wasn't in a mood to hang around and give answers; "Not on your life," he muttered breathlessly to himself, "not on your fucking life." Out of the passageway, and back onto the dancefloor, he even wondered if he shouldn't just leave the place altogether, but no, he knew that he had to find Clodia, and soon – quite apart from anything else, Clodius could hardly have him beaten up then, not in front of his own flesh and blood. Flesh and blood, Catullus thought – not a fortunate phrase. He pushed his way hurriedly through the second door, and found himself, to his surprise, in a marbled hall. The contrast with the scruffy dancefloor he had just left was striking; there were tapestries, wall plants, gleaming oak panels, and all along the banisters, grotesquely carved figures leering from the shadows. The damned in Tartarus, Catullus assumed, though it was hard to tell, since there weren't any lights, only candles, clumped along the staircase at regular intervals, vast and twisted like prehistoric trees, and sprouting up from pedestals carved again with figures of the damned in hell. Suddenly, one of the figures moaned. Oh God, Catullus thought, I've been slipped something. Then he heard a splash of candle wax, and there was a second moan. Catullus walked over to the pedestal. One of the figures had eyes, he suddenly noticed, and they were staring up at him, from painted, chained, depersonalised flesh. Yes, Catullus thought – these are the damned, and this is Tartarus.

There was no Cerberus waiting for him at the top of the stairs, but there was a doorway, glowing dull red. A woman in a black latex ballgown swept out through the door. She had jewels in her hair. So it was true, Catullus thought, the rich really do go to hell – they're the only ones who can afford the price. He walked forwards, eager to relish depravity. He looked around. As on the staircase, weirdly tortured candles grew from painted flesh; a few gold-sprayed figures stood naked on pedestals, or posed like nymphs behind the fronds of plants; two vast statues of Persephone and Dis sat shaded in the gloom. A string quartet played complex variations. In alcoves or around low marble tables, men and women sat talking, while harnessed servants stood bowed behind their chairs. It was strange, very strange, and beautiful. Catullus caught a glimpse of himself in a mirror, and winced at the sight of his diurnal clothes. Thank God for the lipstick and mascara, he thought.

Something tapped him on the shoulder. Catullus looked down. A riding crop.

"It's all right, it's only me," laughed Clodia, as Catullus spun round. "Where have you been?"

"Clodia." He hugged her. "I thought you were someone else. Kiss me."

"But I'll smudge your lovely lipstick."

"I don't care, I need you to kiss me." And so Clodia reached up to hug him, and they kissed, and then Catullus stood back to admire her. "You've lost your stomach," he said.

"Yes." Clodia patted at her corset. "Do you mind?"

"A bit. I liked your stomach."

"It's in there somewhere. Waiting. I had hiccups earlier, so I know it's still there. You can't imagine how awful it was."

Catullus smiled. "Pleasure and pain. I thought that was what leather dykedom was all about."

"Don't be stupid. I'm hardly being a dyke if I'm with you, and anyway, this isn't leather, it's satin, I think. Plus whalebone. Go on, feel it. It's an antique."

"Yours?"

"Yes. It used to be my grandmother's. She wore it for real, every day." Clodia made a face. "Hardcore, or what?"

"But what about –"; Catullus gestured at the rest of Clodia's costume, her boots, her collar, her black laced gloves. "Your grandmother's as well?"

"The gloves were, actually. Don't you remember? I wore them at the ball. But this other stuff, it's Marghi's. She's got a shop. Don't you think I look nice?"

"Yes. I suppose so."

"What do you mean, suppose so?"

Catullus tried to think. He hugged Clodia to himself again, and his fingers stroked the whalebones of her corset, and then, through the satin, her imprisoned flesh. The idea of its restraint excited him. He remembered the night before, how erotic he had found it to bind her into a poem, and now surely, laced into her uniform, she had only turned his fantasy into something physical, so what was he afraid of – his own repressions? Or was he worried because the fetish gear was just that, the stuff of fetishes, anyone's fetishes, and he was nervous that Clodia inside her costume might somehow be less the Clodia he knew? He stroked her hungrily, trying to feel her stomach through the whalebone ribs.

"Well?" asked Clodia, breaking free from him. "Come on, you haven't said. Do I look nice, or don't I?" She took a step backwards and tried to pose, but one of her spike heels slipped, and she twisted on her ankle, and Catullus had to catch her as she almost fell.

He laughed, and told her she looked wonderful. "I just hope it's worth all the indigestion and twisted ankles, that's all."

"Can you believe it," she said, screwing up her face, "I've just been walking about in these? Quick, get me to my chair, before I break my leg or something."

She leant on Catullus' shoulder and directed him over to one of the tables by the wall. "There," she said, pointing. Catullus looked. Leather dykes! Four of them. Once again, he felt woefully underdressed. He lowered Clodia down into her chair, then sat down himself, and smiled round the table embarrassedly. Ariana was back from the gents, he noticed. He couldn't see the Sinex bottle. She returned his smile, and leant over to kiss him. "Do you know everyone?" she asked. Catullus shook his head. "I'm afraid I can't give you their names," she whispered stagily. "In here, you see, we are creatures of the night. We are known only as the Maenads."

"Do you know what a maenad was?" Clodia asked.

"What, me?" Catullus felt insulted. Of course he knew what a maenad was. "Bacchantes. Euripides wrote about them. Wild women who ran about drunk in forests, ripping men to shreds."

"You see?" said Clodia. "I told you he was clever."

"Oh, he is, isn't he?" agreed Ariana. "Very clever." Were they taking the piss out of him? Well, it wasn't his fault – Clodia had asked him the question, he couldn't help seeming like a prig. Fuck them.

"Are you sulking?" asked Clodia wheedlingly.

"No."

"Here, have some Sinex," said Ariana, pulling the bottle from her pocket. "That'll perk you up."

"No thanks," said Catullus. "I need to keep my faculties on duty."

Clodia stared at him. "Why? What's the matter?"

"Well." Catullus wondered what he should tell her. "I saw something I wasn't meant to see, I think. Downstairs."

"Tell me about it."

"I don't think I should."

Clodia took his hand, and slipped it between her thighs. "Was it Clodius?" she asked after a pause.

Catullus stared at her. He shrugged. "Maybe."

"And was he with that soldier, the one he'd been with in Circassia?"

Catullus nodded. "Clodius enjoys – well..." He wondered how he could put it. "Clodius gets a kick from inflicting pain, does he, do you think?"

"Yes, I think so. Well, I always assumed he did. But nothing heavy, just recreational."

"It didn't look very recreational, what he was doing downstairs."

"Yes, but that's only because he's under stress at the moment. It's a difficult time for him, isn't it?"

"What, because he's worried the government might hand him over to Caesar?"

"No!" Clodia laughed and shook her head. "You don't believe all that, do you?"

"Yes, of course. It was on the news. Shouldn't I believe it?"

Clodia raised her eyebrows at him, and shook her head again. "No. Don't worry. I was forgetting you didn't know."

"Didn't know what?"

"I said, it doesn't matter." There was a sharpness to her voice now. Why? "Don't worry about it, anyway," she said, reaching for him. "I promise – he won't mind. But maybe you should have a drink."

"Yes – maybe." Catullus started to climb to his feet, but Clodia pulled him back down.

"We've got a slave," she said, clapping her hands. "Slave slut! Two drinks!"

A bridled servant who had been standing behind Clodia's chair bowed her head and scurried off towards the bar. Catullus watched her go in amazement.

"Who was that?" he asked.

"Didn't you recognise her? It's Marghi." Clodia smiled. "Don't worry. She loves it. It's very convenient. All you've got to do is be rude to her and hit her a bit. It's quite fun." She looked round, as Marghi returned with the drinks. "Quick," she ordered her. "Put them there. Quick, you bitch." Marghi bowed her head again, and retreated. Clodia nodded to Catullus. "Well? What did you think? Pretty fucking dominant."

"Terrifying. Kiss me. I can't bear it."

Clodia reached for his cheeks, and held them tight as she kissed him on the lips. "Think you could do it to me?" she whispered.

"What, be dominant?"

Clodia nodded.

"Yes, why not? I'm always on for being cruel to people, especially if they're not going to answer back."

Clodia smiled. "Would you enjoy it?" she asked.

Catullus stared at her. Her face was flushed, her lips bright red, intoxicating. He felt, all through his flesh, a shiver of devotion to pleasure, a sudden longing for his life, all of it, to be touched by the delights that Clodia would bring, so that nothing, no part of him, would be untroubled by her, so that she would flow through his body like fresh livid blood. "Anything," he whispered, "you know that, anything." He kissed her, breathing in her scent, so that he would never forget. No woman can say, Catullus thought, feeling it thrillingly to be true, that she has been loved as Clodia has been loved by me.

His evening blossomed. He brought himself to be rude to Marghi. He made Ariana laugh. He chatted to a couple of the Maenads. And all the time, Clodia pressed up tightly against him, the pleasure provided so full and sweet that Catullus knew, holding her, that physical experience could fade, and the memory of it still be enough to make him drunk. And yet there would be no parting, only bed, and not even Clodia would fall asleep tonight, not with a corset on, impossible. Catullus smiled, and glanced at his watch. Long gone eleven. And it was only then, with a sudden cold rush, that he remembered Metellus. Shit! He had wanted Clodia to go home early too. He was ill. Catullus wrestled with his conscience; finally, he mentioned that he had spoken to Metellus on the phone. Clodia stared at him, then shut her eyes, and buried her face in her hands. "Oh God," she said, looking up again at last. "I forgot. I completely forgot. How could I have done?" "He's very ill?" "*Very* ill. Come on. I'd better go." She tottered to her feet, and a couple of the Maenads joined her. One of them yanked at the lead attached to Marghi's collar, and handed it over to Clodia. She took it, absent-mindedly, and pulled Marghi after her, across Tartarus and down the stairs. Out on the dancefloor again, Catullus expected her to press on to the far door, but to his surprise she began to dance, so furiously that he was afraid she would slip on her heels again. But she kept her balance, so well that she was able to play with Marghi on the lead, pulling her up close, then dropping her down to the floor, then pulling her up close again and holding her. It was like watching someone with a fucking yo-yo, Catullus thought, and he must have looked jealous, because Clodia stared at him and laughed, then unclipped Marghi's lead and threw it over to him. She tossed back her head and the collar round her neck caught the light. Catullus reached for it. He shook out the lead and snapped the fastening shut. He pulled her towards him, viciously, and Clodia staggered, then fell limp into his arms. He felt her, tried to absorb her, and then he tugged on the lead again, and she started to dance, as fiercely as before, even more fiercely perhaps, and Catullus thought that he was going to melt as he tried to keep up. They danced on, and Catullus could feel his legs stiffening, and then, just when he knew that he couldn't last, Clodia stopped. She gestured with her head to the door, and Catullus pulled her, still on her lead, over to the exit. Clodia leant for a minute against the wall, breathing in deeply, and then she smiled and unclipped the lead from her neck. "Thank you," she said, hugging Catullus. "I enjoyed that." "So did I." "Good." She breathed in deeply again. "Good."

Catullus waited while she picked up her coat and bag, and felt blackness as he understood that she would have to go alone. "Sorry," said Clodia, reading his face. "I don't think we can be together, not until Metellus is on the mend. I owe it to him." A bit late now, Catullus thought, but he nodded, then reached out to hold her in his arms. He had to say something. "I feel almost as though – I'm too sad now – just as I was too happy before. The night has been too full, too much with me. Am I being stupid?"

Clodia nodded and kissed him.

"Don't go," he begged.

"I have to."

"Don't – please."

"Surely you see?"

"Yes, but it's – I don't understand it – it's almost like a presentiment. As though something, a shadow, is crossing our graves." He stared into Clodia's eyes, so blue, like Caelius', he realised as though for the first time, except that Clodia's now were solemn and their gleam had no chill. She left, and Catullus found that he had been almost comforted. But then the shadow fell again, and into his thoughts came the memory of another farewell, when his brother had left to cross the world, far crueller, far more irrevocable that departure had been, and Catullus suddenly ached for his brother to be back. How long would the wait be? A year, maybe two. At least Clodia's absence could be measured in days. Catullus found Ariana and wandered back upstairs, but the Sinex was empty and there was only wine.

It was while he was picking up his own bag, several hours later, that he saw Clodius. Clodius and the two clowns, pushing through the crowds, bearing straight down towards him. Before he had even decided to run, they were onto him, the two clowns taking his arms and dragging him backwards, while Clodius stared at him and followed up behind. Catullus was pulled into a dark corner, and the two clowns forced him down onto a chair. "Outside," said Clodius, gesturing with his head. The two clowns left. Clodius bent down to crouch next to Catullus. He smiled, and shook his head, and then his face froze again.

"You've been avoiding me," he said softly.

"No," said Catullus, "I've just been very busy, that's all. I've been with your sister."

"Yes, I saw." Clodius' eyes hardened, and Catullus kept thinking to himself, he likes hurting people, he likes hurting people. But Clodius didn't move, just kept on staring. "You made a promise to me," he said at last.

"Yes?"

"Yes." Clodius nodded gently. "You promised me that you'd keep me informed about that site of yours. Remember? That you would report anything strange that took place on it? Yes?"

"Yes."

Clodius paused, and stared at his fingernails. Then he looked up again. "Wouldn't you say that finding a semi-decapitated corpse was rather strange?" he asked.

Catullus nodded slowly. "Ye-es."

"Particularly in view of certain circumstances," Clodius carried on. "Which you must have been aware of, as the assistant to a professor of Circassian archaeology?" Clodius began to shake him. "Yes, and now I think about it, you actually asked me about Circassia, didn't you, the last time we met? So why did you do that? What were you getting at?" He was shouting now. He pulled Catullus up from his chair and slammed him against the wall. "A person dies like that –"; he gestured across his face; "- and you don't even bother to tell me about it! So what are you playing at?" He blinked, as though in pain. "What's going on?"

Catullus stared back. He didn't know what to say. And then he saw Pollo tap Clodius on the shoulder, and Clodius looked round, and Catullus was able to take a step out from the wall.

"It's the police," Pollo said.

"What police?"

"The usual."

"Porter?"

Pollo nodded.

"Shit!" Clodius looked around. "Shit! What's he doing here? Following me again, you think?" Pollo shrugged. Clodius swore again, then glanced at Catullus. "Look, go with Pollo, Pollo, stick to him, all right?" Pollo seized Catullus' arm. "I don't want to be seen with him," Clodius shouted suddenly, "not while Porter's here." Pollo nodded, and began to drag Catullus across the dancefloor. Catullus went willingly enough – anything to get away from Clodius. But then he felt a hand on his shoulder, and looking round, he found that he was staring into Clodius' eyes again.

"Listen," breathed Clodius, "someone's setting me up, and I'm going to find out who it is. You understand? I'm going to find out who the hell the bastard is, and then I'll be getting back to you." He nodded and turned, and pushed his way back through the crowds. Catullus breathed in deeply, then stumbled on as Pollo pulled at his arm again.

"Did he say Porter?" Catullus asked.

Pollo looked round and grinned. "You know him, don't you?" he said, still grinning. He opened a door and pointed. "In there," he ordered. Catullus looked. The corridor with the velour wallpaper. He might have known. "How's your back?" he asked Pollo. "Shaping up nicely, thanks," Pollo answered. "Go on, get in."

Pollo followed Catullus and shut the door behind them, then began to lead the way down the corridor.

"Has Porter been shadowing Clodius, then?" Catullus asked, trying again.

"On and off," said Pollo, not looking round.

"Why?"

Pollo laughed. "Because he thinks he might be guilty of some face slashings." He laughed again. "Pretty much the same reason as he's been following you around, I'd guess."

"How do you know that?"

Pollo didn't answer him. Instead, he took a key out from his pocket and walked on down to the very end of the passageway, to the door that Catullus had tried earlier and found locked. Pollo fitted the key and turned it; the door swung open. "After you," said Pollo, leering balefully. Catullus shrugged and walked in. As Pollo followed him, he switched on the light, and Catullus found himself staring at a rack. He glanced round the room. There were cages piled up against the wall, and chains hanging in neat rows. Cruel-looking machines lurked in every corner. Great, Catullus thought. The last place in the world to which he'd have chosen to be brought. A torturer's storeroom.

"Those are for me, are they?" he asked, trying to sound light-hearted. Pollo shook his head.

"No," he said, climbing up onto the rack, "you've got to be rich to afford those." He stretched and opened a small window, right at the top of the wall. "Get up here," he said. He pointed to the window. "You see that? – you're going out through there. And first of all, you're going to hit me on the head with this." Pollo held up a small paddle.

"Really?" asked Catullus. "Why?"

Pollo leered again. "I enjoy that sort of thing, hadn't you realised?"

"No." Catullus shook his head. "The real reason."

"Because I don't want Clodius talking to you."

"Why not?"

Pollo paused, and spat. "I'll tell you tomorrow."

"Why not now?"

"Because he'll be coming back any minute." Pollo pushed at Catullus. "Now go on, fucking get up there."

Catullus looked at the paddle Pollo was still holding in his hands, and decided not to press him. "But this seeing you tomorrow," he asked, as he pulled himself up, "when will that be?"

"Eleven."

"Where?"

"You haven't worked it out yet? Then you will."

"How?"

"You're just fucking question after question, you, aren't you? I said – you'll know. And you'll want to make sure you know, because I've got something which may interest you. I know why your girlfriend picked you up. Remember? That time in her carriage?" He put a finger to his mouth. "No. No more questions. I'll tell you tomorrow." Then he handed up the paddle. "Now, just get on with it and hit me."

"Hard?"

"Enough to look convincing."

"If you say so." Catullus swung the paddle and flinched, like someone afraid to slice an egg. But Pollo swore at him, and Catullus thought that he could hear footsteps, so his second swing was harder, and sent Pollo crashing onto the floor. He didn't wait to see how much damage he had caused. Instead, he threw the paddle down after Pollo, then shut his eyes and jumped, out into the darkness, away from Clodius and Porter and everyone. But for how long, he wondered, as he picked himself up from the pavement. How long would they stay off his back? Please, he thought, long enough for me to get home at least. He began to run down the street as fast as he could.

XV

POLLO

He reached home safely. There had been one scare, just outside the pub where he and Caelius had gone on his first night in Rome; police had been everywhere, but Catullus had managed to slip past through the shadows, and he didn't think that anyone had noticed him. He wondered what had been going on. Probably a fight or something, down in the club. Drugs, maybe.

He climbed upstairs. The familiar creaks. The tatty carpet. So he hadn't been seduced into unfounded pessimism, everything *was* just as shabby and small as he had remembered it. When he switched on his bedroom light, he couldn't bear to look at first; there would be no Clodia, no view of Rome, no beautiful things; just junk, cheap junk, telling him that he was truly home. Then he opened his eyes – and found himself breathing a prayer of thanks to Jez. His walls – they were beautiful! That boy – fine, he was a pain, but he was a genius too, no doubt about it, he was a fucking prodigy. Catullus undressed and lay in bed, admiring the city that had flowered up his walls. Streets, squares, the landmarks of Rome, Jez had melted and twisted them all, so that Catullus could only dimly recognise the city, and found it drifting across his sense of what the real Rome was like. Soon the city outside his windows had been forgotten altogether, and as he began to dream, Catullus left his bed to wander down the streets of Jez's Rome. He was searching for Clodia, but hopelessly, he knew that, for the city was de-peopled. Something was loose, though. Something was hunting him, and as Catullus ran on through the unreal streets, he could feel it nearing him inexorably.

But he never saw it, the thing that had been chasing him. Just as he began to feel its breath on his back, he was woken by the sound of sobbing. He climbed out of bed and hurried into the kitchen, where he found Tubbers slumped over a table, his shoulders heaving.

"Sorry," Tubbers said, looking up, "not taking it like a man, bad display, it's only..." and then, at the thought of what he had been about to say, he choked again. Catullus sat down beside him, and put an arm round his back. Tubbers sobbed on. "I'm gay," he said suddenly, swallowing back his tears.

"God, who isn't in Rome?" said Catullus, squeezing his hand.

"Do you think so?" said Tubbers. "No, rarly, that's – bloody good of you." He smiled, then burst into tears again.

A sudden sheet of understanding lit Catullus' mind. "It's Caelius, isn't it?"

"What?"

"Caelius. It has to be. He's the one who..." Catullus' voice trailed away. Tubbers stared at him. "Caelius isn't my, er, you know," he said at last.

"No?"

Tubbers shook his head. "No." He paused. "Oh no, no. Caelius has never looked at me. It's the Bulldog, you remember him?" Catullus nodded. Tubbers blew his nose. "Bloody good bloke." He swallowed. "He's dead."

"Where?" asked Catullus, cold fear rising like vomit from his stomach.

"The club. You know, he worked on the door." Tubbers blew his nose again. "Was going there tonight, actually. And now we never will. Not ever..." His sentence crumbled away.

"Listen," Catullus said. "You don't have to talk. I just want you to listen, even if it's painful. All right?" Tubbers nodded. Catullus shut his eyes, and leant back in his chair. "This is what happened, isn't it? The Bulldog was found downstairs, in one of the cellars, next to the skeleton in the fibre-glass case. He had been stabbed, and the skull had been sliced in two. Is that what happened? Just nod."

Tubbers nodded. Slowly, Catullus rose to his feet. "Have you got a map of Rome?" he asked.

"No. Think Caelius has, though."

Catullus ran into Caelius' room. The bed was empty. He scanned down the bookshelves, found the city planner, then hurried back into the kitchen. He spread the map out on the table, then fetched a ruler and his notebook. It was going to be a long night, he decided, so he made himself a coffee, and while he was waiting for the kettle to boil, he flicked through his notebook again. He didn't really need to, of course, since the formula was seared onto his brain, but he wanted to check, just to make sure. Yes, there it was, copied down from Varney's book – even, odd, even. Catullus repeated the phrase to himself under his breath, then sat down again by the city map. He found Tallowfield, and put a tiny cross over the site marked as Fairlawns. Then he found the pub, and drew a second cross. He ignored Tubbers, who was staring at him blankly, and reached across the table for the far end of the map. The Dance of Stones, the Dance of Stones, where would that be? Yes, there, on the blank space near the road. Catullus marked a third cross. Then he reached for a ruler, drew a straight line, and began to make some measurements. Even, odd, even. He had needed three murders. Well, he had three murders. Now to find out where the fourth would be. His calculations did not take him long. A few sums, a few subtractions. With a trembling hand, he reached for a pencil. He found his spot. Then slowly, carefully, he drew the fourth cross.

"So you found the place all right?" Pollo asked.
"Yes," said Catullus.
"Been here long?"
"A couple of hours."
Pollo grinned. "I said eleven, and that's what I meant. Eleven."
Catullus shrugged. "I had a rather disturbed night. I wanted to get out of my flat."
"Oh yes? You couldn't have chosen a nicer place, could you?"
"It's very pleasant."
Pollo grinned again, then began to walk away. Catullus followed. Ahead of them was a large shell of concrete and rusty scaffolding, ringed by a fence and scattered piles of bricks. "No one builds in this city any more, you noticed that?" Pollo asked. He pushed at a gate, then held it open for Catullus. "Except them, of course." He gestured towards a shanty town, straggling away across the abandoned site. Dogs were rummaging through the litter, and a few tiny children sat watching them. "You can build with bricks," added Pollo, "but you can't eat them."

"No," said Catullus, still staring at the children.

"One of Clodius', that is, that little saying." Suddenly, Pollo was shouting. "Our great leader, our great fucking leader!" He kicked at a sheet of metal, then picked it up and began twisting it. The sheet was rusty, and snapped in two; Pollo screamed, and rubbed his hands along the two serrated edges. He stopped, and looked down at the blood as it began to flow from his palms. He moaned, and bent his head, then smeared the blood into his hair. He looked up, and saw Catullus staring at him. Pollo laughed. "You've gone all white," he said.

Catullus tried to smile, but couldn't. He stood absolutely frozen.

"Oh, fuck it all, fuck it to fucking cunt hell," said Pollo. He turned, and Catullus followed him, at a safe distance, until they had passed through into the shell of the abandoned building, where Pollo stopped and stood waiting for him. I don't have to do this, Catullus thought. Shall I just turn and run? The sound of his own footsteps echoing across the concrete gave him his answer. Pollo had already moved on again, and was standing next to a shack in the far corner of the building. "Home," he said, pulling open a coloured fabric hanging. The pattern was familiar; Catullus recognised it from Mr Dugbal's sitting room. Circassian. Oh well, he thought, here goes. He pulled at the fabric, and followed Pollo into the shack.

"You remember my friend Lud?" asked Pollo from somewhere in the gloom.

"Yes," said Catullus, straining to make him out. "We met again last night, if you remember." Lud smiled, and Catullus realised that he had never actually heard him speak.

"Sit down," said Pollo, throwing him another sheet of fabric. Catullus caught it, and draped it over a few bricks. "This is just like old times," he said, trying to break some ice. "Like the first time we met. Sitting in the dark on piles of rubble."

"Maybe some of us have to put up with what we can find," said Pollo coldly.

"Yes, of course," said Catullus, kicking himself. "Sorry."

"Exciting, is it, these glimpses of the outdoor life?" Catullus didn't answer, just sat silently as Pollo began to roll a cigarette. He lit it, and Catullus breathed in the smoke. Pot. He breathed in again, deeply, and tried to convince himself that the smoke was calming his nerves. Still no one spoke.

"So," said Catullus at last, knowing that his voice must be sounding frail and distant, "am I going to be murdered, then?"

Pollo took the cigarette out from his mouth. "What makes you ask that?" he asked after a long pause.

"Well..." Catullus swallowed. "I don't know. The other murders. This is where the fourth is due to take place. You must know about that, otherwise you wouldn't have fixed to meet me here."

"I could say the same about you."

"What do you mean?"

Pollo stared at him. "What I mean," he said at last, "is that for a long time, Lud and me, we thought you were the one who was doing all those murders. It seemed strange to us. Everyone you met, they died. So we started following you about, and bit by bit, we found out all sorts of interesting things."

"Like what?"

"Like you dig up the past. Like you have meetings with Clodius. Like you're fucking his sister on the same day you find the body of another person you'd been fucking, which seemed a bit, well – a bit quick off the mark, we thought, didn't we Lud?" Lud nodded. Pollo paused and drew on his cigarette again. "But," he said at last, "but, I knew last night it couldn't be you."

"Why not?"

Pollo stared at him and shook his head. "Come on, you're meant to be the clever one. You were with people all the time, weren't you, last night?"

God, he was right. Catullus allowed a sense of the implications to wash over him. He had an alibi at last. He was safe. He wouldn't go to prison. "So who do you think is doing it?" he asked eventually.

"I don't know who's actually doing it, you know, with the knife, but I do know who ordered them. I've known that all along."

"Who?" Pollo kept on staring at him. Catullus asked again. "Who?"

"Use your fucking brain. Who do you think?"

"Clodius?"

Pollo stood up. "Of course."

"But why him?"

"You know about his ancestor, don't you?"

"Yes. Do you?"

Pollo shrugged. "He's told us about him. We were quite surprised, weren't we Lud, because it made us think, oh yeah, these murders, they're just like the ones his fucking ancestor did, and so we were doubly sure."

"Doubly?"

"Yes." Pollo crouched down again, very close to Catullus, so that their faces were almost touching. "Doubly sure. That's what I said. And you want to know why we knew that Clodius was the killer, right from the very start?"

"Yes. Of course."

"All right." Pollo stubbed out his cigarette, then leant forward again. "Because he told us. Simple as that. When we were in the war, out in Circassia. We had this man we'd captured, and he'd been a historian, just like you. He told us about all these rites, and the god, and how there'd been sacrifices, you know, all that shit, I don't need to tell you about it, and then he showed us the temple, because we'd been camped just by it. And you know what Clodius liked? He really liked the idea that you could kill people to get your country back on its tracks. I can remember him saying, he said, 'fucking hell, that's what Rome needs. When I get back, I'm going to sort this out. There are going to be a few people without faces when I get back.' And then he laughed. Didn't he, Lud? He laughed." Lud nodded. Pollo stared at him, then turned back to face Catullus. "So. What do you reckon?"

Catullus paused. Take things carefully, he told himself. Be tentative. "This prisoner," he asked slowly, "he told you all about the god? About Sesostris?" Pollo nodded. "And so that was when you found out about the even, odd, even – you know – the formula, for working out where to commit the killings?"

"No." Pollo shook his head. "That's the whole point. We only knew about that when Clodius told us about his ancestor. See? If we'd known about it all the time, then we could have stopped the murders, couldn't we? But we didn't know, so we couldn't work it out."

"But now you have?"

"We're sitting here, aren't we? And the point is, because the murders have all followed this pattern, that proves it, that shows it must *have* been Clodius. Because he was the only one who could know about the formula in the first place, what with his ancestor's papers and everything. It's got to be him."

"So what do you want me to do about it?" Catullus asked.

"Go to the police."

"Why me?"

"They wouldn't believe us, would they Lud? A couple of down and outs like us, not a fucking chance." Pollo leant over and stabbed at Catullus with his forefinger. "They're fucking corrupt, incompetent bastards, the police. What's going to stop them from locking us up?"

Exactly, thought Catullus – just what I was wondering. And immediately he tried to think of something to say, so that Pollo wouldn't have time to work out what he had been thinking, but he was too late, his face must have betrayed him. "And supposing – just supposing – you think we might have done the killings ourselves," said Pollo, staring into his eyes, "ask yourself this. 'Why aren't I dead?'"

Catullus stared back at him. "What do you mean?" he asked eventually.

"You said it yourself, this is where the final murder is going to take place." Pollo smiled, then picked at the scabs on the palms of his hands. They began to bleed, and Pollo dipped his finger into the wounds and started to trace a circle round Catullus' face. "If it had been us all along..." He dabbed his finger into his palm again, then ran it along Catullus' forehead, to complete the circle. "We could just get out our knife, and slice along the line." His smile froze and died. "Couldn't we?"

There was silence. A long silence. Then suddenly Pollo laughed, and jumped to his feet. "But we're not going to kill you, because we're not the killers, and now the police know you're not either, you can go and tell them everything."

Catullus scratched at the drying blood on his chin. "Of course I'll go," he said.

"But?"

"But what?"

"Your voice. You sounded like you wanted to say 'but'."

Had he? He had meant to disguise it. "Well, yes," he said, thinking hard about what he could say. "There was one thing." Pollo raised his eyebrows. "You are Clodius' lover?"

Pollo shrugged. "So? You think you can't hate someone you get fucked by?"

"No, of course not."

"He pays."

"But do you hate him?"

Pollo shook his head. "It doesn't matter. I just said."

"I know, I'm sorry." Catullus stood up. He didn't want to watch Pollo become any more angry. "I'm going. In fact, I'll go now."

"Hold on!" Catullus froze. Pollo walked up to him, and pressed a hand on his shoulder. Catullus slumped back onto the bricks. "You've forgotten your reward," said Pollo.

"My reward?"

"Yes. You can't have forgotten, surely not?"

"Oh." He had forgotten. "About Clodia? About why she picked me up?"

Pollo grinned and rolled his tongue over his lips. "That's right. Your lovely lady. Who you danced with so beautifully last night. Clodius' sister." He licked his lips again. "Wouldn't anyone want to know why they'd been picked up by her?"

He nodded to Lud, who felt in his pocket and drew out an envelope. Pollo reached across and took it, then winked as he handed it on to Catullus. "A little token of goodwill. I thought you might enjoy it."

"What is it?"

"A letter, from your lovely lady to Clodius. It's got a photo of you asleep in it. Very beautiful you look too. We got given the letter when Clodius asked us to find you, do you remember? Because his sister wanted to fuck you, and she did, didn't she, right on the floor of a night club. Fucking little tart!" He was starting to shout again, so Catullus pocketed the letter quickly and thanked him, then stood up a second time to leave. "Was she a good fuck?" Pollo asked suddenly, leering in Catullus' face.

"Very, thanks," said Catullus, trying to step past him.

Pollo laughed so loudly that his voice began to crack, and Catullus wondered if he would ever get out. Eventually though, to his relief, he was allowed to walk past, but as he pushed his way out of the shack, he could smell Pollo following him. Catullus stopped and looked round. Pollo was still grinning, spluttering into chuckles occasionally, and staring at him with livid eyes. "Are you going to the police now?" he asked. Catullus nodded. Pollo walked up to him and wrapped an arm round his shoulder. "I'll walk with you, then. To the Underground."

They trudged back across the building site. "Did you know Mr Varney?" Catullus asked suddenly.

Pollo stared at him. "No," he said, looking away again.

"You never met him, in a place like this maybe..."

"No," repeated Pollo, cutting him off. "I said. The only thing I knew about him was he got killed."

They walked on. Catullus wondered whether to press Pollo any further. "I was only wondering," he said at last, "because he used to work here."

Pollo turned to stare at him. "Did he? Where?"

"We'll pass it in a minute. A big office. I'll point it out to you."

"How did you know that?"

"The address. He wrote it in a book he gave me. I went and had a look at it while I was waiting for you."

"So?"

"Well – nothing much. I just think it means I know where Marius was killed, that's all."

"How? You can't know that!" Pollo had begun to shake. But Catullus walked on, not feeling worried now that they had reached the High Street, and he nudged Pollo and pointed up at a building. "Look, there. That developer's office. That's where he worked. I was interested, because I remember Mr Varney telling me that the place where he thought Marius had been killed was quite near his office. He also said that his company had started building on it. So I wondered, could the place where Marius died be the same place where I was waiting for you? It would make sense, after all, Marius as the fourth sacrificial victim. You remember the Circassian legend, who the fourth victim had to be? A man with the power to redeem or destroy the state? Well, Marius certainly had that power. In fact, the more I thought about it, the more certain I became that Mr Varney had really been on to something." Catullus glanced at Pollo. "You're not interested?"

Pollo stared back at him sullenly. "Not really."

Catullus smiled. Come on, he told himself, keep pushing. Pollo had started shaking when he had first mentioned Marius. "And you really didn't know?" he said at last. "That you might be camped on the very spot where Marius died? Or was killed, I should say." He paused. "Sacrificed."

Pollo's eyes darted at him, just for a fraction of a second. "No," he said. "I don't give a fuck about history. It's all dead. Why bother with that shit, what's it matter?"

"Well." Catullus decided to make the obvious point. "It's only what we've both found out about murders in the past that's enabled us to work out who the killer is today."

"That's different, we're talking about things that are going on now. Things that matter. But all this Marius shit, Marius, who is he anyway? Only people like Varney went on about him. And Varney's dead."

That was an odd thing to say, Catullus thought, as he nodded and tried to smile a look of agreement. 'Only people like Varney went on about him.' As though Pollo had actually spoken to Mr Varney, or at least listened to him. Not that it was definite proof that they had met, of course, it was just the way Pollo had said it. Catullus glanced at him, and smiled again. "Yes, you're right," he said. "I'm sorry I went on. It's because I'm a historian, I think everyone must find history interesting."

"Yes, well, I don't. And you've got more important things to do now than worry about some dead fucking general."

They had reached the tube station by now. Catullus bought his ticket, and flashed it at Pollo. "I'm off."

"Don't go to the Aventine Crossroads," Pollo said suddenly.

"But that's where Porter's office is, just round the corner."

"You'll have to go a back way."

"Why?"

"There's a demo on today. Against Caesar. It might get a bit rough." Pollo grinned. "Though obviously, we've got to hope it won't."

"Clodius is leading it, is he?"

Pollo's grin widened. "You might see him." He tightened his grip on Catullus' shoulder. "So don't forget," he whispered, "don't forget." And then he was gone. Catullus stared after him, then began to hurry down the escalators.

"Am I under arrest?" Catullus asked, as Porter came back into the room.

Porter smiled. "What makes you think you might be?"

"Of course. It's standard police practice to have people sit around in pokey shit holes like this for hours. I was forgetting."

Porter smiled again. "The information you brought us was hardly standard," he said. "And we had to keep you in case we had more questions."

"And have you?"

"Yes." Porter held open the door. "Or rather – I haven't. My superiors have."

Catullus sighed, then stood up. "They'd better be *very* superior."

Porter laughed. But he didn't say anything, not even when Catullus tried to press him, and soon he was starting to stride out of earshot. Just like the last time, Catullus thought, as they hurried along yet another nondescript corridor, and Porter's back became ever more distant. They passed through a heavy double door, and down a further long corridor, and then, through a second double door, guarded by two soldiers, the decor suddenly began to improve. Markedly. Very nice, Catullus thought, admiring the cornices and gold-framed paintings. Porter had stopped for him, he saw, outside a beautiful oak-lined door. Catullus reached it at last. "Is this a corridor of power?" he asked. Porter shrugged. "Not as much as it used to be," he said. "Good luck." Then he opened the door , and Catullus walked into the room which lay beyond.

There were four men, their backs to him, grouped by a vast mahogany table. One of them peered round, then leapt to his feet and came hurrying over to meet Catullus.

"Ha ha, welcome, welcome!" chuckled the Great Porto. He held out his arms, encouraging Catullus to admire the room that he had walked into, with its greens and golds, its heavy oak, its age-stained paintings of famous men. "From a Portakabin to the cabinet room! Wherever next, eh?" He held out a chair, then, when Catullus had taken it, hurried back round to his own seat. "So – introductions?"

"Yes please," said Catullus. "But I've already met..." He nodded, as Metellus stared up at him for the first time. God, he looks ill, Catullus thought. "Yes, you know the Minister for Finance," chuckled Porto. "As his house guest. Or should I say, as the guest of a near relative of his. Ha ha ha! As you probably realise, the Minister has made some effort to be with us today." He nodded to Metellus, and Metellus nodded back, but his face stayed wintry and impassive.

Porto continued with the introductions. "His Excellency, our State President, I think you've already met as well. Though you were asleep at the time, I seem to remember noting, ha ha!" Pompey looked up and made a slow gesture with his lips, which Catullus supposed was a smile. Then his head slumped forwards again, and Catullus watched as the President of the Roman Republic built a plane from a paper envelope. Porto cleared his throat. "And have you met Marcus Crassus?" he asked. "Who has just arrived here himself, in fact, so things must be hotting up, ha ha!"

Crassus. Catullus stared at him in fascination. The richest man in Rome! He was vast, as Clodius had said he was, but his flesh struck Catullus as being the stuff of power. "I've enjoyed your poetry," Crassus said in a low growl. Catullus smiled and thanked him, and asked where he had come across it. "My daughter, of course," Crassus said, as though it were self-evident. "And my brother. And your file. Our friend Porto here has a degree of literary taste himself." He laughed, and reached across the table to tap at a brown folder. Catullus smiled at him wanly, and Crassus laughed again. He was sitting quite far apart from the politicians, Catullus noticed. By choice? Yes, presumably, though there was a second reason as well, Catullus suddenly realised. There was a fifth place, between Pompey and Crassus, empty. "Someone else you know," said Porto, who had been watching him.

283

There was the sound of footsteps. Porto twisted in his chair and looked out through a far door. "And here he comes now."

The door was pushed open wider, and Cicero breezed in. "Ah!" he smiled, waving a sheet of paper at Catullus, "our crimebuster! Good to see you."

"Good to see you too," said Catullus. "But I thought you were in prison?"

Pompey grunted, and shifted in his chair. "He still is, officially. Deciding whether he stays there is what this meeting is all about."

"Not at all," said Cicero smoothly, taking his seat. "It is about the future of the Roman Republic. My incarceration or otherwise is purely incidental. Yes," he told Catullus, "I have been set free from prison. Largely thanks to you."

"Oh yes?" asked Pompey, dropping his paper glider. "You received the confirmation you wanted, did you?"

"I did." Cicero held up the sheet of paper he had been carrying as he had walked into the room. "Here it is. Fresh from the fax of the Intelligence Commission. The details of Caesar's engagements and travels."

"And could he..." Pompey asked. Cicero cut him off.

"Yes, he could have done," he said. "Easily." He paused, for maximum effect. "He made a fool out of you."

In which case, Catullus thought, he could empathise with Pompey. "So what's going on?" he asked impatiently. "What's all this got to do with me? I thought I was here to talk about the murders."

"You may be," said Cicero, "perhaps – in a sense."

"What sense?"

"A tangential sense."

"Oh, wonderful."

"Yes, it is," said Cicero, deliberately ignoring the sarcasm. "Because, you see, the question of who committed these murders is important only in so far as it bears on an issue of much greater significance and interest. Do you really think that men such as Crassus and His Excellency the President of the Republic meet to discuss the progress of murder cases? Come, come!"

"Explain the letter to him," said Pompey grumpily.

"In a moment," said Cicero, now fully the lawyer in command of his brief. He reached for a folder and held it up. "This is the report you wrote out for me a couple of weeks ago," he told Catullus. "It was admirably detailed, and achieved precisely what it had set out to achieve, to provide its reader with an account of your experiences at the hands of Clodia Metella and her delightful brother. I read it with great enthusiasm. It provided direct evidence for what had hitherto been only a hypothesis of mine."

"And that was?"

Cicero held up his hand. "All in good time." He skimmed through the report. "One item in particular attracted my notice," he said, looking up again. "The carriage you saw, the one with the eagle painted on its side. Caesar's emblem, I wrote in the margin. Then I sent the report off to the due authorities and back came the reply – no hard evidence. Pure supposition." Cicero flicked the report shut, and glanced at Pompey. "Coincidence."

Pompey shrugged, and patted at his stomach.

"Fortunately for me," said Cicero after a pause, "after this, events began to make my point for me with renewed force. There were riots. The Government was tied by its agreement with Clodius. It couldn't – can't – put them down. This in turn enabled Caesar to claim that Rome was – is – descending into anarchy. It culminated in yesterday's outrageous demand that Clodius – a Roman citizen, after all, alas! – be handed over to Caesar's Commission for trial. The Government refused. Result? Caesar initiates sanctions against us, as from midnight tonight, and Clodius launches another riot. They both seem so determined to bring down the Government that really, one might almost have conjectured they were working together. Except, of course, that this is clearly out of the question." Cicero glanced again at Pompey. "Clearly impossible. Clodius had reached a secret agreement with the Government. He had given his word of honour. He wouldn't go ganging up with Caesar behind the President's back, now would he? That wouldn't be good form. Clodius *is* a gentleman, after all."

"All right, all right," said Pompey, still contemplating his stomach. "Point made."

"Oh, but I don't think so," said Cicero, "not yet. There's an official pardon I want signed." He reached for an envelope – Clodia's letter to her brother. So that was why it had been taken, Catullus thought, remembering how he had insisted to Porter that it had been nothing to do with the murders, and asking to be allowed to keep it. "I hope you won't mind if I read this out?" Cicero asked him. "I would spare your blushes, but I don't want to spare His Excellency's."

"This is from whom to who?" Crassus asked.

"From Clodia to Clodius."

Crassus made a face. "Strictly necessary, is it?" he asked. "Can't stand either of them."

"It's absolutely necessary. It's just about as conclusive as evidence can get."

Crassus grunted, and waved an assenting hand. Cicero turned back to the letter.

"'Dearest, dearest little bro'," he read, with only the faintest curling of a sneer, "'thanks so much for the party. I loved it. It was clever of you to have me pick someone up. You met the one I chose, didn't you? Wasn't he sweet? At first I thought he was the strong and silent type, mainly because he didn't say a word to me the whole journey, but then I met him later and he seemed much more my sort. Also, he seems to have spent the whole ball fast asleep, so that makes him even more my sort – you remember why I married Metellus. Anyway, I think I'm in love with him – not Metellus, the other one, I mean. I took a photo of him, negative enclosed, and have been staring at it wistfully ever since. Where is he now? Could you find him for me? Please, please, please.'"

Cicero paused as he turned the letter over. Catullus glanced at Metellus. His face was still frozen and expressionless.

"Now, this is where it becomes really interesting," said Cicero. "Listen. This is about Clodius' mysterious request to have her 'pick someone up.'" He cleared his throat. "'Did everything go well? You seemed happy. It was lovely to see you all dressed up and looking pretty again, and him too, though he didn't look pretty of course, he never did. It was nice seeing him though. It was funny – having to phone him up and ask if he was coming, and then when he said yes, going out to pick up some other man. Did he think up that signal? Was it meant as a joke? If you see him again, tell him the joke's on him, because it led me to meet my new Dream Man.'" Catullus winced. Cicero glanced up at him, then turned back to scan down the letter. "There's one other thing she writes – let me just find it – yes, here." He began to read again. "'Talking about that meeting in the wood', she writes, 'you asked me if he' – always 'he' – 'had ever worn a dress before. He definitely did once, years ago, when we had that fancy dress thing, do you remember? It was the one where Metellus got drunk and proposed to me and I was so high I didn't think he was serious. I'm amazed you don't remember.'" Cicero lowered the letter, and glanced at Metellus. "I'm sorry, but just for the benefit of Crassus..."

"What?" said Metellus, barely turning his head.

"Do you remember the ball that your wife was writing about?" Pause. "Of course."

"And do you remember a man there who had come in a dress?"

"There were several. It was a masquerade. But the man wearing the most ostentatious dress..."

"Yes?"

"Was Caesar. As I recall."

"Thank you," nodded Cicero, "thank you." He turned to Crassus, then glanced at Catullus too. "You see? Does it make sense now?"

"Yes," said Catullus.

"Expand," said Crassus.

"You," said Cicero. He pointed at Catullus. "You expand. I want to be reassured that my argument is as obvious to someone else as it has been all along to me." He glanced at Pompey. "And it won't do some of us any harm to hear the argument a second time. Just in case any of us were too pigheaded to be convinced the first time round."

Catullus thought. "The 'he' in the letter is Caesar. Correct?"

Cicero nodded. "Correct."

"He tentatively arranged a meeting with Clodius, to be held on his sister's estate during the ball."

"The same ball at which Clodius had also arranged to meet the President of the Republic here," said Cicero at once. "A packed social schedule he had that evening. Sorry. Continue."

"Caesar had agreed a sign, to let Clodius know if he was going to be there. It couldn't be direct, because Clodius was being shadowed."

Cicero glanced at Porto. "Correct again."

"So the agreed sign was that Clodia would pick a man up, anyone she happened to pass on her way to the ball, and that person happened to be me. When Clodius saw my head, that was the signal for him to slip his shadowers, join Clodia in the carriage, and change into his ballgown. In the meantime, I'd been kicked out. But if anyone saw two heads in Clodia's carriage, they'd think that one of them was still mine."

This time it was Porto who nodded. "Which was why we didn't bother to follow the carriage. Most lax, ha ha. We were too busy looking for Clodius at the time, he'd given us the slip."

"Caesar and Clodius met. They agreed whatever plans they agreed. Caesar, of course, was dressed as a woman in the same estate where his wife had been raped. Clodius had insisted on this, I guess?"

"Yes," said Cicero, "I would guess so too. For the same reason that he made you, Your Excellency, turn up to his ball that same evening. To rub your nose in it."

Pompey shrugged. "Yes, yes," he muttered gloomily.

"He wanted to humiliate Caesar as well. What a night of triumph for him! His two enemies! Caesar and Pompey! Both forced to admit that they were grovelling to him. But –"

"Yes?" asked Crassus, leaning forward. "But?"

"But – Pompey was grovelling from a position of weakness. He was grovelling because he felt he had no choice, because he was weak. But Caesar – well – no one would call Caesar weak. Clodius might have done, that evening, but then Clodius' failing has always been over-confidence. He would have been quite capable of not realising that it is possible for people to grovel from a position of strength. And why do people do that? Well, if they're like Caesar, they do it because they are playing a long-term game. Grovel now, to triumph later." He nodded at Crassus. "You see what I mean?"

"Oh, yes," said Crassus. He mopped at his brow. "Oh, yes."

Suddenly Metellus began to shriek. His voice sounded like wire being played on in a gale. "I told you," he screamed, staring at Pompey. "You wouldn't listen, would you? We should never have signed that agreement. I told you." He stood up, and walked painfully, slowly, over to a window. He stared out. At what? Catullus could see the clock tower of the Senate House, jagged against the autumn sky. Everyone was silent, waiting on the dying man. At last, he turned back to face the room. "The police are down there," he said, "rounding up people on the streets. The riot must be over. They must have broken it up." He began to walk slowly back to his seat. "But there'll be more, won't there? We can't afford to pay our people. We can't afford it. And so the more we are squeezed by Caesar, the more we are squeezed by Clodius, and the more we are squeezed by Clodius, the more we are squeezed by Caesar, and soon there won't be a Rome left to squeeze any further. It can't go on! It has to stop!" With a rattling sigh, he slumped back into his chair, and Catullus was afraid that the impact would shatter him into pieces. "What can we do?" Metellus asked despairingly. "What can we do?"

There was a silence, then Cicero began to reach for papers. "Well," he said briskly, "I think there are a number of things we can do. The first is to admit that Clodius *has* been taking us for a ride, and that any concessions we wrung out of him were wholly worthless." All eyes turned to stare at Pompey. "Well?" Cicero asked rudely. "Can we agree on that much at least?"

Pompey sighed, and rested his hands on his paunch. "Yes," he said at last. "I suppose so."

"Good," said Cicero. "And about time. Now, the second stage in our fightback is this. We must find a weakness in this chain that is throttling us. Shouldn't be too hard. In effect, there are only two links – Caesar or Clodius. Which one of these two is the weaker? Fairly self-evident, I'd have thought."

"Clodius," said Crassus.

"Clodius," agreed Metellus.

"Very well," nodded Pompey slowly. "Clodius."

"Good," said Cicero, a smile puffing out across his face. "Any ideas?"

Metellus coughed. "Not while he's here," he said, nodding at Catullus.

Pompey and Crassus both murmured in agreement. But Cicero

raised his hand, and motioned at them to keep quiet. "We've all had a glance over the transcripts of Porter's interrogations this afternoon," he said. "I was wondering if perhaps they gave us any hints as to a possible course of action. Arrest of Clodius as a serial killer and so forth. What do you think?"

"I'm afraid they don't," said Porto unexpectedly.

Cicero stared at him in surprise. "What do you mean?"

"That we don't have much use for the evidence our young friend here so kindly brought us. In the best of faith I'm sure, I hasten to add, ha ha ha."

"Why not?" said Catullus, scarcely able to believe his ears. "You don't believe it? What reason would I have for lying?"

"No, no, no," chuckled Porto good-naturedly. "I'm not saying you've been lying, no, no, those days are long gone. But you see, in our investigation, the facts have been presenting themselves somewhat differently. I mustn't talk too much about sensitive police work, but allow me to say this. We have clues, we have leads, we have a suspect. We are closing in for the, ha ha, kill. And when we do make an arrest, let me assure you, it won't be Clodius." He turned to Cicero. "I'm sorry."

"You're sure?" Cicero asked him darkly.

"Quite sure. I can't say anything else. Don't want to, ha, prejudice the case."

"But..." Catullus stared at him. "But everything Pollo said. Have you looked at a map? Can't you work it out yourself? How do you explain it, the pattern?"

"There is no pattern," said Porto, shaking his head. "If there were a fourth murder, ha, yes, there might be a pattern then. But at the moment, we just have three random killings. And let me repeat, there will be no fourth killing, because soon, very soon, we will make an arrest. We know the guilty man."

"But the pattern – the murders four hundred years ago..."

"The footprints of the past, eh? Ha ha ha! No, no, I'm sorry, but no." Porto shook his head. "You found the body and the skeleton together in the tomb, and so, of course, you wanted to find a broader connection between them as well. Of course. You were shocked and frightened, and then, alas, my own treatment of you, less than sensitive, I'm afraid, ha ha ha..." He shrugged apologetically.

"But it's not just me talking," said Catullus desperately. "Pollo. He knew as well."

Porto raised a hand. "Let me ask you a question," he said. "This formula you talk about – the odd, even, odd formula which lies at the heart of your case – where, ha, *where* exactly did you come across that?"

"Varney's book."

Porto nodded. "Good, good. Now why, when you were with Pollo, why did you choose to press him about Mr Varney?"

"Because I thought that he might have been lying when he said that he'd never met him."

"And what did you end up thinking?"

"I wasn't sure." Catullus thought. "I suppose it's possible. No, more than that. Likely."

"That Pollo had met Mr Varney?"

"Yes."

"And had perhaps learnt about the formula from Varney rather than Clodius?"

"I suppose so."

"And what did you see the implications of that as being?"

"Well – that maybe Pollo had been committing the murders to frame Clodius."

"Yes!" Porto jabbed his finger down onto the table. "Yes! Exactly! But why assume that he had committed the murders himself? It doesn't necessarily follow, does it? Do you see? He had a pattern of three murders, any three would have done, and so he uses them to try and frame someone he may not have liked. Yes, that's possible. But it doesn't mean that he, nor even Clodius come to that, did actually commit the murders. Not when there is evidence, strong evidence, pointing towards a quite separate suspect. And that evidence exists, as, ha, I have told you. And it will be acted on, ha ha, very soon."

"Damn!" Cicero leant back in his chair. "Damn! So that's that."

"Well, it would seem to be, wouldn't it?" said Pompey, stirring restlessly. "On that front. Perhaps we should move on to another. And you," he said, staring at Catullus, "you'd better get out. Thank you for your time and all that, but we have weighty matters to discuss right now. Sorry, Porto, could you ring that bell and ask for the secretary?"

Porto rang the bell. A young woman glided in through the door and stood waiting for Catullus. "I'll be seeing you soon," said Crassus. Catullus looked round, wondering what that meant, but the door was already being closed in his face, and as it slammed shut, the secretary started to lead him away down the corridor. "In here," she said, opening a second door. She sat him behind a desk and made him sign various forms. "These swear you to secrecy," she told him. "If you break your silence, it's a prosecutable offence." Then she rang for a security officer, who led Catullus back out into the corridor. "Hold on, sir," he said, once they had begun to walk down some stairs. "Got something for you." He felt in his pocket and handed over a letter. "What is it?" Catullus asked. The security officer tapped the side of his nose, and then, as though nothing had happened, continued to lead his charge down the stairs towards the street.

Catullus caught a bus, and it was only when he had taken his seat that he pulled the letter out again. It was from Metellus, a very short note. The writing was thin and spidery, and had obviously been scribbled in a great hurry. 'Be kind to my wife', the note read. 'Put up with her. Remember that she herself is not always kind to those she loves. But she is worth it. I still love her very much." And that was it. Catullus re-read the note, then screwed it up and dropped it on the floor. How moving, he thought. And how sad. A dying man, in a dying government, in a dying country, still in love. It can redeem us all, Catullus thought, as he shut his eyes and began to sleep. He hoped. He hoped.

A week later, on the day of Boot's party, Metellus died. Clodia phoned Catullus with the news. She was shuddering, and could barely speak through her tears. "What shall I do?" she kept choking, "what shall I do?" Catullus murmured platitudes, and waited for her to calm down. Her misery surprised him. "He loved me," Clodia tried to explain, "he was kind to me. Even though I was always a bitch to him. I need someone who loves me like that. Who will love me whatever I do. I need it." She choked again. "I'm being selfish again, aren't I? But he wouldn't have minded. That was why I..." She trailed away. Catullus said something softly, he wasn't sure what, something comforting though, and inane. Then he waited for Clodia to speak again. "Everything's dying," she whispered, and Catullus could sense her trying to smile through the haze of her tears. "You mustn't leave me." She laughed. "You wouldn't, would you?" And her laughter choked and rose, then collapsed into tears again. Catullus asked her if she wanted him to come over. Clodia grunted wordlessly, then slammed the phone down.

Catullus felt overjoyed. She needed him, she needed him. Even in Clodia's house, the atmosphere of death failed to cloud his feelings of contentment and relief. After all, he thought, remembering Metellus' note, it was what the dead man upstairs had specifically requested, that his wife be cosseted and made to feel loved. As evening approached, and Catullus saw how desperately Clodia wanted him to stay by her side, his guilt at the prospect of leaving her only served to make him feel even more content, as he looked into Clodia's face and saw that his presence had become her drug. She needed him, she needed him. So when Catullus announced that he had to leave, and Clodia began to cry again, he quickly agreed that she should accompany him. Would Boot understand? He remembered how anxious her face had seemed, at the bus stop, when she had invited him. But no, she was kind and generous, of course she would understand. Catullus took Clodia's hand. "Are you sure you want to go?" he asked. Clodia nodded dumbly. "Okay," said Catullus. "But only if you're sure."

The party, once they had reached Boot's house, turned out to be fabulously vast. Catullus couldn't even find Boot. He had always known that her father was rich, but even so, he thought, staring at the crowds – there was being rich, and there was being rich. "Where's your friend?" Clodia asked. Catullus shrugged. "She must be in one of the four hundred rooms they've got here." They sat down on a step together, to wait for her. Clodia cried once or twice, but mostly just talked. Talked and drank. Catullus could feel his brain starting to spin. He suddenly realised that it was getting on for midnight, and he still hadn't found Boot. He staggered to his feet. "Get another bottle," said Clodia. "I can't move, my legs are full of lead." "Okay," said Catullus, trying to remember why he had stood up. "Okay." He leant on the banister, and found himself sliding down. Then he began to push his way towards one of the champagne bars.

He picked up a bottle, and ran into Camilla.

"Popsums!" she cried, "isn't it all such a riot, don't you think?"

Catullus blinked at her. "Have you seen Caelius?" he asked. There was a pause.

"I had to bin him, I'm afraid," she said at last. "Big elbow time, he was too dull by half. I tried, but really!" She smiled minxishly. "Life is too short."

"Oh, I am sorry," said Catullus, "I forgot. I was just wondering where he'd got to. I haven't seen him for a while, that's all."

Camilla pinched his arm playfully. "There are more important things in life than friends. That's what I've always found." She kissed him and took his hand. "You'll see."

Catullus wondered what he should do, and peered round desperately for Clodia. But he was rescued by a sudden surge of people moving past him, all heading into the main ballroom, and carrying both him and Camilla along in their stream.

"It's midnight," said Camilla, looking at her watch. "Speech time."

"Speech time? What speech time?"

"Oh, he always gives one. About his vision for Rome, that sort of thing. Absolute dullsville, but then, lesson number one for the party animal, there's no such thing as a totally free glass of champers."

Catullus looked around him. People were standing several rows thick against the walls of the ballroom, and in the centre of the circle a microphone had been set up. There was a small crowd standing next to it, quite distinct from the larger crowds, and Catullus wondered who one had to be to join such a gathering. He pushed his way forwards. God, there was Pompey. And there was Cicero. And then Catullus realised that someone was waving to him. Boot! It was Boot! Standing right next to Pompey. He waved back, and was about to step out towards her when he felt a tap on his shoulder. He looked round.

"Listen," said Clodia, "do you know whose party this is?"

"Yes," said Catullus, handing her the champagne bottle, then looking back at Boot and noticing that she had begun to frown. "It's Boot's father's."

"Yes," said Clodia, "but do you know who he is?"

Suddenly, all across the ballroom, a thousand voices dropped away into silence. Everyone turned to face a far door. "No," whispered Catullus back to Clodia. "Who is her father?" And then the far door opened, and a man walked across the ballroom floor over to the microphone, and Catullus understood. "Oh fuck," he whispered, "I didn't know. It's Crassus. I didn't know."

"My husband died today," whispered Clodia back. "What the hell are people going to say?"

Crassus began to speak. He thanked his guests for coming, then introduced a few particularly honoured guests. His mention of Cicero drew an especial cheer, and allowed Crassus to make a jibe against the unions. The attack was soon broadened. He was giving a speech to his shareholders, Catullus realised. He declared war on Clodius. Clodius would be defeated. Clodius would be annihilated. Clodius was threatening the very future of Rome. Clodius was threatening the profits of all Crassus' companies. He had to be stopped, and he would be stopped. "I can't believe I've got to stand here and listen to this crap," said Clodia suddenly. There was a silence. Crassus looked up from his notes, and stared at her. And then all the lights went out.

There was panic for a few seconds, and calls to switch on the generator, and then light was restored.

"You see?', shouted Crassus loudly. "A power strike! But the lights will never be turned off here, nor anywhere else I own! Not even if their leader has to send his own sister to spy on me!"

"He didn't send me," said Clodia.

Crassus ignored her. "Look," he boomed, pointing. "That is a woman whose husband died today!"

There was a low murmuring. Catullus tried to hold Clodia. He could feel her shaking, and thought that she was about to burst into tears. But she didn't cry. "I was invited here," she said slowly, when the murmuring had stopped. She pointed at Catullus. "I was invited by him."

Crassus took off his glasses, and peered at Catullus. "But he was invited by my daughter, I thought. Arabella, didn't you invite him?"

But Crassus didn't wait for an answer, swept a glance of triumph round his audience instead. "Metellus lies stiff in his bed, and what does his wife, Clodius' sister, let us remember, what does she do? Well – see for yourselves!"

"You pompous fucking git," said Clodia suddenly. She left the crowd and walked across to face him. There was silence. Clodia lifted up her bottle of champagne and poured it, every last drop, all over Crassus. Then she smashed the bottle on the floor, and ran from the ballroom. There was another silence. Then there was chaos.

Catullus lifted his head up from his hands. Crassus was being led dripping from the ballroom. The crowds had broken up into a thousand hissing particles. Boot. Oh God, he thought. Boot. He looked round the ballroom again, and then he saw her. Wandering across the floor towards him. Quite calm, she looked. He was surprised. As soon as she was in earshot, Catullus began to apologise.

"You could have told me you were bringing her," she said.

Catullus began to explain, and offer more apologies.

"I still think you should have told me," said Boot, cutting him off. "That's all I'm saying, all right?"

"I'm so sorry. Please, Boot, I really am."

Boot looked at him, then lit up a cigarette. "Well, I suppose my father had it coming. She was right, he is a pompous git. But even so... I mean, it's a bit humiliating, isn't it?"

"What is?"

She bent her head and sighed. "Oh, you know. I mean – I'm not saying it's your fault, well no, of course it's not your fault, if you don't... You know."

"What?"

"Well." She sighed again, and looked up at the ceiling. She swallowed, then shook her head. "I thought I was Lesbia."

Catullus stared at her. "Oh, Boot," he said at last. "I... I didn't know." He reached out to hug her.

Boot stepped back. "It doesn't matter – it's not your fault. It's just it is, well... I feel a bit humiliated, that's all. As I said."

Catullus reached out to hug her again, and this time she allowed him to hold her. Then she broke free and started to hurry away.

"Stop," Catullus shouted. "Where are you going?"

Boot turned. "Well, if you're not interested, I'd better go and get off with one of the maids."

"Maids? What do you mean?"

"That's how I met Mona. Didn't you know? She was a waitress here once." She smiled, very briefly. "See you, perhaps." Then she turned again and was lost.

Catullus drifted despairingly through large crowded rooms. A woman turned and stared at him. "Were you the young man with Clodia Metella?" she asked.

Catullus nodded.

"Well, I think that you'd better go and help her home," the woman said. "Before she does herself an injury."

"Where is she?"

"Out there." The woman pointed. "On the balcony." She turned to her husband. "Really. You would have thought she'd have the decency to go home – at the very least." But Catullus wasn't listening. He was hurrying across the room, towards the large balcony window doors, ignoring all the glances and whispered murmurs that followed him as he ran. He opened one of the doors and looked out. At the far end of the balcony there was a marble seat. Yes, someone was sitting on it, hunched up in a bundle. Catullus smiled.

"Great party," he said. Clodia looked up at him, as he sat down beside her. He held her in his arms. He kissed her lightly on the cheek, then began to stroke her hair.

"You don't hate me?" she said at last.

"No," said Catullus, surprised. "Why should I?"

"For embarrassing you in front of your girlfriend."

"You know she's not my girlfriend."

"No." And suddenly, Clodia began to cry again. She lurched up from Catullus' lap, hugging him tightly and shaking in his arms as he tried to press her, tried to crush her, for he felt renewed by the proof of how much she needed him, how much he needed her. He looked out at Rome, stretching black and lightless from the Palatine, and he could almost believe that it was his responsibility, the responsibility of his love, that it had absorbed the city's energy and soaked up all the light. But no, Catullus thought, love doesn't have to be selfish; it should be a sun, not a black hole, it should give, not just take. And as these thoughts were floating drunkenly through Catullus' mind, suddenly, magically, lights began to reappear all across the city, and it seemed to Catullus that it was because he had allowed them to. "Never worry," he whispered. "Never."

"Not even when I'm shit?" asked Clodia.

"Not even when you're shit." He kissed her, once, twice, countless times. She had stopped shaking now, and her lips were warm. "You've really worried I might give you up?" he asked. "Truly? I love you more than –"; he looked around, up – "more than there are stars in the night, silent up there, looking down at us, at the city, look, we can see it too, look, below us, at all the furtive love affairs, all the lack of joy down there, all the shame. We must never feel shame. Clodia!" He turned her, made her stare into his face. "Do you see? Please. You must."

"Yes."

"There's so little left that is private to us. The world is always around, there, unescapable." He gestured again, at the city below them. "We mustn't let it crush us dead. I've felt, for so long, caught up by events, processes, I haven't even recognised them, let alone understood, and it's so hard, the way things are now, so hard ever to break free. Am I too drunk? Am I making sense? We must be true to one another. Perhaps love is all we have that is purely ours, now, in this age, in Rome."

"Yes." She stared into his eyes. "Yes."

"We mustn't be defeated."

"No."

He kissed her. "Come on."

"Home?"

Catullus nodded. He offered his hand. Clodia took it. Together, arm in arm, they left.

The night wasn't over yet, though. Not altogether. As they turned into the street that led to Clodia's house, a figure stepped out from the shadows and whispered Catullus' name. Caelius. "What are you doing here?" Caelius shook his head. He hugged Catullus, then kissed Clodia, fully, on the lips. "What are you doing here?" Catullus repeated, stepping between him and Clodia, and taking Clodia's arm back again. Caelius started to say something, then shook his head, and took an envelope out from his pocket. "This came for you," he muttered. Catullus took it, and Caelius began to walk on down the street. He was looking very pale, Catullus noticed.

"You've had quite a few people ringing your doorbell," he said at last, watching Clodia as she took out her keys.

"Really? Who were they?"

"Journalists. At least, the one I spoke to was a journalist. You threw some wine over Crassus, or something, is that right?"

Clodia stared at him, then pushed the front door open and walked inside. "It was champagne, actually," said Catullus, following her inside.

"Champagne? Oh, classy." Caelius paused. "They wanted to know who you were too."

"Did you tell them?"

"Yes. I said you were a brilliant poet. Don't worry, I gave you a very good press. I told them to look in 'Alexandrian'."

"Thanks."

"Not at all."

They sat around the kitchen table, and Clodia made chocolate. Catullus stared at his friend, and wondered what the hell was going on. He had never seen anyone look so pale.

"Actually," said Caelius, when he had finished his chocolate, "if you are in tomorrow's papers, you won't be the only one."

"What do you mean?"

"Well, I might be in them too." He smiled feebly. "On the front page, probably."

"Why?"

"God." Caelius ran his hands through his hair. "I don't know how to put it." He swallowed, and looked as though he were going to be sick. He breathed in deeply. "You, um... You've probably noticed that I haven't been around recently," he said at last.

Catullus nodded.

"Well," smiled Caelius, "there was a reason. You see. I've been helping the police."

"What, with legal stuff?"

"In a sense." He paused. "In a sense. Um. You remember that wino who got killed? And your girlfriend? And then there was that apeman in the night club?"

Catullus stared at him. "Yes," he said, very slowly.

"Well." Caelius swallowed again. "They thought I might be able to help with that. They thought... well, actually, they thought I might have done it."

"What? No! The murders?" Caelius nodded. "But – I mean – you're out now. They didn't keep you?"

"No. I'm out on bail. For some reason, they gave me bail." Caelius licked his lips. "But they've charged me. They think I did it. Catullus – I'm under arrest." He began to shake. "They think I'm the murderer. They think I did those killings, and I don't know what to do. Catullus, help me. I don't know what to do!" He screamed. "I don't know what to do! I didn't do it, and I don't know what to do!"

The night held one final shock. Hours later, when Catullus had finally felt able to leave his friend, he remembered the telegram that Caelius had handed over to him. He pulled it out and opened it, and began to read. As he did so, his knuckles turned white, and a film of nothingness began to dance before his eyes.

ATTIS

SUMMER

XVI

VERONA

As Catullus bent down to oil Clodia's feet, the bones of his corset dug deep into his sides. He winced, but was careful not to breathe out too heavily – he wasn't the one who was meant to be in pain, after all. He glanced up at Clodia. She hadn't noticed anything. Her eyes were closed, and her lips slightly parted, as though waiting for a kiss she was afraid to beg. Catullus began to massage the insides of her toes, and Clodia moaned softly, stirring in her harness but scarcely swaying, so tightly she'd been bound, her arms chained high till they almost reached the ceiling, and her feet locked securely into thick leather cuffs. Catullus checked their fastenings, and she stirred again; Catullus pulled on the cuffs sternly, and Clodia relaxed back at once into submissive calm.

He stood up and stared into her face. With a lover's telepathy, she opened her eyes, and met his gaze, before lowering her face as far as the collar round her neck would allow. Catullus smiled. He reached for Clodia's hair, and then, jerking her head back, tied a blindfold over her eyes. He let her head fall again and stood back to admire his handiwork. He felt like a priest, a Bacchic maybe, lost before the sacred beauty of his victim. At the far end of the room, away from windows and the evening light, they were both, sacrifice and hierophant, dyed a dull, near-dark red by the glow of the wall curtains, secret worshippers in some Eleusian cave. Catullus breathed in sharply, then bent to light a candle. He placed it by Clodia's feet, and watched the lambent patterns it cast over her oiled and softened limbs. He lit another, larger, so that her whole body seemed ready to melt, and the black of her collar, and the bands around her wrists, duly deepened in colour and significance. Catullus bent his head. He couldn't bear to look. He was aroused, but in a way he scarcely understood, since what he could recognise as his own lust suddenly seemed, in the context of such ritual, such playing out of depersonalised roles, to be something that no longer defined him as himself. He sighed, and felt his abdomen heave unavailingly against its whalebone vice.

He looked up again and gave Clodia a lingering glance. Then he turned and reached for the long velvet gloves, inherited, like the corset, from Clodia's grandmother. He pulled the gloves up, then stretched his fingers, another person's now, Clodia's perhaps, or those of the society belle her grandmother had once been. He stroked Clodia, and she, her body sensitive to the touch of the velvet, whimpered softly with anticipation.

A flicker of something, some memory or longing, rose from deep inside himself. What was it? – he didn't want to know; the flavour it gave, even adrift in the back of his mind, was touched too recognisably with regret. But Catullus could feel it tempting him, a revelation of something valuable, perhaps, he even wondered, something irreducible, stirring from his unconscious to defy the carapace laced into his flesh. Clodia, sensing his stillness, shifted and moaned. Deliberately, very deliberately, Catullus began to circle her, and Clodia, hearing the click of his heels on the floorboards, tensed and moaned again. Catullus stopped, then reached for a crop. He could scarcely feel it through his gloves. He tapped Clodia gently, once on each buttock, and this time she began to shout out, "No, please, don't, no!" "Sssh," whispered Catullus softly, untying a headscarf from her hair. He rolled it up, then pushed it into her mouth. "Ready?" he asked. "You admit your crimes?" Clodia nodded desperately and mumbled through her gag. "You admit that you've haunted the street corners, and serviced the kerb crawlers, and there's not one Roman you haven't lapped?" Clodia nodded again, so eagerly this time that Catullus would have laughed, were it not for the flavour of that something still stirring in his mind. "Then prepare for your punishment," he said shortly, and rubbed the crop against her cheeks. He paused, and took a couple of steps back.

The birchings were never serious. Clodia, Catullus had long since discovered, preferred the idea of pain to the real thing, unlike the other Maenads, Marghi especially, who liked to have whole strips of their backs taken out. But Clodia – Catullus smiled – she welcomed the rituals of suffering as an anaesthetic, and shrank obstinately, like a child, from even the admission that she might ever have to endure true pain. It didn't exist, she would say, not if you refused to contemplate it. And then, remembering that, Catullus' smile died on his lips, and he felt the sense of loss rise from the back of his mind to submerge him beneath a wave of panic, for his own pain, he knew, his mourning for a brother, despite the passage of time, appalled Clodia and frightened her, not that she was callous, far from it, but that she couldn't bear to acknowledge its hold over anyone she loved. And Catullus, realising this, had felt himself cut off from her by his continuing need to mourn, and found his moods of despair compounded by a fear that he was perhaps losing Clodia, and then his desperation would darken even more.

One final slash, and he dropped the crop. Clodia's back was only lightly marked; Catullus felt a temptation to kiss it, but he knew that such a display of affection was forbidden by the rules, and so he checked himself and turned to reach for a chain instead. He untied Clodia's ankles and wrists; then, jerking her round, he tied the chain to her collar and tugged on it hard to make her fall to her knees. A snap, and her wrists were cuffed behind her back; a tap with his boot, and her legs were opened wide. "Come, you bitch," he ordered with insincere brutality. "Fuck yourself." Clodia did as she was told. Catullus, balancing precariously, placed a heel on her arse, and listened vaguely to the sucking on Clodia's fingers. But he found it hard to believe that he was standing there; the sadness he had sensed at the back of his brain was now so diffused, even to his limbs, even to his toes and finger tips, that he could imagine the emotion as some cloudy perfume, waiting to seep into the night, restrained only by its casket of corset, boots and gloves. And even that, he realised, seemed insubstantial now, for despite its vicious grip, the uniform felt unreal when corroded by grief, just as the role it imposed had long since melted too. Clodia expired; Catullus waited, then shook on the chain, and began to lead her across to the balcony.

Outside, the evening air felt cool on his cheeks. He leaned for a minute against the railing. Open lawns stretched away below him, down to the lake, purple in the twilight, and calm, quite calm. He could just make out the island. The woods looked deep and impenetrably still. The estate was as beautiful, at least, as he had remembered it, for that almost year since his first journey there. Catullus smiled, and turned round to face Clodia, who had slumped down behind him onto the floor.

He paused. "Do you love me?" he asked at last.

Clodia stared at him, then mumbled something from behind her gag. Catullus shook his head, and tethered her by the neck chain to one of the railings. He repeated his question, very slowly. "Do you love me?"

Clodia shrugged, then nodded. Catullus held her chin. "Good." He paused. "And will you always love me?"

Again, Clodia shrugged. She tried to mumble something, and Catullus, relenting, reached across and untied the gag. Clodia breathed in deeply, then shook out her hair.

"Well?"

Clodia stared at him. "It depends."

"On what?"

She made a face. "On how long you're going to leave me tied out here, for a start."

"What else?"

"How long you'll love me."

"Do you think I might stop loving you?"

Clodia stared out at the lake. "I don't know," she said at last. She shook her head. "I don't know."

Catullus was about to say something, to explain how strange he had felt inside, and how now, on the balcony, looking at the lake, his feelings of pain had become a magical mood of regret, for the vividness of his senses on the night when they had first met, never to be experienced in the same way again, never, and yet, there he was, with her, and even as he suffered from the painful clarity of his memories, he couldn't really wish that he was back there, living them out again, not really, not when he could feel ennobled by his mood and yet at the same time hold her and know that she was fully his. He wanted to tell her all this, and had virtually opened his mouth to speak, when suddenly he heard the telephone. He froze.

It came from far away, deep back inside the house. Clodia had heard it as well. "Leave it," she said.

"It might be for me."

Clodia frowned at him. "Why? No one knows you're here."

"It might be for me..." His sense of disquiet had returned. He walked back towards the balcony doorway.

"Where are you going?" Clodia shouted. "You can't leave me here. Wait. I'm tied up. Catullus – wait!"

But Catullus didn't wait. The phone was a long way off, and God knew how long it might have been ringing before he had noticed it. As he ran, he could hear its tone becoming louder and louder, insistent, as though it were an alarm, Catullus thought guiltily, waking him to loyalties and affections that he should never have mislaid. He remembered that evening, months before, when he had read the telegram his parents had sent, and he had never imagined then, trying to spell out the words through his tears, that he might forget all he owed to the sharers of his grief. He reached the phone, and picked it up. "Hello?"

A silence at first, and then the voice he had been expecting. "Hello?" his mother asked nervously. "I was just wondering – could I –"

"It's me."

"Oh." He could almost hear her smile of relief. "Oh, good. I hope I'm not..."

"No, I wasn't doing anything. And I was going to phone you anyway," he lied. "To tell you I'm coming over tomorrow."

"Oh good!" She sounded so happy – just to learn he was coming, at last, that was all it took. "Your father will be pleased!" Then her voice lowered again. "I didn't want to disturb you, because I'm sure you must be very busy." Her whisper lowered even further. "But it's just, your father... He's a bit upset."

"About me?"

"Oh no – no. Not at all." She paused. "It's the memorial – for your brother. It's just been finished. Your father, I think, he's a bit – it brings it all back for him a bit, I think."

"Yes." Catullus shut his eyes. "Of course."

His mother paused again, then spoke firmly. "It's just that I think he would appreciate it if you were here with him. Just for a couple of days. We miss you, you know, we miss you a lot – especially now that..." Her voice caught, and faded into silence. "You do see?"

Catullus stared, very hard, at the tips of his boots, his woman's boots. "Of course. I'm so sorry."

"Oh, please, darling – don't keep saying that. There's nothing to be sorry about. It's just – well – I'm sure you don't mind your parents chasing you up just this once?"

"No. You know I don't. Not ever." Catullus shook his head. "I should have come earlier, I knew this would be an upsetting time for you, but I just – I don't know – I haven't got an excuse. I'm selfish, that's all." He wanted to sigh, but the corset's hold was too tight. "I'll be there tomorrow. First thing."

"Your father will be so happy."

"Yes. And I will too. I can't wait to see you both."

"I'll go and tell him now. Goodbye, my love."

"Goodbye."

"Goodbye." The tone went dead. Catullus imagined his mother walking from the phone, back through the hall, calling to his father, 'he'll be here tomorrow!' He could picture it so exactly – but of course he could – it was his home. His home. And then Catullus shook his head, and remembered that it wasn't any longer, that he lived in Rome now and had made no effort to go back, not for a whole year, not once. He felt tempted to go for a walk, to try and escape his feelings of guilt, but he had no sooner moved than he remembered that he was wearing those fucking heels, and that anyway, he had left Clodia chained upstairs. The thought of her served to lighten him a bit.

When he rejoined her on the balcony, though, Clodia was furious.

"How dare you?" she asked, staring up at him. "How dare you just leave me trussed up like this?"

Catullus tugged lightly at the chain. "It was only for ten minutes."

"That's not the point. It's cold, and I'm naked, and I don't like being tied up."

"Oh, I am sorry," said Catullus, opening his eyes in mock apology. "And there was me thinking you were the same person who'd just asked me to chain her to a whipping frame and do her over with a riding crop."

"That's different."

"Really?"

"Yes. You know it is." She strained at the chain. "Just undo it."

Catullus salaamed, and did as he was told.

"And my hands," Clodia ordered. "My wrists are hurting." Again, Catullus scurried to obey, and Clodia stretched out her arms, flapping her wrists to restore the circulation. She stood up and wrapped herself inside a blanket. Catullus frowned, and realised that he had been infected with a mood of resentment himself.

"You can undo me now," he said.

Clodia stared at him. "No," she said at last.

"Clodia – undo me."

Clodia shook her head. "No," she said again.

Catullus sighed, then had to check himself – that fucking corset, he wanted it gone, immediately! "Look, I'm sorry if I pissed you off, but I had to hurry because I was wearing these boots. All right? Understand?"

"You enjoy wearing them."

"No, I don't."

"Of course you do. Otherwise you wouldn't have gone to such efforts to round up all the gear."

"Not at all." He grimaced a smile at her. "I just wanted to give you a good time, dear."

"Well – now it's my turn."

"Clodia, please. They hurt. I'm very, very sorry I left you."

Clodia shrugged. A thought suddenly crossed her face. "Who was it on the telephone?" she asked.

"My mother."

"How did they have my number?"

"Well, how do you think? I gave it to them."

"Why?"

"Because, if you remember, I originally came down here to see them. A memorial to my brother has just gone up, and I promised I'd spend some time with them."

"So?"

"So – I told them I'd be staying here for maybe a night. It's probably escaped your attention, we've been having such fun, but I've been here four nights now and I'm about to stay a fifth. So – my mother was phoning, not unreasonably, to find out where the fuck I'd got to."

"And what did you say?"

"I told them I'd be there tomorrow morning. First thing."

"Oh, great." Clodia stared at him. "Great. Thanks a lot for telling me."

Catullus narrowed his eyes and met her stare. "Why the fuck should I have told you?" he asked, very slowly. "It's none of your business."

"Of course it is. I've been putting you up."

"Only because you wanted me to stay. And now I'm telling you that I want to go, because my parents need me, and because I'd originally fixed that I'd be with them all week. All right? Is that fair enough?" Catullus stared at her angrily and began to unbutton his gloves. "Now – will you please help me get this fucking stuff *off!*"

Clodia stared out at the lake and lit a cigarette.

"Clodia!" Catullus struggled to reach round to his back, trying to pull at the laces knotted down his spine. He tugged violently, but nothing happened; swearing, he pulled and pulled at the corset's top, but it stayed immovable, and Catullus felt a violent horror at the thought of its presence so tight against his skin, a Nessus' shirt, implacable, humiliating. Clodia, who had been watching him, finished her smoke. "For fuck's sake," she sighed, "come here." She whispered into his face. "Chill." Then she turned him round and began to unknot the corset laces, until finally Catullus could breath again. His stomach had never felt so fat and free.

They made up later, but the quarrel had effectively killed the evening dead. Clodia mewed herself up behind a bedroom door, and Catullus was left alone, to roam long corridors. He decided to take a walk, now that he could at last. He wandered down to the lake, then up again over the rocks to the promontory where Clodius had met Pompey and discussed the fate of the Republic. Or where Clodius had met Pompey, and Pompey had been hoodwinked, Catullus thought, remembering how Cicero had interpreted the meeting, all those months before. And Cicero had been right, the country was disintegrating. But Catullus, staring at the lake and thinking about the chaos that he had left behind in Rome, discovered that he didn't really give a fuck – it was all too complex, too desperate, it hurt his brain. And anyway, Catullus thought, watching the moon's reflection in the lake and noticing that it was shivered despite the calm, he had more pressing reasons for feeling despair. He had lost his only brother. He had behaved with selfish cruelty towards his parents. And he wasn't sure if he really loved Clodia.

There. He had thought it. The unthinkable. He glanced round at the single light shining in the house behind him, then began to walk slowly from the promontory and back around the lake. He had imagined that the admission of his fear to himself might perhaps relieve the sense of gloom in his mind, but he found, on the contrary, that the prospect of not loving Clodia any longer made his future seem even more dreary and grey. He was in the woods now. They lay thick all around him, rich-shadowed, velvet, touched with light from the moon and the stars. A bird sang, from far off. Catullus stopped walking. The air was soft, not only with stillness and the scent of fresh leaves and flowers, but also, Catullus realised, with the memories that he brought to the place, memories that had value because they were touched by Clodia, his love. If he found the woods beautiful now, walking through them, then it was because Clodia had helped to make them so. And similarly, if Catullus shut his eyes and tried to remember the highlights of the year just gone by, he had the impression of a tunnel streaked with whorls and stains, some vivid, some dull, some throbbing with menace, Caelius, Dugbals, murders, Boot, but above all, more vivid than any of these, most beautiful, were pools of rich light, and Catullus knew, without even having to translate them into thought, that they represented his moments spent with Clodia. He opened his eyes, then shut them again, and tried to imagine what a year without those moments might be like. The lights began to dull and melt into a sludge; the tunnel was left featureless; the thought of entering it made Catullus want to struggle, to do anything to escape. So was it really possible – really – that he could allow himself to be not in love with Clodia, that he could face the prospect of such a dreariness? He sighed, and opened his eyes, and began to walk on again.

Ahead of him, there was a small cliff of rock. Catullus left the path and walked to its edge. He looked down and found that he recognised the arbour below. Yes – it was the same place, the place where he had seen the three women in their ballgowns and masks – Caesar, Clodius and Clodia. Catullus edged his way round the cliff, until the rock turned to soil and he could scrabble his way down. He walked back up a trackway, and there, in front of him, was the temple carved from the face of the cliff. It was Circassian, he realised, not Greek, as he had always assumed. Catullus rubbed his fingers down one of the pillars, then walked inside and found a bench. A silence of chalk and earth entombed him.

How he longed for his brother. How he longed to tell him about all his problems and fears, and then laugh, and find that they had disappeared. But it was his brother who had gone. Catullus bent his head forward and buried his face in his hands. From outside the temple a bird sang, from the shade of thick boughs, a wordless threnody of aching grief.

The next morning, Catullus' car wouldn't start. Clodia came out in her dressing gown to watch him as he prodded hopelessly at the engine. There was a sudden fizz, and a jet of black smoke. "Bugger," Catullus said loudly. He kicked the car, and slammed the bonnet down. "Bugger, bugger, bugger."

"Having problems?" Clodia asked sweetly.

"It's only because all the garages were on strike. I knew there was something wrong with it. But what am I supposed to do, if everyone's on fucking strike? It's your brother's fault."

"It always is, isn't it?"

"Yes. Ever bothered to wonder why?"

Clodia glanced at him, then shook her head. "When did you tell your parents you'd see them?" she asked, staring at the car.

Catullus followed her gaze. "About half an hour ago," he said. "Why?"

"Well – if you think it's my brother's fault..."

"You're offering to drive me there?"

"Seems sensible."

"You won't stay?"

Clodia rolled her eyes. "Oh, charming."

"No, I don't mean it like that, you know I don't." Catullus stretched over and tried to hold Clodia. She fought him off at first, but he pinned her down and hugged her tightly in his arms. "I don't want you not to stay, not if you want to, but – you know..."

Clodia stared at him. "No. I don't know. What are you talking about?"

Catullus let her go. "Only that – while I'm at home..."

"Don't worry." Clodia pushed his hands away, and stood up. "I won't embarrass you. I've got a brother too, remember?"

"Clodia."

"No. It's all right." She glanced at her watch. "We ought to go."

"Clodia, wait."

"We haven't got time." She began to walk back to the house, then run. Catullus watched her. Shaking his head, he went to pick up his bags.

The drive, across the downs, past the very spot where the two of them had first met, into Verona and then on again, through a valley of small villages, took much less time than Catullus had imagined that it would. As a result, when he saw his village's name flash past on the side of the road, he was unprepared for his sudden feelings of agitation; the same lake, the same fields, the same houses, the same small shop, all just as he had remembered them, slipping past, quite unchanged by his year away. He felt vaguely affronted. But there were his parents, of course – they had missed him. And now he was back. Clodia parked the car outside his house, and Catullus slammed the door behind him. The noise it made, against the sound of birds and a person talking far off in the fields, was utterly distinctive – no car door had ever slammed like that in Rome. Catullus ran up the front steps and knocked loudly; dogs barked from inside, and he heard the sound of footsteps coming across the hall. For a brief while, he experienced what had once been his everyday as a series of thrilling novelties, and yet he was left without any feeling of disorientation, for the novelty lay only in finding the familiar so reassuring. And when his parents had come to the door, and they had hugged, and laughed, and Catullus had introduced them to Clodia, he found that he didn't mind when his mother asked Clodia to stay. It had been a nervous request, and Clodia had looked at him inquiringly, but he just shrugged and so Clodia said 'yes'. Catullus showed her to his bedroom, almost proudly. "Small but sweet," he said. "Very," nodded Clodia, and lay back on the bed. Catullus kissed her, then leant out of the window. All, all, just as he had remembered it. Tall trees against a warm sky, their branches bending over the garden wall.

It was easy to forget, during the first half hour, that he hadn't come back there on holiday. Out in the garden, with the dogs running madly round and round him, and the comforting smell of warm grass in the air, it was Rome that seemed an eternity away, and childhood, or at least the happiest moments of his childhood, that seemed to have been lived only yesterday. And it was then, as Catullus remembered the summers passed with his brother, that the reason for his visit home came back to him, and all his feelings of comfort stripped themselves away, to reveal the jaws of a trap all the more vicious for its earlier disguise. Again, Catullus felt selfish and ashamed. He stood up, from where he had been lying on the grass, and wandered back over the lawn to the house. His mother was in the kitchen. She had been watching him. Catullus took her and held her, and she slowly crumpled in his arms.

"You must go and look after Clodia," she said at last.

"She's fine."

"And so am I," she said, pulling herself away from his hold. "You're not being kind, leaving her upstairs on her own."

"I said – she's fine."

"No." His mother shook her head. "I'm sure she won't mind later if we want to have a talk, but not now, not when she's only just arrived – you mustn't take your unhappiness out on her. It's not fair."

Catullus wanted to remind his mother that he had just spent four days with Clodia; even more importantly, he wanted to prove that he was sorry for it. In such a cause, he realised, he would happily have sacrificed Clodia for a while on the altar of his repentance – but there was no point in the gesture if his mother was going to refuse any acknowledgment of it. So Catullus went to join Clodia, and he discovered, staring at her, that he passionately wanted her not to be there any more. He tried not to show this too obviously –

his mother was right, after all, he wasn't being fair. But he found Clodia's company a constant strain – all the scenes and objects from his, and his brother's childhood, were new to her, and so he had to explain details that he had been hoping to dwell on in silence, and resanctify. Sometimes, when he was afraid that Clodia might smile at him, he kept quiet about certain memories, an expression of embarrassment that he saw as a betrayal, but at the same time had to recognise he couldn't help. He had changed – the Catullus his brother had known had disappeared. But he hadn't wanted to dwell on such a truth, not now, he thought, not now of all times. So he continued trying to blot Clodia out, and submerge the present at the expense of the past, and of course, with Clodia beside him, he continued to fail.

Afternoon passed, and the evening shadows lengthened. Supper was early – much earlier than Catullus had become used to under Clodia's influence in Rome. But the country air seemed to have liberated long forgotten instincts; Catullus took his place at the table without a second's thought, and it was only the sight of Clodia sneaking a glance at her watch that made him suddenly remember his own urban rhythms. He stared at Clodia again. She sat perched on a wooden stool, trying to look interested in a boiled potato. Behind her, through the window, the sun was setting; her hair, just recently dyed a copper-orange, seemed to glow and blaze. Catullus glanced at his father; he too seemed transfixed by Clodia's hair. He was clearly going to ask her about it. He did, and Catullus winced, as his two worlds seemed set to clash again. But Clodia laughed, and answered with a joke, and his father was charming and witty in return. The two worlds had been bridged, and Catullus felt suddenly proud of them both.

"Well, I think it's a lovely colour," said his mother, joining in the appreciation of Clodia's hair. "Has Caelius got rid of *his* awful haircut yet?"

Clodia laughed, and Catullus smiled. "Yes, he looks very smart now," he told his mother. "But then again, I suppose he's got to. In the circumstances."

"Yes," said his mother slowly. "Poor Caelius."

"Is he bearing up?" asked his father.

Catullus shrugged. "Seems to be. Actually, for someone charged with multiple murders, he seems to be flourishing. Rolling in cash, and when he's not, it's because he's waving it under my nostrils. I'm amazed they haven't locked him up."

His mother frowned at him. "You almost sound as though you think he ought to be," she said.

Catullus shook his head. "No, it's just I'd like to see him sweat a bit, that's all."

"I was wondering about his bail," said Clodia. "Do they usually give it out like that?"

"No," said Catullus. "Almost never for murder. Don't you remember there was all the comment about it in the papers? He's got a curfew imposed on him, but that's about it. I expect it's some cunning lawyer's trick."

Catullus's father snorted. "They're all crooks, lawyers," he said decisively.

"No, but not Caelius, darling," admonished his wife from across the table.

"No, of course not, I wasn't implying that." Catullus' father creased his forehead, and as he always did when he felt suddenly embarrassed, reached for a newspaper.

"Not at the dinner table, darling," said Catullus' mother.

"No, I was just..." He opened and shut his mouth, then shrugged, and dropped the newspaper down by his feet. There was silence. Clodia helped herself to another potato.

The conversation fluttered back to life. Catullus' mother wanted to be told that Caelius was innocent, and pressed Catullus for all the details of the case. Catullus, as blandly as he could, tried to fill them in for her. He kept quiet about his own suspicions, and especially about his dealings with Clodius. This inevitably resulted in a few inconsistencies, and Clodia, picking up on a few of them, offered her own point of view. She seemed to have talked a lot to Caelius just after his arrest, Catullus realised. He hadn't noticed at the time.

"And when does the trial actually begin?" Clodia asked.

"Next week."

"So you'll be back for that?"

"Yes." Catullus glanced at his mother. "I told Caelius I would."

"Yes, yes, of course." His mother nodded. "He'll need you."

There was a brief silence. Catullus' father, who'd been playing with the newspaper, brought it down magnificently onto his table mat. "I think you'll find," he announced, sitting back and nodding his head, "I think you'll find –" He paused. "That Caelius will be acquitted by Cicero." He nodded again and looked around the table. Clodia made a face.

"Is *Cicero* defending him?" she asked.

Catullus' father nodded again. "Oh yes," he said. "Chief counsel for the defence."

"God, I never realised." She put a finger up to her mouth. "Bleaugh."

Catullus' father looked slightly nonplussed. He tapped at his newspaper, as though trying to find some reassurance. "You don't – approve – of Cicero?" he asked Clodia at last.

"No," said Clodia rudely, "I hate him."

"Oh." Catullus' father frowned, and picked up the newspaper again. He ran his fingers down it thoughtfully. "You can say what you like about Cicero, though," he said, more to himself than to anyone, "but he's done a lot of good for this country. A lot of good."

"I think he's been a disaster for this country."

"A disaster?" Catullus' father stared at Clodia disbelievingly. Then, slowly, the memory of whose sister she was dawned across his face. "Well, yes, maybe," he said, trying to salvage at least some point of agreement, "but he is a good lawyer."

"That's not a great reference, is it? You just said it yourself, all lawyers are crooks."

"Yes." Catullus watched his father's smile twitch. Oh God, he was going to make some sly dig at Clodius. He'd mean it as a joke, but would Clodia take it that way? She suddenly seemed to have become rather brittle. Catullus wondered if he should break in with some comment, anything, but it was too late.

"I think you'll find," his father was saying, "that in the state the country's in now, anyone in a position of authority is going to be a crook. Anyone. Don't you think?"

"No," said Clodia. "I don't think that, not if you mean Clodius, no."

Catullus reached across to try and calm her, but Clodia snatched her hand away.

"He's my brother," she said, staring at him.

"I'm sorry," said Catullus' father, clenching his newspaper tightly. "I didn't mean..." He reached out gently, more gently than Catullus had done, and this time, Clodia allowed her hand to be held. "You mustn't think I..." He paused, and tapped the newspaper against a table leg. "I'm sorry," he said again at last.

Clodia stared into his worried face, then back across the table at Catullus. She stood up. "I'm going for a walk," she said. "It's time you talked about your brother." She turned to Catullus' mother. "Thank you for the meal. I hope you'll excuse me." She pushed her way past the table, and then out of the kitchen. She slammed the back door after her, and Catullus watched her running across the garden. Slowly, his father climbed to his feet. "It was my fault," he said. He reached for his newspaper. "I think I'd better go and see if she's..." He frowned and nodded again, then followed her.

Catullus stood up too, but his mother reached across and took his arm. She led him from the kitchen and out into the hall.

"It's getting late," she said.

"So?"

"There won't be any daylight left soon." She stared into his face.

"Clodia was right. It is time to talk about your brother." She opened the front door. Outside, the blue sky was softening into purple, and along the horizon, it was almost dark. "I'd forgotten the time," she said, staring into the dusk. She shut the door behind her, then took her son's arm. She pressed him, and smiled, but said nothing. Catullus looked down at her. She seemed very small, measured against him, much smaller than he had remembered. They turned and walked along a quiet path. The shadows were thick from trees that lined the graveyard. The grip on Catullus' arm became tighter, and he realised, for the first time as a conscious thought, that he was now his mother's only son.

The creak of a wooden gate, the sound of their footsteps along a gravelled path, and then silence. A simple memorial, of freshly cut stone, stood alone in the shade of a yew tree. Catullus read the inscription, and bowed his head. His mother was still holding his arm. He turned to look at her. "I feel – a part of him is here," she said at last. "Even though he is – resting – so far away. Beneath the soil at Troy." She appealed to him with a silent, twisted smile, then stared again at the memorial. "Part of him is still here."

"Yes." Catullus shut his eyes. "What did you find, Ma, at Troy, when you went to see his grave?"

She thought. "That he had died surrounded by compassion."

"Whose?"

"Strangers'."

"You met them?"

His mother nodded. "They were kind to us as well. Very kind. They looked after us, told us everything they knew." She bowed her head, and Catullus waited. When his mother began to speak again, she did not look up. "He had been ill," she said, "for several weeks. We'd had a letter, you remember, he'd described his pains. But he'd gone on travelling. He'd wanted to reach Troy. You remember what he was like, and you too, always interested in Troy. But it killed him."

"How did he die?" Catullus could feel tears starting to prickle underneath his lids. But his voice stayed steady. "What did they tell you, the people who looked after him?"

"Well..." His mother shook her head sadly. "He had been to see the citadel. On the way back, he collapsed in the street. People helped him to someone's room, they called a doctor, but it was too late. Before he died, he whispered something about 'home', and about you, but no one knew what, and they didn't know who you were."

"There was a message for me?"

"Perhaps. But perhaps he was just calling out your name. You were there though, anyway, on his thoughts, at the end." Catullus' mother turned and pressed his hands together, clasped in her own. "He died, and they buried him in a unnamed grave. No one had known who he was, or who we were. Maybe it was better that way. We would never have learned that he wasn't alive. We would always have had that glimmer of hope." She smiled dreamily. "But they found his passport, of course, in the end..."

"And are you glad you went?"

She turned to face him. "Yes. It took us time, to summon the resolve, but in the end – yes. And you? – are you glad that you didn't?"

"To see his grave, and know his bones were under my feet?" Catullus shook his head.

His mother reached inside her bag, and took out a small wooden box. She handed it to Catullus. He unlocked and opened it – there was dry earth inside. He looked at his mother. She nodded. Catullus ran his fingers through the dusty soil, then scattered it so that it fell in a grey arc over the grass that stretched from his brother's memorial. And there it lay, earth from the Rhoetean shore, waiting for the rain that would wash it away.

'What have I lost, brother more loved than life, what have I lost?' Catullus felt the silent question sting his eyes. He stared at the memorial, then bowed his head again.

It was back in the house, though, his presence liberated by the shadows of evening and, perhaps, by the tears shed for him in the graveyard, that Catullus' brother seemed closest to the family he had left behind. When Catullus mentioned this, on their return, to his mother, she just nodded her head slightly, and took him to the bedroom that he and his brother had once shared as boys. She left him there, alone in the dark; Catullus lay on a bed for a few minutes, gathering his thoughts, then walked to the window and swung it open. The silhouettes of trees were still against the burning stars, just as they had been all those years before, when his brother had jumped from the same window that Catullus was leaning against now, and hurried across the lawn, and made his way over the far garden wall. Catullus shifted; the catch was digging into his hip again. He remembered that first night in Rome, how he had imagined his brother as standing silently behind him. He had turned then, but not now – there was no need. His brother wasn't standing behind him, but he was diffused amongst the patterns of darkness and light, and the tricks of the shadows – he was there. In the posters on the wall. In the books left scattered by the bed. In jokes and phrases that Catullus could hear rising in his mind. He was there.

The door opened. Catullus turned round. Clodia. Go away – go away! She stood there, waiting. "Be nice to me," she said at last. "You make me feel I'm in the way."

Catullus stared at her. "You are."

Clodia lowered her head. She walked slowly across the room, then sat down on the bed. "Don't you think," she asked, looking up, "don't you think, it can be very stupid to risk the future for something dead and gone?"

"No." Catullus turned back to stare out of the window. "Leave me alone, Clodia."

Silence. Catullus waited. Had she gone? He turned round, and met her eyes, bright and unblinking, and cold, very cold. "Are you really telling me to go?" she said at last.

"You heard what I said."

Still her eyes glittered and didn't blink. "Fuck you!" she suddenly screamed. "Fuck you!" She began to sob. "Fuck you." The words were swept away on her tears. She stood up, and stared straight into Catullus' face, then ran from the room. Catullus could hear her footsteps as she hurried down the stairs.

For a few seconds, he didn't know what to do. Then, mechanically, he walked over to the door, and pulled it shut. From outside, he could hear the sound of a car starting, and driving away. He returned to the window. The sound of the car faded and was lost in the night. He leaned forward. The catch dug into his hip again.

XVII

THE PALATINE

Heat lowered over Rome in a sullen haze. Driving back into the city, Catullus found that he was tensing almost instinctively, as his memories of Verona began to shrivel under the glare of concrete and stone. There was very little traffic on the roads – the petrol rationing had started to bite – but the city's stillness seemed threatening and angry, and hung in the air like the throb of the heat. Catullus began to notice groups of men on the pavements; some just lounged and stared as he passed; others shouted and punched their fists. Once, as he neared the centre of Rome, he saw someone throw something, and had to swerve; jeers followed him down the road. So Catullus was glad to see the first sign to Tallowfield; it wasn't Verona, but set against the callous anonymity of the rest of Rome, the idea of it suddenly began to seem friendly at least.

There had also been a couple of signs to the Palatine, and Catullus, for a few seconds, had been tempted to turn and follow them. It had only been last evening that Clodia had walked out on him, and he had begun to miss her already. That morning, his parents had driven him to Troy, but there had been no sign of Clodia's car, and the house had been locked; while his father had tinkered with the car engine, Catullus had scanned round the estate, but no, Clodia had gone. So she was back in Rome, and Catullus, leaving the signs to the Palatine behind, wondered how long he should leave her there alone to stew.

The street outside his flat still smelt of tarmac and unemptied bins. Oh well, Catullus thought, remembering the men on the side of the roads, at least he had a home. He opened the front door, and hurried up the stairs to his bedroom. There was a sudden scuffling, coming from beyond the door. Catullus froze. Then, slowly, he inched the door handle down and leant against the door. He walked in. And there, his face inside a large cupboard, and a pile of Catullus' clothes by his feet, was the unmistakable rear of Mr Dugbal.

Catullus took a step forward, and a floorboard creaked. Mr Dugbal jumped and tried to turn round, but his head was still inside the cupboard, so he hit it on a shelf and yelped with pain. His cap fell off; he scrabbled on the floor for it, gathered up a pile of clothes-hangers in his arms, then pressed himself, shaking, against the far bedroom wall.

"I've got to go now," he stammered.

"But what were you doing with my clothes?" Catullus asked.

Mr Dugbal shook his head vigorously. "Not clothes," he muttered. "Clothes-hangers."

"Yes, but why?"

Mr Dugbal shrugged, and stared at him beseechingly. "I've got to go now," he said again. Then suddenly, he began to flit across the room, and before Catullus could shut the door on him, he was out and away. Catullus followed him, asking him to wait, but Mr Dugbal scurried down the stairs, and Catullus gave up the pursuit. He shrugged, and was heading back to his bedroom to tidy up when Tubbers' head popped out from the bathroom door.

"Oh, right," he said. "You back?"

Catullus gestured with his arms.

"Bloody good to see you. Nightmare alley here, though."

"Why, what's the problem?"

"Balloon's gone up rather." Tubbers pulled a face. "Trade figures, inflation figures, bloody everything figures. No bloody good. Inflation, right? – sixty percent. *Sixty* percent. What's a man to do?"

"Surrender?"

"Yah. Exactly." Tubbers nodded and grinned. "They're suspending the Stock Exchange tomorrow, you know."

"That's serious?"

"Rather. Why I've got to go in now, actually."

"But it's the weekend."

"I know."

"God."

"Yah. And I can't find a tie. Oh, *hell*."

"It's Mr Dugbal, I think. I just found him nicking all my clothes-hangers."

"Rarly? Well, bloody hell." Tubbers nodded to himself. "Does that mean you've got any ties left?"

Catullus went to his room and fetched one. Tubbers took it gratefully. "You're right, actually," he said, knotting the tie round his neck. "He takes things from shops and rubbish tips. Caelius saw him. He was coming back with bits of a bed. You still got yours, have you?"

Catullus nodded. "Yes. I probably surprised him just in time. What do you think he's doing with it all?"

"Don't know. But he's up to something fishy in his cellar. Caelius tried to get in there last week, but he was nabbed."

"Oh dear. Caelius getting into more trouble."

"Yah." Tubbers turned away from the bathroom mirror, in which he'd been checking his hair, and nodded. "Exactly."

"How is he?"

"Oh, bearing up, I think. You know what he's like. He never tells me a thing."

"Is he here?"

"No, he's over with his uncle, actually."

"Plotting strategy?"

"That kind of thing. He'll be back soon, though. Kitchen's bloody swamped by his papers."

"That's considerate of him."

"Well, he is accused of murder, isn't he? So bound to have lots of papers." Tubbers glanced at his watch. "Look, got to head. But good seeing you. Catch you soon, okay?"

"Yes, I hope so."

"Good news. Okay. Bye!" He clattered down the stairs, and Catullus, having heard the front door slam, found that he was being drawn, despite himself, into the kitchen. All Caelius' papers, scattered round the table? He couldn't resist the temptation. And there they were, in great piles. Catullus pulled up a chair, and scanned them. Which one should he start with first?

No, he couldn't – no. He leant back in his chair, and was just about to stand up again when he saw something, suddenly, out of the corner of his eye. A letter, on a pile of letters, with handwriting on the envelope that Catullus recognised. He picked it up and stared at it. The handwriting began to shake. Catullus steadied his hand, and slowly took the letter from the envelope. He smoothed it out on the table, then began to read.

His brain seemed to be stopping him from understanding the words. He scanned the letter again. No. Impossible. It had to be a trick. But the handwriting looked like Clodia's. And she had signed it Clodia. And the thoughts and expressions and style were hers. So what had she been up to, writing to Caelius, inviting him to come and stay with her? Catullus checked the date. Autumn. Just after he had moved in to the Palatine. So Clodia had wanted Caelius as well? He read the letter again, very carefully, and was relieved not to find any references to sex. Not that that meant much, of course. Was this what it had been like for Metellus, Catullus wondered despairingly, sniffing for innuendo and always half-expecting to track it down?

And it was as he thought of Metellus that he put the first letter back, and picked up the next on the pile. It was a single sheet, folded in half – a photocopy, Catullus realised, as he studied it. This time there were plenty of references to sex – in fact, there was nothing in it but sex – and it was signed, once again, Clodia. Catullus stared at her signature, and felt cold, very cold. Numbly, he picked up a third sheet, and then a fourth. More sex. Protestations of love. The odd, condescending, comment about a C – Catullus? – yes, the context made that obvious enough. Then complaints; Caelius was becoming cold, remote, he was avoiding her. Then the break; he had told her that he never wanted to see her again. One final letter – so scrawled that it was almost impossible to decipher through the photocopy. Menaces. Vague threats. It was she who jilted lovers, not the other way round; Caelius was in no position to make enemies. Again – threats. Catullus folded the sheet, and stashed it away. Then he sat back in his chair and stared at the wall.

It was impossible. Impossible. Clodia couldn't have been writing those letters, he had been with her almost every day. He studied the handwriting. It looked like hers, but – no – it was impossible. He knew she was mercurial, but – having an affair with Caelius? – she would have told him – she couldn't have kept her mouth shut if she'd tried. But then Catullus remembered the circumstances of his first meeting with her, all the cloak and dagger stuff, the disguises, the assignation with Caesar – she had never talked to him about that. But she had been embarrassed then – well, yes. Exactly. Catullus shut his eyes.

He would have to see Caelius. The thought of him made Catullus shake. But he would have to see him – there was no choice. He would have to find out what the bastard had to say, before he went barging in on Clodia and started screaming at her. He stood up and felt his jealousy as it began to spread through his veins.

By the time Catullus neared Cicero's house, the jealousy was gripping him uncontrollably. He couldn't bear to think of its presence inside him, a black poison, without antidote. Even the idea that Clodia might somehow, some way, still be the Clodia he had known for the past year seemed an impossible fantasy, and a cruel one too, because it tempted him with memories that were now clearly shown to have been misread all along. Catullus tried to picture Clodia, but Caelius' face kept swimming in the way, smiling, laughing, leering. Or worse. Much worse. Catullus quickened his pace.

The Palatine was looking a mess. Groups of homeless people seemed to have moved in and camped out on the roads; there was shit everywhere, bins, papers, tins, even campfires, despite the heat of the afternoon. Catullus was glad that he hadn't driven; he would never have made it through all the tents. What were the super-rich making of their new neighbours? And where the hell had they come from, all these pinched, tired, dirty refugees? – bussed in by Clodius? Or had the tide of human misery risen so far in Rome that it was dumping its flotsam even on the Palatine? Ahead of him, Catullus could hear the chant of slogans, and he wondered if he was hearing the tide's roar. In which case, perhaps there was a sand-castle standing in its way. Catullus turned a corner, and saw that there was indeed, and that it belonged to Cicero.

Good, he thought, staring at the sleek front of Cicero's house. He could identify with the crowd. It was angry, and wanted blood – they could have Cicero's, and he would have Caelius'. "What's going on?" he asked one of the demonstrators. "What's happening?"

"It's the Government," the demonstrator told him, "we want it out!" "The whole fucking lot!" someone else shouted. "Out!" chanted a third voice, "out, out, out!"

There was a great cheer. "We don't want people who should be in jail running the country," said the first demonstrator, trying to explain over the noise. "I mean, look at it, it's a fucking disaster-area. We need change, real change, now!"

"Meaning Clodius?"

"Yeah, maybe. Why not? But just change, basically, that's what it's about."

"Well, I'll pass on your message," said Catullus, pressing forwards.

"Hey, wait!" the demonstrator yelled. Others, seeing Catullus walk up the steps to Cicero's front door, began to shout abuse. Hands reached out to pull him back, but Catullus brushed them away. He knocked at the door, and a storm of booing broke out from behind him. A stone hit him on the back, and he felt someone clinging onto his arm, but then the door opened, and Catullus stumbled through. The door shut behind him again, and the booing sounded suddenly muffled and distant. Catullus blinked and picked himself up.

"Enjoy the welcoming committee, did you?" asked Cicero.

Catullus frowned. "Actually, right at this moment, I can empathise with them. Where's Caelius?"

"Caelius?" Cicero raised an eyebrow at him. "What's Caelius done to draw down your ire? I thought you two were friends."

"So did I till this afternoon. Where is he?"

Cicero shrugged. "In my study. I'll take you to him, if you like." He gestured. "Follow me."

He led the way down a long carpeted corridor. There was an open door at the end, and a desk beyond it, with papers and books and large mounds of files. The study. Catullus began to lengthen his stride. "Steady on," said Cicero, but Catullus ignored him and pushed past. "Caelius!" he shouted. "Caelius! Where are you?" He began to run. Caelius came to the door, then saw Catullus' face and started to back away. "Steady on," said Cicero again, and again, Catullus ignored him. He hurried through the doorway; Caelius had retreated and was up against a window. Catullus walked slowly across the study, until the two men were face to face. There was silence.

"Hello, old chap," said Caelius at last with a faint smile. He lowered his eyes, and glanced at the letters held in Catullus' hand. "Anything the matter?"

"Yes," breathed Catullus. "You know there is." He shoved the letters into Caelius' face. "What the fuck are these?" He unclenched his fist, and the letters fluttered slowly down onto the floor. Caelius knelt and picked them up, then stepped past Catullus and laid them neatly on the table. "You weren't meant to see them," he said casually.

"I'm sorry?" Catullus could feel his anger so physically now that it was almost spume in his throat. "It doesn't matter what you *wanted* me to find out, that's not the point, it's what you *did* that matters, and what you've been hiding from me, not what you fucking *wanted* me to find out!" He picked up the letters again, and thrust them into Caelius' face. "Have you been –"; he paused, and his lips curled with distaste; "having a sexual affair with Clodia?"

"Give me those letters," said Cicero, standing behind him. Catullus shook his head, and continued to stare at Caelius. "Have you had an affair with Clodia?" he asked again.

Caelius' lips whitened. He said nothing, and the silence seemed to last forever, but then he smiled faintly and shook his head. "I didn't think you'd be this annoyed," he said at last.

"Annoyed? *Annoyed?*" To his horror, Catullus could feel tears starting to scratch his throat. He swallowed, and shook his head. "What the fuck did you think I'd be, dancing round the fucking maypole?"

Caelius frowned. "We should talk."

"Yes, I think we should."

"You can't," said Cicero, gliding his way between them.

"What do you mean?" Catullus stared at him. "Why not?"

"Because you're being called as a witness for Caelius' defence."

"So?"

"So – strictly speaking, you shouldn't discuss anything to do with his case."

"But I've been living with him. It's a bit late to say we can't talk, isn't it?" Catullus stared at the letters he still held in his fist. "And anyway, this is nothing to do with his case. It's to do with me, and whether two people I loved have been screwing my life up, and jeering at me from behind my back, and just – fucking everything. So I don't care what the law is, Caelius is going to talk."

Caelius nodded slowly. "I think I should. Uncle? Don't you agree? – in the circumstances – they might require it?"

Cicero sighed, and gestured with his hands. "Well – it's your decision. But I'll have none of it. You'd better go into the garden." He raised a finger. "Two conditions, though. No more than ten minutes, Caelius. I haven't got all day, and we need to go through your statements."

Caelius shrugged. "And the second condition?"

"These," said Cicero, reaching over to take the letters from Catullus' hand.

"They're only the photocopies."

"Doesn't matter. It was foolish of you to leave them lying around."

"Why?" asked Catullus.

Cicero shook his head, and wagged a finger.

"They're not anything to do with the trial, are they?"

"Time for you to go into the garden, I think." Cicero walked over to the door and unlocked it. "There you are," he said. "Ten minutes, Caelius. Do try and be discreet. And you" – he nodded at Catullus – "watch what you do to my client. I don't want a second murder trial on my hands."

He nodded and ushered them out. Caelius led the way across the lawn. "Wait," said Catullus, reaching out to take his arm. "Explain what he was saying back there."

"What do you mean?"

"I want to know what those letters have got to do with your defence."

"I can't tell you that."

"But they're something to do with it."

Caelius shook his head. "I'm sorry, really, I can't tell you. Surely you can see that? I'll talk to you about the content of the letters, because I feel bad about it, and you've got a right to know, but anything else – I can't."

"All right." Catullus stood in his path. "Tell me."

"About Clodia?"

Catullus nodded wordlessly.

"Well." Caelius paused, then stared out across the lawns. "It's not as bad as it probably seemed from the letters."

"What the fuck do you mean? You had – whatever – with her, didn't you?"

"Yes. A few times. But I didn't mean to, really. No, honestly, I didn't. What happened was, you remember that time I brought clothes round for you?"

Catullus thought. Yes, when he'd been at Boot's. He nodded.

"Well – we got on well. You know what she's like, she's funny, she likes being made to laugh. So after I'd gone, she sent me a letter, saying come round again. That was the first one, you must have read it – the original copy."

"Why didn't you photocopy that one?"

"Because strictly speaking it isn't evidence."

"But all the other ones are?"

Caelius shook his head and smiled. "Catullus."

"Well, fine, I don't care about your trial, I hope you're guilty as hell. I just want to know about Clodia."

"All right, where were we? Oh yes – we met up a second time – at the 'Thiasus of Cybele', remember, that club, where I bumped into you? Again, she said, come round, we'll spend some time together, so we did, after I'd been charged. Clodia was upset too, because Metellus had died, and you were – in a state – about your brother, and I don't know, we started trying to cheer each other up, and we ended up in bed. We hadn't meant to, I promise."

"Oh, well, that makes it fine."

"I'm sorry."

"Then why did you do it? Why, Caelius?"

"I don't know. I suppose I quite fancied her. And I was flattered too. Same reasons as you."

"No." Catullus shook his head. No, it hadn't been like that at all. There had been something else, a spark of magic, far beyond the capacity of Caelius' cynicism to extinguish it. But no, what was he thinking? Caelius *had* extinguished it. The spark was dead. Past and future were both dead. There was nothing. He wanted to break for air, but what was there to breathe?

"Are you all right?" Caelius asked, peering at him. Catullus stared back into his eyes, and Caelius had the decency to look embarrassed. "I'm sorry," he said. "Of course you're not." He tried to reach for Catullus' hand, but Catullus snatched it away. "Just get on with it," he said. Caelius nodded, and began to describe the course of the affair again.

"Well – I told myself that I wouldn't get back with her, because I knew how important it all was to you, and I felt a shit, a real shit. But you know what Clodia's like, she can be very persuasive."

"Really?"

"I found she was."

"Oh, well then."

Caelius stared at him, then carried on. "I kept finding I was in bed with her. It was like a farce. We were always listening out for you, and I had to size out the cupboards before we did anything, and, oh – it was awful."

"Poor you." Catullus could barely speak, he felt so frantic with humiliation. Caelius had obviously found the whole thing a scream.

But Caelius was looking sombre now. "Eventually," he said, "I decided that it was all too much, I couldn't bear the feeling of guilt. So I told Clodia I wouldn't be seeing her again – and I didn't. But she wasn't very pleased about it. You saw the letters? Well, first of all she implored, and then she threatened."

"What exactly?"

"Oh, this and that. Vague threats."

"Did she ever say she'd tell me – about you and her?"

"No."

"How odd. She must have known I'd come round and kill you."

Caelius smiled. "I doubt it. She was probably afraid of what you'd do to her."

Catullus thought about Clodia, opening her legs to Caelius and smiling lazily. "Yes," he said slowly. "Yes, you're probably right."

Caelius leant back on a bench. "But I wouldn't recommend anything too heavy, old boy."

"Why not?"

"Well – she's her brother's sister. She's a dangerous woman."

"Clodia? No."

Caelius shrugged. "I wouldn't push her."

It was impossible. Clodia? They weren't talking about the same woman. *Clodia?* "What do you mean, she's dangerous?"

Again, Caelius shrugged. "Just steer clear of her. For the next week or two." He stood up and stared unblinkingly into Catullus' eyes. "I'd really recommend it."

"No."

"Please." Caelius was appealing to him now, he realised, really begging. "Please. For your own sake. You don't know how big this thing is."

"What thing?"

Caelius sighed. "This – thing – we're in. This set up round the trial. I shouldn't be telling you this. But you – me – we're nothing, we're swept up on it, of course, but we're nothing. And the best thing to do, if you've got the chance, is just to keep your head down. At least you've got that chance. Don't ask for trouble."

"And Clodia's a part of it too?"

"I'm not going to say, I can't. But please, Catullus – I know I've been a shit to you, but I did do my best to get out of it. I know you'll find it hard to forgive me, but I'm still... Well, let me put it this way, I still think of you as my best friend. Really. The one I feel closest to."

"Then I hate to think what you do to friends you don't like."

Caelius smiled. "You'll try to forgive me?"

Catullus shook his head. "No," he said slowly, "I'll never forgive you. Never. You're fucking poison. I loved you once, and I loved Clodia, but now you've burnt out my guts and everything." He pushed Caelius' hand away from his shoulder. "I'd better leave you to Cicero."

"I won't be seeing you again before the trial." Caelius swallowed. "In fact, I probably won't see you until you're in the witness box."

Catullus stared at him, then smiled. "Worried I might distort my evidence? Bit of perjury, try and pay you back?" He began to laugh.

Caelius joined in, a little nervously. "No," he said. "But it means – Catullus, listen – just keep away from Clodia. Please. For your own good."

Catullus shook his head. "I suppose I ought to admire you, Caelius. You never give up."

"No, no, it's not like that at all. Just, please – if you do see her, watch what you say. And what she says."

"What do you mean?"

"She can be very clever at keeping things concealed. Very. Maybe you haven't quite realised that yet."

"No." Catullus smiled bleakly. "Maybe I haven't."

He began to walk back towards a gate at the end of the lawn. He knew that Caelius was watching him, but he didn't glance round. He hated Caelius terribly, he realised. But his anger had spent itself, and even the hatred was cold now, numb, as though it despised itself for the worthlessness of its object. Catullus tried hard, but he couldn't even track down a desire for revenge. This surprised him at first, but the thought that Caelius wasn't worthy of his hatred gave Catullus a grim satisfaction, and encouraged him to blank Caelius' face all the more completely from his mind. But Clodia – what about her? Assuming that she had written those letters – *what about her?* Catullus shut his eyes, and imagined his love as a fire, rising high into a darkness, and then pictured his hatred, also blazing high, with coiling, twisting flames, until the two fires seemed indistinguishable and burned like a single pyre against the night. Love and hate. The two emotions that had razed Troy to the ground.

Catullus left Cicero's garden, and began to run down the Palatine Hill. There it was, ahead of him on the street, Clodia's house. A familiar, golden rush of emotion surprised him, and made the succeeding rush of pain all the more winding and fierce. He looked up at the house. Shutters were drawn across the windows, but Clodia's car was parked outside on the road. Catullus glanced at it, then climbed the front steps. He reached for the door bell and rang on it, hard.

No one came. Several minutes passed, and Catullus waited with furious impatience, then rang the bell again. He pressed his ear to the door and heard footsteps. "Come on," he shouted, "hurry!" The door opened, but only ajar, and when Catullus pushed at it he found that it refused to give.

"Let me in, you fucking bitch," he hissed.

"Ooh, nasty," said a voice, not Clodia's. "Don't be so rude."

"Who are you?"

"No," said the voice mockingly, "you're the one outside – who are you?"

"Ariana? Please. It's me."

"And 'me', I suppose, is Catullus, is it?"

"Yes."

"I don't know if I should really." He heard a slithering of chain. "I'm bound to get into trouble for this. But I *do* want to know what it is you've done." The door opened, and Catullus walked in. Ariana grinned at him cruelly. "Is it *really* all over between you?" she asked, prompting him. "Is there nothing I can do to help you make things up?"

"Tell me where she is."

"Are you going to confront her? How simply *dreadful!*" Ariana's grin broadened, and she beckoned coquettishly. "Oh well, if you insist. Follow me."

"She's here, then, is she?" Catullus asked, as they walked up the stairs.

"Oh yes," said Ariana. "Since last night. She came back in an *awful* temper. Something you'd done, she said." Ariana took Catullus by the shoulders and caressed him gently. "Do you want to know what she said about you?" Ariana smiled. "She said you were a cruel, cruel bastard." She widened her eyes in an expression of mock horror. "'Cruel, cruel bastard.' Isn't that awful? What do you say to that?"

"I don't think I'm the one who needs lectures on cruelty."

Ariana's smile and vowels both lengthened even further. "*Really?* Tell me! What *has* she been doing?"

Catullus brushed her away. "You'll find out," he said shortly. "How awful," Ariana murmured. "She's in the bedroom." "I know," said Catullus. Ariana followed him, as he lengthened his stride.

"Clodia."

She looked up. She was by the windows, with a sketch board on her knee. "Oh, hello," she said. "This is early. Come to grovel, have you? I thought it'd take you a bit longer than this."

"I'm not the one who's come to grovel." Slowly, he crossed the room until he was facing her. Ariana followed. "He's terribly cross with you, Clodia," she warned. "I do hope this won't turn into anything upsetting."

Clodia lowered her sketching board, and looked up at Catullus in surprise. "*You're* cross?"

"Cross is putting it very mildly."

"But you were the one who behaved like the total shit last night."

"I'm not here to talk about that."

She stared at him coldly. "Oh?"

God, he couldn't bear it. The accusation slithered out in a sudden rush. "Have you been having an affair with Caelius?" he asked, and he could feel himself starting to shake. "Have you been fucking Caelius?" he shouted. "Have you? Have you? Tell me!"

He stared into Clodia's eyes, but they seemed dead. She rose to her feet. "And supposing I had been?" she whispered slowly. "What business would it be of yours?"

"So you have been?"

Still her eyes looked dead. "Just how did you find out I'd been – 'fucking' – Caelius?"

"There are letters."

"Letters?"

"Letters! Where you write about it. I've seen them."

"Letters." Her eyes slowly widened. "Let me see them, then. Where are they?"

"Caelius has got them."

"Why?"

"I don't know, he needs them for the trial."

Clodia frowned. "Why?"

"I don't know," he said again in a fury of impatience, "and I don't care about Caelius, I just want to know if it's true, did you have an affair with him?" He seized her by the arms, imploring her. "Tell me, that's all you've got to do, just tell me!"

Clodia twisted herself free. "Go away," she said contemptuously.

"Please, Clodia." He was almost begging her now. "Tell me."

"Go away!"

He took her by the arms again. "Please. I'm not the one who should be apologising."

"You don't think so?"

"No. Of course not."

She laughed in his face. "Well, fuck off, then."

"Clodia!"

"Go away!" she suddenly screamed. She began to cry. "Go away, go away, go away!"

Catullus watched her, as though she were trapped behind a layer of thick glass, as though he wanted to rescue her but couldn't break through. He reached out, to try and hold her, but then his arms fell limply by his side and he felt numbed by a pang of love as strong as any he had ever felt, and all the more paralysing because it was also hate.

"I think you should go," said Ariana, from her spectator's position on the armchair.

Catullus didn't look at her. "You want me to?" he asked Clodia numbly.

"Yes. Yes. I can't bear you. Just go."

He couldn't speak, he couldn't move, he could only stare at her.

"Just go," she said again.

"Piss off," said Ariana. "You sad man."

So Catullus turned and left. As he shut the door behind him, he heard muffled laughter. But he didn't care. He walked down the stairs, and reminded himself that it was none of his business now.

The next day, at work, he asked Boot if he could move in with her.

"Of course," she said, looking up. "Why?"

Catullus gave her the whole story. "I can't live where Caelius has lived."

"I see." Boot stared at him expressionlessly.

"I might not be great company, I'm afraid."

Boot smiled slowly at last. "No. I suppose not. Still – my uncle will forgive you anything. His poet."

"You're staying with Aurelius?"

"Yes. My parents just got too – parental – and I haven't got anywhere else to live at the moment."

"You could always..." Catullus ran his hands through his hair. "Perhaps we could look for somewhere, now..."

"You're quick off the mark, aren't you?"

"No, I didn't mean it like that. You know..."

"Yes." Boot smiled self-mockingly. "Of course I know." She took his hand. "We'd better wait though, hadn't we? See what happens? And in the meantime – yes, I'm sure Aurelius will put you up." She turned back to her work. "And I'll like it too," she added, from over her shoulder. "Probably."

"I'm fucked off. I mean, really fucked off."

"Great. There's nothing like someone else's misery to cheer yourself up. Go ahead, be my guest – wallow."

"I'll try not to."

Boot laughed. "Well, we'll see about that, won't we?"

"What do you mean?"

She shrugged. "We'll see," she said, looking round. "We'll see."

Aurelius, that evening, wanted him to wallow as well.

"But of course you must," he insisted, "damn it. Don't hold it in, you'll give yourself a damn rupture."

Catullus shook his head and said nothing. Instead, he tried to concentrate on a radio programme, but it was the news, and Catullus realised that the reporter was discussing Caelius' trial. If he'd been on his own, he would have kicked the fucking radio round the room, but with company, he had to force himself to find the coincidence amusing. He smiled grimly, and Aurelius smiled and nodded back.

"There," he said peremptorily, "keep that grin on your face, flex your backbone and spit it all out. You'll feel better in no time."

"I don't think so," said Furius, who was draped on a sofa. "You, of all people, should understand that grief cannot be tamed by baring your teeth."

"What the devil do you mean?"

"You know."

"Are you daring to allude to Juventius?"

There was a silence. Furius studied his finger nails. Aurelius watched him, then swore and brought his fist crashing down. "I don't object to the experiencing of grief. No, of course not! But what I do object to is the fellow mooning around and feeling sorry for himself, and then keeping quiet about it. For God's sake, he's a poet. Poets are meant to feel miserable. Otherwise, what the hell are they for? What are they going to write about?"

Catullus couldn't bring himself to smile. "Give me time," he muttered.

"Not too much time, I hope. Otherwise it'll go to pot, and before you know it, you'll be feeling cheerful again. No, no! From the smithy of grief you must forge great works."

"It doesn't work like that."

"Well, it bloody well ought to. For Heaven's sake. While you can feel yourself to be interesting. While you can hate and love her at the same bloody time. Write something that will confound the ages."

Catullus shrugged his shoulders. "It doesn't work like that," he said again, helplessly.

Boot nodded. "I thought it was very old fashioned, anyway, writing about what you actually feel." She gestured at Catullus. "And he's meant to be modern, isn't he? That's what he's always saying."

"Exactly!" agreed Aurelius. "He is modern. Which was why this catastrophe had to occur."

Catullus stared at him. "What do you mean?"

"Well, it was so obviously required that Lesbia jilt you. From a structural point of view. So that the parabola of your affair could arc in a satisfying way, that sort of thing. It was the revenge of the text. The philosophers are right after all – language does indeed write us, construct us, compose our plot. So you see, you have no choice – just bloody get on and write."

Catullus did his best. He knew that Aurelius was trying to be kind, and he suspected, as well, that the advice was wise. Despair, unchannelled, might indeed swamp his mind; focussed, it might start to be dammed and held back. When he wrote, Catullus found that he understood why Aurelius still sent his tribute of flowers to the grave of the long dead Juventius, understood the anaesthetic that the flowers had become, though the pain, God knew, might long have faded, and nothing, perhaps, was left there to dull – even so, a drug once taken can be hard to forego. Catullus tried hard with his writing, to make it his own drug. Sometimes, he almost believed that it was taking effect. Sometimes, even more rarely, he dared to think that the poems he was composing were indeed fictions, that he didn't love Lesbia at all, never had done, never would.

Such moods, of course, were hard to sustain. But as days passed, and his longing for Clodia continued numb, Catullus began to hope that real misery, the misery he had always dreaded would devour his life, might instead never descend. It waited in his imagination, of course, a black phantom of despair, casting shadows that would sometimes play across his mind, but these began to lift in time, and the phantom remained what it had always been, a foreboding, nothing more. Sometimes, Catullus found himself worrying about this. What did it mean? That his love for Clodia had been a fraud, worked up by himself into some frantic dream? But no – he was careful not to follow such questionings. If he pushed too far, phantom wings began to stir and beat.

Instead, Catullus kept his mind fixed on other things. Above all, he was glad to be working. Not that it was exciting – just the opposite, in fact. It was dull, very dull. There was no stone circle waiting, of course, no Trojan ruins, that had been clear for months now, even though they had kept on shifting and sieving, and nodding with Doctor Gower, as he insisted that something would come up soon, tomorrow, perhaps, or the day after that. "There's Sesostris," he would say, and take the eagle from its bag. "It's our proof." Well, yes, Catullus thought, but who was it who had found that? Two down and outs – two tramps – two soldiers perhaps, back from Circassia? There would have been plenty of eagle-headed statuettes out there. Catullus shook his head, as he humped a wheelbarrow full of earth. What a waste of time. Not that he minded, though. In his state, it was a positive relief to play at Sisyphus. There was nothing like monotony for lulling painful thoughts to sleep.

On the afternoon before the weekend, though, the bulldozers came. The monotony was lost. "Crassus," boomed Doctor Gower, "it's Crassus!" "Is it?" Catullus asked, looking at Boot. She nodded. "He's had the permission for weeks now," she said. "But I thought if I didn't mention it, nothing might happen." They both stood and watched, as the bulldozers massed on the edge of the dump. "Stop them," shouted Doctor Gower despairingly. He ran forward, flapping his hands, as though the machines were birds on a vegetable patch. "What do you think he's going to do," asked Boot, "chain himself to them?" Catullus shrugged. "What else can he do?" And then he realised. Of course! And as he turned, thoughts of Clodia flooded in on him like sunlight, and the prospect of talking about her, asking about her, sung suddenly from somewhere inside his head. "I've got to go," he said. "There's someone I've got to see."

"Who?"

"Just wait." And he began to run.

Of course, Catullus realised, as he climbed into his car, Clodius might not have been seeing his sister much. He was a busy man – he had a government to overthrow, after all. But just the thought that he might have seen Clodia in the past week made Catullus feel dazzled. Why hadn't he thought of making contact with Clodius before? Because he had closed his mind, because he had virtually convinced himself that he didn't want Clodia back. And now, by accident really, he had found a way to approach her again. He realised that he was sick with longing, nauseous, in his blood, his flesh, his bones. He had to slow the car. A vision from his memory crossed the departed year, and filled his mind with a light that was almost literal, spilling in across Clodia's room, across their bodies, linked, incautious, naked on the floor.

Catullus parked the car. He walked into the Union Headquarters and gave his name. He was taken up almost at once. He knocked at Clodius' door, and walked in, and then thought that a mistake had been made, for it was hard to recognise the man behind the desk. Slowly, Clodius looked up. Catullus stared at him, appalled. This was the hero of the hour, a man who had a state on the run, an entire system of government? The flesh seemed melted away from his bones.

"You." Clodius narrowed his eyes. "Have you found anything on that building site?"

"No, of course I haven't. There's nothing there, is there?"

Clodius' lips flickered faintly at the edges.

"Don't worry, I haven't told anyone." Catullus laughed, emboldened now. "It's only obvious to me because I've met your two fiddling friends. I suppose they were the ones who – discovered – that eagle god. You provided it for them, did you?"

Clodius sunk back into his chair. "Crassus wanted that land. We had to stop him." He shrugged. "It worked."

"For a while."

Clodius looked up at him. "What do you mean?"

"The bulldozers have arrived."

A look of black irritation swept across Clodius' face. "Then they must be feeling confident," he said, and began to grind his fists together. He looked up. "You really haven't found anything?"

"No, of course not. How could we?"

"There might be something out there." Clodius gestured with his hands. "Just because I planted some of the evidence – it doesn't mean all the other evidence has to be discounted as well."

"Does it matter?"

Clodius nodded. He sat back in his seat and reached inside a drawer. "I need to know where these have come from." He pulled out a black figurine and studied it, his eyes slowly widening. Then he placed it in front of him, and Catullus stared at the figure, its familiar black gleam, the curve of its beak. "And this one." Clodius pulled out a second statuette, slightly smaller, and then a third, smaller again, and so on, until there were seven figures in a line on the desk. Clodius stared at them, a look of icy horror in his eyes. "Where have they come from?" he whispered. He reached for one. "And there's more." He pointed at the base of the statue, and handed it to Catullus. "Look. Read it."

Catullus held the statue to the light. 'Beware', he read. He stared at Clodius. "Beware?"

Clodius nodded feverishly. "And then there's this." He picked up the second statue. "'Beware!'," he shouted, without looking at the base. He picked up the third. "'You.'" Then the fourth. "'Are.'" The fifth. "'Going.'" The sixth. "'To.'" He licked his lips, and reached for the seventh. He stared at Catullus. "'Be'," he read, then made a face. "'Be.' Be what? There's going to be another one, isn't there, telling me what I'm going to be. Who's sending me these things?"

Catullus kept quiet. Clodius continued to grind his fists together, then suddenly screamed, and hurled the largest statue against a wall. "It's them," he said, leaping to his feet, "it's them."

"Them?"

"Yes, them! All of them!" He started to pace up and down the room. "They've got something planned, something they think's going to work. They wouldn't have dared let Crassus move in on that land, and Crassus wouldn't have wanted to, not unless they thought they'd got me on the run, and they haven't! We're winning, we're talking about a possible revolution here, so why do they think they've got me on the run? *Why?*" He paused, and leant against a window, staring at Crassus' glass monsters outside. When he spoke again, his voice was measured, calm. "The only thing that worries me – no – let's not beat about the bush – frightens me – scares the shit out of me – are these little statuettes." He bent down, to pick up the figure he had thrown across the room. "But how did they find out about them? How did they know?" He looked up at Catullus, and whispered the question again. "How did they know?"

Catullus met his gaze. "What do you mean?"

Clodius smiled and shook his head. Slowly, he placed the statue back on his desk. "You don't know?" he asked.

Catullus shook his head.

"But you know about Sesostris, don't you? And you've been seen going to Cicero's house." Suddenly he reached for Catullus' neck and pushed him against the wall. "So what's he up to, eh – Cicero? I thought I'd finished him off, but that man needs a fucking stake through his heart."

"I don't understand," Catullus gasped. "You're saying Cicero sent you the statuettes?"

"Yes, he's up to something, he must have done. But how did he know? You've been seen with him. You went to his house. You must have told him."

"Told him what?" Catullus asked desperately.

"About Circassia. Me and what happened in Circassia, you must have done."

"But I don't know what you're talking about, really, I don't."

Clodius paused, and caught his breath. "No," he said slowly. He relaxed his grip on Catullus' neck. "No, perhaps you don't. I'm sorry. I'm a bit – under pressure – at the moment. And anyway," he added, after a few seconds' thought, "you did come to see me, didn't you?"

"Yes." Catullus rubbed his neck. Of course he had – and for a reason too. But how could he ask about Clodia now? He cleared his throat. "You mentioned I'd been seen at Cicero's house."

Clodius raised an eyebrow.

"Well – I expect you'd like to know why."

Clodius raised an eyebrow again, then nodded.

"You know – well, you know about me and your sister. Clodia." Another nod.

"Well – perhaps you also know that Caelius, who Cicero is defending in the trial next week..."

"Yes, yes," said Clodius impatiently. "I know all about that."

"You know he was my friend?"

"Yes."

"Well – the reason I went to Cicero's house was to see Caelius." He swallowed. "You see – I'd just found out that he'd been having an affair with your sister." He looked into Clodius' face. Nothing – just a look of bemusement. And when Clodius spoke, the words sunk like weights into the pit of his stomach.

"You didn't know?"

So that was it then. Catullus shook his head. "You did?"

"Yes. Well – I saw them together. And then Clodia phoned me this week – something about letters? She went on a bit. I wasn't interested, I'm afraid."

Catullus tried to smile. "No. Of course not. Why should you be?"

Clodius stared at him. "I'm sorry," he said simply.

"Don't be." Catullus shook his head. "Don't be. I was just – well, you see – I wanted you to know why I went to see Cicero."

"Of course." Clodius smiled at him kindly and patted him on the shoulder. "I understand, really I do. Would you...?" He gestured towards an opened whisky bottle.

"No. Thank you. I ought to go."

Clodius nodded. "If you insist. And thanks for the warning about Crassus." He scooped up the line of statuettes from his desk and dropped them in a pile on the floor. "I've been running scared from these for too long, you know. Unforgivable." A tremor passed across his face, then vanished. He walked Catullus over to the door. "I'm myself again," he said. "Watch the news tonight."

"Goodbye," said Catullus.

Clodius nodded. "Don't run from phantoms. We both have them. Stand your ground." He nodded again, smiled, then shut the door behind him. Catullus, alone in the corridor, stood frozen. But in his mind, the numbness had melted, and there was nothing now but hatred, blazing hatred. Somewhere from his memories, Clodia appealed to him. Her face was melting. She made to scream, but it was too late. She collapsed away into nothingness. And still the flames burnt on, and Catullus warmed himself by them, and stoked them higher and higher. Pile everything on. No holding back now. As he walked down the corridor, Catullus heard the phantom wings beating again.

That afternoon, the bulldozers were held back by walls of jeering protestors. One machine was set on fire. The police were called in, and shots fired over the protestors' heads. Things were turning ugly. At the last minute, however, the police retired, and the protestors were left in possession of the field. Catullus watched footage of the showdown on the evening news.

Later that night, Aurelius asked to see his writings. Catullus brought them down, and Aurelius read them all. "When did you write this one?" he asked, holding up a scrap of paper.

"This afternoon. Why?"

"It's vile."

"I don't give a fuck."

"Well, you should." Aurlius glanced down at it again, then ripped it into shreds.

"Give it back," whispered Catullus.

Aurelius stared at him, then walked over to a window.

"Give it back," repeated Catullus. "Now. Give it back." The shreds were tossed away. As he watched them flutter, then disappear,

Catullus found that his anger and hatred for Clodia, furious inside him all afternoon, were suddenly now as soft as the breeze, as soft and tempting, for it would be beautiful, Catullus thought, to float on such a breeze, and he found that words of loathing were slipping out on it. "You fucker," he whispered to Aurelius. Obscenities waited on his tongue, waiting to float like the paper shreds, the pleasure of it, hatred, hatred and abuse. "You absolute fucker. For what you've just done, I'd – I'd split your arse for you, I'd stuff my prick down your throat, make you fucking gag, you hypocrite, you fucking hypocrite you shit-pricked hypocrite." Catullus swallowed, then smiled delicately. "You really think you can treat me like that, just because I write down a few rude words. Well, listen!" he screamed suddenly, "listen!" He wanted to sob, but didn't. "I'm writing, and speaking now, to get all the filth out of my brain, all the fucking stinking shit filth. So don't –"; he pointed at Aurelius, who was watching him impassively. "Just don't." He turned, and left the room, and didn't look back.

Later that evening, Furius came to him and sat down beside him on his bed. "I gather you want to split our arses," said Furius softly, stroking his hair.

"No, not now. I don't know what happened. It's gone."

Furius watched him, his pale face motionless. "I'm sure Aurelius would have enjoyed you splitting his arse."

"What do you mean?"

"You upset him."

"I know." Catullus shook his head. "I know."

"Don't you think you owe him something, then?"

"But you..."

Furius smiled palely. "I'm surprised at you. You, with your passion for a single soul. Don't you recognise that passion in Aurelius as well?

"Juventius?"

"Yes, of course." Furius bowed his head. "Of course Juventius. Aurelius doesn't love me. He only loves the glimpses of the dead soldier that he sees in me. And it will be the same with you."

"When?"

Furius bent down, to kiss Catullus' lips. "Tonight. Go to him. Show him kindness. Apologise."

Catullus took Aurelius love poems. "Here," he said, handing over a carefully bound sheaf. "To Juventius. Not poetry of despair, or mourning. Poems of love. I hope they will – I don't know – I hope they will make amends."

Aurelius was kind, kind and gentle. Catullus, lying on his front, played the dead lover. Only when he remembered Caelius, how gentle he had once been, did Catullus feel his own memories start to return. On top of Aurelius, he was himself again, and it was Clodia he had taken possession of, as though she were a slag, just a dirty common slag, fucked for money, then tossed aside, without pain, without rage, only contempt. But there was rage, of course. As Catullus fucked, he could see Clodia clearly when he shut his eyes. He wondered about her letters, about why Cicero was planning to read them out at the trial. He would have to see, wouldn't he? And what would he be asked about, when he was called as a witness? He smiled, as he felt his excitement grow. No – there would be no more mourning, no more pusillanimity. Hatred was a long and welcome pleasure. He was looking forward to taking his place in the witness' stand.

XVIII

CAELIUS

Dawn broke early on the day of the trial, but Cicero had been up long before the first murmurings of the birds outside began to welcome the sun's rays to the square. Light fell across the floor from a gap in the curtains, and cast a line of brightness across Cicero's desk, but still he worked on, and the curtains stayed drawn and undisturbed. "That's good," smiled Cicero to himself once, leaning back in his chair, then standing up to practise his sentence aloud, but otherwise he toiled in silence, and paid no attention to the passing time. Not until he had heard the slamming of a door, and realised that Caelius was up, did Cicero at last lay down his pen.

He was ready. There was nothing more he could do. Have confidence, he told himself – it wasn't his performance that he had to worry about. A second door slammed – Caelius again. Get down and tutor him. He was the one who needed the practice. And then there were the others, of course, just as central, who were beyond overt tutoring all together, and who would only be controlled without their realising it. He dropped his sheaf of notes, and reached across the desk for a magazine. He opened it and read. 'To Lesbia.' Well, it ought to work, he thought. He read the poem again. Yes, it ought to work.

Catullus didn't attend the opening sessions of the trial. He had phoned Doctor Gower late on the evening before, fully expecting to be given permission to attend, but had been told, to his surprise, that it would be out of the question. "Impossible, I'm afraid, dear boy," the Doctor had said excitedly. "You see, something has come up!" Catullus' heart had sunk. Things were always coming up, usually, he had decided reluctantly, from the Doctor's imagination. "What is it?" he'd asked. "Wait and see!" the Doctor had boomed cheerfully, "and prepare to be amazed!" So Catullus, the next morning, found himself standing on a rubbish tip, while across the city the drama in which he felt he had such a central role began without him. He could have wept.

But when Catullus saw what Doctor Gower had been talking about, his regrets began to fade. "Look – here, you see," said the Doctor, standing in a great trench. "Crassus' digger opened this up." He pointed towards a blackened carcass of metal. "It was set on fire

– I expect you saw it on the news – and just in time, I don't mind telling you. Because, you see" – he bent down – "it was just about to smash through this." He pointed, and Catullus craned to look. "See?" Doctor Gower said, brushing away some earth. "Recognise the colour?"

Yes. Yes, he did. "It's blue. Like the stone we found in that wall, ages ago."

"Exactly. But look." Doctor Gower brushed away more soil. "This is much larger. See? This is it, the real thing – a standing stone. We've done it, we've done it by Jove, we've hit the blessed jackpot!"

"We hadn't been digging deep enough?"

"Obviously not! And Crassus – dear old greedy, grasping Crassus! – he was the one who gave us our proof!" Doctor Gower began to laugh, his whole body shaking, until tears were flowing in streams down his face. "So come on then," he finally gasped. "Let's get to work! Where's Boot?"

"Gone to the trial. You said she could last week."

"Did I? Oh well, not to worry. All the more for us, eh? Good-o! Let's get stuck in!" He tossed Catullus a shovel, and together they began to dig. As the contours of the stone became clearer, and its size more impressive, so Catullus found himself regretting his absence from the law courts less and less. "This is what it's all about, eh?" Doctor Gower asked him, "this is what we've been waiting to find!" and Catullus nodded and agreed that yes, it certainly was. Some of the pickets, still clustered on the far road, noticed the signs of excitement, and wandered over to ask if there was anything going on. "You see that spot there?" Doctor Gower asked, looking up from his map and pointing. "Well, get a spade and dig it!" Most of the men laughed; a few picked up shovels, though, and began to drive a trench; when a second stone was found, more men joined in. All in all, Catullus thought as he left the site that evening, it had been an exhilarating day, and he was glad that he had turned up. He had brought his radio to listen to the trial, but hadn't turned it on all day.

Of course, back at Aurelius' house, frustration soon began to gnaw at him again. How could it not have done? – after all, he realised with a sudden sense of shock, these were details from his life up there, on the news, in the papers, topics of general discussion and debate. For God's sake, Catullus thought, it was only a criminal trial – why all the interest? It just made Caelius into a celebrity, damn him. But he'd be sweating underneath it, surely – he had to be. It was impossible to tell from the footage on the news. So Catullus was glad that Boot had gone, and he waited for her to come back each evening and add some colour to the facts.

Yes, Boot reported, Caelius did seem sweaty-pitted. The evidence against him was mounting all the time, and she had begun to wonder whether he might not be guilty after all. It was fairly clear now why he'd been arrested, anyway, and – well – she didn't want to say. And what about Cicero, Catullus asked. Boot just shrugged her shoulders. She wasn't sure. He didn't seem to be taking the case seriously at all. He lounged in his seat, smirking, and even when he did bother to question the witnesses, it was in a strange tone of semi-flippant boredom. Frankly, Boot said, she had been been hoping for something slightly more impressive. She was disappointed.

But Catullus had to wonder. After all, he thought, in a sense, Cicero was on trial as much as Caelius himself – this was his first case since release from prison, and he had a reputation to resurrect. But then why was he allowing the prosecution to make all the running? Or was he? Perhaps there were nuances to his cross-examinations that Boot hadn't recognised, hints of some broader strategy? Catullus couldn't really tell. It was all very frustrating. The week passed, and although finds continued to mount at the site of the dig, Catullus began to wish once again that he was in the court. But he had given his word to Doctor Gower – he wouldn't leave until he was actually summonsed. And it *was* still exciting, being on the excavation site, digging up remains from a subsoil of myth – *of course* it was. But even so, he couldn't stop his thoughts from wandering, and the stones, vast and strange though they were, began to loom less and less as objects in his mind.

Instead, Catullus spent his working hours listening to a radio, and trying to guess the likely outcome of the trial. Not easy – into the second week, and the prosecution seemed ahead on points, but then again, Catullus thought, so they ought to be, Cicero hadn't called his witnesses yet. In print, Cicero's own courtroom style, which Boot had called flippant, Catullus found amused and tinged with soft contempt; his questioning of witnesses seemed to suggest they were a joke. But did this make them any the less dangerous? – not being at the trial, Catullus couldn't be sure. He tried to remember what the various witnesses had actually claimed. There had been the doctor, the round man in the coat who had inspected Mr Varney's corpse – he'd been good value, the trial reports had said. Murmurings in court, pale faces all round. But Cicero had been able to temper the effect by pointing out that no weapons had been found, and that there was therefore no solid scientific evidence to suggest that Caelius might have inflicted the injuries. The doctor had agreed. Again, as the papers had put it, murmurings in court. Similarly, with a whole host of witnesses, Cicero had been able to sow self-doubt, cast insinuations, tinker and fiddle with dangerous claims: had the witnesses really seen Caelius at such and such a place at such and such a time, could they be absolutely sure, didn't they have room for reasonable doubt? Invariably, the witnesses did, and having wrung out an admission, Cicero would smile, sit back and look bored again.

Even so, the sheer weight of evidence was starting to press down heavily. Was it likely that *every* witness could have mistaken Caelius for someone else? Most damagingly of all, there was the evidence of Porter, the police detective. His testimony had been the most detailed and wide-ranging of anyone's; unfortunately for Caelius, it had also proved to be the most unshakeable. Catullus had read transcripts of it with particular interest. Of course, he had already known about Caelius' meeting with Mr Varney, but there had been other details that he hadn't heard before. For instance – Porter had observed Caelius getting his wallet back. It had been on the night of the murder. Caelius had met Mr Varney on the site of the Fairlawns. He had confronted him, vigorously, and then the two men had walked away towards the river front. Porter had lost them. But he had remembered the incident, he said, because Caelius had seemed angry, and Varney drunk, and he had half thought at the time about following them. Did he think it likely that the two men had got into a brawl? Yes, he did, very likely. And what about the second and third victims? Well, yes, in the case of the second, the accused had been seen lurking in the area on the night of the murder. And in the case of the third, the accused had been heard threatening the deceased for several weeks in advance of his actual death. So Porter was convinced that the right man had been caught, was he? Yes – quite convinced.

This was the prosecution's corner-stone, and it refused to be budged. Cicero had tried to shift it, briefly, then given up, as though the effort required wasn't worth his time. But for once, he had seemed unconvincing, and his insouciance forced. As the prosecution's case drew to its close, so also its credibility began to harden, and Cicero's show of confidence came to seem increasingly misplaced, flippant, as Boot had always said it was. Surely, Catullus thought, reading the reports, Cicero had something in reserve – Clodia's letters perhaps? But there were no hints of a strategy that Catullus could discover, not in the transcripts of the trial, at least, and he began to think that Caelius might be convicted after all. Boot, he noticed, seemed convinced already.

On the day his summons came, he asked her if she was going back to work.

"No," she said, looking up surprised. "Why should I?"

"Because I'm not going to be on site tomorrow."

"Well, you won't be the only one then, will you?"

She returned to her paper, and Catullus shrugged. He didn't want to make an issue out of it, so he kept quiet, and the next morning they headed to the law courts together. There were pickets outside the entrance, chanting the usual slogans against Cicero. Catullus brushed past them, and walked inside, to find out when he was due to be called. "Not for a while," an official told him. He was the third defence witness, and the prosecution still had one more witness to call themselves. "Sit in the gallery and wait up there. Don't worry, we'll call you." So Catullus turned and climbed the stairs. He had lost Boot, he realised, as he was shown to his seat. Oh well, he thought, settling down, she'd have to come up to the gallery sooner or later – he'd stay where he was. He leant forward, and watched the court as it assembled below.

Caelius came in last. He looked up and saw Catullus in the gallery. He smiled and nodded, and Catullus gave a short nod back. Then the court settled into silence and the session was opened. The prosecuting lawyer climbed to his feet, and told the senior judge that he had one final witness to call. The judge nodded his agreement, and Catullus sat back and waited while the witness was summoned. Where the hell was Boot? All the fuss she'd kicked up about attending the trial, and now she was going to miss the action. He stared impatiently at the gallery door, then turned round to watch as the first witness came in. She was shown to the stand and took her place. It was only when she began to read out the oath that Catullus recognised her. He leant forward incredulously. Well, bloody hell, he thought. The witness was Boot.

He watched, still stunned, as Boot began to describe her relationship with Mona. She finished her account, and the prosecutor nodded. What about the accused, he wanted to know. Had Mona ever mentioned having sexual relations with him? Boot paused. Catullus held his breath. Then Boot nodded. "They slept together once," she said. And after that? "He chased her. Hassled her. She didn't like it, so she told him to leave her alone." And what had been his response? "He'd made threats." What threats? Boot shrugged. "Threats." She shrugged again. "Just threats."

The prosecutor thanked her and sat down. Cicero rose slowly to his feet. "The deceased – she was your girl friend, then?" he asked.

Boot nodded.

"But she slept with other people as well? Shock, horror – even with men?" The sarcasm won Cicero some laughs. Boot looked pained.

"Yes," she said shortly.

"And you didn't appreciate this?"

"It depended who the men were."

"But you didn't like the accused sleeping with your girlfriend, did you?"

"No." Boot shook her head. "I thought he was a creep."

Cicero nodded to the judges. "No more questions," he said. Boot stared at him, then was led away. The court rose briefly, and the gallery emptied out, but Catullus stayed where he was, hoping that Boot would come and join him by his side. She didn't. Time passed. Down in the court, Cicero was preparing to open his case, and soon the gallery was filling up again. Still no Boot. Catullus kept a seat free, but he didn't expect her to turn up now. Then a hand fell on his shoulder. "We winning?" Catullus looked up. It was Tubbers. Catullus shrugged. "Depends who you mean by we. Just got here, have you?"

Tubbers nodded. "I owe it to him."

"To Caelius?"

"Yes. You read about my evidence, did you?"

"No." Catullus tried to remember. "I must have missed it, I think."

"Didn't say much, actually. Tried to limit it, did the best I could. But you know what these lawyers are like – *bloody* clever blokes. Think Caelius will ever talk to me again? Couldn't bear it if he didn't." He seemed on the verge of tears.

Catullus squeezed his arm. "What were you testifying about?"

"The Bulldog. You remember? Caelius had that punch up with him. And then Caelius said he'd like to kill him? Bloody unpleasant." Tubbers buried his head in his hands. "Oh God. I've rarly cocked up."

"It wouldn't be your fault."

"He is going to be convicted then?"

"No." Catullus held Tubbers' hand. "He'll be fine. Don't worry."

"Oh God. Oh God." Tubbers bent his head forward again. "I'll never forgive myself."

"Ssh." Catullus pointed to the witness box. "Look." Caelius was standing there, taking the oath. Tubbers' eyes slowly goggled. "Come on," he whispered softly to the figure in the box. "Come on." He nudged Catullus. "Look at him," he smiled. "Bloody good, isn't he?"

As a witness, Catullus thought, oh yes – as a witness. Caelius certainly looked beautiful, standing there alone – pale but upright, dress immaculate, face open, brilliant, charming, unbowed, young. He began to speak, and Catullus, watching from the distance of a gallery bench, found himself suddenly moved, quite unexpectedly, by the magic of a voice that seemed to rise from memories of a shared past and return him back to it, to Verona, before they had ever left for Rome. Catullus glanced at Tubbers, who had loved Caelius as well, and still did, and who would never cease to find his love squandered by the man to whom he offered it with such patient hope. Catullus shook his head. No. He had learnt his lesson. No more sirens' rocks for him. He listened to Caelius again, and sometimes found himself straining against his ropes, but the knots remained firm, and he stayed lashed to the mast.

What about the jurors though? Leaping into the sea? Or had enough wax already been poured into their ears? Catullus couldn't tell. Caelius certainly *sounded* convincing. Coaxed by Cicero, he was giving a bravura performance, detailed, witty, self-assured, but with hints as well of a bewildered innocence. No, he insisted, no, he hadn't murdered Varney. In a brawl over a stolen wallet? It was a ludicrous idea. Yes, he'd gone back to the Fairlawns that evening, and yes, he'd found Varney wandering over the tips, but so what? Had anyone *seen* him commit murder? Of course they hadn't – and for a simple reason. He'd never committed anything. Except perhaps the mistake of being rude to the police.

And Mona, the second victim, Cicero asked. Was it true that he had had a relationship with her? Caelius smiled – a sad, rueful, self-deprecating smile. Relationship was hardly the word, he said. A one-night stand – he apologised to the jury – followed by, yes, a certain continuing fondness for her. Nothing more. If she'd disliked him all the time – well, that came as a shock. Cicero nodded. "No great feelings of jealousy then?" he asked. "No sudden frenzy of rage?"

"Of course not." Caelius shook his head. "As I was saying – I didn't even know she'd disliked me so much. It never seemed that way at the time. But if her girlfriend says so – well – I suppose it's true."

"So you didn't go to her flat and kill her in a – what shall we call it? – a paroxysm of crazed love?"

"No."

"But you were in the area on the night of the murder?"

"Yes."

"Would you like to tell us why?"

"A friend had borrowed my car. I thought that he might have taken it to the place where he worked, which was very near Mona's flat. I needed it the next morning. So I took a taxi to try and pick it up, but I couldn't find it. So then I came back. And that was it."

"Your friend can confirm this?"

"Yes. Well – obviously he didn't see me there, because otherwise I could have picked up the car. And I didn't tell him about the taxi. But everything else he'll confirm, yes."

"Why didn't you tell him about the taxi?"

Caelius shook his head and smiled. "I was afraid he'd think I was an idiot."

The court laughed appreciatively. Cicero waited, milking their appreciation, then began to ask about the third victim, Tubbers' friend, the Bulldog. Caelius answered the opening questions soberly, regretfully: he admitted the fracas in the nightclub, and agreed that he might have made a few threats, but only in the heat of the moment, and obviously without any serious intention of carrying them out. Obviously? "Well," said Caelius, gesturing limply with his hands, "look at me." He patted his arms. "The man had sinews wherever you looked."

More laughter. It rippled away, and Cicero, looking like a magician with his hand round a rabbit's ears, glanced across at the jury. "Tell me, then," he said, leaning forwards and staring at Caelius again, "what were you doing on the evening of this third murder, at two-fifteen, the exact moment when the victim's still warm body was being discovered in a Tallowfield alleyway?"

"I was in a rented room in central Rome," said Caelius casually. There was a murmuring from around the court.

"I see," said Cicero. He smiled. "And was there anyone with you in this rented room?"

Silence. Total silence. All eyes on Caelius. He paused, obviously enjoying the mood of suspense, and then nodded. "Yes," he said. "There was."

The prosecutor had already begun to rise to his feet, but Cicero ignored him. "And this person you were with – did he or she have a name?"

"She did." Caelius nodded. "Her name was Clodia. Clodia Metella." He nodded again, then leant back, and allowed the murmurings of disbelief to rise into a storm of noise. The judge hammered furiously and bellowed for quiet; Cicero shuffled his papers; the prosecutor mouthed his protests and demanded to be heard. At last, the noise subsided, and Cicero, with a contemptuous wave of his hand, sat down and waited while the prosecutor made his complaint. "Your honour, this is outrageous," he hissed. "No one was informed of this before. Is Clodia Metella being called?"

The judge looked at Cicero, who rose to his feet and nodded. "My next witness," he said.

The prosecutor looked furious. "Then why hasn't the accused mentioned this before? Why didn't he tell the police, for God's sake?"

Cicero stared at him. "Perhaps, if you'd give me the time, I could put that question to my client himself." He glanced up at the judge. "Your Honour?"

"Yes, yes, let's hear him." The prosecutor opened his mouth again, but the judge brought down his hammer and called angrily for silence. He pointed the hammer at Cicero. "Yes."

Cicero nodded, and turned back to Caelius. "You heard my learned colleague's question?" he asked. Caelius nodded. "Well?" said Cicero. "What were you doing with Clodia? And why didn't you mention it to the police?"

Catullus' concentration, from this point on, became furious. Caelius' account of what had happened that evening sounded convincing – unpleasantly convincing. He had left the nightclub, the 'Thiasus of Cybele', at around eleven o'clock – and bumped into Catullus in the entrance hall. He had then headed on to the room he had rented, and waited there for Clodia. She had arrived several hours later. They had spent the whole night together. Therefore, he added, he couldn't have been in Tallowfield on the same night, and he couldn't have killed the Bulldog. Uproar, again, across the court.

Cicero waited for it to subside. Then, with a nod to the prosecution bench, he repeated his second question. Why hadn't Caelius mentioned this to the police?

Caelius bowed his head and swallowed. "You have to understand," he said, "that it's not pleasant..." He bowed his head again.

"What isn't pleasant?" asked Cicero impatiently.

"It isn't pleasant – having to drag someone else through the mud to save your own neck."

"You're referring to Clodia?"

Caelius nodded. "I didn't want to bring her into all this."

"Into what?"

Caelius sighed, and shook his head. "The 'Thiasus of Cybele', where we'd first met that evening, was a club that – well – it's not a run-of-the-mill place. I found out that it – how can I put it? – it caters to specialised tastes. That was why I left the club without her, you see – it wasn't really my cup of tea. Obviously, my tastes are unrefined." He smiled ruefully, and shook his head, as though mourning the persistence of his damnable middle-class decency. Oh yes, very good, thought Catullus. They'll be loving this in the jury box.

Cicero obviously thought so too. "So let's get this absolutely straight," he said with relish. "You felt that Clodia's association with this club might be damaging to her reputation? Is that right?"

"Yes. It worried me. Particularly, you see, since – no..." Caelius paused, and looked embarrassed. "No, I shouldn't have said that."

"Go on."

"I can't."

"Come on," said Cicero angrily. "What else was it that worried you?"

Caelius appealed to him. "Do I really have to answer this question?"

"Answer it," growled the judge.

Caelius bowed his head. He paused, then looked up again. "I hadn't realised who Clodia was at this time," he said. "In particular, you see, I hadn't realised that she was married. Nor that her husband, Metellus, was in the process of – well – dying."

"Yes, he was, painfully, of a brain tumour." Cicero paused. When he spoke again, he sounded disbelieving. "And Clodia hadn't mentioned this? Not once?"

"No."

"Extraordinary." Cicero shook his head. "Quite extraordinary. And so that was why you didn't mention her name to the police?"

"Yes. Partly."

"Go on."

"There was another reason. I'd rather hoped that she might come forward and tell them herself. Then none of this need ever have come out, because I wouldn't have been charged, would I?"

"But she didn't come forward."

"No."

"Why not?"

"I think that's a question you should put to her."

"Yes, but even so – you must have some idea?"

"No." Caelius shook his head. "Really. I don't know."

"You can't think of a reason?"

Caelius stared at his hands. "As I said – I think you should ask her yourself."

"Well, that," said Cicero, with a glance towards the jurors, "*that* is exactly what I intend to do." He turned back to Caelius. "Your last chance – you've got nothing more to say on this matter?"

Caelius shook his head. "Only that I'm innocent."

"Something Clodia will confirm?"

"Yes." He paused, significantly. "If she wants to."

Cicero nodded, then turned to the judge. "No more questions, Your Honour."

"Good," said the judge. "Then let's call it a day." And the court duly rose, amidst a hubbub of suspense.

Catullus, that evening, went with Boot to the pub. "An eventful afternoon," she said, taking his arm. "I watched it all on the news."

"I wish you'd come up and sat with me," said Catullus after a slight pause. "I kept a place for you."

Boot glanced at him. "I'm sorry. I couldn't."

"No. No." They walked on in silence for a few minutes. "I do understand," said Catullus at last. "I think. Catharsis, that sort of thing."

Boot shrugged. "If you want to put it like that. Yes. Which was why I hadn't wanted to tell you. Actually, I'd been hoping they'd call me while you weren't there."

"Why? Because Caelius was my friend?"

"Why do you think?" She looked up at him. Catullus suddenly

felt conscious of how warm she was, how close her face was to his own. He looked away. There was another silence. "No," said Boot at last, "it was a sort of exorcism, I suppose. Or a last funeral rite. I'm glad I had the chance."

"Even though Caelius has turned out not to be guilty?"

She stared into his face. "You really think so?"

"Yes." Catullus stopped and shut his eyes. When he opened them again, Boot was still looking up at him. "Yes," he said again, "he isn't guilty. He's got his alibi, hasn't he?" He paused. "He was with Clodia."

They both stood still. Boot hugged him, then stepped back and took his hands. "Tomorrow," she said, "when you have to go into the stand – then maybe that'll be your chance to exorcise..." Her voice trailed away. She didn't finish her sentence. Instead, she allowed herself to be pulled by Catullus until she was holding him again. Her eyes were closed, he saw. For a second, his lips hovered. When he kissed her, she welcomed him, passionately.

The next morning, Catullus waited outside the courtroom, staring up at a television screen. Clodia looked tired, he thought, watching her give her evidence, tired and depressed. Good. He tried to convince himself that she might be losing her looks, but couldn't – even haggard, Clodia was beautiful. He'd always wanted her, always found her desirable. No, Catullus told himself, staring down at the floor – be obdurate. Remember everything the bitch has done.

A door swung from behind him, and there was the sound of footsteps coming out. "What is it?" Catullus asked, looking up as the official hurried past him. "Second witness just finished," the official said. "Watch out, you'll be on in a tick."

Catullus stood up. As he did so, the door behind him swung open again. He turned round. Oh fuck. She was coming out. He stared. She glanced at him, then looked straight ahead. She brushed past him, and walked quickly down the hall. Another door swung open, then shut, and she was gone. "You're on now," said the official, from behind Catullus' back.

Thoughts of Clodia were still thumping in his heart as he walked into the court-room. He looked around. Everything seemed so much larger, more grandiose, than it had done from the gallery. People were talking in excited whispers, and the prosecutor was smiling, Catullus noticed. He glanced across at Caelius, then at Cicero. Both sat impassive. The judge called for silence, and Catullus read his oath. He finished. Eyes, from everywhere, bored into him.

Slowly, like a cat stretching after a nap in the sun, Cicero rose to his feet. He smiled at Catullus, kindly. "Just for form's sake," he said, "let's go through all the evidence. Just for form's sake." He smiled again. Then, point by point, the cross-examination began.

Catullus found the questions easy enough at first. He was asked to give a brief account of his friendship with Caelius, and of his move to Rome. He was asked to confirm the details of Caelius' meeting with Mr Varney, and then to say whether he had indeed, as had been claimed, borrowed Caelius' car on the night of the second murder. And had he left it parked near the site of the victim's house? Yes, agreed Catullus, he had. Because he'd been working there? Yes.

"Good," said Cicero, "good." He glanced at the jury, then turned back to face Catullus. "Well – so much for the first two killings of which my client has been accused. Fog really, that's all they've been, drizzling away over the contours hidden below. Thank you – we have some light at last – let's see what it illuminates." He glanced at his notes, then stared up again. "So – the night of the third murder." He folded his arms. "Tell us what you did."

Catullus tried to remember. He'd met Caelius. He'd met Clodia. And then he'd gone home.

"But that was unusual, wasn't it?" asked Cicero.

"What do you mean?"

"On a normal night you would have expected to go back with Clodia, wouldn't you?"

"Yes."

"Tell us why."

"I was living with her."

"In what sense?"

"In any sense you care to mean."

The prosecutor stood up to a background of whisperings from around the courtroom. "Your Honour," he protested, "this is all irrelevant. What has it got to do with the case we are meant to be discussing?"

"A great deal, Your Honour," said Cicero calmly. "Everything, in fact."

"Well," said the judge doubtfully. "You had better hurry up and prove that."

"Oh, I will, provided my learned friend manages not to interrupt me."

"Very well." The judge waved his hand. "Objection overruled. Continue."

"Thank you, Your Honour." Cicero bowed his head, then returned to Catullus. "Describe for us, please, the course of your affair with Clodia Metella."

Catullus did so.

"Passionate then?" asked Cicero. "Passionate love?"

"Of course. I've just said."

"Right, so we're clear about that – you're speaking here as someone who was in love – passionately in love – with Clodia."

"Yes," said Catullus impatiently. "For God's sake."

Cicero gestured to him to calm down. "All right, all right. Now then – let's get back to the night of the murder. You parted from Clodia."

"Yes."

"On her prompting or yours?"

"Hers."

"And what reason did she give?"

"She said that she wanted to be with her husband. He was ill."

More murmurings. Cicero ignored them. "But that's strange, isn't it?" he said. "Because the accused, I think you heard Caelius, he claims that Clodia had in fact planned to spend the night with him. Not with her husband at all." Cicero paused, and glanced down at his papers. When he looked up again, his question was simple. "Do you believe him?"

Catullus gripped the edge of the witness box. "Yes," he said at last. "Regrettably, I do."

This time, the court did more than murmur. Cicero waited until the judge had quietened the noise. "I don't think you were here for the evidence that Clodia gave just now, were you?" he asked. "You see – she denies that she spent the night with Caelius. She claims that she did indeed return to her husband, even though she has no one to corroborate this." He paused, and his face looked grey with sweat. "So – in your opinion – who is telling the truth? Clodia? – or Caelius?"

Caelius. Of course it was Caelius. But to say that – to pronounce those three syllables – what would die once he had spoken that name?

"Come on," said Cicero. "Your answer, please."

Catullus swallowed. "Caelius," he said. As the courtroom erupted, he saw Cicero breath in deep with relief. Caelius too was mouthing a silent prayer of thanks. This is my revenge, I suppose, thought Catullus. But there was no sweetness, not that he could taste. At that moment, Catullus would have given anything to take those three syllables back.

There were a few more questions. Cicero wanted to know about anyone who might have been following him and Caelius; Catullus mentioned Lud and Pollo. And who were they? Did he have any idea? Catullus described what he knew of their history. Cicero looked pleased. "They had been in the Circassian war then, you say? Serving under whom?"

"Clodius."

Cicero looked round the courtroom triumphantly. "Clodius," he repeated. He made a note of the name with great ostentation. Then he glanced up at the judge. "No more questions, Your Honour." He sat down.

The prosecution's questioning was brief and uninspired. Thank God, thought Catullus, as the session came to an end – he couldn't have faced a second Cicero. He walked out from the witness stand, and wondered what he should do – watch the trial, head home, or get stupidly drunk? But his mind was made up for him by the wholly unexpected appearance of Doctor Gower, whom he found sitting on the bench in the passageway outside. Catullus stared at him in surprise. "What are you doing here?" he asked.

Doctor Gower looked up. "I'm an expert witness," he said.

"Why?"

"Haven't the faintest."

"How odd."

"It is rather, isn't it? Damn odd. Glad I bumped into you though. Need you to do me a favour."

"Of course. What is it?"

"The stone circle. Go there and keep an eye on it. The bulldozers have come back."

"What about the pickets?"

"Oh, they're still there too, but you're the one who'll know what's got to be preserved. Just until I get back from the court. Please?"

"Of course. I'll go there right now. And what about tomorrow?"

"It's a public holiday. You won't get bulldozer drivers out on a public holiday. And anyway, I'll be there tomorrow. No, it's just for this afternoon. Thank you." He mopped at his brow. "You've set my mind at rest. Thank you."

"Not at all." Catullus smiled. And he meant it. He needed a sense of purpose. Anything to keep his mind from what he had said that afternoon.

The next morning, the day of the public holiday, Catullus was surprised to learn that the trial was continuing unadjourned. He wandered down to the law courts and took a seat in the gallery. The prosecutor was summing up his case, clinically, point by point. There was too much evidence, he was arguing, too many witnesses, for Caelius' presence at each murder to have been pure coincidence. As for the pretended claim to an alibi – well, he wasn't going to dignify that little fiction by even discussing it. No, the verdict was clear – guilty. Everything pointed to it. It had to be guilty. One final appeal, impassioned at last, and he finished his speech. Cicero just smiled.

All morning, he had been lounging lazily in his seat, as though too bored to pay attention to his opponent's arguments. Even when the judge called on him to deliver his own speech, it took Cicero time to rise to his feet. He stretched, then turned to the jury, and smiled confidingly.

"Gentlemen," he said, "I offer you my commiserations. Suppose there was someone in this court who wasn't obsessed by the minutiae of law, who didn't study it every day – just suppose. I think he would wonder why it was this case, and this case alone, that had to be held on a public holiday, and he would probably assume that the defendant's guilt was absolutely certain. But wait – he asks someone about the details of the case. He discovers that the accused, a young man with a brilliant future ahead of him, is almost certainly innocent – and that furthermore, he is being attacked through the influence of an upper-class whore. So what is he to think then? Probably that the schemes of the rich can be pushed too far – and almost certainly, gentlemen, that you have been dealt a very raw deal indeed, since you have to sit here during a holiday. So, as I said, you have my commiserations. But please – don't take your resentment out on my client – he didn't choose to be here either, remember."

There was an amused stirring from the jurors. They were obviously hoping for something good – the reference to a whore had woken them up. But Cicero, having flicked his spot of mud, seemed reluctant to dirty his hands any more: he began to describe Caelius' background, his good name, his many talents and achievements; then, in a bored way, he began to answer the evidence that the prosecution had produced. "All these details, of course, are merely academic," he said at last, glancing sympathetically at the jurors, as though apologising for a speech that had been necessarily dull. "The charges against Caelius are so clearly fabrications that really, it seemed a waste of time to deal with them. And yet – it had to be done. After all – Caelius is on trial, and if we had failed to realise who lay behind the charges, then, who knows? – you might have been sufficiently convinced to find him guilty of crimes committed by another man." He paused. "And woman as well, of course." He smiled and shook his head. "But there we have it, don't we? – my client's real crime – he slept with the wrong type of woman. That is why he's standing here today. He slept with a prostitute. Now, I can't approve of that – of course not – promiscuity must always be condemned. But you'll agree, I think, that on the scale of things, it is a lesser crime than the savage murder of three people – and especially so when there are extenuating circumstances. And these circumstances are?" He paused, and smiled round the court. "Well – these circumstances are what lead us to the very heart of this case."

Everyone stirred. The judge had to call for silence before Cicero could continue with his speech. Cicero himself seemed to relish the fuss.

"So then," he said, when the court had finally settled again, "the night of the third murder." He began to review the evidence that he had presented earlier, to insist that it did indeed provide his client with an alibi. "For essentially," he argued, "the whole trial devolves itself upon a single question – which witness do you believe? Look at the choices. There is Caelius, a young man of proven integrity, great talent, an excellent record. Or" – Cicero gestured contemptuously with his hands – "there is Clodia Metella, who has been described by her own regular sex-partner as a liar and a slut. Difficult, isn't it?" Cicero nodded at the jury. "All right, then. Let me help you. What about Clodia herself, what exactly *has* she been claiming? That she spent the night with someone other than Caelius. Who? Her regular lover? – no, we've heard from him, and he's denied it. Her brother perhaps? – no, she didn't spend the night with him either, not that time. Who was it then? Someone unlikely, someone a woman like Clodia rarely met." Cicero pretended to think, then put a finger up. "I've got it! Her husband!" He laughed. "Her husband." Then his laughter died away. "No, not really funny, I'm afraid. I knew Metellus. He was a good man. He worked hard to serve his country, and I think... Well – no one could want a better epitaph. But his death was wretched – neglected by his wife, in a house filled with her lovers, wracked by agonies that no doctor could understand. Strange – the way he died. And then, on the very day of his death, remember how Clodia mourned him? – she gate-crashed a party and threw wine over the guests. If she behaved like that on the day of her husband's death, then how can we doubt Caelius when he says that she spent the week before with him?

"Not that I'm blaming Caelius too harshly for that. I said earlier that it was wrong to sleep with prostitutes – yes, of course it is. But you also have to ask yourselves this. What if the prostitute comes in the guise of an intelligent, upper-class woman? What if she arranges to meet you in a sex-club, and then comes along dressed as the commonest sort of tart? And above all – *above all* – ask yourselves this – what if she is the pursuer, and you're the poor pursued?" Cicero smiled tolerantly. "Gentlemen, my client's a philosopher – but not that much of a philosopher. He was tempted, he fell, and – very well – so he has suffered for his lapse. That's why he's here today, after all, sitting in the dock. But please, come on – enough is enough. He fell into a honey trap. That, I think, is punishment enough in itself.

"No." Cicero shook his head. "No, no, it's the wrong person who is being tried here today. And so, bearing that in mind, I hope you'll forgive me if the tenor of my speech starts to change a bit now. You know the old cliché – the best form of defence is always attack. Well" – he nodded his head – "I am now going to attack. For clearly, if

Caelius was set up, then the person who framed him is the person who is guilty of murder, and my client can be freed without more ado." Cicero glanced up briefly at the television cameras. "Let's look at the facts, then, and follow them through."

Catullus clutched at the gallery railing. He had been appalled and exhilarated by the assault on Clodia, but now, with this new development in Cicero's speech, he was starting to feel unsettled. What about the letters? There hadn't been a mention of them. Cicero's argument seemed to be taking no account of their content at all. Instead, the speech was tracking different prey. "So who was Clodia working for that night?" Cicero asked. "Who was he – Clodia's pimp?" He paused, to glance at the cameras again, before turning to the jury with a quiet smile. "It seems to me that there is a single candidate – Clodia's lover." Up in the gallery, Catullus felt his heart start to melt. But Cicero shook his head, and coughed apologetically. "Oh, sorry," he said. "Did I say lover? I'm always making that mistake when I talk about Clodia. I meant brother, of course. Clodia's brother. Clodius. That's the man she would prostitute herself for."

There was uproar in court. Cicero, who would have been disappointed if there hadn't been, quietened the storm and then glided fluently on. "Of course, some of you will think that I'm just pursuing a vendetta here – far from it. Indeed, just the opposite – since my feud with Clodius is so well-known, I wouldn't dare bring accusations against him unless I had cast-iron proofs to back them up. And believe me – oh yes, believe me – I have those proofs." He began to detail them. Catullus listened astonished. For he was hearing the case that he had taken to Porter all those months ago; there they were, the same arguments, Circassia, the ritual killings, the formula. Only the murderer's identity had been changed – in Cicero's argument, Lud and Pollo served as mere accomplices, Clodius' thugs. Cicero expanded. "We heard from Doctor Gower how the murders follow a certain pattern. Four hundred years ago, Clodius' ancestor killed a man on the Fairlawns. Clodius decided to emulate that deed. One night, he lay in wait next to the sacred spot, and saw two men, Varney and my client, arguing over a wallet. My client took his wallet and left – Varney, though, was drunk, stayed out on the Fairlawns, and – well – we all know what happened. But you see, this was the crucial point – Clodius had seen my client leave. He had his scapegoat. And so Caelius was trailed and spied upon, and the plot conceived that has led to us all being here today."

Piece by piece, Cicero built up his jigsaw. For a second time, he reviewed the details of the case, but now with the assumption of Clodius' guilt, and the jurors, Catullus noticed, seemed much less inclined to fall asleep. "Of course, it's not my job to prosecute," Cicero kept insisting, "that will be for someone else," but he ignored his own injunctions cheerfully, and prosecuted on. He knew that he was winning, and when he discussed motivation, the climax of his speech, he began to leave even the ostensible details of his case behind. Caelius' compulsion to slice faces off, he noticed almost in passing, had never really been explained – what had the prosecution suggested? – that it had been an attempt to make crimes of passion look like the work of a lunatic? "But for God's sake," Cicero snorted, "we have a far more likely suspect who *is* a lunatic." It was insanity that made Clodius kill, insanity that made him follow the logic of a twisted religious rite. How, Cicero didn't know, but in Circassia, Clodius had clearly broken down, something in his mind had twisted out of shape. "I don't say that in any mood of triumph," he claimed, "I'm not gloating over an opponent's mental state. No – just the opposite – it is Clodius' mental state that prevents me from considering him an opponent at all. But he is a dangerous man. A very dangerous man. He has killed three people – unchecked, he may kill more.

"And yet" – Cicero turned to the cameras – "that is not the worst." He glanced at the jury again. "Gentlemen, our country is on the verge of terrifying crisis. It must confront questions it had thought answered a long time ago, when fundamentals we think of almost as defining Rome – free speech, democracy, the rule of law – were first established. For now, from the dark margins of our minds and our past, ghosts arise, to threaten this heritage, and force ourselves, all of us, to decide – do we surrender to these spectres, or do we fight? This isn't a political trial, and a man's innocence remains at stake – but still... there are great issues riding here on any verdict that you reach. Caelius won't mind me telling you that. He knows what we are up against. I called Clodius insane, and so he is – psychotic, mentally sick. He has killed three people – he has put an innocent man in the dock – four human tragedies. But there is also a national tragedy waiting to happen, and you, now, when you reach your verdict – this is your chance perhaps to put it in reverse. So save Marcus Caelius – yes, as you must, because his innocence shines out, and that is the specific issue before this court. But think what else you might be saving here as well – think very hard. This is your chance, gentlemen. Please, I beg you – don't waste it." And with that, Cicero finished his speech, and sat down at last.

As he did so, across Rome, unmarked lorries began to move in from the outskirts. It was announced that an emergency meeting of the Senate would be convened. And Crassus, who had arrived in person to see the Dance of Stones, ordered his bulldozers to level the site.

Half an hour after retiring, the jury assembled once again to deliver their verdict. Not guilty. Caelius was free.

XIX

AETOS

Catullus grabbed Caelius as he walked from the law-courts down an empty side-street. "Congratulations," he whispered, pushing Caelius hard against a lamp post. "Tell me why you did it."

Caelius stared at him coolly. "Did what?"

"Those letters. Clodia's. They were never mentioned."

"So? Did I ever say they would be?"

"You implied."

Caelius laughed, and shook his head, which meant that he didn't notice the fist aimed at his face until it was too late to duck. He staggered, and put his hand up to his nose. Blood trickled over his fingers; he dabbed at his nose again and looked at the gore with shock. "Why did you do that?" he asked slowly. "You want to be careful. You're no bouncer."

Catullus smiled bitterly. "Oh, I wouldn't worry about me. You've inflicted quite enough damage on me as it is."

Caelius blew a stream of blood from his nose onto the pavement. Then he looked up again. He stared into Catullus' face. "Damage," he said at last. "You mean Clodia, I suppose?"

"Of course I mean Clodia. Those letters, Caelius, which I oh so conveniently found waiting for me on the kitchen table, and which led me to stand up and inform the entire fucking nation that I thought she was a – what did Cicero say? – a liar and a tart." His fingers had grabbed Caelius' shoulders again. "But she's neither, is she? Because those letters were fakes. You never had an affair with her. I can't believe what you've done." He relaxed his grip. "What I've done." His arms fell to his sides. "Why, Caelius? Tell me why, please."

Caelius stared at him, then, as though as his eyes were sinking under the weight of Catullus' fury, he looked down at the pavement. "I had to win, didn't I?" he said at last. "But I'm not the one to tell you why. Come with me." He took Catullus by the arm. "This way."

Catullus shook himself free, then followed silently. Down a side-street alone again, Caelius turned and asked Catullus if he recognised where they were.

Catullus looked around. He could see a door with a little brass sign next to it. He shook his head. "The Police Complaints Department."

Caelius smiled. "Exactly. And this time, of course, you really do have some complaints to make. Follow me."

Inside the doors, they were met by Porter. Caelius whispered something. Porter glanced at Catullus and frowned, then waved them on. "He seemed very affable," Catullus muttered, "considering he thought you were a serial killer."

"Ah, yes," grinned Caelius, looking back over his shoulder, "but I was acquitted, wasn't I? Come on. No time to lose."

And on they went, up stairs, through doors, along passageways. The decor began to change, as it had done the last time Catullus had visited the complaints department, when he had been taken to Pompey's cabinet room. They were in the same corridor now, he realised. Caelius stopped outside a door, and pressed his ear to the panelling. "Yes, this is the one," he said. He knocked. The door was opened, just slightly at first, then flung wide open. "Ha ha!" chuckled the Great Porto. "Come in do, come in!"

Caelius brushed past him. "Where's my uncle?" he asked.

"He's through there. Getting changed. Ha ha. He's in a bit of a hurry, so best not to disturb him, eh?"

"I want him to talk to my friend."

Porto glanced at Catullus. "Not sure he should be here, don't you think, Caelius, walls have ears and all that, ha ha ha."

"I don't care," said Catullus.

"He's right," said Caelius. "He deserves it. He's had his life pretty well messed up by us, after all."

"Oh, come, come. Ha ha! Having your life messed up is an occupational hazard, I'm afraid, of being alive."

Catullus sat himself down behind a desk. "I'm not leaving."

Porto shrugged. "Very well. I've warned you, though – Cicero won't be best pleased."

Cicero wasn't. "What are you doing behind my desk?" he shouted at Catullus as he came hurrying into the room. Caelius explained. "No," said Cicero, shaking his head, "out of the question." He pointed to the window, and the crenellated spires of the senate house. "You have no idea what's breaking. I'm sorry, there isn't the time."

"I don't think you understand," said Catullus, holding him by the arms. "You are going to make the time." Cicero looked startled, and tried to break free, but Catullus wouldn't let go.

"See?" said Caelius. "He's pissed off. I told you he was."

Cicero frowned. Then, slowly, his features began to relax. He shrugged. "I suppose you did win us the trial," he admitted at last. "A magnificent performance."

"Magnificent?" Catullus wanted to scream. "How could I have been magnificent, when I didn't even know what the fuck was going on?"

Cicero smiled. "But of course you didn't. It wasn't your performance I was complimenting, it was my own. It was – well – magnificent."

"Tell me about it."

"If you'll let me..." Catullus released him, and Cicero sat down behind the desk. "Now then," he said, politely. "What was it exactly you wanted to know?"

"Was I set up?"

Cicero nodded. "You were."

"Did – I can't bring myself to say his name... Did your nephew have an affair with Clodia?"

"He didn't."

"So I've behaved like an utter tit?"

"You have." Cicero smiled, and then, seeming to think that Catullus might hit him, put his hands up to equivocate. "There were extenuating circumstances, of course. You were tricked, but a tit? – no, maybe you weren't an utter tit. We have excellent forgers, you see, here in this department."

"The letters?"

Porto put his hand up. "We have, ha, a little man, he sits in a room and forges all the day long."

"The first letter you saw," Caelius explained, "that was genuine. She really did send that to me. But the rest, the photocopies..."

"The incriminating letters."

"Yes, the incriminating letters – they were fakes. Designed to lead you on."

"Which was vital, you see." Cicero leant back in his chair and stretched. "Such a clever plan we'd come up with, but dependent on you – on your jealousy. But I knew that you were a passionate man. I'm an admirer of your poetry, you see, and I was fully confident that you could be pushed over the top."

Catullus shook his head, stunned. He tried to think what to say. "Why?" he stammered out at last. "I don't see..."

"Clodius," interrupted Cicero. "That's why. He's destroying the country. We had to destroy him. As simple as that."

"Why not arrest him, then? Why this round-about way?"

"Remember what happened before? The rape? We had him then, the evidence was all secure, but he broke free, and all because he'd had enough time to prepare. Not this time though!" Cicero laughed with glee. "Destroyed before he even knows what's hit him!"

"So Clodia..."

"Clodia – I'm sorry about. More for your sake than hers, though, I have to admit. I never really believed in her as a Lesbia."

"So what are you saying, that Caelius, you didn't even – not once..."

Caelius shook his head. "I'm sorry."

"Oh, don't be sorry, I mean, for fuck's sake, it's not as though you were really screwing her, is it? No. Thank God. She was innocent all along. What a relief. Thank fucking God."

Caelius gestured. "I've said I'm sorry."

"That makes it fine, Caelius, just fine. So what *were* you doing on that night of the third murder?"

"I was in a rented room, as I said. With a girl I'd picked up."

"Who?"

Caelius shrugged. "A girl."

"What, a Mona?"

"If you like."

"And what about Clodia?"

"With her husband, I suppose, looking after him. Doing what she said she was doing."

Porto stuck up his hand again. "She was. I can confirm that." He noticed Catullus' glance of distaste, and smiled. "She was seen returning alone to her house."

"Why? By whom?"

"By whom? Can't you guess? Ha ha ha! How terribly amusing! By us! We thought you were the murderer! Ha ha! We kept a watch on Clodia's house all the time, just to keep a track of your comings and goings. No, no, now don't get cross. You should be grateful. It was because we were spying on you that we knew you couldn't have committed the third murder. Otherwise it might have been you in the dock, and not your friend, ha ha!"

Cicero nodded. "So, you see, we knew that you hadn't been with Clodia that night. And Caelius – well – he'd been with his tart. A profitable conjunction of coincidences."

"And this girl, the one who'd been with Caelius, she confirmed this?"

"Oh yes," chuckled Porto. "Otherwise we would have arrested him. Ha ha!"

"Really?"

"Yes, maybe. It had to be one of you two. Either that, or someone was trying to frame you."

"Who?"

"For God's sake!" Cicero brought a fist down onto his desk. "You answered that question yourself in the witness box. Clodius, Clodius, Clodius!"

"I never said that."

"You did. Those two men you saw, following you around..."

"Yes, but they weren't Clodius."

"But they work for him, don't they? Now come on, show some

common sense. You may feel aggrieved about what we've done, but look into your soul, look very deep, and ask yourself – what else could we have done? As I said – if we'd attacked him directly, he would have stitched up the trial."

"But instead you were able to stitch it up yourselves."

"Because we had no choice! Because at the moment, it's destroy or be destroyed, and I've learnt that the hard way, let me tell you. I know what we are up against here, so please" – he made a sweeping gesture with his arm – "no more! Please! It's your – what? – your duty to understand."

Catullus shook his head. Duty? *Duty?* "You really think that fixing the law will help preserve the rule of law, do you? That's the theory?"

Cicero stared at him. His face was red with anger, but when he spoke, it was with the hiss of water turning into ice. "Your platitudes reflect your ignorance and self-satisfaction. Please understand that I do not willingly use the tools of my enemy, nor do I enjoy trampling on standards that I have devoted a lifetime to upholding. But perhaps it has escaped your attention – it is not Plato's Republic out there at the moment. You are a student of history. I'm sure you will appreciate Rome's tradition of appealing for sacrifice. I am sorry that you have lost your lover, but at least you have retained your self-respect."

"While you've sacrificed yours for the good of the nation? Such nobility."

Cicero clenched his fists. "Please," he said slowly, "do not debase your intelligence by resorting to cheap sarcasms."

"Sorry – it must be you. You seem to have debased everything else you approach."

Cicero closed his eyes. Distantly, from the Senate House clock tower, a bell tolled. "I must be going," Cicero said, opening his eyes and staring at Catullus again. "The session will be opening."

"What session?"

"The one that your evidence has helped to precipitate."

"Oh?"

"Yes." Cicero glanced at Porto. "Tell him."

Porto hopped and grinned. "Caesar," he said, waving a faxed sheet of paper in the air. "He's mobilising troops on the frontier. High noon," he whispered, then giggled.

"What has this got to do with my evidence?"

"Because your evidence had destroyed Clodius, and Clodius was Caesar's ally, fostering the internal dissent in Rome that has always been Caesar's excuse for claiming the right to interfere in Roman affairs. See?" Porto giggled, then nodded at Cicero. "But ask him. He's the statesman."

"Well?" said Catullus. He waited, then asked again. "*Well?*"

Cicero nodded slowly. "Yes, that's about the sum of it," he said. "So you see – you are a figure of Homeric proportions, indeed."

"What do you mean?"

"That your love for a woman brings war in its wake."

"And that's meant to comfort me, is it?"

"I thought it might. Knowing your love of the classics. Don't you find that it gives you an insight into the psychology of the ancient heroes?"

Maybe, Catullus thought, maybe. Yes, actually, he would happily burn a city down for Clodia right now, if it would help to bring her back. But he shook his head and turned away from Cicero's smile, for it was dangerous, this banter, it would sterilise his hate. Cicero opened his mouth again, but Catullus cut him off. "What's to stop me telling people all this?" he asked. "Your perjury?"

Cicero shrugged. "Who'd believe you?" He smiled. "Clodia might, of course. Good luck to you."

"Truth, you see," said Porto, "the old problem. What is truth? Something absolute? Or maybe, ha ha, it's as shifting and transitory as our own feeble minds. In which case – the whole basis of your complaint just shivers away."

Very politely, Catullus took him by the throat. "Would an assault on a policeman be a shifting illusion, do you think?" Porto gurgled a chuckle. Catullus stared at him, then sighed, and let him go. "I'm starting to see why they put Socrates to death." Porto chuckled again, and looked pleased with himself.

"I'm going," said Catullus. "I can't stand the sight of any of you any more."

"Wait," said Caelius, as he opened the door. "I'll come with you."

"No."

"You'll get lost."

"Oh, fuck me, you are at home in the corridors of power now, aren't you, Caelius? But of course you are. You must be important if you can sacrifice your friends with such ease." He looked at them all, Caelius, Cicero, the Great Porto, then slammed the door behind him and began to hurry down the corridor.

The door opened again. Catullus looked round. Caelius. What the hell did he want? Catullus quickened his pace, but Caelius ran and took him by the arm. "You weren't mollified then?" Caelius asked. Catullus made no answer. "Look, I'll say it again, okay? – I'm sorry. Really. I'm really, really sorry."

"Don't bother, Caelius, you're shite at this sincerity lark."

"That's not my fault, must be something to do with my face. Because I am sincere." Caelius waited for Catullus to say something, so Catullus brushed him off and walked on down the corridor. Caelius hurried, and caught him up again.

"Okay," he said, "carry on a vendetta against me, I can't complain, I suppose. But there's one other thing."

"Yes?"

"Just for a few days, watch your back. Shadows in the night – you know."

"*What?*" Catullus stared at him in disbelief. "Are you telling me that Clodius is still out there?"

"Yes. As I said – just for a few days."

"Oh, great. Fucking great." Catullus gestured with his hands. "Why?"

"Because that's the way things work. The police have got to have time to check out the evidence. Can't have it looking like they had it all along."

"Oh no, we can't have that. And what if someone else gets slashed up in the meantime? What if *I* get slashed up?"

"He's being shadowed."

"What if he slips them?"

Caelius shrugged. "As I said – watch your back."

"How can you do this to me, Caelius? I mean, fucking hell, this is *dangerous*." He paused. "Still – you have arrested those tramps, haven't you?"

Caelius twisted his mouth and looked embarrassed.

"You haven't?"

Caelius shook his head. "We don't know where they've gone. They've vanished." He lifted a hand, and patted Catullus' shoulder. "But look, don't worry, they might be nothing to do with it."

"Of course they're something to do with it. They're the fucking killers."

"I don't think so."

"What do you mean?"

"We – well, I say we – the police – don't think they'd do anything without Clodius' instructions. And if Clodius is being watched, then we'll know if he has any contact with them. See?"

"You make it sound so simple."

"Well, what else can we do?"

"Get out there, find them, and lock them up. They're dangerous as hell. I know, I've met them."

"As I said – we're trying." He pointed to a door in the wall. "This way."

Catullus followed him down some stairs. "And in the meantime," he called after him, "stop practising all this psychological warfare on Clodius, that's dangerous as well."

"What do you mean?"

"It just makes him even more fucked off. Don't do it."

"No, no, hold on, I meant what psychological warfare? What are you talking about?"

Catullus remembered Clodius' face, his look of icy panic, and the eight statuettes in a line on his desk. "The messages. On those statues. Don't send him another."

"What messages?"

"Oh, come on, Caelius. The ones on those statues of Sesostris. He showed them to me. What was it? – 'Beware, you're going to get – blank.' Don't send him the last statue, all right, that's all I'm saying. It's cracking him up."

"But I don't know what you're talking about."

"The statues. You know – with the eagle heads."

Caelius looked puzzled. "Someone's been sending them to him?"

"Yes, you – well, Cicero, I mean. Or Porto..." Catullus' voice trailed away. "You really don't know anything about them?"

Caelius shook his head. "No. Really – nothing to do with us." He held open a door. "Here you go. The road's out there."

Catullus leant against a wall, and breathed in deeply. "Then who is it?"

"I don't know."

"Oh God."

"Does it matter?"

"How can I tell? Clodius seemed to think it did." Catullus walked out onto the pavement. It was dark. Black clouds lay piled above the silhouette of Rome, and a wind, blowing litter along the empty street, made Catullus shiver. "I should think it does matter actually, yes," he said at last. He looked over his shoulder. "Anything to do with Sesostris seems to matter."

"Well – as I said, old chum. Watch your back."

Catullus stared at him coldly.

"What are you going to do now?" asked Caelius after a pause.

Catullus stared at him again. "What do you think?"

"See Clodia?"

Catullus nodded shortly. "Yes. If I can."

"Good." Caelius looked at his feet. "Well – best of luck."

That was too much. Catullus turned, and began to hurry down the street.

"There won't be any buses," shouted Caelius after him.

"What do you mean?"

"They've been cancelled. All transport's been cancelled. You'll have to walk."

"Why?"

Caelius shrugged. "This is a crisis."

"Oh, of course it is. I was forgetting." He walked on.

"Watch your back!"

Catullus turned the corner.

"I'm sorry for everything! Goodbye! Goodbye!"

He may have shouted something else. If he did, Catullus didn't catch it. Caelius' voice was lost on the wind.

He had been right about the public transport, though. The bus stops at the Aventine Crossroads were empty, and there was a metal grille across the entrance to the Underground. No one was around, except for two men in a large, unmarked car, and when Catullus looked at them and gestured with his arms, they pretended not to see him. So Catullus walked, down roads denuded of traffic, past boarded shops and black-windowed offices, through a city emptied of all noise it seemed but the wind, which whirled and shrieked through the darkening streets. Catullus remembered the city painted on his bedroom at home, depopulated, impossible, and now, hearing the wind at his back, he remembered his nightmares, how he had dreamt himself lost in the city, searching for something while an unseen beast pursued him through the streets, drawing nearer and nearer until Catullus had felt its breath, and screamed, and woken up. He shook his head, and smiled, then recalled a philosopher's phrase, the description of Rome as a web of dreams, where ancient occurrences are attached to the present day, and Catullus, whispering the sentence to himself, couldn't help glancing round at the street behind. There was nothing, of course, only darkness, and litter in the wind. Catullus hurried on.

He reached the Palatine and began to climb its hill. The streets were less empty now – he could see policemen, and drivers in vans, and the same unmarked cars that had been parked by the Underground. One of the policemen stopped him, and asked him where he was going; Catullus pointed vaguely, and the policeman waved him on. He crossed Cicero's square; more people, protestors this time. Further down the road, there were orange pinpricks of flame, lights from the shacks of the homeless, like the campfires of some army besieging a long-ago town. Catullus picked his way across the square, and turned into Clodia's street. He looked down towards her house – it loomed dark, featureless. He began to run. There were a few people gathered outside her door, he could see now, but when he looked up at the windows again, they were as black as before, and he knew that Clodia wasn't there. But he ran anyway, and when he reached her house, he brushed past the men sitting on the entrance steps and knocked furiously on the door. "She's not here," said one of the men. Catullus ignored him, and knocked a second time. "Clodia!" he shouted. "Clodia!" "Didn't you hear me?" the man said. "She's not here." Catullus stared at him wildly, then began to pound with his fists.

One of the other men stirred and stood up. "Hold on," he said. "Aren't you the one from the trial?" He peered at Catullus. "Well, fuck me, you are." He pushed a microphone into Catullus' face. "No," said Catullus, brushing at it, "no." But the men ignored his protests. Microphones, questions, demands for a statement. Catullus screamed out Clodia's name one last time, then began to run. Shouts from the reporters followed him down the road, but he didn't listen, the blood in his ears was pounding too hard, and still he ran, on and on, until the night was silent again, and he realised he was lost.

He stumbled on through the unfamiliar streets. Memories of his nightmare began to return. Clodia, he had to find her. She had to be made to forgive what he'd done. But where was she? – he didn't know. The streets continued empty, and beyond every corner Rome waited for him, too vast to be searched, to be understood.

A signpost pointed him back towards the Aventine Crossroads. The club, he realised, the 'Thiasus of Cybele', of course – ask there. He began to quicken his pace again. Damn, he thought, why hadn't he looked there in the first place? – he might have spared himself a trek. He passed the Senate House, and glanced up at the windows. They were blazing with lights, and outside, on the roads leading into the House, men could be seen, building barriers across the gates. Catullus hurried on, keeping to the shadows. Above him, the street lamps flickered and sparked; a few went dead. As Catullus reached the Crossroads, all the lights in Rome blacked out.

He crossed the road, not bothering to look for traffic, and walked down the steps that led to the 'Thiasus of Cybele'. The entrance door was shut, and there was no sound of music coming from beyond it; the lights, like all the others across the city, were off. He knocked, without much hope, and waited. Nothing. "Shit," he whispered under his breath – what was he going to do now? He kicked at the door, then began to walk away, but as he did so, he heard something, a movement, coming from inside. He hurried back to the door. "Hello?" he called. "Can I come in?"

"No," said a voice. "We're shut."

"I don't care. I need to come in. Please."

"Go away."

"Is that you, Marghi?"

There was a silence. "What if it is?"

"I need to talk to you. About Clodia."

There was another silence. Then Catullus heard the sound of a key being turned. The door opened very slightly. Marghi stared at him, then whistled. "Well, I'll say this for you, you've got a nerve."

"Can I come in?"

"No, you can't. Fuck off."

"Please." And Catullus began to explain. Marghi listened until he had finished, then shook her head. "I don't believe you," she said. "It's impossible."

"You really think so? Impossible?"

Marghi thought. "Well, you were a fuckwit then, weren't you?"

"Yes, which is why I need to see Clodia now, to make up for it."

"No hope."

"I can try." He waited. "Please, Marghi. Please."

She sighed. "Come on, then," she said. She opened the door, and Catullus walked in, blinking as he tried to adjust to the dark. He heard a drawer being pulled out. Then something was thrust into his hand, a card.

"Here," said Marghi. "Come back tomorrow. She'll be here then. Give this in at the door."

"You don't know where she is tonight?"

"Look – don't push your luck, all right?"

"All right, all right." Catullus glanced down at the card. He could make out words now – 'Cybele the Castratrix'. "What is this?" he asked. "Sounds a bit ominous."

Marghi snorted. "Only if you've got balls."

"Well, exactly."

Suddenly, there was the sound of footsteps from outside. Marghi, who had been about to say something, put a finger to her lips. "Sssh." She bent down and leant against the door, while someone knocked on it, then stood back and began to shout.

"Let me in! Come on! You've got to be open!"

Catullus' heart stopped. "It's Clodius," he whispered in a low scream. "Oh my God, it's Clodius." Marghi shook her head, and pointed to her lips again. "Clodius, is that you?" she asked quietly.

"Yes." He paused. "I was told to meet someone here."

"Well, you can't, can you? We're shut."

"Can I come in?"

Marghi shook her head. "Sorry, there's no light."

"Damn." Clodius paused. "He definitely said to meet me here."

"Who?"

"Pollo. You know, the..."

"Yes, I know him. Of course I do. But like I said – he's not here tonight."

There was another pause. "I'm finished," said Clodius suddenly.

"You know that? – finished. I don't know what the hell's going on here. I'm just... I don't know. I don't know what I'm going to do."

Marghi looked at Catullus and twisted her mouth. Then she turned back to the door, and opened it wider. "Do you want to come in?"

"No!" Clodius said with sudden violence. He pointed back up the steps. "I've got to go. I don't want to wait here, I don't trust these shadows. You never know what might be waiting there, do you?" He stared around. "Good night," he whispered urgently, "good night." He began to hurry back towards the steps.

Marghi watched him disappear. She turned to Catullus. "Go on, you too. Get out. I don't want to have anything to do with this."

Catullus waved the card she had given him. "Tomorrow?"

She nodded. "Tomorrow, late. Now get out." She pushed him, and the door slammed shut. Catullus slipped the card into his pocket, then began to creep back up the stairs. At the top, he looked for Clodius. Gone, it seemed. Catullus began to walk along the pavement, keeping to the shadows, careful not to let his footsteps sound above the moaning of the wind. He turned a corner, and looked around again. Still all clear. Then the wind fell suddenly, and Catullus heard something – a footstep perhaps. He froze against the wall, and stared behind him. Nothing but shadows, thickening into black. "Who's there?" he whispered. There was no answer, and the wind began to scream again, as though in mockery.

On the far side of the crossroads, a man had lit a small fire. He was crouching over it, feeding it with scraps of newspaper, trying to keep the flames alive in the face of the wind. Flickering touches of orange lit the pavement, and the shadows around it were edged with red; Catullus stared into them, and realised that there was a second man, on the margins of the light cast by the fire, standing on the kerb and looking around him all the time, obviously waiting for something, or someone, to appear. Catullus strained with his eyes: yes, the man was Clodius. Catullus breathed in deeply, and listened to his heart. Could Clodius see him? No, clearly not. Not if he stayed in the shadows. He pressed himself tightly against the wall again. Then suddenly, something touched him on his back.

Catullus spun round.

"Sssh," whispered a girl's voice, "he'll hear you."

"Oh, fuck!" Catullus patted at his heart. "Who the hell is that?"

"Can't you see me?"

Catullus looked. There was a face, he could just make it out, pale, delicate. He frowned. "Vanessa?"

"Yes." She pointed to Clodius. "I've been following him."

"Why?"

She shook her head, and pointed again. "Look."

Catullus stared. Nothing, just the flickering of red shadows. He turned back to Vanessa. "What are you doing here? What will your father say?"

Vanessa looked into his eyes unblinkingly, then she shrugged. "I don't care."

"But it's dangerous."

Her eyes widened. "Of course it is." She looked back across the road at Clodius. "Otherwise I wouldn't be here, would I?"

Suddenly, she pointed again, and this time Catullus did see something. A figure, passing through the red shadows cast by the fire, and then gone. Catullus blinked. Were his eyes playing tricks? No, there had been something there, he was sure, but it had looked strange, wrong somehow. Then Catullus realised – its height. The figure had been too tall. Taller than any human, at least. Catullus glanced at Clodius. He had seen the apparition as well. He was staring into the shadows with a look of open-mouthed horror. Then he began to walk towards the spot where the figure had vanished. He looked around, and must have seen something, because he turned and hurried down a side-road.

"Come on," said Vanessa.

"Wait," whispered Catullus, as she scampered across the road. "Vanessa, wait!"

"Come on!" she hissed.

He ran, and caught her up. "What was that thing?" he asked.

As she looked at him, he could see her eyes glittering. "It's happening," she whispered. "Just like my dad always said it would." She began to run faster. "I can't talk any more. I've got to save my breath." She looked over her shoulder. "And if I can't keep up, you'll make sure you follow him. Promise?"

Catullus nodded. He wanted to ask her more, but as he opened his mouth to speak, he turned a corner and saw Clodius, standing only a few metres ahead of them. He pulled Vanessa against the wall, and felt her freeze in his arms. "There," she whispered. Catullus looked. Beyond Clodius, at the very end of the street, stood the same black figure he had seen before. It turned, and as it did so, Catullus saw that its shoulders seemed stooped, and that it wore something, a hood, pulled close over its head. But the glimpse, again, was momentary: no sooner had Catullus seen the figure than it was gone, and the winds screamed as though they had swept a ghost away. Clodius shook and muttered to himself loudly; then he began to hurry down the street, and Vanessa tugged at Catullus' sleeve. "Come on," she whispered, "we mustn't lose them." She began to run through the shadows, and Catullus followed her, a few steps behind, careful not to make any noise that might alert Clodius. But their quarry stayed transfixed by his own pursuit, and never looked round once. Gradually, Catullus dared to close in on him.

As a result, he was sometimes able to catch further glimpses of what seemed an impossible phantom, a Circassian god, returned a second time to haunt a stricken Rome. It was hard, though, to keep the figure in sight, and even Clodius, so much nearer to it, had to stop sometimes to scan different roads, or search the shadows of a park or square. A second's movement, a glide across an open space, and the figure would reappear, just long enough for Clodius to see its silhouette, before it floated back into the darkness again. The pursued, Catullus realised, was beckoning its pursuer on; and yet Clodius seemed reluctant to press the chase too far, as though content to follow wherever he was led. But Clodius was not content; far from it; his face, when he turned, bore witness to that. It was frozen, and Catullus, from the shadows, wondered what terror might lie beneath such a look of ice.

The chase itself was draining. Sometimes Catullus would glance round, to check that Vanessa wasn't falling behind, but she would stare at him unsmilingly, and point, motioning him to keep his eyes straight ahead. So the pursuit never flagged, and still the spectre danced on the remote margins of the visible, and Clodius tagged it with the same unchanging pace. They were leaving central Rome now. They crossed the Tiber, and the swirling waters that had carried Varney's corpse, and then on, past empty store houses and through derelict estates, where windows grinned like the teeth of skulls, and still on, into the urban wastes. A couple of twists, up a side-road, down into a high street, and they were back again in a Rome where not all the buildings had disintegrated into rubble, but Catullus, glancing round, felt no sense of relief. He had been to this place before, he realised. He could recognise the tube station; he could recognise the street: he knew where they were going. Ahead of him, Clodius turned again. Catullus followed. Soon the offices and shops had been left behind, and the road itself petered away, into the wasteland Catullus had been expecting, for it was here, months before, that he had sat with Pollo in his half-built shack. Across the site, Catullus could make out the wire fence he remembered from his visit before. There was a great rip in it now, he could see; standing in the gap was something hunched in black. It turned, and disappeared. Clodius followed it. "Be careful," Catullus whispered to Vanessa. She glanced at him, and nodded. So she had been here too. Catullus squeezed her hand. Then he led her over the rubble and on, through the fence.

Clodius was standing ahead of them, inside the ring of concrete and scaffolding. Catullus inched forward. At the far end of the shell, brought to bay at last, the phantom, the god, the whatever, was waiting. It turned and faced Clodius. Neither of them moved, neither spoke. Then, suddenly, Clodius pointed and screamed: "I know who you are! Don't think you frighten me, because I know who you are!" The cowled figure stood motionless. Then slowly, with sacerdotal elegance, it raised its arms. They were tiny for its body, joined halfway down, barely able to reach the hood to draw it back. The creature inclined its head, at an angle, like a bird watching prey; its fingers reached the hood and pulled it down. Two cold eyes glinted from the dark; the creature bent back its neck, and an eagle's head showed in profile against a grey concrete wall. Then the creature turned, and stared across the rubble at Clodius. From behind the scimitar curve of its beak, the eyes gleamed again, brilliant, dead.

Suddenly, Clodius began to laugh. Gravel crunched under his feet as he walked across to where the eagle-man stood. There was silence again; then Clodius pushed at the creature, and it stumbled and fell. "You can flutter and float like a ghost," Clodius said, "but you never could take a punch." He kicked the figure once, twice, then stood back. "Did you really think I didn't recognise you?" He bent down, and pulled at the eagle's head. Something snapped; Clodius tugged at the head again, and it came off in his hands. He held the mask up and stared at it; then dropped it into the dirt. "Get up," he said, tugging at Mr Dugbal's chest.

Catullus glanced at Vanessa; she met his eyes briefly, then turned back to watch her father. Mr Dugbal tottered to his feet; he walked across to his mask and tried to pick it up, but Clodius kicked it from his hands, and the mask bounced across the rubble. Clodius kicked it again; the beak snapped off. He stamped on the mask until he had flattened it, then turned back to face Mr Dugbal.

"Broken, I'm afraid." He paused. "Your own creation?"

Mr Dugbal said nothing.

"Suited you, actually. Better than your own stupid sheep's face, anyway."

Again, Mr Dugbal kept silent. Clodius stared closely into his eyes.

"Come on," he said at last, "where are they? The other two. I haven't got all night. Where are they?" He waited, but Mr Dugbal just shook his head and tried to walk away. Clodius grabbed him by the arm. "This isn't the time for living in the past, don't you see that, for God's sake?" He pointed back towards the city. "It's now that matters. Now, and the future." Almost gently, he took Mr Dugbal's hand. "We must be ready. Changes are going to happen, great changes, and very soon. You shouldn't have brought me here tonight. This wasn't the right time." He spun round, and suddenly shouted at the darkness. "I said, this wasn't the right time!" He waited, but only the wind moaned in answer. He dropped Mr Dugbal's hand and walked back towards the centre of the ring. "Where are you?" he shouted. "Come out, I know you're there!" He listened. A stone fell. Clodius ran towards the sound. But there was nothing, just a pile of bricks, and Clodius couldn't see into the darkness beyond. He wiped at his face and muttered something. Then he turned round, and looked for Mr Dugbal. His eyes widened as he scanned the concrete rim. But there was nothing to be seen. Mr Dugbal had gone.

Slowly, Clodius walked back to the centre of the shell. He stopped. Silence. Then he bent down and picked up the ruined eagle's head, and nestling it in his arms, began to walk towards the tear in the fence. It was only when he heard the violin that he stopped and looked round again. At first, he seemed to doubt that he had heard anything at all. The wind was shrill: it was hard to be sure that they were really notes of music on its swirl. But then the wind dropped, and the notes became unmistakable, as beautiful amidst concrete and mud as they had been beside the lake of Clodia's estate. Catullus watched as Clodius stared into the darkness, and clutched at his ears. "No," he shouted, "I said no, not now, no!" He ran towards the music. There was a pile of scaffolding ahead of him. He clambered up it, and peered over the top.

The crowbar caught him on the side of the head. There was a thud. Clodius spun, and seemed to be reaching for something, his fingers grabbing and scraping at air, his whole body stretching in a gymnast's arc. Then he fell. He bumped down the scaffolding, and came to rest on the concrete floor. A shape followed him, leaping down from the top of the scaffolding pile, and landing next to Clodius' black-stained head. Catullus stared. Yes, it was Pollo. Clodius groaned, and Pollo bent down to cradle him in his arms. He sang softly. Then footsteps crunched from behind him, and he looked up again.

He stared into Lud's face. "Not dead yet," he said. Lud nodded. They were both wearing their costumes, Catullus realised, the boots and green trousers he remembered from the ball, and Lud was wearing make-up. But it was a woman's, not a clown's, and when he moved, it was with a parody of feminine grace. Pollo, by contrast, wore no make-up, and had grown a beard which curled to his chest.

"Water," he said brusquely. Lud handed him a bucket. Pollo emptied it over Clodius' head. "He's opened his eyes," he said, nodding. "He's coming round." Clodius began to vomit. Pollo waited, then bent down and settled his burden so that Clodius' head was on his lap. "Bit sore?" he asked, dabbing at the wound. Clodius retched again, and Pollo spluttered with delight. "Oh, you're going, aren't you, you're going! But listen." He bent his head down to Clodius' ear. "Are you listening?" He jogged Clodius' head. "Are you listening?" Clodius groaned. "Good. Because I want you to understand why it's all worthwhile."

Pollo bent down close again. "You know what I've done? I've only gone and phoned your friends. And you know what I told them?" He began to hiss with laughter, and had to pause, to wipe away a froth of spit from his mouth. "I've told them to come here, to this very spot, where they're going to find you dead. Very dead. They'll be here any minute." Pollo cocked his head. "What's that you're saying? 'Why is this good news?' All right then, I'll tell you why it's good news. It's good news because I've told them we're from the fucking army!" He spluttered again. "Which we were, of course, weren't we, we all were, once upon a time." He shook his head. "Which means, the point is, you – me – Lud here – we've all recognised those army trucks, haven't we, those cars, we've all seen them waiting around in Rome today? What were you planning to do about them, eh, you great fucking leader of the people, you? Lead the masses in a glorious struggle, you at the forefront, eh? But supposing the masses had told you to fuck off? – which they might have done, I mean, when you see people with guns, it can make you reluctant to rise, can't it? We all remember that. So it might have been a problem for you, that's what I'm saying here."

Pollo nodded to Lud, then whispered into Clodius' ear again. "They need something to get them going." He paused. "A sa-cri-fice." Clodius began to moan and twitch. Pollo shook his head, but his expression now, Catullus could see, was almost one of tenderness. He felt in his pocket and drew something out. A tiny black statue with an eagle's head. "Beware, beware," he murmured, "you are going to be – what?" He smiled, and looked at the base of the statue in his hand. "Going to be what?" He read the statue's base again, then placed it next to Clodius' head. He kissed the dying man on his lips, then stood up and stared into his face. "It's time," he said. In the distance, torches were waving. Voices could be heard. Pollo grinned. "Time."

Lud had gone to fetch the axe. He handed it to Pollo, who felt the edge with his finger. He licked at the blood and nodded, then pushed Clodius over onto his side. "Sleep well," Pollo whispered. He stood back. Then he raised the axe, and swung it down hard.

The voices and torches were drawing nearer. Lud tapped Pollo on the shoulder and pointed, but Pollo didn't look up. He had sunk onto Clodius' body, and lay there without moving, as though he had fallen asleep. Gradually, he stirred. He reached for the statue, which had been knocked over by debris from Clodius' skull. He cleaned it, then rolled Clodius so that he was lying on his front. Suddenly, Pollo laughed. "Fucked!" he shouted, reading from the statue's base. "Beware, beware, you are going to be – fucked!" He undid Clodius' trousers and pulled them down. Then, gently, he pushed the statue into Clodius' anus, until only the base could be seen sticking out. Pollo sat back. He laughed and laughed. Tears began to stream down his face.

Lud shook him. The torchbeams had reached the outer fence, but still Pollo refused to stand up. Instead, he clung to Clodius. Lud began to run. Pollo turned Clodius over, and stared into the mess that had once been his lover's face. Lud looked back, and waved frantically, but Pollo shook his head. He bent down, to kiss the wound, a long, lingering kiss of farewell. Blood ran in gouts through the curls of his beard.

Catullus held Vanessa tightly in his arms. She was shuddering. "Come on," he whispered, "we've got to get out of here." He glanced across at the gap in the fence, but the men with their torches were already spilling through. "We'll have to go this way," he said, pointing to the far end of the site. "Hope there's some way out." He pulled on Vanessa's arm. "Come on!"

They began to run. Then a gun shot rang out. Catullus turned round to look. Pollo fired again, into the wind. He had been surrounded by a ring of men. "You've got me," he shouted. "You've got me!" He placed the gun barrel in his mouth. A third shot rang out. The back of Pollo's head disintegrated in a shower of blood and bone.

Vanessa screamed, and began to sob uncontrollably. The men looked up. They began to run across the site towards her. "Come on, for fuck's sake!" Catullus screamed. He could see Lud, waiting by a gate in the fence, holding it open. He yanked on Vanessa's arm and together they stumbled through the darkness until they had reached the fence. Catullus pushed Vanessa through the gate, then followed through himself and slammed it shut, but Vanessa wriggled from his grip and unslid the bolt again. "Dad!" she screamed. Catullus looked. Mr Dugbal was running across the site, his hands flapping as though he were trying to fly. "Dad!" Vanessa screamed again, and ran towards him. "Come back," Catullus yelled, "he's making it, come back!" Mr Dugbal reached the gate, but Vanessa, following him, twisted and fell. Catullus reached for her. "My hand," he shouted, "take it!" He pulled her up. He pushed her towards the gate, and bundled her through the gap, but it was while his back was turned that he felt the blow to his head. For a brief, brief fraction of a second, his world turned white. Then it began to spin, and then there was nothing at all.

XX

LUD

Beyond red mists of swirling pain, there was a city. Catullus blinked. The mists didn't clear. Instead, the buildings themselves seemed to be phantoms, crimson shadows that bred from his wound like the miasmas that hang over swampy plains. The blood was still damp: Catullus could feel it in a gash across his head. He tried to touch the wound, but his hand refused to move, and the red clouds thickened as they swept before his eyes. He looked at the city again. He found it hard to believe that anything could really be there, for whenever he tried to fix the limits of a building or the skyline, shapes would reproduce themselves endlessly away, as though the architecture were nothing but the contours of some impossible trick of his mind. There were pyramids and tower blocks, hanging gardens and vast concrete bowls, grotesque mausolea and radio spires; Catullus wanted to struggle, for the confusion of the architecture was suffocating him, and he had to know that he could wake from it. But again, when he tried to move, the clouds from the margins of his eyes began to thicken; the redness deepened to purple, then black; he surrendered to the clouds as though they were chloroform.

He woke again. There were voices. He tried to listen. He found it hard at first, for sounds too, like the buildings he had seen, seemed unreal when experienced through the fumes of his pain. But he concentrated, and gradually the syllables began to make sense. Vanessa. She was talking. So she had escaped from the mob.

"You can't leave him here," she was saying.

Somebody muttered something.

"No!" Vanessa said. "You can't. Get him to a hospital." Catullus heard her stamp her foot. "Dad!"

Mr Dugbal stammered. "B-b-but..."

"Dad!"

"No." There was a pause. "No, he can't. Not yet. He must stay here."

"Why, Dad? Why?" There was silence. "Dad, I want to know why! It's not like he was really working for that man who chased you last night, is it? But that's what you told me, and it was a lie, a lie! But I found out months ago, yes, that's right, I knew what you were doing, because I followed those other two round, and I listened to them, and I knew what you were doing, that you were going to kill that man you killed yesterday. Yes, I knew, Dad. And now, Catullus, you've got to save him, because he was hurt when he saved me. You've got to, Dad. It won't be fair otherwise." Suddenly she screamed. "Dad!"

"No, Vanessa," said Mr Dugbal with unusual firmness. "He's got to wait."

"Then I'll get Mum."

"She's out."

"Where?"

"With that man from the graveyard over the road."

"Then I'll get Jez. I'll get anyone."

"No, you won't. Just stop it, Vanessa." Catullus heard movement. He opened his eyes, very narrowly. Mr Dugbal was hurrying up some steps. There was a door at the top, which he locked, swatting at Vanessa as he did so. Then he turned. Catullus shut his eyes quickly. He could hear Mr Dugbal walking back down the steps, then across the room to stand next to him.

A hand settled lightly on the side of his cheek. Then it touched the wound, and Catullus flinched, and opened his eyes.

"Is it very painful?" Mr Dugbal asked.

Catullus tried to nod, but couldn't.

"I have..." Mr Dugbal felt in his pocket. "I always found, with my own – sufferings –" He held out a pill, and nodded. "Try it."

Catullus licked at Mr Dugbal's palm, then forced himself to swallow the pill. He shut his eyes again.

In the background, Vanessa had begun to shout at her father, but Catullus found himself floating away from the noise. Soon, the pain too was starting to empty out, like dirty water leaving a sink. Catullus tried to lift his hand. It moved. He opened his eyes and looked at it, then raised his arm. He checked with his brain. It didn't hurt. He stood up and looked around the room.

They were in a cellar. It was large and candlelit. In the middle of the floor, built up on a large board of wood, was the city he had seen earlier, through the red mists. Catullus stared at it. He had been looking at a model. He bent down, and realised that Mr Dugbal had built it entirely from waste – bed springs, old shoes, clothes hangers. The detritus, though, had been transmuted into something marvellous and new, for nothing ugly had been used that did not now contribute to the splendour of the cityscape, or enrich its detail and complexity, or leave Catullus feeling overwhelmed. "It's wonderful," he said, looking up and shaking his head. "It's unbelievable."

Mr Dugbal smiled nervously. "Of course it is unbelievable," he said. "It is not a real city."

"Does that matter?"

Mr Dugbal nodded.

"Why?"

Mr Dugbal smiled again. "Because..." His voice trailed away. He swallowed, then tried again. "Because – it would not have been built if the real city was still alive."

"Why – what happened to it?"

"It was bombed," said Mr Dugbal simply. He sat down and buried his face in his hands. Catullus watched him, wondering, then turned back to the model. There were flags, hanging from poles or loops of thread. Catullus peered at them. He began to laugh.

"What do you find funny?" asked Mr Dugbal, looking up in anguish.

"The flags – you made them from my flatmate's ties, didn't you?"

Mr Dugbal leapt to his feet. "Don't laugh," he pleaded, "don't laugh!" For a few seconds, he stood paralysed by his emotions, then he threw himself at Catullus, his hands beating the air. Catullus beat him off, but as he did so, he felt his wound turn cold, and blood began to trickle down the side of his face. Trying not to stagger, he reached for Mr Dugbal and held him by the arms. "Let me go," Catullus whispered. "Your key – give it to me."

Mr Dugbal whimpered and fluttered. Catullus strengthened his grip. "The key," he said again. Then he felt something pulling his own arms back. He looked round. He was being held by Lud. "Where the hell did you come from?" he asked in a low scream.

Lud gestured towards a corner. As he did so, Catullus shook himself free and made a run for the steps, but when he reached the door it refused to give. He looked back down at the cellar. Lud was staring at him. "What are you going to do with me?" Catullus asked. He waited, then pushed at the door again, but the effort made him dizzy and his legs gave way. Lud walked up the steps and took his hand, then led him back down to the cellar again.

Catullus sat on a chair and mopped at the stickiness he could still feel oozing from his head. He felt sick. "Let me go," he said at last. "Please."

Mr Dugbal stared at him. "I'm sorry," he said.

"Why?"

Mr Dugbal nodded at his model. "You might prevent the atonement."

Catullus stared at him in bemusement. "What, for your city?"

"No." Mr Dugbal shook his head frantically. "Not for my city. Never my city. For the cities of Circassia, don't you see that?"

"No."

Mr Dugbal looked at him in surprise. "You mean, you don't remember? The fire descending from the hills and skies? The bodies of children buried under rubble? But you must do. Surely you do. In Circassia, the bombed cities, you must remember."

Catullus shook his head gently. "I was never in Circassia."

"But I was! – with my guns! Pointing into the valley from the hills, bang, bang!" Mr Dugbal shivered. "Yes sir, no sir, shoot them, bang!" He turned back to Catullus. "Don't you see?" he asked despairingly. "There was a sheet of flame, and it devoured the city. Bone or brick, it ate them all."

Catullus stretched out a hand, to try and calm Mr Dugbal's shudderings. "But I don't understand," he said, after a decent pause. "What has this got to do with me not being allowed to go?"

"Because you might talk about him!" said Mr Dugbal frantically. "Say that it was us!"

"Who's him? Clodius?"

"Yes, yes," muttered Mr Dugbal, nodding his head. "Him!"

"And he commanded you in Circassia, didn't he?"

Mr Dugbal nodded again.

"Tell me about it."

But Mr Dugbal shook his head, rocking himself as he began to hum. Catullus groaned. He looked around for Lud, who had hidden himself in the shadows again. Vanessa pointed him out.

"He won't tell you," Mr Dugbal said, looking up. "He never speaks."

"Why not?" Catullus glanced back at Lud. "Is he dumb? Did he have his tongue ripped out?"

"No, no, no. But he never speaks a word."

Lud smiled to himself. He walked across to Mr Dugbal, and held him by the hand. He looked deep into Catullus' eyes, and Catullus began to hallucinate, that he was dead, that Lud and Mr Dugbal and Vanessa were all dead, that they were locked in the cellar for eternity. He wanted to get out. He had to get out. "I'm leaving," he said suddenly. He tried to walk back towards the stairs, but with each step, he seemed to be wading through mist, and he couldn't do it. The effort was killing him. No, that was an unfortunate phrase. Just keep the legs going, he told himself, and it will all be okay. But his limbs wouldn't hold him. He was going to fall down. So this is what it's like to die, he thought.

He must have been caught by Lud, because when he woke up again, he could feel no bruises, and he was lying in Lud's arms. Catullus stared up at his face. Lud looked pale, he could see now, very pale, behind the woman's make-up that had streaked with his sweat. Catullus tried to catch his eye, but Lud wasn't looking at him. Instead, he was staring at Mr Dugbal's model, and there were tears, a meniscus of them, caught between his lids. He was humming something softly to himself. He blinked, and a single tear rolled down his cheek.

Lud wiped at it, then looked down into Catullus' face. "I will talk to you," he said.

Catullus had never heard such a strange voice. It was foreign, he realised, but that didn't explain the lightness, the thinness, the hint it had of something beyond the human, like metal fragments, perhaps, hanging from a tree, disturbed by the breath of a sacred breeze.

"I will talk to you," he said again. He frowned, as though concentrating on the shape that the words made on his tongue. "I will tell you all that I can." He looked across at Mr Dugbal. "After all – locked down here, sealed inside the earth – why not? We have wronged him enough." He turned and stared down at Catullus again. "I always knew that it was you I would tell. So I am ready. I have prepared for this moment. I will talk to you."

He wiped at his cheeks. The make-up smeared, but in the candle light, Lud's skin looked as though it had been sprayed with fresh paint, or moulded from clay to make an idol's mask. Catullus shivered. Lud glanced at him, then coughed, and began to speak again.

"You will realise, of course, that I am not a Roman. Also, you must understand, my habit of speech has atrophied over the years somewhat. You will therefore have to excuse any infelicities I commit while using your tongue. But I would rather, while I speak, that you did not interrupt."

"You speak very well."

Lud didn't answer. He turned to look at Mr Dugbal's model, and clasped his hands together. Only after a minute's silence did he turn round again.

"It was – what? – two decades ago, I think, that I began my work. Yes – I should begin with that." He nodded to himself. He muttered something, under his breath, as though rehearsing words that he had already prepared. "My work, then." He nodded again, and now he began to speak with fluency. "I was, like you, an archaeologist. So long ago! I graduated, from the university of my native city, in the north of Circassia. I took a job, and travelled to the far south, to the deserts where the first cities in the world had once stood. Eridu, Uruk, Ur – to have these syllables as dust under my feet!" He smiled, then shook his head, and corrected himself. "Dust and stone, I should say – for beneath the sands that whipped so scorchingly across the empty plains, there were walls, temples, homes even, still preserved – the common bones of all our many civilisations." He smiled again. "I was young, of course, very young, and the excavation to prove the existence of these cities of the plain had begun long before I joined it – but it was only once I had arrived there that finds, true finds, began to be made. So I felt, in a strange way, that the cities belonged to me – or that I belonged to them, I should say. Very soon, I was almost in love with the idea of what we were excavating. It mattered to me, a great deal, that evidence showed the cities to have been peaceable. More than that – that they had been communities of equals, without castes, or kings, or warrior gods. Instead, the temples we found were open to the skies, and on tablets the gods were spoken to as friends.

"And yet the cities had been burnt. I remembered the boast of the Great King, Tiglath Pilesar. 'I took the cities of the plain. I destroyed them, I razed them, I beat them down. I served them with salt. I made their destruction so complete that it was as though the cities had never been.' These words haunted me. Years passed. More and more remains came to light. I tried to convince myself that by rediscovering the cities, I was defying the Great King who had claimed to have exterminated them so utterly. And yet I could not convince myself. I could not escape the truth – the ruins were a graveyard, a meaningless jumble of dust and bones. Amidst the vast waste of the sands, what dignity could such feeble heaps of brick possess? Finally, I began to notice the stones we had unearthed were being eroded by the wind. I decided that I could not endure to stay and watch the cities' second death.

"So I left the ruins behind. But the memory of them endured, and so did the sense of desolation with which they had inspired me. I fell into a profound despair. I returned to my own city, far in the north, but even there, I seemed to feel the desert wind against my cheeks, and see nothing around me but a necropolis. My nightmares began to mingle with the hours I spent awake. I was sickened by dizzying distortions of time and space. Ziggurats seemed to rise in the dry heat, and swirling pageants from history, Assyrian armies, cruel-faced men of war with burning torches. Doctors prescribed travel, a change of scene. I left Circassia behind. I travelled to the West, to Athens, and beyond.

"I reached Rome. For a couple of years, I settled here. I began to feel myself heal. I was seduced by all the pleasures your city had to offer, and gradually, I fell in love with the place that offered them to me – of course – I was happy. I found work, with an archaeologist, who claimed that the old legends were true, that Rome had indeed been founded by the Circassians. I believed him. I needed to. I was no longer afraid to remember the ruins in the desert, because it seemed that here, in Rome, what they had represented was still alive. Of course, I could see that even so, things were far from perfect – I could see the dirt, the poverty, the decay. But I didn't care. Not then. I thought I understood. Perhaps I did understand. I believed, you see, that a city must be defined by its potentialities. Rome was like a dung-heap, from which flowers could grow. And so I loved it.

"Then an opportunity arose. My superior, the archaeologist, had some excavations he needed to undertake in Circassia. I was happy to return. Why not? We would be going to my native city. I felt that there was nothing any longer to fear. We travelled there together, and then on, up into the fastnesses of the northern mountains, to the long abandoned site that had once been Dumutsi-Bau. I remembered the hill from my childhood – but had never dreamt then, when I had walked across the mountain side, that an ancient city lay in ruins under foot. But there had been legends, rumours, peasants' tales – and it was my superior's style to follow up such beliefs. And, of course, with Dumutsi-Bau, he was proven triumphantly right. We found the temple site, and the traces of the eagle's cult – you will have read Doctor Gower's account, of course?" Lud glanced at Catullus, who answered with a nod. Lud smiled. "It was a strange place. A very strange place. But I was happy there. And when the dig finished, I decided not to return back to Rome.

"We had been staying in a village, a few miles down from our excavation site. I had met a girl there. We married. Doctor Gower went home – and so did I, back to my native city. The nightmares stayed away. I loved Aliya very much. We had children, two daughters, whom I also loved very much. I found a job at the museum, as a curator of antiquities, and I focused, of course, on the finds from Dumutsi-Bau. I even wrote a monograph, on aspects of the cult of Sesostris Aetos. I had noticed, you see, that the eagle had been represented as female. This intrigued me, since, as you will know, in most cults, the eagle is associated with the male. I even offered my own solution to the problem – wrong, of course, quite wrong. But the paper made me a name, and I was invited to write a book on the subject. My research began to intensify. At the same time, my wife bore me a third child, a son. My cup of happiness was full.

"Then the troubles began – the coup, the first stirrings of civil war. I wasn't worried, not at first. It all seemed so remote from us. But the fighting grew worse, and began to spill out from the capital. External pressures developed. Rome had her oil supplies to worry about – the warnings became progressively more stern. I knew – I knew – that she would have to invade. A peace-keeping mission." Lud laughed faintly. "Even then, though, I did not worry. I still had my affection for the time I had spent in Rome. And I was a historian, I couldn't blame her for behaving as she had to behave, a great power in precipitous decline – it was written into her genes." He laughed again. "No, I had my wife, my children, my museum – what did I care about politics?"

He shook his head and frowned, staring at the model. "At first Rome was welcomed – it seemed that she had won. Circassia's friend. But right from the start, there had been opposition, from the various factions, from the army – whatever. The Circassian resistance retreated north. They reached my city, with the Romans chasing hard. Then I was afraid, of course. I didn't want my home to be a battlefield. But the Romans came in overwhelming force, and with devastating speed – the Circassian fighters had no chance against them. For one sickening day, it seemed as though they would stand their ground – but no – they saw reason – they continued their retreat. The next morning, the Romans entered the town.

"I had three soldiers billetted on me. I didn't resent them. They were from Rome, after all – I knew their language, the way they thought. Furthermore, I could recognise them as the expressions of a historical imperative, one far beyond their own control. Circassia had disintegrated into a mere chaos of factions – I felt no true loyalty to her. My city was all I cared about. So I made the soldiers feel welcome to my house. Soon, in a certain sense, we were almost friends.

"There was a captain, a young patrician, of the sort I had never met during my own humble sojourn in Rome. He was from an ancient family, and had all the menacing charm of a man born to power. Nevertheless, he claimed to have turned his back on his own class. When he discovered that I was a historian, he told me with pride that his own university thesis had been on the establishment of the tribunate. He added that when he returned to Rome, he would seek to relinquish his own patrician status. In confidence, he told me that he was thinking of entering union politics.

"I didn't doubt him. Despite his views, however, day to day, he was far from treating his colleagues as equals. As a result, it was hard for me to get to know them well. With one, though, I did make contact, and we became good friends in the end. He was the captain's orderly, a big man, but shy, sensitive. I discovered that he played the violin. Sometimes, he would give my wife recitals. I would join him. Amongst other things, I taught him to play music from her village, high up in the hills. When we performed the songs for her, I would notice that there were tears in her eyes. She became fond of the soldier, he of her. But I had no reason to be jealous of my new friend. I had already long guessed that he was more than just the captain's orderly.

"The third man I never knew." Mr Dugbal bowed his head. "He was shy too, and very distant. I hardly ever saw him, he kept himself to himself. He was good with my children though, and allowed them to play with his guns. Sometimes, he would make them things, little contraptions, toys on wheels. I learnt he had a family, back in Rome."

Lud paused. He glanced at Mr Dugbal, who was stroking Vanessa's hair. Lud nodded, then turned back, and cleared his throat. "The occupying army stayed all summer. Gradually, though, with winter drawing in, the resistance fighters began to return. There were car bombs. Snipers. A patrol disappeared, others were stoned. The nights became colder, and I advised Clodius to leave while he could. He shook his head – then, in turn, he advised me to leave. Rome would never abandon her peace-keeping role, he told me, not to a terrorist campaign. It surprised me to hear him call Circassians fighting in Circassia terrorists, but then I remembered that despite all his fine words, he was instinctively Roman, with a Roman's belief in his right to interfere, to order other people, other countries, around. I realised that he had told the simple truth – Rome would never give the city up. So I feared the worst. It was then that I sent Aliya and our two daughters up to the hills."

"But my son was ill, too weak to travel. My son!" His voice squeaked; he paused, and bowed his head with embarrassment. "My son," he said again, and his thin voice stayed level. "I grew frightened for him. The fighting became worse. The Resistance had brought back artillery, and they began to fire their shells towards the Roman positions. I asked Clodius to leave – the soldiers' billets were all well known, and I was afraid of attacks. Clodius refused – he had his orders, he said. I pointed to my son, and appealed, down on my knees, but still Clodius said it was impossible. And I knew, in my heart, he was right. I remembered that cruel Roman proverb, 'Woe to the conquered'. I accepted that Clodius was not going to disobey orders for my sake.

"So when the car bomb exploded outside my house, I didn't blame the soldiers who had been its target. My son was injured, not fatally, and the three soldiers drove him and me to the hospital. I stayed there overnight. In the morning, I was advised that I should go. There was nothing I could achieve by staying there. Reluctantly, I did as I had been told. As I left, I noticed bands of men standing with guns on the pavements.

"They were from the Resistance, of course. Doubtless, they thought they had made a shrewd move by seizing the hospital. It had a commanding position in the heart of the town, and there was no chance of the Romans shelling it. No chance at all! I returned to my house. From the roof, I looked down towards the river, and saw a pall of smoke hanging over the centre of the town. There was gunfire, and the thud-thud-thud of the Roman heavy guns. The museum was hit – I saw it collapse as easily as though it had been a chocolate egg. In another part of the town, a fire had begun. I didn't know then what was burning. I found out later that it was the Roman supply depot. I couldn't smell the dying men, trapped inside it, nor could I hear their screams. But I could watch, appalled, as the fire began to spread.

"I tried to return to the hospital. It was impossible. The Romans refused to let me through their lines, and I didn't know where Clodius was. I returned to the roof of my house. The fire was out of control now. Nothing could be heard above its blaze, and there was the sense of a lull in the combat. I was wrong, of course, but even so – it was oddly beautiful, watching the flames as they spread, destroying with such grace, such ease. Then, above the crackle, I heard a droning. I looked up into the sky. There were dots on the horizon. They disappeared, behind the smoke, and the droning began to shake in my ears. There was a whirring, and then a vast explosion. The town below was lit by a flash of white. The bombing had begun.

"It destroyed the ancient heart of the town. It also destroyed the hospital. Flattened it. The fighters inside it were killed. So were the staff. So were the patients. Everyone died. Everyone. The bombers left, and the army moved in, retaking what had once been the centre of the town, and which was now just a mangled ruin of corpses. I ran screaming through the rubble. I never found my son, but he was dead, no doubt about it, he was dead. As I picked hopelessly through the rag doll bodies of other people's children, I felt a sense of hatred grow inside me so powerful that I could no longer recognise myself. I left the hospital, feeling that I had to cry, or my chest would split in two. But I choked my emotion back, and the tears froze, and my thoughts began to be lined with ice. I had a gun. I went back to my house, and rummaged it out. I slipped it into my pocket. I found Clodius. He was kind to me, or as kind as he could be, feeling the shame that he did. He spoke of his sense of guilt. I told him not to be foolish. I wasn't blaming the Romans – it had been the fault of the Resistance. Clodius nodded at this. I asked to see the general of the Roman forces. I had information for him. I wanted revenge on the madmen responsible. Again, Clodius nodded. He said that, yes, of course, he would take me to the HQ. We arrived, and he spoke to the sentries. I wasn't searched. I was taken into the presence of the Roman general. I told him that he was guilty of the murder of my child. Then I took out the gun and shot the man dead.

"I was seized at once, of course. I spent a month in the military prison. Outside, the cold became worse. People began to die. Outbreaks of cholera were reported, in the city first of all, and then spreading further, towards the heart of Circassia, and west, towards

Troy. Beyond Circassia, in the outside world, moral fury at the bombings began to undermine any legitimacy the army might once have commanded as a peacekeeping force. The authorities, feeling the pressure that was ultimately to drive them from the country altogether, decided that I should not be left in army custody. It was proposed that I, and other political prisoners, be brought to the capital and placed in civil detention. A convoy was readied. We were loaded onto an army lorry, and the convoy drove off. We passed through the centre of the city, still desolate and charred, then on. We reached the outer suburbs. It was there that the first lorry hit a mine.

"At once, we were attacked. The soldiers were picked off, one by one, with rifle fire. The prisoners were set free, and the arms seized. The surviving trucks were detonated. Then we vanished, back into the maze of streets where no Roman would dare follow us, and it was as though the convoy had never been. All part of a policy, the commander told us, of placing the city under renewed siege. Later, when we were alone, he told me that his own child had been killed in the bombings, and that he had attacked the convoy only so that he could shake my hand. I felt embarrassed, and proud, to have inspired such a man. He asked me what I would do. I said that I wanted to head for the mountains, to find my wife and daughters. He told me that a group of his men would be crossing the mountain range, into Elam, to pick up supplies. We left the next morning.

"It was hard-going from the start. We were careful to keep away from the roads. Instead, we skulked through the foothills, and then, when we reached the mountains, began to clamber up along shepherds' tracks. As we climbed higher, I would look down and see the road following us, winding distantly up cliff-faces, or disappearing through precipitous ravines. Ahead, far ahead, the snow peaks gleamed, and I thought of my wife's village, nestled at the base of the highest pass. I would quicken my step and hurry, to reach the next brow, and then beyond, the next after that. And so it went on, for almost three days, until at last we were barely a few hours away.

"It was then that we heard the faint grinding of trucks far below. We were in the clouds by now, so we began to weave our way down, from crag to crag, until suddenly the cloud broke, and we could see the road, just below us. There were trucks, three of them – Roman. The men I was with were disturbed. 'Where are they going?' they wanted to know, 'what are they doing?' They explained to me that a road-bridge ahead had been detonated – there was no way that vehicles could reach the pass. 'Maybe they don't know that?' I suggested, pointing at the trucks. 'Maybe.' The men shrugged. 'Maybe.' They had brought ponies with them. From the back of one of the animals, they unloaded various metal parts. They fitted them together. One of the men nodded to me. 'Let's give the Romans a little hint they should be heading back.' He loaded the missile. There was a thud, then a screech. An explosion echoed round the mountain pass, followed by a second. Then there was silence. When the smoke lifted, the last lorry in the convoy had disappeared.

"The Romans from the other two lorries tried to pursue us. They scrambled up the mountainside, fanning out, but we had already long disappeared, back into the soggy grey of the clouds. Eventually, we heard the muffled choking of engines again. 'They're heading on,' one of the men whispered. He was excited. He wanted to take out another truck. But the commander shook his head. 'We should find out what they're up to,' he said. 'They must be insane, after what we did to them back there.' So we hurried on, the road below us, and the lorries always toiling far behind.

"It wasn't long before we reached the point in the road where it dropped away into a rubble-filled chasm. My companion tugged at my sleeve. 'Look,' he said proudly, 'they'll never mend that.' I gathered that he had been responsible for detonating the bridge. He looked round, back down the mountain side. We could just hear the Roman trucks, from beyond a sharp bend in the escarpment road. They hadn't seen the drop that lay ahead of them yet. The first Roman lorry appeared round the bend."

"No!" shouted Mr Dugbal suddenly. He stood up, patting at his chest. "No!"

Lud stared at him. "The first Roman lorry appeared round the bend," he said again. Slowly, Mr Dugbal slumped back into his chair. Lud carried on. "There was a sharp curve. The lorry swung round it. It began to pick up speed again. The front of the second lorry appeared. Then suddenly, for no reason we could see, the driver in the leading lorry slammed on his brakes. It screeched to a halt. There had been no warning. The second driver swerved. The lorry's wheels spun, trying to grip into the track, but there was nothing to hold except loose pebbles and stones. The road was narrow – the pebbles showered into open air. The lorry teetered, its wheels still spinning. We didn't see it fall, but we could hear it, crashing into the mountainside, and then exploding with a distant roar. A faint plume of black smoke drifted up from the chasm. My companions cheered in disbelieving joy.

"We watched the men from the first lorry clamber out. There were four of them. They peered over the edge, then one of them began to shout at the other three. He pointed at the road ahead. He clambered back into the lorry, and the other three followed. They looked reluctant – I wasn't surprised. The lorry choked back into life. It began to drive on up the road. All the men around me smiled.

"We crept down towards the road, until we were just a few hundred feet above the ruined bridge. The cloud was following us, and I could only just make out the muffled silhouette of the lorry as it rumbled up towards the drop. I wondered if the men inside the truck would notice the ruined bridge. They did, just in time. The lorry shuddered to a halt. The four men climbed out and peered over the edge of a second precipice. Their backs were turned to us. There was a whispered clamour from the men around me. The commander of our group shook his head. 'Not in the back,' he said contemptuously. 'We are men of honour.' He asked for a rifle. One was handed to him, and he aimed at the truck. He fired three times, puncturing the tyres of the three wheels on show. With a fourth shot, he punctured the petrol tank. 'There,' he said, as the four men below us peered vainly into the clouds, 'walk back, soldiers.'

"Everyone laughed. As we pressed on, my companions stayed in high spirits, but I was starting to grow nervous now – the closer we drew to my wife's village, the more concerned I became to know that she and my daughters were all safe. I began to think that I was recognising features of the path we were taking, but the mist was so thick that I could never really be sure. And so I hurried on, and while the others joked, I stayed preoccupied with my own thoughts and anticipations. But at last we reached a cave, one I remembered from my courtship, and I knew for certain that Aliya's village was now only half a mile away. We crowded into the cave. My companions insisted that we ate together, one last time, and I agreed – of course – how could I have refused, after all they had done for me, guiding me there? We sat together for an hour, chatting, making our farewells, and then at last, it was time to break up. My companions were heading on upwards, towards the pass, and so I waved them off, until they had vanished into the cloud. Then I turned, and took the path that led down towards the village and my family. I started to run.

"Ahead of me, the mists were growing Stygian. I shouted out, hoping that someone from the village might be coming up the track. But there was no answer – only a grey dripping from the leafless trees. Everything was stagnant, sodden – dead. I called out again, but the mist was so thick now that it just swallowed my words. Once, I thought I heard a noise – a twig breaking, someone hurrying through the trees. But there was no one I could see, and I didn't want to waste time blundering in a wood, not when I was drawing so near to my goal, with the path direct ahead. I pressed on. I reached a curve in the track, where I stopped, and strained to look ahead. I remembered the vantage point from walks with my wife – on a clear day, I would have seen the village spread out below. Now, though, I could only just make out the buildings nearest to me. They loomed faintly, like icebergs in a northern ocean, and although I waved, I knew that no one in the village would see me through the mist. I turned, as the buildings themselves began to fade, and a black curl of cloud thickened before my eyes. Suddenly, though, just ahead of me, I saw someone. I called out to him. He made no answer. Instead, he faded back into the cloud, and when I ran to where he had been standing, there was no one there, just dank trees. But I was sure there had been something. I was badly shaken. The something – I'd imagined it, of course – but – the something had worn an eagle's head."

Mr Dugbal stood up violently. "There, you see," he said, pointing at Lud. "He saw it! He saw it too! Remember that!" He stared into Lud's eyes. "Don't go on," he begged. He gestured at Vanessa. "Please."

"Your daughter," Lud whispered softly. "Your dear daughter, who you love so very much."

Vanessa stared at him wide-eyed. Mr Dugbal began to cry, and reached out for her, but Vanessa pushed him away. "What is it?" she asked. "Dad. What does he mean? Dad!"

Mr Dugbal was sobbing. He shook his head.

"You never told her?" A smile cracked the mask that had been Lud's face. "All this time, and she never knew? Well, well. Just think. The little girl, who never knew why her daddy came back from the wars so changed."

Vanessa stared at him. "What do you mean?" she asked desperately. "What had Dad done?"

"'What had Dad done?'" Lud spat the words out. He began to repeat them, over and over again, chanting them with the rhythm of an executioner's drum. "What had Dad done, what had Dad done, what had Dad done, what had Dad done!" The death roll stopped. Lud shut his eyes. When he opened them again, he had plastered the mask back across his face.

"I walked down into the village," he said. "Everyone was dead. Aliya, I thought, Aliya – please. But she –": Lud sighed. "She was dead. Someone had laid her out on the floor. Our two girls had been placed on either side of her, so that when I first walked in, I did have – just a fraction of a moment – when I thought perhaps – perhaps... But then I saw that the blood on their backs was still damp."

Vanessa was staring in horror at her father. "It was you?" she whispered.

Mr Dugbal reached for her despairingly. "Go away!" she wailed suddenly. "Go away!" She ran to the door again and pulled on it, but it stayed locked as before. She called for her mother, but no one came.

"Say it's not true," she said at last, appealing to Lud. She pointed at her father. "Not him."

Lud stared at her. He smiled, as though Vanessa had asked him a clever riddle. "My mind," he said thoughtfully, "in that – dead place – seemed suddenly very clear. I left my wife, my two daughters. I walked back outside. There were bodies in the street. The mud was oozing red as the mist drizzled down. I stood, staring at the desolation, and then, just by my feet, I noticed a corpse in uniform. I rolled it over. The man had been a Roman, an officer. He had a bullet in his forehead. I bent down and looked at his shoulders. There were more pips there than Clodius had ever worn. I remembered the man from the truck, ordering his three companions to drive on. I was sure then who the soldiers had been. Clodius – the army had sent him to bring me back. It had been his fault that I'd been introduced to the general, and so it had become his duty to go and flush me out. All three of them, the soldiers who had been billeted with me, they would all have known that I would head for my wife. So up they had driven, in a convoy of trucks, with an officer to make sure that they did their job. I saw it all. I understood. They had been frightened. They were alone in the mountains. They had seen one lorry incinerated. They had seen their own lorry wrecked. They had been expecting terrorists round every corner. They had been frightened. And somehow, in the grip of this fear, they had shot a village of innocent people to death."

"And the eagle," Mr Dugbal whispered. He glanced at Vanessa. "Tell her about that."

Lud's mouth twisted. "Oh yes. How could I forget?" He smiled politely at Vanessa. "Your father had seen a god. As he was driving up, he had seen it standing straight in his path. He had braked, and that was when the second lorry had plunged over the edge. So – you see – he'd been hallucinating."

"Not hallucinating," Mr Dugbal protested. "You had seen it too."

"We had both been hallucinating. There had been nothing there, only mist on the breeze. I had told you about the god, you knew you were driving towards his sacrifice ground, and so you hallucinated."

"But why?" Vanessa appealed again, "I don't see *why*."

Lud buried his face in his hands. His whole body shook, and Catullus thought that he had begun to weep. "Why?" he asked, looking up. His thin voice caught, but there were no tears in his eyes that Catullus could see. Lud shook his head. "I was beyond the stage of wondering why. A darkness had fallen on the village. I had no time to probe questions of evil or fate. I had no time to worry about *why*."

He paused, shivered, as though he could still feel the mist against his throat. "I stamped on the officer's face," he said, nodding. "Crushed it. Then I walked back in to where my family lay. I gathered together food, supplies. I kissed my daughters, and then Aliya, my dear wife. I took the golden grasshopper from her neck. I packed her violin away. I stared at her face one final time. Then I sprayed the house with petrol, and watched it as it burnt. I felt that the world was dead. I waited until the flames had eaten up the pyre. The mist settled on the embers like a mould.

"It was dark now. I wondered what to do. I couldn't stay in the village. Then I remembered Dumutsi-Bau, a few miles further on. There had been a hut there, just by the site. I would spend the night there. And then – I didn't know. Find Clodius, the other two – kill them. I didn't know.

"I began the climb. There had been two paths to the ruins – I took the less obvious one. As I scrabbled up the mountainside, I began to notice that the cloud was thinning, and then suddenly, ahead, I saw the glimmer of the moon. I looked behind me: a silver mist was lapping at my feet, and an ocean of cloud, deepening into blue, stretched away towards the far south. I felt an intense agony, to think of all the beauty in the world that my wife would never see. For the first time since I had discovered her body, I was able to cry. Breathing in the clearness of the night air, my grief seemed purged to a new purity. Hatred and pain thrilled through my blood.

"Ahead of me, I recognised a silhouette of rock. Beyond it, sheltered in a hollow, were the temple ruins of Dumutsi-Bau. Staying in the shadows, I climbed the rock and looked over the brow. The sacred site lay moonlit below. I clambered down towards it, running across the silver grass. Then I heard a shout. I looked round. There were three men, waiting amongst the graves, down in the very depths of the hollow. One of them shouted again. I recognised Clodius' voice. 'Stop!' he called. 'We don't mean any harm. Stop!'

"I began to run. 'No!', I heard Clodius scream. 'Put it down!' I looked over my shoulder. Pollo was aiming a gun at me. I stumbled, and ran on. There was a shot. I heard the bullet whistle over my head. 'All right,' I shouted, 'all right!' I turned round, with my hands in the air. I heard a second shot. The bullet hit me. I clutched at the wound. Blood was everywhere. I felt myself melting into a pool on the grass.

"Someone picked me up. I wanted to know where I was being taken. No one would answer. I looked up, to see for myself. The mountain had gone. Instead, there was a tower, but I knew that was impossible, unless my nightmares were returning to haunt me again. I stared up at it, appalled. The brick was made of cloud, and its summit seemed to lie beyond the stars. We were on the lowest rampart, we were smaller than the smallest block of masonry, we were lost amongst a heartless infinity of steps. There was a chamber portal ahead of us.

On either side were statues of grotesque gods. There was no part of their bodies that was in proportion to the rest. They seemed to grin at me, and chatter, and then we were past them, into a passageway that shrank around us, and I struggled, because I thought I was being taken to my tomb. I screamed – and my voice rose like a fissure through the ceiling above. The temple cracked to the very summit. It shattered and collapsed in a whirlwind of dust.

"I was dying, I knew. I could feel the whirlwind behind my back. It swept me through strange worlds and times, until I was delirious with the impossibilities I had glimpsed, and I knew that the whirlwind was my own ecstasy. Its swirl began to thicken and dip. I was sinking. I was on a bed. Ease felt sweet through all my limbs. I looked about me. I was in a cave, and the shadows were the source of the strange comfort I could feel. In front of me were four figures, muffled in grey. I called out to them – my son, my daughters, my beloved wife! They bowed their heads. I tried to stand. Their faces – I had to see their faces. I called out to them, but they stayed where they were, and their faces were hidden behind funeral cloth. An imp, a loathsome imp, was in my way. He was naked and fat, with breasts that lolled in an epicene fold. He took a step towards me. 'No,' I shouted out, 'no!' He smiled, and his lips were like soft putty. I never saw a person I hated so. He bent forward, his lips parting in a damp smack. But he was changing. I stared into his face. My wife. She smiled, and I began to cry, for I had thought that she was dead. She brushed her cheek against mine. We kissed. And then I felt the pain again rising between my legs.

"I cannot describe it. I was in hell. I rose to consciousness through a sea of red flames. It took me days. At last, I opened my eyes, and I knew where I was, but the pain didn't go, it will never go. 'I should have died,' was the first thing I said. I looked around me. I was in a cellar. I remembered it. I had excavated it, years before. There were paintings of dancing figures on the wall, and skeletons, embedded into the rock of the floor. The front of their skulls had all been sliced away. 'Not here,' I said, looking around. 'But Fate has brought you here,' a voice said. 'Here, and nowhere else.' I stared up. There was an old man. He had long white hair, but no beard, and he wore a peasant woman's dress. The skirts were spattered with brown whorls. 'My blood?' I asked, pointing at them. The old man nodded. I dared to look down at the source of my pain. There was nothing I could see – my groin was swathed in bandages. 'There will be a time for everything,' the old man said. He bent down and gave me something to drink. He began to fade. For the first time, I was able to sleep and dream of nothing.

"But then, and every time, I woke to the same agony. I would scream, and ask to be killed, but always there was only the old man's smile. 'Suffering is the path to relief,' he would say. 'Peace and distress have met in you, be content.' I would howl at him. He would shake his head and hold my hand, or give me more of the medicine. 'You will be healed,' he told me once. 'The pain will fade.' I asked him how the hell he knew. He smiled, and rose to his feet. He lifted up his skirts. Then I saw that what I had already suspected was true. He had no testicles. I stared at the pink scar. Then I sobbed, to think of what I had become. But I had known it all along. Again, I shouted out for death.

"But the old man had been right – the pain did start to fade. I told him. He smiled. 'Of course,' he said. 'Why?' I replied. 'Why 'of course', why? I know about medicine – the loss of blood. Why 'of course?' The old man stared at me. 'Don't you see?' he asked. He looked surprised. He pointed at the wall paintings. 'And yet you understand these, why they are here, you have talked about them in your delirium.' He began to mumble about the deep mysteries hidden in the images – I lost interest, began to drowse, fell back to sleep. But the old man was patient. When I woke again, he started his ramblings for a second time. I had no choice but to listen. He talked about truth, and union, and the transcending of opposites. 'For there must always be conflict,' the old man said, 'and yet beyond the irreconcilable lies reconciliation. Here lies the key to our sacrifice. Beyond the clinch of man and woman, oppressor and victim, slayer and slain, waits the dark mystery of all-redeeming love. It is this which creates from what it also destroys. It is this which justifies the universe. And it is this to which you now bear witness, my friend.'

"I had no time for his gibberish. I told him so. But always, that infuriating mystic smile! He stayed oblivious to the hatred I felt for him. He talked on, telling me about what I already knew, the myths of Sesostris, the rituals, but all the time there was the difference that he believed in what he spoke, with a luminosity I longed to frustrate. But in vain. Instead, it was I who felt the darkness lapping at my soul. He dared to tell me that the deaths of my family had been ordained. Four people killed – four victims sacrificed, he said, to summon down the god! I stared at him with loathing. Where was the god then, I asked. The old man kissed me on the lips. He whispered the secrets of death in my ears. The legends I had read in my books had been nothing, barren allegories, a veil cast before the glory of truth. That truth was love. I was to affirm its triumph. I had become an incarnation of the god. He nodded inanely to himself. He was very tired, he said. He had been waiting for me a long time. Now that I had come, he could die at last.

"'Yes,' I whispered. I stared at his neck. I longed to feel it in my hands, and watch his eyes pop as I twisted it round. I wanted to hear his gurgle of surprise as he realised the kind of god he had annunciated. For there would be no golden age under my reign. Instead, as I felt my strength start to return, I discovered that my hatred was coursing with that same pristine fury that I remembered from the mountainside, when I had broken through the cloud and seen it stretching from my feet, out across a dead village, a dead country, a dead world. The old man clucked on. I ignored him. I began to dream of a godlike revenge – fantasies of destruction, cities drowning in lakes of flame.

"I was encouraged by the discovery that I had a slave. Pollo had deserted, and stayed camped out in the ruins. He came cringing like a dog to lick my hand. He confessed to the madness that had come on him. I listened as he wept and stammered. He hadn't known what he was doing. He hadn't known. It had been the mist, he told me, it had come from hell and rotted his brain. He begged for my forgiveness. I refused it. But I enjoyed seeing his contemptibility. I asked him what had happened. The officer, Pollo told me – as I'd suspected, he had been afraid of terrorists. He had been the one who had fired the first shots. Pollo and..." Lud glanced at Mr Dugbal. "They had both joined in. Only Clodius had kept his head. He had tried to stop the massacre. Then he had been touched by the madness as well. He had shot the officer between the eyes. I was disappointed to hear that. It blunted the purity of my right to revenge. I found that I hated Clodius most of all.

"When I was ready to walk, we left. The old man followed me down the hill, weeping. He begged me to stay. I laughed in his face. I ordered Pollo to throw him down a gully. We walked on, and the old man's cries were lost on the breeze. I was pleased with Pollo. He had changed. I took pleasure in forcing him to confront his guilt, and grovel before it. Something had broken inside him. I would twist it, dislocate it even further, as though it were a fractured bone. The pain was brutalising him. His gentleness died, the more his mind became self-hating and disturbed. Only his love of music survived. I gave him my wife's violin. I made him practice the songs he had once played for her. Down on the plains, this bought us our food.

"We headed westwards. We arrived in Rome. Pollo played a Circassian dirge outside this very house. You wouldn't let us in at first, would you?" Lud stared at Mr Dugbal. "Afraid for your family. I was pleased to see it. Pleased to see what you had become – a cringing, broken insect, a wreck. I gave him the grasshopper, to make sure that he stayed that way. Show it." Mr Dugbal shook, and fumbled inside his robes. The gold caught the candlelight. "Good." Lud nodded. "My second slave."

Catullus felt his head, gently, being lowered onto the chair. Lud had stood up. He walked over to the model and leant against the board. "I waited. Rome failed to recognise the brooding god her own slums were sheltering. But Clodius though – did he pierce the darkness? Was that what he was fighting against? Perhaps." Lud reached for a stick. "But too late." He brought the stick down, viciously, onto the gossamer town. "Clodius is dead." He slashed a second time. "The sacrifices have been made, the ritual has been obeyed." A third slash: the model lay in ruins. "And now?" Lud asked, staring at the debris. He swept it onto the floor with his stick. "We shall see what we shall see." He shook his head. Suddenly, he looked tired again. His shoulders slumped, as he shut his eyes. He whispered softly to himself again – "We shall see what we shall see."

There was silence.

"And us?" Vanessa finally dared to ask.

Lud stared at her. "Us?"

"Are you going to kill us?"

Lud sighed, and shook his head.

Vanessa pointed at Catullus. "And him? Can't you let him out? He's going to die. Do you want that?"

Again, Lud sighed. He looked unspeakably weary now. "No," he said. He crossed the room. Catullus felt his hair being stroked. He groaned – the pain was returning. Lud whispered into his ear. "If I told you that I saw my old self in you, would that help explain?" Catullus shuddered. "No," he answered. Lud kissed him. Catullus shuddered again, and tried to beat him away.

But Lud had already left his side. Catullus stirred. He raised his head. Lud was gliding up the steps, then he paused, a phantom silhouette against the door. "Whe... whe.... where are you going?" Mr Dugbal stammered. Lud shook his head. He unlocked the door, and pushed it open. "Wait!" Mr Dugbal called. Lud disappeared. The door swung shut.

But Vanessa had heard voices. She ran up the steps, shouting. "Mum, Mum!" The door slammed open. Mrs Dugbal stood framed at the top of the steps, with Mr Smallpiece hovering behind. "I see *he's* been back," Mrs Dugbal said. She snorted. "Met him on the way out." Down in the cellar, Mr Dugbal nodded and shook. Vanessa pulled on her mother's hand, and led her down to Catullus' side. Mrs Dugbal inspected his head. "What's been going on, then?" she demanded. "And what are you still doing here? You should be in a hospital."

"We were locked in," said Vanessa. She shivered. "By that man. And Dad."

Mrs Dugbal shook with anger. "Well, go on then," she rasped at her husband. "Make amends – pick him up."

Mr Dugbal shrank. "I think – no – I..." His voice trailed away.

Mrs Dugbal stared at the sexton. "You."

"Oh dear. I'm sorry." Mr Smallpiece patted at his back. "This isn't what it used to be, I'm afraid."

Mrs Dugbal raised an eyebrow. "I've seen you bend it." Mr Smallpiece chuckled in embarrassment, while Mrs Dugbal gave a bellow of contempt. "Men!" She bent, and Catullus felt himself being scooped up in her arms. "You shouldn't travel," Mrs Dugbal said, peering at his head more closely. "Come on, I'll take you up to your bedroom for now. We'll get a doctor in when you've had some proper rest." She carted him through the house. Catullus felt himself being put to bed. Anxious faces stared down at him. Jez was there. "Are you dying?" he asked.

Catullus smiled.

"Does it really hurt, does it?"

"Leave the poor man alone," said his mother." She turned back to face Catullus. "Now then, you," she said. "Try and get some sleep. In the meantime, is there anyone you'd like us to get in touch with? Anyone you'd like to have come here?"

Clodia. He tried to whisper her name. Clodia. Mrs Dugbal nodded her head. "All right," she said. "Don't talk, we'll find someone. You!" she said, prodding Vanessa, "close the curtains. You!" to Jez, "give that glass of water here. And you," to Mr Smallpiece, "turn that light out now." She shooed everyone out from the room, but as Mr Smallpiece was leaving, she took him by the hand and held him in her arms. They kissed; then Mrs Dugbal turned back to Catullus. "Try and sleep," she said. She shut the door behind her. Left alone, Catullus began to sob.

XXI

ATTIS

Catullus couldn't remember falling asleep. As he ran through the marshes to the temple steps, he was afraid that he might still be awake, that everything he was doing might be real. He reached the top of the steps. Clodia was waiting for him. He approached her. She turned her back. He wanted to know what he ought to do, there was something, he was sure. He looked around. There were corpses, shot through with bullet holes, everywhere. Clodia shook her head. She walked away. Catullus shouted out that it hadn't been him, he hadn't shot the village dead. He stared after her. She was gone. Catullus was terrified that it might be forever. Was it really possible, that he might not be asleep? He seemed to be dreaming someone else's tale. He struggled. As he woke, everything came back to him.

He opened his eyes. The room was dark. There was a woman, her back turned, sitting in a chair. For a second, Catullus hoped that it might be Clodia. He sat up. Boot looked round.

"Feeling better?" she asked.

Catullus didn't know. He frowned. His thoughts felt like a slurry spilling out beyond his skull.

Boot walked over and sat next to him on the bed. Catullus stared up at her. "I've seen – heard – terrible things," he said calmly. "But I'm fine now." He tried to stand up, but Boot held him in her arms. "Your head looks fucked," she said.

"It doesn't feel it, actually," said Catullus, lying.

"I think you should rest."

"I've been resting." Catullus looked out of the window. "What time is it?"

"Late."

"There, you see. I've been asleep the whole day." He broke free from Boot's embrace. He stood up, and staggered, then held himself straight. When he dug his hands into his pockets, he could feel the invitation that Marghi had slipped him the night before. "I need to get to a hospital," he said. "I've got to go now."

Boot stared at him. "I wouldn't recommend it."

"Why not?"

She gestured towards the window. "It's not very pleasant out there."

"What do you mean?"

"Well, you know what happened with our stone circle..."
"No."
"You're joking. You must do."
"No, of course I don't, I've been lying here all day, haven't I? Tell me! What's happened?"
"Dad's bulldozers wiped it out..."
"*What?*"
"Wiped it out. And then the pickets wiped out Dad's bulldozers. And then there was a bloody great riot, and the whole area got sealed off, and it sounds like there were hundreds dead, but it's impossible to know exactly."
"Why?"

Boot smiled. She reached across for the radio, and switched it on. There was a crackle of static. She flicked through other stations, but still the same crackle. "See?" she asked, looking up. "And it's the same with the TV."

Catullus stared at her stupidly. "But I don't understand. What's going on?"

"How am I meant to know, there's nothing on the radio, is there? That's the whole point." She smiled at him. "Come on. Lie down. Cocoon yourself in my loving embrace."

"No, I can't, I feel..." It was so hot. He leant out of the window. Everything seemed wrong. His head was spinning. He felt the card in his pocket again.

Boot touched him on the shoulder. "Dearest," she whispered, "dearest."

"I'm sorry," said Catullus, turning to face her. She looked so scared, so full of love. "What can I say?" If he didn't suppress his guilt, he would be drowned by it. He tried to concentrate, but he was sinking, he knew. He had to get away.

Boot led him to his bed. "Just lie there," she said. "I'll go and see if the phones are working." Catullus heard her leave. He shut his eyes. Images swirled unbidden through his mind. Boot's face, imploring him, melted into Lud's. Clodius' body lay amongst corpses in a street. Bulldozers loomed through a slush of rock and blood. Across them all, the heavy shadow, beating, of an eagle's wings. With an effort of will, Catullus summoned up Clodia, but when he reached for her, she turned her back on him again. "No!" Catullus shouted out, twitching, opening his eyes. "No." He mopped away his sweat. It was so hot.

Boot came back into the room. She was holding a tub of water. "I've rung you a taxi," she said. "It'll be here any minute." Settling down, she began to wash the blood from Catullus' hair. "I gather I'm not meant to ask you where you got this," she said.

Catullus stared at her. "Who told you that?"

"The woman who phoned me, your landlady."

Catullus nodded slowly. "Well, she was right. I'm sorry. Not now, I can't talk about it." Boot shrugged, and began to hum. When she had finished washing Catullus' wound, she held him in her arms. "You will be all right, won't you?" she asked suddenly. Catullus nodded. Outside, a car drew up in the street.

Catullus walked downstairs without any help. The Dugbals were waiting for him by the front door. Mr Dugbal tugged at his sleeve and handed him an envelope. Catullus opened it, and saw pills inside. "For your head," whispered Mr Dugbal, nodding and shaking. Catullus smiled at him faintly, and slipped the envelope into his pocket, before clambering into the back of the cab. Boot joined him, but Catullus kissed her and shook his head. "Don't worry," he said, "I'll be fine. Honestly."

"It's no problem."

"But I feel it is. Please, Boot, please. You've done so much for me, I'll feel bad, dragging you miles out of your way."

"But it's not miles."

"Please. I'll feel better. Really."

Boot frowned. She looked hurt. "All right," she said at last, and climbed back out of the cab. She reached into her pocket. "Here," she said, pushing a bunch of notes into his lap. "For the fare." Catullus handed the money back, then, filled with mute shame, pulled her towards him and embraced her again. He shook as he held her. "Get well," she said softly, kissing him on the lips. "See you soon." She broke free suddenly and shut the door behind her. "All right," she called out to the driver, and tapped on the window. Catullus stared behind him, as the car pulled away, and Boot disappeared.

"Hospital, then?" asked the driver.

Catullus looked round. "No," he said. "No, the Aventine. The Crossroads."

"Can you afford it?"

"Yes." Catullus opened his wallet. "Here," he said. He tossed a note at the driver. "And another. And another. Have it all." He emptied out his wallet. "All right?"

"All right." The driver glanced in his mirror. "Just checking. Petrol's pricey nowadays."

Catullus slumped back. His head had started to throb again. Guilt and desire felt dry in his throat, and when he swallowed, he found it hard not to retch. "But I've got to have her," he told himself, 'I've got to', and suddenly, the idea that he might not risk everything to win Clodia back seemed ridiculous. She would understand. He would hold her, and her skin would seem so golden and warm, after such a long time, and such bitterness, all resolved, laughed away, and then he would kiss her, and even as he felt the touch of her lips against his own, he would think of how infinite a woman she was, and the thought would not cause him pain, as it caused him pain now, but would be the index of his happiness, yes, even of his security. He smiled at the thought. She would have come back to him. She would have left his hold, and then returned to it, and despite all her variety, she would never leave that hold again. And then Catullus shook, as he realised with new force what he had done to her, and could feel his hopes calcifying.

He began to choke on them. He looked at his palm. There were spots of blood. A sudden despair settled across his mind, and he could feel all strength draining out from him as the blankness drizzled down, grey, impenetrable, deadening. He couldn't move. Desire remained, but no potency; he was weak, weak, there was nothing left, Clodia and Boot, he had been vicious to both, contemptibly, and now he was alone. He moaned with fear. "Clodia," he found himself muttering, "Clodia." He shivered with disgust. The driver was staring at him. "I must look obscene," Catullus thought, and then he realised that he was still muttering out loud, and shaking, and that his throat had caught, and he needed to be sick. "Stop the car," he whispered. He pushed the door open and leant out. He stared at the tarmac. It smelt of filth and heat. A spasm of revulsion filled his stomach, and he began to vomit. He stared at the mess, and was sick again. Then he shut his eyes, and felt the wind blasting hot against his cheeks.

"Sure you don't want to go to a hospital?" the driver asked.

"No." Catullus breathed in deeply, then looked up. The car was parked by the kerb of a bridge. Ahead of him, Catullus could see the Tiber flowing, black at first, then greasy with streaks of orange and red. There were flames on the bank, a long way down, but lighting the horizon with a sullen glow. Catullus gestured at them. "What's on fire?" he asked.

"Golden Quay," the driver answered, unemotionally.

Catullus looked again. He could just make out glass towers amongst the flames, ghostly shapes of black above the orange haze. "What started it?"

"Clodius," said the driver. "He's dead."

"So – what, it's his supporters..."

"Over there, see?" The driver pointed down the road. "See the road blocks? They've got them all round here. People are worried the trouble's going to spread."

Catullus looked, across the river, towards the far bank. On one side of the road stood the Senate House; on the other, the government ministries. In between was a barricade. "How am I meant to get through?" Catullus asked.

"Ask politely," said the driver. "Shut your door, and I'll take you up."

Slowly, he drove the car across the bridge, stopping again just before the barricade. "Good luck," he said. "But I wouldn't stick around here if I were you, specially not in your state. Do you want me to wait?"

Catullus shook his head, and climbed out of the car. He stood, watching it, as it drove away. Then someone shouted at him from the top of the barricade. Catullus looked up. A man was nervously waving a gun at him. "Where are you going?" the man asked.

"The Aventine Crossroads," Catullus said.

"Why?"

Catullus paused, and thought for a few seconds. "To visit the Police Complaints Department."

"Oh, right, right, fine, up you come then." The man gave Catullus a hand. "Most of you lot left already though, haven't you?" he asked.

"I don't know, I've been away." Catullus pointed to his scar. "Active service."

"Oh well, you've missed a lot, then. Yes, they've all gone. Went when the ministers went. All evacuated themselves. Rats leaving a sinking ship, you know. We must have got the the short straws, eh?"

"Looks like it." Catullus smiled. He jumped down from the barricade, and waved cheerily. "See you, then."

"Yes." The man gripped his rifle. "See you." He turned back to watch the bridge, and Catullus felt himself start to shake again. The show of bravado had left him feeling drained. He stared ahead. The streets were empty, although he could see more barricades by the Senate House. What was he doing here? The club wouldn't be open. No Clodia, just a fucking riot, and him feeling like death already. He slunk down towards the Aventine. He looked around. There was no hooded figure in the shadows tonight. Catullus swore at himself again. What *was* he doing? Feeling shit, he thought, feeling shit. He bent double, to make himself vomit, then stood up again and breathed in hard. He'd come this far. He walked slowly down the steps, towards the club's front door.

It opened, suddenly. Someone was flung out, hitting Catullus, and sending him sprawling onto the steps. He groaned. His wound felt sticky again. Blood started to drip down the side of his face.

"Poor baby, baby's got a scratch!"

Catullus looked up groggily. "Camilla."

"Poopsy." She smiled at him. "Excuse me." She kicked the door. "Inadequates!" she screeched. "Pitiful inadequates!" She turned round again and beamed. "So sorry. I *do* apologise."

Catullus pointed at the door. "Is it on then, the party?"

"Yes, but you don't want to bother with that, popsicle, *really*, it's shudder time with a big S, a no go zone for ravers like us, *absolutely* nothing city."

"But it's on?"

Camilla shrugged.

Catullus staggered to his feet. "I'd better go, then." Camilla held him by the arm. "No," she said decisively, shaking her head. "I think not. You need a ticket, and you won't have a ticket, because only the most grim sort of lesbian gets tickets for a *bomb out* like that. Look at me, darling. I haven't got one. But then – that's because I'm beautiful."

Catullus showed her his invitation. Camilla goggled at it, and Catullus smiled faintly. "Goodnight Camilla." He pushed the door open and left her standing. The door slammed shut behind him again.

He looked round. It was dark – no lights, only a few scattered candles. He could just make out a woman, in a red bustle-dress, leaning against the entrance till. Her eyes were narrowed.

"Ariana." Catullus took a step forward.

Ariana folded her arms. "You shouldn't be here," she whispered slowly.

"I've come to see Clodia."

"I said – you shouldn't be here. Go away. I've already had to throw that other bitch out."

"But I've got a ticket." He waved it in her face. Ariana snatched it from him. "No," she said. "No." She stared at it, until her eyes had become slits. "You should still go," she said at last. "Clodia won't want to see you." She reached for his testicles and began to squeeze. "Go away," she smiled.

"Please," said Catullus. "I'm feeling shit."

"Good."

"Please." He tried to push her, but she reached for his hair and twisted down his head. "Don't jostle ladies," she hissed, "not if you haven't got the strength for it." Catullus could feel his wound start to bleed again. His head swam, and he slumped onto the floor.

"Leave him." Catullus looked up. Marghi was pulling at Ariana's arm.

"But he's a bastard," said Ariana.

Marghi shook her head. "No, he isn't. And he's got a ticket, I gave it to him." She knelt down. "Are you all right?"

Catullus nodded. "I feel a bit odd. I need some water."

"In the shop." Marghi helped him to his feet. "Come on, this way."

Catullus staggered after her. "Is Clodia here?" he asked.

"Why, do you think she'd want to speak to *you?*" laughed Ariana lightly. "She thinks you're a *bastard*. Chuck him out, Marghi, he's going to ruin the whole night."

Marghi stayed silent. She led the way into her shop and sat Catullus down. He stared around. In the candlelight, everything looked stranger even than he had remembered it. Lines of rubber clothing hung wetly, like membranes, Catullus thought, recently dissected and slung up on hooks. The idea made him shudder. Sweat prickled across his face. "You look dreadful," said Marghi, handing him a glass. He drank the water gratefully. "I feel dreadful," he said.

"Go home, then," drawled Ariana.

"Here, take this." Marghi offered him a pill. Catullus stared at her, then swallowed the pill down. He remembered the envelope that Mr Dugbal had given him. "I've got these as well," he said, emptying the contents out. "Are they good?" Marghi asked. Catullus nodded. Marghi shrugged. "Well, why not?"

Catullus took one. He lay back. The room began to swim. He felt worse. He tried to concentrate, and realised that Ariana was talking about him.

"Not like that," she was sneering. "Just *look* at his clothes. You can't let him stay like that. It's not fair on everyone else. We have all made *such* efforts."

Marghi stroked the front of her rubber vest. "What do you suggest, then?"

"Well, look around you!" Ariana gestured with her arms. "There must be something for him here."

"But he's ill."

"And he makes me ill, lying there in those *horrific* clothes. Here." She reached across to a clothes rack. "What about this? He'll look lovely." She held up a short black dress. "Captivating."

Catullus tried to sit up. Marghi helped him. "What do you think?" she asked.

"It doesn't matter what he thinks," Ariana snapped. "He's got to wear it. Either that or he goes. And you know that everyone else will agree with me, this is a special night, we only have it once a year."

"Why are you so jealous of him?" Marghi shook her head. "I don't understand. It's not as though Clodia's been leading you on, he's not taking her from you or anything."

Ariana bared her teeth. "Don't believe all the gossip you hear."

"It's not gossip I've been listening to, it's you, tonight, it's like you're on fucking heat."

"The reason I'm insisting he goes is because I care about something you wouldn't understand, Marghi, and it's called style. So."

She stared at Catullus. "Are you going to leave?"

Catullus shook his head. He reached for the dress. "I'll put it on."

Ariana's smile broadened, but her rictus was set. She watched, as Catullus stripped, then pulled on the dress. When he met her stare, she looked away.

"See," said Marghi. "He must love her."

"Yes." Suddenly, Ariana twirled, holding up the hem of her dress, speaking in a mock-falsetto. "A girl's got to live in hope though, hasn't she?" She laughed. "And at least it's not as though you're prettier than me." She turned and hurried from the room. Catullus stared after her.

"I had no idea," he said.

Marghi shrugged. "Girls with dicks. What can you do?"

"*Really?*" Catullus stared at her. "I had no idea," he said again.

Marghi grunted. "I'll tell her. Might even cheer her up." She took him by the arm. "Come on, don't worry about it. Let's go and see if Clodia's here. You feel okay?"

"Yes, yes, fine." He felt as though he were a beam of light. "Fine."

"I told Clodia."

"Thank you, Marghi. Thank you so much."

"She will be coming. It's hard for people this year, what with all the stuff going on in the streets outside. But don't worry, she'll be here. If I were you, I'd just take it easy and wait."

She led him up the grand staircase. "Where are the men," Catullus asked, "the ones with the candles on their backs?" Marghi shook her head. "No men tonight. Not unless they look like women."

"What about me?"

Marghi made a face. "Just be glad there's a power cut on."

Catullus nodded. He was. He didn't want to be pointed at, recognised as an alien. He slipped through the crowds and sat in the dark, away from the wash of the candlelight. Pain was starting to swirl through his head, until he could no longer be sure that it was pain at all. Marghi left him. Catullus sat back deeper in his chair, and scanned the room. The very thought that he might catch sight of Clodia lay like a weight across his chest. He breathed in deeply, but the weight remained, pressing on his heart, constricting him, while the lightness in his head spiralled on beyond control.

From across the room, someone waved. Catullus looked up, his heart breaking its bonds. But it was Ariana. She pointed, and said something, and the people around her began to laugh. Catullus stared at them, not with resentment, but with careful concentration, trying to anchor his mind to the details of their look. Ariana shook out her hair. She couldn't really be a man, Catullus thought, it was impossible, and at once he felt his mind lurch unpleasantly again. He stared at other women, their clothes, their faces, the curves of their breasts, and dizzied himself with imaginings of distorted flesh, concealed but tumid beneath the outer show, breeding under carapaces of rubber and skin. Everything was obscene. The place bred revulsion. He couldn't stay. He stood up, and felt his own skirt loose against his thighs. As though he were floating, he made his way through the crowds.

He found a fire exit, and pushed the door open. There was a metal escape outside. Catullus sat down and felt the night air hot against his legs. Shouts were rising from the street below. Catullus peered down: there was a line of policemen holding riot shields, blocking off the street, and then, at a safe distance from them, scattered groups of men, jeering and whistling, skimming stones. Catullus leant his head against a railing bar. He was staring at the front of the Police Complaints Department, he realised. Its windows were black. Its roof was framed by an ugly red glow, which rose from beyond it into the sky.

The door behind him opened.

Catullus looked round.

Clodia.

Blood started thumping loudly in his ears.

"Marghi saw you go out here," Clodia said at last.

"Yes." He stood up. He held out his hands. She pressed them, and allowed herself to be pulled across to him. She stared into his face. "Clodius is dead," she said at last.

"I know."

"How do you know?"

"I saw it."

"Tell me."

And so Catullus did. He told her everything. Clodia kept very quiet, nodding occasionally. Catullus finished. He stared at her, at every detail of that much loved, remembered face. He was afraid to ask if she had forgiven him.

"Of course...I know – well..." he said at last.

She smiled. She stroked his hair, then frowned, as she studied the scar. "You shouldn't be out with something like this," she said.

"I had to see you, though. I mean, not wanting to sound romantic and excessive, or anything, but – no – fuck it – I do want to sound romantic and excessive. I would have done anything to see you tonight."

She stared at him. "So I see." She laughed. "You look ridiculous."

Catullus smiled. "Don't you like it? Marghi lent it to me."

"I can tell." She pulled him close against her. They embraced, and their lips met, and, suddenly, as his fear ebbed away, Catullus felt himself lost to his thoughts, which still swirled but in a haze of light now, rising in golden patterns through his mind, through his body, up, into the night, emotions of excitement and drunken relief. The pain from his head was gone – there were only her fingers on his naked thighs, her lips against his own. Intoxicated with the pleasure and his sudden sense of joy, Catullus imagined himself made from the air of Rome, warm, rich against the skin, full with the touch of Clodia, and he laughed, and hugged her, and kissed her again, a thousand times. Even when shots rang out from the street below, he didn't stop, it would have been beyond him. But Clodia froze. He tried to hold her down. But she pulled her mouth away and scrambled to her feet.

"Look!" she said. She pointed. "Catullus, look!"

Reluctantly, he peered down into the street. "Shit," he whispered. He tugged at Clodia's hand. She sat down beside him again, and they both stared below. Armies of men were coming down the road, chanting, waving banners and flags, flooding towards the barricades. The police fired a second volley of shots, high, into the air. A few men turned, or waited on the side, but the main phalanx of marchers continued unperturbed. There were more shots, answered by a low growl of anger that began to surge and roar, as men broke from the front ranks and ran on down the street, towards the police and their barricades. They hurled themselves onto the row of waiting shields. Desperately, in terror, the police fought back, and a few men fell, as bullet shots rang out again. But there was a second roar, and the surge continued undimmable, as the police fell back, clambering behind their makeshift wall, struggling to avoid a hail of firebombs and bricks. There was the sound of breaking glass. Catullus looked across the road, at the Police Complaints Department. More windows were being shattered. A few men forced their way in through the doors. Deep inside the blackness of a second-floor window, Catullus saw the sudden spurt of an orange glow.

Clodia hugged him. He could feel her shaking. She kissed him urgently, again and again. More shots rang out, as the barricade was stormed. There were cheers when the men began to pull it apart.

"I see you made things up, then," said Marghi, joining them on the escape.

"Yes," said Catullus. He smiled, but Marghi was no longer watching him. She stared at the eddying of men below. "Looks serious, doesn't it?"

Clodia nodded. "It's sort of exciting, though."

"Oh yes, very." Marghi pointed back inside. "Actually, people are talking about going and joining in."

"Really?" Clodia looked interested. "Bit dangerous, I'd have thought."

"Well, yes. Exactly. But people are worried about their bikes."

Clodia put a hand to her mouth. "Oh God! Are they all right?"

"They were when I left them."

"What bikes?" Catullus asked.

"The bikes we all came on," Marghi explained. "It's what this evening's all about. We have a good time, then we get on our bikes, and have an even better time, rubbering up the roads. It's sort of tradition, isn't it?"

Catullus looked down. "Bit crowded for it tonight."

"Yes." Marghi nodded gloomily. "Which is why people want to look after their bikes before they get nicked, see, that's the whole point."

"Where are they kept?"

"There's a sort of parking place under the club." Clodia reached across to stroke Catullus' head. "Aren't you ill?" she asked. She frowned at his wound again. "I don't think you should go out in a riot with that. You're covered in blood."

"I feel fine," Catullus insisted. It was true. He felt more than fine. He stared across the road. There were flames now all along the building's lower levels. Papers had begun to flutter through the night, tossed from a window on the highest floor, a soft rain blessing the crowds below. Catullus watched the papers as they fell. His own limbs felt just as light. There was a crash, as part of the barricade was cleared. Catullus turned to watch it, and felt a nervous excitement like fever in his blood.

"Really. I feel fine."

Clodia looked at him uncertainly.

"Come on," he said. "We should hurry." He followed Marghi back into the club. It was empty and dark. Marghi pointed. "This way." They hurried down the staircase and across the main floor, then out, down some further steps and into a cellar, concrete, without lights. Catullus blinked. Rows of motor-bikes loomed from the shadows, their riders sitting or leaning, just shapes. "Is the grille open?" Marghi asked. The woman nearest to them shook her head. "Well open it then." The woman climbed off her machine. Catullus watched her. She was dressed in red rubber, with black boots and cap. She walked down the cellar, into the dark and Catullus heard her winching the entrance grille open. There was a glow of fire from the street outside. Engines roared into life. The bikes began to move. "Come on," said Clodia. "My one's over here."

She climbed on to it. Catullus perched behind her, hugging her back. The metal felt cold against his legs, and he shivered with pleasure. In front of them, bikes were still nudging their way out. None of the riders wore helmets, none of them had changed out of their party-wear. Rubber, leather, red silk, all gleamed in the fire's half-light. Catullus looked for Ariana, and saw her, skirts hitched up, hair flowing, riding her bike a few ranks ahead. She drove up the ramp and disappeared, out into the street. "Okay?" Clodia shouted. "Here we go!" They picked up speed. They hit the ramp. Up they drove. There was the roar from thousands of people in the street, and the darkness reddened to a fiery haze. They passed the grille. Catullus felt himself buffeted by heat. "Okay?" Clodia shouted again. He hugged her tightly. She blew a kiss back. Slowly, she threaded her way through the crowds.

Catullus looked behind him. The roads were swarming. One side now was a stretch of flame, and the light it cast was hectic and deep. Excited faces gleamed with sweat. Men punched the air, or waved banners dyed the colour of blood. Some were crying. There was a sudden roar, of anger and pain. The crowds began to fall back. A lorry, lit with torches, could be seen driving down the street.

Catullus shouted the news into Clodia's ear. She pulled her bike in and looked round. They both stared. The lorry was drawing nearer. As it passed, people were running up to touch its side. Some screamed, or threw themselves down onto the ground. There was another roar, sweeping along the road, up to the barricades and beyond. Catullus was deafened.

"It's my brother," said Clodia suddenly.

Catullus stared at her. "How do you know?"

"Who else would it be?" She turned the bike round. "Clodius!" she shouted, "Clodius!" She drove down the street. Catullus recognised Norris, the aide, standing on the back of the lorry. Something had been laid out next to him, a body. Catullus stared at it. No attempt had been made to conceal the horror of the wound. Clodia leapt from her bike. She jumped onto the lorry and stared appalled at what had once been the face of her brother.

She knelt down and embraced the corpse. Then she looked up, to ask Norris a question. Catullus saw him nodding in reply, and saying something. Clodia began to sob. She hugged her brother again, then jumped from the lorry back onto the road. "They're taking him to the Senate House," she shouted.

"It's guarded," Catullus shouted back.

Clodia shrugged. "So were those barricades up ahead."

"I suppose so. What are we going to do?"

"Be his escort. Come on. Let's get some of the others back."

They drove down the road towards the barricades. Clodia beckoned to other bikes she could see, then turned round again, and sped back to the lorry. The bikes formed a line on either side of the hearse, which rumbled on, inexorably. It passed the barricades, almost flattened now, and turned the corner to the Senate House. Catullus craned over Clodia's shoulder to look. Fires were burning everywhere, on the pavements, in the squares. Outer gates had been stormed. Inside the main wall, a line of soldiers was holding the final barricade, against desperate, overwhelming odds. As the lorry drove towards them, the besiegers paused, and a silence fell, across the flickering desolation of the Senate House square, so that only the crackle of flames could be heard, and the roar of the funeral escort and its hearse. One of the soldiers aimed something. "Get away!" Catullus shouted suddenly. He pulled on Clodia's arm. "Get the fucking bike away!" Clodia swerved, as a thump sounded across the square, and the lorry was enveloped in a sheet of fire. There was an explosion. "Clodia! Are you all right, please, tell me you're all right!" Clodia nodded. Catullus kissed her desperately. She was shaking in his arms. "And you?" she asked. "You have to be. Oh God, oh God." She began to cry. Catullus held her even more tightly, and felt her tears against his cheeks. He stared at his arm. It didn't look burnt. It ached, just a bit, and his head again as well, and he supposed that he ought to be more conscious of the pain, but there was nothing he could really feel except exhilaration, wild and passionate, rising higher than the flames consuming Rome.

Other bikers gathered round them. "Are you all okay?" Marghi shouted. Catullus nodded back. "Bit of a fucking close one that, eh?" Catullus nodded again, and suddenly began to laugh, with pleasure at being alive, and delight at having Clodia wrapped in his arms. Marghi stared at him. "Sure you're all right?" Catullus smiled at her, and kissed Clodia on the lips. "Never better," he said. He pointed towards the Senate House. "I'm just enjoying the view."

They all turned and watched. The final barricade was being overwhelmed. Flames began to lick up the Senate House front, and a section of the wall collapsed into the road. "All right!" Marghi shouted, punching a fist into the air. "All right! Let's speed!" There was an answering roar from the line of bikes, as they followed Marghi across the square. Catullus watched them go. Clodia hadn't moved. He kissed her again, and she met his lips greedily, reaching to stroke his naked skin, holding him as though afraid he might burn away.

There was another crash of falling stone. Catullus glanced up. Lumps of masonry lay shattered in the road, glowing red-hot. A shower of ash hung where the wall had been. Through the crack in the Senate House, Catullus could make out beams, arching over emptiness, the ribcage of some dead and gutted beast. People began to cheer. Catullus looked around, trying to see what was happening. A man pointed. Catullus looked up, and then he understood. Flames had reached the top of the highest tower, curling round it and spitting out, over the roofs and crumbling stone, tendrils of a banner planted in the night. There were more cheers, and the crowds began to move, not away from the wreckage, but towards it, through the smoke and the withering heat. People climbed up onto the barricades. Catullus watched as they began to jump and dance, and the sight of them, silhouettes against the wall of flame, seemed to madden the crowds into frenzies of their own. All around, men, women, possessed by the night, writhed in an empassioned moan of need, as though the sight of such destruction, such beauty, such power, had aroused in people the fear that their lives had been nothing until then. Catullus stared across the heaving, flame-lit sea. In the shadows, he could see a figure standing, head cowled. It turned. Catullus watched the figure as it passed away.

"Clodia," he whispered.

She stared into his eyes.

"I think we should go. We should leave Rome."

"And go where?"

"Anywhere. The country. Just ride. But leave Rome."

"All right," she said calmly. She smiled. "Now?"

He laughed with happiness. "Yes. See where we end up. See where the road takes us."

Her eyes gleamed. She nodded. She choked her bike back into life, and wheeled it round towards the main road. Slowly, she steered it through the crowds. "Just wait," she said suddenly. She jumped off her bike and bent down in the street. The remains of the lorry were scattered all around her. The debris was still too hot to touch, but Clodia scraped some ash with the tip of her boot, and nudged it into a riding glove. "Look after this," she said. Catullus took the glove, then pressed himself to Clodia's back again. She wove the bike on. The road began to broaden and the crowds thin out. There were more barricades, but again, they had been flattened, and were no problem to cross. Beyond lay the bridge. With a sudden roar, Clodia accelerated, then, once over the Tiber, swerved to the right. Ahead, the road stretched empty along the river's southern bank.

Catullus glanced back across at the Senate House. It was now wholly consumed by fire. The Tiber boiled with its reflection, blood red, flowing on through Rome towards the ocean's deep calm, but turbid now, Catullus thought, turbid now. A wail of sirens rose faintly through the night, the gods mourning as they abandoned Rome.

"Hold on!" Clodia shouted. "Here we go!" She picked up speed. There was a junction ahead. Catullus read the sign – they were coming up to the motorway. Across the junction, up a bridge, and there it was, broad, empty, theirs. More speed. Catullus held to Clodia even more tightly, feeling her breasts through the leather of her jacket, rucking up his skirt as he pressed her with his thighs. He looked down at the grey suburbs, then up again, at the road, disappearing ahead. Sometimes the moon would be reflected on its tarmac, a mirage of silver, and Catullus, if he stared at the gleam for long enough, would find a blissful sense of freedom starting to quicken through his blood. Then he would kiss Clodia's hair, or try to reach for her cheeks, and she would laugh, and speed on even more.

They passed a tank, on the furthest outskirts of Rome. It had clearly been abandoned. Equipment lay scattered across the road. A few miles on, there were trucks, and more equipment, and then another tank. They had left Rome now. Catullus glanced back. The horizon was lost behind a crimson haze. Ahead was the moon-gleam on the empty road. There were hills in the distance. Catullus pointed at them. Clodia looked, then nodded. She left the motorway. The roads were narrow, and began to wind uphill.

Slower now, the bike climbed the country lanes. Catullus lost all sense of time. The stillness of the heat, under the trees, across the folding contours of the hills, enraptured him, so rich in solitude and colour it seemed, and Catullus felt that at last he had understood, some secret, some insight, far beyond thought, an emotion breathed in on the country air, touching sensations made tender by its first kiss, sweet shivers of joy. On a night such as this, long ago, he would have walked barefoot with his brother through the grass of his home. And now, with Clodia, something more. He kissed her softly on the back of her neck. She glanced round at him, and stopped the bike. There was a fork ahead. "Which way, navigator?" she asked, "I'm lost. And tell me again, what exactly is it we're looking for?"

Catullus stroked his finger down the curve of her back. The feel of the leather was strange, exciting. His finger seemed to thicken the further it stroked. It reached the plastic of the motorbike seat. Catullus rolled off the bike. He lay in the grass.

"Which way?" Clodia asked again. She clambered off the bike and stood over him. "Decide, lover."

He stared at the forking of the roads. There was a sign, illustrated – an observatory set against a background of stars. Catullus remembered having seen it somewhere before. It stood by the road that led uphill. Catullus pointed. "That way."

Clodia waited. "All right, then. Come on." She took him by the hand. Catullus smiled. He pulled her down. He felt her. He stroked his cheek against the grass. Clodia pulled his skirt up, high, above his hips. She must have removed her trousers and pants. She took him. Catullus gouged his fingers deep into the earth. The pleasure was like nothing he had ever known. He looked up at the trees. They grew and moved, their boughs heavy with purple leaves, while the sky vibrated with the pulsing heat. Catullus scratched at his wound.

The blood felt thick as it began to drip and spill. He smiled at Clodia. She had the weight of a dream. She leant back, and the sky dipped low. There was a soft, sweet pain as it touched him, then abandon, flowing out, himself too, flowing away, nothing else, nothing, just the openness, and he felt himself slipping out and beyond.

"Catullus."

He looked up into her face. There was nothing more beautiful.

"Catullus!" She bent down. He tried to touch her but she seemed so far away. When he clutched with his fingers, there was nothing to hold, Clodia's body was as thick as air. He saw her lips moving, distantly, and her words as they fell through a labyrinth of glass. He shut his eyes. He couldn't understand. "Catullus." Whispered in his ear. "I need to move you, my dearest, I need to get you on the bike. Please, dear God, please, oh my God. My love."

There was a strange sound, coming from the sky. He opened his eyes. A plane, he could see it through the leaves. Heading towards Rome. "Look," he said. "A plane." He felt an arm, lifting him up, and then he swam through the air towards the motorbike. He needed to speak, tell Clodia that he wanted to stay lying on the grass, staring at the leaves, that they had been so strange and full of life, but when he tried to move his tongue, it wouldn't stir. There was a deeper droning, from above the trees again. More planes. Catullus glanced up, and the darkness began to spin, and he choked on a gurgling moan of fear, as something started to crush his head. Clodia, she was there. He slumped forward against her, and the pain became a fog.

He could only dimly make out her head. It shimmered, as Clodia herself had always done, beyond his comprehension, beyond his reach, this woman, on whom he had sought to build his defiance of the world, even though, for him, she had never been real, not real as the world was, and yet now he could touch her, and the world was gone. Thank God. He reached out to touch her. Thank God. He felt her hair, and saw, with sudden illumination, that she had dyed it dark again. It swept the back of her neck, as it had done long before, beside the lake.

Dimly, Catullus heard the motorbike start. Then nothing, except for the feel of Clodia's back, and the pain, thickening and pressing him down. Where were they now? He tried to look. A building, a dome, set against the stars. Back came the fog. He felt Clodia's hands against his chest. She was whispering softly, nonsense, in his ear. He wanted to cry, because when he looked at her, he couldn't see her face, she was muffled in grey, a phantom shape. He tried to hold her, but the cloud, the hopeless cloud, it wouldn't let him, and he tried not to think, as the pain rolled on.

"Catullus."

Where was the voice coming from?

Where had he been?

"Catullus. Look at me." Clodia. She touched his lips, to keep his head down. He was on a mattress, he realised. He stared at her.

"My love. Listen. I've got to go. Can you hear me?" Catullus tried to open his mouth. Clodia smiled. "Good. Because – I've got to leave you, now, as soon as I can. The nearest hospital is almost twenty miles. I've got to get there, because – you're not well, my dearest. Do you understand?" Catullus frowned. Clodia touched him on the lips again. "You're safe here. You're with a man, he knows you, you'll be all right. I promise." She kissed him. "Please, be all right. Please." She kissed him again, and stood up. Catullus found his voice. "No!" he shouted out. Pain split through his skull. "No!" he shouted out a second time. Clodia stood in the doorway, looking back at him. "I won't be long," she said. She turned and left, and the door slammed shut.

Catullus slumped back onto his bed. The mists rolled across his thoughts again. He struggled to sit up and melt them away.

"Lie back," said a voice. "I did not bring that mattress up just so that you could leave it."

Catullus opened his eyes. He was lying under a gleaming white dome. A telescope pointed towards the stars. Titus was sitting next to it, dwarfed by its size, watching him.

"I feel fine," said Catullus.

"Of course you don't." Titus stood up, and cracked his fingers in alarm. "Now whatever you do, you must stay still."

"What's the matter with me?"

Titus stared at him, and frowned. "I couldn't say," he said at last. "I am not a doctor of medicine."

"But Clodia – why has she gone?"

"Because – as I said – I am not a doctor of medicine."

"But..."

"But what?"

The words bobbed out on a surge of fear. "Out there, there were planes, hundreds of them flying over, I heard them. It can't be safe. Can it?"

Titus sat down again by his telescope. He sighed. "There is a comet I am tracking, through the icy wastes. In thirty, forty, fifty years' time, we will see it, a short blaze, here on Earth. Then it will vanish back into the emptiness of deep space. It will return here again – when? – in a thousand years' time. We will all be dead. We might as well never have been born."

Catullus clutched at his stomach as he tried to speak. "So?" he said at last. "So what?"

Titus sighed again. "I was hoping," he said, standing up, "that the banality of my argument would offend you less here, in the observatory, where we can seem so very close to the chill of space. I remember how we argued on the matter before." He walked across to Catullus' bed. "My point is simply this, I suppose, that we should never fight our need for calm. Inner calm, you see? There is nothing else in life that is worth the pain of our desire." He paused, to thread out hairs from their caking of blood, to smooth down the folds of Catullus' skirt. "I don't understand, you see, this lust you have – everyone has – for experience. What is the point of it? You want something – you have the craving – so long as it is not satisfied, the craving is your life. Then you satisfy it, and what do you demand? – something else to crave. Always this panting thirst, never quenched, degrading yourself. No wonder you look – well... Can you not be happy with peace of mind? I don't understand it. Lie back, Catullus. Enjoy your rest." He looked into his patient's face, then sighed. "I am sorry. I must sound banal, after all. But it is what I think. I am sorry."

Catullus swallowed. He needed to concentrate. "When Clodia went..." he whispered. He stopped. He tried again. "The planes."

"It is her risk. She wanted to take it. It is not yours."

"The planes..."

"It is not your problem. You do not need to know."

Catullus tried to sit up. He moaned, "I do, I do, I do, I do..."

"No."

"I do." Catullus steadied himself. "Can't you see? Please! *Can't you see?*"

Titus frowned. He stood hunched in thought for a long time. "Very well," he said at last. "If you really want the news." He walked across to a panel of lights, and flicked up a switch. Voices, noises, crackled. "The planes are heading towards Rome," said Titus, turning back to face Catullus. "Caesar's armies have crossed the frontier. If your lover rides hard, she need not meet them. But she knows that. I told her before she left."

"No."

"It was her decision."

"No." He felt desperation cramping his lungs, but he could speak now, he suddenly found, because he had no choice. "I must get her back. A car – if I had a car, I could catch her, she's only got the motorbike." He appealed to Titus. "Please. Your keys. She hasn't been long. And look, I'm all right now." He stood up. "You see?" He crossed to Titus and took him by the arms. "Or if you're worried, you could drive me. Please. But we must go now, we'll lose her." He yelled out. "Please! We've got to go now! *Please!*"

Titus stared, impassively. "You are very ill."

Catullus strengthened his grip.

"You are hurting me."

"I'm sorry. I need her back."

Titus gnarled his fingers together as he frowned and thought. "It means so much to you?"

"Yes." Said with patience. Yes, yes, yes.

"But really – I think, really – you are not well."

Catullus shook his head. "If I don't have her back, I will die."

Titus nodded slowly. "Maybe." He cracked his fingers again. "I can't tell."

"But I can."

A long pause. "Maybe," he said again. Another pause. "All right," he agreed at last. "But this is your decision, it is what you want." He felt in his pocket for his keys. "I will drive."

With great application, Catullus walked down the stairs. Outside, though, on the gravel front, he was surprised at how weak his legs still felt. He staggered, almost fell – Titus supported him. Catullus looked up, as though affronted, and snatched himself free. He walked on again, a few further paces. Then he did fall. Titus never said a word. He pulled Catullus up, and helped him over to the car.

Catullus lay back in his seat. Titus sat down beside him, holding the wheel. He glanced round. Catullus nodded. The effort made him break out in sweat. Titus turned the ignition key. He glanced round again, then began to drive. With careful speed, the car slipped down the hill.

"Faster," Catullus managed to whisper.

The car increased its speed.

Catullus watched the road ahead.

Clodia.

Where was she? To have lost her again, so soon. She couldn't be far ahead.

Clodia.

Catullus strained to look through the windscreen. Nothing. Only the country lanes, and trees gentle in the windless air. Catullus mopped at his brow. He was flooded with sweat. He peered ahead again, and then he saw her! "There," he whispered. Titus looked. He shook his head. "There's no one."

Catullus frowned. It was true, the lane was empty. But she had been there. "Faster," he muttered.

The road opened out. "Look," said Titus. He pointed. Catullus stared. Down beyond the hills, on the open land, vehicles were moving, tiny dots of light. "Towards Rome," said Titus. "Caesar." Catullus nodded. "Faster."

A plane screamed overhead. Then there was a silence which hummed in the ears. Above it, Catullus could hear his heart pumping blood, like the throb of sperm, or a funeral tattoo. He couldn't be sure that it wasn't his pain. His thoughts were trapped between the beat. He began to fade away from them.

He looked up. He could see her now. She was standing alone, in the middle of the road. "There!" he screamed. He tried to reach for the steering wheel. "You'll run her over, you fucking fool!" She was caught in the lights. Titus swerved. A shape was rumbling out from the dark. There was a bump, as the car hit a verge. A tank, its gun, just a blink. Then a jolt, and Catullus heard the crash, as he felt his skull hit the window screen. Silence, blackness. Catullus opened his eyes. He could hear a wheel spinning, through empty air. He reached for the door. It opened. He staggered out.

Birds were singing. Almost morning. Catullus walked down the road. He stared around. Clodia wasn't there. If she had escaped the tank, perhaps she had fled into the woods. He should follow her, to bring her back. He looked for the woods, but they had disappeared. The hills were bare. The road stretched over them, white, carved from chalk.

He heard a noise. He glanced round. A carriage was rattling towards him down the track. Catullus stood on the verge, and waited calmly as the carriage drew near. It began to slow. The horses neighed as the coachman reined them in. A paw from a hoof, a harness chink, and they were still. Catullus stared at the coach. It was painted gold and black. A door swung open. Catullus looked inside. He smiled with relief. He clambered in.

The door was shut behind him. The coachman flicked his whip. The carriage was soon just a vanishing dot.

ALLISON & BUSBY FICTION

Simon Beckett
  Fine Lines
  Animals

Phillip Callow
  The Magnolia
  The Painter's Confessions

Catherine Heath
  Lady on the Burning Deck
  Behaving Badly

Chester Himes
  Cast the First Stone
  Collected Stories
  The End of a Primitive
  Pink Toes
  Run Man Run

R. C. Hutchinson
  Johanna at Daybreak
  Recollections of a Journey

Dan Jacobson
  The Evidence of Love

Francis King
  Act of Darkness
  The One and Only
  The Widow

Colin MacInnes
  Absolute Beginners
  City of Spades
  Mr Love and Justice
  The Colin MacInnes Omnibus

Indira Mahindra
  The End Play

Henry Miller
  Quiet Days in Clichy

Adrian Mitchell
  The Bodyguard

Susanna Mitchell
  The Colour of His Hair

Bill Naughton
  Alfie

Dolores Pala
  In Search of Mihailo

Matthew Parkhill
  And I Loved Them Madly

Boris Pasternak
  Zhenia's Childhod

Ishmael Reed
  Japanese by Spring
  Reckless Eyeballing
  The Terrible Threes
  The Terrible Twos
  The Free-Lance Pallbearers
  Yellow Back Radio Broke-Down

Françoise Sagan
  Engagements of the Heart
  Evasion
  Incidental Music
  The Leash
  The Unmade Bed

Budd Schulberg
  The Disenchanted
  Love, Action, Laughter and Other
    Sad Stories
  On the Waterfront
  What Makes Sammy Run?

Debbie Taylor
  The Children Who Sleep
    by the River

B. Traven
  Government
  The Carreta
  Trozas

Etienne Van Heerden
  Ancestral Voices
  Mad Dog and Other Stories

Tom Wakefield
  War Paint